Fantasy

The Blood
Of
Azar

For my sister...
Who was born with Elven Magic

The city of Azar was cast in the shadow of the volcanic mountain of Mt. Ire. The darkness of night complete, though sleep eluded much of the cities people through the screams of those who were enduring the strange plague that had befallen the empire.

A woman walked into a nearby tavern within the city, the dark walls lit with lanterns that hung from the ceiling in even distances from its center. She walked up to the bar and took a seat next to a small group of men who were talking heatedly among each other. She ordered a small but simple meal which she picked at passively as she listened.

"No, I don't think that's true," the man nearest to her argued.

Another man in the group, a man with a ragged black beard and thick eyebrows, drew his scowl in deeper and shook his head, "It is," he grumbled, "it has to be. The king died less than a month ago and already she's hanging all over that man."

"That doesn't mean they were together before his death," he said unhappily, "Maybe it just worked out that way."

The bearded man snorted and took a deep swig from his lager and set it back down on the bar with a thud, "No, I think she's had an interest in him for a while. He's a wizard after all and now they're making decisions about the empire together. That kind of thing doesn't just happen because the king died."

Another man on the far side of the bar leaned in and nodded, "It seems suspicious to me," he said, and dropped his voice lower, "that he would die of the plague when the goddess Fantasy herself made him a pendant to heal the sickness…"

The bearded man agreed quietly, "I heard that too."

The man closest to her at the bar looked into his drink and frowned, "No," he mumbled, "she did make it, but it never got to the city. What I heard is Fantasy's father was bringing it to the city himself to keep her away from the plague, but he died along the way."

"How?" the man at the end of the bar asked.

He continued to look into his drink, "I don't know for sure, but what I heard is that he was murdered for the pendant. No one knows where it went."

"That would sure be a thing to find," one of them interjected.

"Yeah it would," he agreed sternly, "too bad it wasn't in time to save King Edward."

They all grumbled their agreement and held their drinks in the air in respect. They all drank from their glasses and sat quietly for a moment.

The woman pushed her half-eaten plate of food away from her on the bar and rested her chin on her hand. She glanced over at the group of men and asked, "So when did the plague start here anyway?"

The group looked over at her all at once, taken aback by the question. The man sitting next to her drew down his brow and said, "About two months ago. The king was one of the first to fall ill... Where are you from?"

She smiled politely, "I'm not from anywhere."

The men studied her quizzically before a sharp crash stole their attention towards the front door of the tavern. An armored man burst through the door and staggered into the room, his face sunken and grim. He swallowed hard and glanced around at the patrons of the bar as he spoke loudly and clearly, "The queen is dead."

There was a general uproar, some saddened, some confused, but many of the voices around them were angry.

"What happened?!" one of the men shouted.

The lieutenant bit his lower lip and shook his head, "We're not sure yet. The royal sorcerer claims it was the same plague that took the king..."

The uproar intensified.

The woman at the bar slid down off of her stool and stood next to her seat uncomfortably. She glanced over at the group of men who were now hotly arguing amongst the chaos of the room.

"How are we supposed to believe him? The man's a psychopath!" one of them shouted.

The bearded man worked his jaw angrily as he muttered through clenched teeth, "She wasn't even sick. She spoke with the city this week! Something foul is going on around here."

"The sorcerer can't be king... can he?" the nearest man asked, looking between the others anxiously. A flutter of fear flickered between them in a sudden understanding.

"General Armond would be able to handle him," the man at the far side said.

The woman laughed softly and the men looked back to her again. She looked between them, "This general Armond... is he a great wizard, or an alchemist, or a necromancer?"

"No," he answered uncomfortably.

She smirked, "Then how exactly would he be able to control a wizard with a blood line pure enough to be a royal sorcerer? That kind of power isn't easily subdued."

The man looked among his group and fell quiet.

"The king still has three sons. It may not matter," the nearest man said quickly, trying to ease the fears of his companions, "One may still be a baby, but two of them are close enough to the proper age, maybe the wizard's council and the royal court will decide to crown the eldest a year early."

"Doubtful," the woman said, shaking her head, "it seems at this rate that none of them will become king."

The men looked at her with wide eyes, horrified by the thought, "Why would you say that?" the nearest man asked angrily.

"I've seen this kind of thing happen before," she said darkly, "and it's never a good thing for the royal family. The children will all be dead within a year."

"Nothing like this has happened before," the bearded man argued, looking her over suspiciously, "and you're hardly out of your thirties, how could you have seen anything even remotely similar before?"

The woman split a one sided smile, "Looks are often deceiving..." she took a slow step towards the door, "I'm leaving the city before the riots start."

"Riots?" one of them asked.

She nodded, "If I'm not wrong, things will get worse — quickly — and I don't want to be here when it does."

"You can't know what will happen unless you have something to do with this," the bearded man said, his eyes narrowing down at her.

She brushed away the glare with a gentle wave of her hand,

"No, what good would it do me to warn you if I were?"

"I suppose…" he said slowly, "unless you are smarter than you want us to believe."

"I am," she assured him slyly, "but I have no intention of, nor any inclinations towards, regicide."

"So you say," the bearded man said, getting up off of his stool and towering over her like a mountain as he set his glass on the bar behind him while keeping his eyes on hers, "but you seem to have a pretty strong feeling on how this is going to go."

She looked at him, unimpressed by his size, and shrugged, "Even you three," she said, nodding to the men on either side of him, "have figured it out already, even if you won't admit it out loud. Why should my saying so make me guilty?"

"Riots and the death of the king's sons? Sounds like more than speculation to me," the man said, taking a heavy-footed step closer to her.

She stood her ground and craned her neck to keep eye contact with the man as he loomed over her with dark eyes, "I already told you that I'm going to leave. I suggest you not get in my way."

"You're not going anywhere," he said, as he wrapped a massive hand around her upper arm in a vice like grip.

She looked down at his hand disgustedly and back up into his rugged face. In a brisk flash of movement her knee made contact with the man's groin, buckling flesh and involuntarily seizing his body. As he began to sink to the floor in agony, her free hand hit his throat and clenched his windpipe, her fingers sinking deep into the meat of his neck. She took in a deep breath and brought her face in close to his, listening carefully to the movement of the tavern, "I'd rather not kill anyone today… I'm leaving now, and you're just going to have to be okay with that."

She let go of his throat and tore her arm from his fingers as he sputtered, gasping at the air and doubling over to hold and protect his groin.

She glanced around the bar, ignoring the stares, and turned from the tavern and out into the night.

Within the week, the death of the king's eldest two sons stoked the fire of the people's suspicions. On the day of the second son's death, Venhow, the royal sorcerer was crowned king and the city of Azar glowed with the dancing fires of the revolt and the castle erupted in fire and magic.

The smoke that rolled off of the city plumed up into the sky along the side of Mt. Ire and was mistaken by many in the distance as the rolling rage of the volcano, rather than its people.

The infant prince was gone, and the new king's iron grip on the empire intensified for the next fifteen years.

Chapter One

Thick, damp air clung throughout the dungeon, fogged with the smell of sweat, blood, and decay. Beads of water glistened on the floor. The sweltering heat expanded in the chamber like a hot breath that filled the prison with ever rolling, stagnant air.

Twelve lamps were mounted along the walls that lined the cells of the prison, flickering light against the stones and reflecting bright coins to the damp floor below. The heavy oak door at the end of the narrow hall was ornate with unconventional carvings and covered in filth. The door clattered as it swung wide and three beings entered into the dungeon, the sound of their footsteps causing a fearful stir within the cells as they passed.

A tall and slender man of pale complexion with a narrow masculine face and eyes as cold as steel, strode first from the doorway. He was dressed in a black suit that was well fitted and armored at the shoulders and draped in a thick, grey, Elvin cloth. His eyes were deeply sunken, and as grey and as dark as the depth of the room itself.

He stepped forward confidently and swiftly. Small pools of water parted around his steps as he narrowed his eyes fixedly on a cell near the back of the passage. Following him were two towering Keernith Goblins in full uniform, their immense size was merely a suggestion of their brutality as they hunkered into the room. Their deep green flesh and knotted features caught the shadows and were sharply distinguished in the flickering firelight of the torches.

The taller of the two guards hunched his head down to his chest to avoid colliding with a rusted hook that hung high from the ceiling. The other guard barely cleared the space with the tips of his elongated ears grazing the metal.

The armor in the uniforms was thick and heavy but was carried as easily on their backs as if it were cloth. The length of their arms were extreme and they reached low against their bodies. Their fingers, like long roots with four gnarled joints, gripped as strong as iron at the weapons on their sides. Their backs stooped beneath the weight of their bodies and their waists held three curled Keernith blades.

Venhow reached the cell with the guards trailing closely behind him. He glared through the bars at a figure that was lying curled on the floor against the far corner.

She was old, frail, and deadly thin, trembling against the wall. Copious amounts of mud coated her worn and ragged cloths as well as her olive skin, spotted with age. Her hair was knotted and matted so thickly with filth that her natural hair color could barely be recognized. Only the smallest amount of greying blonde was left uncoated with dirt.

Venhow gestured towards the door with a graceful flick of his wrist and the taller of the two guards, Maurik, pulled a key from his belt and unlocked the door. Venhow stepped into the cell, not bothering to close the door behind him. He looked down at the woman at his feet and waited for her to respond to his presence.

She slowly turned her head and looked weakly up at him with wide blue eyes. She pushed herself upright from the wall to see him better and scowled as her cataract fogged eyes found focus on his face.

"Leda," Venhow said clearly, his voice shaking the air around the cell, "it's been over a year. Do you really want to suffer any more for the sake of a traitor?"

Her nostrils flared and her brow crumpled angrily but she lacked the energy to do more than scowl. Her eyes burned into his, "He's no traitor," she said.

"No?" he said, with amusement in his voice, "A man who would turn on his family and his people to fight for the enemy, how is he not a traitor? He betrayed you. He left you to die," she turned her face from him and looked bitterly at the wall as he spoke, "When I became King, I sent my armies to kill those who have killed our people, our people Leda," he emphasized, leaning forward into her glare, "and your son led the revolt. He killed my men. He's a murderer and a traitor."

She swallowed hard to regain her voice and allowed her heart to settle, "You're no lord. And you don't command any army to whom my city would fall. My son is a hero," she gritted her broken teeth, the muscles in her face deepening the lines in the aged wrinkles of her face, "You've drowned yourself in dark power. Your army's not human," her eyes shifted from Venhow's increasingly hateful expression towards the guards at the door of her cell and shouted with what strength remained of her voice, "they're Gorks!"

Maurik and Gher each reached for their weapons, their long fingers wrapping quickly around the hilt of their blades. They snarled darkly, the blue gums of their mouth showed eerily from behind their forest green flesh and their teeth glinted against the sharpened white points of their dagger like teeth. Venhow gestured for them to stand idle and reluctantly they released their weapons.

"No need to be hateful. Human or not, they are alive and loyal and an army to be unmatched." Venhow looked down on her and his eyes narrowed, "They follow me."

"I can't understand why," she hissed.

"I have taken land and power and I'm running Azar with pride and promise for greater things. They have made it so, and so it is. I respect them and in turn they respect their king," Venhow said, with a sidelong glance behind him. The goblins grinned again, turning to one another in approval.

"Because they don't know any better," she said, and pursed her cracked and split lips, the creases around her mouth deepening, "you've fooled them all."

"I don't have a reason to lie to them," he said dryly, "I already have their loyalty and their respect. I'd like yours as well."

"I have nothing but hate for you—" she said, through gritted teeth, "—contempt — absolute loathing!"

"That's because you listen to lies," Venhow said, his expression darkening, "In my service all are equal and everyone is taken care of the way that they deserve to be. They are given what they earn and all power is divided amongst all who are loyal. It's the way it should be."

"You lie to them," she insisted, "They fight and die for you and you turn them away at the first sign weakness. You kill your own army and you slaughter the innocent. Is that how it should be?"

"You're misinformed, Leda. I am King. I am ordained to rule and I simply want to share this prosperity with those who need it," he said, gesturing with an open hand, "My army is loyal and treated well and the only people who die in my attempts to clean and reinvigorate the world are those who attack us first."

"No. Your armies kill, fight, and die alone because you don't care for anything but yourself," she spat, scooting across the grimy stone floor of the cell and sitting up straighter to see him more clearly, "We fight for freedoms and for *rightful* kings. *We* don't kill our wounded nor do we invade other countries and boundaries because we think it should be ours."

"But the lands that I take, are mine," he said clearly.

"They are not!" she shouted, smacking the floor bitterly.

"You don't seem to understand me very well..." Venhow said darkly, crouching low to meet her eye to eye.

"I do understand," she corrected, "You dabble in darkness and gather bloodthirsty minions to do your every bidding. We don't make others do our dirty work and we don't leave because we're afraid. We will see it through to the end and we will have our victory even if it must be in death."

"You make it sound so... noble," Venhow said slowly, and he looked back at the guards for a sweeping second and then back to Leda, "Death. Perhaps, but you do have traitors and bloodthirsty men yourself. War makes everyone think that they are the heroes, that they are doing the right thing. Do you feel like a hero? Am I the villain here, really? We're all wicked in our own way. Your son's treachery put you here. Is that noble?"

"It's not the same," she hissed.

Venhow smirked wickedly, "And why is that?"

"We were being surrounded," she said sharply, "There were women and children that had to be taken care of. They had to leave. He led our people from danger at any expense necessary. He was expected to do the right thing. I believe he did."

"How long would it have taken to come back for you? Would those seconds have changed anything?" he looked down the end of his nose and raised a mocking eyebrow, "Are you not one of the women that needed help to flee the *brutality* of it all?"

"Those moments must have been crucial," she whispered, looking down to the stone solemnly, "I know he only did what he had to," her demeanor changed rapidly back into a scorching and murderous anger, "Which wouldn't have been necessary if you hadn't sent your Gorks to ravage our peaceful little city to begin with!"

"Say it again human," Gher growled deeply. His voice grumbled and cracked like the groaning of the earth itself, "Say it again and I will tear your limbs off."

Venhow held up a hand to silence him but a greasy sneer of pleasure curled upward on his thin lips, "I had heard tell the people there were forming an army of their own to stop my progress. I acted preemptively with the intent to stall further bloodshed. I was correct, was I not? There was an army."

"Thirty men is not an army! It was hardly enough to keep the people safe from the wild animals that lived around us. You came for Armond, not for the army. We had just enough to protect ourselves."

"To protect everyone except you," he said quietly, with a cruel smile.

"There wasn't anything more that he could have done," she said insistently.

"Maybe he just didn't notice you weren't there with them. Maybe," he suggested snidely, "he tried but was unable to find you. Or perhaps he just left you to die."

"Our people were dying. His priority was to them, not me," she said, her aged expression placid, "He saved more lives than I'm worth."

"How many lives are you worth?" he asked, and his eyes narrowed. Leda scowled, tight lipped and bitter, breathing heavily as he leaned forward, resting his arms on his crouched legs, "Would he give up anything at all to get you back, or are you just a casualty that he will get over in a few days?"

"My son loved me."

"Did he?" Venhow asked sinisterly, his cold eyes lingering on her stoic appearance.

"And I love my son. I would die for him and I would die for any one of the children and women that he saved," she said firmly.

Venhow smirked, looking around the cell impassively, "You are a righteous heroine now aren't you? Lying in a dirty cell in a cold stone room, starving. That makes you better off than them doesn't it?"

"I am better than you," she retorted, her anger heating, "I'm glad to be in my cell starving on this floor. At least I am not living under you. I've not sold my soul to you. I'm not serving you or your hateful, deceiving, malevolent, homicidal Gork—" Venhow's hand struck across her face hard, throwing her head solidly against the stone beside her.

She clung to the wall and trembled as her eyes flooded with dark watery shadows and dancing lights.

He smiled cruelly, his voice echoing his enjoyment of her sorrows, "I thought we made it quite clear that racist remarks are inappropriate my dear. Don't let it happen again." Maurik and Gher straightened up satisfactorily, their ears pressing against the ceiling and their eyes peering down at her.

Leda touched her head where it had hit the wall and felt the hot knot beneath her fingers and the stream of blood that drizzled down her face. She withdrew against the wall and looked away from his icy stare.

"It would be wise to answer me today," Venhow said, all of his tolerance with the situation vanishing from his voice, "I'm tired of arguing with you... Where is Armond now?"

"He's gathering an army," she said, and looked back to him, turning her head from the wall as a thick dribble of blood dripped from her chin, "He will kill you."

Venhow blinked and tipped his head slightly, his face contorted in disbelief, "Did I hit you so hard that your brain jarred out of place? You know that I can do *far* worse. I suggest you tell me where he is, him or the child."

She pressed her lips together tightly and scowled, "No."

"Tell me," he demanded, as his fist climbed back over his shoulder, the back of his hand creaking against the black leather gloves that stretched across them so tightly.

"No," she hissed again.

Venhow took in a sharp breath and punched the side of her head, her skull cracking against the stone as it was caught between his fist and the wall with a wet pop.

"Where are they?" he shouted, as he reached out and took a handful of her grey hair and wrenched back her head, forcing her to look into his eyes.

She closed her eyes against the pain and fogginess of her thoughts and he shook her skull sharply until she opened them again. "The child died a long time ago..." she mumbled through the pain, working another bloody chip of her molar out of mouth and letting it fall off of her bleeding lip.

Venhow stared at her closely, trying to discern lies from the truth, "And Armond?"

She lifted her fogged blue eyes to his and said weakly, through rapid breaths, "I won't tell you."

He tightened his grip on her filthy hair to pull harder against her scalp and he gritted his teeth, "Do you intend to die for the very man who abandoned you?"

"Always," she whispered, blood running down the lines of her aged face.

"He knew you would be brought here. He knew you would suffer and he knew you would likely die. He has made no sign to try to find you. There have been no sightings and no rescues. You can't survive here much longer. It doesn't have to be this way," he leaned in just low enough to meet her eyes and tightened his grip on her filthy hair, "you just have to tell me where he's gone."

"If I do, you'll kill him," she said.

"Why would I kill him?" he said, with a sadistic grin, "He's valuable. He knows of the whereabouts of the other armies, of the Nelwin, Dwarven, Elvin, and Terith leaders. He knows of the other rebellions and future plans. He knows about the allegiance of the Trolls and southern forest Brutes. It is knowledge that would benefit me. He would be rewarded for the information, and both of you would live through this war."

"You lie," she said, biting back her pain as another chip of her tooth worked its way out of her mouth through a new flow of blood which she allowed to slide from the corner of her mouth.

"I'm not as ruthless as you would like to believe. I'm not the enemy here," he said, letting go of her hair in disgust.

She pulled her head away from him and scowled through her pain, "I know you lie. You're afraid of him and the influence he has. You would make an example out of him. You would break him and beat him, but you know as well as I do that it would do you no good with him. He's stronger than I am. I will say nothing and so you will you get nothing from him!"

"You won't tell me?" he said, his scowl deepening.

"I'll die first," she said, swallowing fear and being sure to speak clearly. She held her head high, her features firm as she glared back at him.

Venhow stood slowly, his brow knitted together as he recognized the glint of an unbreakable spirit. He stared down at her and raised his hand at his side and made a distinct flowing gesture with his right hand, as if he were balancing a marble between his knuckles and failing to keep it centered. He poured his magic through the motion and a dim light began to materialize and grow rapidly within his overturned hand, and he said, through gritted teeth, "A King is meant to serve his people."

He flicked his hand quickly and the light elongated down the end of his fingertips in a flash and the piercing light was replaced by a spurt of blood which showered the cell and everything that it could reach.

Her body slumped lifelessly in the growing pool of her blood as it seeped from a dark and penetrating hole in her chest, marked only by the fragments of bone that stuck out from the ragged remains of her flesh.

Venhow turned from the scene and stepped back out into the hall between the cells, pulling off the Elvin cloth around his shoulders as he went. He used the grey cloth to wipe away the blood on his face and arms, the magic in the cloak soaking up every droplet it came in contact with. Quickly, the draped cloak became rich with red stains and the stench of blood. He held the cloth out to Gher who took it from him with a green four knuckled hand and went into the cell to finish the job that he had been brought to do.

There was a clamor in the stairwell and Venhow turned towards the commotion in time to see the Keernith general rush into the corridor of the dungeon. His eyes met with Venhow's and he quickly dropped down to one knee and threw his gaze to the floor. The goblin, even down at his knees, came just shy of meeting Venhow's gaze.

"What is it Skemir?" Venhow asked casually, as he stepped forward to meet the general at the door.

Skemir stood slowly, breathing heavily, and looking disheveled from his usual prestige. He straightened the chainmail around his green neck and spoke in a voice like groaning branches in a high wind, "My lord, there was a incidence at the prison camp concerning a Nelwin leader, a thief, and a dwarf lord from the southern kingdom."

"And?" Venhow said angrily, locking his jaw as he looked over the general's crooked posture.

The general licked his lower lip with a dark blue tongue and grumbled tensely, "They escaped. The dwarf lord and the two Nelwins are all gone. We're sending our best trackers after them as we speak."

Venhow thought for a moment and nodded, "Do what you have to. The Nelwin leader has caused me trouble in the past. He's too intelligent for his own good. I should have done away with him when he arrived in my dungeon last time," he said bitterly, with a quick nod of his head, "Find him. Kill him on sight, and as for the Dwarf, find him a cell. Imprison him in the darkness without food until I've spoken with him."

Skemir nodded, his armor clinking as he took a short step back, "And the thief sir?"

"He's worthless to me," Venhow said, with an unconcerned flip of his hand, "find him and make an example out of him in the city so that the people can watch."

"Yes, Sir," Skemir said, glancing around the cell tentatively, "There is a slight problem, however."

"A problem?" Venhow asked, turning his head towards Skemir with sharp eyes, "Is it something that you're incapable of handling yourself, General?"

"No my lord, but—"

"Have you developed sympathy for them?" a dangerous fire burned in Venhow's voice and he stood motionless, observing Skemir closely.

"Not at all," Skemir said reassuringly, shaking his head rigorously, "it's just that the absence of dwarf lord is causing uproarious problems within the camp. There is a distinct hazard with keeping him within the prison for too long."

"Hazard? This is my prison," Venhow snapped, gesturing back to himself as vein distended in his neck, "I should be feared for it. They should not be able to cause problems because one man is in a cell! Do as I say!"

"Yes sir," Skemir said, staring at the floor.

Venhow spotted a strand of hair knotted against the leather of his glove and he picked it away disgustedly before looking back to Skemir, "How long have you been my General?"

"Ten years," he answered quickly.

"Do you wish to extend that record Skemir?"

The general looked up suddenly, his yellow eyes wide, "Of course I do. I'm more passionate about my work than any other Keernith that you'll find. I've always followed you."

"And until recently you had not given me any trouble. You had followed orders without question, reported information that no other man has ever been able to retrieve and carried out deeds that to this day go unnoticed. You're among the best that there is, however," Venhow said, his expression falling darkly, "your age is beginning to show in your ability to handle complicated situations."

"I retain the strength of my youth," he assured him, "I'm no less able. I can take care of it."

Venhow looked at his glove again, checking for another hair and seeing none, "If that's so, then why did you bother me with this?"

"I merely needed your clearance. I would like you to approve of my request — from the humble stand of such a loyal General," he added, with pleading eyes, "Please allow me to imprison him in the city of Azar, not the camp at Tetrach."

"Which is why I told you to find him a *cell*," Venhow said, his dark voice deepening dangerously, "You need to listen to me more closely."

Skemir swallowed hard, "A cell in this dungeon?"

"Yes. Again, general, if you cannot handle it, I will find someone else who can. Do you understand the severity of your current position? Three escapes and riots," Venhow said grimly, "You're lucky, that you still are graced with the blood that fills you."

Skemir dropped like a stone further down on his knees and bowed as low as he could, the end of his nose rested only a few inches from Venhow's shoes, "Please. I will take care of it. I'll not bother you with meaningless matters again. I'll handle everything that I can before I bring it to you. I promise my lord. Spare me."

"This once," Venhow warned.

"Thank you. Failure will not happen again. Neither from me nor my men," Skemir said, glancing up from the floor to see if it was acceptable for him to move.

Venhow did not react.

Skemir shifted up to a kneeling position and paused, unwilling to test his luck further.

"Good," Venhow barked, "What are your orders? Repeat them."

General Skemir locked eyes with him, "Find them. Restrict the Dwarf Lord to the dungeons of Azar until you see him. No mercy. Eliminate the others, make an example of them."

"Make them suffer," Venhow added spitefully, "and I have also decided that I need another wizard at my side."

"Who?" Skemir asked.

"Walt," Venhow said clearly, "He should be back to his home within the next two days. Fetch him for me."

"I'll send someone to escort him immediately," Skemir promised.

"As for the Nelwins, I want you to find Priie," his eyes pierced into Skemir's golden eyes with clear meaning, "Keeping her hidden of course."

"Always," he nodded.

"Send her with the alpha trackers. Tell her to be quick and to report directly to me the moment it is finished," he glanced into a nearby cell and watched as another prisoner made eye contact with him before he scrambled back into the shadow of the corner. Venhow looked back to Skemir and added scornfully, "and increase patrol around the camps. If your men can't keep even the Nelwins in check, I may not have any use for them at all."

Gher passed them slowly, the bloody cloak wrapped tightly around a small and limp frame. He shifted the body on his shoulder and walked up the stairwell and out of sight.

Venhow turned to follow him back to the surface level but stopped in the doorway. He turned to Skemir and stared at him warningly, "I would suggest you not let anything of the sort happen again, for your sake."

Skemir nodded once and bowed low once more as Venhow passed through the doorway and vanished up the stairwell.

Chapter Two

Their heavy breath mixed with a rush of leaves and sharp brush that whipped by painfully with resistant whispers of where they were. Shards of dry air rubbed coarsely against their lungs as they ran near exhaustion, their muscles ached and burned.

Nedtedrow stopped, leaning against a small tree for support and gasping for air. His clothes were dark and torn in places from the brush and struggle of escape, his hair was dirty and slightly mussed. He was built slightly heavier than most, with an average form of face. He sank to the ground and let his mind race for ideas.

Bolzar slid to a hesitative stop, looking back at Nedtedrow who knelt panting on the ground looking disheveled. He went back and crouched beside him.

"We can't stop here," Bolzar said breathlessly, looking around through the darkness, "they'll find us. We have to keep moving until we get somewhere safe."

"We can't run forever," he replied looking up into Bolzar's strong and determined face. "I can't go — much further —without a little — rest. — Let me catch — my breath — at least."

"We have to stay ahead of them," Bolzar snapped, his eyes darting around through the darkness, "Get up."

"We are ahead of them!" Nedtedrow argued, gasping as he held a hand up into the air, "Just give me a moment."

"You know that they'll catch up with us quickly if we don't move," Bolzar looked around through the forest and the blackened shadows of night nervously, "We're not that far ahead."

"Then I'll just have to catch up with you," Nedtedrow breathed, bent over with his hands on his knees wheezing slightly.

"I'm not going to leave you here, so get up!" Bolzar said as Nedtedrow groaned as he pushed himself up onto his feet. Bolzar turned and started off, keeping a steady clip and moving further and further ahead into the dark brush.

Nedtedrow grunted with effort as he tried to keep moving. The air in his lungs scraped away at his insides with each struggled breath. He stopped again and looked around. It took several moments before Bolzar reappeared, looking angry for having to backtrack once more.

"Do you want to die?" Bolzar said sharply, his dark blue eyes glinting with adrenaline.

Nedtedrow shook his head, "I can't keep running."

"You can and you will," Bolzar said, grabbing Nedtedrow's upper arm in an iron grip, "Our lives depend on us moving forward. Move or you will die."

"You are mistaken," Nedtedrow said, holding an index finger up for effect as he heaved through exhausted breaths, "I will die if I keep moving. Not the other way around."

"You're just lazy."

"I'm not lazy! You are just freakishly energetic."

"You spend your life wallowing in goods that aren't yours. You eat yourself fat on sweet bread and salted meat and you think you're not lazy?"

"No. I'm comfortable," he said, patting his somewhat rounded belly.

"The Keernith aren't. They're fit. They are trained as warriors from birth. They'll kill you if they find you, and they *will* find you if you don't move," he said looking out to the hills once more, "I guarantee it."

"Yeah, well," he paused trying to think of something to retaliate with while stalling for time to take a short rest, "They would be sure to kill you first, so I would have a little bit of time to bask in what lazy life that I have left," Nedtedrow replied with an exhausted half smile.

"That's not funny, there's too much at stake for you to be goofing off!" Bolzar yelled.

"I thought it was funny," he said shortly.

"This isn't a joke Nedtedrow."

"No," Nedtedrow agreed as an idea popped into his head and he quickly rattled, "but this is. — A Dwarf walks into a mine and spots a satyr holding a potato. The Dwarf had never seen such a bizarre thing and —"

"—Nedtedrow —"

"—so he asked the Satyr 'What are you doing?' and the Satyr replied 'Doing what exactly? Doing in the mine or doing with your toys?' The Dwarf looked puzzled —"

"—Shhh —"

"—and said loudly, 'that isn't a toy, it's a potato," and the Satyr grinned and said, 'Well —'"

"—Stop yourself! There isn't any time for this and it isn't funny."

"It's a little funny but you have to hear the end of it."

"No I don't. This isn't the time or place for that!"

"No, it isn't, but I figure that we're dead anyway," he said bitterly, "might as well make a good time of it." he paused for a seconds silence, "Ever heard that one?"

"Not from anyone with any amount of education."

"Come on, don't be such a stiff. You aren't dead yet. Try to enjoy something before you die, really. You can be such a letdown sometimes."

"We are not going to die."

"Where are you getting your information from? Because it looks to me like we are," Nedtedrow looked out through the pitch black inkiness of the forest with his arms out dramatically, "In the middle of hog jumping nowhere, running nonstop for over a day and a half with trackers and goblins in our footprints behind us. Pretty damn dead to me."

"We can survive. We just have to get to Gommorn. It is only one day away. Just one more day," Bolzar breathed hopefully, "But if we stop they'll catch up with us, and then we don't have a chance."

"No, we can't survive if it's going take another day to get to Gommorn," Nedtedrow retorted grimly, "They'll catch up with us in a matter of hours. They're already faster than us and then *that* will make us dead. You are supposed to be the scholar here and I figured that one out! We're running out of options. There is no way that we'll make it to the city."

"And so what do you suggest?" Bolzar said arrogantly.

"Hide."

"They're bringing trackers! Find any hiding place and they will find it before we can pull the brush away from the entrance. We have to get to Gommorn! It is the only safe place!"

"Except that we can't get there!" Nedtedrow shouted bitterly.

"Now see here you fat stupid twerp of a thief," Bolzar said taking a fistful of his shirt and pulling him closer, "I've done a lot for you through our lives but I won't die for you."

"Didn't ask you to," Ncdtcdrow said, with a noncommittal shrug and a scowl.

"But, I'm sure as hell not going to let you choose death!" Bolzar pulled on his shirt and drug him to his feet again, "We're going to keep moving or I swear to the Goddess I am going to—"

A wolf howled in the distance and they both felt the color and warmth drain from their faces. Their voices stalled and they stared to where the sound seemed to come from. They looked at each other with the same level of fear and apprehension.

Bolzar let go of Nedtedrow and they both ran as hard as they could, panting as they tore over stones and fallen logs.

A second howl reverberated over the forest and the sound put panic in their steps until the voices of goblins were close enough to be heard muttering in the distance.

They were closing in.

Bolzar resignedly shifted his eyes around the woods searching desperately for a place to hide. The only choice that had caught his attention and Nedtedrow followed his gaze up the nearest tree.

Nedtedrow shook his head sharply knowing that the goblin's height would give them a huge advantage at spotting them.

Bolzar's expression was fixed and determined as he pushed Nedtedrow towards the tree. They hurried silently as they could to the trunk looking up at the nearest branch. It was almost seven feet in the air, and neither of the short Nelwins could reach it alone. Bolzar did not hesitate however, grabbing Nedtedrow, picking him up around the knees and lifting him as high as he could.

Nedtedrow wavered once or twice before stabilizing against the trunk. He reached up for the branch and was relieved to feel the bark of the limb under his fingers. He struggled to pull his heavy body up to sit on the branch. Flipping his leg over and hoisting himself into a stable position he reached down for Bolzar's outreached hand. Their fingertips barely reached each other's.

Bolzar jumped to get a good grip on Nedtedrow's hand, grasping it briefly and nearly pulled him out of the tree with the jolt of the catch. Nedtedrow let go of Bolzar's hand in order to remain in the tree and stabilize himself once more.

He braced his feet against the trunk of the tree and made another reach down for Bolzar's hand.

The third and final howl stabbed the air, so much closer than the last that the sound of it made him jump in his skin.

The sound was quickly accompanied by the distant rustle of moving brush. His heart skipped and he and Bolzar locked eyes for a long second.

"Sorry," Nedtedrow whispered silently and he withdrew his hand from Bolzar's reach.

Bolzar's brow crumpled painfully with anger and betrayal.

A low grumble of voices could be heard closer now and Nedtedrow turned his face away from the hurt in his friend's face, and overtaken by his fear he turned up the tree, reaching for the next branch.

Nedtedrow began to climb the tree as high and as quickly as he could move until he ran out of branches and could barely see the ground through the leaves. He could still vaguely make out the form of Bolzar at the base of the tree and wondered for a moment if he meant to reveal his hiding place because of his cowardice.

Instead, Bolzar gave him a final glance and ran as quickly as he could to the northeast toward Gommorn. Nedtedrow heard another howl and now from his perch could see the wolves darting through the forest several strides ahead of a tall Keernith in black armor with waxy pale skin that made him look unnatural.

Following along with the Colonel was another Keernith goblin slightly shorter with a sharply hunched back and abnormally long fingers. Two river goblins dwarfed alongside them holding the leads to the trackers. It came down to a total of four goblins and two wolves. They heard the commotion of Bolzar's sudden steps and they began to run in his direction.

Nedtedrow froze, afraid to move, and afraid to breathe for fear of them noticing him. Instead they ran by his hiding place, ducking the branch he had used to get up the tree, and running to where Bolzar had vanished from sight.

He still did not move.

For several long minutes he sat motionless watching where he had lost sight of them. A long time passed but he listened through the noise of the woods waiting. Far away he heard the excited yelp of the trackers until the wolves' howls turned into vicious snarling and sharp barks.

A short while later a shout in the distance was followed by sharp yelp and a guttural scream that rattled the air. When the scream died away there was nothing but silence and Nedtedrow's heart sank with shame and self-loathing.

He had killed his friend through cowardice.

The heartache panged in his chest and he did what he could to push it aside. He waited for the return of the goblins anxiously for fear that his life would soon come to an end as well.

The quiet dark of the air was interrupted by a soft fluttering sound just behind his head. Nedtedrow jumped and spun his head around, losing his balance if only for a moment to come face to face with a very small fairy.

It beat its luminescent blue and white wings and began to sing in a high whirring tune. Nedtedrow's heart skipped a beat at the loud sound and he puckered his lips quickly and blew a gust of wind into the fairy's wings. She spun in the air and sank three or four feet into the leaves of the branch below before she flew off looking rather offended.

Relieved that the quiet had now returned he refocused on the location of his pursuers. He stared into the dark until the inkiness of the air began to filter softly with the light of dawn. His eyes ached with the strain of focusing so hard for so long.

He lowered his guard now that the sun began to rise and no sign of them had returned.

He rubbed at his sore eyes and then slumped his aching back against the trunk of the tree now feeling the full effects of his aching muscles and minor injuries. He swallowed hard, staring off into the deep orange in the skyline. His fear for his life began to dwindle for the moment and his heart sank once more into grief and shame.

He leaned quietly against the nook of the trunk between the tree branches for support. His chest felt heavy and he could feel a thick slab of sorrow in his throat. He shook his head feeling the blood throb in his temples rather than focus on the sting in his eyes.

Slowly he started to make his way down the tree, which was more difficult it seemed than climbing up a few hours before. The last branch in the tree he had to jump from to reach the ground, catching himself short of cracking his head on an exposed root. He slowly got to his feet and headed to in the direction of Gommorn, taking a detour that he thought would keep him far from goblin territory.

The thick brush and thorns slowly began to clear as the sun rose and he traveled into the waist high grass of a thinning forest. The trees surrounding him were supple and young, yet still towering amongst the wildlife. He could hear the panicked shuffle of brownies in the grass but he couldn't quite see them. He kicked at the grass a few times making sure that he did not step on one and cause a swarming effect. Brownies were aggressive after all.

A call of a griffin cracked into the air like a screaming whip. Nedtedrow spun around and spotted a nest in one of the older saplings, the heads of three baby griffins popping up from inside the large nest.

"Sure Nedtedrow, escape to be eaten by a wild animal, that's just great..." he muttered nervously. He moved a bit faster through the woods hoping that he would not come across the mother griffin along the way.

He could just make out the edge of the trees at the furthest reach of his vision. He spotted large white piles of stones and the edge of the woods. Ignoring the brownies at his feet and the potential for becoming griffin food, he ran towards the stone wall.

The wall was a natural formation, not a created piece. There were hundreds of smooth looking stones stacked upon one another, overgrown with sand moss and small shrubs. He ran his hand along one of the largest stones and felt its cold and neatly coarse surface. He was unsure of where he was, but he knew that snow stones were a sign of fertile land and life.

He looked around, squinting at anything that could be an indication of a village or a city. Something moved just over a hill beyond the wall of stone and Nedtedrow's stomach churned. Whoever it was moved too gracefully and looked too beautiful to be natural.

He swallowed his fear for a moment. They were not an enemy, or else, they did not appear to be hostile. Usually something would have happened, an arrow flying through the air, a mystical light, a shout for backup, anything.

It was still quiet. Nothing had happened yet.

He cleared his throat forcefully and shouted, "Hello? Could you tell me where I am?"

The figure did not reappear nor did he get a response.

He shivered involuntarily and took in a deep breath. He grabbed the top of one of the stones and began to climb so that he would be able to reach the top of the hillside. The rocks were slick with moisture and moss. The occasional briar weed would catch on the tattered strings pulled loose from his shirt sleeves. His foot slipped once or twice on the climb, but he was able to stay upright and keep from tumbling down the stony edge.

Finally his feet reached ground again and he trudged carefully up to the top of the hill. "Hello?" he said, looking down the other side. There didn't seem to be anyone nearby, at least on foot. Perhaps he imagined it.

He looked closer at the surrounding area and saw a house on the side of the next hill in front of him about half a mile away. Beyond that, there seemed to be more homes, the rest of them however were in a flatland beyond that hill. Nedtedrow thought for a moment about the direction he went in and what kinds of places were in the area. He must have been mistaken, or he had traveled further than he thought the night before.

This was not a rebellion alliance, nor was it a stand for the high power. It was too small to be either. Just what the town was Nedtedrow was unsure of, but his eye drifted to the little home on the hillside and his fingers itched with the need to fill his pockets.

Chapter Three

Oswald sat bolt upright in bed, wiped the cold sweat out of his eyes, and attempted to peel the drenched shirt from his back. Silent, forgotten tears dampened his face. Shaking off the sorrow in his throat and choking back memories that simmered in his mind, he took in a deep rattling breath and threw the covers off his bed. The sheets crumpled lazily into a heap on the floor.

A soft summer breeze drifted indolently in through the open window, embraced with secrets of the early morning. He flipped his legs over the side of the bed, exposing his bare feet to the cold as he walked across the room. He looked into the dresser mirror and saw his bright bluish-grey eyes looking back at him, glistening with the past. His pale reflection stared back at him with a frozen look of grief and exhaustion. He was fine featured, his face long and thin like his mother's, with a similar ivory complexion.

He ran his fingers carelessly through his deceivingly thick, curly red hair. Wisps of short curls entangled his fingers in a kind of living knot. He jerked his hand loose, making his hair stand up on end, hopelessly wild and sticking out in odd places. At an average height and fairly thin, Oswald fit the stature of the elves with little discrepancies beyond his slightly shorter ears and red hair.

He hung his head slightly and closed his eyes, brushing his own reflection out of his mind before returning his attention down to the top of the desk.

He looked down at his hands and he stared at them in an almost alarmed way. They were not stained red and they were no longer their smooth childlike selves. It had been many years since he had to relive his past through his nightmares.

His heartbeat slowed after a few deep breaths and he sighed heavily and reached out past his reflection.

A small glass fairy atop a petal lay still as stone on the oak dresser, lifeless and dull in the faint light.

Oswald wrapped his long fingers around the figurine and held it up close to his face. A scratch on its right wing had blunted the effect that the fairy had at first glance. Frowning, he took the chain and gently wrapped it over the mirror's edge, letting the figurine rest delicately against the wooden frame. He tore his eyes away and went to the window where the night waned slowly into a faint shade of dawn.

At first he believed it had been his haunting memory that had awoken him, and then he heard the quiet sound of far distant music filtering through the woods.

Oswald shook his head sluggishly in realization. The Salwin Festival.

He yawned for a moment and pulled out one of his dresser drawers, gazing down at the dim assortment of clothing. He searched the drawer for a moment and picked out a dark brown shirt, which he quickly slid over his head. He straightened the cloth and carelessly snatched a lighter set of brown pants from the same drawer. Hopping on the spot, he struggled to get his foot through the pant leg. Untangling his toes from the cloth, he slid the pants on completely, adjusting his shorts beneath them.

Trudging groggily through the house, he picked up an oblong reddish purple Peta fruit from the bowl by the kitchen door and stuffed it in his mouth. With each bite juices threatened to slip out from between his lips, but he managed to keep from making a mess. The skins stuck between his teeth, and he picked at them with his tongue for a moment before swallowing what was left of the sweet and slightly tart fruit.

He snatched up a small bronze key from the corner of the dresser and stumbled groggily from the room and out of the house.

The outside air was brisk and cool, but hinted of the intense heat that would bake through the canopy of trees by mid-day. A large gnarled oak tree towered outside of the tiny house; its twisted branches reached far beyond the shade and up into the faintly orange sky.

Music drifted over the hills to him with the scent of baking pie and fresh cider traveling along in its wake. He breathed in deep wanting to eat more than a bit of fruit. Work, however, called louder than a slice or two of not-quite-baked pie and he turned out towards the workshop.

Oswald shut the door behind him and walked around the oak to where a small wooden shed sat, propped up by a slightly larger building. He tucked in his shirt carelessly as he made his way to the shed, eyeing the old handle and rusted lock. He slid the key into the lock and snapped it open easily, letting it slip from the latch and hit the ground with a defying thud. The door creaked open grumpily and folded back to allow passage.

"Hey! Oswald!"

Oswald turned to look behind him and up the hill where a tall, skinny man stood waving his arms. Oswald hurried up the hill reluctantly, wanting to get back to his daily routine. His mind churned, thinking of the amount of work that he had to finish and how badly he wanted to fill his orders for the week. The man jogged gracefully down the hill to meet him halfway.

"Hey, what are you doing?" the man asked brightly.

"Working. Good to see you are back," Oswald said, with a half-forced smile, hiding his exasperation. He shook his hand and nodded out of what little respect he did have for the man who stood before him.

The man's name was Grimb. He was the husband of Narish, a seamstress who lived on the opposite side of the town, and he was a valued messenger between the Elvin villages. He had a nicely sun-kissed tan and was lean with very long ears and dark eyes to match his short, fine hair. Grimb was often gone for months at a time and never seemed a day older than the day that he left. Such was his gift in life. Oswald wasn't as lucky; every year it seemed like he aged a bit more than the rest of the Elvin world. Grimb, on the other hand, was flawless.

"Why are you working? It's a holiday. Come join us in the celebrations." Grimb clapped him on the shoulder and tried to encourage him to move up the hill with him.

Oswald shook his head and slid out of his reach. "No thanks, I really have to get a few things done."

"Nonsense," he said loudly. "It's the Sal-win festival. You should be with the village. Eat some food, dance with someone. Be social."

"I would love to, Grimb," Oswald shrugged and glanced back to his tool shed for a second, trying to buy himself some time, "but I'm backed up with work. There really isn't any way that I will catch up if I don't work on it today. Besides," he said, "the festival is for the harvest, and I'm not exactly a farmer. Come back and get me when we have a shoemaker's party."

Grimb dropped his shoulders and frowned for a second. "It isn't all about the farmers. It's about the people here and is the most fruitful time of year. We should enjoy it and that includes you," he looked off into nowhere for a second and his smile returned, "You should at least get something to eat before you start your work. My daughter has been waiting for you to come back, you know. She wants to finish playing that board game you made her this spring."

Oswald's bitterness melted slightly with the slab of guilt that slid down his throat. He hadn't really talked to anyone in several days. He loved his work and rarely thought to leave it for socializing. It had probably been months since he had made a day to spend playing with the children or listening to the music the people often played.

The thought of the pile of work waiting for him slid into his mind again. He looked back again to the shed and hung his head for a second. "I really shouldn't. Tell Missy I will see her soon. I might be able to drop in later this afternoon, but I do need to get those orders filled before the farmers get back into the fields."

"Most of the farmers won't go back into the fields until spring. If you don't want to go, then don't, but from what I hear, you need not to spend so much time in the workshop."

"I—" Oswald dropped his shoulders, unable to think of anything to argue his point.

"Everyone here knows how important your work is, to you and to everyone around here. Hell," Grimb said, with a shrug, "I wouldn't be able to do my job so well without you. I've never found a shoemaker that can make a shoe fit as well or last as long as you can. You are the best at what you do, Oswald, but you can't make your job your life."

"Says the man who's only here three months out of the year," Oswald mumbled childishly.

"What was that?"

"I said," Oswald paused, "that you're right, but you also have a reason to keep your work from becoming your life." He pointed back up the hill to where Grimb had appeared. Another figure stood in the shadows, looking down at them.

Narish was tiny. She had dark hair, bright eyes, and a beautiful face. She was curvy and soft looking, but her figure was currently distorted with extra layers of clothing and a protruding pregnant belly. Grimb waved up at her, and Oswald could almost feel her smile back at her husband. Their connection was always strong; they were truly built for one another.

"Everything alright?" Grimb asked. She nodded down at him and motioned for him to come and join the festivities. He waved back at her again in acknowledgment and turned back to Oswald, "She is great, isn't she?"

"Lovely," Oswald agreed honestly. "She's always exceptionally kind to anyone and everyone."

"That she is," he smiled, "Missy is just like her too."

"When is the new baby due?"

"The last month of autumn," he said proudly.

"Looking forward to it," Oswald said, in a half-truth. He loved children, but never really was able to take care of or even be around babies. Children were easy; make a game and play until everyone is tired, take a break for lunch, and then find another game and play some more. Babies were loud and all too fragile; they were soft and quite simply too hard for him to understand.

Grimb seemed to drift off into thought before remembering why he was there.

"Come and join us, just for a minute. I'm not here very often. I have to leave next week and I probably won't be back for another month."

Oswald shook his head slowly, "Doesn't leaving all of the time bother you?"

"It does sometimes, but I have to. I run fast so I can get home sooner."

Oswald nodded, "I understand how that is. Get done what you have to so you can do what you want to," he pointed his thumb over his shoulder at the workshop.

Grimb sighed slightly. "Are you going to come and get something to eat at least?"

"I just ate, but I will try to come up in a few hours for lunch."

"Alright. If that's what you have to do." Grimb shrugged disappointedly and turned back up the hill with a sharp nod. "I expect to see you later then."

Oswald raised a hand in confirmation and trudged back down the hill.

The small shed was full of hooks and tools that hung from the walls as neatly as if they were on display. Tools with sharp rotating rims and thick cutters cradled themselves along the wall. A set of hinges that were used for rolling prints onto fabrics and skins sat detached from their counterparts. A bench near the door held a few wire instruments with varying designs and sizes as well as a small burnt-out torch. Several long blades, sharp and dull alike sat side by side on a shelf directly along the back wall, handles hanging just an inch off of the edge to reveal an assortment of numbers that accompanied each blade.

Oswald retrieved a dull blade with the number nineteen etched in the iron handle as well as a very short and well sharpened blade numbered four, piling them up in his arms. He took a final look around the shed, snatching up a rawhide hammer from the right wall and a small bucket of thick, dark, sloshing liquid before walking back out of the building. He kicked the door to the shed shut with his heel and walked around the corner. He stepped into the second wooden building through a high open archway.

The shop was crowded with counters and shallow dishes of water. The smell of hot leather greeted him in a comforting kind of familiarity as he stepped around to his work area.

A strip of dried skin hung from clips on the wall along the ceiling where the sun bleached out its imperfections. A large pile of treated leather was stacked neatly at the far end of a stained and worn U-shaped counter that wrapped around a swiveling chair in the center of the room. A dozen or so horsehair brushes lined a shelf just off to the side of the archway.

Oswald placed the rawhide mallet and the bucket of stain on the counter beside the pile of treated leather and laid the two blades on the opposite side. He went back to the archway and picked up a wide brush off of the shelf before returning to the work bench. He slid the chair up closer to the bend in the counter and took a seat.

The pile of leather slabs stuck together from the morning dew. It took a few minutes for him to work the pieces apart, laying them evenly along the entire surface of the bench. Slowly he stained the leather, brushing the dye as evenly as he could along every inch of each slab. After two coats on each side and a couple of hours of soaking, the leather was a crisp and clean color of auburn, ready to be scraped with the dull blade and worked into a soft and useable leather rather than its current stiff and unyielding form.

The heat of the day waned into late afternoon, and the weather outside was beginning to darken with storm clouds, thickening the air with moisture. A low and quiet thunder rumbled in the distance, crawling slowly across the mountains.

"Mr. Bawshade," A voice called from the path, "are you there?"

He smiled softly and set down the short cutting blade that he had been working with. He called back over his shoulder, "Yes, Laurie, I am," and grabbed a cloth from a drawer to his left. He dipped it in a pan of water and scrubbed at his dyed and sticky fingers with the wet cloth. He set the cloth down in a separate pan of water which almost immediately began to soak up the deep color of the dye.

He got up out of his chair, grimacing lightly at the stiffness in his legs from sitting for so long. He shook his left foot, trying to shake away the sleep in his muscles without success.

Footsteps gently shuffled through the leaves and undergrowth from the path. Laurie appeared around the edge of the archway and a wide smile slipped across her face. She was elegant, with long blonde hair pulled back in an abundance of braids, tied off with a strip of white silk. Her green eyes glinted with an unnatural kindness. She wore a fine and simple dress laced in soft shades of coral peaches and beige that distinguished her features.

She stepped in the shop and looked around at the mess before deciding that she didn't want to take the chance of staining her clothes and stepped back beneath the arch. She looked Oswald over lightly, taking in everything from his stained fingers to his messy hair. She grinned and said, "Good evening, Mr. Bawshade. How are you?"

"There is no need for formalities, Laurie," he pressed politely, returning the smile. "It's just Oswald, and I am doing quite well today, thank you. How is your father?"

"Oh," she said, as if remembering the reason that she had come, "he is much better. In fact, he asked me to come by and pick up his boots for him. He plans to be back in the fields by Sunday to clear the space for the chicken coop," she looked down at her purse, an old fashioned crimp with a silver string, and began searching around in it for a large gold-rimmed silver coin, "You do have them finished, don't you? He said that they should be ready by now."

"Yes, as a matter of fact, they are," Oswald said, turning away from her. He headed around to the back of the shop to where a large chest stood in waiting. He opened it and retrieved the high boots from within, admiring his own work and craftsmanship. He took a quick glance at the other pairs of shoes that lay within the trunk, awaiting their owners to take them. He stood up slowly and slid the lid back onto its latch. He inspected the boots quickly for the hundredth time and turned back to Laurie, holding them up for her to see.

They were stained dark brown and laced with black leather strips, strengthened with starch. They were made especially for farming work. The soles of the shoes were brown rubber, bought from the stock he had purchased as the Pewins headed south through the village earlier that year. His store of rubber was slowly diminishing. It would be a journey that would take couple of days to get more and he had been putting off the trip.

He smiled broadly at her and held them out for her to take. "I finished them yesterday morning," he said proudly, as they slid from his grip and into her arms. "Tell Keiosh that he may want to flex them for a day before he wears them for work, so they won't wear at his heals."

"I will," she said. She looked them over for a moment before adding casually, "They look really nice, by the way."

"Thank you very much," Oswald said, giving her an eloquent bow. "That means a lot, coming from you."

She blushed slightly and held out the gold-rimmed coin, which Oswald took, slowly looking over its symbols. He smiled at her again, unable to help himself, and slid the coin into his back pocket. He snapped his eyes back to the floor, realizing that he had been staring, and forced his attention back to what he had been doing previously, looking over the pattern that he had only just started to cut out.

"Well, I'll leave you to your work, then. Are—are you coming to the festival later? Dad's going to play the violin."

"I don't know. I would like to, yes—but—" Oswald stammered, fighting his force of will, "—I will surely try. I'll see if I can't find you if I get there."

"Alright then. Thanks, Mr. Bawshade." Laurie looked over the boots again and turned away from the shop.

"Call me Oswald," he called insistently after her as she walked down the path. He watched her carefully until she had vanished around the bend and forced himself to return to his work, though his mind drifted away to other things.

He returned to work slowly, paying close attention to the fine details of leatherworking.

Oswald blinked away the strain in his eyes and looked up from his workbench, dragging his mind away from the thoughts of what could be.

His work began to take shape, the beauty and perfection of exact cut sand stitches weaving into the fabric of time as it passed without his notice. Darkness had drifted beneath the canopy of trees and the moonlight could only just glimmer against the occasional patch of earth, but the gloomy haze of night was not the reason that he had stopped so suddenly.

He glanced up out of the open archway as a shadow crossed through his property. He froze for a moment, completely still in his seat.

The thought crossed his mind that he was seeing something that wasn't there. He thought too that the shadow could have been an animal of some kind but a feeling crept into his skin and he wasn't convinced. He watched it closely as it moved again and knew immediately that it wasn't just a trick of his mind.

Someone had just crept from the shadows of his home towards the tool shed, using the darkness as camouflage. The intruder looked thick and yet not too tall.

A falling tool from the shed echoed in the stillness and Oswald got up silently, picking up his large scraping knife as he headed to the front of the workshop.

He stepped to the side of the archway of the shop and looked over the surroundings quickly.

Everything else seemed still.

Quiet rummaging sounds and shuffles could be heard from beyond the door to the tool shed off to his left. The door was ajar and a figure could be seen moving, but the darkness veiled the identity of his thief.

Without thinking, Oswald strode quickly and deliberately to the door of the shed and slipped in behind the intruder, weapon in hand. The sudden action startled the man standing in front of him.

Oswald's heart sank coldly into his stomach.

The figure turned to face him and then stood upright, inching foot by foot until it was towering over him, nearly tripling the height that he had first judged him to be.

The goblin was massive with broad shoulders and an arched back that just kept his head from colliding with the ceiling of the workshop. Sharp cheekbones lined its face with the glimmer of angled knife like teeth. Its long hands were grasping something, but the object did not register in Oswald's overall picture of the beast.

Oswald felt his body lock up in fear. He had only heard stories of the Keernith goblins, and none of them were good.

The goblin curled back its lips in disgust and swiftly struck Oswald with an empty hand across the side of his head. The power behind the blow was enough to lift him up off of his feet and Oswald felt his body hit the ground before he had even felt the pain of the strike. Stars danced in front of his eyes, and he saw the goblin raise one of the picks from the wall and pull it over his head with its green face twisted. Oswald felt his mind blur before darkness swept his vision.

He was certain he was dead. He could feel the cold of the earth against his chest and the side of his face. A weight pressed him into the darkness, and his limbs felt numb and useless. He realized that he was not breathing, but after a moment of wordless thoughts Oswald took the most painful and difficult breath of his easy life.

His heartbeat pounded in his head. Dull knives raked at the inside of his skull and his body was cramped, pulsing with the struggled beats of his heart. He cried out and forced his eyes open.

He tried to move and felt a heaviness across his body, a weight that pinned him painfully against the ground. Through the shadowed haze of the darkness he could still see movement and he waited for another blow that would finish him.

He tried to crawl away and felt a bony hand on the ground beside him. He pulled his arm away from the long fingered green hand and realized that it was sitting still beside him. He trailed his eyes up the dark figure from the hand and realized that the heaviness pinning him down was a body lying across him.

Startled, he mustered the strength to force the figure off of him and saw that the movement had come from his right side. A man's face looked down at him with mingled surprise and pity.

Oswald looked at the man, having difficulty focusing on him through the pain and the darkness. He shook his head trying to clear away the fog and sat up, regretting his effort immediately.

"Who are you, elf?" the man demanded.

Oswald thought for a moment, and frowned, "Who are *you*?"

"I asked you first!"

"I live here," Oswald said, confused and slightly irritated, "This is my property. So, who are you?"

"I am the guy that just saved your stupid ass."

Oswald gingerly touched his head, feeling a sticky mass where he would usually find thick curls. He started to panic.

"That isn't yours. Relax." The man stood, though he was not much taller when standing than Oswald was while sitting on the ground. "Name's Nedtedrow."

"His?" Oswald asked, gesturing to the motionless goblin.

"No!" Nedtedrow said, looking offended. "That's my name. Aren't no goblins named Nedtedrow, genius. What's yours?"

"Oh, um," he closed his eyes and slowly he began gathering thousands of questions but pushed them aside, "I'm Oswald."

Nedtedrow snorted. "Really? Well, that isn't your fault, is it?" he put a firm hand on Oswald's shoulder and helped lift him from the ground, though Oswald wavered dangerously on the spot. Nedtedrow shook his head. "You've got the balance of a one-legged frog, Oswart. It is a wonder you can walk at all on those lanky things."

Oswald steadied himself on his feet and gritted his teeth. He caught glimpses of the chaos of the tool shed through the dark as he rocked back and forth on his heels, his head swimming.

"I'm staying with you tonight."

"Why?" Oswald asked more sharply than he had meant to.

"I just took out a goblin four times my size, and I don't have a place to stay. You owe me."

"Fair enough," Oswald mumbled, still wiping the fuzz from his thoughts. "You can sleep in the guest room for tonight."

Without a word of thanks, Nedtedrow turned and walked out of the tool shed. He went around the large tree and towards the house shaking out his shoulders every now and to loosen up his joints.

Oswald shakily and tenderly took a few steps towards the house, feeling the weak tremor in his knees. He followed the stranger into his own home with questions burning in his head.

Chapter Four

There were too many questions, no answers, and no current will to pursue them. Oswald could barely focus on his reflection in the mirror or the water drawn from the hot spring in his tub.

He was matted and smeared with a deep purple substance that he assumed to be the blood of the goblin. The blood was caked with dirt and pieces of early autumn leaves. Dark circles ringed beneath his bloodshot eyes, and a small split in the side of his head had clotted already. He could almost see through the paleness of his face.

He picked up a wash cloth and dipped it into the warm water before dabbing at the small cut on his head. Once it was clean, it didn't look as bad as it had at first glance. He rinsed out the rag and finished cleaning up the clots of odd purple blood.

He hardly remembered going to bed, but his dreams were filled with blood and large dark figures in the night.

A crashing sound woke him late in the morning.

He rolled out of bed with difficulty. His body ached and his head lightly throbbed. He walked to the kitchen and was startled to see that Nedtedrow had made himself at home so quickly. Something was cooking on the stove, and there were bowls and food laid out almost everywhere.

Nedtedrow was standing on a chair at the stove, prodding the sizzling contents of the pan with a wooden spoon. It sizzled and he grabbed a biscuit from the plate on the counter and stuffed the entire thing into his mouth.

Oswald took in a deep breath and stepped into the hurricane that once was an organized and clean kitchen.

"You're still here," Oswald said amusedly, looking over the mess and already trying to figure out how to fix it. He leaned on the doorframe.

"F'ere a prob'em wit tat?" he asked through the biscuit that was forcing his cheeks to pouch out on either side.

"No, not at all. I actually wanted to figure out exactly what happened last night. It doesn't make sense."

"Sur' it does."

"Then explain it."

"It's a long story, really," Nedtedrow said, swallowing away the pieces of biscuit in his mouth, "And what makes you think that I wouldn't stick around for breakfast?"

"It is just that I've never seen anyone like you around here before. I didn't really expect you to stick around."

"Like me?" Nedtedrow asked with a raised eyebrow.

"Yeah, no one comes through here but the Pewins and the elves that live nearby. I—well, to be quite blunt, I haven't seen anyone of your particular…stature before." Oswald pushed himself away from the doorframe and stepped into his disheveled kitchen to stand beside the cluttered table.

"Well, that's what war does, elf. It forces people to move further and further out. I won't be the last non-native to pass through here, I assure you."

"But we don't have anything to do with the war here," Oswald said casually, crossing his arms across his chest and lowering his brow seriously, "We're secluded and peaceful. This land has been ours for, well, a thousand years or more. We aren't a concern to anyone."

"Not for long anyway," Nedtedrow snorted.

"What do you mean?" Oswald asked as he uncrossed his arms and stepped closer to Nedtedrow slightly taken aback by the sudden change in the tone in his voice.

"This place won't exist if things don't change. This whole town is going to vanish," Nedtedrow looked away bitterly and shook his head as he added salt to the pan he was cooking in, "I've seen it happen before."

"We aren't involved," Oswald insisted. "This whole war is about who rightfully owns the throne of Azar. We are four weeks away from there on horseback. It's too far for us to worry about. Besides, it's a civil war."

Nedtedrow nearly choked on another bite of biscuit. He coughed and his coughing turned into laughter. It was a hard, forceful, mocking laughter which sprayed crumbs across the counter. Oswald's brow crumpled disapprovingly.

"Am I missing something?"

"If you really think that's all there is to this war," Nedtedrow said, swallowing what was left of the crumbs in his mouth, "then you are a fool."

"This isn't about the throne?" Oswald asked curiously.

"Not exactly."

"Not exactly, or no?"

"It just isn't about the throne. That was a child's tiff. That was over years ago," Nedtedrow eyed another biscuit but seemed to decide against it, turning his attention back to the cooking food in the pan.

"Grimb hasn't said anything about that," Oswald said, looking to the table beside him and brushing away a small pile of crumbs and watching them flip off the varnished wood to the floor.

"Who the living hell is Grimb and why do I care?" Nedtedrow said, sounding irritated at the change of subject.

"He's the messenger for the area," Oswald frowned.

"For the area?" Nedtedrow asked with a raised eyebrow. "If you are this poorly misinformed, then I wouldn't expect anyone else that lives 'in the area' to know any better."

"We aren't hermits. We would have heard something before now."

"Apparently not," he retorted with a derogatory sneer, "since you're drawing a blank for the last twelve years of history."

"Then what is the war about?" Oswald asked trying to push away the frustration of Nedtedrow's sullen attitude.

"This isn't about the throne of Azar. Venhow has that already. He was crowned king before any of this war started. This is about everything else."

"Everything?" Oswald asked incredulously, "That's hard to believe. I don't think that there is anyone who really wants everything."

Nedtedrow tipped the pan of food and turned the mixture as he stared off into his own mind. He took in a deep breath, "He does."

"That's impossible. No one can have everything."

"Impossible is what he likes, and it hasn't slowed him down yet." Nedtedrow sighed heavily, looking grim for a moment. "His army is moving like a swarm of locusts. He already has more than most people thought he would ever get."

"How?" Oswald asked trying to understand the situation.

"He has no problem killing anyone who thinks that he doesn't have the right to rule. Everything he has," Nedtedrow said slowly, turning his eyes away from the cooking food to Oswald and studying his face closely as he spoke, "he took from small areas and innocent people like your little place here."

"He shouldn't be that big of a problem though," Oswald said, letting his head roll with questions. "No army would think that he should own it all."

"You really don't get it, do you?" Nedtedrow shook his head disbelievingly and stirred the meat frying in the pan.

"I guess I don't." Oswald pulled out a chair and was disappointed to see a pile of dishes sitting in his usual place. He put them on the table and took a seat.

"Venhow isn't just a king. He's a sorcerer, and a damn good one," he said, shifting his weight on the chair from one foot to the other uneasily.

"So? I'm sure there are lots of other wizards out there that could do the same thing."

"No, there isn't. Magic is genetic and it's dying out. All sorcerers anymore are human, and most of the humans want to share the power that Venhow is collecting. That's why they all support him."

"So, what then?" Oswald asked disbelievingly, "They think that he's going to share the land that he takes or power over it?"

"Don't know. Anyway, it doesn't matter. They want to be on the winning side," Nedtedrow frowned darkly, looking over his shoulder at Oswald, "Guess who's winning."

"They aren't winning. The war has stayed in the west," Oswald said, sitting up a little straighter in his chair.

"Why do you think I am here?" Nedtedrow said sharply, turning to face Oswald his face disbelieving, "Why do you suppose that a Keernith was sneaking around your secluded little village? The war found you, whether or not you understand the seriousness of it."

"I thought you were just a traveler."

"Technically, I am. I was on my way to Gommorn."

"Gommorn?" Oswald said, trying to figure out how he ended up here, "That's over a hundred and eighty miles from here. What are you going there for?"

"Are you kidding me?!" Nedtedrow looked suddenly angry. "There is no way I'm still that far away!"

"Maybe you got turned around," Oswald suggested.

"I don't get lost!" Nedtedrow spat, rubbing at his forehead as he tried to figure out why he was still so far away.

"Apparently you do if that's where you were headed."

He gritted his teeth and threw the spoon into the pan with a loud clatter, "Bolzar said we were only a day away. That bastard was going to make me run another three days straight!"

"Who's Bolzar?" Oswald said curiously, looking up at the sudden outburst uncomfortably.

Nedtedrow paused for a minute. "He was a friend of mine. We were traveling together."

"Where is he?"

"Dead." Nedtedrow's shame and anger deepened, and he picked the spoon back up and violently stabbed at the pan. The contents jumped into the air and were now beginning to smell vaguely burnt. "The Keernith goblin in your shed had friends and they were quicker than I was." Bolzar's look of betrayal flittered across Nedtedrow's memory.

"Oh," Oswald looked up suddenly and his stomach churned, "I'm so sorry!" he watched sadly as Nedtedrow stared intently into the pan of cooking food with a distant expression.

Nedtedrow sighed and looked towards the wall, "Me too."

"Why would they attack you?" Oswald asked gently.

"We were from Saffermine."

"So you're a Nelwin?"

"Wow, you figured that out really quick." Nedtedrow rolled his eyes. "Venhow's army flooded through our city and captured all of the leaders and strategy keepers for the races and the generals of the armies that fight against him."

"You're a Nelwin leader? Or are you one of the generals?"

"Neither. I was taken by accident. I was in the wrong place at the wrong time, but they found that I wasn't invaluable, which is why I'm still alive." Nedtedrow picked up the pan of food and flipped the entire contents onto a large glass dish, not bothering to do anything with the dirty pan. He climbed down off of the chair with the plate of food and joined Oswald at the table, dividing the mildly burnt breakfast between the two of them.

"Thanks," Oswald said, looking at the food. He hoped it tasted better than it looked.

"Not a problem."

Oswald took a bite and was surprised. It was good. He shoveled down a third of the plate before letting the questions continue to flood out of his mouth. "So how did you end up here?"

"We were in the dungeons of Azar for a while," Nedtedrow said, "then transferred to a holding camp in Tetrach. We were interrogated, evaluated, and most of us were killed," he stabbed a slab of meat with his fork as he spoke, "A few prisoners, including Bolzar and myself, escaped about four days ago. I don't know where our other companion went."

"How'd you escape?"

"We took advantage of a once in a lifetime opening."

Oswald waited for more of a response, but it was quickly clear that he would get no better answer than what was just given. "So," Oswald thought aloud, "you're the reason the goblin was here. He was looking for you?"

"Yeah," Nedtedrow said, not looking up from his food and shoveling in a large bite. "He a'tchully found me. I should t'ank you. Your timing is incre'ble."

"You were in my tool shed?" Oswald asked as he fished a small bite onto his fork and stared at it for a second.

"Yeah," he said shortly, working the large bite of food around in his mouth thoughtfully.

"Why?"

"I was hiding, obviously," he took another bite of what looked like a meat covered noodle and continued, "He had me cornered under the shelf when you came in. You aren't much of a hero, though, are you? Seizing up like that?"

"He wasn't exactly what I was expecting. I thought it was a Pewin looking for tools to pawn at the market."

"You should have seen your face," Nedtedrow snickered.

"How did you kill him, anyway?" Oswald asked, doing his best to ignore the mocking expression.

Nedtedrow shrugged arrogantly and smiled, "I put a pick in the back of his head."

"He was almost ten feet tall!" Oswald argued, "I couldn't have even reached his head. There's no way you could have done that."

"Go see for yourself."

"I think I will." Oswald took a final bite before getting up and heading for the front door.

Nedtedrow stood up quickly, a sharp flash of alarm across his face. "You know what? We'll both go have a look in a minute. How does that sound?"

"Fine, meet me out there."

"Hey, wait, I'll go with you now. Slow down." Nedtedrow rushed ahead of Oswald towards the door, threw it open and scuttled outside.

"What's your hurry? He's dead, isn't he?"

"Of course he's dead!" Nedtedrow called back sharply. "I just remembered that I left some things in there that I have to get," he vanished around the corner of the building and was down the hill and into the tool shed before Oswald had the chance to respond.

Oswald could hear him in a frantic scramble, and curiosity got the best of him. He glanced around the corner and a strange and grizzly sight greeted him along with the powerful stench of blood and the beginnings of decay. The Keernith's body lay sprawled awkwardly and rigid on the ground. A large pick that was rusted with years of misuse was now neatly burrowed into the back of his head, and at least ten tools were scattered like confetti around the floor of the shed. With closer inspection, the back of the Keernith's knees were cleanly gouged of tendons with a single clean cut. Nedtedrow was right. The goblin lay in a shallow pool of congealed, dark purple blood.

Nedtedrow was on his knees in the middle of the mess, quickly picking up scattered items from the ground and tossing them into a unique looking box.

Oswald spotted a glass figurine on the ground as Nedtedrow scooped it up into his hand, "That looks familiar, where did you get that?"

"I bought it!" Nedtedrow replied hurriedly. He reached for another item on the ground which glittered subtly. Oswald recognized it without hesitation and dove for it. He caught the chain and snatched it out of Nedtedrow's hand. Carefully, he stepped out of the tool shed and into the fresh air where the late morning sunlight was inching closer to mid-day. He looked closer at the figurine. The scuff on the fairy's wing confirmed its identity.

"This is my mother's necklace! You stole this from my house!"

"I did no such thing!" he argued, pointing to the goblin. "I was keeping it safe from him!"

"You little liar! He was after *you*, not my things. What else did you take from me?"

"Nothing," he said, gathering the box of trinkets up into his arms like treasure.

"You stole that box, too! It's Narish's. I recognize it. You looted the entire town, didn't you?"

"You keep accusing me of stealing things. You should be nicer to me. I saved your life, remember?" Nedtedrow kicked the goblin lying face down at his feet. He scowled up at Oswald and stepped outside the shed.

"You said yourself just an hour ago that it was an even trade. He would have killed you if I hadn't showed up. Isn't that right?"

"Well yes, but I could just as easily have snuck out while he killed you."

"You wouldn't have gotten very far."

"Yes, but—" Nedtedrow paused. He looked up at Oswald, whose face was distorted with shadows, accusation, and anger. Nedtedrow crumpled his expression into a thoughtful scrutiny. "You remind me of someone."

"Don't change the subject, you weasel. Give me the rest of my things and return everything else that you took."

"Hey, you have your necklace back. Stop attacking me. I didn't take anything else from you or anyone else. This is mine. Yes, I took the box, I needed something to put my things in, but I promise you I left something of equal value in its place."

"What did you leave?"

"Just trust me. It's worth what I took." Nedtedrow locked eyes with Oswald and after a tense few moments, Oswald seemed convinced, if only just enough. His expression softened lightly but the similarity of his face did not ebb from Nedtedrow's mind. "You really do remind me of someone."

"Who?"

"I don't know. I can't seem to place it. I don't like it, whatever it is," he paused again, "Do you have a brother?"

"No. I'm an only child."

"Who was your father?"

Oswald shrugged. "I don't know. It was just me and my mother."

"What was her name?"

"My mother? Emily Bawshade."

"Nope. Doesn't ring a bell." Nedtedrow stared for a few long seconds, tracing the lines of Oswald's face with his eyes.

"What?" Oswald asked.

Nedtedrow shook his head. "Never mind. Maybe you just have one of those faces," He turned away with the treasure box in his arms. He started back to the house, glancing at Oswald twice along the way. "We should get moving."

"What?"

Without responding, Nedtedrow vanished into the house.

Oswald followed, only mildly disconcerted. He sighed as he reentered the kitchen, noting the bulging mass of dishes on the countertops and the crumbs that were strewn throughout. It took a moment of scrutiny before he realized that Nedtedrow wasn't there. Begrudgingly, he turned from the mess, willing himself not to turn around and clean the filth behind him.

He loosened his grip on the fairy necklace and looped the chain around his neck, so that the fairy rested peacefully on his breastbone. "Nedtedrow?" he went into the hallway, noticing the small drips of goblin blood on the carpet, no doubt from what had drizzled off of his clothing the night before. He cringed.

Oswald looked through the living room which had tracks of mud through it but otherwise was empty and untouched. He moved through the house, listening and turned down the hall and peered into rooms as he went. The guest room not only was mildly disheveled but also was void of the Nelwin hurricane from Saffermine.

Oswald's room was the only one left unchecked.

"Nedtedrow, I don't want you in there!" he said forcefully. He looked around the corner and was irritated to see his room had been disorganized and peeled away from its usual nature. He spotted Nedtedrow elbow-deep in his dresser, throwing clothing into a bag taken from the closet.

"How exactly am I supposed to pack if I am not in this room?" Nedtedrow asked, heaping another armful of clothes into his satchel.

"You thief! Stop packing my things! These are *my* things!"

"I know," Nedtedrow said, rolling his eyes. "What do you want? To be naked or dirty all the way to Gommorn?"

"I am not going to Gommorn!"

"Yeah, you are," he said, matter-of-factly. He stood on the tip of his toes to gather the rest of what he could from the top drawer.

"Quit packing my things!" Oswald shouted. "*You* are going to Gommorn, not me, and you are not going to take my clothes with you."

"Look," Nedtedrow said, zipping up the bag, "if you don't go, you and half of the people in this town will be dead within two days."

"What are you talking about?!" Oswald shouted snatching a book out of Nedtedrow's hand as he started rummaging through another drawer.

"The Keernith."

"What about him?"

"The death of a Keernith guard won't go unnoticed for long. They'll come looking for him," Nedtedrow started throwing more items out of the drawer looking for anything useful as Oswald continued to occasionally snatch things out of his hands, "and when they find his body in your shed, they will kill you. And then they'll take out their anger on this town."

"Stay out of my stuff," Oswald snapped, kicking the drawer shut and nearly catching Nedtedrow's fingers in the wood as the drawer slammed into place, "And I didn't kill that goblin!"

"No," Nedtedrow agreed pulling his hands away from the drawers with his eyes narrowed up at Oswald, "but that's because you're a pansy."

"I was startled," Oswald protested.

"You startled yourself into a situation where you would have died," he said firmly, turning out of his reach and looking underneath the bed for something that might be useful to pack.

"So did you," Oswald said, reaching down and jerking Nedtedrow out from under his bed, "and my people shouldn't die because you decided to ransack the village."

"That isn't the point," Nedtedrow said desperately, a vein standing out brightly against his temple. He pulled away from Oswald again, pulling his shirt out of his hands as he turned to another set of drawers, looking back at Oswald firmly, "They would blame you all the same and wouldn't care who really did it. And anyway, this little village would make a great outpost for their assault on Cauldridge. They would take it anyway, just a few years earlier than they would have."

"What if they never find out what happened to the guard?"

Nedtedrow opened a drawer and once again began throwing items around the room, "They will."

"I'll bury the body, then," Oswald decided. "I'd have to get rid of it anyway. I can't just leave him in my shed."

"It wouldn't matter," Nedtedrow insisted as he moved on to the next drawer, "Their trackers would find the body and then trace it back to where it came from."

"Maybe I would have enough time to—"

"It wouldn't even buy you a full day."

"Well, maybe I don't need a full day," Oswald said, fueled by the increasing sense of determination and speed at which Nedtedrow was packing, "I just need a few hours so that I can…do something, anything. I can't leave my home."

"You won't have a home when they get here," Nedtedrow said, grabbing something out of the bottom of a drawer and opening the bag to stuff it inside.

"What if I could stop them?" Oswald asked trying to rack his head for answers

"You couldn't even stop *one*, elf," Nedtedrow said sharply, standing up and opening his hands to his sides, "How do you expect to save your entire village from ten or twenty?"

"I'll think of something," Oswald insisted.

"If you don't have a plan now," he shook his head and looked around the room quickly, "then it won't do you any good to have one later. Trust me."

"You're a terrible cynic."

"No, I'm realistic," Nedtedrow said, in a lower tone, "Optimism gets you killed."

Oswald stood in the doorway and watched Nedtedrow continue to shuffle around the room, looking for more things to shove into the bag, which was now full to bursting at the hem.

Oswald had not yet thought of the consequences of the body which lay in his shed, merely of the shock that had come with it and the realization that—in the real world—horror was growing into a war for all life within his sight, as well as those which were beyond the furthest reaches of his travel. He thought of the town and his heart grew densely cold.

"I can't leave these people here. We need to get everyone out."

Nedtedrow stuffed another item from the bedside table into the bag, now fighting for a place to cram it into. He stood up, heaving the bag up onto the bed and looking solemn. "You can't get them all to leave. This village will die, and there isn't anything that you can do. We have to leave now!"

"I'm not going to leave them without even a warning."

"They won't believe you."

"They have to."

"I've watched a dozen villages just like this one die in a matter of hours," Nedtedrow shouted, his eyes burning into Oswald's, "There will be *nothing* left when they get here! I'm sorry, but there is nothing that you can do to stop it now."

"Watch me," Oswald said, determined. He grabbed the overstuffed rucksack and shouldered it. The strap on the bag dug into his shoulder with the weight of its contents.

He turned back around and tore through the house. He shoved open the door and left his home, standing just outside the house under the shade of the large tree nearby.

Oswald looked around. The sky was beginning to fill with clouds, spotty grey and white forms which were emerging from the west. He tried to smother the rush of panic that hit him as he turned to face the village. He wasn't sure what he was going to tell them.

A sound far in the distance echoed into the hills. It was strange and unrecognizable, sounding like an injured griffin's caw, though he knew that wasn't right. He thought about stopping at Grimb and Narish's home, but then a thought came to him and his stomach dropped sadly.

They wouldn't listen.

He swallowed his uneasiness and a face flittered across his mind's eye. Laurie. He should start with Laurie and Kieosh. They would believe him, or at least they would give him a place to start.

The path to the village was a dirt strip lined with the occasional pair of marking stones, which increased in number the closer he got to the village center. The first of the houses came into view over the second hill, and the village lay just beyond it. It was a small cottage that was built with white limestone and oak. It was quiet, and the occupants were not there, so Oswald quickly passed by it.

Before long, he reached the village. All of the homes faced a natural spring in the center, surrounded by wildflowers that formed a perfect circle. The heart of the village had become the place for festivities, harvest rituals, and celebrations. Few people were outdoors; the Sal-win Festival had been the day before, and sleep always followed it in abundance.

A child sat by the spring, her feet in the water as she peeled the petals from one of the pink rosary flowers that grew wild around it. Her little dress was damp at the bottom of the lace hems. Oswald thought to himself of the days when he played in the spring as a child, and he was suddenly remorseful, knowing that he would probably not get to see the spring again.

"Tina, princess," Oswald said, as calmly as he could, "you need to go home. Tell your mom and dad that they need to start packing. Oswald said so, okay? Tell them I will be by to explain. Can you do that for me?"

Tina looked up at him with strings of hair in her face, her smile gone. She nodded twice and dropped the remains of the flower to the ground beside her.

"Go now," he said, and she promptly pulled her feet out of the spring and made her way in the opposite direction.

He wondered to himself if she would actually know what to tell her parents, or if she would remember to tell them anything at all. As he passed by the spring, he thought of her and the fear she would endure so young. She did not leave his mind until he had followed the path beyond the home of Narish to the end of the road where a familiar house replaced his somber thoughts.

Laurie's home was just south of the village. It was one of the largest homes, lying on the outskirts by the small wheat field which fed the town through winter. The house was well decorated with ferns and flowers. A rich color of mahogany with stone-lined walls and windows made up a house twice the size of Oswald's.

He could hear music from the open window, and he was relieved by the sound.

He sighed heavily, trying to relieve the tension in his expression and the weight in his heart. The knock on the door seemed hollow, though the sound was quickly stifled.

Laurie answered the door in a casual, soft blue dress that brushed against her ankles. Her hair was up in a bun today, high on her head and decorated with ribbon as usual, though today the ribbon was midnight blue. She looked surprised as her eyes fell on him, and she raised an eyebrow at the rucksack hanging on his shoulder.

"Mr. Bawshade?" she asked, looking over Oswald's shoulder at the stillness in the woods. "What brings you here?"

"It's Oswald," he said, much more seriously and sharply than he had meant to. "There's a problem."

Chapter five

Laurie looked suddenly concerned and stepped back away from the door.

Oswald walked into the foyer.

She shut the door behind him and led him down a narrow and cluttered hallway, decorated with an assortment of antiques placed on the wall in a random pattern.

They turned the corner at the end of the hall and into the den area where a large table was set with a new linen and surrounded with six ornate chairs. She offered him a seat and he took a moment to respond, wondering how much time he had and how to address the problem.

He removed the rucksack from his shoulder and placed it in one of the empty chairs, taking a seat next to it. He looked down at the table for a minute as Laurie took a seat across from him, concern etched deeply into her face. "What's happened Oswald? Why have you packed your things?"

Oswald sighed again. He pulled his eyes away from the intricate wood grains of the polished table and met her eyes. It was quiet for a while. Oswald gripped the fairy around his neck before stumbling through a recount of the night before, strained and blubbering with few sentences uninterrupted with long strings of silence. When he was finished she stared at him, the worry replaced with disbelief and mistrust.

"We have to leave the village today. If we don't ... everyone will die." Oswald looked away from her face unable to keep eye contact with her. The longer he had continued to talk, the deeper her frown had creased. She clenched a fist and stood from the table.

"You should leave. I want nothing to do with this," Laurie said, gesturing towards the door. "I won't have you lie to me and I will not be tricked into leaving with you."

"No, you don't understand!" Oswald said, taken aback and suddenly angry, "This isn't a joke. I'm not trying to trick you. I don't want to leave either but if we don't, then we won't get the chance to."

"You're ridiculous. The Keernith are nowhere near here. The war is locked in the west and the Nelwins aren't fighters. They are knowledge seekers, not warriors. Read a book sometime."

"Books don't have the answer to everything and apparently things change quickly under pressure," his heart leapt frightfully, "And I suppose people do too. This isn't something I would believe if I didn't know it firsthand."

"I never expected you to be like this Mr. Bawshade. You always seemed like a nice stable hardworking person, but I guess you never really know someone. You're a liar and I want you out of this house." she flushed red high in her cheeks and when Oswald did not make a move towards the door she shouted. "Get out!"

The music that had been all the while drifting throughout the house in a gentle flow stopped with a tuneless screech. Oswald picked up his rucksack from the chair and put it back on his shoulder.

Kieosh stepped into the room with a slight limp and stern face, violin gripped in his left hand. His large white eyebrows were knitted together and the lines in his face were deep and unsettling. His winter blue eyes were seeing through him deep into the wall beyond. "Laurie what's wrong? ... Oswald? What's going on here?"

"He won't leave," Laurie said flatly.

Kieosh spotted Oswald's bag and his eyebrows slid even tighter towards one another, "What are you up to boy?"

"Sir I need to get everyone out of the village. The war has come closer. The Keernith are going to destroy our village in the next day or so. We all need to leave."

Laurie's face softened slightly and Oswald couldn't tell if she had begun to believe him or if the support from her father had calmed her. She opened her mouth to speak but said nothing more than a soft 'no' before again drawing into the silence.

"You have to believe me. We don't have enough time to squabble over what you believe or what you want. We have to do this. We don't have a choice." Oswald locked eyes with Kieosh and he seemed unresponsive to his plea, his expression did not change and Laurie had resolved to stare at her father for guidance.

"What makes you think that you're right?" Keiosh grunted.

"I have a dead Keernith in my tool shed. It's a long story, but I was attacked. It was following a Nelwin and long story short, we have to leave or they'll come back for revenge and we will all die."

"I don't know what you are thinking, but they aren't going to hurt us. We haven't done anything."

"That's what I said at first," Oswald said, lowering his eyes.

"What changed your mind?" Keiosh said, looking bored. Laurie crossed her arms and pursed her lips obviously waiting for the absurd conversation to end.

"I was there."

"Is anyone else going?" Keiosh asked firmly.

"No. I haven't gotten to anyone else yet, I came here first," Oswald readjusted the strap against his shoulder nervously, "I hope everyone will."

"Not likely."

"Please, Kieosh," Oswald begged, "Believe me."

"Whether or not I believe you doesn't matter," he shook his head and the age lines in his face deepened, "We aren't leaving."

"If you don't you'll die," Oswald stressed looking around and trying to find a way to convince them

"You talk a lot about death for such a young man. You also know nothing about the nature of death or the nature of our people. All you do is work and sleep. It isn't natural," Keiosh eyed the bag over Oswald's shoulder disapprovingly, "What is natural, is death. I was born here and for whatever reason, I will die here and be comfortable doing so."

"Please, in all respect, Sir, I suggest that you leave, if not for you than for your daughter." Oswald's eyes burned into Keiosh's and they locked there for several bitterly long moments swelling with unspoken disagreement.

The old man's tired face hardened and he sighed. Without answering one way or the other, he turned away and limped back to the room from which he came. Only a moment after Kieosh vanished the music resumed its tune, though a bit louder than before.

"You have your answer. Leave." Laurie turned to the hallway as well, waiting at the doorway for Oswald to follow. He shifted the bag on his shoulder and felt heaviness in his chest and found it difficult to breathe properly. As he passed an open window he tried to breath in the fresh air to reassure him that everything would work out in the following hours. It was then that he noticed a familiar stench in the air but was unable to place it.

He followed Laurie to the front door pleading her with his eyes to believe him. She opened the door and they both heard the same noise in the same instant. A scratching howl that seemed uncomfortably close to the hills in which the village lay. Oswald recognized the sound as the same cry he heard leaving the house just a couple of hours before.

It was much closer.

His heart leapt into his chest when it was followed by a blood curdling scream in the distance and then a shout, "Oswart!" he looked around quickly and Laurie suddenly looked frightened, her eyes on the pathway leading from the village. Nedtedrow scrambled over the top of the hill nearly tripping over his own feet as he slid down to where Oswald stood with Laurie.

"It's gone! We have to leave now!" Nedtedrow shouted in a panic.

"What's gone?" Oswald asked, looking around for something obvious to be missing. There was nothing.

"The Keernith's gone!" he said franticly.

"What? How?" Oswald turned his attention now to the woods, suddenly very conscious of the familiar scent of the goblin's flesh and the new sound that had been growing steadily nearer.

"I don't know, but I'm leaving!"

"Wait just a second, we're coming with you." Oswald looked at Laurie. Wide eyed she just stared into the horizon like a doll, frozen in a moment of absent thought.

"I'm not waiting. I value my life too much." Nedtedrow said, as he readjusted the treasure box beneath his arm and ran past Laurie's house into the wheat fields. He vanished into the high field of mature wheat and was heading directly towards Gommorn, away from the approaching sounds.

"Laurie, we have to leave now. Please, I can't just leave you here to be killed. Please!" Oswald begged now sounding desperately fearful.

She looked around ashen and stunned and finally nodded.

"Okay," she said weakly, "Let me get my things."

"I don't think we have time. We have to go now." he reached for her arm and she shrank away from him just enough to be out from his reach.

"I need clothes," she said, turning back into the house quickly, growing paler as the seconds passed. She shut the door, if only partially as she swept inside. Oswald could hear her rummaging within the house. The shuffling from within was quickly overtaken by a deafening howl, now so close that he jumped at the sound.

He looked to the top of the hill and he felt his heart stop cold in his chest. A tracker wolf, larger than any wild beast he had ever seen crested the hill and leered down at him with eyes as brightly gold as the sun. Its grey and white coat was lightly matted with what looked like tar and blood though it was patterned evenly across its body. Its large brow was marked with a symbol that seemed to be cut into the animal's fur, bearing a circle with an intricate and indistinct pattern.

It snarled down at him, poised with its shoulders arched and its teeth barred. Oswald stepped back quickly towards the door, reaching behind him to push it open, unwilling to let his eyes leave the tracker's. It snarled darkly and leapt from its place on the hill, bounding down the dirt path with ease.

Oswald turned around and ran the few feet to the doorway and dove into the house. He grabbed the door handle and tried to slam it shut. He quickly noticed that there was something in the way of the doors latch and strained against it.

He pushed harder on the frame and saw the snout of the beast creeping into the house through the gap in the door. The tracker snorted and wedged in a little further, its foul breath creeping in before it. Its lip shoved upwards against the bridge of its muzzle, revealing its teeth and their massive size.

Oswald felt the bag at his shoulder fall out of place, sliding down his arm. He dropped the bag and put more force against the wood of the door. The tracker snarled and a long string of bloody saliva dripped from its white fangs.

In a panic he drew up all of his strength and pressed his weight against the door more forcefully, pushing off the wall behind him with his feet for more support. The beast snarled and

Oswald could see that the door was pinching the trackers snout in the small space.

Unsure of what else he could do, he brought a tight fist down on the top of its exposed nose repeatedly until he felt it retreat and hurriedly latched the door shut.

Before he had thought of what he was doing, he felt himself locking the door, hoping that the small bolt would hold against the animal. There were no sounds outside that he could make out through the door but he knew that it still lingered beyond the mere inch of oak that separated them.

Laurie came around the corner; her arms full of clothing that were bunched up into her arms like a small mountain. She stared at him, her face was an ashen grey and her eyes seemed to dart from one corner of the room to the other.

"Why aren't you still outside?"

"Trackers are out there. I don't know how we are going to get out." Oswald backed away from the door letting his eyes drift back to the latch several times as he searched for answers.

"What's a tracker?" she asked shakily.

"It's a *very* big wolf."

"We're trapped?" she looked weak and for a second Oswald thought that she was going to faint. He shook his head trying to reassure her and trying to keep her from fainting.

"No. We aren't trapped. We'll get out, I'm just not sure how yet." It took him a few moments listening intently to the sounds outside before he realized that the music within the house had stopped, but Kieosh had not reappeared. He backed into the hallway, his eyes still flickering to the door.

Another sound, much different from the Trackers howl, shook the ground at their feet. It was a deep thundering sound coming from the direction of the village circle. He had never heard anything like the sound before. It was like the roar of high winds mixed with the crackle of thunder.

Laurie swiveled on the spot looking at each room with horror.

"The back door," she said, with a revelation, "Maybe the back door." she rushed past him and into the den where she too vanished into unknown rooms. It was only a moment later that she ran back to the hall, leaving a trail of fallen clothing behind her and a rigid fear in her eyes. "Something is gnawing on the back door."

Oswald went back to the front door and unlocked it. If the tracker was at the back door, surely it would be preoccupied and the front could go unnoticed. He quietly opened the door a crack and peered out. He could see nothing, but his vision was limited. The smell of smoke lingered outside and he pulled the door open a bit further. Another tracker stared at them angrily from the woods, guarding the building.

He dared to open the door another inch and the other tracker lowered its head, eyes still locked on him, hair raised and ears laid back flat against its skull. It barred its teeth and launched from its hiding place towards the house. Oswald slammed the door shut again and locked it in time to feel the animal's weight thunder against the door with a wood splintering crack. Its claws were scratching on the wooden frame above his head on impact and sank to the ground as it began pacing before the door.

He looked back over his shoulder and felt all of his ideas fall out of his head. He looked down to his bag and picked it up off the ground, throwing it back over his shoulder as his eyes searched the room.

It was a moment of anxious thought before they heard shouting from the town, screams that pierced the air like cold daggers. He looked towards the town though he knew he was unable to see it through the wall. Laurie looked suddenly less like fainting and seemed more alert. She dropped her clothing and ran around the hall to the next room over. Oswald followed.

A window was on the far end of the bedroom and the two of them stared out in shock.

The hills were clouded with smoke, dark and heavy, hanging above them in the air like an ominous cloud. Narish's home was nearest and was not only on fire but roaring so violently that bits of the walls were being thrown away from the building's structure with unimaginable force. Pieces of the building were landing yards from their original place, charred and smoldering. Beyond that there were mounds of orange flames and debris so thick that only a few homes could even be seen.

A tall figure emerged from behind what was left of Narish's home. It was hunched and lanky with green flesh that was hidden by thick coats of soot. Its armor was tarnished and dirty but still caught in the light of the bright light of the fires.

The Keernith leered in their direction and picked up a piece of the burning home beside him. Flames still licked up what could be recognized as a piece of windowsill which he held like a club in his long gnarled fingers.

Oswald grabbed Laurie's shoulder and pulled her quickly away from the window. They exchanged looks, hers apologetic and his concerned. He pulled her back out of the room and to the kitchen which he found by accidently turning the corner a door too early.

The kitchen was nearly pristine though the image of Narish's home flittered in his mind's eye and he saw what would soon remain of this room, charred and undistinguishable from any other room in the house, or in the village.

He thought for a moment of his own home and he felt vaguely ill. Surely it too was on fire and probably would be burnt to the ground without the means for rescue. He could see his own kitchen and the dinner table and the ornate chairs that were carved by his grandfather. They were gone, ashes and broken remains of their former selves in his mind's eye.

He thought also of his workshop and the trunk of shoes he had finished that had not yet found owners and the time and effort spent to make them. His heart sank heavily for a moment.

He shook away the image and woe with a little difficulty and spotted a collection of kitchen knives in a box near the spring well. He ran over to it and found the sharpest blades in the box, handing one carefully to Laurie.

She took it but did nothing more. Her eyes drifted down to the blade and disgust wrinkled her nose. "I can't fight. I can't do this! This isn't right!"

"Do what you have to," Oswald said sternly, an anger beginning to well up in him. His grief slid across his throat and festered in his stomach as a burning rage he had never felt before.

"I can't!"

"Just protect yourself!" he shouted, his eyes burning into hers. Laurie shrank away from him, holding the knife too tightly and so close to her body that he doubted anything could pry it away from her. A crashing thud reverberated through the house and a dark guttural growl inched closer from the den. Oswald pressed a finger to his lips. He took a tighter hold on the knife and stepped as quietly as he could towards the hall.

The growling seemed to be lurking throughout the house slowly creeping from one room to another. The tracker was gradually moving away from them, deeper into the house, and he gestured for her to follow him. He stepped out into the hallway and moved into the foyer once more, stepping over the pile of clothes in the doorway.

He unlocked the front door and listened again for movement. The tracker didn't make a sound and its footsteps still sounded heavy and steady in the outer reaches of the house. A soft crackling sound popped in his ears and he looked around one more time.

Nothing.

He pulled the door open slowly, grateful for the silent hinges.

The tracker in the house must have been the same one who had been watching the front door. There were no trackers in sight.

The window at the front of the house to his right was open, the same window that had been lulling soft music earlier had allowed entrance to that beast. The windowsill had gauges in it from the claws of the tracker and a tuft of fur on the latch of the window.

Oswald looked around for a second, the smell and sight of the dense smoke almost overwhelmed his senses. The clarity of the world around him would rise and fall with the strength of the smoke and the direction of the wind. He walked outside and gestured for Laurie to follow once more. She didn't move.

He turned around and looked at her, following her gaze upwards to the roof which was billowing smoke from beneath its gutters. Silent tears were running down her face. Oswald reached out for her and she hurried out to follow him.

Oswald remembered the Keernith and his eyes sharpened. It wouldn't be gone.

The tracker within the house howled and they stifled a panicked cry as they ran out towards the woods next to the open field, which also was a canvas for the fires of hell.

Everything was on fire, burning around them. Even the tree that they leaned against for protection from the heat felt hot to the touch. The smoke began to scorch in their lungs and the intensifying heat brought them to the ground, gasping for air and clinging to the coolness of the earth.

Screams suddenly began to cut through the smoke and through the sound of the crackling, angry fire. Another howl slid down through the hills. Oswald watched through the soot as Laurie's house second by second began to collapse beneath the fire that now not only rolled from the roof but licked at its walls. A window in the house broke and a shout from inside curdled Oswald's stomach.

"Daddy!" Laurie clawed at the ground, fighting against Oswald's grip as he tried to keep her back into the shelter of the woods. She jerked free of him and in one hard kick she was gone, enveloped in the mid-day darkness that hung in the air.

"No! ... Laurie, get back here!" Oswald got up and followed her, the knife in his hand slick with sweat and his eyes were burning so badly that he couldn't keep them open for more than a few seconds. He felt the violent intensity of the heat from the house before he had even reached a point that he could see the fire burning from it.

"Laurie!" he shouted, coughing so hard that he gagged on the soot in the air. Weakness set into his mind and he realized that he was having trouble thinking straight. The roar from the fire was overwhelming to the senses and he couldn't hear or see anything else.

The house groaned desperately for a moment and something from within cracked suddenly and violently. Oswald heard a shrill scream and could feel and hear the house falling in before him. "No!" he felt his way through the hot wooden wall and fire to where the door hung open at an angle. He got to his knees, and looked into the billowing smoke and saw nothing but fire. "Laurie?" he waited for an answer, but only heard another piece of the house fall in on itself. His heart wrenched his stomach with fear. He stood quickly looking for another way in.

Remembering the window to his left he moved towards it. He reached into the open window and felt nothing but heat and flying ashes, but he couldn't see any flames. Suddenly something small and solid made a sharp contact with the side of his head. His eyes blacked out the world for a second with the shock. He withdrew his hand from the window and paused for a second looking around.

Deciding to ignore the pain he lunged forward, towards the window and rubble but something caught his pant leg about mid-thigh and pulled him off balance. He turned quickly and saw nothing at first. It tugged again and he spotted Nedtedrow below the heaviest of the smoke, one of Oswald's shirts wrapped and tied around his mouth.

He waved a hand quickly and gestured towards the woods where he had run off to earlier. Oswald shook his head, "Laurie's still in the house!"

Nedtedrow tightened his grip on Oswald's pant leg and shook his head slowly as the flames began to lick at the window in front of them. He pulled hard at Oswald and reluctantly he stepped away from the house. Another loud crack of splintering wood echoed in the roar of the fire and the front of the house collapsed in flying ash and hot embers.

Half-dragged, Oswald ran from the village through the black walls of rancid smoke. He didn't pay much attention to where they were going, the last image in his mind was of black smoke, and hot flickering fire and what was once a yellow painted home.

His feet felt numb and after a while he felt his feet catch on the uneven path and he pitched forward, his pack flying off his back and rolling ahead of him. He hit the ground hard, gasping and coughing, the now fresh air so clear in his lungs that he wanted to breathe in forever. His eyes watered with the force of his cough. Finally his lungs cleared of the soot enough that he could breathe freely.

He looked up from the ground, dizzy and shocked. Nedtedrow was the only one that he could see. He was covered in soot from his nose up to his hair, the shirt he had tied around his face had kept quite a bit of the ash from getting to his mouth and nose. His clothes were shaded black and grey as well. He was sitting against a large tree breathing heavily and looking exhausted.

Oswald looked around again, he couldn't see anyone, but he could look up through the canopy in the trees and see the smoke and ashes being pulled up into the air. "Where is everyone?" Nedtedrow did not look up from the bare spot on the ground in front of him. "Where did everyone else go?"

"They didn't," he said quietly, "Nobody else got out."

Oswald looked at him emotionless for a moment, unbelieving. It wasn't possible. There were two hundred people in the village. "Someone else had to have gotten out. They aren't dead."

"You were in the last house on the outside of the village and I don't know how you got out alive."

"I can't be the only one to get out. Why would I get out and no one else? It isn't right. You're not right, you can't be."

"I'm sorry. You must have some purpose I guess." Nedtedrow had a tone that seemed out of place for him. It was like pity but somehow held a tone of suddenly found respect. He seemed solemn, but too calm to seem real. Oswald didn't respond.

Nedtedrow stood up and walked towards Oswald, still looking anywhere but at his face. "Give me your hand."

Oswald looked down at himself and noticed a large piece of skin was hanging off the outside palm of his right hand, it was a clean cut but the open flesh was filled with ash. He couldn't remember getting hurt.

Nedtedrow grabbed the hand and turned it over, "Don't move. This is going to hurt." Nedtedrow picked up the knife on the ground next to them and quickly slid it across the loose skin and cut it free. Oswald flinched but it wasn't as bad as it had looked a moment ago. A clean shred of the shirt that had been an ash cover was tied around the wound. "That should do for now," he said, "I'm going to go get some water." he looked away and left Oswald in the shade of the woods.

The distant crackle could still be heard and the occasional piece of burning ash would drift down from the black cloud above. Oswald's mind was blank. The horrors of the day flashed in and out of his mind's eye and when the visions of the fires had faded, the faces that he knew took their place.

Slowly, it sank into his heart.

Grief flooded his chest, trapping air deep within him. They were all gone. He would never see them again. His friends would never speak again, would never run, fight, or dance. The children would never play again. Missy, she was so small and her laughter was so fine and so light. He wouldn't hear it again. Narish was gone and her baby had gone with her. Grimb.

The village would never again hear the sound of music during the harvest. He choked on the slab of heartache in his throat and swallowed hard trying to force it away. Two hot tears welled in his eyes and streamed away, carrying soot away with them. He thought of the children that had been playing in the fountain and the distant laughter he heard just days ago. He heard the hollow echo of voices drifting over the hills to his modest home which was now no more than charcoal and stone.

His mind conjured darkness, burned bodies and graves that would never be built. He thought of lonely hearts and somber souls that would never be realized. No one would know what had happened but him. He was the only one to know the people who would never be seen again. The people he loved and would never see again. His heart suddenly skipped with fear and sadness.

Laurie's green eyes would never look into his. Her hair pulled up in ribbons would never graze the wind. He hung his head low, his chin resting on his chest. His heart sobbed and his eyes burned. There were no tears left in him, the fire had burned them away and his soul grieved harder because he had none left for her.

His mind's eye conjured shadows and her elegant features haunted him, her sweet face, bloody and burned, would be the last vivid image of her that he could imagine. He pulled at his hair angrily trying to scrape the images of the dead from his mind and pull away the rage inside him which rampaged suddenly and beat against his chest without rhythm or limitations.

The anger within him tore at his heart until the pain and confusion was too much and he screamed into the dirt at his feet, curling into his knees and fighting for breath against the smoke in his lungs. His body shuddered and his voice gave way to a hoarse, dry scratch. He looked up slowly and out into the quiet and empty wood.

The pain melted all at once, replaced by a void of numb and empty fog.

He stared out through the trees, hearing nothing, seeing nothing, and though he knew it was callous, he couldn't bring himself to feel anything anymore. His heart couldn't take the strain. He couldn't deal with it all.

A deep dull throb rose up behind his eyes and over the crown of his head and he forced everything out of his mind.

Chapter six

Nedtedrow knelt by the stream which was churned and muddy, but cool to the touch. The cold felt like nothing else at that moment. It was refreshing, energizing. He cupped his hands and dipped them into the water trying to filter out as much of the silt as possible. He pulled up a scoop of light brown water and splashed his face. The water ran down his cheeks, neck, and chest making his skin sigh with relief.

He went to scoop another handful and saw the black streaks in his palms and washed them away before repeating the process several times. After a while of kneeling by the creek his clothing was soaking wet and his hands finally came from his face clean. He looked into the slowly moving current and saw that most of the ashes were gone and he looked like himself, tired, but Nedtedrow once more.

He looked over his shoulder back down the path that he had taken. It was quiet, and the skies were dark with towering plumes in the distance. He turned back to the water and drank a few mouthfuls before reaching for the remaining shreds of the shirt. He dipped it in the stream and did his best to rinse it as clean as he could.

He made sure it was as soaked as it could get and pulled it up into a ball in his hands. He started heading back to where he had left Oswald, leaving a thick drizzle of water on the shrubs around his knees. He crested the hill after a few minutes and saw Oswald, exactly where he had been. Nedtedrow wasn't even sure that he had moved at all.

"Hey, Oswart," he said, trying to sound stable, "Here, clean up. We need to move, we're still too close to stay long."

Oswald reached out blankly for the wet cloth looking almost confused. He wiped down his face slowly, getting everything but a pair of streaks beneath each eye which didn't look like they would come off for a while. He didn't make eye contact with Nedtedrow and stayed eerily silent.

After a deep rattling sigh, he stood up and picked up the ash covered bag from the ground ahead of him. He shouldered the pack and started towards Gommorn ahead of Nedtedrow who could do nothing but trudge along behind, smothering blame beneath his cowardly heart.

It was quiet except for the occasional snap of twigs or the brush of leaves against their steps. It was a deep silence that lasted until the orange in the sky deepened, the smallest hint of sunset visible through the branches of the canopy along the horizon.

Their feet ached and their backs were stiff, but neither stopped though their bodies were begging for them to rest. Nedtedrow's stomach rumbled and Oswald coughed throughout the last several hours, finally spitting the last of the black mucus onto a rock along the path they were making. Occasionally Oswald would hang his head low at the front of the pathway and his shoulders would shudder lightly through the silence. Nedtedrow kicked at the brush when he noticed, trying to make noise and distract himself from the heaviness above him.

They walked at a fast pace, clearing ground but neither was entirely sure exactly how far they were able to walk for the day. All they knew was exhaustion and the weight they carried.

When the sun had finally set, hours passed quickly and the moon had risen high enough that it could cast its own silver beams of light and spotty shadows on the ground around them. Griffins cawed to each other deeper into the woods and small owls swooped down into the heavy undergrowth to fly off with dinner dangling from their talons.

The air grew colder as they came to a place where the trees thinned out enough that measurable light fell down on the two of them. A large sycamore tree loomed a few yards ahead of them, its branches hung low to the ground and the roots lifted around it in small stoops.

Oswald walked up to it and stopped with a sigh. He let the heavy bag fall away from his shoulder with a dead thump against the ground.

The wind was still and there were no sounds from the world around them. He took another quick sweep of their surroundings looking for any sign of movement or life.

Deep into the darkness, far enough in front of him that it was difficult to make out, was a glimmer of red on a large form. He stood as still as possible watching it for several minutes. It didn't move or make any audible noise and therefore he decided that it was harmless and exhaustion took its toll on him.

He looked down at the base of the tree by which they had stopped and saw Nedtedrow within the tangle of roots and weeds. He was already asleep.

Oswald's heart hardened for a second staring down at the small man who had cost him so much simply by existing. He was unsure really how much he liked or trusted the Nelwin and whether or not he should leave him to lay there and continue forward. Would it make his journey easier or safer without him?

Anger roared in his stomach for a brief moment as he thought of everyone and everything that was gone because of this one small thieving little mooch.

He thought of how much of his life had been changed by one day and one action.

He closed his eyes for a moment and sat down on the other side of the tree, his every muscle sighing relief as he leaned back against the trunk. His thoughts continued to wander on, bitter, lonely and angry until sleep snuck into his guarded mind and he drifted off into a restless and nightmare filled world.

Screaming and the smell of smoke woke him suddenly in the early hours of dawn. The scream he quickly discovered was in his mind and the smoke was simply the smell of ash on his clothing.

He took a deep breath to slow his heart which was drumming in his chest uncomfortably. He shook his head, waking up what was not startled awake by his nightmares. He leaned around the tree and saw that Nedtedrow was still there and had adjusted himself to use a large wide root as a pillow. It seemed that his anger had ebbed, but had not yet completely vanished.

He wanted to get away from him for a while.

There was enough light from the almost morning sky that he could now make out what he had seen when they had stopped that night. Off in the distance was a large heap of white boulders that had formed into a hill-like mound in the middle of the clearing around them. On the side of the rocky hill's face near the top was a red glint.

Curiosity and the will to get away from Nedtedrow lifted Oswald from the dusty earth and pressed him forward into the grove towards the strange formation. His feet still ached but he ignored it and brushed forward through the weeds.

The birds had noticed that light was growing slowly in the cool air and they had begun to twitter themselves awake in the treetops. A small yellow bird swooped from its early morning perch and landed on the white rocky hill. A shudder rippled through the air and the bird flew away startled, and crashed with batting wings against a nearby tree before dropping like a stone to the ground.

Oswald stared at the still bird, confused and looked back to the hill of strange stones.

He stopped short of the mound and stared at it wondering what had caused the strangeness in the air. Nothing moved and he noticed with interest that there were no living things on the hill at all. No weeds, no moss, not so much as a fallen leaf lay on the white stones.

The closer he got, the more the air seemed to thicken with static and slowly it drew the hairs on his arms on end. The thought crossed his mind that this must be a living thing and not simply a pile of rocks.

He looked up to the crest of the mound to what had caught his eye to begin with. The red glint seemed to be a sword, half buried in the stone, sticking out at a crooked upward angle. It looked as though it had been planted there deliberately.

He reached out carefully and touched the nearest stone. It was warm as if it had been sitting in the sun for hours though the sun had not even begun to peak over the hills yet.

The rock was rounded nicely and felt coarse and solid like sandstone. A strong vibration shot up from the stone and startled him. The feeling of the vibration remained for a few moments and made his fingers go numb for several long seconds. He looked down at his hand and saw that it was covered in white dust. He brushed it off on his ash covered shirt and stared transfixed at the rock he had touched.

He looked around again and he felt compelled to get up to the sword near the top of the hill. It felt like it was calling him, pulling him forward with an invisible rope. Taking a deep breath, he reached out a single finger and touched another stone. It felt the same, hot and coarse. After a second it shocked him too, but the effect of the dust on his hands lasted almost twice as long. The numbness in his finger began to ache when feeling began to return and he stood up straight and let ideas run through him.

He stepped up to one of the larger flatter stones and slowly placed the sole of his shoe on the top of it. He waited patiently and nothing happened. He took another step up to the next sturdy place so that each foot was standing on one of the stones. He waited and again nothing happened.

Not wanting to touch any more of the rocks with his bare hands he judged each step carefully so he wouldn't slip and touch anything with his flesh. Transfixed on the placement of each step, he came up to the sword quickly and realized that it probably was not the smartest thing that he could have done. Going down would not be as easy, and he hadn't even thought about the idea that the sword was not meant to be touched.

Either way, he decided he had made it this far and the anger and grief that had been shoved aside in his mind was pressing for him to do something reckless. He looked carefully at the blade of the sword and how it was stuck. It seemed as though it were forged in the rock, the two appeared at first glance to be one in the same. There were no gaps in the rock and it was not stuck between stones. It had been driven into the large venomous stone with extreme heat and force.

Without giving it a second thought he grabbed the hilt of the sword. It felt hot. It was not like the odd stones that had mounted the hill which felt sun warmed, but as if it were radiating heat from a fire. As hot as it was, however, it didn't burn him.

He felt like it was his. He earned it, like it had been waiting for him all this time.

Oswald pushed on it to see if it would budge. It didn't, but he didn't really expect it to. He found stronger footing and wrapped both hands around the hilt and began to pull it up.

"Hey! Stupid Elf! Oswart, get down!" Nedtedrow was huffing quickly towards the hill and bobbing like a wobbling top in the grass.

"It's Oswald," he corrected dryly and returned his attention to the sword, readjusting his grip on the hilt.

"You don't know what you're doing! You're going to kill yourself!" Nedtedrow reached the bottom of the white stone hill where Oswald stood and began pacing back and forth at its base wringing his hands occasionally, his eyes wide.

"I seem to be doing alright so far," Oswald answered. He felt his fingers against the hot metal and heaved upward on the sword and felt it move, if only a fraction and his heart leapt up into his throat with excitement. He shifted his footing on the rocks and glanced down at Nedtedrow.

"Idiot!" Nedtedrow shouted, darting his eyes around the mound and increasing the speed of his pacing, "I don't know how you got that far!"

"I'm taller than you," Oswald said sharply. He tried again to pull the sword out, locking his shoulders and bending his knees a little for leverage. He pushed against the sword and felt it move. It shifted almost half of an inch and the rock that it had been fused with began to crack. The small fissures around the sword blade elongated down the face of the bolder, splintering outward in a widening pattern.

Nedtedrow clenched his jaw in frustration as the sound of the cracking stones began to echo in the stillness of the dawn, "Smartass! What are you trying to do? No one gets up this hill and sure as hell no one gets down!"

"Then what's your problem? If I'm going to die getting down from here then I might as well try to get the sword out since I'm already here," Oswald watched as one of the cracks in the stone near the blade widened and he crouched again for another tug on the sword, "You might as well start moving. Gommorn is still a few days away."

"You don't understand Elf, this was built as a marker when the war started. It's cursed!" Nedtedrow pointed to the sword angrily and then waved his hand quickly, gesturing for Oswald to follow him, "Get down!"

"If it's cursed—" Oswald said, readjusting his hands on the hilt again and straining against the sword one more time, "-then I wouldn't have — been able — to get — up — here!" A loud cracking sound broke into the air as the cracks in the stone suddenly traveled along the full length of the bolder. The sword gave way from the rock, the length of the red blade freeing itself into the morning air with a dry ringing sound that clashed with the continuing crack of stones.

He felt his footing soften beneath him and what had been stable ground beneath his feet shifted loosely. The rocks all at once beneath his feet began to crumble, splintering and crushing into dust and gravel.

Nedtedrow gasped as the splintering stones began to fall. He turned on the balls of his feet and ran back into the woods. He reached out, grabbing the bark of the nearest tree and swinging his body around it, putting the trunk between himself and the rockslide. He moved tighter against the tree, dodging the pieces of falling poisonous rock as they beat against the ground and rolled away into the brush of the woods.

Oswald gripped the sword tight and stumbled as each rock that had formed the hill broke into rubble beneath him and rolled towards the forest floor. He lost his footing, quickly readjusting for the sliding stones and slid down the rock that had been solid only a moment before. He felt his feet come out from underneath him and he hit the side of the hill. He landed on his back and the turning stones flipped him over into the chaos. He felt himself being tossed around, rolling and tumbling in a cloud of white dust and broken stones.

He slid into the grass at the forest floor, hearing the clatter of the rocks beat into the ground around him. When he felt his body slide to a stop he waited for pain, a report of his injures, but felt nothing but the dusty grass against his face.

He opened his eyes and saw that he was lying in dirt and grass with the gleaming rust colored red blade sitting inches from his face. He wondered for a second if the stones had made him numb and if so, how much pain he would find himself in when it wore off. He tried to move and to his surprise he found that he could. He touched his legs, chest, arms, and face and could feel them all.

The hill behind him was now a mass of grey and white pebbles and a small cloud of white dust that was beginning to settle.

He grabbed the sword and stood up. The heat from the hilt seemed to give him energy and he couldn't help but grin. He had never done anything so stupid in his life and he had ignored the danger of it until it was over. Now he realized that it was probably not the smartest thing that he could have done.

He pushed himself up and stood, reaching down to pick up the red sword. The hot metal of the hilt greeted him again and he turned the sword over in the dim morning light.

He laughed. He couldn't help himself. He knew the second he saw the sword that it was something he had to have and now that it was his, he felt the triumph of his prize. His own quiet laughter echoed before the commotion of the rockslide had settled down enough for the birds to resume their songs. He felt safer being armed with his new sword. The fact that he didn't know how to use it didn't mean anything to him, he was simply happy to have it in his hand.

The top of Nedtedrow's head popped around the trunk of the large tree, his eyes sweeping around anxiously. He glanced down into the center of the white pebbles and broken stones, and saw Oswald, holding the red sword.

"Hey Oswart, you dead?"

Oswald looked down to the mess that he had created and the powdery white dust that settled around him and shook his head, his laughter dying slowly, "It's Oswald. And no."

Nedtedrow tilted his head and stared at him as though he would at any moment burst into flames, "Are you dying?"

Oswald thought for a second checking himself once more for numbness or wounds. "No," he called again, dusting himself off and admiring his newly found prize, the hilt of it radiating heat all the way up into his arm.

"That's good," he said cautiously, "Feeling dizzy?"

"No." Oswald said, shaking his head.

"Numb? Sick?"

"No," he said again, more firmly this time as he kicked aside a small stone and watched it skip a few feet away.

"You sure?" Nedtedrow asked, stepping partially out from behind the tree, slowly and deliberately placing his steps. He watched his footing, making sure that his steps fell between the stones that had come to rest on the forest floor.

"Yeah, I'm fine. Why do you keep asking?"

"Oh, it's nothing much," Nedtedrow said sarcastically, as he crawled out fully from behind the tree and stared at Oswald from a safe distance, "You're just lying in poisoned rock dust, is all. Stupid elf. You never seen venom stones before?"

"No…" Oswald said. He looked around him elated to have succeeded in such a brainless quest and still somewhere deep within his heart, disappointed that he had survived it. He pushed thoughts aside with a sigh and started walking towards Nedtedrow.

"You sure you're feeling alright now?" Nedtedrow asked, taking a cautious step backwards as Oswald came closer.

"Fine," he assured him, "I'm not hurt."

"Awful stuff those stones," Nedtedrow insisted, obviously not wanting to come within arm's reach of Oswald or the stones that he carefully maneuvered around as he backed up another step, "Had a cousin who fell on some once when traveling. Got an excellent pair of boots out of the whole thing. Lost a cousin though. You sure you're not dead?"

"Great story," Oswald scoffed disapprovingly, "Yeah, I'm sure I'm not dead." he picked up his arm and drove the sword into the ground beside him with a satisfying thud. Nedtedrow's gaze was immediately drawn to the sword, fixated as though he were in a trance. "You can't have it," Oswald said preemptively.

"Hey!" Nedtedrow said, shaking his head sharply, "What makes you think that I would take that thing?"

"Just a feeling," he said dryly, "and all the same I'm not going to let you touch it. No offense."

"No," Nedtedrow agreed, his face fallen, "I don't think I could if you gave it to me," he stared at the sword and swallowed hard before letting his eyes wander back up to the chain around Oswald's neck, "That necklace on the other hand, I would take in a heartbeat."

Oswald tucked his necklace under the collar of his shirt and frowned down at Nedtedrow. He then followed Nedtedrow's gaze back to the blade of the sword. He noticed an etching along the face of the blade on one side and recognized it as an Azarian script, which was very similar to the dialect of the Pewins.

It was clear, deep writing that caught the light of the rising sun in the same way that glass catches the intense flicker of a fire.

The words danced in the light.

Not but He who Breathes veined Magic and those Whom are Born of the Blood Following

Can hold the sword which is Blessed of Deadly Poison and Forged in Hellfire.

"What's that supposed to mean?" Oswald asked. Nedtedrow looked at it inquisitively and reached out a finger to it. Oswald scooted it a few inches away just out of his reach.

"Look," Nedtedrow said impatiently, "I ain't going to take the damn thing. It's too heavy for me to carry very far and I think there's something wrong with it."

"What?" Oswald turned the sword over in his hands and saw nothing wrong with it at all. He brushed off a little remaining white dust that was stuck to it. Nedtedrow backed away quickly and held his breath until the dust settled and let out an explosive breath looking offended. Cautiously he came forward again and Oswald examined it once more. There wasn't so much as a scratch on it.

"It might be cursed," Nedtedrow said tentatively.

"What makes you think that?" Oswald asked annoyed.

"One," Nedtedrow held up fingers as he counted and looked back to the mound of broken stones behind Oswald, "It was stuck on the top of a mountain of venom stones. Two: It has a red blade that won't tarnish and it's engraved in Azarian. Three: It was put there by the King of Azar himself."

"This is King Edward the Second's sword?"

"Venhow's sword!" Nedtedrow snapped angrily, "You don't listen to me at all do you?"

"You said it was put here at the beginning of the war, right?" Oswald asked looking it over.

"Yeah! I did, but King Edward was dead a year before the war started," Nedtedrow shook his head and gestured sharply to the sword in Oswald's hand, "Venhow put that sword here as a marker. He wanted his army to hold everything from Azar to this province to Cauldridge and around to the Eastern coastline."

"You're sure about that?" Oswald asked looking the blade over thoughtfully.

"Yes."

"This sword? And you say that it's cursed?"

Nedtedrow shrugged, "It might be. People say that it is. Everyone and everything that has tried to get up to it has died before reaching the top."

"It wasn't hard to get to," Oswald insisted looking back over his shoulder, "I just had to keep my footing solid on the way up."

"Those stones kill everyone." he said seriously. He eyed the white dust that still coated some parts of Oswald's clothing and backed away again.

"They just make you numb for a minute or two." Oswald argued, following Nedtedrow's gaze and brushing at his shoulder casually.

"No," Nedtedrow said, backing away another couple of steps as Oswald brushed himself off. He held his breath again as the dust settled and he kept his distance as he continued, "Just to breathe the dust will kill almost anything. They are absolutely deadly … to everyone but you apparently."

"That doesn't make sense."

Nedtedrow clenched his jaw and looked Oswald over slowly, "Neither do you elf."

"Why do you say that?" Oswald asked curiously.

"An orphaned, red-headed elf that makes shoes in the middle of nowhere, wears his mother's necklace, survived an attack from a tracker, escaped a Keernith Goblin from under his nose while in a burning building, is immune to venom stones and was able to get a sword that no one else could ever even get to," Nedtedrow frowned seriously and shook his head, "No, you're right, you are a run-of-the-mill kind of guy I could've run into just anywhere."

"Smartass," Oswald muttered.

"Elvish freak."

They frowned at each other and Oswald held out the sword again, looking it over closely, "Then what exactly is this sword?"

"Only one way to be sure," Nedtedrow said. He slowly reached out again with one stubby finger and lightly touched the hilt of the sword briefly. He quickly jerked his hand back with a sharp yell, looking down at an angry blister that was rapidly forming on the end of his index finger. He shook his hand hard and met Oswald's confused gaze, grinding his teeth through the pain of the burn.

"What just happened?" Oswald asked, looking down at the blister. He gripped the sword tightly tried to understand why the sword had burned Nedtedrow.

"It's… It only…" Nedtedrow stared at the blade and then looked up at Oswald with a fixed expression, "Never mind."

Something in Nedtedrow's eyes changed. He returned to meet Oswald's stare and paused with a distant shrug. He suddenly looked uncomfortable but brushed the expression away as quickly as if it had been a pebble tossed from his shoe.

"Well," Nedtedrow said, in an over-the-top bouncy kind of way, "This will either be very good for us, or very bad. Nothing left but to find out which I suppose. We should get moving. You make too much noise Oswart."

"Oswald," he corrected.

"Who?" Nedtedrow asked ignorantly.

"Never mind." he rolled his eyes and readjusted his new sword in his hand. They walked back to the sycamore tree that they had slept under and Oswald picked up his pack from its place against the uplifted roots. He shouldered the bag full of clothing and whatever else must have been crammed into it up onto his back and started off towards the east.

Nedtedrow scooped up the box that until just now Oswald had not fully realized that he still had. He stared at Narish's box and he decided not to say anything about it as the two of them pressed forward into the woods.

At midday the brisk cool breeze died away into a dry heat with brutal sunlight beating down on their heads. They weaved through the woods trying to stay in the shade as long as possible, only to be forced onward into clearings and rocky hillsides. Nedtedrow puffed along beside Oswald, pausing now and then before running to catch up with him every hour or so.

That night they stopped and slept against a large oak tree along the edge of a dry creek bed, but their sleep was short lived.

A howl woke them through the night.

They weren't sure what had made the noise, whether it was a wolf, a youthful dragon, or a hippogriff, but the sound was enough to snap them back into action. They leapt to their feet and ran until dawn when their feet began to rub raw against their shoes and their muscles started to seize with effort.

They slowed down, not having heard the sound again since they had been startled awake, and tried to pace themselves through the wilderness. They cut through dry land and rocky paths, dreading the mid-day heat.

When the sun was nearing early evening once again, the pendulum of sunlight began tipping behind them into the westward sky. They stopped at a wide barren strip of land that stretched like a penciled line, drawn in the earth over the hills and out of their vision.

They were getting close.

They had reached the Wanton Roads.

Exhausted, Nedtedrow plopped down onto the ground and lay in the dusty earth trying desperately to catch his breath in the center of the road.

Oswald on the other hand was feeling much better than he had the day before. Whether it was the events from the previous morning that had weighed him down yesterday, or if it was the energy forcing heat into his arm through the sword that made the trip seem easier today, he wasn't sure. Either way, he did feel well enough that when the sound of trickling water caught his attention he had enough energy left to search for it.

"Where — you going?" Nedtedrow panted.

"To find some water." Oswald crossed the road to the woods on the other side and left Nedtedrow to lie in the dirt while he went to find the source of the running water.

It was not far off of the road that he found it. It was a stream that was heavy with a fast paced current. It was fairly clear and deceivingly deep, at least for such a narrow stream. He dropped his things on the ground beside him and knelt beside the water.

His reflection was broken in the churning movements cast by the roots and rocks in the creek bed. He looked tired and hungry, still slightly dusted with rock remains and ash. He removed his shirt and tossed it into the grass beside him. The sun shone down on his pale exposed shoulders and back and he took a deep breath and soaked in the sunlight.

The water was cold on his skin but with the heat of the day and the brightness of the sunlight, he did not find it unpleasant in the least. He cupped his hands in the water and rubbed it into his hair and washed his salt ridden body. He caught sight of himself again noting that the cut on his head was healing quite rapidly and that he looked much healthier without a dirty face.

There was a rustle of brush behind him and he turned, expecting to see Nedtedrow hobbling down to join him. Instead he saw the figure of a beautiful woman up near the top of the hill half hidden by trees. She was tall and strong with chestnut colored hair and perfect ivory skin which faded casually back into the chestnut body of a mare.

She looked back at him, her attention sliding once to the sword and back into his eyes. Her own limpid amber eyes were so captivating that he was unable at first to notice that she had no clothing covering her but a thin strip of tightly pulled leather across her chest. Her aura and presence drew his attention completely. It was difficult not to notice the wildness and the intelligence in her gaze and he had to tear his eyes forcibly away from her to keep himself from staring. As he did so he heard a swift movement and looked up again to see what little could be caught of her flicking tail as she vanished over to the other side of the hill.

The sounds of hooves drifted away with her.

He wondered distantly if she had been a figment of his imagination or if he had really seen what he thought he had. A centaur. He had never seen one before and he stared transfixed on the spot at which she had vanished.

Satisfied with his short wash in the creek, he decided to get back to the road with Nedtedrow.

He stood upright and stepped rather clumsily along the bank where he rummaged for dry clothing trying to remember the details of what had happened. He slid on a dry shirt and clean clothes in a haze of distant thought. She had seemed analytical of him at least, but why had she said nothing and why did she leave so quickly?

He wondered about her for as long as it took him to reorganize his things packed among the mess of wadded clothing stuffed into the bag. He stooped down and filled the water bladder that he had found in the bag with the cold water from the stream.

He stoppered the bladder and set it aside as he washed the soaked rag that had bound his hand and replaced it over the shallow wound in the palm of his hand.

He thought again about the centaur and wondered why she had stared at him so intensely, and wondered too what she was doing this far from the coastline. When no answers came to him, he shouldered the bag again and picked up his sword. He headed back towards the road, all the while looking off to where she had gone and seeing no glimpse of her.

Nedtedrow was still lying in the middle of the road, looking up at the sky with his mouth hanging open slightly. The remains of a crumbling biscuit was stuck to his lips and a smear of jam lingered on his fingertips.

"Where did you find a biscuit?" Oswald asked as he stepped out of the woods and back onto the dirt road.

"Huh?" Nedtedrow looked away from the inside of his eyelids over to where Oswald stood, clean and suddenly hungry.

"Food. Where did you find it?" he repeated.

"I uh," Nedtedrow licked the jam from his fingers as he thought about the question, "bought it from a passerby."

"You have money?"

"Okay, so I didn't buy it exactly." Nedtedrow sat up in the road and licked the crumbs off of his lips and wiped his sticky hands on his filthy pant legs, "I more kinda bartered for it."

"What did you give them?" Oswald asked curiously, reaching a hand up to his necklace for reassurance and feeling the lump of it against his breastbone.

Nedtedrow paused thoughtfully, "Well, I uh…"

"You stole it." Oswald finished sharply.

Nedtedrow frowned and held up a hand to stall any further accusations, "Technically I did swap for it. There were a few rocks and a nut and —"

"And you stole it."

"Yeah, I suppose I did a bit," Nedtedrow admitted half-heartedly, "But only a basketful … and some coins."

"A basketful?" Oswald asked disbelievingly, looking around for the basket.

"And some coins," he nodded, "and a pair of earrings."

"You stole earrings?!" Oswald scoffed and threw his hands up in frustration, "Why do you need earrings?"

He shrugged deeply, "Might be able to get something for them when we get back to the city. You never know. This one time when I lived in the Shye province there were these two rich folk that moved in across the street and they had the biggest dog I had ever seen, it was twice my size at least," he said, making a wide gesture with his hands, "I noticed — being the responsible man that I am — that the man's wife dropped a rather elegant emerald pendant. Well, in my haste to return it to its rightful place I caught the attention of her dog and was chased off the property and a few miles down the road. There was a river. I'm not the best of swimmers so halfway across the river I threw the pendant on the bank so that I wouldn't drop it. There was a strong current and I about drowned when I found the bank again only to find that the dog was waiting for me on the other side. Well, a pair of ripped pants, one sock and two deep scars later I found myself at a pawn market," he shrugged exaggeratedly and gestured with a pat on his pocket as he spoke, "The pendant was a fake but I still got a pretty twenty silver pieces out of the deal."

"What does that have to do with anything?" Oswald asked, staring blankly at Nedtedrow.

"Anything as lovely as these," he reached into his pocket and then held up the gold earrings obviously where Oswald could get a good look at them, "are going to be worth the trouble."

"So that was worth it," Oswald said disbelievingly, "really?"

"Sure. I would do it again. Actually, that reminds me," Nedtedrow wiped his hands on his pants again, mingling what was left of the jam with the caked dirt that clung to him. He stuffed the earrings into his pocket and fished out a button that seemed to match Oswald's shirt.

Oswald checked his shirt over twice. It was not missing a button. "Where did you get that?" he asked exasperatedly.

"I noticed that it matched most of your ugly ass clothes so I got it for you."

"Thanks," Oswald said sarcastically, retrieving the button, "How thoughtful. So you took a button too?"

"For you," Nedtedrow said, taken aback, "Next time I just won't do anything nice for you then."

"Nice?! What about those people?" Oswald exclaimed, "They needed these things."

"No they didn't and I didn't take everything," he said, crossing his arms defensively, "just what I could snatch from the back of the wagon. Just a couple of things."

"Is that all?" Oswald rolled his eyes.

"Yeah. Well," Nedtedrow paused and thought for a second running over the ordeal in his mind for a second, mumbling to himself, "food, coins, earrings, a button, oh! And a rag." he pulled it from his back pocket and held it up smiling broadly. It was dirty with black and red patterns on it.

Oswald sighed and shook his head, "Why would you take that?"

"I dunno," he said absently, looking over the cloth, "Seemed like a good idea at the time."

"Are they going to kill you if they figure out you robbed them?" Oswald asked looking over the small assortment of stolen goods.

"Probably not," he said, with a reflective frown, "It was just an old man and his pregnant daughter. I'm not worried."

"You robbed an old man and a pregnant woman?" Oswald let his mouth fall open in disbelief and disgust before snapping it shut again and shaking his head slowly, "You're awful."

"Hey, we've got to eat too. I didn't take *all* their food."

"So where is the rest of it?" Oswald asked.

Nedtedrow licked his lips guiltily and opened his treasure box holding out a single slice of bread towards Oswald and what looked like a spoonful of blackberry jam in a small jar.

"Is that it?"

"Hey," Nedtedrow said indignantly, "you were gone for a long time and I was hungry. Didn't know when you were gonna come back, or even if you would."

Oswald frowned and dropped his bag back on the ground. He sat on it, feeling the lumps of clothing and random items within it stick uncomfortably against his backside. He reached out and took what remained of the food from Nedtedrow with a sour expression.

He tucked the sword tightly beside him and ate what he had been given. He was disappointed with the means of how the food had been gathered but his body was happy to have something to fill his rumbling stomach.

The jam was tart and sweet and the bread was dry, both variables contributing to the thirst that followed. They emptied the water bladder between the two of them and rested in the late day's heat, falling asleep along the side of the road for the night.

They woke before dawn and started off again towards Gommorn.

The winding road slid out in front of them as they started along their path, kicking up the dirt of the road into a red plume along behind them as they went. They both knew that they would make better time on the even ground, away from the steep inclines and rocky fields of the dwindling forests.

They knew that the road would lead them directly into the city and it took a lot of the arguing out of the travel as they went.

Chapter Seven

The heat of the day cooled once more and the darkness of the night overtook the defining characteristics of the road. The moon replaced the sun's light, making the rocks and roadside weeds shine with a halfhearted dusty hue. The red blade of the sword hung lazily at Oswald's side, the heat rising from it warming his fingers.

Oswald stopped for a second. Voices were traveling on the wind from over the next hill, mumbles against the breeze, shouts and laughter. Nedtedrow stopped next to Oswald and paused for a second too and listened.

"Finally," Nedtedrow said, smiling broadly with a relieved sigh, "Gommorn."

Nedtedrow readjusted the box in his arms and broke out into a sprint. Oswald followed until they reached the top of the hill.

The city seemed to suck the breath from his chest. The sight was unlike anything that he had ever seen. It was so unlike living in his little village and different than any city he had come upon on his travels to and from the Pewin market.

This was a real city.

It lay in a huge valley, hills on every side of it, cradling it like an egg. The city stretched from the base of every hill around to each one of the others. Lights were flickering in windows everywhere, spotting in and out of the homes and buildings through the darkness.

"Wow," Oswald muttered.

"It's something isn't it?" Nedtedrow said fondly.

"It's enormous," Oswald said, looking over the overlay of structures that reached out into the darkness and deep into the valley, "I've never seen anything like it."

"It's my home away from home."

"I never would've dreamed that it looked like this. The valley is incredible. The city itself is … is so different than Elvish designs. They're so unorganized," he said, with both interest and some form of discomfort, "It looks like they build the houses crooked on purpose."

"They do. They get more land if another house can't be built next to it. Also it's easier to hide between buildings this way," he said, with an unconvincing smile, "The entire city was built by people who were fleeing from someone, either the war or from other people," he looked up at Oswald with raised eyebrows, studying his face in the dark, "It's a city for people like us. Everyone's different and no one has gotten here without a story."

"There are so many," Oswald said, overwhelmed by the size of the city's shadow branching out through the valley.

"Yeah there are."

"They have a lot of stone buildings here," Oswald said curiously, spotting a nearby home and marveling in the fine molding of the stones.

"Some of them even have steel in the walls," Nedtedrow nodded. His face fell sadly, "Stone houses don't burn."

The largest building lay on the far side of the city and was several times larger than any other building he could see. It caught his eye in the moonlight, reflecting a light white-green color against the vast field of homes. Lights glowed from the rooms atop the building, overseeing everything. He wondered what the building was for, but before he could ask, Nedtedrow was headed down the hill.

Oswald followed after him, "So who gets to live in the stone houses?"

"Whoever builds them," Nedtedrow said obviously.

"Everyone here has built their own homes? Is that why it's so random looking?" Oswald asked as he spotted a home at the city's edge that had no windows at all and was made entirely of stones and mortar.

"Uh-huh."

"Is there a carpenter that lives here anywhere?" Oswald asked, suddenly wondering where he was going to stay now that he was actually here.

"No," Nedtedrow said shortly, his attitude towards Oswald changing with every step closer that they got to the city's edge.

"There isn't a carpenter anywhere in this huge city? That doesn't make any sense. There has to be one somewhere."

"No," Nedtedrow assured him, "If you're lucky though, you might get help."

"What do you mean?"

"Make some friends and you might get a sturdy place to live," Nedtedrow said, turning away from him as they walked.

"But I can't build a house!" Oswald said, alarmed with the thought, "Isn't there anywhere for people to stay here?"

"No," Nedtedrow said, with a shrug, "There isn't, and as for building a house, you'll just have to learn how."

Oswald sped up, trying to make eye contact with Nedtedrow as they moved their way down the slope of the massive hillside, "Can I stay with you for a while?"

Nedtedrow snorted, "No."

"Do you even have a house here?"

"Of course I do. It's just *my* house," Nedtedrow said, holding up a hand quickly as he looked over at Oswald, "Nothing personal."

"I let you stay with me, the least you can do is return the favor until I have somewhere to be," Oswald argued, suddenly feeling a ball of anger ignite in him.

"The least I can do? I'm doing the least I can do," he insisted, "But I guess we'll see what happens when we get there."

At the bottom of the hill Nedtedrow turned to Oswald and he spotted the sword. His eyes lingered on the red glint of the blade and he looked suddenly alarmed, his eyebrows drawn together and his eyes opened wide, as if suddenly remembering something very important.

"Hide that sword," Nedtedrow ordered suddenly, "Don't let anyone see it!"

"Why?" Oswald asked looking down at it through the darkness.

"Just trust me and do what I say," he said flatly.

"Why would I trust you?" Oswald asked, narrowing his eyes at Nedtedrow's attitude.

"You just have to argue with everything I say don't you?" Nedtedrow spat.

"It's part of my nature," Oswald retorted bitterly, "All I want is an answer and a place to sleep."

"I have a house across the way here. But you have to hide that sword!" Nedtedrow began to look around nervously the longer that they stood at the edge of the city, his eyes flickering to the sword occasionally.

"Just tell me why," Oswald said obstinately, tightening his grip on the sword.

"Because I value my life," Nedtedrow said, lowering his voice and putting a hint of urgency behind his tone, "You have to learn to just trust me."

"You haven't exactly given me a lot to trust you by."

"Hey I warned you of what was gonna happen. I got you food today. I got you here and I kept you from diving into a collapsing building. There is no reason for you *not* to trust me." Nedtedrow stomped his foot and looked around quickly again before glaring up into Oswald's green eyes.

"You tried to rob me. I know you've robbed other people and you're the reason my people are *dead*."

"Hey," Nedtedrow snapped angrily, squaring up his shoulders and taking a heated step forward, "I didn't want that to happen any more than you did!"

"You didn't try to stop it!" Oswald spat.

"Because there wasn't anything that I could've done about it!" Nedtedrow shouted sweeping his eyes along the hillside before bringing them back to meet Oswald.

"You didn't even try!" Oswald said, stepping forward slightly with his arms outstretched, the red blade catching the moonlight.

"What did you want me to do? Go door to door prophesying death?" he exclaimed, throwing his arms up into the air, "You ever noticed that doesn't work? People say you're crazy, don't believe you and if you insist on it, they flog you and throw you out of town! You think I haven't tried to stop it before?! Nothing ever convinces people that they aren't safe until they can't get out!"

"Yeah, like you have ever tried to help someone else," Oswald said doubtfully.

"I've lost people that I cared about too!" he said, burning his eyes into Oswald's.

"Did you try to help them?" Oswald asked with a hint of cruelty in his voice, "or did you just let them die too?"

"I do what I have to do to stay alive!" Nedtedrow shouted.

"That's what I thought. You're a coward. I could have saved her!" Oswald shouted painfully, "I could have saved her! You didn't let me!"

"I saved your life!" Nedtedrow argued, his brow creased darkly and the lines around his mouth drawn tight against his jaw, "She killed herself by going back in there."

"I could have pulled her back!" Oswald contended heatedly.

"You would have been burned alive under that house," Nedtedrow said angrily.

"I should have. Everyone else did!"

"So you wanted to go with them?" Nedtedrow asked confused, he shook his head and put his index finger against his temple before dropping his hand and continuing, "There's got to be some reason you lived through that. You can do something to help. Find a reason to live and help us end the war. That's what the rest of us are trying to do."

"I'm alone," he reminded him painfully.

"We are all alone," Nedtedrow gestured to the forest of homes behind him furiously, "Everyone here is alone. We are all going to get the revenge we are looking for. It is just going to take a while. You have to want to fight for it! Don't dwell over it. You can't change it!"

"It's still your fault," Oswald said sternly, "You shouldn't have brought that down on my home."

"I didn't know there was a village out there!" Nedtedrow said with a sharp shake of his head, "I was lost in the middle of nowhere!"

"Bullshit!" Oswald retorted angrily, sweeping an arm down and smacking the box from Nedtedrow's arms, "You could've skirted the village, but instead you decided to rob the town blind!"

Nedtedrow watched the box fly out of his hands and crack heavily on the ground at his feet, the latch snapped and came slightly undone, scattering various baubles across the shadowed hill.

"You killed hundreds of people because you wanted a couple of trinkets," Oswald snapped disgustedly.

"*I* didn't kill them!" Nedtedrow said, screwing up his face as he looked at the scattered items, his jaw clenched, "The Keernith army did!"

"And *I* will never let my guard down again because of it."

"Stupid elf!" Nedtedrow spat, the veins in his neck pulsing with each stressed beat of his heart, "You just want to die don't you? Do you realize what will happen to you if they see this sword? Not that you care, and that's just fine with me, I don't owe you anything."

"You owe me everything!" Oswald roared, the pounding of his heart in his chest making his body ache.

"You want everything?" he asked skeptically, "You said yourself that no man can ever want everything."

"I changed my mind recently," Oswald hissed.

"You want it all? Then take it!" Nedtedrow stooped down and picked up the box, hurling it at Oswald's face.

Oswald moved, but was too slow and the corner of the box hit him square in the shoulder before flipping up over his arm and landing on the ground behind him. Sharp, electric pain, shot through his arm and up into his back. He sucked in air sharply, gritting his teeth through the discomfort as it ebbed away. He grabbed his shoulder, hilt still in his hand and stared down at Nedtedrow angrily, all of the blocked and suppressed anger and grief swelling back up into his fatigued mind with each passing moment.

The hilt of the sword suddenly trembled in his hand and radiated more heat than it seemed was possible. He thought for a second that it would burn him, but instead the warmth overtook him and his pent up anger exploded.

He dropped the sword, casting it off to the side, and dove at Nedtedrow, his hands wrapping around the man's throat. He pulled him closer and forced eye contact, "It's your fault she's dead! You killed her!"

He tightened his grip painfully and felt the blood rush in his head like a drug, feeding the beastly anger within him. His eyes were cold and wild, burning with an intensity that fogged over the glossy light in his emerald eyes until they were like sheets of ice over a boggy moor.

Nedtedrow dug at Oswald's hands fearfully with his nails, carving away thin scrapes of skin. He buried his index finger in between Oswald's hand and his throat and loosened his grip enough that he was able to pull himself free. He took in a cold breath and balled his hand into a fist, swinging upward and feeling his knuckles make contact with Oswald's stomach.

Oswald doubled over with a huff and Nedtedrow took the moment of hesitation to hurtle himself forward, catching around Oswald's middle and throwing them both to the ground in a fury.

Nedtedrow felt a fist dig into the side of his ribs hard and he swung blindly. He punched Oswald in the face with a surprising amount of strength behind it, the flesh swelling at the instant of impact.

Oswald was pulsing with so much anger he didn't feel the pain, just the jolt of each hit as every impact thumped sharply at his face and chest. He grabbed the front of Nedtedrow's shirt and lifted him from the ground for a moment, his weight straining against the neck of the shirt. He grimaced and threw the Nelwin into the ground beside him as hard as he could.

Oswald knelt in the dirt and scrambled so that he could look down at him directly, pinning his shoulder to the earth and breathing heavily. The faint taste of blood filled his mouth from both a fresh split in his lower lip and a place on his tongue that he must have bitten during the tumble.

Nedtedrow grabbed Oswald's wrist and used it as leverage as he kicked up into his stomach from his place on the ground. Oswald doubled over in sudden agony, feeling the stabbing ache of the kick radiate from his gut to his back.

Nedtedrow freed himself from the entanglement of bags, limbs, and clothing that engulfed them and crawled towards the nearest house, clawing at the ground. He kicked at the ground, trying to get to his feet to put some distance between the two of them.

Oswald reached out and caught his ankle as he stepped away. He jerked at his leg, pulling his foot out from under him and dragging Nedtedrow back to the ground where they tossed in a furious knot of fists and knees and kicks.

Oswald dodged a swing at his face and caught one of Nedtedrow's arms. He tightened his grip on it and twisted his arm at an awkward and painful angle. He pressed at the twisted arm harder and felt the flesh begin to give in to the pressure.

Nedtedrow writhed and tried to move his arm as it strained under Oswald's weight. He screamed as he felt the bone begin to move from its usual place. Tears welled in Nedtedrow's eyes from the pain in his arm and from the wide-eyed fear that drew in the dry night air, making them water more.

Nedtedrow could feel the bone of his upper arm bend beneath the muscle and his heart flipped in his chest making his stomach churn violently. The back of his mind urged him to try again to free himself. In a final effort he swung as hard as he could with his free arm and made contact with the left side of Oswald's face.

Oswald's grip failed and his head spun. The small amount of light the moon had to offer suddenly faded away into blackness and bright flickering stars in front of his eyes. He fell over and hit the ground as his arms collapsed beneath him, the world spinning as his anger ebbed. His head ached and his body realized all at once that it had been damaged. His muscles burned and his skin was hot to the touch and tender with large bruises forming everywhere. Knots could be felt on his arms, chest, and face. His head and neck throbbed with his heartbeat and his mouth felt as though it were full of needles. He felt with his swollen tongue and found a tooth that had chipped in the back of his mouth.

He rolled over onto his back and watched the lights fade and the world come back into view slowly.

Nedtedrow was stooped over him breathing heavily and looking stern. He was holding his arm tightly and his breaths were short and sharp, "Go ahead... blame me all you want." he picked up his box and returned to stare at Oswald lying on the ground exhausted and dazed, "But I didn't tell her to go back into that house. You had already saved her and she *chose* to go back."

Oswald watched Nedtedrow step over him and walk away between the nearest two homes and vanish. He watched the stars in the sky fade in and out through the dark and closed his eyes from the pounding in his head.

When the will and strength returned to him, he sat up slowly and gathered his scattered belongings. The sword had cooled down to a soft heat and looked almost menacing in the night, its red blade and etchings standing out from the darkness. He opened his bag and rearranged the items inside it so that the sword fit as well. He closed the bag and watched the fabric strain against the seams.

He stood up carefully trying to keep his head from spinning and shouldered his bag. With a sigh he looked around at the edge of Gommorn and had no idea where he was going to go.

The large white-green building crossed his mind and the curiosity lured him forward. He noticed after a few blocks into the maze of buildings that one of his knees hurt and wondered where in the fight it had gotten hit. He shrugged off the pain and wandered past house after house of dark windows, occasionally spotting a half-burned candle in a window.

The smell of cooked food hung nearby and voices caught his attention. His stomach growled pleadingly and he followed the smell of meat and spices to where music and loud disruptive voices clamored from a large, high roofed building. A sign outside hung over the door like a swinging branch.

The Burning Mill

A loud scuffle from inside broke out and Oswald found himself staring at the swinging door to the pub apprehensively. His stomach growled again and he decided to brave the riot to find something to eat. He pushed open the door in time to see two giant men holding a skinny black-haired boy, the two of them holding the kid up at the shoulders and running at the door. Oswald stepped back in time for the boy to be hurtled from the pub and out into the alley where he skidded to a halt.

Oswald looked at the two men alarmed as they turned to stand on the inside of the doorway. The door swung shut and Oswald looked back at the kid sprawled on the rocky path. He was a young human boy who looked hardly more than a child.

Oswald stepped up to the boy and looked down at him, "Hey, are you alright?"

The boy looked at him quickly, almost startled. The boy had a large black eye and a nose that looked like it had been broken once before. His ears were large and rounded, sticking out from his head unusually. The boy's hair was black as ink and straight with dark eyes to match. He sat up and looked Oswald over for a few seconds before smiling wide, showing the place where one of his back upper teeth should have been, "You too uh?"

"Me too, what?" Oswald asked looking down at the boy.

The boy pointed at his own black eye and back to Oswald, "D'ey kick ya out fer fightin' earliers' too?"

"Uh," Oswald touched the swollen hot lump on his eye and knew it must look bad by now, "No, I kind of got in a little fight outside of town."

"Ah. Ya new here?" he asked.

"Yeah."

"Name's Matrim. S'ur name?"

"Oswald."

Oswald held out a hand to the kid who took it and jumped to his feet energetically. He kept hold of Oswald's hand after getting up and shook it enthusiastically. "Good ta meet cha'." Matrim tossed his head from one side to the other, cracking his neck loudly with a sniff. He looked at Oswald with a half-smile half-sneer and brushed at his lip the thumb of his hand, "You got a lil' bit a' blood jus' there."

Oswald reached a hand up and wiped at his chin. A streak of dried blood flaked away after a few tries and Matrim seemed satisfied with the fix.

"Musta been quite a rustle ya gotcha self into."

"Yeah." Oswald shifted uncomfortably, "It has been a long and very hard couple of days. I didn't really think about what I was doing."

"I nevah do." he said, nodding back to the bar, "An' I totally get the whole bad day thing. Ya gotta get it all out there somehows. Knock a couple heads, ya know. It's the o'ly way to get betta sometimes."

"I usually don't. This actually is the first real fight I have ever been in," Oswald said, licking the split on his lower lip and cringing at the taste of iron and the pulse of pain beating in the cut.

"Done a real numba on ya's though. Ya get a few good shots in youself?" Matrim asked with a mischievous grin that once again showed the gap in his molars.

"Not that I'm particularly happy about it," Oswald said, with a short nod, "but yeah I did."

"Good," he said positively, "Ya feel betta?"

Oswald thought about it for a second and nodded, "I do."

"So whatcha get so upset 'bout then uh?" he asked, backing up to the nearest building and leaning back against the wall to make himself comfortable.

"I…" Oswald looked down at his feet for a minute and felt his throat tighten up a little and cleared his voice of cracks before answering, "I was fighting with the guy that I met before my village was attacked."

"So?" Matrim shrugged, "What for?"

"They were after him. Trackers hunted him down to our village. No one else made it out but me and him."

The boy looked up noncommittally and readjusted himself against the wall, "Ya made it though. Wa's the prob'em?"

"I lost everyone and I took it out on him."

"D'he do it?" Matrim asked with a frown, and made a sharp gesture with his hand pointing out of the city aimlessly.

Oswald closed his eyes, and sighed heavily, "No. It wasn't his fault really." Guilt slid around in his stomach and a hot shame burned up into his cheeks.

Matrim nodded slowly and pursed out his upper lip knowingly, "Did somthin' similar myself couple 'a years back. It sucks," he looked down at his knobby fingers and began to pick at his nails, "I lost my sis and my pop on 'a same day. I'm 'lone now too. It's' not so bad af'ta a while. Ya learn ta move on."

Matrim pushed himself away from the wall and walked back over to Oswald with a supportive smile, and thumped him on the back heartily.

Oswald felt a bruise under the place where Matrim had thumped on his back and he grimaced lightly, working his shoulder to try and distract himself from the ache. His stomach grumbled suddenly with the luring smell of food he had not been able to eat.

Matrim looked at Oswald with raised eyebrows, "Ya hungry?" Oswald nodded "Come wit' me then, I'll feed ya. Got some cornbread n' mead at the house," he gestured for Oswald to follow and without another word he turned and headed down the nearest alley and around a corner.

"That's very kind of you," Oswald said humbly. He followed through the dark, having a hard time keeping up with the boy through the maze of crooked homes, "but why are you helping me?"

"'Cause i's the right thing ta do," he answered with a shrug and made a gesture with his hand for Oswald to hurry up.

It wasn't long before they stopped in front of a very small wooden home with lop sided windows. The boy smiled proudly and opened the door. Oswald stood in the doorway for a second before seeing a flicker of light as Matrim lit a candle on a short-legged table by the window. It lit up the room enough that Oswald could see that there were only three rooms total in the house. The kitchen had a two person table and two old chairs, an icebox that looked unused, two cabinets and another candle which was lit only a few seconds after the first.

It was extremely simple, but effective.

"Welcome to my home. Dombret dea a subra, bro."

"What?" Oswald looked up, confused by the foreign dialect.

"Where ya from Oz?" Matrim asked, surprised by his lack of understanding.

"The Tradewind province, a village called Neion."

"Nevah heard of it."

"It was a fairly secluded place and we didn't get many travelers. The only person that ever really left the village was our messenger, Grimb."

"Grimb, Grimb..." Matrim repeated quietly, "Sounds famil'a. Can't place a face though. Do I know 'em?"

Oswald raised one eyebrow unsure if he was actually meant to answer the question or not, "I don't know."

"Eh..." Matrim shrugged, digging into a very empty cabinet to pull out a loaf of cornbread wrapped in paper. He set it down on the table and took a seat. He unwrapped the bread and picked off a large chunk of bread and handed it out to Oswald who took it gratefully, but not wanting to eat very much of the kids food.

He sat in the chair opposite him and waited as Matrim took a similar sized chunk of bread for himself before taking a bite. The bread was dry and had large grains in it, but otherwise was very good and Oswald was more than happy to have something to eat. He had never been quite so hungry in his life.

"So where are you from then?" Oswald asked picking another piece off of his slice of bread.

Matrim rolled the piece of bread in his mouth into his cheek, which made his accent thicker and harder for Oswald to decipher, "Me? I'm from da Rio Alto n' da nor'tern mountains. Big cities up d'ere ya know."

"That's really far from here," Oswald said, swallowing the bite of cornbread and looking the kid over curiously.

"No shit. Took me n' the rest the survivors from the south side a' town ova' a month to get 'ere," he shoveled another bite in his mouth and shook a string of hair out of his eyes.

Oswald tried to get a better look at Matrim through the dim light of the candles, "How old are you Matrim?"

"Huh?" he looked up from his bread and smiled, "Oh, you can call meh Mat if ya like, some folk does," he popped the last bite of cornbread in his mouth and licked up the crumbs off his lips. He slicked his hair back out of his face with one hand and looked at Oswald, "Ya really wanna know?" he looked up as Oswald nodded, "I'm fifteen. Been 'ere tr'ee years now," he looked up at the ceiling ponderously, "House is still standin'."

"It's cozy," Oswald agreed finishing his final bite as well. He was still hungry but didn't dare take a bite more.

"Yea, yea. S'bit small I know. Still. Home's home."

"That it is. Speaking of..." Oswald paused for thought, "Do you happen to know a Nedtedrow or where he might live?"

Matrim leaned forward intensely, his dark eyes a sudden sharp reflection of the candle on the table between them, "What? You lookin' for that 'lil shit too? Damn, I havn' seen him in months a' least."

Oswald paused at the sudden venom in Matrim's expression, and looked around the room passively, "Do you have any idea where he lives?"

Matrim shook his head disappointedly and sat back in his chair, "He ain't dere. I check e'ery now n' again."

Oswald felt the hot throb of the bruises and swelling on his cheek and he looked around the empty room, "Could you tell me where it is anyway?"

"Sure. It's 'bout ten houses east, then count fi'ty north. It's a big house," he pointed blindly as he spoke, gesturing in what Oswald hoped was the right direction, "The buildin' is half stone to 'bout ches' high and the rest is cherry wood. Fairly unique."

"Thanks," Oswald said, trying to map the route in his head.

"Aint nobody there though. I checked yesta'day. S'far as I know e's dead," he shrugged, "Bolzar's missin' too. It's really Bolzar's house but that thief took it e'ery chance 'e got."

"Took the house?"

"Bolzar let 'em. If he didn' wanna, he wouldn'a got it, but he nevah asked I'll tell ya that."

"Nedtedrow didn't have a house of his own?"

"You kiddin'?" Matrim scoffed, "He was as lazy as a slug. Moochin' freeloader. Not ta mention d'ey spen' most of the last few years in Saffermine, no sense ta build one 'ere ya know. Las' I heard it was taken ova' though. Don' hold me to that. Wasn' there myself. "

"If you see him will you let me know?" Oswald asked.

"Sure," Matrim said, "What you want I should do 'bout it when I do?"

Oswald tried to decipher what Matrim had just said, but couldn't figure it out and after a frustrated pause he asked, "What did you say?"

Matrim rolled his eyes a little while trying to be polite, "Where can I find ya?"

"At The Burning Mill," Oswald said, before he had thought about it. He wondered if he would even be able to find the place after wandering around in the dark.

"Sure, sure," he agreed, "I'll find ya."

He thanked Matrim and sat back in the chair thoughtfully. His bones ached and his muscles were tired, his mind fuzzy and his eyes were heavy. He had to find somewhere to sleep and he didn't want to take advantage of the hospitality that Matrim showed him.

He got up slowly and stretched, glad for the piece of bread in his stomach once more, "Thanks again Matrim. I'm sure I'll run into you again soon."

"Yea, sure, no prob'em. I'll see ya 'round Oz."

Oswald left the small house and softly closed the door behind him with a polite final nod to Matrim who had gotten up and was putting out the candles.

Oswald was so tired that he was having trouble keeping count of the houses as he passed them. He got to where he thought the house should be and looked around. There were no half stone houses in sight and the night was wearing down at his bones. He sat down on the grass-grown gravel and had resigned to sleep in the street.

He had dozed off for an hour or so when a loud crashing sound woke him with a start. He sat up, pushing himself away from the wall in the dark of the alleyway and looked around. After the fog cleared out of his head from the little bit of sleep he had gotten, he began to recognize Nedtedrow's voice.

"I've got to get a set of keys someday." Nedtedrow's voice sounded frustrated but didn't seem very far away. The night swallowed the half stone house and he couldn't see its defining features. Oswald got up and wandered around until he found the house and a drunken Nedtedrow three buildings further east.

Nedtedrow had an empty logger in his hand and was turning the knob on the door repeatedly. It didn't budge.

Oswald walked up to him cautiously, "Hey, Nedtedrow. Where've you been?"

Nedtedrow turned and stared at him for a few minutes before crumpling his forehead in recognition, a deep frown setting into place, "Oswart... What? You didn't get enough earlier? You here to take another shot at me?" Nedtedrow threw the logger at Oswald who didn't have to move at all to avoid it. It landed several feet away with a dull thud.

"I'm sorry," Oswald said genuinely, looking back at the empty logger on the ground, "I didn't mean to take everything out on you."

"No? I don't know about that. I think you did," Nedtedrow dropped his hand from the doorknob and rubbed at his chin sharply, "You think that I'm a heartless coward of a thief, don't you?"

"No," Oswald said, looking him over as he stumbled forward off the stoop of the building and into the alley in front of him.

He scowled and looked up at him, throwing his arms out wildly as he continued, "Yes you do! You know why? Because I am... I can't help it!"

Oswald swallowed uncomfortably, "That isn't what I came here for."

"Then what?" Nedtedrow snapped.

"I just meant to apologize."

"Yeah, right. You were trying to break my arm a few hours ago," he rubbed at his arm and looked down at the ground, "you were holding me responsible for everything that has gone wrong in your life. Now you're sorry?"

"No I didn't... Well," Oswald paused feeling uneasy, looking back at how he had reacted, "I did a little, but I am sorry ... I just had to do... something. I was so angry, but it really wasn't you ... okay, maybe it was a little bit, but mostly I was just mad. I'm used to having more control over my life than I've had over the last few days."

"So you decided to try and break my arm? You stupid Elvin pinch! I should —" Nedtedrow pointed at Oswald angrily and a pale complexion slid over him and he looked like he was going to be sick. He shook his head and recovered after a second and took an unstable step forward, clenching his jaw tightly, "I should rat you out!"

"For what?" Oswald asked blankly.

"For being who you are! I could be hung for bringing you here!" Nedtedrow panted as he ran a hand through his hair, his eyes wide, "You are going to get me freakin' killed!"

"What are you talking about?" Oswald asked confused.

"That sword! That goddamned sword, Oswald!"

"Hey! You said my name right," Oswald proclaimed, elated for a fraction of a second.

"Don't — don't change the subject elf! I won't die for you, you got that? I won't!" Nedtedrow scowled, breathing heavily as crept closer with heavy steps, "I — I wouldn't even risk my life for one of my closest friends. So... What makes you think that I would save you again? Huh?"

"I'm not asking you to."

"Yes you are," he insisted franticly, "You have no idea what I would be doing for you if I let you stay here with me. They would kill us *both*!"

Oswald drew down his brow and looked past Nedtedrow down the alleyway to the darkness and back, "Who are they?"

"The generals. The people who live here and anyone else that found out."

"What about the sword is so important Nedtedrow? What aren't you telling me?" Oswald shifted his bag on his weary shoulders and pulled the contents closer to his body.

"That," he said, pointing to the bag impatiently, "is Venhow's sword."

"So?" Oswald shrugged, "You said that already."

Nedtedrow shook his head disbelievingly and darted his eyes from Oswald's face to the bag slung over his back, "No one is supposed to be able to hold it except for him and his bloodline."

"What?" Oswald asked dumbfounded, trying to make sense of the news. He shook his head with a disgusted scowl.

"No one else can hold it," he assured him, "It's cursed!"

"But I'm not related to him! That's ridiculous!"

"Is it?" Nedtedrow asked, his eyes bulging and his skin waxy from the alcohol and panic fluttering through his chest. He lunged forward, more quickly and steadily that Oswald had expected, and seized the strap of Oswald's bag. He jerked on the strap and pulled him down to meet his eye level, "Who is your father then half breed?"

"I'm an Elf."

"You are a bloody mutt! You're half human! I saw the difference in your face the day I met you!" Nedtedrow said sharply.

"So what if I am? That doesn't make me related to Venhow. My mother would never have been with someone like that."

Nedtedrow snorted and let go of the bag, shoving Oswald back up to stand straight, "Let me tell you something. Your mother has traveled the world. You don't know because she didn't live long enough to tell you, right?"

Oswald readjusted the bag on his shoulder indignantly, a hint of warning in his voice, "That's my mother Nedtedrow."

"Does that make my point less valid?" Nedtedrow held out a hand as he continued, "Your mother died right before the war started didn't she?"

"I —" Oswald began.

"— You what? You never thought about it before?" he dropped his hand bitterly, "How old were you Oswald?"

"I was only a child."

"How old were you?" he demanded.

"Ten. But I don't understand what that has to do with —"

"And what happened that day?" Nedtedrow asked coldly, "She didn't just die did she? She was murdered, right?"

Oswald glared down at him, a fire flickering in his chest, "Hey, you don't know anything about me or my mother so how dare you think that you could tell me about my life!"

"But she was killed, wasn't she?" he said, squaring his shoulders defensively as he stepped back.

"Yes, but that doesn't prove anything. People are killed every day," Oswald said bitterly, "That doesn't mean that —"

"Doesn't it? Then explain to me where she lived before she found that village."

Oswald's frown deepened, "Why?"

"She has traveled farther than anyone I have ever met. You don't find jewelry like that anywhere I've ever been," he said, pointing a stubby finger at Oswald's chest, "And I gotta tell you, I have been almost everywhere."

"This?" Oswald put a hand on the fairy figurine.

"Yeah that," he said obviously, with a tone of contempt, "It's a handmade item from a sacred grove on an island off the southern coast. Not just anyone goes there. You can't buy those on *any* market and you should keep that to yourself too while you are at it! So long as you're here you should hide everything about who you really are."

"I'm an elf from a little town in the middle of nowhere! What's there to hide?" Oswald asked, a frustrated flush of color rising up into his cheeks.

"You are a damned freak!" Nedtedrow shouted. He took in a deep, slow breath and looked down at the rocky alley floor, gesturing sharply with his hands as he grumbled, "I should have known better. I knew I recognized your face and I ignored it because I didn't think it was possible either. That damned sword and your damn face should have told me right then and there to leave you where you were. You wanted to die and I should have let you."

"I'm not his son!" Oswald yelled angrily.

"Then whose son are you?" Nedtedrow retorted, snapping his eyes back up into his face.

Oswald paused with a scowl, "... I ... I don't know for sure."

"You don't know?" he said, rolling his eyes, "Then what makes you think that you're not?"

"Because," Oswald said defensively, "I'm not like him!"

"Then you had better stick with that and keep your face hidden elf," Nedtedrow said, with his eyes narrowed through the darkness, "You'd better not lie to me, and for your sake you better be different from him."

"I'm nothing like he is."

"I hope you're right," he looked at Oswald sternly, his gaze steady, "I'll help you but I won't die for you." Nedtedrow heard his voice echo back and the sound of it had the same tone as Bolzar's had. His face fell painfully and he pushed away the memory.

Oswald watched as Nedtedrow turned and walked unsteadily away from him, staggering drunkenly around to the side of the house and out of sight.

A sharp crashing sound rattled down the alley, followed by the raining tinkle of broken glass. A deep thud echoed from within the house and was followed by a low and stretched out groan. After a few loud curses from the nearest window, shuffling footsteps made their way towards the front door.

The lock rattled and the door swung open. Nedtedrow's turned without so much as another glance and vanished into the back of the home. With only a second's hesitation, Oswald pushed the door open a little wider and wandered in behind him.

He dropped his bag in the first room he came to and fell asleep on a bed far too short and narrow for long Elvin legs.

Chapter Eight

Oswald woke late in the day to a quiet and empty home.

He wandered around the building, taking in the strange architecture and the unnatural neatness that made him feel uneasily at home.

The ceiling looked lower than he was used to, but he was still able to stand up straight when walking through the doorways. The walls were painted and were an even shade of beige. The stone part of the walls could be seen from the inside as well as the out. The stones were even and thickly mortared until they too were even with the walls.

The furniture was neatly adjusted in each room and there were no disturbances of the precisely placed items except in the empty bedroom at the back of the house. The floor was littered with broken glass, a few drops of blood and a bed that had obviously been slept in. Nedtedrow was gone. If not for the night before Oswald would have been startled by the sight, but instead he ignored the chaos and made his way into the kitchen.

It was twice the size of the kitchen that he had back in Neion. The cabinets were dark, lining the floor all the way around the walls. A sink sat against the nearest wall and looked like it had been made of shell. Oswald realized all at once the value of the home and the work that went into it. It looked like Nedtedrow hadn't been the last one there as the room was still tidy.

Oswald walked up and opened the nearest cabinet and was surprised to see so much food. There were sealed and labeled cans and jars filled with everything. He flipped through door after door of cabinets to see much of the same. Jam, jelly, apples, peaches, peta, pawpaws, dates, nuts, sugar, flour, spices, soup, corn, wheat, beans, crackers, oil, rice, and some jars filled with more of that burnt noodle breakfast Nedtedrow had made for him among even more mysterious foods.

Oswald thought about Matrim's empty cabinets and made a mental note to bring him something in return for his hospitality.

He picked up a jar labeled Peach Oats and closed the doors. He dug around the kitchen for a few minutes before finding a fork and returning to the jar sitting out on the counter. He struggled to open the jar but finally felt the metal seal pop loose and dug in. It was sweet and crunchy with peaches and candied chunks of oats and wheat. He finished every bite of it and felt so much more comfortable with something real to eat and a full stomach.

Not sure what to do with the empty jar and the fork, he set them carefully in the grey oblong sink.

The only two rooms left unexplored were near the front of the building.

The one at the corner was locked. Oswald wrestled with the handle but it wouldn't give and there were no keys lying around that he could remember seeing when wandering around the house.

The other room next to it was a small washroom with a stone bath that drew Oswald in. Warm water was welcoming against his skin. As he sat in the tub, he thought over what Nedtedrow had said and his eyes locked on the fairy necklace which had belonged to his mother, lying in a heap of fine chain curled over his dirty clothes.

It didn't seem very special, it had always been around. It was only a piece of jewelry that meant something to him and only that because it was the only thing left that had belonged to his mother. She had never said anything about anywhere other than Neion, the little village that he had hardly strayed from throughout his life.

Oswald tried to remember anything, any mention of his father but couldn't recall a single moment in which he ever came up in conversation. He couldn't even remember asking about him. His family, small as it was with only his mother and himself, always was complete. At least it was until the day she died.

The image of his mother, sprawled across the back stoop in a pool of blood with a deep wound burrowed in her back, flickered gruesomely into his mind. The door was open with one of her feet still inside. Broken glass filled the hallway behind her and blood trailed through the house to where she lay. The fairy necklace had been clutched in her hand, not worn, and was scuffed and damaged.

He always thought that it had been a monster that killed her. Only a monster could. He tried to remember more, what the village had thought of it, what people said happened, anything, but nothing surfaced. All he had to remember of that day was that he had been off playing in the woods and then had heard something and had come home in a rush to find her already gone.

Oswald splashed a cupful of hot water over his head and wiped the water out of his eyes, careful not to hurt his black eye or busted lip. As he washed he found more bruises, some dark and large, others could only be felt and were no more than faint lumps of warm flesh.

He looked down at his hands and decided that he would prune up if he stayed in the bath any longer. He dried off and drained the bath. His bag of clothes were back in the room he had slept in and he peeked around the doorway.

The house was still empty.

He went back to the small bedroom and over to his bag. It was stuffed full and it was the first time he actually looked at what had been packed. There were three pairs of pants, four shirts, undershorts, a candle holder, and what coins had been on the dresser or what seemed to be half of them. Oswald suspected Nedtedrow but didn't much care as of the moment. There were also three of his hundreds of leatherworking tools, two scraping blades, a roll of cloth that must have been in the bag before it had been packed and the rust red sword glinting at the bottom.

Oswald stared at it curiously. He reached out a finger and touched the blade. It was warm, sleek and flawless. It was also strange. The etchings caught the light and he read it again:

Not but he who breathes veined magic and those whom are born of the blood following can hold the sword which is blessed of deadly poison and forged in hellfire.

He thought it over and shook his head. It couldn't mean what it says. He wouldn't give it up because it was supposedly cursed. It hadn't caused him any trouble at all and it didn't matter who was supposed to have it.

It was his now.

He paused for a second and put his mother's necklace in the bag with the blade. If Nedtedrow was right, then he probably shouldn't wear it.

He got dressed and repacked everything but the clothes he had been wearing before. He went through the pockets and found the coin that Laurie had given him for the shoes he had made for her father and put it, along with the coins he had gathered from the bag, into the pocket of his clean pants.

Curious of the white and green building he had seen when entering the city the night before, he decided to try and find it.

The air was cooler than the day before and the sky was blotched in light grey clouds that strung from one side of the horizon to the other, lining the cavernous valley that cradled the city.

The wind was brisk and rose and fell slowly like sleeping breaths from the trees themselves. The glowing bulb of the sun which hid behind the ribbon of clouds was high. It was early afternoon and he realized that the days were passing quickly. He frowned for a moment and headed out of the door.

Oswald put the wind at his back and headed towards what he believed to be the center of the city. He wasn't sure if he was going in the right direction or not but he didn't have anything else to take up his time.

He noticed along the way that there were very few Elvin homes.

The homes surrounding him as he wove between the alleys and paths of the uneven city were each captivating and very different. Some were nothing more than wooden shacks, rickety and drafty, sitting crooked against the walls of other buildings nearby. Some of the homes were elaborately designed with high walls and strange shapes. Often, the styles and materials shifted with the motion from one home to another. He rarely saw two homes side by side of the same style or makeup.

One home in particular caught his attention as he stepped gladly out of the wind and into an adjacent alleyway. It was eccentric and oddly creative. It's make up was unremarkable, a sandstone base with light birchwood walls which held up a mahogany colored wooden roof. What caught his attention was the odd proportions of the building itself. The walls were nearly three times as high as many of the homes around it and built into an octagonal shape. The windows were too high to see into and the door was also much taller than it should have been. It was extremely narrow at the bottom, only two feet wide at the ground and broader than was usual at the top.

He stared at it for a while wondering who would build such an odd home, or else who would need a home to be built this way. As he considered the answer he took a quick glance around him and realized how few people he actually had passed so far along his short quest and wondered curiously where everyone was.

The city wasn't deserted, obviously. There were voices carrying through the winding trails of alleyways from somewhere off in the distance and the faint sound of children playing trailed along behind him on the winds. He thought for a fleeting moment that he must have been in the quiet part of the city when a loud crashing noise shook the earth beneath his feet.

He swiveled towards the sound and listened carefully. There were no screams, no sounds of alarm or any other signs of distress. It seemed like no one even noticed the ground shaking thunder that had just overtaken the city.

With a final look back at the towering and inexplicable home he headed towards the source of the crash. After several minutes of weaving through the labyrinth of the city he saw the white and green building he had been looking for, looming over the city from afar. The closer he got to it the more magnificent the building appeared. It was the largest building that he had ever seen in his life, and the closer he came to its base the more he was awed by its sheer size and craftsmanship.

It was an old fashioned building which was blooming with unmistakably dwarven architecture. It was easily eight floors high with only ten large windows between them, all of which seemed to be blocked out of view by large heavy objects. The six pillars at the entrance were placed in a semicircular pattern and carved with encroaching vines from the staircase upward to where each pillar met with a different animal. A bucking Pegasus defended the pillar to the far right. At its side was a clawing griffin and then a large bison, head down in a charge. The far left pillar was defended by a chimera and each head wrapped the pillar to watch in full circle. The next pillar had a striking basilisk and next to it was a raging phoenix. They surrounded a wide stairway that led to the door which in itself was a massive structure. It was high enough for any of the tallest races to clear with a comfortable space above them and wide enough for ten people to walk in shoulder to shoulder.

Oswald climbed the stairs and stood before the doorway, like a child in its wake. He touched the cold green limestone and traced his fingers over the antique dwarven scroll etched on its surface.

He couldn't read it.

It was an ancient dialect, too old for him to understand. He admired the stone and how perfectly smooth it was after all this time weathering the elements.

Suddenly something heavy crashed into the door beneath his hands from the other side. He felt the limestone give with the force and was sure he heard it crack and spider across its frame from the inside. He stumbled back shaken and felt the foundation of the building tremble as whatever had made contact with the door thundered to the floor and bounced briefly before rolling back deeper into the building.

Quickly he turned from the building and ran down the steps to the ground, glad to put some distance between himself and the distressed explosions coming from within the old building. Someone nearby chuckled and Oswald turned to see who it was that had been watching him, suddenly feeling unexplainably foolish.

At the base of the stairs a man stood leaning on the pillar that was ruled by the fearsome phoenix. He was a skinny older man with short salt and pepper colored hair and a narrow face hanging with age and difficult days. He was about Oswald's height and from his profile had broken several bones in his face throughout his life.

The man shook his head slowly with a smug grin and stuck the end of a large cigar in his mouth. He fished a single match from his jacket pocket and struck it on his belt which was a rough sand textured grey and the match lit. He worked for a moment at lighting the cigar, the wind kicking at his face as he tried. When it billowed with smoke, he dropped the match and put it out with the tip of his worn shoe. He replaced the empty place in his hand with the now billowing cigar, holding it loosely between his thumb and index fingers.

"You haven't been here long, have you boy?" he said, through the streaming cloud of smoke that floated away in the updraft. His voice was gruff and low and reflected the stony grey bands in his eyes.

"No," Oswald replied still staring apprehensively at the building.

"Everyone seems to do that exact same damn thing when they first get here," the man chuckled.

"What is this building?" Oswald asked taking another step away from it and looking over the immensity of its structure.

The man puffed on his cigar and surveyed Oswald closely, "It used to be the community building back before they gutted it. There used to be living quarters on the top floor, a dance hall, a huge kitchen and nightly private rooms. It was a hot spot for travelers, and large parties. You know, things like weddings, festivities, fancy things and such."

Oswald looked back at the magnificent building as something exploded within its walls and looked at the man with wide startled eyes, "So what is it now?"

"Military research mostly," he said, tapping on the cigar and following the fall of ash from it with his gaze, "No one gets in there but the generals anymore."

"Research?" Oswald asked, pointing a thumb over his shoulder and gesturing back at the huge door and the sounds from within, "What kind of research does that?"

"Explosives," he said casually, taking a long drag on his cigar and speaking through the smoke, "they are developing new weapons."

"How do you know?" Oswald asked.

"Huh? Oh," the man pulled himself away from the pillar, stuck his cigar between his teeth, and held out a thickly calloused left hand with a smile, "Brigadier General Loch at your service."

Oswald took his hand and shook it heartily. He let go and suddenly his eyes were drawn away from the man's face and to his right arm, or what little remained of it. He had little more than half of his arm above the elbow. His jacket was rolled up and wrapped around the stump of his arm and crisply pressed and pinned. Oswald stared for a second before realizing that he was doing so and promptly looked back at Loch's face.

"I'm sorry," Oswald said, a little ashamed at himself.

Loch laughed heartily and took the cigar out of his mouth with a grin, "Don't be. I won that fight," he puffed on the cigar for a few seconds surveying Oswald closely with curious eyes, "So what's your name?"

"Oswald Bawshade."

Loch nodded slowly looking down at the ground at Oswald's feet, "Bawshade huh? I met a Bawshade once," he ashed his cigar again before looking back up, his face drifting in memories.

"You know a Bawshade?"

"Yeah, a long time ago. It was tragic really. His name was Nicholi. Familiar?" Oswald shook his head. Loch shrugged and continued, "I met him on the side of a road on the way to the coast. You think you're related?"

"I don't know. Probably not," Oswald shrugged.

Loch nodded and blew a dark plume of smoke over his shoulder and watched it dissipate into the ether. He looked back at Oswald and gave him a half smile, "Do you have a place to stay yet?"

"I'm staying with a… friend for now."

"At least you have that," he said, with a stained smile, "A lot of people that end up here sleep on the streets for weeks before they are able to get a place to live."

Oswald did feel more grateful towards Nedtedrow at the thought of sleeping in the cold nights that crept closer to autumn. He looked at Loch seriously through the new plume of dark grey smoke and asked, "Is there anyone who could help me build a home? I have no real construction experience. I would probably end up crushing myself under a piece of roof eventually."

Loch chuckled at the ridiculous image of Oswald pinned under a thin board of pine and flailing like a trapped spider, "It isn't impossible. There's a chance you might be able to get someone's help if you offered them the right price. What can you do?"

Oswald smiled proudly, "I'm a cobbler."

Loch raised a bushy grey eyebrow, "Well that's something different. I don't think that we even have a shoemaker in the city."

"Well," Oswald said, thinking of the burnt remains of his old workshop, "You have one now. And, not to be conceited mind you, but I'm not just any shoemaker. I'm one of the best there is."

"Is that so?" Loch snorted.

"I could prove it," Oswald said, with a genuine smile, "If I make you a pair of shoes will you help me?"

"Build a home?" Loch asked, curling his lip up in an amused and dry expression.

"Yes."

"I doubt you're thinking very straight boy. I'm old and I can't do that kind of work anymore," he lifted the stump of his right arm and shrugged, "glad you think that I could help though, but I can't exactly hold a nail and hammer anymore. I would buy a pair of shoes from you though if you're willing to make me a pair. I do need new ones. You got a shop yet?"

"No," Oswald shook his head.

"Then I'll tell you what," Loch said, dropping his arm to his side and allowing the cigar to smolder, "I'll point you in the direction of someone who will help you for a good pair of shoes."

"That would be great," Oswald said hopefully.

"Have you been down to the market yet?"

Oswald shook his head slowly, "I don't even know where everything is. I'm wandering around today trying to get a grip on the city. I've never been here before and I just got here last night."

"Last night..." Loch paused for a grim moment, the lines of his face deepening, "then you must be from either Neion or Ladar am I right?"

"Neion," Oswald replied remorsefully, "how did you hear about it? I'm the only one who got out of the village."

"I didn't think that anyone did," he said darkly, "and I know because it is my job to know. I keep up with everything that goes on with the war," he finished the last drag of his cigar and put it out on the ground beside the discarded match. "Alright, I'll give you the quick layout of the city." He got down on one knee, supporting himself with the relics of his right arm against his leg. He began to draw in the dry ground at the base of the steps. A rough layout of the city formed and Oswald began to get a good idea of what the city consisted of.

"This," Loch said, pointing at the drawn figures in the sand, "is the marketplace, and we are here at the community building. It will take you about half of an hour to get there if you hustle," he scratched his head and continued, "Over on this side of town is The Burning Mill and The Stone Hand and over here is The Unicorn Horn. All taverns with good food and rough people."

Oswald mentally mapped his way back to Nedtedrow's house and tried to figure out how to get from one place to another from there. On the map Loch drew, there was a large space off to the side of the city away from everything else. "What is this?" he asked pointing it out in the sand.

"That's the cemetery."

"Oh..." he said, suddenly once again reminded of his loss.

Loch noticed the subtle change in Oswald's expression and his face fell slightly. He turned his grey eyes back to the blank space on the map that he had drawn into the sand. He took in a deep breath and looked back up at Oswald knowingly, "You should visit it if you get the chance to. It's the only cemetery where humans lie next to goblins and elves are buried next to the dwarves. Everyone is the same once they're in the ground no matter how they treated one another during their lives. Death is non-discriminatory, as we all should be," he grunted and pushed himself back up onto his feet, "Well, I hope I was some help to you Oswald. I should probably be getting back into the building with the other generals before something goes wrong." As if on cue the ground shook with another explosion. Loch buttoned his jacket surprisingly quickly with his one hand and nodded politely at Oswald. "It was good to meet you."

"And you!" Oswald said brightly, "Thanks for everything. I really appreciate all of your help."

"Not at all," he said, "The man you want to look for is a merchant blacksmith. He's one of three in the marketplace, but the only one who sells tools and animal hides as well. His name is Mich. He's a Southern Brute, a big guy with copper skin and black hair who has a booth in the middle of the market. He should be there until dusk."

"Thanks again, General."

Loch nodded again and straightened his shirt, "Good luck to you," he turned and climbed the stairs to the massive stone doors and vanished into the community building.

Oswald looked down at the map one last time before he started sprinting off in the direction of the market. He lost interest in the diversity of the homes around him after the first few minutes and slowed down occasionally to catch his breath. He stopped in front of a cottage-like hut to rest for a moment and read the sign on the door.

Ollie Yewler, Dwarven and Nelwin Seamstress

Everyone seemed to have been able to rebuild their lives in this city and Oswald suddenly really wanted to be back at a bench and making shoes again. More than a home, he wanted his shop back, knowing that he needed a way to make money so that he could continue to eat. He had money, but knew that it wouldn't last him very long.

An old dwarf woman came to the window of her home to water the flowers in the window and looked up at him and smiled. She had long white hair and the wide forehead and broad nose of the dwarves. She waved at him politely and stepped back into her home.

Oswald waved back at her, happy to see more friendly people in the city and started his way back towards the market. The sounds of people got louder and louder as he got closer to his target.

Finally he came around the corner and looked on at a huge line of tent-like buildings which stretched far enough that the last of them were lost in the sea of people. There were huge crowds weaving in and out of the kiosks as the merchants shouted out the curios and commodities that they were trying to sell to the buzzing hoard around them.

Oswald forced his way through the crowd. Everyone was shoving, shouting, and fighting to get to where they wanted to go. He suddenly felt uncomfortable as he waded from tent to tent, shoulder to shoulder with busy and bustling people. Trying to get more space between him and the others he dove from one side to the other taking advantage of the spaces and small paths that were created.

The shops were selling everything. Most of them were food merchants, selling salted meat, fish and bread. Others had varieties of vegetables, some of which he'd never even heard of before. There were a few shops selling fruit but the fruiting season was almost over.

Many shops were selling jewelry and clothing and the others were few and far between. He passed one shop selling all kinds of weapons, knives, swords, shields, sickles, axes, and gaucho bolas which covered every inch of the table up front. Another shop was selling musical instruments, another furniture.

"Griffin hide! Deer hide! Sledgehammers and vices!"

A booming voice overtook all of the other merchant's calls and Oswald tried to figure out where it was coming from and followed it. He pressed his way forward until he saw a huge man, very tall and heavy, wearing a white shirt with plenty of dark grey and black smudges. He had dark copper colored skin and shaggy black hair that was short but wild.

"Saws here! Picks and rabbit hide! Ten coppers a piece!"

Oswald stepped up to the shop and looked inside. There were piles of random animal hides on one side of the table, some with fur and feathers and some without. Tools were strewn about and lying everywhere from one side of the tent to the other. A bench setting against the back of the tent was littered with all kinds of small tools and knives with piles of griffin feathers piled high beneath the chair in front of it.

"Are you Mich?"

He looked down at Oswald, looking surprised at the sound of his own name. He stared at his new guest and examined his face trying to recall if they had met before. When he couldn't place Oswald's face he said in a voice naturally louder than it should have been, "Depends on who you are."

"Oswald. General Loch sent me here. He thinks that you can help me."

"Brigadier General Loch?" The man raised a thick black eyebrow, allowing a stream of light to catch at his dark eyes in a curious glimmer.

"Yeah," Oswald nodded.

"Well," Mich looked around as if Oswald had just told him that he were born of royalty, "If the good General sent you to me then it's my duty to do what I can. What do you need help with?"

"I was wondering if you could help me build a house."

Mich suddenly looked disappointed, "That's quite a task elf, and I don't know that I can. I run this shop from noon to sundown every day and it's the only way I can make a living for myself."

Oswald frowned disappointedly, the split in his lower lip burning and he nodded at Mich in understanding, "So you can't help be build a home?"

He sighed, "No, little man, I really can't. I'm sorry."

Oswald looked at the empty grassy area beside Mich's shop and an idea struck him, "Well if not a home, could you help me build a shop?"

Mich followed Oswald's line of sight to the small empty lot and smiled, "That might be more possible. What do you sell?"

"Shoes."

Mich stared at him through the dark windows of his eyes, visibly planning the shop's layout and needs with his gaze, "Where do you get them?"

"I make them," Oswald said pleasantly.

Mich laughed, a deep booming laughter that Oswald could almost feel hit him like a moving force, "Is that so? You any good?"

Oswald returned the smile slyly, "The best."

Mich burst into laughter again and nodded cheerfully, "Alright, alright. Let's see what you can do." Oswald ducked down in the crowd and untied one of his own shoes. He removed the shoe and placed his bare foot on the cold ground in the shade of the tent as he stood up. He handed it over to Mich whose face shifted slightly. His eyebrows rose and his grin slid down into an impressed pucker. He turned the shoe over in his hands checking each seam, "That's a really nice shoe. You made this?"

Oswald nodded and reached out to take the shoe back, "Two years ago."

"This shoe is two years old? I don't believe that," Mich said, and handed it back to Oswald, grinning once more.

"You don't have to believe it. I know it is," Oswald put the shoe back on, his cold toes grateful for shelter. He stood up straight again and looked up into Mich's large, kind face.

Mich considered his options for a moment and said, "Alright shoemaker, you make me a pair of shoes like those and I will make you a shop. Deal?"

"Deal," Oswald said brightly.

Mich snorted loudly and spit into his hand, holding it out to Oswald.

Oswald leaned back away from him and stared at the dripping glob in Mich's hand apprehensively. Oswald tried not to look disgusted as he reluctantly spit into his own hand and shook hands with Mich. His hand was just over half the size of the blacksmiths' and several shades lighter. He peeled his hand away, a long string of spittle finally breaking apart in the air between them. He couldn't suppress the revulsion on his face any longer and he hastily, though discreetly, wiped it off on the side of his pant leg.

Mich looked over his shoulder and back to Oswald, "Have you got a place to work?"

Oswald thought of the pristine house that Nedtedrow was graciously letting him live in and then of the dark sticky stains and mess that coated his workshop back home, "No, I don't."

"You can use the bench," Mich said, nodding back to the feather laden worktable at the back of his shop.

"Thanks," Oswald said, looking around Mich's bulk to the bench, "What do you want your new shoes to be made of?"

Mich's face lit up like a child finding gifts on his birthday, "You can use anything?"

"Pretty much."

"Can you use this?" Mich picked up the black griffin hide that had been sitting on the top of his merchant table and smiled expectantly.

Oswald looked at the leather, taking it in his hand and measuring its thickness and strength, "Yeah, I can. I just need a pot and some rubber. I think you have everything else that I need back there already. Do you know where I can get those?"

"You have any money?"

Oswald dug into his pocket and pulled out the handful of coins he had gathered from the bag that morning. Mich reached out and grabbed the gold rimmed silver coin sitting in his palm. Oswald jumped for a minute not willing to part with the last piece of Laurie he had, but stopped himself as Mich turned it over and pocketed it. "I know where to get those," he said, and stepped out from his place at the merchant table, "I'll be back. Watch the shop for me will you?"

Mich wandered out of the back of the tent and vanished in the bustle of people and shops.

Surprised at Mich's sudden disappearance, Oswald jumped behind the table and looked around, panicked at the swarms of people. He thought for a second and looked down at the goods and then to the other merchants who were all shouting and trying to sell their wares.

Oswald cleared his throat and began shouting what Mich had been announcing as he had approached the tent.

"Hides! Tools! They will meet all your working needs! Ten coppers a piece! Rabbit hide and sledgehammers!" Oswald felt a sudden surge of comfort as people stopped to see what he was selling.

Chapter Nine

Venhow sat in a large, black, stone chair. The light of dusk lay warmly across his desk, streaming in from the window off to the right of his chamber. The light glinted sharply off of the obsidian figures on the desk, basking in the final glow of the day. He picked up a hand written report from Skemir about the state of Azar and the reassurance of their new system of patrol.

He smiled as he read, pleased with the new measures taken and the sudden lack of revolts in the city. Azar had become once again quiet with fear and despair.

It was comforting to him to know that there would not be any more problems for a while and that he could focus on the more pressing matters of the trial before him.

A strong, sharp knock on the chamber door caught his attention and he turned towards it. With a quick flick of his wrist, the door swung open, untouched. A tall, thin Keernith stood in the doorway. He was in uniform and promptly bowed as Venhow caught his gaze. He stood straight again and walked directly up to the front of the king's desk and dropped to one knee, "My lord," he said, in a strong voice that shifted like water.

"Ah. I was wondering… My lovely Priie." Venhow sighed with a smile, "I wasn't sure when you would return with the good news."

The goblin stood up and frowned, nearly pouting. It spoke suddenly in a high pitched and soft voice that could unmistakably entrance any unwary man, "How did you know it was me?"

"My dear, no goblin I have ever known stands that straight," he relaxed back into his chair and watched as the Keernith's green skin faded and shifted into a smooth silver white. Its ears shrank to about half the size that they had been and the goblin itself shrank and curled. The body bend inward as the skin and bones shifted before it unfurled gracefully into a small, delicate, and feminine figure.

Priie arched her thin back and flexed her glossy translucent wings in a long stretch as if she had been curled into a ball for several days. She opened her eyes and smiled affectionately. Her large, almond shaped eyes were a deep shade of summer violet and her hair was an untamable mass of pearl white waves and tangles.

"I'll have to work on that then wont I?" she stood straight and started extending her arms above her head and spreading her fingers out in a wide palmed stretch, "But the goblins have such terrible posture. It makes my back ache to stand that way for very long."

"I don't blame you. I can't exactly criticize your talent, regardless of what gives you away to me. No one else notices that you stand straight and all that really matters is that you're able to get the job done," he smiled calmly, "And you always do." Priie hung her head slightly but he didn't seem to notice, "Speaking of, come now and tell me the good news."

Priie hesitated for a moment, her cunning purple eyes dimming at his sharp gaze, "My lord..." she paused again, "I do have good news, but not all of my news is good and much of it is unexpected."

Venhow's smile drooped, "Tell me the Nelwin is dead, Priie."

"He may have died from blood loss," she said hopefully, her face brightening with shame, "but we've not been able to find his body. He vanished from under us."

Venhow's face contorted bitterly and his voice sharpened, "What was that?" he suddenly sat upright in his chair, his eyebrows knitted.

"He got away," Priie muttered meekly, looking down at the floor, "We couldn't find him."

Venhow's nostrils flared and his expression slowly became frozen and stony, "You were supposed to take the trackers. You were supposed to have killed the leader and brought me the other. It was a simple task that I sent you to do specifically," he leaned forward intently, "So where are they now?"

Priie swallowed hard and shrank back a bit, "We did bring the trackers! We had him pinned in the woods. Shevia caught him before we caught up to her and he struck her with a stone. She was knocked out and her mate refused to press forward until she woke up... The Nelwin ran off and it was a while before the trackers would move again."

Venhow drew his brow in even tighter, deep lines etching between his eyes as he brought his eyebrows down angrily, "He knocked my best tracker unconscious with a *stone*?"

"It surprised me too," Priie said, she looked at the floor unable to keep eye contact with the icy chill of his gaze.

"Weak," he murmured under his breath, "she has become weak," he pulled away from his thoughts on the tracker, Shevia, and his anger flared again making his chest heave as he brewed over the situation, "Why didn't you go after him?"

Priie looked up with a hint of fear, "We did. When the trackers were moving again, they became distracted. They had found a new trail. They brought us South. I stopped in the village they led me to and I went to find the thief. I sent Colonel Roche with the trackers to search for the blood trail of the Nelwin leader."

"So where is the thief?" Venhow asked looking around the empty room.

She brushed a wild wave of white hair out of her face and avoided his eyes as she mumbled, "He's either dead or gone."

"Are you really becoming so worthless Priie?" he seethed, flexing his fingers before balling his hand into a fist on the desk. He tightened his fist until the skin around his knuckles paled like bleached bone, "Come closer," he demanded.

"No. Please…" She said, her fine wings fluttering with fear. She bit her lower lip and tried to word the new information she had for him, "That, my lord, is where I have good news."

Venhow clenched his teeth but uncurled his fist slightly, "You lose the prisoner and you have good news?"

"Yes," Priie smiled daringly and Venhow raised an eyebrow, intrigued by her sudden change in demeanor, "I found the Nelwin thief in a small tool shed in an Elvin village. I had him pinned against the wall but I was interrupted," she paused giving him the opportunity to speak and when he didn't and showed no change in his expression she continued, "I heard someone coming and came face to face with an elf."

"An *elf* stopped you?" he asked dangerously, his eyes narrowing darkly.

"It wasn't the elf…" she said thoughtfully, "…And it was."

"What are you talking about?" Venhow asked impatiently.

"The elf had my attention for only a second and the Nelwin slit the back of my knees and put a pick in the back of my head," she rubbed the back of her skull as if she could still feel it, though she knew that she couldn't. She dropped her hand and looked back at Venhow longingly, "I was there for a little more than a day before I could get up again. The Colonel and the trackers joined me shortly after I woke and we took the village."

"You took it?" he asked approvingly, tilting his head to the side slightly as he looked her over carefully, "Very good. Any survivors, prisoners?"

"Yes and no," she said, thinking of how to word what she wanted to say.

Venhow pressed his lips together bitterly, "There either were, or there were not, any survivors. I will not tolerate any more of your round about answers Priie, you'd better start making more sense," he interlocked his fingers on the obsidian desk and looked through her with the intensity of his stare.

"Let me explain," she said quietly, tucking her wings against her body slightly as she took a tentative step closer to the edge of the desk, "the trackers started to hunt the Nelwin thief again. He was still there. We were burning the homes along the village and made sure that no one could get out. The smoke confused the trackers a bit but they helped us keep people in the homes as they burned. When I came to the last home I saw the elf was in it and I felt the need to make sure he would die."

"I do adore your sense of revenge," Venhow relaxed slightly, his furry of annoyance laying stagnant in his chest.

Priie smiled pleasantly, "I set fire to the house and set the trackers on them. I was sure they were in there. The trackers thought they were also… but when the fire died out by sunset we searched and the elf was gone. His body was not in the home with the other elves. The thief was gone too. It haunted me."

"It should," Venhow said blankly, "Failure is not met with welcome here."

"It wasn't the failure that troubled me the most, it was the elf. He shouldn't have gotten away. There was no way that he could have escaped me. And his face…" she said, looking at him fixedly.

Venhow unlocked his fingers and sat forward to the edge of his stone chair, "Do you know him?"

"No." Priie grinned mischievously, "But I know your face," she walked forward and leaned across the desk, with a full lipped smile and searched her eyes across his features lustfully, "I know it's every line; it's every bone and contour... And I had never found another with the same face as you until this week."

Venhow's eyes darkened dangerously and his posture changed. His shoulders squared, pressing against the back of his chair and he lowered his head slowly, with his face angled down. He looked at her through his eyebrows, daring her to continue, "Where are you going with this?"

"He had your face, the bastard half breed son of an elf," Priie said, and bit her lower lip excitedly, unfazed by his hateful expression.

She began to warp her flesh into a longer feature. Her skin darkened slightly, her torso flattening and elongating into a male Elvin frame. She began to look much taller and less frail, her white hair tinted until it was shaggy, short, and red with looping curls that wrapped around the lengthening ears. Her eyes slid from violet to emerald green and her face shifted evenly.

Oswald stood in front of the desk grinning down at Venhow whose expression sunk deeper with dark lines and an unmatchable anger drowned in hate.

"You watch yourself Sprite!" he spat, "Pick your words carefully. I take care of my own problems and you accusing me of otherwise is dangerous."

Oswald's figure crossed his arms and slid one side of his mouth upwards to his ear smirking, leaning his hip on the edge of the obsidian desk. Oswald's voice spoke slowly and clearly, "Do you think that I'm mistaken?"

Venhow stood up in a swift motion and swept around the desk to stare at Oswald's face closely. Priie took a step back weary of Venhow's intent. He scrutinized Oswald very closely, looking over his every feature. He looked over his jaw line, his cheekbones, his red curly hair, his nose and the sloping lines of his shoulders. His face twisted hatefully the longer that he stared. Finally his cold grey eyes met with Oswald's green ones and his heart flared with a sudden rage.

"NO!" he screamed ripping his attention away from Priie and her new form. His mouth locked shut tight. His teeth clamped together shooting pain through his jaw and cracking one of his rear teeth.

Priie frowned and shrank fluidly into her usual form. Her arms wrapped around her small frame protectively. She hadn't expected the fiery rage that burned across from her. She had expected praise for finding him, and his sudden forceful pacing around the room began to make her nervous. She pulled her wings close to her body and made sure that she had a good distance between her and Venhow.

"Where?!" he howled, rounding on Priie with his arms to his sides and his hands balled tightly, "Where did you find him?"

"A little nowhere village called Neion," she said cautiously, her violet eyes wide. She held herself tighter, folding her arms against her body and standing with her legs close together.

Venhow screamed angrily again grabbing the back of a nearby chair and flipping it over to the ground with a violent crash which echoed in the still room. He kicked the chair, watching it slide across the floor. Unsatisfied with the amount of damage he rushed forward and picked it up with a snarl and threw it brutally across the room where it came to a crunching halt against the stone wall. Priie hunched down beside the desk to get away from him but the movement only caught his attention.

He turned towards her sharply and in only a few long strides he was on her. He wrapped his iron like hands around her throat in a death grip, being sure that his fingers were just relaxed enough that she could fight for breath. He adjusted his thumbs over her windpipe and could feel the air scraping through her neck and the heavy pulse in her veins. His eyes burned into hers, "You'd better not be lying to me Priie! If I find that you are lying I will kill you myself!"

Priie beat her wings franticly and pulled at his vice like hands trying to pry him off of her with absolutely no change in his grip. Her large eyes pleaded with him and she tried to shake her head while fighting for breath. He lowered his face down to hers, inches away from the end of her nose, feeling her fought breath brush his lips as she struggled. He screwed up his face and threw her to the ground. She hit the stone floor with a hard crack and curled away from him with her hands over her head.

He knew she wasn't lying and his heart thundered.

"It doesn't make sense," he growled, "I took care of that problem years ago. I killed that worthless child *and* his mother! There's no way that he survived. He's dead. He died by my hand years and years ago and I do *not* make the mistake of leaving anyone half-dead."

Priie coughed and sputtered on the floor, trembling. Venhow continued to pace around her. She slowly and cautiously pushed herself up to her feet pressing one of her cold hands to her burning throat the other holding the pain in the back of her head. She forced herself to breath normally for a few minutes before daring to speak, knowing that he expected her opinion the moment she was able to use her voice again.

She cleared her throat a little and said meekly, "Were you sure it was the right child?"

Venhow looked back at her and a flicker of doubt crossed his face, "He was outside her home... He was the right age." His eyes darted back and forth searching a faded memory for confirmation that would not come.

"It must have been the wrong child..." she suggested comfortingly. Her curiosity bubbled to her lips before she had thought of what she was saying, "Why does he bother you like this? I thought when I saw him that he would just make a good fear ploy and that you could just take care of two problems at once by killing him in Azar. I never imagined his existence would make you so... livid."

Venhow frowned and put his face in his hand, rubbing at his jaw, "You don't understand what this boy is capable of."

Priie let go of the hot knot on the back of her head and rubbed at her fingers nervously, "Do you know that he's dangerous, or do you just think that he may be?"

"I don't know," he said quietly.

"What about him concerns you?"

He looked over his shoulder at her and then out the window in front of him, the orange of the setting sun enveloped in shadows and the haunting whisper of night, "If he is who we believe he is, then he has magic in his blood."

Priie smiled uneasily, "But he's a half breed, he has no chance to match the power that you have," she said flatteringly, trying to win back the affection he had shown her when she had arrived, "Elves can't even use magic. Maybe that part of him will not allow the magic in his blood to surface."

"Never assume that the enemy is weaker than you. That's how you lose your life in war and how you lose respect," he turned away from the window looking troubled now that his rage had ebbed away. He played the day he visited Emily, the day he had to rid himself of her in his head. He realized his mistake at once. The child he had killed had dark eyes. Emily had green eyes. His stomach turned. He should have noticed then.

"I still don't see the problem," Priie said softly, "You have wizards at your beck and call. There are a dozen men with magic in their blood that will live, fight and die for you."

"They're pathetic. With the exception of Walt, they're such weak spell casters they can't even heat their own bath water, much less fight with magic. My bloodline is pure and are born with powers greater than many wizards even hope to attain."

Priie shrugged gently and took a timid step forward towards him, "But, he's just a half breed with no knowledge of his power."

"He doesn't know?" Venhow said, looking at her hopefully.

Priie smiled again at the sound in his voice and said, "No. He actually fainted when I turned to face him in the tool shed."

Venhow's face split into a sudden smile and he actually laughed at the news, relief swelling in his lungs, "After all of this time he still can't use magic... Maybe you're right. He may not be so hard to get rid of after all."

"Other than evading the trackers, he has nothing," she said, trying to encourage his good mood.

He ran a hand through his fine hair, thinking, "Yes, and why is that? Are the trackers losing their touch or are our targets smarter than we think they are?"

Disappointed by the response she fluttered her translucent wings gently and muttered, "I don't know."

"We'll have to test them to see if it's the trackers fault or if there is something more going on here."

"At once," Priie smiled, "I need to know what's going on as well."

A sharp knock at the door drew both of their eyes to the sound. Venhow heatedly threw his arm out wide and the door exploded open. Skemir stood in the open doorway looking alarmed at the sudden crash.

"I'm busy!" Venhow said, annoyed, "What do you want?"

Skemir froze, thinking of whether or not he should leave and return later. Looking at the pieces of splintered wood on the floor and the door leaning crooked against the wall beside him, he decided that the damage had been done and bowed slowly, "I'm following your orders your highness. You wanted to know when Walt arrived. He's here."

Venhow breathed deep and closed his eyes trying to keep his mind on how to fix the sudden explosion of bad news. "Very good," he said, nodding to the General before turning his attention to Priie, who still looked a little apprehensive, "Perhaps Walt will be able to shed some light on the trouble."

Priie nodded and the general stood up with a straight face and square shoulders. He turned from the wrecked room and began to make his way down the spiral staircase and into the darkness.

Venhow gestured for Priie to follow him and turned from the mess. As he passed through the destroyed door, a small meek looking old man warily sauntered into the chamber and began cleaning the mess as if he had been summoned by the noise.

The spiral staircase that led down to the lower floors of the building was lit with torches along the stone walls. Their steps echoed as they spiraled downward to the lower level of the citadel, the occasional red glow from the westward sky filtering in through high windows.

Skemir led them through the cold and empty corridor to the great front door which was opened by two Keernith goblins as they approached. They passed through the doors and out into the frigid evening air.

Azar lay before them down at the base of the mountain. It was vast and as still as death. Homes stretched beyond the trees and into the depth of the forest where lights circled in the evenly gridded weaving of the city streets. Patrol had increased and Venhow smiled, watching the lights pass in and out of sight through the trees and between the buildings which lay at his feet. Skemir cleared his throat quietly and politely, waiting for Venhow to turn back towards the path ahead of them.

He did so quietly, the winding dirt path down the mountain laden with the first of the early fallen leaves of autumn. It was otherwise clear of brush and weeds, a clean path that wound through the thickening blanket of trees as they made their way silently towards the base of the mountain.

"Disguise yourself," Venhow said to Priie, as lights began to peek through the branches ahead of them. Priie fluttered her wings nervously before nodding to him with a smile. After only a few steps, Venhow was suddenly followed by a short heavy woman with grey hair and an old face lined with age. She smiled playfully up at him and waddled along behind the leading party.

The small collection of lights flickering at the end of the trail crept closer and a group of people became visible through the rapidly darkening eve. Five men stood in the clearing facing the trail. Four of them were tall and burly standing behind the fifth. The fifth man was rugged and shorter then Venhow, with wide shoulders and a narrow chest. His face was shaggy and unshaven with straight mousy brown hair that fell around his shoulders in strings.

Walt looked up from the ground as Venhow came into the firelight, his dark brown eyes glinting like amber in the torchlight. "You sent for me?" he breathed in a raspy voice. His lips were thin and pale and hardly moved when he spoke.

"Yes I did," Venhow said, drawing himself upright as he stepped up to greet him, "I trust you had no trouble getting here?"

"Of course not."

Venhow looked to the four men standing behind him and back Walt, "Who are your escorts?"

Walt looked behind him as if he were refreshing his memory, "They are McCormick's sons. Roger, Dowling, Harvey, and Bow. They wish to join your efforts here in Azar."

Venhow looked them over, checking their expressions at the proclamation. He nodded slowly, "Then, you're welcome here," he gestured for Skemir to lead them up the mountain to the old citadel and turned back to Walt, "I'm glad that you could get here so quickly and on such short notice. Your loyalty means a lot to me."

"You didn't call me here to talk politics," he said bluntly, his eyes lingering on the old woman that was Priie, "I've been traveling for well over a week. I wish you would get to the point for now so that I can get a full stomach and soft bed."

Venhow agreed curtly, "I understand. I'll be brief for now," he followed Walt's gaze over his shoulder to Priic and added, "And she won't cause you any trouble I assure you."

"There is something strange about her," he grumbled.

"Yes, there is," Venhow said warningly, "and you'll leave her be."

Walt turned his back to her and snapped his fingers on each hand at the same time. An intense white flame burst into the air and burned between the fingers of his upturned hands, hanging in the air in front of him. He held it out to Venhow who held up a hand to decline it. He drew the flame back against him, warming himself with the white fire, "I'd feel more comfortable discussing things with you if you would dismiss your deceptive shadow with the men and your general."

Venhow stared at Walt, his expression stony, "Your comfort is rather demanding this evening," he said, he looked back at Priie and tipped his head in the direction of Skemir and the McCormick brothers who were walking away further up the trail. She obeyed, disappointedly looking at her hands, trying to figure out where her transformation went wrong.

"You obviously need my help or you wouldn't be humoring the demands of my comfort," he said observantly.

"I need your advice this evening," Venhow said tentatively, "Tomorrow I will need your expertise, and in the future I will require your service." He walked forward, closing the distance between them and watched the glimmer of the flame reflect in the intelligence of Walt's eyes.

"I'm willing to give you my services as you need them or I wouldn't have come," Walt said, as he brought the fire closer to his face and breathed in the hot dry air that pulsed from it. Sufficiently warmed for the moment he opened his fingers and let the fire drift out in front of him a few feet, where it hung in the air as a bright source of light and heat for them both. He took in a deep breath, his narrow chest expanding under his dark robe, "What advice do you need from me?"

"It's a personal matter… and a potential threat."

"What about it?" he said irritably.

"Fine," Venhow said darkly, staring into the fire, unable to make contact with the abrasive wizard gaze, "I'll start with general questions. The first is, can elves use magic if they are born of magical blood?"

Walt looked suddenly into his eyes but Venhow stared determinedly into the fire refusing to answer the silent question.

He rubbed at the stubble on his chin and worked his mouth curiously, "I do think that it's possible if given the right conditions," Walt said slowly.

Venhow's heart ran cold, "Which are?"

Walt frowned and dropped his hand to his side, putting his hand into the pocket of his robe, "To be born of the two magical worlds can potentially give the offspring an advantage over that of the purely magical bloodline. If an elf is in fact born of magical blood it may be more powerful than the magic of humans."

Venhow's eyes widened slightly, "How is that possible?"

"Elves at one time had magic themselves," he said, staring intently at the deepening lines of Venhow's face.

"I'm aware of that," he said sharply, "but how did that magic become lost?"

"Four hundred years ago the elves angered the goddess Fantasy by taking her creations and changing them to make them more elegant; more powerful; more beautiful," he fidgeted with something in his pocket as he spoke, "The goddess was jealous of their powers, which were greater than that of her young and underdeveloped gifts at that time. She was a wicked and envious child in that life, envious of the elves grace, and in her rage she banned the use of their magic by binding it to the earth."

"Was the magic drawn from them and into the earth or was it locked so that it could not be used?"

Walt raised an eyebrow, his face placid, "Does it matter?"

"Yes, it's very important."

"Then I must say that it was a combination of the two. Their children were born and raised as their magic was absorbed by the working of the world," he looked down to the ground at his feet, "Soon they forgot how to use the magic of their ancestors and some forgot that it had even existed. The death of that particular incarnation of the goddess Fantasy and her rebirth brought peace, but it was too late. The magic was lost."

Venhow mulled over the history and tried to figure out the meaning of it all, "So the magic is gone?"

"Yes and no," Walt said impatiently.

Venhow frowned, disappointed with the direction of the conversation, "You give me few straight answers."

"You ask questions that have no direct answers," he snapped, "I'm giving you what information that I have at my disposal."

"Then please," Venhow said, trying to keep still as his stomach turned, "tell me if the magic of the elves can be returned."

"Elves cannot remember how to bring out the magic of their ancestors but that doesn't mean that it's unable to surface if it is given magic that is fresh to ignite it."

"What do you mean exactly?"

"I mean," Walt said darkly, thinking of how to carefully word his response, "that if a half breed child is born of the ancient elven magic and of human wizard blood then the old magic will likely surface along with the new."

Venhow swallowed back his nervousness and cleared his throat, "What are the chances that this magic will never surface?"

"That would depend on the child," he said clearly, "As with humans, some are born with magic, many will never be able to use it at all and some have to work to attain it, but this is a strange situation that you have brought to me with very serious questions. I wouldn't want to make any assumptions."

"Which is why I seek your council specifically Walter."

"How kind," Walt said, sounding bored and put out by the lack of information that he was being given in return for his wisdom.

Venhow noticed the tone in his voice and sighed deeply, "All in due time. Another question that I have for you is if such a person existed how is it that they would be able to elude my finest trackers?"

"Meaning that such a person does exist," Walt said, with interest. He chose not to push the matter any further and answered with a bit more stagnancy in his voice, "Trackers are difficult creatures. It would depend on their training and on the distance of their prey."

"This person was within a small village. They had him and then he was gone without a trace to be followed."

"Interesting," Walt said, taking his hand form his pocket and brushing his fingers sitting against his bristly chin, "I'm not sure how that would happen without very strong magic."

"How strong?" he asked uncomfortably.

Walt looked at him with a hint of danger in his eyes, locking his attention seriously on the illumination of the small fire across Venhow's face, "Neither you nor I would be able to cast such a spell."

"Do you mean to say that he may have magic that he's unaware of?"

"*He,*" Walt said glad to catch slips of information, "probably didn't cast it either. It's my educated opinion that it was the goddess herself who would cast such a spell."

"Fantasy?" Venhow said angrily, "Why would you think that?"

"It's what she has been doing with her birthright for the last forty years or so," he said, reaching out for the drifting flame and drawing it in a little closer, "Ever since people have found out that her will is to save the vulnerable as her current mission in this lifetime, she has been flooded with requests for safety. Making protective charms that is. It could even be old magic but I do think that it was hers."

"What kind of charms?" he asked, trying to keep track of the information.

"Glass charms. Rings and arm bands mostly," he said dryly, "There aren't many of them that exist anymore. Knowing what she does, she chooses who needs them against who wants them for ill purposes. There haven't been very many who were deemed worthy of that protection."

"Would he have such a thing?" he asked.

"Seeing that you are hunting him, of all people," Walt said quietly, with a grim and unpleasant smile, "I would think that he would need it above anyone else."

"How would he have known?" Venhow asked, more to himself than to Walt, "How would he have gotten to her? How would he have gotten it at all?"

Walt drew his fire in further with one hand, holding it above his palm like a candle, "He didn't."

"What?" he asked suddenly confused at the short answer.

"He didn't get it from her. There is also a good chance he didn't even know about it. Fantasy stopped making concealment charms many years ago. He isn't very old I assume? …"

Venhow drew his eyebrows so far down in thought that his eyes nearly vanished from the light of the fire into the shadows. Unexpectedly a woman's face drifted in and out of his mind with sudden understanding.

Emily.

She would have known the dangers and would have been prepared against them. She meant to protect that child. She would have traveled any distance to find him safety.

No. Perhaps he was giving her too much credit. She had been a simple woman who appreciated the common comforts of life. He thought for a minute that she was not driven enough to have traversed the grasslands of the midworld to reach the seashore to ask for something that she may not even get. Perhaps it was older than the child. Older than Emily. It seemed unlikely but nothing else he could bring up in his mind was able to explain the events that had come to pass.

"What do I do about these charms? He's far too much of a threat not to find."

Walt shook his head and looked out towards Azar looking exhausted, "You need to wait until he feels safe. Only when he lets his guard down will you be able to find him."

"Just wait?"

"Yes," he said shortly, looking back into the white fire.

"If I'm nothing else, I'm patient," Venhow looked back at the city with a new wave of plans rushing into his mind, "We have a long day ahead of us tomorrow and a lot of planning to do, my old friend. Let's get you a meal and someplace befitting for you to sleep. You may have your choice of anything that I have. You only have to request it, and it's yours. I'll be at the citadel as always."

Walt softly threw the fire ahead of them towards the city and it drifted off as if it were a boat rocking on a murky sea. They followed it towards the dancing lights of circling torches that lined the border of Azar each lost in the turmoil of thought that the night brought them and following the light of the fire which would lead each of them to where they wanted to go.

Walt followed the fire towards food and warm shelter with questions boiling like oil in his head. Such questions would be answered in time. He trusted that it would come sooner rather than later as Venhow strode silent alongside of him.

Venhow's thoughts spun in circles. The trouble that cocooned him was beginning to ache his bones.

He shook his head slowly. He had to focus on what he had to do now.

There was one final task before night would bring him to sleep. The dwarf lord still breathed easily in the dungeons. He still gave hope to the people.

It had to end and he wanted answers.

Chapter Ten

Oswald blinked down at the tangle of leather and tools in front of him, his eyes straining against the enveloping darkness. He looked up from the workbench and over his shoulder. Mich was stuffing everything into a trunk beneath his merchandise table, wrapping up shop for the evening with considerably less leather to repack.

"I should have these done by tomorrow night," Oswald said, rubbing at his eyes from staring so intently all day. He set his tools down and scooped up everything except a simple scraping knife to put in the trunk with everything else.

"Tomorrow?" Mich said, sounding surprised as he looked up from the trunk, "You'll really have them finished that fast?"

"Yeah. It usually just takes me one full day," he said, stretching his arms and shoulders, "but I got started late today."

"You are something else Oswald. I've got to say I've never met an elf like you around here. Every elf that comes through here is uptight and self-righteous. It's good to see someone laid back with some good talent come by for once," Mich said standing up straight, his full height looming like a mountain beside Oswald.

"Thanks," Oswald said, thinking of everyone that he had known. He had never really thought of them as being pompous or lazy but now that it had been brought up he agreed with Mich. There weren't many elves who appreciated hard work above leisurely music or home comforts.

"Not at all," Mich said, looking up at the sky searching for the tell-tale stars that told the time of the night. He found one particular star through the gathering clouds and guessed it to be only a few hours until midnight. He had stayed at the shop longer than usual, keeping Oswald company, "Where are you heading now?"

Oswald's stomach growled and he tried to remember in what direction the taverns were in, "The Burning Mill I would suppose. At least for now."

Mich raised an eyebrow, "A little man like you in an angry place like that? What do you want to do there?"

"I just want to get something to eat mostly," Oswald said, stepping out of the tent and into the streets of the marketplace.

Mich watched him, with concern in his heavy voice, "There are lots of places here that have good food that aren't quite as dangerous... Why do you want to go there of all places?"

"Well," Oswald said, looking around at the rapidly emptying street, "honestly, I told a friend of mine that I would meet him there sometime soon and while I'm there I'm hoping to find someone else."

"And who would that be if I might ask?" Mich asked, reaching down a final time and rearranging the last of the items in the trunk so that the lid would shut properly.

"He isn't exactly popular around here but I'm hoping to meet up with a Nelwin named Nedtedrow," he looked up and down the street through the darkness wondering passively if he would be able to find his way around the city, "He wandered off this morning and I'm not sure where he went."

"Humph," Mich snorted, "Not sure how to help you there but I suppose that's as good of a place to look as any. Watch your back when you're there. I can't do much with an injured colleague and a half finished pair of shoes now can I?"

Mich closed the trunk and locked it, throwing the key down the front of his shirt and smiling up at a single passerby who slowed down as he passed the tent. The man stopped at the mention of the Nedtedrow and took a few steps back so that he faced Oswald directly, his eyes widening as he looked over his face.

"Did you just say you were looking for a man named Nedtedrow?" The man asked. He was short, a Nelwin, with blond hair, a rounded chest and an able-bodied build which made Nedtedrow look all the fatter. He looked strong and quick witted for the most part but he had a thickly bandaged hand and a sharp limp which he attempted to mask by taking short strides. Aside from the hidden injuries, he was the healthiest looking Nelwin Oswald had ever seen in the city.

"Why? Do you know where he is?" Oswald asked.

The man shook his head, "No I don't."

Oswald looked the man over curiously, "So, you know him then?"

The man frowned, his blue eyes surveying Oswald's features with a weary glance, "I do. I haven't seen him in a little over a week. Where are you meeting with him?"

"That depends on who is looking for him and why," Oswald said, trying to protect his thieving friend from watchful eyes.

"I'm an old friend of his from Saffermine," the man said, rubbing absently at his bandaged hand, "I was hoping that he was alright. Do you know where I'll be able to find him?"

"No," Oswald said, judging the Nelwin and wondering if he was really telling the truth, "but he's staying at a house on the far side of town. I doubt that he'll go back there anytime soon though," he pointed out in the general direction of the house and left his conversation there, telling the stranger a half truth. He was certain Nedtedrow would go back to the house at some point within the night but he didn't expect to find him there until very late. He thought that there was a better chance that he would find him where there would be food, loot, and beer aplenty rather than at a dark and empty house.

"Thank you," the man said to Oswald, looking as though someone had just told him a confounding secret. He took a step back still staring at Oswald for a brief second longer and then smiled at Mich politely as he made his way straight towards an alley nearby.

Mich smiled, looking a little confused, "Why did you send him that way?"

"Because," Oswald said, staring after the limping stranger, "I don't know who he is, and as I've said before, my friend is not well liked."

Mich grunted and shook his head, rolling his massive shoulders to stretch his back between his shoulder blades, "Then you may need friends who are of a better sort. I wasn't kidding when I said that the Burning Mill isn't a friendly place. If your friend's really there than I suggest that you find him and get out of there fast. It usually isn't too bad until Lord General Ramif gets there and has a few drinks, but once he gets warmed up you don't want to be anywhere near the place."

"Why? Is he mean?" Oswald asked turning away from the stranger and back to Mich.

Mich laughed, his huge chest pulsing with each breath, "He's something. He ... well," he paused, "to be blunt about the subject, he's short, even for a dwarf, and he has a temper to match."

"So he's just angry," Oswald said, sounding nonplused.

"He isn't *just* angry," Mich said, leaning on the merchant table making it groan under his weight, "He's always in a fit of *rage* and very violent. Never underestimate the power of an angry dwarf, no matter how short. That's some of the best advice you'll ever get around here," he looked around at the darkness and sighed, "Just be careful. I'm going to head home. It's getting late." He checked to make sure the key was nestled in the pouch of his shirt and stood up straight, weaving out of the tent and into the street.

"What time should I be back tomorrow?" Oswald asked, as the thought popped up into his head.

He looked back over his shoulder and smiled at the elf, "Mid-day. It takes me most of the morning to hunt down new hides to sell. They don't just leap out of the ground and onto my table you know."

Oswald smiled and gave him a short wave as he turned to leave, taking long strides and vanishing between two homes further down the road.

Oswald sighed and took a glance up at the sky. There were very few stars visible through the clouds, making the night much darker than it had been throughout the week. He looked back towards the far side of the town and started down the road in the direction that he expected the tavern to be in.

As he came out of the marketplace, the wind found him with the smell of rain and the cut of cool air. He brushed the longer curls of his hair out of his eyes when the wind whipped them around into his face. The breeze was pleasant but gusts that broke down through the valley carried the heavy whispers of distant storms. He wove through the city, passing quiet homes and dark windows as he strained his tired eyes in the dark alleys.

After a time, he heard the sound of loudly chattering people and soon after he could smell the cooking food ahead of him. He stepped out into a familiar street and looked down the road towards the noise. The swinging sign to the Burning Mill tossed back and forth in the wind.

He walked up to the building and heard not only talking inside, but shouting and the occasional tinkling of glass and the scrape of chairs on a wooden floor. Hesitantly, he pressed a palm flat on the door and swung it in on its hinges.

The two huge men that had thrown Matrim out into the streets the night before were standing on either side of the door, arms crossed and looking grim. They didn't so much as give Oswald a second glance as he slid into the chaos of the warm tavern.

The tavern smelled like cooking pork and spices but was also beleaguered with the smell of sweat and sharp drinks. He looked around. The place was as full as Oswald thought that it could possibly be. It wasn't just full of any kind of people, however, it was every kind of people.

There were mostly very large men scattered throughout the bar. Some were in uniforms and armor but the rest were dressed in leather or thick skins and cloth. They drew his attention first because of their sheer size but also because of their faces. None of them looked as though they would look in his direction sooner than they would kill him.

He thought about leaving.

"Hey, Oz!"

Oswald looked around the room and after a few minutes of searching through the sea of men, he spotted Matrim at a table against the far wall. Quickly, he made his way over to the table, careful not to touch anyone in the bustle or do anything that would bring attention to him. He reached the table and quickly slid into the chair opposite Matrim, looking around for a final sweep of the room.

Matrim's black eye had shrank so that it no longer swelled against his cheek and the flesh had become a sick shade of deep blue. He smiled, again showing off the missing tooth in the back of his mouth. His hair was greasy in the plentiful lighting of the tavern and Oswald could see now that his hair was cut unevenly as though he had done it himself with a dull knife in the dark.

"I was wonderin' if ya was goin' ta show er not," Matrim said, with a playful smile as he looked around the room.

"I've been busy down at the market," Oswald said, his eyes darting around the room restlessly. His watchful eyes landed on a man sitting at a table nearby and stuck as if he were transfixed on the strangeness of him. The man looked like and elf but he was obviously not. His skin was dark and a grey-brown in color with a texture that looked rough and stuck out as if he had been coated with ruffled feathers made of stone. The man's face was sharp and unnatural, like a roughly carved mask which had adhered to his skin.

"What was ya doin' there?" Matrim asked.

Oswald tore his eyes away from the man and back to the scraggly boy in front of him, "Oh, I was trying to figure out where everything was here and came across a merchant who is going to help me build a shop."

"Really?" Matrim asked with an impressed eyebrow raised. He shrugged and put his hands behind his head and leaned back, "I guess dat makes sense. You's easy 'nough to get 'long with. Ya mus' make friends quick."

"Kind of," Oswald said, his gaze flickering inadvertently back to the strange man before returning, "I'm making him a pair of shoes in return."

Matrim nodded absently and turned around obviously to see where Oswald's eyes kept drawing to. He turned back in his chair with a strange expression on his face. He nodded again and looked at Oswald, waiting for him to ask the question that he knew was hovering over his head. He didn't ask. His shame was still high over staring at Loch's arm and his long ears reddened.

"D'at dere fella's Bore." Matrim said. Oswald looked confused, unsure if anything he just said was supposed to be actual words, "The man's name's Bore," he repeated looking impatient. He put his hands back behind his head tipped his chair back away from the table a little, "He's cool. He's an elf too."

Oswald looked at Bore who leaned forward to grab his lager, creaking like an old door as he did so. He only vaguely resembled an elf. He had the elongated ears and the facial features in a way, but they were distorted beneath the strange skin. His appearance was so odd that it was hard for Oswald to see him as alive and all the more difficult to see him as an elf.

"What happened to him?"

Matrim frowned and tipped his chair back on two legs, rocking back and forth casually with a sad look in his eyes, "He spent 'bout six months in that city by Mt. Ire."

"Azar?" Oswald asked trying to remember which mountain it sat on.

"Yeah," Matrim plopped his chair back onto all fours with the clatter of the wooden floor. He leaned forward, dropping his hands from behind his head and putting them back on the table and tapped a long finger on the grains of the table, "Azar. Anyways, he used ter be a big weapons designer in the west. He made sommit that can 'splode things from a distance," he said, with wide eyes making big hand gestures as he did so, "but what he was buildin' was killin' Venhow's men. So he took ova' his town and den took 'em back to Azar."

"Venhow took him?" Oswald clarified.

"Yeah."

"Over weapons?"

"O'course," Matrim nodded, "He cain' have his army fallin to pieces on 'em now can he?"

"I expect not," he looked once more back at Bore, "but why—"

"—I'm gettin' 'ere!" he shouted with a flail of his right hand, "Anyways, He was taken ta the city and tortured."

"Tortured? Why?" Oswald asked horrified.

"Well," Matrim looked up at the ceiling hoping to pull invisible words out of the air as they passed over his head, "from what I can fig'a is Venhow wanted ta know how ta make dat stuff too. But 'dere's also rumors dat Bore was friends with a man named Armond."

"Who's that?"

"Armond's a guy that Venhow's lookin' for," he said, glancing around the room, "He's afraid of 'em."

"Venhow is afraid of Armond?"

"Well," he said, pausing for short time thinking, "I s'pose dat he is more intimidated by him d'en scared."

Oswald studied the grains of wood on the table, "Why would a wizard be intimidated by one man?"

"I dunno. He jus' is. The guy's jus' 'nother army honcho 'ere in the city but he knows a lot 'bout the war right now. He's pertty talkative I guess and 'e gets ta know a lot'a important ranking people," Matrim flipped his hand in the air dismissively, "He's jus' a general of some sort... I haven't met him myself. Bore's a good guy though."

Oswald thought about it for a second and looked over Matrim's shoulder again, "So he was taken because they thought he knew where Armond was?"

Bore put a long arm in the air and shook it with a loud snapping sound that broke against the walls of the room like the crack of a whip. He put his arm back down and a tall skinny man brought him another logger and left him be.

Matrim shrugged with his palms up, "How shud I know? Anyway, when dey had him 'dere and he wouldn' tell 'em what dey wanted to know, dey forced him to take a marsh orb," Oswald's eyebrows knitted together. Matrim mistook the confusion for sympathy with an agreeing nod and continued without waiting for a response, "He *still* wouldn't say nothin' to 'em so Venhow gave him *another* one and 'e writhed and froze up lookin' like dat. D'ey thought 'e was dead and threw him down Mt. Ire. He woke up afta' a few days, wandered off an' ended up 'ere."

"What are marsh orbs?" Oswald asked finally able to talk and interject into Matrim's continuous string of information.

"Huh?" Matrim looked up from the table and looked surprised, "oh. I keep forgetin' that you aint from around 'ere," he held up a hand with his thumb and forefinger about an inch apart and continued, "D'eys is little crystal things, d'ey are round an' green with some liquid white-ish grey stuff inside it. Not sure where they're formed es'actly but I know it's somewhere in the bayou," he dropped his hands and looked down at the grains on the table, suddenly stiff and unwilling to look up from his own fingers, "It kills folk if they eat 'em. It's a slow death, horrific… a torture all its own. It can be drawn out wit' magic so dat da pain can last fa weeks 'fore folk die of it."

"But he's alive," Oswald said, bemused and trying to absorb the details of the story, "Is there a way to reverse it or something?"

"Nah…" Matrim began tracing the grains in the wooden table with a short grubby finger, "It effects some peoples differ'nt. Most folk die and there ain't nothin ta be done 'bout it. Bore's differ'nt 'cause he got somethin from a wizard 'efore he was born. His momma was blessed a some sort. Some folk think that dem who survive marsh orbs like that get immortality, but no one knows. He got turned to wood. A livin tree. Ain't many of 'em who do change that way that have lived through the change though, 'e may be the only one. He seems to do alright all the same. He's a good guy."

Oswald grimaced at the thought of what he had just been told and he felt suddenly cold. He hadn't realized how terrible the world had become because of the war, a war that a week ago he hadn't even known had been a threat. He hadn't understood how sheltered his home had been from everything else and he wondered for a fleeting passage of time how they had gone so long without knowing what was happening around them. He hated the thought that one man could gather a following so great that there was an actual possibility that every province would bow to him eventually.

He stiffened in his seat a little and made a quiet vow to himself that he would never kneel before such a man.

He opened his mouth to speak but he couldn't think of anything to say and so shut his mouth again. His stomach rumbled and he looked back over his shoulder at the bar behind which a pork roast turned over a pit fire. Wanting to get away from the dark subject and sorry that he had asked, he got up and went to the skinny old man at the counter.

"What do you have?" Oswald asked looking back over the counter and into the open area beyond it.

"What do you want?" The old man asked, leaning his rail thin forearms on the counter. Oswald thought for a minute that he looked too frail to even put his own weight on his arms but the man seemed to manage, his face looking younger than his grey hair and thin frame suggested.

"That would depend on what you have and how much it is," he said, surprised.

The man scowled and said, hatefully with narrowed eyes, "We either got it or we don't. What do you want?"

Oswald paused, "A plate of pork and some bread," he decided, sure at least that they had both things. The man's expression didn't so much as flicker as he and turned towards the kitchen behind him. Oswald wasn't sure if he had meant to ignore him or if he had gone to get what he had asked for. A short while later, the man returned with what Oswald had asked for.

"Eight coppers," the man demanded with an open hand. Oswald dug around in his pockets for the change Mich had given him from the gold and silver coin spent that afternoon. He counted out the coins, placing them in the man's hand, and took the plate from off the counter.

The food was piled high on a round and depressed wooden plank with just enough rim to hold the food on. There were strips of pork in all sizes which let off a sweet and salty smell into the air. He hurried back to the table with Matrim and sat the food down in front of him.

"Eat up," he said, taking a pinch of the meat off the plate for himself. It was juicy and sweetened with honey and oils. He had never had pork cooked like this before. He quickly decided that he liked it and the two of them dug into the plate.

Matrim ate more of the meat than Oswald, but didn't reach for the loaf of bread. Oswald was too full to eat it as well, so it sat on the plate untouched. The two of them sat listening to the rumble of noise in the room. People of every race sat and laughed in voluntarily segregated tables around the room.

Oswald tried not to stare at Bore as his eyes drifted past him once more.

His attention shifted as a tall, dark skinned woman walked by the table with an immense cat at her side which was growling quietly. The cat was large and grey, its shoulders arched as it walked with heavy steps alongside its owner with its head down and its attention fixed.

The woman had broad shoulders hidden by a generously thick, dark blonde braid. She had sleek clothing that hung nicely against her. She had wide hips with a narrow waist and long, thick muscular legs.

She was oddly beautiful but his attention was not drawn by her body or her cat but by what hung from the calf of her left leg. It looked like a fat string of large, round, rust colored beads which got gradually smaller down towards the end and was about a foot or so long. It hung loose but Oswald noticed with a sick feeling that it was not tied around her leg, but dug into it, pressed into her muscle like a barbed pin. Her slightly aggravated flesh held the odd thing in its place. He put a hand up to his mouth and could not take his eyes away no matter how hard he tried to distract himself.

The woman stopped and it took a moment for Oswald to realize that she was staring back at him. She didn't look happy.

"If you want to keep your face the way it is," she said, leaning in closer to Oswald so that her water clear, blue eyes were drowning his, "then keep your attention on someone else." She stood straight again and looked down at him grimly.

Matrim laughed quietly, muffling the sound through his hand, cupping it over his mouth.

Oswald went red and abruptly turned his head away from her, her eyes too sincere for him to doubt her threat. Matrim laughed harder and for a second he thought that he might fall out of his seat.

When Matrim's laughter died away the woman had already vanished from sight completely. Oswald shook his head slowly his heart beating harder than he felt that it should have. The woman went to the counter at the front of the tavern and didn't look back at him.

This was a strange place.

The tavern hushed all at once and both Oswald and Matrim turned to look at the door searching for a reason for the stillness. A middle-aged man walked into the building. He was only a few inches taller than Nedtedrow with long, dark black hair that was sleek and shiny, and pulled into a pony tail at the base of his neck. The man's face was cleanly shaven to his chin where a beard that matched his hair began. It was braided at his chin into a long but thin and finely groomed trail that sat at the top of his barreled chest.

He was a Dwarf. He wore bands of red and black cloth over chain mail armor and thick black pants that looked like they could be made out of ox hide. His shoes were thick but were quickly wearing down at the front and looked like they might have been made from the same hide as his pants.

The man glowered across the room and turned to the bar, hoisting himself effortlessly into one of the highest stools at the counter. Before he had even spoken a word, he had a dark colored drink in a metal cup on the bar in front of him. As if given the cue, some of the people abruptly left the building and everyone else continued talking, though not nearly as loudly as they had been before.

"Is that—?"

"Ramif," Matrim finished with a nod and a mischievous grin. He snorted arrogantly and leaned back in his chair.

Oswald watched from across the room as Ramif took a long drink from the metal cup, draining it and setting it back down with a clatter. He knocked on the bar and another one was brought to him.

Oswald looked back to Matrim, "Is he really as bad as people say that he is?"

"Nah! Not at all," Matrim said, smiling wider, "he's got a tempa', I'll admit dat. He's a tough fighter too an' he's got a mean right hook," his hand reached up to his bruised eye and then he slid his hand down to his mouth and stuck his finger in the place where his missing tooth should have been, "But I gotta say he's mos'ly talk."

"In my experience 'mostly talk' doesn't leave marks like that on anyone," Oswald said, with a raised eyebrow.

Matrim looked disappointed and leaned forward over the table, "It really depends on what time a' the *day* it is when ya try ter push his buttons."

"Why would you want to make him angry at all?!" Oswald asked flabbergasted.

"Because," he said, with a chuckle, "it's really funny!"

"How would that be funny?" Oswald asked unable to find any humor in it.

"Oh, no, you gotta see dis," he said, grinning madly, "jus' watch."

Oswald watched as Matrim pushed back his chair and stood up, "What are you doing?"

Matrim walked away from his seat at the table and before Oswald could reach out to try and grab his arm, he dove between a group of people standing close by and made his way across the room in a blink. Oswald tried to see over the group of people to where the boy had vanished but he had to lean forward to get a good look at where he was.

Matrim had walked up to the counter and leaned against it. He looked over at Ramif who was staring into his drink and doing his best to ignore him.

Oswald couldn't hear what Matrim was saying, but the longer that he talked, the darker the look on Ramif's face got. His brow crumpled into deep lines and his eyebrows sank down his face, hiding his eyes from view as a deep shade of red rose from his neck up into his face. He tipped the metal cup back, draining it, and all at once he launched himself off of the stool and into Matrim's chest.

The two of them hit the ground with a loud thud and the bar erupted with noise, cheering and random insults and curses which seemed to fly overhead at the two of them rolling in a wave of fists.

The crowd pulled together so that Oswald couldn't see what was going on between them any longer. It was only a few seconds before the crowd moved again, but for different reasons. Ramif and Matrim were now on their feet and moving around the room as they tried to get in good shots at each other and dodging others. They moved closer to the table that Oswald sat at and immediately he was uncomfortable with the closing distance.

The large cat, which was a few tables away, snorted and hissed as they got closer. They seemed to notice the cat and they were suddenly on the other side of the room and back on the floor again.

The two big men who had been standing frozen at the door now swiftly moved into action. They were on the two in a matter of a few steps. The larger of the guards had Ramif by the shoulders holding him in place and the other had picked up Matrim around the middle as if he were a bag of rice.

Matrim caught Oswald's attention, hanging under the man's arm like a doll, and gave him a quick grin and a nod looking for approval. He didn't have time to get a reaction before he was turned from the room and tossed out into the street as he had been the night before. Oswald no longer wondered how or why Matrim had such a crooked nose and so many bruises. It looked like something he did often.

Now that it was over, nearly as quickly as it had started, people relaxed a bit as if someone had called out the all clear signal and they all moved back to their respective tables. Ramif shouldered roughly out of the bouncer's grip and moved back to his stool at the bar angrily.

Oswald sat alone at his own table just long enough for his heart to calm a little. The woman who had passed him earlier walked by his table again, stopping only a few feet or so away.

"Trunts!" she cursed under her breath, "I leave for two seconds and they take my seat! What makes them think that they can sit there? I sit there every night. Every night!" she grumbled a little more, her voice quiet and frustrated. She dropped her shoulders with a drink in one hand and a small plate of food in the other.

Oswald cleared his throat. She looked back at him with narrowed eyes.

"You could sit here if you like," he said, trying to sound friendly. She didn't seem to like something in his tone and she looked around the room trying to find another seat. Everyone had moved, and now that the number of people standing around to watch the fight had dwindled away and they had gone back to their tables. She was left standing, and there were no empty seats.

With an unwilling sigh, she rolled her eyes and took Matrim's seat, dropping her things on the table. Oswald moved the empty plate and the bread out of her way and she scowled at him for moving his hand closer to her. Her cat pulled the hair on its back up on end and growled deeply again, this time its eyes locked on his.

He pulled the plate of bread closer to him. He wasn't hungry but he picked at the loaf of bread in front of him, trying to make himself more comfortable with the tension in the air around him. When she had finished her food to the last few pieces of meat, she handed the last couple of strips down to her massive cat.

Oswald dared to look away from his plate and back up at her, "What's your name?"

She looked at him from under her narrow eyebrows and didn't answer right away. She studied him for a second and finally said, "Satomi," she looked down at her cat and stroked its large head, not asking for his in return.

"And your cat?" he asked, trying to keep the conversation moving unable to take the thickness in the air any longer.

"This is Ember," she said, much more pleasantly.

"He's big," he said, trying not to sound as nervous as he was. Truthfully he would have left when she sat down, but the sight of the cat had unnerved him and he was afraid to pass it on his way out; so he had been waiting patiently for her to finish her meal.

"She," Satomi corrected scratching behind the cats ears, "is a wild cat that my people raised to protect my family. She is very big," she agreed.

"She has a beautiful color coat," Oswald said, watching the cat almost as intently as it watched him. It was grey striped with light and dark ribbons that wrapped around its body and face. Its flicking tail was so dark it was almost black.

"She does. It is a rare pattern too. It marks her as mine," she took a drink from the glass that she had brought from the counter, looking more relaxed. She set the glass down and returned her attention to Ember.

Oswald noticed a necklace hanging around her neck, made of silver and molded into a symbol he recognized. It was a silver triangle, intricately woven in tightly knitted and curved patterns. At its center was a single silver ivy leaf caught in the talon of a crow. He recognized it from a book Grimb had brought after a particularly long trip he had taken when he had to deliver a letter brought from further north by another messenger who couldn't make it all the way down to the Brutes territory. Oswald eyed the pendant and cleared his throat, "You're a member of the Naddow family."

Satomi let slip an unplanned smile, her eyes still on her cat.

Oswald saw it. She was much less threatening when she smiled. It gave him enough comfort with the situation to see how lovely she really was. He also noticed, now that he had looked at her for a little while, that she was tall. She was even an inch or so taller than he was, with rich copper skin and even features. She was a Southern Brute. He had known that from the symbol, but it had taken him a while to see it in her face.

Oswald took yet another quick sweep of the room.

Bore was gone, leaving him the only elf there. The rest of the swarm was made up of Southern Brutes, Dwarves, and a few northern men. He felt singled out but when his eyes landed on Satomi again, she smiled, not at the cat or at anything around him, but at him. He smiled back, glad that she didn't want to rearrange his face anymore.

Chapter Eleven

Oswald walked out of the Burning Mill, grinning from ear to ear, despite the fight that broke out between groups of humans which grown into a vicious brawl as he stepped out the door. The air was as bitter and brisk and it cut the heat away from him as he had taken the first step away from the shelter of the building.

He stepped out into the street and started heading towards the house, listening to the rush of his heart beat as the sounds from the tavern drifted away, smothered in the wind.

He smiled to himself. He felt good. He couldn't feel the bruises that covered his body or the cutting cold of what he could only assume was part of the usual valley air. He was lost in his own mind's eye with the vision of Satomi burned into his memory fresh and bright.

She was so different, so strange, so powerfully captivating and so beautiful. She didn't seem to have much of a sense of humor that Oswald had been able to find as they had talked, but he thought that perhaps it was a cultural difference.

He thought about it, and nodded to himself. Her culture was foreign to him but it wasn't hard to figure out as he met more and more people from the south. It seemed that the Southern Brutes valued power, work, and strength over humor. Mitch was another example of that. He had not been a welcoming person at first but quickly became much friendlier as he had talked to Oswald throughout the day.

It hadn't taken too long for Satomi to decide that he was not worthless. She was reluctant to talk with him and seemed bitter about her lack of respect from anyone in the tavern. He wasn't surprised. There wasn't much respect in that room anywhere for anyone.

She seemed almost aggressively shy, brandishing her strength and her short temper to keep people away from her, but she had not stayed that way for very long. She had smiled and been more open to talking with him after he had recognized her family crest and even more so when he had stared down a drunken man who had come by the table.

Oswald shook his head and blinked hard, thinking about the stupidity of it, glad he hadn't gotten into a fight with the man.

The man had been twice his weight and a few inches shorter with arms as thick as a dinner plate is around. He had come over and taken a hold of Satomi's upper arm with the crude charm of a troll. Before he had thought about what he was doing, he had been on his feet, eye in eye with the man. To his surprise, the man snorted, letting go of Satomi's arm and had turned away to go back to his table.

At the time it had seemed like the right thing to do.

Looking back on the short incident, he realized how lucky he was not to have had his arms broken in a bar brawl with a group of drunk and angry men. All the same, he still had his arms and they were still in one piece. Best of all, Satomi had immediately showed him gratitude insisting that it hadn't been necessary but thanking him anyway by buying him a beer. He didn't like beer, but found himself drinking it anyway and happy to do so.

They had talked for a while, trading general stories about where they were from and the usual conversational questions. Age. Family. Interests.

He enjoyed listening to her and he wasn't sure how late in the night it was when she had politely bid goodnight and went up to the upper floor of the building to where she had a room rented above the tavern. He had watched her until she and her cat vanished up the stairwell behind the counter.

It had been an interesting night and a long, eventful day. He found himself smiling down at his feet as he walked. He noticed that he had not been counting the buildings as he had left the Burning Mill and had missed the turn that would lead him back to the house. He turned to backtrack to the right path and again went back to thinking about the woman who he couldn't get out of his mind.

He traced her features in his mind. Her skin was unique. It was a soft light copper brown that was shared by all of her race, but her skin in particular looked more evenly shaded and healthy. She had a wide bridged nose and strong features that were very different than the elves but well complemented in their variations. She had narrow cheekbones that sat higher on her face than he was used to and fuller lips that lined a characteristically strong and feminine jaw.

Her hair was long and very thick. It was a deep blonde which wound into a loose braid that hung down to the middle of her back in a precise and fitting way. Her braid was tied at the end with a sharp metal-spiked black band which swung gently as she turned her head. It had made him nervous at first, but he soon realized it must have been something she wore every day and was used to. She had habitually moved it out of her way as she leaned back against her chair each time. He wondered to himself what would happen if she forgot to move it out of the way.

Shaking his head as if trying to shake the image out of his eyes he tried not to picture the wounds such an accessory would inflict. He realized that it must have been the entire point of the hair tie though, why it was a hair tie and not something else that would be more useful, he didn't know. He shrugged it away and his attention slid back to her graceful good looks.

He was distracted almost immediately by the image of what had been dug into the calf of her leg, the long rust orange thing which was buried into her muscle. He hadn't asked about it. He didn't want to offend her and he was certain that she knew that it was there. It bothered him a little and he wasn't exactly sure why.

No, he did know why. It was an invasive thing that was causing obvious discomfort and he could think of absolutely no reason for it. That's why.

Suddenly his mind flipped to her eyes. Her eyes are most of what was so captivating about her. They were such a deep endless shade of mid-day summer sky blue that he almost couldn't breathe at the memory of them. They were haunting. They were just like Laurie's eyes but a little darker...

Laurie.

His smile sagged. He had nearly forgotten her. It had only been a few days and already he had nearly discarded her memory for someone new. He had been in his own world and had deliberately blocked out everything. He had decided to forget her.

No. He hadn't decided, his mind had just done it.

The shock faded and withered into the gaping hole in his heart which sank deeper into the depths of his miserable longing of what he had pushed aside. He hadn't thought of anyone throughout most of his day, and only had when prompted.

He was suddenly disgusted with himself. Was it so easy to shrug off and forget the people that were important to him? He stopped walking and put his face in his hands, looking down through his fingers to the ground. He stood there, his mind blank for a short time before a thought wriggled its way into the void that he had been basking in. The thought made him feel worse.

What if they hadn't been as important to him as he thought that they had been? He had grieved for them the night after it had happened, but had not done so since.

There were so many people, so many faces that he had known that were gone. Many of those people helped him when his mother died and others had helped to teach him how to make a living doing whatever he had wanted. They were encouraging and protective of him.

It had been Keiosh that had taught him how to plant a garden and work with ground tools. It was Narish who had shown him how to work with fabrics. It was Grimb who had brought him books from faraway lands and had taught him how to read maps. He had showed him how to understand other dialects and speak some of the Eastern languages. Although on him, they were wasted skills.

He had always preferred to make things rather than farm or travel. He had even taught himself how to work with leather over the years with results that had brought him interest and praise from the people of Neion. Nevertheless, he found it troublesome that he had been able to brush them all away and out of his mind only a short time after losing everyone he had ever known.

And Laurie.

He had never been able to spend as much time with her as he would have liked. She had always been social and busy, visiting people and playing her father's violin. He too had always been busy, although what kept him busy weren't people but his work. His hobby. His workshop. He was too occupied with his shop and didn't spend the time with the people of his village even when he did have the opportunity to. Now it was too late.

He had felt singled out, different, and lonely for many years. He had felt this way ever since he could remember, but it had become more distinct after his mother died. And now there wasn't anyone left who even shared his culture, more or less what desperation he was in.

Gommorn was a huge city full of people who had suffered loss, but none of them had comfort to offer him. He was truly alone. Oswald felt a deep burn behind his nose and in his eyes which he swallowed hard to try to relieve.

Thunder rolled quietly overhead.

Oswald looked up for a second blinking away the tears that were trying to surface against his eyelids and saw nothing but the inky, black, night sky. He looked back down to his feet and kicked a rock in the middle of his path. It skipped up the road with a gentle clatter and bumped softly against the side of a building.

Oswald noticed, as the rock came to a stop, that he was already at the house. He looked at it for a minute through the dark to make sure that it was the right house and recognized the strange pattern of the stones by the door. He stepped up to the door, not sure if it was unlocked or not, and reached out for the handle. He stopped as the sound of dark angry voices met his ears. He paused and realized that it was coming from within the house.

His eyebrows knitted together as he listened. One voice was Nedtedrow, and the other was a stranger. He couldn't hear what they were saying from where he stood and he decided to try to find a better place to hear what was going on.

He hunched near to the ground beneath the low windows of the house, nearly crawling on his hands and knees as he crept around the alleyway between the house and the neighboring building. It was the same narrow passage that Nedtedrow had stumbled down the night before. It wasn't more than a dozen steps before he was crouching beneath a window where the voices seemed closest to.

He listened, but still couldn't clearly make out what they were saying and an idea came to him. He slid his hands slowly over his head to the seam of the window, against the sill. Trying to make sure that his hands were out of view from the window itself, he worked his fingers against the frame and felt it slide a little. He paused and the voices inside didn't seem to realize what he was doing. He slid the window open a fraction more, just wide enough that he could slip the first knuckle of his index finger beneath the window.

The voices drifted to him more clearly and he thought he recognized the stranger's voice. Daring to take a peek to calm his curiosity, he straightened up enough that his right eye could peer over the edge of the window.

The two of them were in the den of the building and standing tensely out of each other's reach. Nedtedrow was standing nearest to the window, lit by a candle sitting on the table against the wall. He was staring blankly at the other man.

Oswald flicked his attention to the stranger and saw that it was the fit blonde Nelwin that he had talked to, if only briefly, in the market that evening. It seems that he had found Nedtedrow without too much trouble. He looked angry and was leaning heavily with one arm against the back of a chair, taking the weight off his bad leg.

"You don't know what it cost me!" the man said sharply.

"What makes you think that I wouldn't know?" Nedtedrow looked hurt, distant, and desperate, his eyes wide. Even from the distance Oswald could see that his hands were shaking down at his sides.

"You don't think of anyone but yourself," the man spat, breathing heavily, "You never have! I dared to trust you with my life and you had the gall to turn away from me. You're a sad excuse for a living thing and a disgrace to our people."

"I didn't have a choice," Nedtedrow said, almost pleading.

Thunder crashed loudly overhead and Oswald jumped at the sound, his heart pattering against his chest. He quickly sank to the ground fearing that they would have spotted the sudden movement.

He waited through the silence as they looked out into the darkness to nothing. They didn't come to investigate but Oswald didn't have the courage to stand back up and look through the widow again. He listened instead.

"Of course you did. You chose to let me die to save your sorry hide."

"Please," Nedtedrow said, pausing for a long time through the quiet, "you don't understand what was going through my head. I don't think before I act. I—"

"No you don't. You never do think do you?"

"You know you're like a brother to me. I had no idea. I never thought … It — it was just too late when I realized—"

"That what?" The man suddenly sounded dark as if he were fighting with the demons within him, his anger flooded to dangerous levels, "that you are a worthless coward who would sell his friends to the enemy for a short rest in an elm tree?"

"I thought that you would be able to keep ahead of them," Nedtedrow muttered.

"No, we would have had enough time to get away if you hadn't stopped in the middle of everything to tell nasty jokes about satyrs! We would've had time, but when the time came that it was too late to run, you left me out in the open."

"I know I'm a coward," Nedtedrow's voice cracked and came painfully out of his throat, "I never meant to be. I wish I had your bravery but I never have. Even when we were kids I never had the strength that you do. The only way I've ever survived life is by hiding. I've never been fearless like you."

Oswald felt a small pang for the pain that he heard in Nedtedrow's voice, but he didn't move from his hiding place beneath the window. A droplet of rain fell through the darkness and landed on the knee of his pants.

"That is no excuse," the stranger barked.

"It's the only one I have."

"Do you have any idea what I've gone through for you?!" the man roared, "*Because* of you?!"

"I do," Nedtedrow choked out.

There was a pause and the stranger lowered his voice dangerously, "I don't think that you do."

"Bolzar," Nedtedrow said quietly, "I know what I've done. I know how awful it must have been. I really do."

"You meant —" Bolzar hissed, "— to kill me."

"I never meant that at all," Nedtedrow insisted, "I was just afraid… I didn't want to go back to Azar… I didn't want to die. I lost track of what I should have done."

"Look!" Bolzar demanded and Oswald felt his face run cold, thinking that he had been spotted, but when he demanded again for Nedtedrow to look, Oswald felt compelled to do the same. He turned around and took a deep breath and he peeked back through the window.

Bolzar had moved forward a step or so, and was down on one knee, holding up the fabric of his pants, exposing his bad leg. He was holding a bloody bandage with one hand. In the glint of the candle lights around the room, Oswald could see that there were mangled strips of flesh which were gouged out and missing from his leg in wet and dark gashes. The gruesome wounds looked like they were barely beginning to heal.

Bolzar stood up with difficultly, not bothering to re-bandage his leg, and Oswald could see the bare muscles work with the movements. He felt his stomach churn sickeningly.

"Do you think that's enough? Here," Bolzar now ripped his shirt over his head and tore bandages off of his hand and upper arm, "look at this! These are the wounds I suffered for your cowardice!" Similar wounds were on his arm, deep slits and torn flesh, but it was his mangled hand which he held up close to Nedtedrow's face.

He had only three fingers on his hand and was missing a chunk of his palm. The only fingers remaining on his clotted and crushed hand were his thumb, index and middle finger, his ring and little finger were gone without any trace of remains, "This was your fault!"

"I— I'm sorry..." Nedtedrow stuttered.

Unable to look at the gruesome sight any longer, both Oswald and Nedtedrow turned away from the sight.

Oswald slid back to the ground with a hand over his mouth as if given the comfort that perhaps it would keep him from being sick. Rain began to patter around him lightly with the sound of dry and thirsty ground soaking up the drops of rainwater.

"I never wanted you to get hurt," Nedtedrow's voice said, carrying an unexpected strength to it which must have come from the accusation.

"Then you would've helped me..." he said sharply, "I've *always* helped you. Our entire lives, that's all I've done is help you!"

"I can't repay the debts that I owe you," Nedtedrow said remorsefully, "You've taken care of me all of my life. I won't be able to do the same for you. I try to help and it doesn't work."

"But you didn't even try!"

"If I could do it again," he said slowly, "I would have done things differently."

"Well you can't take it back," Bolzar said angrily.

"I didn't say I could. I just wish that I could."

"It's too late for your pathetic whining. You've cast your stone through the ice, now you'll just have to fall with it."

"No..."

"No, what?!" Bolzar yelled.

"I didn't mean for things to happen the way that they did!" Nedtedrow said cogently.

"Did you even look at me as they tracked me down, or did you just turn your head away?" he asked accusatorily.

"I thought you were dead..."

"That is not an answer to my question."

"I grieved for you for days!" Nedtedrow pleaded, with a sudden strength in his voice, "I have suffered like you can't imagine with the guilt of it all. I could hardly breathe from it."

"You suffered?" Bolzar snorted, "Well, here you stand. Apparently you were able to breathe. It's a wonder that you have the capacity to feel the guilt of it, more or less the grief from your own stupidity."

"My *stupidity*," Nedtedrow said, suddenly sounding affronted, "is what got us out of that camp in the first place."

"That was luck. It never should have worked and you didn't plan it. It just happened and we took advantage of the opportunity."

"You still wouldn't have gotten out of that camp without me," Nedtedrow said stiffly.

"I would have eventually."

"How?" Nedtedrow asked.

"I would've done whatever I had to," Bolzar said grimly, "I wasn't going to stay there."

"And if you'd gotten those wounds fighting your way out of the camp, you would have shown it with pride and been happy to have gotten away with them!" Nedtedrow shouted prudently.

Silence rang in the room for a while and Oswald felt the rain fall heavier. His clothes stuck to him with the chill of the rain and the night. He pulled his knees up to his chest and crossed his arms trying to conserve the warmth. He wondered for a minute whether or not he could sneak into the house and out of the rain without alerting Bolzar and Nedtedrow of his presence. Deciding that he probably would not be able to sneak in, he pushed the curly strings of wet hair out of his face and blinked away a drop of rain that slid down his brow and into his eyes.

"But that isn't how it happened. I got out of Tetrach unharmed. The only reason I got hurt," Bolzar warned, lowering the tone of his voice to a seething rage, "is because I was betrayed."

"What is it that really bothers you?" Nedtedrow asked sharply, "that you were hurt, or that you weren't the unchallenged hero for once? Was it that you didn't have a head on a pike when you got back? Is that what you are really upset about?"

"No."

"Really?" he asked lowering his voice, "because it seems like there's something else there but you are not saying it."

"You were supposed to be my brother! We protect each other!" Bolzar screamed, his voice booming against the sound of the storm. Bolzar's uneven steps could be heard from inside the room, but they stopped shortly after they had started. His voice dropped low, and he said through the hiss of gritted teeth, "I should kill you Nedtedrow."

"Then why haven't you?" Nedtedrow asked seriously, "You must have come here for a reason. I assume that's what you came for, or is this just another empty threat from a big brother? It was either that or you really did want to hear the end of that bad joke," he said humorlessly.

Oswald could feel the tension in the room. He shook drops of water out of his eyes and wiped the running drops from his face. His clothes were soaked to the skin and the cold had soaked deeper into his bones. He shivered and looked into the room. The hairs on the back of his neck stood on end from the uneasy and stagnant silence.

His eyes landed immediately to the long knife which was held in Bolzar's damaged hand. His heart leapt. He hadn't been joking when he had threatened to kill Nedtedrow.

Oswald swallowed back the fear in his throat and he suddenly realized how Nedtedrow had become his friend. He didn't want him to get hurt, especially when he had been the one who had directed Bolzar to where they had been staying. He thought about shouting to distract them, but thought better of it.

"Give me a good reason not to kill you," Bolzar demanded.

"I don't have one."

Bolzar took a long powerfully determined stride and had his good hand around Nedtedrow's throat and pinned him to the nearby wall, looking down at the knife in his hand. Nedtedrow choked against the pressure against his throat and his face reddened.

Oswald saw the knife come up, the tip of the blade sitting directly over Nedtedrow's heart.

Oswald's heart leapt in his chest at the sight of the expression on Nedtedrow's face. He couldn't wait the argument out any longer.

He swept away from his hiding place and moved down the alley to the next window. He slid around to the back of the house where broken shards were all that remained from the window that Nedtedrow had shattered the night before. He slid it open, surprised that it made little to no noise, and easily slid into the open space.

His foot landed carefully on the fallen shards of glass on the floor by the bed, the rain that had come into the window made the floor slick. He kept a tight grip on the window until he had found solid footing, and quickly, silently, he ran into the room across the hall.

He tossed a lock of wet hair out of his face as he dove down for his bag. He reached into the folds of the fabric and it wasn't a moment before the warmth of the sword found his fingers and absorbed the cold from the rain in a single moment. His fingers wrapped around the hilt and his heart pounded.

He drew the sword from the bag, the red blade reflecting dully in the dim light that had drifted into the room from the den. He heard Nedtedrow grunt deeply and draw in a sharp breath. Fear flooded him. He hoped that he hadn't been too slow to act when he could have.

He quickly came out of the room, rounding down the hall, his wet shoes slipping slightly against the floor. He thundered into the den, and knowing where they had been standing, took up the sword in both hands. He swung down, the blade stopping short of Bolzar's wild and wide blue eyes, holding still in the air. The red blade rested short of the base of his chin by only an inch.

Surprise and an unbridled fear whitened Bolzar's face in a look of nightmarish horror.

Oswald's gaze flickered to Nedtedrow who was pale, but didn't look to be harmed. The blade in Bolzar's damaged hand still sat frozen, pinned against Nedtedrow's flesh where a shallow prick had been made and small bead of blood pooled. A heavy drip of water fell from the end of Oswald's nose but he paid it no heed. His voice came dangerous and deep, the final and only warning that he would give, "Back up."

He complied, taking a weak step on his bad leg and pulling the knife back down to his side but his grip on it seemed to have turned to iron. "Hurt this man," Oswald said, shocked by the threat in his own voice, "and I will kill you myself," he paused to judge the impact that his threat had, and when no one had so much as blinked he tightened his grip on the hilt of the red sword, "Get out."

Bolzar promptly stumbled backwards, afraid to turn his back on the razor red blade of the sword. He flared his nostrils and took in a shaky breath as he turned into the depths of the house. The sound of his footsteps tore through the building before they dove out the front door and into the rain. In a heartbeat he had vanished into the darkness.

It was a full minute or two before he realized that he had the sword still hanging steadily in the air in front of him and he lowered it. The pain in his fingers from the death grip that he'd had on it screamed in his joints.

Nedtedrow groaned.

Oswald's attention was suddenly drug back down to the room he was in, "Are you alright?" he asked, looking Nedtedrow up and down intensely.

Nedtedrow closed his eyes slowly and shook his head, "You've just killed us both."

"What?" Oswald said confused, "I just saved you. He was going to kill you, I heard him say so."

Nedtedrow rubbed at the small puncture wound on his chest frowning, "he always says that he's going to kill me. I get death threats from him like this every year and he ain't killed me yet."

"How would you know that he wasn't serious this time?" Oswald asked taking a hand off of the hilt of the sword and wiping away a trickle of water from his face as a stream ran down from his soaked hair.

"He might have been I guess," Nedtedrow mumbled unhappily, still rubbing at his chest, "I never really know."

"Then what do you mean I've killed us both?"

He gestured with a lazy flop of his hand to the sword and grimaced, "He's gone to get Lord General Ramif. They'll be looking for you... and me," he added.

"If the sword is what you say it is, then why would they even be interested in finding *you* at all?"

"Because you're with me," he looked tired and suddenly older than he was, "Oswald," he said gravely, "you can't stay here. They'll be here to find you within the hour. You have to leave. Find somewhere else to stay tonight, hide, and in the morning you need to leave Gommorn."

"Leave? Where should I go?" Oswald asked, looking from Nedtedrow's world weary eyes down to the sword in his hand.

"Go south," he suggested, looking down at the floor sounding defeated.

Oswald frowned, "Why are you doing this?"

"Because," he said, looking fixedly out through the floor and into the earth itself, "I'm not gonna let anyone else die because I want to run away from my problems. Don't argue with me for once. Just leave."

"What about you?" Oswald said, feeling foolish and realizing the significance of his warnings about the sword and regretting not listening to them. He regretted, too, the trouble that he had brought to one of the only real friends he had left.

"I'll stay here. I wouldn't get far. Too many people know who I am around here and I'd be spotted. If I'm not with you, then there's a chance that you won't get caught," he caught Oswald's expression, "Don't worry about it. It is too late to do anything about it now." Nedtedrow looked over to the window and saw that it had been opened, if only a crack. He looked up at Oswald but said nothing, looking exhausted, "Take anything that you need. As much as you want."

"I'm sorry," Oswald said quietly, his head spinning, "and thank you."

He took in a deep breath and went back to his bag, making room for a few shards of flint, a couple of candle sticks and three jars of canned food. He zipped up the bag and hid the sword in the folds of his jacket before taking up everything he had and running back out into the rain and murky darkness. He was alone once more, gone again without another word to the man whose life had cost the lives of many.

Chapter Twelve

Oswald's breath rose in the air in front of him, a dim fog through the darkness and the cold rain. He shivered against his wet clothing, the exhaustion of the long day setting into his skin and hazing his mind into a whirl of both real and imagined shadows, threats and strange visions in the darkness. He realized he was walking almost headlong into a crooked wall down the alleyway and abruptly turned to avoid it.

He wasn't sure where he was going to go but he knew that he needed sleep and most of all he needed to get out of the rain and into something dry. He sniffed through the cold and brought his arms tighter around himself, holding the sword against his chest and trying to draw in what warmth that it gave off.

Rain continued to spray down from overhead. Drops ran down his back and through his hair, slipping down into his face and chilling pain into his busted lip. He stepped out of the alley and realized that he was standing in the middle of the street.

He squinted through the darkness and the drizzle and saw that he had already crossed a good part of the city. He was standing back at the marketplace. It was still and lonely looking, each tent and stand was bare and echoed with the sound of the storm. Mich's tent was nearby. He wandered the street for only a few minutes before he found it and stepped around the empty table and under the canopy of the tent.

The cold air seemed even deeper out of the rain, Oswald frowned. He had been hoping that being out of the storm would warm him up. He set down his bag on the lightly damp ground and placed his sword on top of the bag. He walked over to the table and looked up at the canopy. Sure enough there was a blanket of tarp that had been rolled up against the roof. He reached up and pulled it loose of its ties and the fabric folded down to the ground, shielding out the rain and the wind, making the tent impossibly darker, but a little warmer.

He sniffed again, pushing the water and hair out of his face. He looked back at his bag and opened it, fumbling in the darkness.

He found a piece of flint and after a little bit of searching found one of the candles.

Sparks briefly lit the tent with each strike of the flint. It took a while for the sparks to do anything other than flash in the darkness. Finally success came to him and the wet wick of the candle lit into a tiny delicate flame which very slowly and tentatively grew into a respectable sized glow and a good source of light.

He sheltered the tiny flame and stood up, bringing the candle over to the work bench that he had been using throughout most of the day. He set it off to the side where it could give off just enough light that he could see into his bag.

Oswald dug through the clothes and found a few articles of clothing that weren't as damp as the others. Eager to get out of the soaked clothing, he changed. The lightly damp cloths were a relief from the cold, if only just. They shifted around him uncomfortably but he knew that he would be dry before dawn. He flattened out his wet clothes, not wanting to put them with the rest, and set them to hang over the edge of the merchant table to air out and maybe dry a little.

He looked around in the semi-darkness. It was too cold and damp for him to sleep comfortably and his nerves were on edge as his thoughts ran circles over everything that had seemed to plague him over the past week. The week now seemed like months. He could hardly remember what it felt like to have slept well.

If he couldn't sleep he tried to think of something to take his time. He looked back to the work bench and decided to work on the shoes he had started. If he couldn't stay to finish them for Mich, it was the least he could do to finish them now.

He looked at the trunk and remembered that everything was locked inside. He thought for a second and went back to his bag. Finding the three of his remaining leatherworking tools he picked the one with the sharp and narrow tip on it. He needed something else... He looked around and saw the scraping knife and a strip of wire that he had left on the bench that evening. He went back and got the wire.

Kneeling beside the trunk he began picking randomly at the lock, feeling the gears and metal bars within it. He had never actually picked a lock before but he knew the concepts of it and had heard of it being done. It seemed like he had been picking for an hour when he finally heard a click and the ring of the lock popped open.

The trunk creaked open and Oswald grabbed an armful of the leather that he had been working with, a few of the tools that he didn't have and needed to finish the shoes with, the copper bowl full of black rubber, a shallow pan, and the half made shoes. He took everything to the workbench, closing the trunk with his foot as he turned back to his work.

In the candle light he organized everything that he needed, setting the shoes in front of him and picking up the narrow tipped tool that he had used to pick the lock with. He set it on the edge of the roughly cut leather and began beating the flat top with a rubber hammer, punching holes along its edges. He beat holes around the shape, each one the same as the other, perfectly spaced and sized even through the flickering shadows from the candle.

How had he gotten himself into this? It was so strange.

There were customs and cultures surrounding him that he was so unfamiliar with, not to mention the world outside of his own which had rules of its own. He had never heard of the sword sitting behind him until it was in his hand. He had never seen anyone like Bore, cast into a living tree because of magic that he had never even heard of, and he had never been in a fight or traveled further than the Pewin market. He had never been stuck in the rain with nowhere to go and he had never feared for his life before he had awoken that morning only a week ago. He half wished that he hadn't woken up that day, but he had.

Lighting flashed across the sky. It flicked a bright spark of light through the canopy overhead, casting everything in a faint blue brightness, if only for a second. He paused, waiting for the thunder. It grumbled quietly over the hills of the valley.

He set the punched piece of leather aside and pulled the last untouched piece towards him and began to make a perfect replica of the one before it, down to the number, size, and placement of the punctures.

As he punched the last hole into the new strip of leather, he paused with the hammer hovering in the air and the tool sitting in its new groove.

What if Nedtedrow was lying to him? What Bolzar really had been trying to kill him? What if that had been what

Nedtedrow had wanted? He had seemed tormented by something that Oswald simply didn't understand. He had seemed hollow and remorseful.

Oswald understood his feelings, even if he didn't understand the situation. He felt much the same now, with the hovering shadow of not only his own woes but the troubles of others and what little control he had over anything that happened in his life. And Nedtedrow...

He realized that he still had his tools hanging in the air and gave the tool a final beat into the leather before setting them aside. He picked up the pieces that he needed and matched up the materials where they needed to fit, forming a more solid shape that resembled a good work boot. He held the pieces there with one hand and with the other picked up a thin strip of hide that was stiff and stripped thin. He began looping it tightly through the holes that he had just made, stringing the pieces together in a water tight twine of griffin skin. He continued to weave the shoe together.

Why had Nedtedrow insisted to stay in the house when he knew that trouble was moving in his direction? He had said that he wouldn't have gotten anywhere even if he had tried. Oswald didn't believe that. He went looking for him and couldn't find him, nor could anyone else who he had asked. He could hide easily if he hadn't wanted to be found. So why did he decide to stay?

The tenebrous idea that Nedtedrow had made up the threat slithered into his mind and swirled in his thoughts like an immeasurable mist. Maybe there was no danger. What if he just wanted to get him out of the way for some reason?

He couldn't think of why that would be, but the longer that he thought of it the more possible it sounded. A small ripple of anger fluttered in his veins. The candlelight shuddered.

He pulled tight on the last loop of the shoe and made a small tight knot which tucked neatly into the sole of the shoe at the toe where it would not be noticed. He picked up the shoe and held it up to the candle to see it better. He half smiled at his own work and set it aside, picking up the other pieces to the shoe's pair and a twin strip of leather to begin looping the pieces together to match the other. He struggled with the task a little, fighting each prick in the leather with the strip to force it through to make a tight loop.

He pulled at the twisted strip of hide a bit harder than he should have as the thought of Nedtedrow turning him away for some unknown reason surfaced again. He had sent him out into a storm alone with nowhere to go after he had just saved his life. He had tried to make it sound like he was doing it for Oswald's own benefit. He had believed him, but now he questioned the honesty of what he'd been told. How much danger was he really in?

He wondered in silence as he finished tying together the second shoe and inspecting it too by candlelight with an approving nod to himself. He set it aside and reached for the metal bowl of rubber and the shallow pan. He needed a small fire. He looked back to the trunk, grabbing the dwindling candlestick and taking it with him.

There was nothing in the trunk he could burn without feeling bad about doing so. He looked around, behind the trunk and beneath the table were a few logs of wood covered with another smaller piece of canopy; no doubt set aside for the cold of the coming winter. He grabbed two of the medium sized logs and one very small rod of wood and pulled them out. They were damp at the bottom where they had sat on the ground, but otherwise seemed to be fairly dry. He was grateful for that.

He set the two big logs next to each other about a hand's width apart and held the little one up over the flame of the candle. He held it there watching the flames lick up the bark until it had started burning promisingly. He set it down between the other two logs and set the bowl of rubber to balance on top of the two bigger pieces, hovering over the little log and the tiny fire by a few inches. He could smell the rubber beginning to melt and burn slightly at the bottom of the bowl and he turned back to the bench.

He set the candle down where it had been a few moments ago and he looked around for a second. The fire was crackling and casting a fair amount of light. He blew out the stub of candle and could smell the smoke of the fire filling the tent. He tossed back the corner of the tarp hanging from the canopy out into the cold open storm. The smoke was gently pulled from the tent through the gap into the night and Oswald shivered with the breeze that replaced it.

He went back to the bowl of rubber and the fire and sat on the damp ground close to the licking flames, holding his hands out to the heat. He soaked up the radiating warmth from the fire through his fingertips and up into his arms. The chill of the air loosened around him and he waited for the right time to move the bowl from the fire. More than once as he sat there he had to force dark and desperate thoughts from his head.

The burning stench of rubber intensified and Oswald grabbed a scrap of raw leather reaching quickly into the fire to grab the bowl with it so as not to burn his hand on the hot metal. He poured the rubber into the pan sitting nearby and set the bowl behind him. He grabbed the shoes and set them in the hot liquid and waited for it to settle into the creases and pockets of leather to seal it.

Once it started to cool and harden a little, he pulled the shoes from the pool and began to shape the forming rubber with the flat blade of a nearby tool. It firmed quickly as he shaped the rubber.

At last the shoes were finished. Oswald inspected the shoes in the light of the fire and smiled slightly. He got up and gathered the tools and other items that he had pulled out of the trunk and put them back. He did one last check and closed the trunk. He closed the lock back into place with a metallic snap.

He set the finished shoes on top of the trunk and made sure they were out of sight from anyone unless they were crouching in front of them. Satisfied with the work, he went back to the fire, his eyes drooping. He was exhausted.

He sat in front of the smoldering coals and what was left of the fire. With a toe he pushed the remaining corners of the wood into the glowing coals where they smoldered quietly. He lay on the ground and listened to the patter of rain against the roof and on the ground outside. It seemed to be letting up.

His eyes drooped heavily and he felt the tired blanket of sleep slip over him.

Dreams haunted his restless slumber.

The misty haze of shadowed figures crept through the winding vines and mountainous forms of a sea of stones. They darted in and out of the shadows with sharp whispers and wide searching eyes. They had to find it. Life hung in the balance like a leaf dangling on the last branch of the great oak. The storm would take it and ruin the world. Menace slithered like a low bellied snake towards him. His chest heaved with the fear and the feeling of hate the welled up around him like a fog. It was a fire that burned through the contagious corners of his knowing mind.

Something was wrong.

He snapped awake, taking in a startled breath and sitting up like a shot. The heel of a foot landed powerfully square in the center of his chest, throwing him painfully into the ground, his head smacking into the solid earth. The air flew from his lungs and lights sparkled in his vision as the world began to refocus. The foot that had kicked him back to the ground was still on him. It pressed heavily against his breastbone and pinned him down like a bug.

A sharp and authoritative voice slashed through the stillness, "Find it!"

Oswald took in the deepest breath that he could with the pressure on his chest and looked around through the dark. It was lighter than it had been before he had fallen asleep, but it was not yet morning.

Three men were with him in the tent, fully armed and draped in light armor. A lantern swung by the arm of one of the men and the other was spotted by the glint of a dagger.

The man that hovered over him and had him pinned to the ground was a human, burly and broad shouldered with white-silver scars across his forearm in a crooked line. He had light brown hair that hung just above his shoulders in a disheveled hustle and unshaven stubble across his chin. His brown eyes darted around them like a birds eyes watching the darkness, ever vigilant for anything out of sorts.

One of the other two men was a Nelwin and the other was a Dwarf. After a minute or two of watching them tear through his bag and search the work bench, he recognized them both. It was Bolzar and lord general Ramif.

"It's here," Ramif announced. His voice was powerful and strong, each word running smoothly into another. Even in the low tone it boomed around them like dark wind, a force all in its own.

Ramif's hair was pulled tight into a pony tail at the base of his neck and the hair slid over his shoulder as he leaned over the ground where the sword lay. Ramif reached out for the sword. Oswald spoke before he thought, "No, don't touch that!" The foot on his chest stomped against him, throwing the air out of his lungs in a huff.

"Keep your tongue still or we'll cut it out," the man said. It was then that Oswald noticed that there was a sword point at his throat. He wasn't sure how long it had been there, but now the sight unnerved him.

Ramif's hand wrapped around the hilt of the sword and he promptly screamed. He quickly released the sword and tore his hand away from it, the hilt sticking to his searing flesh for an excruciatingly long second before it clattered back to the ground with a heavy thud. His hand shook with the pain of the burns and he rounded on Oswald, the long braid on his chin whipping around with his inky black hair.

"What magic is this?" he demanded. A drop of blood dripped from the end of one of his fingers as he stepped closer, glaring down at Oswald menacingly.

The sword at Oswald's throat slid dangerously closer.

"I don't know," Oswald said, straining against the pressure on him, "I tried to warn you. I'm the only one that can hold it."

"You lie!" Ramif said darkly. The man slid the sword away from Oswald's neck and let Ramif move forward, grabbing him around the neck of his shirt and pulling him closer, "This can't be Dashai. That sword is cursed. No one can get it. Now tell me the truth."

"I swear," Oswald said, looking over to the sword on the ground, "I found it on the way to Gommorn and pulled it off a pile of stones. I haven't done anything to it. I just found it this way!"

"Don't lie to me!" Ramif shouted, slamming a knee into Oswald's stomach.

Oswald thought for a second that he would be sick from the impact but he took in a deep breath and steadied himself. "I haven't lied," he wheezed.

"The sword of Dashai can't be taken from the venom stones without magic *and* the blood of the Kebana family. You are an elf and therefore lying to me in one way or another. It isn't possible," Ramif grumbled, pulling Oswald in closer, "so talk!"

"I don't understand it either," Oswald said, trying to pull away. Ramif's grip was iron tight and he couldn't move so much as an inch in his grip, "I just found it and took it with me. I didn't have anything else and it seemed like a good idea at the time. I didn't mean to take anything important."

"It can't be done," he protested shaking Oswald a little.

"It can," Bolzar said flatly. Oswald looked over to Bolzar. He had almost forgotten that he was there. His eyes landed on the fairy figurine necklace hanging from its fine chain in Bolzar's hand. It swung back and forth lightly, catching the light of the lantern that he had in his other hand.

"What is that?" Ramif asked, his eyebrows drawn together tightly.

"It's a pendant of Fantasy," Bolzar said firmly.

"What?!" Ramif suddenly looked ravenous. He threw Oswald to the ground, "Grater, keep him there." The human took a single wide step forward and replaced the sword at Oswald's throat.

"It's old, but I know Fantasy's work when I see it," Bolzar said again, holding the fairy pendant higher.

"How would he get something like that?" Ramif asked snatching the figurine out of Bolzar's newly wrapped, three fingered hand. He leaned over to the lantern and studied the figurine.

It was dancing.

The light patter of rain outside kept its beat. The fairy slowly bent and stepped over the glass leaf, turning and swaying to the sound of rain in a graceful pirouette, "It is…" Ramif whispered. He stared, transfixed by the figure in his hand, "What are the properties of this one?"

"I don't know," Bolzar said quietly, "I haven't seen but one of them in my life. There's no way to tell what it does without days or even years of watching it."

"But…" Ramif turned back to Oswald, "how did …"

Bolzar leaned closer to Ramif and lowered his voice, "Look at his face. Look at him really close."

"Why?"

"Because I want to know if you see what I do there."

Ramif frowned, the lines in his face deepened by the shadows cast by the lantern. He took the lantern from Bolzar and handed the fairy figurine back to him. He slowly stepped back to Oswald and gestured for Grater to stay where he was. The blade didn't as much as twitch in the air at Oswald's neck. Ramif leaned in close to Oswald, holding the light up over his head as he did so.

Oswald flinched against the light in his eyes and blinked away the strain. It seemed like everything had frozen, no one moved and it seemed as though no one had even taken a breath since Ramif had taken the lantern. When his eyes had adjusted to the light, the darkness resumed its hold on him as Ramif stood up straight and swung the lantern away from him.

"Lord General?" Grater said tentatively.

Ramif had his back to everyone, looking out into nowhere, his head down. It took a moment before he crouched and it was evident that he had moved to study the sword more closely. His chest swelled and fell more deeply and his breaths could be heard over the sounds of the sprinkling rain.

"Ramif? Am I right?" Bolzar asked sounding worried and apprehensive.

Ramif kicked at the sword and flipped it over to its other side, reading the carved inscription along the red blade. He stopped and stood up slowly. He stood rigid in the light cast from the lantern, "I'm afraid so," he nudged the sword with the toe of his shoe again, stalling for time to think, "This is the sword of Dashai."

"How can we be sure?" Grater asked.

"Bring him here," Ramif ordered.

Grater snapped down and had a strong hand around Oswald's upper arm before Ramif had even finished his sentence. Oswald was hauled to his feet and tossed forward to where Ramif stood with a dagger now out and in his hand. Oswald now had both a sword at his back and a dagger pointed at his chest.

"Pick it up," Ramif said, nodding to the sword at his feet.

Oswald hesitated unsure of what he should do. He could try to fight them off when he picked it up but he was sure that swinging a sword wildly and untrained at two sword masters seemed somehow foolish. He thought that if he could knock Grater to the ground that he could probably outrun Ramif, but he couldn't be sure. His mind raced but he couldn't think of anything that would get him out of the situation.

"I said pick it up!" Ramif shouted.

Oswald sank down to the ground and reached out for the sword, disgusted by the thin layer of scorched flesh that hung burnt on the hilt. He grabbed the sword, his fingers tightening around the comforting warm metal under his hand. He picked it up off the ground, the weight of it balancing in his grip. He stood up straight and looked around at the men surrounding him.

They seemed to be waiting for something that didn't come. When nothing happened, Ramif's face flooded to a bright red, Bolzar and Grater's faces on the other hand went sheet white in an instant.

"You took the sword of Dashai from the venom stones?" Ramif asked trying to clarify something that remained unsaid.

Oswald nodded.

"By your own hand?"

He nodded again.

"How?"

"I don't know. I just pulled it out. It wasn't that hard."

Ramif forced himself to breathe slowly, "And the pendant from Fantasy... Where did you steal it?"

"I didn't," Oswald insisted.

"Don't lie to me!" Ramif bellowed, his voice echoing in the stillness. He shook the dagger in his hand and set it against Oswald's ribs threateningly. Oswald tightened his grip on the sword and whitened his knuckles. It didn't go unnoticed. Ramif looked back behind him, snatching the now mostly empty bag from the ground, "Put the sword in here."

Oswald did so reluctantly and watched the sword as it, along with the bag, was set out of his reach.

"Now don't try anything stupid and tell me the truth," Ramif hissed, "Who did you take that pendant from?"

"No one!" Oswald said insistently, "It was my mothers. I took it when she died. She had said it was meant to defend me from demons."

The three men in the tent all looked up suddenly, exchanging odd glances. Ramif's brow drew down and he clenched his jaw, "What?"

Oswald shrugged lightly, looking around with wide eyes, "I don't know. I was just a kid but that's what she always told me."

"Who was she?" Ramif asked sternly.

Oswald thought about asking a few questions of his own but the sharp points of the blades at both his chest and back discouraged him. He decided not to press his luck and he swallowed to answer, "Emily Bawshade of Neion in the western province."

Ramif's eyes shrank to slits as he scrutinized him, "and your father?"

Oswald shook his head, "I don't know."

"Yes you do," Ramif said, his face distorted with a bottomless hate, "I can see it in your face and the sword betrayed you. Just admit who you are and we'll make your death swift."

"My death?!" Oswald said startled, his eyes opening wider. His heart thundered against his ribs with the pulse of shock that washed through his body.

"Tell me your family name."

"Bawshade!" Oswald said fearfully, his eyes pleading, "My last name is Bawshade. I don't know who my father was!"

"I can see it in your face!" Ramif shouted.

"See what?" Oswald asked shakily, he cleared his throat and crumpled his forehead in worry.

"The face of your father," Ramif breathed darkly, "*HIS* face. You're the mirror image of Venhow Kebana, the false king and warlock of Azar. The hateful bloodstained murderer," Ramif took in a deep breath, pressing the blade of the dagger painfully against Oswald's chest, "The same man who cut out the heart of my wife and laid it in my worthless hands," he twisted the blade, cutting a fine layer of Oswald's skin, "My revenge will not be with mercy."

"I am not that man!" Oswald said, horrified at the image, "I had nothing to do with that! I'm so sorry that happened to you. Even if he were my father, even if I knew who he was, I wouldn't hurt anyone! I don't know that I could even if I had to. I swear on my life!"

"I hold you to it," Ramif snarled.

Bolzar snorted and gripped his good hand tight around the glass fairy in his fist, "He had that blade in my face before I even knew that he was in the house. He would have killed me if I hadn't gotten out of there," Bolzar said definitively.

"Is that right?" Ramif said, with a sick curl of a smile.

"I was defending someone," Oswald pleaded honestly.

"Who?" Ramif demanded suspiciously.

"Nedtedrow."

Ramif narrowed his eyes bitterly, "He's just another traitor and a thief."

"He's a friend of mine," Oswald insisted, "and a good man."

"Like you?" Ramif asked mockingly, "So should he die too?"

Oswald shook his head emphatically, "No."

"You'd defend him?"

"Yes," Oswald said quickly, "I already have."

"By trying to kill our best strategist?" Ramif accused, looking back to Bolzar.

Oswald looked around the tent breathing heavily, feeling the points of the blades against his back and chest, "I didn't try to kill anyone!"

"So you didn't have that sword at his face?" Ramif asked, nodding with his head down to the bag on the ground with a fiery glare.

"No..." Oswald shook his head, "I mean, I did, but I wasn't going to hurt him!"

Bolzar's frown deepened and he stepped closer, "He threatened to kill me. He even said he would do it himself."

"Is that so?" Ramif growled.

"I — I did say that but ..." his voice drifted away weakly at the burning stares of the eyes surrounding, the sword at his back pressed harder against him and he winced at the pressure of it, "I wouldn't..."

Bolzar shook his head, making eye contact with Ramif, "There is no doubt in my mind that he had full intention to kill me."

Ramif smiled wickedly, "And so the axe falls," he pulled his knife away from Oswald's chest and made a swift gesture with the blade. Following the silent command, Grater sheathed his sword and quickly seized Oswald. He wrapped his arms tight under his grip, like a bundle of twigs in twine.

Oswald felt his hands wrench up behind his back and tie together with a thick rope. The knot of the rope was pulled so tightly that a dull pain grated at his wrists with the pressure.

"What's going on?" Oswald asked trembling slightly.

"This will be your last dawn," Ramif's expression sagged with the dark eyes of revenge, craving blood in a wild and savage way. His gaze tore at Oswald's face seeing only the hateful etched face of the enemy.

"Why?" Oswald cried out, fighting against Grater's stony grip, "I didn't do anything!"

"Yes you did," Ramif argued quietly, "You drew a sword on a Nelwin leader. You threatened to kill him. You assisted a traitor and a thief. You are the heir to that wicked throne. Darkness runs in your heart and magic in your blood. You are a danger to the people of this city. You are a murderer at heart, and for your crimes you will pay. Your head will fall at sunrise and your blood will bring us a new day," he took in a deep breath through the pounding of his heart, "Today you will die."

Chapter Thirteen

Oswald opened his mouth to argue, to try and save his own life, but a strip of fabric wrapped around his mouth, gagging his words into a muffled whimper. The edges of his mouth were drawn back painfully and he couldn't move the fabric out of his way to say so much as his own name. He was struck across the back of the head with something dull and heavy and he suddenly felt the cold earth against his face and the warm trickle of blood in his hair.

His vision came in and out of focus and he felt a hand grip the scruff of his neck and haul him halfway onto his feet by the collar of his shirt. He was promptly shoved forward by a large hand and he stumbled blindly and clumsily out of the tent and into the luring early morning light.

It was still dark outside but the sky glowed soft green in a whisper of first morning light. The rain had stopped. He stood with his knees weak and trembling as he held up his weight. It wasn't a breaths rest before the small precession of weapons and strong hands pushed at his back. The man named Grater now had a fistful of his shirt at the shoulder, and held his sword at the ready in his other hand. Bolzar walked quietly with the group, holding his wounded hand with the fairy pendant clutched against his chest and he was slowly falling behind them with his muffled limp.

Ramif marched forcefully alongside Oswald and he could almost feel the bitter hate that radiated out from his clenched hands a few feet away. Grater released him suddenly and Oswald felt a foot kick at the back of his shaky knees and he collapsed with the abuse. He braced for the impact with the road, unable to catch himself with his hands tied behind him. He hit the ground hard with his shoulder. His cheek and chin scraped on the rocky path with the impact.

He opened his eyes in time to see Ramif smirking and Grater's big hand reach down for him again. He was pulled across the ground for several feet as they kept moving, hauling him along. The gravel tore at his skin as he was dragged without pause before he was able to get his feet beneath him and get back up to his struggling feet, kicking rocks out of place as he tried to find his footing.

They forced him through the city, around corners and through narrow lanes, but all the while sticking to the rock paved roads leading intently inward to the heart of Gommorn. The houses became closer together and more uniform in shape and placement, setting in more even lines the further into the city that they went.

He thought franticly of ways that he could escape. He thought of trying to push over Grater and make a run for it but being bound and gagged would make his escape more difficult. The thought of trying to grab the sword of Dashai from the bag around Ramif's shoulder but he couldn't think of how that would do him any good either. He could fight them, but he also knew that if he were to try, that it would only take one swipe of the sword, any one of the swords, to stop him still in his tracks.

He watched the ground at his feet, his head buzzing and spinning with the lightheaded sickness that washed through him. He wasn't strong enough to pull away from the thick arms or the strong hands of Grater and he wasn't fast enough to outrun or out skill a Dwarven General. The Lord General.

He was tired and weak. His body had never taken so much violence or had endured so much damage as it had in the last several days. He was sore all over, aching, miserable. His eyes drooped and he could still feel the droplets of blood slipping slowly from swollen cut on the crown of his head down to where it cooled and stilled behind his right ear in a wet mass of curly hair.

He was shoved again and he staggered, catching himself before he lost his balance. He didn't want to fall again. He wasn't sure, if he were to fall, whether or not he would be able to get back up.

Oswald looked around as the light of morning began to brighten the air of the city. The sky faintly took on the hue of a thick crimson droplet of fresh blood. The horizon was bleeding in a thin line that pooled on the distant hillsides and the horizon of the mountain range. The color wavered in a pool which rippled against the tiny remaining puffs of cloud and brightened in the mist that hung over the city.

The buildings of the city had suddenly thinned out to nothing. A large expanse of land had been cleared ahead of them in a massive circle. In the center of the clearing there was a chest high platform with a wide base and sturdy build. On the platform was a block that was too tall to be a place to stand and too short for a podium.

Oswald feared, as he stared at the block, that it would be the last thing that he would ever see.

They marched him forward to the platform, and with a single heave he was half lifted, half shoved, up onto the wooden frame. Grater clambered up after him, followed by Ramif. Bolzar stood wearily in front of them on the ground, looking pale and strained but pleased with the night's justice.

"Go and get the other officers," Ramif said, down to him, "and then send for my son. I have a job for him."

Bolzar nodded and jogged off clumsily. He was landing heavily on his good leg and limping gingerly on the other as he went off through the labyrinth of homes in the direction of the community building.

Ramif took a handful of Oswald's hair, the cut on his head digging painfully into his skull, and dragged Oswald to the block in the center of the platform.

Oswald was shoved hard, his torso forced to lie across the angled and risen shape of the block, his face staring down at the grains of the oak wood that made up the platform. He was horrified when he realized the height of the platform was perfect for his body to lean across with his knees on the boards and his shoulders hanging over its edge. His head was left unsupported and the dark brown stains in the wood in front of his face made his whole body revolt in a desperate wave of nausea.

Two metal bands, one and then the other, clipped down over Oswald's upper arms locking him down to the block that he was pinned across. The bands immediately made his shoulders ache. His hands were still tied behind him and the sharp pressure of the bands holding him down twisted his shoulders and elbows because of the unnatural angle. He tried to move to relieve the pressure without success. He couldn't move anything but his head and ankles.

Ramif turned away from Oswald, knowing that he would not be able to get away, and instead turned his attention to Grater.

"Take this," he said, holding out the bag that the sword was sitting in, "and show Armond. Tell him to come here, we have an execution to deliberate."

"Yes sir," Grater said, with a quick bow. He jumped down off the platform in front of Oswald. He shouldered the bag with Oswald's sword and gave him a brief unreadable look before heading in the opposite direction that Bolzar had gone.

People began peeking out from their doors and windows from the houses surrounding the circle. Some stepped forward into the clearing but others drew the blinds of their windows and pretended that they didn't know what was going on just outside of their homes. Oswald's neck began to ache from holding it up at the angle he needed to look around, so he hung his head down but the stains on the floor below him made his heart race.

He felt a hand thump down on his back and Ramif's low smooth voice sank down to him in an icy drip, "The trial is a formality," he whispered with an evil grin that could be heard in his voice, "because when it comes right down to it, I'm the judge *and* the executioner. I am the Lord General and my word is law around here." He laughed quietly to himself and Oswald's last string of hope broke, sending his heart tumbling down into his stomach.

He heard Ramif walk away from the block, pacing back and forth behind him on the wooden floor of the platform, mumbling incomprehensibly to himself as he did so.

Oswald's knees and his lower ribs started to hurt from the pressure of his weight against the hard surface and he tried to put more pressure on his toes, but he couldn't move enough to help much. He lay there listening to the clop of Ramif's footsteps and watching the unsettling crimson light of sunrise darken the bloody stains in the wood as unknown minutes drifted by in time.

After what seemed like only a short while, people began to circle around the platform, some of them climbing up to stand with Ramif, and others muttering in groups on the ground. Soon there was a clamber of voices around the city's circle. The voices that were the loudest seemed to come from behind him as the officers gathered to the trial site.

Grater came back to the platform and hopped back up to join with the officers. He was followed by a tall blonde man with deep blue eyes.

Armond was thick and muscular, with wide shoulders and masculine features that could have been cut from fine stone. His rich, blonde, hair was cut short against his head and the fine muscles of his jaw worked underneath his skin as he surveyed the group. He had a regal air of self-importance about him that parted the gathering sea of people as he made his way through.

He leapt up onto the platform without much trouble and mingled into the group. He set the bag with the sword down in the middle of the floor in front of the gathered men. They turned to look at the sword as it hit the floor and slid from the bag enough that the red blade and part of the engraving could be seen. The voices quieted to near stillness before flaring up into an angry roar of disagreement.

Bolozar hobbled up to the group with the last of the officers and a boy that looked no more than ten years old. The boy had thick black hair like Ramif and the same sharp vigilant eyes but the rest of his features were softer and more approachable, either due to his youth or his resemblance to his mother, as there was nothing soft about Ramif. The boy looked up at Oswald from the ground with a curious expression, looking almost sympathetic.

"Dad!" the boy hollered over the noise.

Ramif made his way through the pressing crowd to the edge of the platform, looking down at his son with a solid look. He held out a large bell that had been brought by one of the last officers to arrive and leaned down over the edge and handed it over to the boy, "I need you to run out into the city and call for a trial of execution for the son of Venhow. Gather anyone who has anything to say for the elf. You got that?"

The boy promptly grabbed the bell, eager to have something to do that didn't involve staying in the circle. He nodded and without a minute to waste he turned and began shouting at the top of his lungs as he ran, "Trial at city heart! Elven execution! Trial! Trial!"

Ramif made a kick at Oswald's leg as he walked by, heading back into the bustle of the crowd behind him. The officers were circled around the sword and arguing about whether or not it was what they thought it was or how it happened to come into the hands of an elf.

Ramif held up a hand into the chaos and one voice at a time, it fell down into the quiet hum of the crowd around them.

"One at a time," Ramif said loudly, looking around at the circle of men.

An older man with gray hair that was thin around the sides of his head held up a bony finger with a quizzical expression on his face and asked, "I don't believe I heard you correctly. My hearing is going. Did you say that this elf is the son of Venhow?"

"I did," Ramif said, with a nod.

There were murmurs around the circle and another man, younger and short with shifty eyes raised a nervous hand to the group, "How can you be sure?"

Ramif stepped forward to the bag on the floor of the platform and reached down, pulling the bag out from under the sword and freeing it so that it could be easily seen by everyone around it. It clattered before resting still with the red sunrise deepening the color of the engravings to a liquid bloody scrawl. "Not but he who breathes veined magic and those whom are born of the blood following can hold the sword which is blessed of deadly poison and forged in hellfire," Ramif read aloud. He looked up at the concerned faces, "He had the sword when we found him."

"How do we know that he didn't steal it from someone else?" Someone asked.

"No one else can touch it," he said definitively. As if they didn't believe him, two of the younger officers leaned forward with an outstretched finger to the metal and before Ramif could shout his angry disapproval, the boys touched the blade and shouted almost simultaneously, withdrawing their hands with bloody boils on their fingers. He shook his head slowly, rolling his eyes, "As I was saying," he looked to the boys, "anyone who touches the sword gets burned." He held up the palm of his injured hand where he had grabbed the sword before and some of the men flinched at the sight of the weeping wound.

"Then how does he have it?" one of the two boys asked holding his burnt finger to his lips.

"He can hold it."

"How is it that he can hold it then?" Oswald recognized the voice and tried to place it. He strained his neck and looked up and saw the missing arm, now recognizing Brigadier General Loch. He was standing off to one side and looking down at Oswald, instead of at the sword.

Ramif smiled grimly, "As I said, he is the son of Venhow Kebana. The sword of Dashai cannot be held by anyone but a magical born male of the Kebana bloodline."

"Yeah," someone said, from the far side of the circle, "but elves can't use magic, besides, why would a member of the Kebana family come to Gommorn?"

"Because he's stupid," the youngest Lieutenant said, with a snicker that rippled through some of the others in the group.

"For refuge," General Loch said quietly, "and the elves could use magic at one time. Their blood carries it naturally even if they can't use it like most magical races."

The crowd roared up all at once and it took a few minutes to quiet down once more.

"And why would he need refuge?" Ramif asked angrily. The crowd silenced to the stillness of placid water, they held in a collective breath, listening intently.

"From people who would try to kill him for no real reason," Loch said boldly.

"No reason? The sword is reason enough!" Ramif thundered, "He brought it and held it at the throat of a Nelwin Tactile war leader!"

Loch looked from Oswald, pinned against the block, to Ramif, his voice low, "Why would he do that?"

Ramif glared at the old man, "he claims that he was defending a friend."

Loch frowned, "That isn't illegal."

"Bolzar says otherwise and I'm more inclined to believe our men over a stranger, don't you agree?"

"Only when prejudice isn't involved," Loch reached across his torso and grabbed his stump of an arm casually, his face creased in determination. The officers around finally dared to breathe and some of them argued amongst themselves with whispers of confirmation as if they weren't sure they had heard it right.

"Prejudice?!" Ramif roared, "What are you talking about?"

Loch dropped the arm across his chest and dug out a cigar from the inside pocket of his jacket, pointing with it as he talked, "Yes. You have a personal vendetta against this man and it has nothing to do with what you are claiming to be an attempted assassination. He said it was in defense of someone else. There's something else there."

"The facts are all against him!" Ramif said sharply, holding up one finger at a time as he counted them off, "He's the son of the enemy's ruler; he had the sword of his father in hand while trying to kill one of our leaders; he has shown violent tendencies and a murderous intent and he has dark magic in his blood."

"Can you prove *any* of that?" Loch asked.

Ramif paused lowering his brow and looking through his bushy eyebrows, "There are witnesses."

"Who? Where are they?"

Bolzar thumped on the platform with his fist, unable to climb up onto the platform to join the group with his bad leg. Attention refocused to the ground where Bolzar stood, holding up the fairy pendant dangling from his hand, "I'm Bolzar Nolerkin the third of Saffermine, Tactile war director, strategist, and leader of the western Nelwin province. I'm the man who was at the end of that blade this night and I give you my word that he had full intent to kill me had I not left when I did."

"Who was it that he claimed to be saving?" Loch said, almost disregarding Bolzar's claim altogether, hearing the loophole in his promise.

"A thief and a traitor," Ramif said.

Loch stuck the cigar in his mouth and dug out a match, striking it against the armored shoulder of the man next to him and lighting it. He puffed at the cigar and tossed the match off the side of the platform. He took the now lit cigar from his mouth, holding it between his middle and forefinger, "Where is he?"

"We don't know," Ramif said venomously.

"Find him," Loch said, "It's the only way to be sure."

Ramif clenched his jaw and straightened his posture, his barrel chest rising and falling with his heavy breath, "Are you giving me orders *Brigadier* General?"

"No sir," Loch said, with a shrug. He puffed on the cigar, looking back at Oswald with fatherly concern and unease, "But it would look to be in your favor to have the evidence to condemn someone *before* their execution."

Ramif huffed and turned around to look out at the ever growing crowd, "If he truly saved the life of a man to get into this situation, I would think," he said, glancing back to Loch, trying to appease his discomfort, "that the man would return the favor if called upon, if offered amnesty of prosecution, correct?"

"If he comes forward he won't be put on trial alongside the elf?" Loch asked in confirmation.

"No," Ramif agreed, "On my honor he will leave with pardon of past crimes."

Loch nodded slowly, "Then I would think that, yes, the man would come forward."

"So be it then," Ramif turned to the people gathered around the circle and with a deep breath, he shouted, his voice resonating across the clearing, "Good people of Gommorn, as you are well aware, we are gathered for a trial of execution. This man," he waved a hand back behind him to where Oswald lay bound without taking his eyes away from the crowd, "has been accused of a list of crimes against the city and our people. There is doubt among some of the generals as to the truth of one of his accusations. Our predicament can be solved by one of you," he paused and some of the people turned to look around at each other. After letting his voice settle he continued, "He brought a sword to the throat of one of the war room leaders with intent to kill."

A rush of voices stabbed at the air with shaking fists and jeers with obscene gestures of hate. Ramif looked back at Oswald a moment, letting the words soak into the minds of the angry shouting mob. The uproar died down as quickly as it had risen with the open hand of their Lord General, "He claims to have done so in protection of another," the uproar rose and fell again, hearing the slight mocking tone in Ramif's voice, "With the gracious offer of amnesty," he called, "that man is summoned to step forward and proclaim the truth of this story. To come forward and save the man who has already protected him."

There was a cautious stillness as eyes slid over every face in the crowd. Ramif smiled satisfactorily when no voices rose into the air. He opened his mouth to speak when the crowd bustled a little and he snapped his mouth shut again with narrowed eyes. Oswald looked up hopefully.

"Dad," it was Ramif's son, "There are people still coming. They should all be here in a few minutes," he was breathing heavily with the effort of running around the city shouting. He put his hands on his knees, bell still in hand, and looked back up at

Oswald, "You should ask again when they get here. Give him another chance."

"Isaiah," Ramif said, with a tinge of red in his face and a warning tone in his voice, "You have done your job. Now be silent." Isaiah shrank back into the crowd looking embarrassed, twisting at the hem of his shirt as he tried to catch his breath.

Ramif pressed his lips together as he thought. He gave a short nod and shouted back across the crowd, "We will make this offer but one more time before the verdict is called and this man is put to death. Spread the word. If such a man exists he has one more chance to save the life of this elf," he turned his back to the crowd and faced the circle of officers again.

They seemed to be pleased with the decision.

Loch took a deep drag of his cigar and let it out with a low rattling breath, speaking through the black plume of smoke, "So… about this list of crimes…"

Ramif grunted, "I have gone over them."

"But in that so called 'list' you gave us, there was only one crime and even that crime," he gestured to the throng of people around them, "has its doubts."

"He is the son of Venhow," Ramif snarled.

"Being the bastard son of an evil man doesn't condemn the boy," Loch said, as if it were the most obvious thing he had ever said.

"Is he though?" Ramif asked bitterly.

"You just said that he was," Loch said, with a raised eyebrow as he ashed his cigar.

"No," he paused, "I mean, what if he isn't a bastard son? What if he is like his father? What if he has the power to overthrow the city?"

Loch snorted through a new plume of smoke, "You would kill a man over a paranoid 'what if'?"

Ramif looked around at the swarm of men on the platform. All of them were watching him, "Of course not! I just want it to be considered as a possibility as you try and protect a violent stranger."

"I defend him," Loch said, pausing intently between his words, "because there is no evidence to condemn him to death."

A voice came from off of the platform behind them, "What about this?" Bolzar was holding out the fistful of fine silver chain and the fairy pendant for everyone to see. Some of the officers looked awed by the object, others shrugged in disinterest as if it were no more than a pretty rock plucked from the river.

"What is that?" The blond man, Armond, finally spoke. His voice was thick and clear in the air around them, with the practice of a man who had been speaking in public his entire life. He uncrossed his arms and stepped forward to the edge of the platform and shrank down to one knee. He started fingering the necklace with genuine interest, turning it between his thick fingers to inspect each corner of it, his eyes glinting.

"This is a pendant of Fantasy," Bolzar said, his eyes moving one by one, meeting the gaze of each man on the platform, "it was found in his things when we caught him hiding this morning."

"That can't be a pendant of Fantasy," one of the Nelwin officers said definitively, with a shake of his head, "there aren't hardly any left in the whole world. Wizards search their whole lives to find one and never do. Why would an elf have one?" Some of the others agreed without even giving it a closer look.

"This is no ordinary elf," Ramif insisted, "which is why we are in trial over him, not over this pendant."

"But what if it is real?" Another officer chimed.

"I believe," Armond said, sliding the pendant from Bolzar's hand and standing up, "that this is in fact the genuine craft," he walked around the circle, holding it in his wide palmed hands to show each of the men standing.

"It is!" Ramif said, louder than he had meant to. He was losing his temper. No one was listening to him. He had never had so much trouble trying to finish a trial before, but now all of the sudden, they were rising up against him with doubts and questions, "I have seen its telltale properties myself. It dances."

"Under what circumstances?" Someone asked.

"I'm not sure what triggered it," Ramif said, forcing himself to calm a little, "It was either the shedding of blood, the storm, anger, fear, or the darkness. We would have to watch it to find out."

Armond wrapped his fingers around the pendant with a cautious hunger in his eyes, "What are its gifts? What spells are on it?"

Bolzar shook his head, "We don't know. I think it has to do with a concealment charm, but it's very complicated. It would take me years to figure it out."

"How did he get it?" Armond asked.

"He said it was his mothers. We believe he may have stolen it. His mother was no one of consequence and therefore would not have been given one," Bolzar said, and looked over at Oswald and then down to the wooden grains of the platform.

"His father was a man of merit though..." Armond said, more to himself, "but Fantasy wouldn't give it to a man like that. I refuse to think it would fall into his hands that way."

"This isn't about the necklace!" Ramif roared stepping up and snatching it out of Armond's hand, "We are in a trial!" The officers straightened a bit looking indignant.

"Get on with it then," Loch said, looking livid. He knew how the trial would end no matter how much he argued against it. He sucked down the rest of his cigar and threw it down to the platform to sit and smolder. The creases in his face were deep and well shadowed in what is left of the nighttime air as the sun finished peeking over the horizon, the sky now a brilliant orange red.

Ramif looked back to the crowd. It had nearly tripled in size. He decided that he had given the elf all of the time that he was willing to give him and he stepped up and addressed the people again. He brought his hands up high into the air for silence.

"The time is now upon us! If the man on trial is innocent, then let the man he saved come forward to repay his debt. He will not be prosecuted for his testimony or previous crimes should he speak the truth of the last night's events. Step forward now if you care to speak for this man's life," Ramif looked out almost daring someone to make a move forward.

The sea of people parted with a ripple as they moved away just enough to let a man through the mass. Oswald strained his swollen, puffy eyes and could just make out the short plump figure of Nedtedrow at the front of the platform. He looked solidly up into Ramif's face with matching malice.

"I speak for him," Nedtedrow said placidly. Oswald's heart could have leapt from his chest with hope. He wanted nothing more than to have the gag torn from his mouth so that he could express his gratitude to the odd little man, "He did brandish the sword against Bolzar in my defense."

"Explain," Ramif snapped shortly.

Nedtedrow pressed his lips together thoughtfully and glanced over to Bolzar, "That's hard to do without causing more problems."

"You will tell the officers what happened or your testimony is null," Ramif ordered.

Nedtedrow looked down at the ground and shuffled his feet, kicking at a clump of thick weeds at his toe before swallowing his apprehension and continuing with a nod, "Bolzar and I were once friends. In haste to save my own life, I left him to die. When we came back to Gommorn—"

"—We who?" Ramif clarified.

"Oswald and I—" Nedtedrow pointed, "—when we arrived here, it seems that Bolzar had survived the attack when we fled Tetrach, and he hunted me down. He was threatening to kill me and had a dagger at my chest when Oswald came in," he paused, licking his lips in thought. His mind focused in on the frighteningly menacing glare that he had seen on Oswald's face when he had appeared, seemingly out of nowhere, to come to his aid, "He only wanted Bolzar to leave. He had the sword out as a warning."

"Is every word of this true?" Ramif warned.

Nedtedrow hesitated but was able to speak with clarity, "Yes."

"What is your name?" Ramif asked lowering his brow.

"Nedtedrow Kin of Saffermine."

Ramif opened his mouth to contest the story but he was cut short as a furious and frantic shout broke the air and the crowd parted again, more quickly and with a wider birth for the kid plummeting his way through the people around him.

"Nedtedrow?! Ya thievin' troll!"

Matrim darted to the front of the platform in a streamline of focused anger. He came to a screeching halt at the platform and had his hands wrapped around Nedtedrow's shirt front before he had even looked around to take in the scene around him. He caught Nedtedrow's concerned and weak expression and it cut through his impulsive anger like a thin wire wrapped around clay.

Matrim followed Nedtedrow's line of sight and the color promptly drained from his face in shock.

"No," Matrim whispered in a full breath of disbelief, "Oz?" he stared at Oswald, tied down and strapped to the executioner's block, blood matted in his red hair and scrapes and small cuts torn all across his chin and bound arms, "Hey!" he let go of Nedtedrow all at once, completely forgetting the reason he had plowed forward angrily to get him in the first place, "Hey! Wha's he doin' up there uh? Get 'em down!" he pointed put at Oswald looking like a man in righteous anger rather than the young boy he really was.

"Mat," Ramif growled, obviously well acquainted with Matrim, his face flooding with warning, "mind your place or I will have you locked in the cells again for the day."

"Wha's stoppin' ya?" Matrim yelled, his arms open wide in mock welcome, "He ain't done nothin' wrong! Get 'em down!"

Ramif locked his dark eyes on Matrim with a grim scowl, "He's on trial and you will mind your place!"

"Wha' for?"

"Right now," Ramif bellowed, "his defense is slipping. Mind your tongue or the trial will end immediately with my verdict!"

Matrim shuddered for more reasons than the cold. He visibly tried to restrain himself from speaking by biting his lower lip. With clenched fists, he remained quiet.

Ramif sighed and looked out once more, "The reliability of the testimonies of these two men are unreliable. Is there anyone with honor that can speak for the elf?" his shoulders slumped when another voice broke the crowd.

"I can," Satomi called holding up a hand and shouldering her way forward to stand in front of the Generals. Oswald looked up to her, his heart thundering. The symbol of her necklace introduced her and no one asked for her name, "The elf has good intentions and a strong will. I don't think that he's a threat or a danger to the people of this city."

"What makes you think that?" Ramif snapped.

"He had the intention to protect me from haughty and insistent men at the Burning Mill yesterday evening," Satomi said, crossing her arms.

Ramif narrowed his dark eyes, "Why?"

"For no other reason than to do what he believed was proper for a man in his position to do," she said, looking slightly annoyed with having to argue with the general.

"Are you certain?" Ramif asked looking down on her from the platform with a knowing and suspicious stare, "How long have you known this man?"

"Not long," she admitted, with a glance up to Oswald.

"Then how do you know that he was not intending to do more harm by drawing your trust?" Ramif asked with a smirk as the mob of people began bustling with whispers and nodding heads, "Did you also know that he is the son of Venhow Kebana?"

"No," she admitted again.

The gathered people hissed and cried out, many of them calling for Oswald's blood. Ramif let the wild chaos escalate into a rush of angry noise and held up hand, "Quiet!" The voices died down but more reluctantly than they had before, "I have decided, on behalf of the safety of people of Gommorn," he paused knowing all eyes were on him and each ear was pricked to hear his every breath, "that magical blood of such heritage cannot stand to weak arguments. Murderous intent cannot be dismissed as poor judgment. I have decided that he cannot be set free to harm, betray, or bewitch anyone else."

Cheering erupted at the proclamation and Ramif reached over to the nearest General and drew the sword from his scabbard.

The man did not protest.

"This isn't right," Loch grumbled to Ramif as he moved closer to the executioners block.

"It is my decision to protect the people of this city," Ramif said with finality.

"Are you certain this is the right way to protect them?" General Armond added, looking over to Lock and back to Ramif.

"The responsibility of this decision rests with me and me alone. You are all excused," Ramif muttered to the men with a hard stare at Loch and Armond. They turned, one at a time leaping off the platform. Loch and Armond were the last disapproving faces to leap down and then only Ramif and a trembling Oswald remained.

Ramif held the blade high into the air, looking to the crowd, and the explosion of cheering rose with the tip of the sword to the morning sky. "This day," he shouted triumphantly, turning to Oswald's upturned face, "our fear of this wicked man dies! This day, a father will lose a son and the city of Gommorn will gain the upper hand in this war!"

The people cheered again as he stepped closer to Oswald, looking down into his fearful and forlorn face with intensity and finality.

"This day, justice will be done!" he lowered his voice so that only Oswald could hear him, "Die," he commanded as he drew the sword up over his head, the sunrise glinting on the blade as it rose to its peak. Oswald heard cries of panic and a handful of protests through the bellowing of the people and in a moment with absolute power of will and brute force, the blade fell.

Oswald turned his face away from the blade closing his eyes tight and bracing for impact and waiting for death to come crashing down over him.

The screams and scuffles continued for what Oswald thought must have been the longest second that had ever passed the world and all at once, it stopped. He heard a wet thump and felt something warm ooze down the back of his neck, blood dripping onto the floor beneath his now wide open, glazed eyes. His head was not on the ground and for a horrifying split second he thought that one chop would not have done it and he felt sick at the idea that he would have to endure another.

When a few seconds passed by, he realized that the blood was dripping, not from his neck, but onto it. Rivulets were drizzling onto the nape of his neck and sliding around his throat to dabble onto the oak boards. The blood was not his. He wasn't hurt.

Daring to look up, he met the eyes of a centaur. Her chestnut colored hair and amber eyes gave her away as the same centaur he had spotted, if only briefly in the woods a few days earlier.

Up close she was almost an unnaturally perfect figure of beauty. Her face was flawless and eerie. She had a faded and distant expression, as if she were lost into another world through her mind. She was far from what seemed natural and the strangeness of her lingered. The serine quality of her presence was haunted by the wildness of her eyes. They were, at that moment, nothing more than the eyes of an angry wounded animal and they betrayed the calm expressionless porcelain face.

He looked out to the parted swarm of people where her path had been torn. People were scattered around the city circle, some on the ground nursing bruises and others standing pressed together tightly as if they were afraid to return to the path that the centaur had carved.

A congealed drip of lukewarm blood landed in his hair and he grimaced with the feel of it cooling against his scalp.

Oswald looked up over his head, afraid to see what was dripping blood so insistently onto the back of his neck. It was not Ramif as he had expected, but the centaur who lay at the end of the sword's blade. She had it gripped tightly in an outstretched hand as if she had caught it in mid swing.

It looked as though she had.

The meat of her hand was gored deeply and Oswald thought that for a minute he could see the bones in her palm. The blood dripping down on him was running down her arm in a steady trickle from the gaping wound.

She did not release the blade.

Ramif looked stunned for a moment but his open mouth snapped shut and the surprise faded back into its usual angry, shadowed set. His fingers wrapped tighter around the hilt of the sword, his knuckles were white with the force he pressed against the metal.

The centaur lowered her head and torso, pulling at the sword as she straightened her back and trotted her hooves to add to the force against them. With her mangled hand she tore the sword from his hands, nearly pulling him off of his feet and into the crowd of people. She took the sword from her tattered hand and brandished it in the other, pointing its bloody blade at Ramif. The tip of the sword was as steady in her hand as it would have been while lying on the ground.

She spoke, her voice as smooth as fine silk and wavering like ripples in a pond, "I am Olivia. I have been sent with a message and direct orders. You will release Oswald Bawshade, the last remaining elf from Neion."

"On whose authority?" Ramif asked, straightening his back and squaring his shoulders, staring at the point of the blade.

"Mine," she said placidly.

"You said you were sent with orders! Who sent you?" Ramif demanded angrily stomping his foot down on the boards uncomfortably close to Oswald's leg.

"I was sent on the command of the great goddess Fantasy herself," a hush fell around them. She held up her head high and said a bit louder, "He is innocent and will not be harmed."

Everyone stopped and shifted their eyes to exchange looks with each other, unsure of what to do or who to believe. Everyone seemed to be holding their breaths as Ramif and the centaur locked eyes with a silent challenge to one another. Neither moved or showed any sign of backing down for a long time. Finally Ramif took a step backwards with loathing in his eyes.

"Release him," she said slowly, her eyes burning on her emotionless face.

"No," Ramif growled.

"Release him, or you will replace him," she said flatly.

Ramif watched as the sword inched closer to him and he looked briefly down at Oswald and back to Olivia, "How can I be sure that your word is her word?"

"Because," she hummed dryly, "my word will be proven when she arrives."

"She's coming to Gommorn?" Ramif asked and suddenly sounded apprehensive. He looked as though he had been struck open palmed across the face.

She nodded slowly and then with a graceful and all too slow tip of her head she gestured back to Oswald straightening her arm and leaning the risen and bloody blade closer to the hollow of Ramif's throat.

"This man is under the direct protection of the Goddess until she arrives to speak with him herself," she recited, her eyes bright and intensely locked into Ramif's as if she could stare into his soul, "If you wish to disregard her orders, I have orders of my own to dispatch you."

"My duty is to the people of this city..." Ramif muttered, the bloody sword reflecting in his eyes, "I only meant to protect them."

"You meant to have vengeance for your wife's death, but knowingly against the wrong man," Olivia said, her voice suddenly cold and her eyes darkened expressively, vivid against her stoic features, "Your wife deserves justice... not this."

"I ..." Ramif began slowly, stung by the words in the air and pausing to look down at the platform unable to find words in the pain.

"You will release him," she ordered calmly.

He scowled up at her, the fight nearly gone from his movements. He reached over to the metal rings binding Oswald to the executioner's block, all the while keeping his eyes on the centaur. He fumbled with the latch and felt the ring slip free from the iron pin. He pulled the metal bands away from the block, freeing Oswald from their grasp.

"Untie him," she ordered in her otherworldly tone.

Ramif's face contorted and he tugged more brutally at the knot that was binding Oswald's hands than was necessary.

The rope fell away from him and Oswald tried to move his arms only to find that, like his legs, they would not respond. He lay against the block and tried to move.

Inch by inch he was able to bring his violently shaking hands up to his mouth and he pulled the gag away, letting it fall to hang around his neck. He tried to lather up enough spit to wet his dry, aching mouth, but his tongue seemed to be unresponsive as well. He summoned up as much strength as he could and pushed his body up away from the block to stand on weak legs. His knees trembled like a new born fawn's but he held up his weight, even if he didn't trust himself to take a step.

In a heartbeat, Matrim had pushed through the chaos and clambered up onto the platform to stand next to Oswald. Matrim suddenly looked like he had been sick and hadn't slept in weeks, though his lips were curled lightly into a grateful smile. He put a hand on Oswald's shoulder reassuringly with a relieved sigh.

Olivia lowered the sword and turned to address the city, her hooves readjusting on the ground, "The goddess Fantasy will be here at the third dawn. At first light on the third day she will come from the south with news and blessings for the people of Gommorn. Make your preparations. Fantasy is traveling."

The stale quiet over the city broke and people began to move. Some turned on the spot and ran back into the city. Others looked excited and began quickly talking with other people standing nearby. They had begun to disburse amongst themselves with the new and thrilling news.

Only a handful of people remained standing around the platform. Matrim, Olivia, the three generals, Ramif, Loch, and Armond, Bolzar, Nedtedrow and Satomi were all that remained, looking at one another in a stunned pause.

Oswald looked groggily over to Olivia and saw the mass of blood stringing down her arm and then to the exposed tendon of her hand.

The darkness swallowed him in a wave, it rolled over his vision into the rush of panic. A sick feeling crept in his stomach. He gagged sharply on the vomit rising up in the back of his throat and choked hard trying to keep it down. His head swam and the world spun as if he were a balancing top on a tossing sea.

He took in a deep breath. His stomach churned again and the world around him slipped through his fingers like patch of dense fog. He tried to take a step through the feeling but his legs buckled beneath him. He crumpled like a pile of bones, toppling off the platform and out of consciousness.

Chapter Fourteen

The world shimmered. It was a mirage in a sea of watery air which was also the darkness of the otherworldly. Dreams danced in his head. They were strange dreams, vivid and fluid with unfamiliar voices that called out to him by name with distorted faces that grinned like demons in the dim flickering light of a grand fire. He felt a dreadful horror and a prolonged feeling of death and sadness. There were odd sounds of rejoicing and the calamity of boarded windows and doors.

There was pain in his shoulders and wrists as well as a burning ache in his knees and back as if the fluids of each of his joints had been mixed with sand. He imagined that he knew what it must feel like to be a rock on the bed of a river, beat down with each moving flow of air and water passed over him. He felt as though he had been trampled.

He imagined centaurs, a sea of them, an army galloping into the forested hills with bloody blades held out before them like proud flags and trophies. They called for him to rise up with them, to fight the war with the ferocity and fearless lack of pain that they had. He turned away from the centaurs for fear they would drag him into battle.

Oswald felt a hard surface beneath his head and body. His feet hung over the edge of the hard place into thin air and he realized that he must be lifted up off of the ground. The air around him was cold and stale. He felt something warm heat the skin of his face before leaving and coming back to return its warmth once more. The warm thing that dabbed his face made a light pain zap through his chin and cheek.

He groaned and thought he heard his name. When he heard it again he knew it wasn't a part of his strange dreams and he opened his eyes, blinking against the light that met him through the window beside him. He shook his head and blinked hard trying to shake away the grogginess and the remnants of his waking dreams.

Matrim's face came into focus. He looked better than he had from the last of what Oswald could remember. His hair was slicked out of his young and gangly teenage face and he had more color in his skin than he had before. He was smiling with the dark space of his missing tooth showing proudly and it looked like the yellowing bruise beneath his eye was healing well.

"Hey Oz," he said excitedly, "Guess what?"

Oswald raised an eyebrow and picked himself up onto his elbows. He realized he was in Matrim's tiny, cold and drafty house. He was lying on a wooden bed that could have easily been mistaken for a table with a thin cloth draped on it except for the old flattened feather pillow that was almost hammered level with the boards. The window next to him did, unlike those in the front of the shack, have glass in its frame. He was sure it was warmer in here because of it and the sunshine blazing though the glass felt good against his face.

"What?" Oswald said, surprised to hear his voice sound so deep and so gruff with stress and sleep. Matrim smacked him playfully with the warm damp rag that he had been cleaning Oswald up with. It was tainted with blood that had been mopped up off of his face and out of his hair.

He dropped the rag into the bucket of water between his feet and grinned knowingly, "You're still alive."

"Really?" Oswald asked groggily, "I wasn't sure."

"Ya gave it 'ur all though."

"I wasn't trying for that," Oswald said dryly, as he pushed himself further upright.

"You scared me too man," Matrim said, looking down solemnly for a second before bouncing back up with his usual attitude.

"I scared *you?*" Oswald said, thinking about the strangling fear that had choked the last comprehensible thoughts from his head when he was strapped to the block.

"Yeah," he said, as if it were the most obvious thing he had ever said, "I lost everyone I ever had like that. My dad, my uncle, my sis… I don't know if I could handle losin' anyone else …"

Oswald felt a sort of regard for the boy. He was an only child. Most, if not all, elves were. He had never imagined having a little brother but he supposed that if he were able to choose one, Matrim was definitely an interesting person and someone who was easy to like. He smiled.

Matrim cleared his throat, "Glad ya's alright. I thought ya was gonna die fer sure."

"Yeah," Oswald looked down and flipped his legs over the bed to sit up all of the way, grimacing through the dull pain and agreed bitterly, "Me too. The Lord General seems to be a bit bigoted. I think that you guys need an executioner who is open minded enough not to kill innocent people."

Matrim raised an eyebrow and frowned with a one shouldered shrug, "Atch'ully, he ain't dat bad. Usually he's pretty fair. He's hard ta get along wit' and has a great right hook when he's pissed," he said, touching his jaw, "but he's never done nothin' like dat 'afore."

"You like him?" Oswald asked, confused, "But you fight with him for no reason."

"I don't have to like 'em to know dat he's fair at trials," Matrim said, as he kicked the bucket of water under the lip of the bed and out of the way.

"Fair?!" Oswald exclaimed, "He almost killed me for no reason!"

Matrim shrugged, "Don' mean he's a bad guy."

"That's hard to believe somehow."

"I dunno," Matrim said, creeping a guilty sneer onto his lips, "I guess it's jus' you. Must be somethin' 'bout ya face he don't like."

"Ah," Oswald said, throwing a hand up in the air dramatically, "well, at least it's just me," he smiled at Matrim, unable to ignore the odd mocking look on his face, "At least I don't have to worry about that now."

"Yeah," Matrim laughed, "now you jus' gotta worry 'bout everyone else lookin' at dat ugly mess."

Oswald reached out and smacked Matrim's shoulder, "At least I don't look like you."

Matrim raised an eyebrow and looked over at him amusedly, "If ya did look like me ya'd be a lil' less ugly, now wouldn't cha'?"

"What do you mean?" Oswald joked, "You have more bruises than teeth!"

"Look who's talkin'" Matrim said, shaking his head and gesturing to the blue bruises coating Oswald's face and arms.

He took a few steps back and grabbed an apple from the bowl on a small bench against the adjacent wall. He tossed it at Oswald who caught it in both hands reflexively without thinking. His shoulders shocked him sharply with the movement and he caught himself halfway through a grimace and tried to recover a smile. Instead it looked like a facial spasm and Matrim laughed again.

"Smooth," he said, with a short nod. He grabbed an apple for himself and dug in hungrily. He sucked on the bite of apple in his mouth for a minute before saying casually, "Ya got a few visitas when you was out. Oh! An' that horse lady told me ta tell ya when ya got up dat yous suppos'ta go ta meet your teacher tomorrow mornin'."

"What?"

"Lots a' people came by when you passed out. Everyone thought you needed ta be somewheres' else," Matrim pushed the bit of apple into his cheek and gestured with the rest of the apple as he spoke, "Nedtedrow wanted ya to be brought back to Bolzar's ol' house but I fig'yad since you was charged for threatenin' him, that wasn' the best idea. So's I convinced 'em to let ya come 'ere. When ya got 'ere, people kept bringin' ya stuff and wantin' to talk to ya 'bout Fantasy."

"I don't know her," Oswald said, at the pause and the expectant look on Matrim's face.

He shrugged again and continued, "Anyways," he held up the apple in his hand, "dey brought ya some stuff to make up fer the whole trial thing," Oswald snorted disapprovingly but Matrim continued talking, unfazed, "And 'a horse lady came by an' said somethin' 'bout ya needin' ta learn how ta use that sword right from General Armond."

"Who?" Oswald asked, still trying to wipe away the fog from his head, "He's the guy you were telling me about yesterday, right?"

"Yeah," he said, and leaned back against the table comfortably, pondering his next bite of the apple as he turned it over in his hand, "He's the big blonde guy at the trial who was lookin' at ya necklace like it was the last piece a' gold on the planet."

"My necklace!" Oswald shouted, his hand shooting up to his chest as if he expected it to be there, "Where is it?"

"R'lax," Matrim muttered and dug into his pocket, "The horse lady got it and gave it ta me when wez got ya back 'ere," he pulled it out in a mass of wound and tangled chain around a glass figurine and held it out for Oswald to take.

Oswald set the apple in his lap and grabbed the necklace. It was a mess of small silver links and he began unknotting the necklace, relieved to have it back in his possession. He was glad too that he would be able to wear it now that everyone knew that it existed and that he was out of the trial.

He picked at a tight ball of knots in the chain and watched it unravel one loop at a time. After a short struggle, it was in one fine loop and he slipped it over his head, the fairy resting in its usual place.

"So," Oswald said slowly, staring at the necklace for a minute more, "what exactly is going on?"

"I just tol' ya. Ya supposed ta go and train with General Armond in the mornin'. He's supposta' always be outside the city to the north at dawn."

"Why?"

"Cause he likes it," Matrim said, with an exaggerated shrug and an annoyed sneer, "I dunno do I?"

"No," Oswald said, shaking his head to correct the misunderstanding, "I meant why am I learning to fight?"

"I dunno that too," he said bluntly, as he took another wet bite of the apple, smacking his lips.

"Then what *do* you know?" Oswald asked glancing out the window into the late afternoon light

"He took ya sword and e'll give it back when 'e sees yas tomorra."

"How did he get it?" Oswald asked with a frown, perplexed as he remembered the strips of flesh burned from Ramif's palm.

Matrim drew his eyebrows together thinking, admittedly Oswald realized that it had been an odd question for anyone who didn't know about the sword to hear, "Well," he answered, "'e picked up a stick and kinda poked it inta an old green bag. He was gonna give it ta me but the horse lady tol' 'em to keep it tonight."

"Why?"

"Wha' makes you think I know these things?" Matrim said, his voice sharp and frustrated, "I'm just tellin' ya what I saw."

"Alright," Oswald said, now rolling the uneaten apple in his hands, "Sorry. What else did I miss after I fell?"

"Not too much. I already told ya most of it. Lots a people do want ta talk ta ya. Most of 'em say they know ya but if they didn't know ya name I sent 'em away. Most folk is expectin' ya at the Burning Mill at some point tonight."

"Who?" Oswald asked curiously.

"I aint no good with names," Matrim said, looking down at his feet for a second before taking another bite of his apple, "but, there was an ol' general with one arm... Loch I think... and a big Southern Brute lookin' guy who was grinnin' and hoppin' 'round a lot and wearin' nothin' but slacks and a nice pair a boots — Weird dude," he looked up at Oswald and shrugged habitually, "nice though. I wan't sure he knew ya but he did know ya name. There was Nedtedrow and Bolzar too. I turned 'em away. Dey was arguing something fierce but I suspect that's nothin' new," he turned the apple over, rolling it with his fingers to find a new angle to get a good bite, "Uh... and there was another Southern Brute. A girl with spikes in her hair, a big cat and a rust colored brain leach on 'er leg."

"A brain leach?" Oswald asked horrified, "What in the name of hellfire's a brain leach?"

"It's what it sounds like," Matrim said casually, "I've only eva' seen dat one."

"But what is it?" Oswald asked disturbed by the thought, he remembered the string of rust colored beads that were embedded into the back of Satomi's calf.

"It's a pet.... kinda'," Matrim said, rolling his eyes as if Oswald knew nothing, "it's also a kind a' parasite... I suppose it's both," Oswald opened his mouth but couldn't find anything to say. Matrim sighed and continued, "It knows stuff dat it takes from other people and shares it in exchange for their owner's blood. It's good for keepin' stuff secret."

Oswald started to ask why but realized that he had been asking that one question more than he would have liked to and stopped himself. He supposed that he would just have to accept the oddity for now. He looked out the door frame and tried to peek out into the street. It was bustling with people who were moving more quickly than people usually would.

Matrim followed his gaze and smiled, "You feelin' up to movin' yet?"

"Yeah," Oswald said, slipping off the table-like bed and standing on legs that were still not up to carrying his weight without protest. His knees shook for the first few steps but with each following stride, he felt stronger. The two of them stepped out into the street and almost immediately a voice shot out from down the street.

"'Oy!" Another human boy, about Matrim's age but taller, with brown hair and a pox-marked face was waving his arms up over his head, "Mat! There's somethin' in your trap outside the city!"

"Right," Matrim shouted back with a hand in the air. He turned back to Oswald with mischievous eyes that could have been his usual expression, "Hey I gotta go 'n see what I caught. D'ya think ya can manage not dying without me today?"

"I'll be fine," Oswald assured him.

"Cool," Matrim said, starting off down the road at a trot, "I'll meet up with ya after a bit, eh?"

"Alright," Oswald nodded. Matrim, with a hop in his step, sped down the road and out of sight.

Oswald watched him vanish around a corner and looked towards the Burning Mill, looking for his route but instead he realized that the rushing people in the streets had stopped in their tracks. They were staring at him as if he were an angry ghost or a shadow of death that could strike them down with a single thought. Everyone was frozen with wide eyes and curious faces. He wondered why everyone had stopped, but didn't dare ask anyone.

He tried not to make eye contact with the strangers as he walked with his head down towards the tavern. After a minute people began to move again behind him, but with much less energy than they had before he had stepped into the street. It seemed like a long and lonely walk, which really only took a few turns and a few minutes for him to reach his destination.

The sign of the Burning Mill hung still over the door and the smell of smoking fish and meat met him at the entrance. He pushed the door open and glanced at the guard that was standing just inside the door. The guard looked down at him for a second and quickly ripped his eyes away as if he had seen something that he was not supposed to and he stared determinedly at the opposite wall.

Oswald hesitated but stepped into the tavern. The air stiffened with each passing second as he approached the bar and looked around the room for anyone he recognized. Slowly, one head at a time, people turned to look at who had just walked in and fell silent. He tried to ignore the eyes on him and looked at the barman whose face had changed from the disdainful and bitter look from the night before, to an apprehensive pause that drew his old thin face and eyebrows together.

"We…" The barman started, speaking as though the words were burning his mouth, "We can't have you in here without—" The man stopped and looked up with his beady eyes widening slightly.

A large, long fingered green hand landed onto Oswald's shoulder, gripping it with an odd pressure and a low and grating voice came from high above his head, "That's alright Mill, he's with me."

Oswald's gaze slid from the deep moss green skin on the four jointed, long fingered hand, to the long thin green arm attached to it and then up to the unmistakable face of a Keernith goblin hovering high above him and looking down to meet his eyes. His face was thin and narrow with high cheekbones and big sunken blue eyes that looked out of place on his sharp features. His nose was long and hooked which hovered just above his thin blue lips. His smile parted and a sharpened line of pearly white, angled, demon like teeth, which shone down at him in a grin that made his blood run cold.

Oswald realized that he was holding his breath and let it out slowly unable to take his eyes off the goblin. No one else seemed to be upset by the appearance of the goblin as he led the way to a table in the back of the room with his huge hand on Oswald's shoulder the entire way. Oswald's heart thundered almost painfully and he thought for a second that he was going to faint again but when he began to feel sick they had reached the table and he was half helped, half forced into the seat.

The goblin took the seat on the bench across from him and curled down, his back arching impossibly until he was comfortably eye to eye with Oswald. He smiled again and Oswald thought that he had to be dreaming and that he still hadn't woken up from that morning. He mentally tried to wake himself but was unable, staring into the light blue foggy eyes of the Keernith across from him.

"I'm Fretcritck Letkerthern," The goblin said, holding out a bony massive hand across the table, "but everyone calls me Fred. People have trouble pronouncing my name right."

Oswald tried to hold back his fear as he held out a hand to shake with the goblins. His hand was completely enveloped with the abnormally long and thin fingers. He was surprised to feel that the boney hand was warm as he shook it. He pulled his hand back trying with everything that he had not to pull it away quickly or to let his voice betray his fear.

"Fretcritck," Oswald repeated, glad to hear his voice was steady. He jumped when the goblin laughed, his voice hitting the air like clattering rocks with a rich sound beneath it.

"Not bad," he said, and straightened up just a little in his seat, "but just call me Fred. I'm used to it, and having had to use it for years, I have to say that it has grown on me rather charmingly. I like it."

"Okay, Fred," Oswald said cautiously, not sure what he should be saying. He looked out into the crowded room hoping to see someone familiar, but didn't. He turned back to the goblin, still not used to the look of him, "What can I do for you?"

"Oh," The goblin said, looking surprised, "Nothing. I was just hoping to talk to someone interesting for a change. I don't meet many elves, not to mention anyone at all who got out of an execution quite like that."

"I didn't expect that," Oswald admitted looking fixedly at the table.

"You should be a little happier about it I would think," he said, with a low tone, "Is everything alright?"

"Fine," Oswald said quickly, feeling the air catch in his throat. He stared at the table.

"Look at me," his deep voice grumbled.

"I… uh…" The rows of sharpened teeth glinted behind his blue lips. Oswald blinked uncomfortably feeling like he was being watched through glass, "have never really…"

"Met a goblin?" Fred finished not looking offended, but disappointed. Oswald shook his head not wanting to keep eye contact for very long. Fred sighed with a massive breath, "I would have thought that you would be more open minded to different people with how you were treated this morning."

"I didn't mean to offend you," Oswald tried to assure him, looking up to take in a little more of the goblin's appearance with what he hoped would look like compassion.

Fred was about two and a half feet taller than Oswald and was grossly thin. He closely resembled a massive skeleton with thick green leather, pulled tight over the bones and what muscle could be seen with his movements. He tried to remember the other Keernith he had seen and realized that they had all been wearing armor and he wasn't sure if they were simply supposed to be built like this or if Fred was unhealthily skinny.

Fred raised a hand and brushed at the air nonchalantly, "No worries. I suppose there aren't many people like me around here. At least you didn't run from me. Some people do until they get used to me."

Oswald shook his head trying to look casual himself while noting that the thought had crossed his mind when he had first seen the goblin, "It isn't anything personal, it's just that the last time I saw one of your kind—" Oswald's voice failed at the look that burned out from Fred's slightly foggy, crystal blue eyes and the creases that formed around them.

"I'm well aware of what happened," he growled.

Oswald's heart thundered again as fear rose in him once more, the look on Fred's face more dangerous than the sword that had been his fate that morning. He considered running now more seriously than he had before, but was afraid that the act itself would bring him harm by offending the goblin further.

"How do you know what happened?" Oswald asked quietly, his hands shaking under the table.

"Because I've heard it again and again," he bellowed suddenly, the blue of his lips and gums darkening with his anger, "Death follows my people as they abuse the rights and gifts given to us. Greed and power over others corrupted them. Joining with that man who is ravaging everything barren in this world!" Oswald backed away from the table as best as he could without getting up, not trusting his legs to obey him if he stood. Fred looked at the wall with menace and added, "It's despicable!"

"I wasn't suggesting—" Oswald began but Fred cut him off.

"We aren't all like that!" he snapped. He reached up with a deep breath, visibly trying to calm himself and scratched a long, pointed ear. He dropped his hand and looked back up with soulful eyes that Oswald hadn't really seen behind the fog before, "I'm sorry that many of them are though," he said much calmer, "my brothers among them, and I'm sorry that you were a victim. Not just from whatever happened to you before, but this morning too. I know what it is like to be shunned for something that you can't change."

"What do you mean?" Oswald asked relaxing a little with Fred's sudden tone change and the misty, kind, eyes that he had suddenly realized were not so different from other people that he knew.

"As much as I hate the man who is your father, you are no more like him than I am like my brothers who have joined him," Fred said, with a wise nod as if agreeing with himself that he had said the right thing.

"Thank you for understanding," Oswald said, pausing a moment, "How many brothers do you have?"

"Three younger brothers," he said deeply, "and each of them chose power over freedom. When I say brothers however I meant my tribe, not just my family. There were thousands of us."

"Where are you from?"

"The Harpsure Mountain range. We lived in the mountains for a long time. A lot has changed in my life."

"Like what?" Oswald asked cautiously.

Fred licked his thin blue lips with a narrow blue tongue and stretched his hands out on the table looking at them as he spoke, "The life, death and rebirth of the goddess. The fall of Azar. War mostly. When the army came to the mountains, they offered us goods to trade first. We were happy to trade as most people won't talk to us, more than less trust us with goods. We made great machines for them."

"What kind of machines?"

"Whatever they asked for," Fred said grimly, "usually weapons and carts with gears for rough terrain, sometimes we made well pumps and sometimes we made things that should have never been thought of. We were builders, craftsmen, miners and mechanics, we were respected by the army..."

"You just made whatever they told you to?"

"For respect and support you would be surprised what people will do."

Oswald chewed on his lip thoughtfully, "When you got them what they wanted, what happened then?"

Fred lifted his eyes from his hands and gritted his razor white teeth, curling a lip back in thought for a moment, "They offered power, money, food, and land if we would join them. Most of us did. Those of us who didn't, stayed home, gathered together and had to try harder to survive. Maria and I were gathering rock wheat when our brothers came back. They asked again for us to join them. When we said no, they came back with men and dogs, they killed as many of us as they could."

"I'm sorry," Oswald said uncomfortably, regretting the path of the conversation.

Fred shook his head with a sigh, "I don't know how they could do that... kill their own families... something changed when they left home. Maria and I were two of six to survive the raid. The others went to a sister tribe to the east, I had the feeling that the army would follow us there too so I insisted we come to Gommorn."

"Did they?" Oswald asked.

"Did they what?" Fred said, looking up from his fingers again and studying Oswald with curiosity.

"Do the same thing in the east?"

Fred frowned, "I believe they did, though no one would know for sure without going into the mountains," he curled his four knuckled hands into large fists and pulled them down into his lap and off of the table, "I hope they found refuge somewhere."

"I do too," Oswald said genuinely.

Fred smiled, his sharp teeth gleaming, "Thank you."

"I'm sorry I was afraid of you," Oswald said, with a small smile, now much more comfortable somehow around Fred than he had been.

"Well," Fred said pleasantly, bearing his knife-like teeth with a crooked smile, "I'm a scary guy," he chuckled deeply and sat up straighter in his seat giving a long stretch with his arms in the air which was interrupted by a familiar voice that came suddenly from beside the table.

"Move over," Nedtedrow demanded at Fred who raised his eyebrows and did so without a word of protest. Nedtedrow had crept into the tavern without attracting any attention. Oswald was half surprised to see him, and more so when he and Fred began a mini, playful, shoving fight that ended when Nedtedrow toppled off the bench and hit the floor with an ungraceful thud. He scrambled back up with a short snort and a smile. Fred chortled deeply.

Nedtedrow sat up high, looking all the smaller next to the massive goblin who was easily three times his size. He looked smug and smiled at Oswald, "Hey Oswart. You look awful."

"I thought it was Oswald," Fred said, sounding embarrassed and confused.

Nedtedrow rolled his eyes, and said with a short sigh, "It is, I just like to irritate him when I get the chance to."

"Oh," Fred said, sounding more comfortable knowing that he wasn't mistaken.

"Anyway," Nedtedrow said, shoving the goblin again with an elbow, "I see you got your necklace back."

"Yeah," Oswald said, touching the fairy on his chest, "glad to have it back on actually."

"I would say so," Fred said, looking at it regally, "It's a precious thing. There aren't many of those left. What does it do?"

"It dances when it rains," Oswald said dully.

Fred raised an eyebrow, "They all dance, that's what identifies it, but what does it do? What are its properties? What magic does it have?"

"I don't know," Oswald said, with a shake of his head, "Maybe nothing."

Nedtedrow and Fred exchanged looks before shrugging off the question as if they both thought that Oswald did know but just didn't want to answer.

"Oh well," Fred said dismissively, "I guess it doesn't matter if it's yours anyway," he yawned, his narrow sharp teeth glinting in the light, "My wife has a charm too. Not a Fantasy charm," he added quickly, "But one that was enchanted by the elves seven generations or so ago."

"Your wife?" Oswald asked. He felt slightly ashamed. He had never imagined the Keernith race to value family in the same way as everyone else.

"Yes," Fred said, sitting back a little, "Her name is Maria."

Oswald was going to ask more about her but Nedtedrow seemed much more interested in this new article, "You say she has a charm? What kind?"

Fred smiled, "It's a lovely thing. It's a wooden carved griffin. It's supposed to repel sickness and promote healing."

"Does it work?" Nedtedrow asked.

"You can never be sure, but I can't ever remember a time when she was the one who came down with a fever. So I would think that it does."

People in the bar began to quiet down again a little and Oswald looked up to the door, expecting to see Matrim stepping through. Instead Satomi walked in and was looking placidly at the table Oswald was sitting at and strode up, her long braid swinging behind her, the spikes sticking through the knot menacingly.

"Oswald," she said sharply, and threw up a hand. Oswald fully expected to be smacked across the face with the way that she had postured but instead he felt a walloping pain of impact burn across his face so intensely that he was blinded by it for a few long seconds. She had punched him in the nose with all of the potent strength that she had. Oswald cupped a hand up to his freely bleeding nose and felt it to be sure it was where it should be. He wasn't so sure that it wasn't cracked.

"What was that for?" Oswald demanded angrily through the fountain of blood streaming down his face. He could hear Nedtedrow snickering from across the table.

"Because you startled me," she said angrily, and Oswald felt a pang of elation that momentarily ignored the stabbing pain in his nose. If she had been scared, then that would mean that she must be interested in him on some level. He tried to breathe in to respond but coughed on the blood running into his mouth.

"Mostly," she said, with her hands on her hips, "that was for making me look bad. How could you pass out like that after I stood up for you? — and in front of the entire city no less!"

She took a seat next to Oswald without asking and handed him a cloth.

She had planned this.

He took it and tried to mop the blood away from his face.

"You punched me in the face because I fainted?" Oswald asked incredulously with a hint of frustration in his voice.

"Yes, well, mostly anyway," she said, able to smile now that her deed had been done, "There's also the almost dying thing and not telling me who you were."

"I didn't know it was important," Oswald insisted.

"I suppose not," she said, with a shrug, "You just almost died over it."

Oswald felt his swelling face and added, "No one in this whole city is even going to know what I look like without a puffy face and a black eye."

"It's an improvement I'm sure," Satomi said, sounding more honest than Oswald would have liked, "it shows character and strength. Besides, it's the only thing on your skinny body that looks threatening."

Fred had a hand over his thin mouth and was trying to hold back a snort of laughter with some success, the grin of his pointed white teeth and blue gums showing between his abnormally long fingers. If anything he looked more like he was thinking of something else amusing but distant. Nedtedrow however, openly roared with laughter as Oswald still tried to see through the dancing lights in front of his eyes and failed to stop the flow of blood.

"Go get cleaned up," Satomi said lightly, "there's a fountain out back of the building. When you're done you can come back and sit with me. I'll get us something to eat."

Nedtedrow tapped the table with a pudgy finger, a grin, and short laugh, "I like her."

Chapter Fifteen

Through closed eyes the world spun around him, each land and province slipping around through his thoughts like water beating over stones in the riverbed. He saw mountains pass by him and cities slip into and out of his line of sight. The valleys and rivers pulled past him like pulled threads. The desert expanded and shrank away and the ocean turned in on itself. He suddenly saw nothing but the darkness and he opened his eyes.

Nothing.

An angry fire began to boil in his chest and he closed his eyes again, feeling the magic tear through his body and send sharp slits of magic into his mind. The world passed around him quickly and again he was back in his chair, staring at the back of his eyelids.

Venhow let out a roar. His rage a full bolstering inferno.

"Why can't I find him?" he demanded.

Walt shrugged passively, "It's hard to say why. Maybe he has better control over his magic than your little companion is aware of."

Priie huffed, hiding in a disguise of the little old woman once more. She waddled slowly over to Venhow, standing next to the obsidian desk and tried to meet his gaze but he ignored her, leaning back in the stone chair.

"I would be much more comfortable," Walt said, his eyes landing on Priie with a little bit of disgust in his ragged features, "if your skin-changer would at least be honest with me."

"Meaning what?" Venhow asked warningly.

"I already know it's a skin-changer of some kind. I don't much care for them to begin with, but if you insist that it be here with us, then at least show me enough respect to not try and fool me with it."

Venhow looked back at Priie thoughtfully and nodded, "Fine, but you won't expose her presence to anyone else."

"Why not?" Walt asked curiously, looking the old woman over before looking back to Venhow.

"Because she is valuable to me and no one but my head guards have ever seen her true form. I have to keep it that way for my own reasons."

"Fine," Walt said annoyed, "just quit insulting me with the disguises."

Priie frowned and twisted her shoulders uncomfortably, shaking off the form and quickly fading down into her frail thin form, her very pale skin and glimmering white wild hair. She unfolded her wings and beat them a few times to get comfortable again. She crossed her arms bitterly with a look of distain and looked away from Walt, offended.

"A sprite," Walt said surprised, his bigoted expression suddenly brightening with interest, "I thought that there weren't any of you left."

"There aren't" she replied bitterly.

"How old are you?" he asked intently.

"Not too old," she replied with a sneer. She fluttered her wings and moved closer to Venhow, refusing to make eye contact with Walt any further.

"How did you find her?" Walt asked attentively.

"She found me," Venhow said, brushing off the question, still absorbed in his own problems. He grabbed the bridge of his nose and pinched it softly trying to focus harder, "I don't understand. There isn't anyone who has been able to hide from me for this long. Everyone has given in eventually, including you."

"I'm also not threatened by you," Walt said, with a sly smile behind his narrowed eyes, "If I were then perhaps you wouldn't be able to find me either. It depends, I suppose, on how much he knows and whether or not he is afraid of you."

Venhow closed his eyes again and paused. Priie and Walt exchanged doubtful expressions, hers palpably anxious and his jaded. They watched patiently for a minute and when he came back around he snapped his eyes open and slammed his fist down on the desk, making all of the items on the desk jump and rattle. Priie startled as the sound, and inched away from the desk slightly.

Walt rolled his eyes.

Venhow caught the doubtful expression and his anger found a target, "Explain it to me then. Why? You're supposed to know everything, you sure want everyone to think so anyway. Suddenly you don't know? Tell me Walt, why can't I find him?"

"We have already discussed this," Walt said dismissively.

"Fantasy?" Venhow asked offhandedly.

Walt shrugged with one arm as he tucked his hands into the sleeves of his robes. He looked around with a pause and as if he had seen the word floating by and plucked it out of the air he answered, "Potentially."

"Why do you insist on that?"

"Because," Walt said dryly, slipping a hand out of the sleeve of his robe and straightening a figure on the desk, "he has to let his guard down eventually. He has to sleep sometime, but even with all that, he still can't be found. That is unusual at best."

"I have to find him," Venhow grumbled angrily, getting up from his chair and looking around the room, surveying the artifacts and racking his brain, "There has to be something, some way to find him."

"I'm sure there is, but obviously your way isn't working."

"Then what do you suggest?" Venhow snapped.

"You need something more powerful if you want to see into magic like that," Walt said, as he moved to the next item on the desk and picked it up, looking at it carefully before setting it back down exactly where it had been before.

"Like what?" Venhow asked as he stepped around Priie and began to pace.

"You need something that can work around magic," Walt said slowly, as he thought, "something unaffected by it so that the magic cannot interfere..."

Venhow thought for a moment and an idea occurred to him, "Yes, I do," he went to the tall row of cabinets along the far wall and threw open the furthest door. He reached up to an iron plate and pulled it down off of the shelf. He moved over to the cabinet and started pulling out vials and boxes of herbs and potions. He brought them back to the obsidian desk and laid them out.

He put a carefully mixed pile of herbs at the center of the plate and took a vial of black liquid from the assortment. He pulled off the stopper and breathed it in deeply before deciding that the potion had gone bad and trading it out for another vial. The second had a better concentration to the sour smell and was poured over the herbs which began to sizzle like meat in a pan.

Venhow quickly found another container with a thick mash and opened it to the air beside him recounting the steps in his head.

"This *is not* what I had in mind," Walt said firmly, apprehension seizing his thoughts, "I was meaning more along the lines of a blind tracker or a guard with a brain leach."

"No," Venhow said decidedly, "I need this."

Walt shook his head emphatically as he picked up the mix of herbs and the pulse in his temple quickened, "They may be slow and may not work but they're safer. You should try them first."

"But this *will* work," he said, as he put the lid on the desk and began mixing the paste rapidly with a man root.

"I don't think the risk is worth it," Walt insisted.

"I do," Venhow said flatly, "They can find him and kill him with or without Fantasy's protection. They're the only sure way to get this over with now."

"At what cost?!" Walt said alarmed, not believing the irrationality of the new plan.

"Give me your hand," Venhow said, pulling open a drawer and reaching into the desk. He pulled out a silver dagger, the bright metal glinted in the light. Emerald stones glittered at the hilt and the tarnished creases of the intricate carvings caught the shadows in contrast.

"No!" Walt said sharply, his eyes angry, "I won't call them."

"Priie," Venhow rounded on her, the dagger shone maliciously in his hand and a wild hunger festered in his eyes.

Priie brought her hands to her chest tightly and shook her head, afraid of the blade but far more frightened of what he planned to call up from the underworld.

"*You* call them if you want them here," Walt demanded, his rugged face carved resentfully.

"I can't," Venhow said lividly, "The Grimms and I have a... previous history," he worded his statement carefully and looked down at the blade in his hand, "I need blood," he looked around the room absently. Slowly a cruel smile slid across his face. He gestured at the door with his hand and it swung open. He looked back at Walt, "Find the Keernith General, tell them to bring me the Dwarf lord."

Walt, looking appalled by the idea, "That isn't necessary."

Venhow narrowed his eyes darkly, "So you are volunteering then?"

"No," he replied shortly.

"Then get the Dwarf lord," Venhow ordered.

Walt pushed a stringy piece of brown hair out from in front of his face bitterly and started walking down the spiral staircase, his footsteps echoing behind him as he went. After some time, a loud procession followed back up the staircase and Venhow tightened his grip on the dagger.

A very large Keernith goblin slouched into the room, his long arms and four knuckled fingers dragging a tied and noisy dwarf. The dwarf was struggling to keep his footing, being held up nearly off of the ground by his upper arm as he was brought further into the room. Walt sauntered into the room behind them unhappily.

The goblin threw the dwarf lord out onto the stone floor where he hit the ground hard at Venhow's feet. The guard looked around the room and shuffled back out the door, closing it behind him.

Venhow smiled wickedly down at the man. The dwarf had dark brown hair and a thick beard lined with streaks of new grey hair. He was filthy and bruised, freshly blinded in one eye which wept a thick yellow fluid down his cheek. His hands were tied behind his back, his wrists bloody and raw. His legs were burned in various places and it was difficult for him to roll into a position where he could see with his good eye.

"Hitch," Venhow called down to him clearly.

The man's face went white behind his beard at the sound of his voice and he turned his head further, his good eye a dark blot in the chaos of pain and filth.

"What do you want now?" The dwarf asked shakily, "I've already told you how we got out. They were moving towards Gommorn, I fell behind. I don't know anything else."

"Oh," Venhow said, with a sick smile admiring his own handiwork, "I bet you do… but that isn't why you're here with me now."

Hitch licked his broken lip and cringed at the taste of filth and crusted blood, turning his body slightly by pressing on the floor with his shoulder. He winced, and said in a desperate whimper, "T-then what do you want?"

"I want you to call someone for me," Venhow said, and tilted his head to one side, allowing the dwarf to see him through his good eye.

"What?" Hitch asked quietly. He shuddered suddenly with a stabbing pain as it pulsed through him and he doubled over into a ball on the floor. He tried to support himself as best as he could without the use of his hands and started breathing heavily as he looked around.

Venhow patiently waited for the pain to pass before smiling down at him again, "You are going to call the Grimms for me."

"NO!" Hitch tried to back away, kicking at the floor but was unable to move, his one eye open wide.

"It's not so bad," Venhow smirked stepping forward and hovering over the dwarf with the silver blade easily visible in his hand, "If you cooperate with me, you might even get to live a while longer, if you don't I'll call them anyway and you'll die now."

Hitch shook his head violently, "I don't want anything to do with this. Please, why do you need me for this?"

"I need blood for an offering," Venhow said, as he thumbed the length of the silver dagger.

"H-how much?" Hitch asked shakily and grimaced as jolts of pain shot through his body.

Venhow raised his eyebrows and spoke slowly and clearly, "A little if you are willing to make a deal for me… all of it if you aren't."

Hitch arched his back and screamed with another jolt of pain as it passed through his grievous wounds. He panted a moment on the floor before he was able to remember what they were talking about. He sat up straighter with his nostrils flared and his teeth gritted, "I won't make a deal. I would rather die."

"A king's purpose is to serve his people," Venhow said placidly. He reached down and seized the front of Hitch's shirt and hauled him halfway off of the ground, dragging him over to the desk. Venhow grabbed the container of paste and scooped out a large sliver with his fingertips. He reached down and smeared the paste on the floor, filling in a wide circular area and covering as much of the ground as he could.

He wiped the remaining paste across Hitch's neck and snatched the plate of still sizzling herbs and threw it to the ground, the plate smashing into the center of the paste covered stone. A dark foamy smoke started to roll out from where the two concoctions met.

Venhow grabbed Hitch again, looking into his mangled appearance with satisfaction, the fluid from his weeping eye reflecting grossly in the light, "Last chance."

Hitch took in a deep breath as though to answer and spat in Venhow's face.

Wet strings of blood and spit hung from Venhow's cheek. Horrific loathing took over and he threw Hitch as hard as he could onto the ground at his feet listening unsatisfactorily to the sickening crack of his face on the stone.

Hitch grunted and moaned through the broken bones in his face, blood dripping from his mouth and nose. Venhow stepped forward, his heart thundering as he lifted his foot from the ground. He stomped hard on Hitch's exposed lower back and felt something give within his body.

Hitch screamed into the floor, matted rivulets of fresh blood garbling his voice as it echoed off of the walls.

Venhow dropped to the ground, putting his knee square in the center of the dwarf's back with all of his weight. In a swift and calculated movement he took a handful of his beard and slid the blade along the dwarf's jawline. He sliced the beard short and uneven and cut a small chunk of his face away as he did so. He threw the handful of beard and flesh aside and stifled another scream from Hitch as he pressed his knee into his back harder and forced the air from his body. He quickly snatched a handful of Hitch's hair and jerked his head back, hard, towards his body at an extreme angle.

He tightened his grip on the blade and brought it around to the side of the exposed throat beneath him. Angrily, he stabbed the blade into the flesh and violently tugged at the dagger feeling the blade shudder as he started tearing through tendon and sinew. A thick spray of blood arched across the floor in spurts as he worked the blade.

It stuck in the flesh and he turned the blade slightly feeling a hot wave of blood roll over his hand. He tugged again and felt

Hitch's windpipe pop and then give. A sudden wet gurgling sound sucked at the air desperately.

He readjusted his grip on the hilt of the dagger which was slick with blood as new gushes and spurts poured out from the wound, and ripped the blade through the last few inches of muscle and flesh to a renewed bout of bloodshed.

Venhow pulled harder on Hitch's head to expose the wound further and listened for several long minutes as the gurgling sound slowed down and the pool of blood grew larger.

Hitch took in a final weak breath which bubbled in the flow of blood before fading away.

Venhow let go of the handful of hair and dropped Hitch's lifeless head facedown into the pool of rapidly cooling blood. He threw the bloody dagger aside and watched it skid across the floor before he turned back to the circle of blood.

The thick foamy smoke that had been rising from the circle turned red and rolled out more vigorously than before. He stood up like a man who had become accustomed to having blood on his hands and rolled his shoulders back, his eyes fixed on death. He stepped over the cooling corpse of the dwarf, leaving bloody footprints in his path as he walked around the obsidian desk. He quickly seated himself in the large stone chair, breathing heavily and noticing every drop of blood than slid from the tips of his fingers as they fell to the floor.

The pillar of red smoke began to roll so heavily that it started to accumulate against the high ceiling and the room hazed with the fog of it. Priie and Walt both shrank back to the edge of the room where the walls gave them little comfort.

As the source of the smoke began to fade away, a figure could be seen beginning to stir in the bloody pool. A long, black, skeletal arm reached out from the center of the circle and clawed with long talons at the stone as it began to climb out. Its head rose out with a shoulder. Its face, distorted and flattened, twisted in maliciously.

Blood coated its skin and bony body as it rose up, but as it cleared the pool the red tinge crisped and charred into a burnt and brittle charcoal black that coated its every inch. Barbed spikes rose up on its back, the end of every barb dripping liquid smoke that broke into the air around it as it moved. It pulled its legs from deep in the pool, its clawed feet clicking wetly on the bloody stone as it rose up to full height.

The black coloring of its body looked dry and burnt, as though it had been set on fire, smoke seeping out from its skin and filling the room with the smell of ammonia which mingled sharply with the already heavy stench of blood and smoke in the air.

It took a heavy step that sounded like its bones were filled with lead, its clawed feet leaving a sick trail of blood as it walked a few steps into the room, its small yellow eyes finding Venhow through the smoke. It curled it's scorched black lip up in disgust at the sight of him and its voice sounded like disturbed gravel when it spoke, "Called to turn yourself over, did you?"

"Hardly," Venhow replied with a placid expression, "I need your services."

"No," The Grimm said sharply, "Not for you. You didn't follow through on the last deal. You cheated."

"It isn't cheating, it's assurance," Venhow said, and sat back in the stone chair, feeling the final drip of cool blood drip thickly from the end of his middle finger.

"Whatever you want to call it," it grumbled, "We never got our side of the deal."

"I didn't feel it called for such drastic measures," Venhow said with a smirk.

"Of course not… You aren't the one being cheated out of a thousand years," The Grim said, with a darkness in its yellow eyes. It stepped closer to the desk and let out a breath, heavy with smoke.

"I need a man killed," Venhow said, dismissively.

"I won't do anything for *you*," it said definitavly, "I don't care what it is."

"What if I found you a soul?" Venhow interlocked his bloody hands thoughtfully across his chest.

The Grimm looked down at the horrific scene that nearly covered the room wall to wall and sneered, "It looks like even they don't want to make deals with you."

"I could find one," Venhow assured him, "and it wouldn't take me long."

The Grimm shook its smoky head, "No, not even for a hundred souls. Not for you."

"There has to be something you want," he said, sitting forward slightly in his seat, "Everyone wants something."

It chuckled sinisterly and its bright eyes lingered beyond its line of sight beneath the desk, "I will take the dagger strap around you calf and nothing less."

"No," Venhow said flatly, "That would hardly be worth it for me now would it?"

"Worth it?" The Grimm scowled and held out a long taloned forearm and gestured back to itself with a claw, "You owe us! Your life is mine! I want that article."

Venhow shook his head calmly, "That's the only thing that keeps you from touching me... and I will never remove it. I will be buried with it and you will never touch me, even then."

"Where are the gauntlets?" The Grimm asked, suddenly more aware of the room, taking a quick glance around. It spotted Walt and then Priie and dismissed them as harmless.

"Stolen," Venhow said bitterly, "Many years ago now."

The Grimm let out a smoky breath and chuckled to itself, "You don't have your sword either, now. You must be so frustrated."

"Dashai is in a safe place," Venhow said placidly, "I've meant to go and retrieve it."

The Grimm's sick chuckle exploded into mockery. Its loud booming voice grated painfully at everyone's ears and echoed off the walls. The echo gave the sound an unearthly nature as it reverberated. Venhow didn't as much as flinch at the sound. "Oh, how nice," it said, enjoying the game, "You'll be so angry. It is a real pleasure to be the one to tell you... It truly is..."

"What?"

"Dashai isn't yours anymore," it said, as it grinned.

"That's impossible," Venhow said unfazed, "I'm the only one that can wield it."

The Grimm cackled again, delighted in the turn of events. It lifted a hand and picked at a broken tooth with a razor sharp talon, "That's funny, I wonder how it moves every day without you."

"It's in a mound of venom stones. You're trying to get me wound up," he said, with a raised eyebrow, "It won't work."

"Don't believe me?" it said, flexing the barbs on its back tauntingly, "Then check for yourself."

Venhow paused for a moment and closed his eyes, drawing magic into his mind's eye and watching the landscape below him. He saw the mound of pale white stones standing bare in the forest, a crumbled heap of powder and gravel. The sword was gone. A sharp flash, a brief flicker of a vision, snapped into his head and he saw a red headed elf with the red blade in his hand. He opened his eyes to an electric jolt of pain in his head and a rolling mixture of anger and fear.

The Grimm laughed again, both at his pain and at the shock on his face, and grumbled happily, "Isn't that disappointing?"

Venhow's face slowly contorted, curling up into a hateful snarl, enhanced by the few small flecks of blood on his face. His breathing became deeper and more irregular, his voice dark with loathing, "I want him dead..." he whispered, his voice getting louder with every breath, "Kill him... I NEED him DEAD!"

"It is a shame that you and I don't do business," it snickered in absolute delight.

"I didn't ask for your business... I demanded your service!" his face was livid, his bloody hands shaking angrily and it was everything he could do to keep his magic in check as it threatened to set the room on fire around him.

"You aren't in the position to demand anything from me," The Grimm rose up taller and took a few heavy, clawed, steps forward until he was staring down at Venhow with contempt, only a breath's width between them as it leaned over the desk.

"Don't push me, or I will be," Venhow promised.

It looked down disgusted, no longer amused by the conversation, "You are worthless without your weapons. Just another mortal bag of meat," it said, looking Venhow up and down, its glare stopping down at the hidden dagger strap at his calf, "I would mangle you in a heartbeat, tearing your muscle from bone and stringing your guts from your belly... but I can't... and you can't touch me without your artifacts..." it said, through gritted teeth letting its beady yellow eyes drift through the room, "But I can," it paused hungrily with a taunting talon touching its blackened cheek, "kill them..."

It turned away from Venhow and locked its eyes on Walt and Priie, pressed against the far wall. It took in a deep breath, black smoke rolling out of its open mouth as it breathed, a greedy satisfaction in its eyes, "You even care about the little one, don't you?" it said darkly, "How sad…" it dropped to all fours, a guttural growl rising from somewhere deep in its gut.

Venhow launched out of his chair as the Grimm turned.

There was a sharp scraping sound from somewhere in the room as the Grimm launched, its clawed back legs leaving deep gouges in the stone as it kicked off from the ground. It passed through the wall above Priie's head as if it had not been there and rounded back through, catching her from behind, tearing a wing with a sharp talon as it dove back into the room. It pulled her to the floor, its mouth opened wide, teeth lengthening from behind its charred lips.

Priie screamed and turned her head away from its gnarled face, throwing her arms up around her head and trying to curl her body up defensively. The Grimm dove its head down with its teeth bared for the kill. Smoke rolled and it stopped short of her throat with a surprised look on its face, unable to take in a breath.

Its body jerked and suddenly was thrown aside, hitting the floor with the weight of a bolder. The Grimm looked around, stunned, and its eyes landed on Venhow.

He was standing over Priie with a sharp fingered gauntlet enveloping his right hand and a dangerous expression on his face.

"You said they were stolen… I know that they were stolen… How?" The Grimm asked tilting its head and pushing itself back up onto all fours. It grunted hatefully with its eyes on the gauntlet and began pacing around the side of the room watchfully.

"Half of it was stolen," Venhow corrected flexing his bare left hand.

"Clever," it said, touching its charred throat and sliding its eyes to Walt, "I don't suppose you have the other half?"

"I wouldn't tell you if I did," Walt guaranteed him his every fiber braced in apprehension of another attack.

"I suppose you wouldn't," it said, debating on whether the risk was worth the kill.

"You won't touch them," Venhow said firmly with no hint of doubt in his voice.

"Then since we have no business here," The Grimm said sauntering placidly back into the now cold and thickened pool of blood, "I have to be back to run the wheel."

"We do have business," Venhow said sharply, "I have a job for you."

"No," it said, through a fresh plume of smoke, "we don't." The Grimm stomped in the puddle of blood and suddenly its body dropped through the pool as though the floor had given way beneath it and it was gone. The floor was solid once more and the smoky fog that hovered in the air began to fade away.

The room was suddenly quiet, smears and trails of blood on every inch of the floor, the overwhelming stench of iron, ammonia, and blood hanging in the air. Priie took in a sharp breath and nursed her torn wing, looking up at Venhow with wide eyes.

He looked down at her for a second and then back at the claw marks torn into the stone. Hitch's body lay awkwardly among the carnage.

Walt and Venhow exchanged looks, "Everyone wants something..." Venhow repeated, staring at the place where the Grimm had vanished with renewed determination.

Chapter Sixteen

Oswald doubled over as he was thrown back onto the ground, hitting a root as he landed flat on his back. Every ounce of his breath was forced from his lungs as the root slammed into his ribs. The force from the blow made his stomach lurch up into his throat as he gasped for breath on the ground. Bright orbs of light danced in front of his eyes for a moment before fading away to the sight of a blade coming down at him through the air.

The tip of the shining blade cut through the air as it made its way down to where his head lay, the destination of the glistening steel marking its intended path towards the space between Oswald's eyes.

Wide eyed, Oswald threw his weight to one side, the clinking of his chain mail scraping against the hilt of his sword as he rolled over it to evade the strike. He had hardly moved his head out of the way when the blade made contact with the earth with a resonating thump, spewing clots of dirt and grass up into the air before sticking into the ground.

Oswald scrambled to his feet, the hilt of his sword biting into his fingers with the force of his grip. Its red blade glistened for a moment in the sunlight before Oswald brought it up over his shoulder and took an open strike at the man at the wielding end of the claymore.

Armond eyed the movement and released the claymore, leaving it stuck into the ground at an angle. He stepped back quickly, throwing his arm free of the first swings path and with purpose, he drew a short sword from its scabbard and blocked Oswald's second attempt at reaching the armor against his body.

The clatter of steel on steel as the blades made contact with one another in the morning air resounded against the surrounding trees and bounced back to double the sound of each strike.

Oswald grunted with effort as he pushed with his sword against Armond's, trying to throw enough force into him to put distance between their strikes. The strength of a shoemaker, however, was little match against the strength of an experienced general.

Armond braced his sword against Oswald's and threw his weight forward, pressing the broad side of Oswald's sword against his chest and overbalancing him.

Oswald stumbled but spotted another opening as he began to fall back, quickly he decided to strike rather than brace himself from his fall. He swung the glinting red blade in an arc and felt impact shudder through the steel as it met with the side of Armond's chest plate. He hit the ground, holding his sword up towards Armond who was smirking lightly and looking down at the scorched scratch in the armor plate.

"Interesting decision," Armond said, and he lowered his sword in response. He reached a hand down to Oswald and effortlessly picked him up off of the ground.

Oswald panted, most of his energy expended by the short mock battle, dropping the tip of the sword to the ground letting it rest for a moment. He brushed his hair out of his face and a red curl bounced back into place above his eyebrow. A droplet of sweat dripped down into his eyes, stinging lightly. He blinked hard and shook his head, feeling the wind against his dampened brow.

"Ready to try again?" Armond asked, more of a demand than a request. He wasn't even winded despite the heavy armor pressing against his shoulders.

"Can't I just have a minute to rest?" Oswald asked through heavy breaths.

"The enemy won't let you stop for breath, nor will I," Armond said bluntly, and brought his short sword up to the ready.

Oswald tried to do the same and his arms protested the movement. A shrewd snicker sounded off from up in a nearby tree. Oswald looked up to Samuel, Armond's son who was sprawled out across a thick, low hanging branch and looking smug.

Samuel's dark hair and pale blue eyes were deeply in contrast to Armond's blond hair and deep sapphire eyes. Samuel, Oswald guessed, was around seventeen years old. He was a lean build, tall and strong, with an attitude that Oswald suspected came from having such a prestigious father. Samuel rolled over on the branch, crossing his arms and resting his chin on the back of his hands, his legs and elbows hanging freely in the air, "You're pathetic," he chortled.

Armond frowned deeply at his son with a look that was nothing if not disappointed, "Get down here," he demanded.

Samuel rolled his eyes and slipped down from his perch, "Yes sir?" he asked airily.

Armond shook his head and flipped the sword in his hand holding the blade carefully and holding the hilt out to Samuel, "You think you can do better? Then you teach him."

Samuel looked up, wide eyed, and shook his head, "No, I meant him. That isn't what I had in mind."

"Then what did you have in mind, besides being disrespectful?" Armond asked with his eyes stony.

"I was just thinking out loud," Samuel said passively, "I didn't want to offend you, dad. Can't I just go hunting with the other men? Please?"

"No," Armond said sharply, holding the sword towards him more forcefully.

"Why not? There's a flock of green dragons grazing just outside the valley!" Samuel said, and pointed off in the general direction, "Matrim caught one in a trap last night and is down at the Burning Mill eating like a king and wallowing in the money that he just made. Why do I have to be here for this? I'm a great hunter!" he boasted, "I could get two or three down before the flock heads South. Do you have any idea what kind of money that would bring in down at the market?"

"Matrim needed the money *and* the food," Armond said forcefully, "You don't. You have never in your life been in need of anything."

"But I could—"

"—No." Armond said sharply, and dropped the hilt of the sword into Samuels hand with a look that would not tolerate any more argument, "Now, be useful and show him what he did wrong. You think you're so much better, show me that you know what *you're* doing."

Samuel wrapped his fingers around the cool metal and took the sword as Armond stepped back. He frowned at the sword and glanced at Oswald with a crumpled brow and looked back to his father, "Dad—"

"—Now!"

Samuel sighed and readjusted his grip on the hilt. He stepped back and swung the blade in graceful arcs, looping it around his back, over his shoulders, and into the air before catching it once more and assuming a fighting stance.

Oswald swept the sweat and hair out of his face once more and picked up the tip of his sword from the ground. He brought it up and across his body and bent his knees slightly, waiting for Samuel to make his first move.

Samuel rolled his eyes again and stepped forward without intent to strike. He brought himself up, chest out and with the command of a born leader, he shouted, "Fix your stance! Feet apart, toes forward!" Samuel hit the side of Oswald's foot with the broadside of his sword.

Oswald adjusted his footing.

"Keep your back straight and eyes on me!" Samuel commanded.

Oswald looked up from his feet and did as he was told.

"Arms engaged," he said sharply, demonstrating the positions, "Sword up! Tighten your grip!"

Again, Oswald corrected himself.

Without warning, Samuel took a step back and attacked with the force of a hurricane, his blade swinging masterfully in the air with deadly accuracy.

Oswald had barely enough time to react to each swing, only blocking each strike with the very tip of his blade as each blow came closer and closer to his center. He hadn't the time to make a strike himself before Samuel was at his face, his free hand wrapped around Oswald's chainmail shirt and the tip of the blade pointed squarely at the hollow of his throat. Oswald had no idea what just happened, but he knew he would have been dead if Samuel had any less control over his own swings.

Samuel let go of the fistful of chainmail, lowered his sword, and said casually, "Good." Oswald was surprised by the encouragement. Seeming to recognize the expression, Samuel continued, "You kept your footing. This time look for weaknesses in my defense. Exploit it if you get the chance."

Again, Samuel attacked without warning and without giving Oswald the opportunity to ready himself.

Oswald brought the sword up to block with hardly a second to waste. He felt the air cut as the tip of Samuel's blade grazed the chain-mail at his shoulder. He blocked another strike, his muscles beginning to tremble with the effort. He watched Samuel's movements, trying to find an open place.

There was none.

It wasn't more than a few minutes before Samuel again had cleared the distance between them and was too close to swing at with the sword. He did the only thing he could think of and let one hand go of the hilt of the red sword and threw a punch, surprised when he felt his knuckles connect with Samuel's stomach.

Samuel gasped and doubled over for a moment before quickly composing himself. He stood straight once more, though now breathing heavily, and put a hand on the place he had been hit. He nodded and dropped the tip of his sword, "Good...Good, If you'd had a dagger..." he trailed off catching his breath, "See what good form and stance can do?" he stretched his back and stuck the sword into the ground an inch or so. He let go of the hilt and the sword wilted a little, leaning to one side in the ground.

Samuel turned to Armond with his arms out, "Can I go now?"

Armond sighed impatiently, "Fine. Meet us at the Burning Mill at sunset."

"But it takes at least—" Samuel started with sharpness in his voice but then quickly stopped himself and with disappointment on his face he nodded respectfully, "Yes sir."

It wasn't long before Oswald was sore, tired, and could hardly lift the sword anymore. His bones ached and his muscles strained, his body felt bruised and scraped raw from the light armor and the constant humiliation of being thrown to the ground.

Hours passed and it wasn't until it came time for another round and he simply couldn't make his arms move to block one of Armond's swings, allowing it by way of exhaustion to smack his chest plate with full force, throwing him to the ground again, that Armond finally decided that enough was enough. He let Oswald lay there on the ground for several long and restful minutes before helping him to his feet and nodding that the day was finished.

Oswald put his sword in its new, black, leather scabbard, resting against his hip. He looked down at his raw and swollen hands with distaste, opening his palms and stretching his fingers to relieve the discomfort.

Armond looked up and said surely, "Go ahead and take your armor off. We're done today."

Oswald shrugged out of the armor one exhausting piece at a time and tossed them into a pile at the base of the tree Samuel had been lying in.

"You can leave those there for now. I'll have someone put them away for you. You did very well today. You learn fast," Armond said, looking at him through the corner of his eye as he too shed his armor and looked relieved to be rid of it. Armond straightened his shirt, pulling the wrinkles from the cloth and letting the sweat dry off of it, "I don't know that I've ever trained anyone who picked up on proper forms and footing so quickly. You'll be a force to be reckoned with on the battlefield someday."

"Thanks," Oswald said reluctantly, "but I hope never to be on the battlefield."

Armond looked at him for a long moment, "Things have changed over the years. No one hopes to be on the battlefield, but many see it anyway. My only hope," he said, picking up the bag with the training equipment and starting down the dirt path, "is that we know enough to survive it. Come on now, I'll buy you a drink and a proper meal, it looks as though you've been without for a while."

"Thank you," Oswald said again, quietly following along behind. He watched his feet as he trudged along the path, feeling the tired numbness in his thighs and calves, his arms seemed useless and hung at his sides, too tired to even sway with his steps. He watched the dirt pass under his shoes along with the occasional rock and twig scattered along the trail. He was looking forward to getting something to eat and drink but in the back of his head he wondered if he would be able to get up when the meal was finished.

The dirt trail suddenly turned rocky as he entered town and he looked up to see where he was. He didn't look to be far from The Burning Mill and was fairly sure that he knew the way there, which was good because it seemed as though he had been walking too slowly for Armond, who had let him fall behind far enough that he couldn't be seen ahead of him, and was now lost in the sea of crooked homes and pathways.

Oswald thought about food and what he would be able to eat when he reached the tavern. He missed the purple Peta fruits that grew on the trees back home. He thought perhaps that they could grow around here too, but had yet to find a tree, besides they were pretty much out of season by now.

He took in a sharp breath as he stepped on something wet and lost his footing. He slipped and his feet threw out in front of him and his backside hit the gravel. His body stiffened with the soreness from his training and with a grunt, he tried to push himself back up to stand. He put his hand behind him and his hand landed in whatever it was that he had slipped on. Whatever it was, was cool, sticky, and wet. Disgusted he looked at his hand, hoping it wasn't what he thought it was.

It wasn't.

His hand had landed in a small pool of something purple. It was a deep purple, thick and sticky with an irony stench to it that seemed familiar. All at once it sank into his memory. Full realization hit him and he remembered the thick purple blood clotted in his hair from back home. It was Goblin blood. He stared.

Goblins...

"Oh, no..." Oswald said to himself, quickly getting to his feet and starting into a full run down the pathway, all tiredness forgotten, *Fred.*

He ran around the corner, desperate to catch up with Armond. He couldn't see him anywhere. He accidently clipped someone as he rounded a corner but was too concerned with the blood on his hand to stop and apologize. He took another corner to get back onto the main roadway and could see the Burning Mill in the distance.

The cold air braced his lungs and his feet beat against the stone road. He put his arms ahead of him as he reached the front door and slammed into it, throwing it open and nearly falling into one of the guards at the door.

"What's your hurry?" The man grumbled darkly and snatched the back of his shirt and stopped him from going any further.

The dim lighting took a moment for his eyes to adjust to. People were staring at him. He turned to the guard who had ahold of him, "I need to find — General Armond," he gasped.

The guard's face creased unhappily, "He hasn't been here today."

"Or...Fred," Oswald asked shakily, "Have you seen Fred?"

A chair scraped across the wooden floor, "I'm here," came a deep grinding voice. The guard let go of the back of Oswald's shirt and stood nearby suspiciously. Fred uncurled his back and stood at his full towering height, the fierceness in his features still something that Oswald was not accustomed to. He walked across the room a few long strides and furrowed his brow as he came to a stop in front of him. He reached a long boney arm out and touched Oswald's shoulder, "What's wrong?" his voice rumbled softly.

"Are you alright?" Oswald asked, looking him over and still trying to catch his breath.

"Fine," he said cautiously, curling his back and lowering himself to meet Oswald's gaze evenly, "Why do you ask?"

Oswald opened his hand, only now realizing that he had been clenching his fists, and held his palm upward for Fred to see. It was still stained a deep purple and the blood had begun to clot and dry, "I slipped in a … puddle—" Oswald said, looking up at Fred's face and his voice fell short. All color had drained from Fred's usual deep green complexion and a look of bottomless horror overtook the place that concern and curiosity had held moments before. Fred's mouth dropped open and he mouthed wordlessly for a second. In a sudden flurry of movement, he threw Oswald out of the way and blasted out of the tavern in two wide steps.

The noise in the tavern erupted all at once and people started moving about nervously.

Oswald didn't stay. He pushed his way past the guard and tore after Fred, his heart thundering. Oswald watched as Fred turned just shy of the secondary road and cut between homes. He could barely keep track of where he was, following short flashes of long green limbs as he continued to find shortcuts to his destination, weaving endlessly through narrow gaps between homes and only occasionally finding solid footing.

Fred was fast and knew where he was going, Oswald hadn't a clue and as he turned a corner that he thought Fred had taken and he found himself in an alleyway alone. He listened to what he hoped was the sound of heavy footsteps.

On instinct, Oswald backtracked and took another path, happy to see a very large footprint in a patch of dirt among the stones and followed the point of the print. It wasn't long before he spotted Fred through a lengthy gap between houses and was back on track. He jumped a stack of logs piled nicely in the alleyway and sped down a path too narrow for Fred to cut through. He spotted Fred's unusual form ahead of him, finally catching up to him.

Fred didn't hesitate or even really notice that Oswald had been able to keep up with him, instead he stepped up to a very tall and strangely shaped house and rushed inside, leaving the door ajar behind him.

Oswald noticed with a churn in his stomach that there was a dark purple stain on the doorjamb and heavy purple droplets on the ground at his feet.

He could hear the deep rumble of Fred's voice from within the building but couldn't understand it through his own heavy breathing. He tried to quiet his heart and his breath as he stepped up to the doorway and peered inside.

Most of the home seemed to be made of large cut stones with the occasional wooden dividing board or support structure. It was a dark home, with strange metal ornaments hanging from the walls and from the very tall ceiling. A table was in the middle of the room covered in tiny metal gears and some things that Oswald didn't directly recognize.

Once his eyes adjusted, he saw what he had been looking for. Fred was kneeling on the floor in front of another goblin, who was sitting in a stone chair, bent over one knee and breathing heavily. Fred was speaking but even when Oswald held his breath he couldn't understand what was being said and he guessed that it must be the Keernith language. He leaned into the doorway a little, not wanting to assume that he was welcome and cleared his throat lightly.

"Is everything okay?" Oswald asked nervously.

Fred rounded on the spot, his features contorted in rage and pain but the look subsided immediately when he saw it was Oswald. Fred looked from the floor to Oswald and back to the goblin in the chair several times before he gestured with a light curling of his fingers, "She's wounded."

Oswald looked between the two goblins cautiously, "Can I help in any way?"

"I don't know," Fred said, turning back to the woman.

Oswald stepped into the room gingerly. The goblin woman sat up slowly in her chair, a hand wrapped tightly around her thigh, and a blood soaked towel between her fingers and the wound. Her features were nothing that Oswald had imagined. She was smaller than Fred, though not by much and her face was softer, though no less fierce. Her cheek bones were less pronounced and her lips seemed fuller. Her eyes were larger than Fred's and she had hair, very fine, short, dark blue hair, no more than three inches long. Her body looked much the same as Fred's in shape, at least from what he could see of it. Tightly stretched, leathery, green skin over dense tendon, muscle and bone, giving her a skeletal look beneath the cotton shirt and pants she wore.

"You're Maria?" Oswald asked, recalling Fred mentioning her name before.

She nodded lightly.

"What happened?" he asked stepping further into the dark room, trying to get a look at the hidden wound. Maria looked nervously to her husband and didn't answer.

Fred looked worried and angry, a look that didn't seem out of place on his features, but was unnerving.

"We need to stop the bleeding," Oswald said, mostly to himself and an idea crept into his mind as he spoke, "I think I can stop it quickly, but I need to see it first."

Maria grimaced as she began to pull the fabric away from the large open wound as it stuck to her wound. The gash itself looked to be a single clean cut of some kind, deep and open, muscle bared and blood seeping readily into the gap between her torn flesh.

Oswald drew his sword slowly, but in a flurry of movement and pain, he found himself sprawled on the ground with Fred standing menacingly between them.

Oswald clutched a place on his chest where Fred had hit him. "I won't hurt her! I swear!" Oswald said, through gritted teeth. He sat upright and gripped the hilt of his sword tighter than was probably necessary, "I just want to try and stop the bleeding."

Fred huffed uncertainly and stepped back to his wife, letting Oswald get up from the floor. Oswald felt the bruise forming against his breast bone as he shifted the weight of his sword. He took a firm but careful grip on the guard of the sword and held the base of the hilt out towards Maria. He gave both Fred and Maria an encouraging look that he hoped looked more sincere than frightful and gently pinched her wound closed with his left hand as he slowly and forcefully drug the hilt of the sword across the entire length of the gash.

Maria let out a chilling scream.

Oswald felt another impact to his chest, his feet lifted off from the ground. He hit the floor hard, smacking the back of his head against the stone floor. Long fingers seized firmly around his throat as the last breath of air flew from his lungs with the impact on the ground. The grip around his neck tightened quickly and his throat closed off from the pressure.

He could feel the blood in his head begin to pool with the pressure and his skin felt tighter across his scalp as the vision began to fade from his eyes. His heart thundered in his ears as he fought for breath. He heard a voice but couldn't understand it, either because of the desperate drumming in his head or from his fading consciousness.

Something gave in the iron grip and he was able to take in a breath, cold and jagged. He felt Fred's hands leave his throat and again, he found himself on the floor. He gasped and was relieved to feel the cold air hit the walls of his lungs as he coughed violently against the floor. The pressure in his head, along with his vision, gradually returned to normal with each thunderous beat of his heart. When he was able to stop coughing and the pounding in his ears had subsided, he realized that Fred was talking to him.

Red faced, exhausted, and now with a splitting headache, Oswald sat upright on the floor, not bothering to get up again. Fred was kneeling next to his wife, inspecting the wound and looking flustered and sheepish, "I thought you were hurting her," he grumbled to the floor, decidedly not making eye contact, "but you were right… The wound sealed and the bleeding has nearly stopped…"

"She needs herbs," Oswald croaked, the use of his beaten voice making him gag and bringing on a new coughing fit before it subsided again, "or it will get infected…" Oswald took a generous moment of silence and a few minutes to recover before pushing his body up from the ground for the hundredth time that day, thinking to himself that if he were to land on the ground again, he would simply stay there until morning.

He looked over at the wound, now sealed shut from the burning magic of the sword and holding together nicely. It was still bleeding but it had slowed enough that he was no longer concerned, although he was unsure how much blood she had already lost.

Oswald took a few unsteady steps and knelt next to her in the chair, noticing the seep of purple blood that was oozing between her thigh and the chair, "I need to know what kind of wound this is so I know which herbs that I have to find..." he said gently. Maria whispered something but Oswald couldn't hear it. She glanced at Fred again looking worried. "I *have* to know what herbs you need," Oswald repeated quietly.

"I was gathering pine nuts at the edge of town. I was attacked... it's a sword wound," she said meekly. Immediately Oswald understood her hesitation. Fred roared, letting out one deep rumbling scream at the doorway that rattled the walls, the muscles and veins in his body tense and trembling.

"WHO?!" Fred demanded loudly with a certain primal wildness in his eyes.

"It was an accident, treacle, please," she begged, still holding the wound and sounding weak and exhausted, "please..."

"WHO?"

"A couple of boys, Brutes, from the North end of the city. They were just teenagers, they didn't know who I was and—" Maria shook her head desperately reaching out her long thin arm and only catching air as Fred rounded from the room like a beast and tore out the door into the city, "No! Fretcritck, PLEASE!"

Oswald stood in shock next to Maria, breathing heavily until her trembling grip on his arm tore him from his own thoughts, "I don't know you," she said quickly, "but my husband seems to trust you. Please," she begged tears welling in her large indigo eyes, "don't let him kill those boys. Whatever you do, please, please, don't let him hurt anyone... please..."

"I won't," Oswald heard himself say before he had considered what that may entail. He was easily half the size of Fred, but he had to do something. He tried to give her a reassuring look but was caught by the distress in her face, "We'll be back soon," he promised and raced out of the door after Fred and headed North through the city.

It wasn't hard to find the path Fred had taken, unlike before where he had simply been in a hurry, now there was a warpath, and the people in the street who had seen him pass by looked scared. People gladly pointed him in the right direction when he wasn't sure and after twenty minutes or so of tireless chasing, he heard shouting in the distance.

Panting, he followed the sounds and finally found where Fred's warpath had led them. Fred was towering over a large heavily built middle-age man, he was copper skinned with black hair and dark eyes and had arms as thick as Oswald's thighs. Oswald recognized the man from the Market; he had never spoken to him before but knew that he was one of the local blacksmiths.

The two men were shouting and it was only after he had reached the porch that he saw the two teenage boys behind their father, cowering with their backs against the front wall of their home. The boys were young, maybe thirteen and sixteen by Oswald's best guess, and they looked absolutely terrified, and rightfully so.

Outrage boiled against Fred's skin, flushing his completion to a deep forest green. Sweat beaded against his shoulders, face and neck and his eyes were fixed and destined for murder. Fred's heartbeat could be seen from feet away, pounding in the veins in his arms and neck; his teeth, sharp and long glistened against his bared blue gums. His four knuckled fingers were balled into fists that could rival stone and every breath he took rattled with the purity of his rage.

"Move…" Fred commanded sharply, dragging the V from his demand against his lower lip, his sharpened teeth tearing his open a jagged wound on his lip, though he didn't seem to notice.

"What *is* this about?!" The blacksmith roared back squaring his broad shoulders and doing his best, though failing, to match the goblin's immense height.

"Your sons tried to kill my wife!" Fred spat, a spot of blood from his lip trailing down his chin.

"Maria?" The blacksmith asked, losing the color in his cheeks as he said so.

"Yes," Fred's murderous gaze swept from the blacksmith to beyond him where the boys looked on in horror.

"My boys?" The blacksmith turned his head to look back but only for a brief glance as Fred tried again to work his way past the blacksmith to where the boys stood.

"We didn't know, honest," The oldest boy pleaded, seemingly finding his voice, "We had never seen her before and she came up behind us and we were startled…" Fred tried again to reach them and was just held off by the Blacksmith's quick movement.

"We're sorry!" they pleaded, "We're so sorry!"

The blacksmith turned to look at his boys once more and Fred didn't miss the opportunity again, he threw an arm against the blacksmith and threw him across the porch and out into the street. In one stride had closed the gap between himself and the boys and had his hands around the oldest boy's throat.

"FRED!" Oswald screamed, "Maria is DYING!"

Fred stopped in his tracks, frozen. He loosened his grip on the boy, though ever slightly, and Oswald was relieved to see the boy was able to catch a breath.

"I need your help to find that herb or she will die *tonight!*" Oswald lied, "We need to go NOW! Please help me find it! I can't do it myself!"

Fred let go of the boy who scrambled back against his brother protectively, looking terrified but relatively unhurt.

Fred turned towards Oswald dumbfounded for a moment and wavered in the air unsteadily like a dead tree in a high wind. He steadied himself against the railing of the porch and looked more and more lost as the thought sank deeper into his mind. Oswald watched as the fire that roared within him was snuffed out. All of his anger was gone, taken from him in an instant. After a few raspy breaths he stepped off the porch weakly and his eyes glazed.

"She's dying?" Fred whimpered, "My Maria is dying…?" his face contorted painfully into an unmatchable and torturous expression that Oswald never wanted to see on another living thing for as long as he lived. Fred had been broken by three words. He looked like a man with nothing left, torn and lost to the emptiness.

Oswald took in a strong breath and shook his head, "If we find the WhimsMoss she needs she will be fine. Alright?" Fred nodded absently and Oswald wasn't so sure if he had heard him.

"WhimsMoss?" the younger of the two boys asked cautiously, "I know where the WhimsMoss is growing this time of year."

Fred looked over his shoulder slowly with wet eyes, "Where?" he asked gently.

"There's a patch of it growing not far from here," the boy pointed down a narrow alleyway, "it grows in the Fer trees by the Widow Home from now until the mushrooms grow in early spring, after then you can't find it near town."

"Thank you," Oswald said, tentatively reaching up with an unsure hand and placing it up on Fred's back and giving him a gentle push in that direction.

They started walking East towards where the boy had pointed, moving slowly at first but once the shock of Oswald's words had worn off of Fred's mind they sped into a gentle run. As not to pass the plant, and they both became more aware of the trees they passed and were keeping an eye out for the small creeping yellow and green vine.

They passed the Widow Home after what seemed like far too long and Oswald spotted a lonely vine wrapped around a particularly large Fer tree, "There it is," Oswald said, pointing to a branch too high for him to reach.

Fred eagerly reached up and ripped the leafing part of the vine from the branch. He looked at the WhimsMoss distantly, gripping it tight in his fist. He took in a shallow tired breath and stooped down to look Oswald in the eyes. His eyes reflected the sincerity of a tired soul and a hopeful half smile came to his face. He licked his lips and wiped the drizzle of blood from his chin, just now realizing that he had hurt himself earlier. He held the vine out for Oswald to take and asked flatly, "Maria is going to be okay isn't she?"

"Yeah," Oswald said, taking the vine and trying not to look guilty, "This is just to keep the infection out. She should be fine with rest," Oswald braced himself, hoping that he would not have to endure the wrath of the giant goblin before him. He took in a deep breath and met Fred's eyes, pleading for understanding, "I had to say something.... I'm sorry."

As if the world fell off his shoulders Fred hung his head and let out a breath as though he hadn't been able to breathe out ever before. Oswald expected anger, but when Fred looked up again, instead he looked grateful. He nodded and gave Oswald a small smile.

"Thank you," he said softly, "for stopping me... and for saving my wife. If you hadn't come to get me when you had and if you hadn't stopped her bleeding, I may not have even had a chance to save her. You forever have my gratitude." He stood upright again and started off in the direction of his home. Oswald followed along behind him and pulled the leaves off the vine and rolled them in his hands releasing their sap until they were a wet sticky mass of mulched leaves.

Preoccupied with his task, he was surprised when he looked up and realized that they were not only back at Fred's home but that it was dark, the evening sky had come and gone to the stars of night without his notice. Fred opened the door to his home, a candle had been lit and Maria had apparently found the strength to move from her seat. Her chair was empty and the candle was burnt down to half on the stone table in the center of the room, her bloody clothing had been discarded and the remains of fresh bandages were lying on the table.

"Come in," Fred offered and waited for Oswald to enter before closing the front door, "wait here a moment." Fred went into the other room and went up a flight of stairs to the room above. Oswald stood in the quiet and continued to mash and roll the leaves in his hands waiting. After a while Fred called for him to come upstairs. The bedroom upstairs was small, but warm, with a single bed and a chair.

Maria was lying down in clean clothing on the bed looking pale and unwell but not altogether as bad as Oswald had expected. She woke up for just a moment and thanked him quietly before closing her eyes back and drifting into her world of dreams. Oswald hoped that they would be restful dreams for her.

Oswald held out the WhimsMoss mash to Fred, "Next time you change the bandage put this underneath against the wound, put water in with it if the leaves dry out before then. You shouldn't need more than that."

"Thank you," Fred said, taking the herb, "do you have anywhere to stay?"

"I think I'm staying with Matrim tonight," Oswald said distantly, not entirely sure of his answer.

"Hmmm," Fred thought, "you are welcome here. It isn't much but it is out of the cold."

"Thank you," Oswald said, as he wiped the remains of the WhimsMoss sap from his hands and onto the leg of his pants, "but I need to get something to eat and I was supposed to have met general Armond hours ago."

"You're exhausted," he said, with weary eyes, "rest here."

"Really," Oswald said, trying to look more alert than he truly was, "I'll be fine. I have to go to the Burning Mill before I can rest," he said, with a smile as he subconsciously rubbed at his aching joints, knowing that if he stopped he would not get back up. "I hope she heals quickly," Oswald added and turned to go back down the stairs, now suddenly realizing the weakness in his knees and fighting to stay on his feet.

Oswald reached the small adjoining room at the bottom of the stairs and paused a moment as Fred called after him, his deep voice drained of energy, "If you ever are in need of anything... come to me. There aren't many people that would have done that for me. If, you ever need anything...." Fred's voice trailed off and Oswald understood the meaning. He nodded, more to himself, and left the home being sure to close the door behind him.

A long stretch of road, a meal and an explanation of the evening is all that stood between him and sleep, and it hardly seemed like anything against the day that he had behind him. He was looking forward to a good night's rest.

Chapter Seventeen

He woke up, the cold clench of bitter air on his face and the sunlight just visible in the beads of dew on the window beside him. He turned and lay flat on the hard board of his bed and sighed.

Matrim lay sleeping across the room on a new pallet of blankets he had bought from selling the dragon hide and meat he had caught the night before. A fresh pile of fruit lay in the bowl on the table alongside a bright green dragon's brow scale, as large as the palm of his hand and elegantly diamond shaped.

Oswald sat up quietly and winced at the tension in his body. Everything ached. He touched the fairy necklace against his chest to be sure it was still there and reached a hand up to his face. He recoiled at his own touch, his face was sore and burning with the combination of injuries. It seemed like the swelling had gone down, however, with the cool morning air.

He slid off the stiff bed and limped slightly. He stretched out the tired and sore muscles in his legs and he staggered his way to the table and picked up a key fruit, bright yellow and sweet. He picked up his sword with the black scabbard and strapped it onto his waist. Carefully he made his way to the front of the shack, taking a bite of the fruit and trying not to wake Matrim as he did so. He wiped the drip of juice from the fruit off his chin and stepped out onto the cobble street.

There were few people moving about at this time of morning, most of them seemed to be merchants, gathering their wares and rolling their carts to the market, those who weren't looked like huntsman, coming into town from the valley forest with their kills. Very few were just early risers eager to wander the city.

Oswald rolled his shoulders, trying to loosen them as he walked, occasionally taking a bite of the key fruit as he went. He found his way to the path that lead back to the clearing after what seemed like a very long walk.

He looked down at the ground and saw the small pool of dried blood he had slipped in the night before and sickeningly wondered how Maria was feeling today. He passed the first tree out of the city and continued to where the pebbles turned to dirt in the path. He started up the slow incline and over the hill to the place where he was meant to train.

His muscles protested the thought of going through it all again, but he ignored the discomfort in his body and kept walking. He thought for a moment about his appearance and guessed that he looked like a terrible mess, he hadn't looked in the mirror for a few days. He needed a bath and clean clothes but he figured he could sort that out after training. His clothes and belongings had vanished from the green bag at some point during the trial.

When he crested the hill he was surprised to see how many people were already there. Yesterday it had only been Armond, Samuel and him, today there were five. Loch, Fred, Armond, Samuel, and Ramif stood at the tree, adjusting their armor and talking among one another cordially.

The sight of Ramif fueled a pyre of loathing somewhere buried in Oswald's chest, the aches in his shoulders and the scuffs on his body burned with disgust.

Fred was the first to spot him, standing up straight and making the small assemblage around him look like children in comparison. He waved kindly and smiled, his thin blue lips curled on his bony face, the sharp ends of his teeth shining. The others, one by one, realized that Oswald had arrived and also turned to greet him. Everyone except Ramif, whose face was frozen with contempt and acknowledged him only with a small tug at the end of his braided beard and a scowl.

Oswald wandered down into the group, pitching the pit of the fruit out into the thicket of brush as he went. Loch gave him a hard pat on his back and Samuel put out a hand for Oswald to shake as he had done the day before. Armond smiled, a wicked deception in his eyes.

"What's going on?" Oswald asked tentatively.

"We were waiting on you," Fred said, and scratched at his bony shoulder.

"How is Maria this morning?" Oswald asked.

"She's tired and weak, but eating and moving well," Fred said gratefully.

Armond grabbed Oswald's shoulder and said with a sharpness, "You lied to me."

"About what?" Oswald asked, concern running through his beating heart as he tried to remember what he could have possibly lied about.

"You failed to tell me the whole story last night, Fred was kind enough to fill me in," Armond said, looking smug.

"Fill you in on what?" Oswald asked, and looked from one face to another in the small assembly. They all stared back at him amusedly.

"Maria," Armond said flatly, "I'm impressed. You only told me that she was hurt and that you made a poultice."

"I didn't do much else," Oswald said, mildly confused, "That's what happened."

"You also neglected to mention taking a beating from Fred — twice, or that you were able to keep up with him at a run afterwards," Armond raised an eyebrow and smiled lightly, "No small feat for any man. You protected two young boys. You also kept quiet about your knowledge of healing, or how you used your sword to cauterize the wound. I'm thoroughly intrigued. You're a puzzle that I plan to solve one day."

"That was nothing," Oswald said honestly, his brow furrowing in concentration, "Anyone could have done that."

"No. Not anyone could have," Armond assured him.

"Nor *would* many," Fred said, his low voice beating the air.

Loch fumbled in his jacket for a moment and reached through the group holding out a thick cigar to Oswald, "Take it."

Oswald was surprised by this motion, "I shouldn't."

"You deserve one," Loch said, still holding it out for him to take.

"No, thank you. I really can't take your cigar," Oswald said, as politely as he could manage. He never was a fan cigars but the offer made him feel good somehow.

"Well then," Loch said brightly, "I won't force you," he pulled the cigar back and looked at it as though thinking of lighting it, but instead he put it back into his pocket alongside the others, "But you have surely earned some respect around here."

"Enough," Ramif barked, shouldering his short, broad, frame into the tight circle, "We're here to train him, not baby him," he looked sternly around the group and fixed his dark eyes on Oswald, "Get your armor on."

The circle broke slightly, and Oswald backed away and shrugged into the armor that waited for him. The group dissipated into a low businesslike conversation until Fred bumped into Oswald playfully as he finished tying up his armor and drew the curved blade of his sword.

"I'm fighting you?" Oswald asked, a little surprised.

"Of course. It's my way of saying thanks," Fred said, with a sharp-toothed grin, "How better to learn defense against a Keernith goblin then by sparring with one?"

The two squared off, and Fred waited patiently for Oswald to draw his sword and gave him a short nod as he watched for his first move. Oswald came forward hesitantly, unsure where to strike at the massive form and tightened his grip on the hilt. He saw an open place at Fred's knees and he took a quick swing.

Fred's curved blade snatched at the red metal and hissed as it tangled against the cross guard. Oswald was surprised at the knotting of metal and the sword was instantly ripped out of his hands with a single sharp tug. Fred smirked and unhooked his blade from the red sword and let it fall onto the grass at his feet.

"Try again…" Fred said, with a smile.

Oswald moved his feet as quickly as he could manage and he swung the sword hard and felt the heat of the magic strengthen his arms. Sweat rolled down into his eyes and he felt the blade make contact with the Keernith iron shield.

Fred lunged forward, a rampaging beast in size and ferocity, towering over him like death. Oswald readjusted his footing as he backed away, afraid to get too close to the wicked, curved, goblin blade and its formidable master.

He blocked blow after blow, the group behind him trying to shout encouragement that did him no good in the moment. He tried to take another shot, but Fred's size alone gave him the high ground in every fight.

"Close the distance!" Ramif roared into the clatter.

Oswald hesitated, wondering for a moment if Ramif just wanted him to die in a training accident and was telling him stupid advice on purpose.

He blocked another blow and decided that distance wasn't doing him any good either. He waited for another swing and dove inward, twisting his body away from the arching blade. He felt the air cut against him in warning as he crouched low, grabbing Fred's ankle and slipping between his long legs, now standing at his back. Oswald pulled hard at the foot in his hand and felt Fred's footing give. He hadn't been fast enough to correct for it and Oswald watched, surprised, as Fred fell forward and hit the ground. He took advantage of the moment, releasing Fred's enormous foot and swiftly pointed the sword at his back.

"Wow, Nice!" Samuel said cheerfully. The others nodded in agreement, entertained by the mock battles. Fred rolled onto his back and looked up at Oswald with a prideful grin.

"Never had that happen before," Fred said honestly, and the grin became vicious with a glint in his eyes, "And it will never happen again." He curled his body quickly and was on his feet before Oswald could even offer to help him up.

Fred chuckled deeply and turned towards Oswald, flexing his four knuckled fingers against the hilt of his curved blade. He turned his shield closer to his body and without mercy he charged again, his eyes livid with the challenge of a fight. He was enjoying the battle more than seemed was normal.

The look on Fred's face put Oswald off guard. He blocked a blow from the curved blade and had no opportunity to do anything more than block one strike after another with the flurry of his movements. His energy was waning, whereas Fred seemed to be fueled by the violence.

Like he had promised, no opening was given for Oswald to get around him this time. He postured and swung with the speed of dragon fire.

Oswald tried to draw up his arms for another block but was too late. Fred broke through the defense and the full force of the blow contacted the armor at his upper chest, the sound of metal scraping on metal shrieked against the bone of his skull. He lost his balance and Fred took up a foot and flatly kicked him square in the gut just hard enough to send him into the ground gasping for breath.

The next thing he saw was the glinting curved blade at his chest and Fred's self-satisfied expression hovering over him.

Oswald dropped the back of his head against the ground, resting for a moment, the sweat drying on his brow in a sudden breeze. He tried to catch his breath but heard laughter on the hill behind him. He didn't really care. He was too tired to care. Eventually he turned his head to look at the generals.

Loch was puffing on a cigar, looking amused, and Ramif's expression was the same as it had been all day long. Full of bitterness. In the distance Samuel and Armond were talking and Oswald expected he was trying to get out of having to stay and help train again.

He looked back to Fred who had extended a hand to him. Oswald took it and was nearly jerked to his feet with Fred's strength.

Fred shook his head, the veins in his long pointed ears showing darkly in the bright sunlight, "I think I'm done for the day," he said, looking down at Oswald, "I'd like to check on Maria." He started removing his overly elongated armor and piling it to the side. When he was finished, he raised a hand to the generals who each nodded respectfully in recognition of the gesture before he turned back to Oswald, and said matter-of-factly, "It has been a *long* time since I was the one knocked to the ground."

With that, he nodded a goodbye to Oswald and started wandering off towards the city.

Oswald put his sword in its scabbard and felt relief from the weight of it and his muscles sighed with the short rest. Armond came back down the hill without Samuel, who seemed to have wandered off into the woods when given permission to leave. He reached into the large pack at his hip and pulled out a wrapped loaf of rye bread, a wedge of cheese, an apple and some dried meats. He tore off a piece of bread for Oswald and handed him a few strips of the meat, he offered Oswald the cheese which he politely declined, but he happily accepted the apple. Armond dug into the bag and pulled out more apples and then moved between the generals, splitting the rest of the simple meal evenly between them.

Oswald went to the hillside and sat beside Loch, happy to have a moments rest.

Loch finished the last drag of his cigar and put it out in the ground between them and then turned his attention to his food taking up the wedge of cheese that he had chosen and chewing on it thoughtfully.

The food was good, but Oswald's stomach churned slightly, tired and hot from the hard day of training. He slowed down with eating the bread and bit into the apple instead, happy to have the cold flesh of the fruit in his mouth. Fruits always seemed to make him feel better. The group was quiet as they ate, each more interested in quieting their stomachs than filling the air with conversation.

They finished eating and the food had settled enough that conversations started to roll between the generals casually and about people that Oswald had never met. He felt like he was unwelcome in the conversation and he was comfortable with that for now. He lay on the hillside resting, not wanting to expend any more energy than he needed to, knowing that he would have to get up and fight again at any moment. He was grateful however that a decent time had passed before anyone tried to make him get up, he figured that they knew he needed the rest and allowed him to do so.

Eventually the conversation turned to him, "You ready to face me?" Loch said, with a hint of concern in his voice.

"Yeah," Oswald said, trying to pry his heavy eyes open into the daylight. He forced himself into a sitting position and shook out some of the sleep fogging up his head, "I'm training with you now?"

"Only if you can handle it," Loch said and looked him over slowly, his brow crumpled.

"What do you mean?" Oswald asked.

"You are learning impossibly fast and you took a clever shot with Fred," Loch said, with a one armed shrug, "but I don't know if you're ready to fight me."

"It... seems...." Oswald trailed, trying to form a sentence that didn't sound derogatory.

"What?" general Loch asked sharply.

Oswald paused and took in a short breath, "Wouldn't it be an unfair fight?"

"Unfair how?" Loch asked, his face hardening into an expression Oswald hadn't seen on him before. The other generals leaned over to look at Oswald quizzically.

"Well," Oswald paused deciding on the frank conversation, "You only have one arm."

Laughter erupted from the three men, Armond out of amusement, Ramif in mockery, Loch out of boastfulness.

"That is the only reason it's even close to a fair fight," Ramif chortled, turning his nose up arrogantly and smirking over to Loch, who nodded in agreement.

"Sorry," Oswald said, feeling the bruise in his cheek throb as his face tried to flush with embarrassment. He looked at the grass between his legs and decided to pick at the blades for a moment as the laughter died down, "You ready to start then?" he mumbled.

"I am," Loch said, reaching for his scabbard on the hill behind him, "That is if you are sure you can keep up."

"Or would you rather fight me?" Ramif asked with a tone of viciousness in his voice.

Oswald thought for a moment, he could either train with Loch for the afternoon and he had a feeling he would regret it if he did, or potentially have the opportunity to get some revenge on Ramif.

Oswald wondered which of the two he would take the least amount of damage from. He wasn't sure, what he was sure of, however, was that he craved the satisfaction of getting a few blows in if he could fight with Ramif. He knew at the same time that with Armond and Loch present, Ramif wouldn't try anything that would really hurt him.

"I'll fight General Ramif," Oswald said, trying to take a tone that he hoped wouldn't offend Loch. He didn't look offended but had an odd expression on his face.

"I don't think that would be wise," Armond said, looking from one to the other.

"Why not? The boy wants to learn from the Lord General. I can teach him," Ramif said, with hunger in his eyes.

"Because I don't think that's what either of you have in mind," Armond said flatly.

"Nor do I," Loch agreed.

"I think I can handle it," Oswald said, trying to sound determined and not losing eye contact with Ramif. He had a sudden rush of energy at the prospect of getting even and the sword at his side suddenly felt warm against him.

"Just one round should be more than enough," Ramif said, getting up off of the ground with the presence of a man who was more comfortable in armor than in his own flesh. He put on his helmet and rolled his shoulders before marching powerfully down the hillside.

Armond and Loch exchanged looks but did not protest.

Oswald got up and adjusted his scabbard against his hip and felt the energizing warmth of the hilt respond somehow to his touch. He didn't have time to think about it for long. He straightened his armor at his shoulders and picked up his helmet and put it into place as he followed Ramif to the base of the hill, the fire burning in his chest.

Ramif turned and drew his sword, the ringing song of freed steel singing in the wind.

Oswald drew his sword, the red blade glinting eagerly.

The two of them locked eyes and their breaths stilled for a moment, a tension in the air that was tangible, drawing them to the fight with a force beyond nature.

Ramif's eyes narrowed and he took a solid stance. The glint of his armor bobbed in the sunlight with his breathing, his burned and bandaged hand white knuckled against the hilt of his sword.

Oswald planted his feet hard to the ground with his toes pointed forward and his knees soft. He licked his lips and they each began to circle one another, sizing each other up on even ground. Their steps were deliberate and well placed, there was no misstep or falter with either party and their eyes never wavered from one another's.

Ramif must have sensed a weakness or an opportunity because he made the first move, swift and smooth. The arc of the blade was graceful and showed his mastery. When Oswald was able to make the block, the strength behind the blow startled him, rattling the bones in his arms.

The surprise must have shown in his face because Ramif began to close the distance between them with the first strike. Oswald blocked another and felt pain well up in his elbows with a sharp jab from the sheer force of the onslaught. The blades met once more and Ramif's face came close enough to Oswald's that he could see the hate in his eyes, and could see the pain behind them.

"I will teach you—" Ramif growled through gritted teeth, "—How you will die."

Oswald felt his rage well up into his throat and his blood heated. The warmth in the blade responded again, sending energy into his body like lightning. He shoved Ramif away from him and surprised himself at the distance he was able put between them. Ramif roared and dove forward with a well-placed swing that missed Oswald's face by no more than the width of a coin.

Oswald watched the sharp tip of the sword pass between his eyes and pass down out of sight from the helmets range of view. He threw his arm out of the way and fought to keep his stance. He heard something in the distance make a loud and sharp sound of protest, but neither Ramif nor Oswald acknowledged it.

In an instant Ramif was on a rampage, swinging in an endless loop of painful and powerful blows, though with each strike that the blade received in defense, it sent a surge of warmth and energy through Oswald's body. He backed up and reveled in the intensity of the blade in his hands and watching every small move that Ramif made.

He saw a small open space in Ramif's defense, it was only there for a heartbeat, but Oswald acted instantly and accurately. His heart thundered and skipped as the blade caught its target, catching Ramif below the shoulder hard and he drove it upward with a definitive force and will. The blow pulled Ramif off the ground and sent him flying back to land flat on the upraised root of the tree. Oswald tried to take advantage, but was not fast enough.

Ramif hit the ground with a grunt and rolled, getting up to his feet as smoothly as though he had planned the fall, though the air of astonishment about him gave him away.

Ramif recovered in an instant and was full of renewed rage that threw him into a whirlwind of violence that Oswald was fully unprepared for. The first few swings he was able to block by the narrow width of the blade. The overwhelming anger that emanated from Ramif seemed to score the air, and the depth of his eyes chilled Oswald's heart.

Oswald winced as he felt a wicked strike land down hard against the armor plate of his shoulder, in half a blink another blow hit him in the chest followed, what seemed instantly, by another across his helmet. He landed on his back on the ground once more and his eyes got wide, fear replacing his anger.

Ramif raised his foot and stomped forcefully on the armor plating of Oswald's chest. His sword was raised again, pulled high over his head in both hands and in one swift blow he brought the sword down at Oswald's face.

The tip of the blade swung down towards Oswald's left eye and landed with a thick dry sound into the ground. The edge of the blade was close enough that any move of his head would press his skull against the razor edge of the sword. He realized in that instant that his helmet was gone and he thought that he must have lost it in the last strike or sometime during the fall.

Ramif hovered over him with a heavy iron clad foot on his chest, looking down into his face repulsively. Oswald realized that Loch and Armond were only a few feet away with their own swords in hand looking shocked and completely silent, afraid to intervene and afraid not to act.

Ramif stepped off of Oswald's chest but did not remove the sword nor release it. He leaned down into Oswald's face, the single braid of his beard resting on his metal breast plate as he said in a low tone, only a few inches away, "It is but from the grace of the goddess that you breathe. I don't understand why. But I tell you this now, you will respect me or you will die in this war."

He plucked the sword from the ground at Oswald's head, nicking his ear just enough to sting as he did so. Ramif sheathed his sword and walked away, taking the dirt trail to the city without another word.

Loch leaned down and helped Oswald to his feet with an unreadable expression painted on his narrow face, "The Lord General really must hate you. You should probably stop pissing him off."

Oswald straightened up and let go of Loch's hand gratefully and reached a hand up to his but ear gingerly, "The feeling's mutual," Oswald admitted, "Why *does* he hate me so much?"

"Because he hasn't decided who you are yet," Loch said tensely, and tilted his head to examine the wound as well, "He will."

"He's so angry," Oswald said, as he took his hand from his ear to examine the bloody drip on his fingertips, "How do you know if he will or not?"

"Because he's a good man," Armond interjected.

"I haven't gotten to see that yet," Oswald said angrily, and wiped the blood from his hand on the grass.

"I suppose you do bring out the worst in him," Loch agreed, "But I never want to hear an ill word about him." His eyes looked stony and Oswald got the feeling that there was something that he just didn't understand about Ramif. He decided silence was the correct response.

Armond stooped down and snatched up the training bag from the ground with the bustle of cloth and the clink of his armor. He untied the leather strap that held the bag closed as he walked. "That's enough," he said, holding open the bag for Oswald's sword to be placed in, "Give me your sword. We're done today."

"But it's just past midday," Oswald said, not exactly wanting to continue, but curious at the sudden change of plans.

"You have done plenty in the past two days," Armond said surely, "You need to rest."

Oswald eyed the open bag, "Why do you need my sword?"

"Because you won't be needing it," Armond said, and nodded to the bag, "You can have it back in a few days."

Oswald reluctantly untied his scabbard form his hip and placed the sword in the bag, unhappy to part with it.

The sword made him feel whole, as if it had become a piece of him. The sword and he had seemed to have come to some kind of understanding and it comforted him just to have it at his side. He watched Armond close up the bag carefully, the bright red blade stifled by the scabbard and shadows.

He sighed and started pulling off his armor, throwing it into the pile where the noticed that the helmet had landed, and shook his head slowly, "Tomorrow then?"

"No," Armond said, as he shouldered the bag warily.

"Why not?" Oswald asked curiously.

"We have to prepare for Fantasy's arrival," Loch said, and looked at Oswald's ear again with a disappointed frown, "We won't have time for training."

"Can I have my sword then?"

"You won't need it," Armond said sharply.

"What if I wanted to train on my own?" Oswald asked.

"You shouldn't. You should rest and make your own preparations," Armond insisted.

"What is there to do?" Oswald asked, rubbing at his shoulder, suddenly aware of the new bruise and trying to loosen up the joint.

Armond suddenly looked stern, a flicker of disbelief in his emerald eyes, "The Goddess herself is coming to this city and had the will to stay your execution and provide her protection to you. You can't think of anything you want to do before she arrives?"

Oswald thought about it a moment and felt sheepish, "Alright. Another day then."

Loch thumped him on the back as he passed by, taking the trail from the clearing. Armond nodded shortly and followed after him, "Leave your armor, I'll put it away this evening."

"Thank you," Oswald said, looking down at his sweat soaked clothes. He was unsure what he had to do first, but he knew that he had to get cleaned up and he needed new clothes. He also wanted to find Nedtedrow.

Chapter Eighteen

The next morning was colder still, Oswald's breath fogged in the air as he walked the back road into the East side of the city. His eyes slid from building to building looking for the stone and oak home he and Nedtedrow had stayed in somewhere nearby. He thought for a while and decided that it was unlikely that Nedtedrow was even awake at this time of morning and that it was less likely that he would be out in the city. He wasn't sure where else to start looking.

He turned another sharp corner, stepping over an empty flower pot in the alley, moving forward because he had no other ideas.

The morning light began to cast narrower shadows in the wake of the strange buildings. A glint of sharp gold light reflected against his right eye and he looked back at its source. It was a piece of glass, the shard of broken back window from Bolzar's house, propped up against the foundation of the home at an odd angle. He had accidently found it again.

He crept slowly around to the front of the building with doubts riding heavily in his mind. He stopped at the door looking around awkwardly. The sound of a scraping chair from inside the house confirmed that at least someone was awake. He swallowed and knocked sharply on the door.

There was a pause and uneven steps that made their way to the door. The lock clicked and Oswald's stomach dropped as Bolzar's solid face and freshly trimmed blonde hair appeared through the crack in the door. They locked eyes and stared at each other.

After a long, empty silence, Bolzar opened the door, "Come in."

Oswald hesitated, but stepped in through the open door, picking at his nails nervously. The house was exactly the way it had been the first night he had seen it, pristine and orderly. "Thank you," he said, and turned around, hearing the door click shut behind him.

Bolzar limped lightly past him and gestured with his good hand to a chair sitting the living area. He walked on into the back of the house where Oswald knew that the bedrooms, the locked room and the washroom were.

He walked back to the chair and sat in it rather uncomfortably. The chair was built for Nelwin legs and he felt scrunched up into a ball. He shifted in the seat and stretched his legs out in front of him a bit, hoping that he wasn't being rude by doing so. The blood flow in his legs began to stall and he wiggled his toes trying to make his blood circulate, a vague numbness starting to take its place. He wiggled again and decided the chair wasn't going to happen. He got up from the seat and walked over to a clear spot across the room and made himself comfortable on the floor instead.

Finally Nedtedrow came in, looking wide awake and only a little uncomfortable. He looked from Oswald on the floor, to the few chairs in the room and seemed to understand with a hint of amusement. He pulled a hand out from behind his back and threw a jar at him. Oswald caught it with surprise and looked it over. It was a jar of peaches and oats. He grinned widely, "Thanks."

Nedtedrow walked over and held out a fork which Oswald took gratefully, "You're early," Nedtedrow said, with a smile.

"You were expecting me?" Oswald asked.

Nedtedrow nodded, "Eventually."

"How did you know I was coming over?" Oswald pried at the lid of the peaches until he heard the seal break, "I never said where I was going."

"I figured that you would either get in trouble and need help, or that you would do something weird or great and want to brag," Nedtedrow said, with a half-hearted shrug.

Oswald frowned, "That's not exactly what I wanted to hear."

"So which is it?" Nedtedrow asked, taking a few steps back, his arms crossed as he looked him over thoughtfully.

"Neither," Oswald said indignantly fishing out a bite of the peaches, "Why would you think that?"

"Well then, what do you want?" Nedtedrow asked curiously as he flopped down into the chair that Oswald was unable to sit in.

Oswald swallowed the bite of peach and picked a piece of oat from between his teeth with his tongue. He poked at another peach in the jar with his fork, "I was wondering if you had any idea what happened to my things after the trial."

"Which things?" Nedtedrow asked defensively.

"My clothes," he said, taking another bite and trying to feel the fairy around his neck without being obvious about it.

"Oh," Nedtedrow said comfortably, "there's one outfit you left here. It's clean now."

"Just one?" Oswald asked regretfully.

"Yeah," he said, and stretched his legs out in front of him and placed his overlapped fingers over his rounded belly, "It's not like I can wear them."

"They've been missing since then," he set the jar down on the floor in front of him and shook his head, "I need new clothes."

"What do you want me to do about it?" Nedtedrow snorted.

"Nothing unless you know where I can get new ones," Oswald shrugged.

"Have you been to the market?" he asked obviously.

"Not recently," Oswald said slowly.

"Why not?"

"I've been busy," Oswald said, half truthfully. Mostly he didn't want to go back because he was in no hurry to mentally relive being drug through the street. The thought of the market kind of made him anxious.

"Well," Nedtedrow said, with a shrug, "What are you waiting for? The shops are going to close early today and won't be open at all tomorrow and maybe not the day after that."

"How much are clothes there?" Oswald asked as he picked the jar back up and shoveled in a few large bites.

Nedtedrow shrugged exasperatedly, "I don't buy elf clothes. I don't know."

Oswald finished the last of the peaches and oats and shoved the jar aside. He reached into his pocket and counted out his remaining coins. Three coppers, a silver, and a nickel. It wasn't a lot, but he figured it should be enough for clothes. The thought crossed his mind that he had to buy food too and he knew he needed to make more money somehow. Too many people had been too kind to him. He looked at the peaches uncomfortably trying to think of a way to return the favor.

"I need to get cleaned up before tomorrow too," Oswald said uncomfortably.

"No kidding," Nedtedrow said, sitting upright in his chair, "I thought you looked bad a few days ago, but whatever you've been doing isn't good for your face."

Oswald scowled slightly, "It's not as bad as it looks."

"I doubt that," Nedtedrow said, with raised eyebrows and taking count of the bruises and wounds that were visible, "I heard you got into it with the Lord General."

"This wasn't him," Oswald said, touching his nose carefully.

"I know, I was there when Satomi hit you," Nedtedrow said and waved his hand dismissively. He pointed to the side of Oswald's face with a short cringe, "I meant that one."

Oswald reached up and touched his temple. It was tender and hot to the touch and he winced, "It must have been when he sliced my helmet off," he said to himself.

"Ramif?" Nedtedrow confirmed.

"Yeah," Oswald said, dropping his hand into his lap.

"I suppose that's why your ear's cut too?" he said, with another gesture to the dried blood around the slice.

Oswald nodded, "Same fight, different stroke."

"Making friends everywhere you go huh?" Nedtedrow said, with a playful grin.

"You could say that I suppose," Oswald said, as he fought to return the smile.

"You also stink," Nedtedrow said bluntly.

With a sigh Oswald rolled the coins in his hand, "Any chance I can use the tub here?"

"After we talk," Bolzar said.

Oswald spun around and realized that Bolzar had been leaning on the frame of the wall behind him. Oswald wondered how long he had been there.

"Okay…" Oswald said apprehensively. He looked back to Nedtedrow, "Can you buy me some new clothes?"

"Hey, I don't do charity," Nedtedrow said, and he held up his hands and shook his head.

"No," Oswald interrupted holding out the handful of coins, "Buy them *for* me."

Nedtedrow raised an eyebrow and got up from the small chair quickly. He walked over and took the coins from Oswald's hand with a glint in his eyes, "Sure. What kind?"

"Just something better than this," he said, pulling the filthy shirt away from his body.

"Yeah," Nedtedrow said, pocketing the money and heading to the door, "Yeah, sure thing."

"—Nedtedrow—" Bolzar and Oswald said at the same time. The two of them exchanged their train of thought with the same expression and Oswald continued, "*BUY* them for me."

"I will," he said, feigning innocence, "I'll buy them. I promise," he opened the front door and they could hear him talking to himself as he walked away from the house, "—Buy clothes… I'm going to go and buy some nice elven clothes… I am supposed to buy them… coming back with clothes... Just clothes… getting clothes… maybe toffee…"

Oswald dropped his shoulders and hung his head for a second, feeling suddenly like he had made a poor choice. He grabbed the empty jar and the fork and went to stand up.

"Stay there," Bolzar said, and limped forward and took the dirty jar and fork from him.

"I was just going to put it in the sink," Oswald said, not wanting Bolzar to have to clean up his mess.

"I know," Bolzar said, as he looked back over his shoulder, and he nodded for Oswald to sit back down. He limped back out of sight and Oswald heard water begin to run and assumed that he had decided to wash the jar.

Oswald lowered himself back to the floor and sat with his legs crossed. The clinking of glass came and went followed by silence. After a few quiet minutes he started picking at his nails again, trying to occupy his time.

Bolzar came back with a small box and took a seat in the chair, placing the box on the table beside him. He sat up and winced, taking his wrapped three fingered hand in the other, guarding it through the pain. He took a few deep breaths and looked up.

Bolzar waited patiently, and when Oswald didn't speak, he looked up at the ceiling in thought, "Nedtedrow and I grew up together. Our parents were friends so we saw each other almost every day," he paused, "His father left when we were young and his mother died when we were still in school. I was a few years older than him and my family cared for him, so we took him in."

He looked around the room as he spoke, not wanting to look at Oswald, "He always was my little brother, really. I took care of him. I taught him. I fought with him — a lot. But mostly, I protected him," he made a face like he was chewing on the inside of his cheek and continued, "When the plague took my parents, it was just us. I went into the army, and Nedtedrow... well, he started this kleptomaniac compulsion of his. It got worse all the time. It seemed like he really wasn't able to help himself... Anyway after a few years I was promoted, then again. When the war got close enough that we were getting concerned about invasions, our generals were coming to me for advice. I was good at what I did, even then. For a while we were able to hold them back, but it only takes one mistake."

The scent of ashes and blood filled Oswald's head through his memories and he nodded slowly, "One can be enough," Oswald agreed.

"A year ago," Bolzar started, his eyes finally falling to Oswald, his eyes burning intensely from across the room, "I made that mistake. The army got through an area I had overlooked. They took the generals, they took me, and by accident they took Nedtedrow because he was running an errand for me and had come back into the war room without knowing that they were already there," he rubbed at the bandages around his hand, too far lost in memory, "They threw us in caged metal carts, exposed to the elements, and took us to Azar. No food and no water for over a week. One of the generals died on the way there and they threw his body out onto the trail and walked over him like a pile of shit. I worked with that man. He was a good man..." Realizing that he had started to drift off topic he looked back down at his feet and composed himself, "We were in the city dungeon for a while. I didn't count the days, we never saw the sunlight so we couldn't if we had wanted to. All I knew was Venhow tortured us whenever he felt like it. I tried to protect my brother but I couldn't do anything. I don't know what he said to save himself, what information he traded for his life, but they didn't kill him. They didn't kill me... No one else came out of that dungeon."

Oswald looked away for a moment, unable to hold the intensity of Bolzar's stare "What did you tell them?"

"Everything. Anything. Whatever I had to say to make them stop. It got so bad after a while that I dreamt about Venhow's face, his face and his hands," he said, his face distorted in horror and hate, "Sometimes I even saw him when I was awake, whether he was there or not. I heard screams every night in my head, sometimes mine but usually they were Nedtedrow's. After a long time they put us back on the prison cart and sent us to another prison, a control camp for prisoners of war. Even after they sent us to the control camp and we didn't have to see him anymore, the nightmares and the hallucinations stayed," he swallowed hard, "Nedtedrow still screams at night sometimes."

He shook his head pushing away the horror. He rubbed at his forehead and continued, "There was daylight, water and food at the camp but there was no freedom whatsoever. We shit when they told us, we slept when they let us and we worked the rest of the day. If we weren't working we were confined to individual cells underground without any light and with more restrained rations. We worked just so that we could be out in the daylight," Bolzar rested his hands on his knees, looking as if just telling the story was exhausting him, "Twice we were flogged for no reason. We were there for over 8 months. Nedtedrow's compulsion is what finally saved us."

He reached over and picked up the small box, "We were thrown in our cells for the night and the guards were working in groups of two, which was very unusual. Nedtedrow snatched this pocket knife from the new guard's pocket right before he closed his cell," he reached into the box with his three fingered hand and pulled out a steel ring with a small pocket blade latched onto it, "He waited until everyone was in their cells asleep and picked the lock to his cell, and then mine. He was afraid to take too many people so they wouldn't notice us leaving, but we had made friends with a Dwarf lord named Hitch when we were there and we woke him up so he could leave with us. The three of us made it to the fence and I don't know how we made it, but we squeezed under the razor wire and got away without anyone noticing."

Oswald watched as Bolzar stared at the little blade for a long time in silence before slowly putting it back into the box and snapping the lid shut, "We made it to a nearby town and got supplies by explaining our situation. Most people were glad to help but we had to keep moving. We knew that Gommorn was the only place we could go. We traveled for three weeks when we heard the first tracker howl... We ran. We don't know when he fell behind or whether he took a wrong turn in the dark or what happened, but when we stopped for a short rest Hitch wasn't with us anymore," he looked haunted by it and shook his head, "That's when Nedtedrow made his mistake. The trackers were closing in on us, and we didn't have time to look for Hitch. Every time we stopped they got closer. I told Nedtedrow that we had to run the rest of the way and he wasn't happy about that. We were exhausted and he wasn't exactly in the best shape of his life," he licked his lips and his eyes darted across the floor, flickering through his thoughts, "They got close, really close, and we had to hide, but the only place was a nearby tree and the branches were too high to reach so I gave him a boost. The trackers were right on top of us and when they howled Nedtedrow panicked. He kept climbing up the tree and left me on the ground. He left me to die. I didn't have a choice so I had to keep running, but I didn't get far," he rubbed his leg gently, "The tracker pinned me down another mile or two down into the forest. It grabbed my leg when I tried to crawl away, I turned over and it gouged me with its teeth and claws and went for my throat but I was able to block the bite away from my neck... and it took my hand instead," he flexed his three fingers looking at them as if he could still feel the rest of his hand.

"How did you get away?" Oswald asked quietly.

Bolzar jumped a little, startled at the sound as if he had forgotten that he had been talking to someone. He looked up, "There was a heavy stone nearby. I grabbed it while she was tearing my hand away and I hit her in the head with it. I had to swing a few times but she finally was out cold. I meant to finish her off when I heard another howl in the distance. I knew I couldn't survive another attack and this time I knew that I was far enough ahead, but I was also injured. I ran... as best as I could... until dawn when I came to a crossroad and found a wagon, a man and his sister traveling to Gommorn. It was beyond fate. They gave me a ride the rest of the way here."

Oswald remembered the deep meat of the wounds, wrapped and hidden beneath Bolzar's bandages and felt his heart sink, "I didn't realize how much either of you had gone through."

"We've all been through a lot," Bolzar said dismissively, looking as though he were trying to lock away the feelings and memories again, "But now you at least understand why I was so angry with him... and so afraid of you. You look just like him, you know, Venhow... except for the eye and hair color, that is."

"I'm not angry," Oswald said with a pause, "not anymore. I just didn't want anyone to get hurt. I didn't know you wouldn't kill him... you looked serious."

"I was serious," Bolzar said darkly, dropping his eyes to his feet, "I don't know if I would have done it or not."

"I don't think you would've," Oswald said, shaking his head, "Not now anyway."

Bolzar shrugged deciding not to think too far into his own actions, "Nedtedrow and I have been talking about you."

"Hopefully good things," Oswald said doubtfully.

"For the most part..." Bolzar said slowly.

"What did he say about me?" Oswald asked curiously.

"That you act without thinking a lot," he said, looking back up to Oswald with an eyebrow raised and an odd expression on his face. He sat up straighter in his chair.

"Only recently," Oswald said unhappily, as he tried to stretch out the cramp in his bruised shoulder, "I'm sorry that I threatened you. I didn't know what else to do and it seemed right at the time."

"It's alright," Bolzar assured him with a distant frown, "it probably was the right thing to do," he mumbled as he continued to gently rub at his wrapped hand. He looked out the window nearby thoughtfully, "Go ahead and run your bath. Nedtedrow should be back with your clothes soon."

"Should be," Oswald said hopefully, and pushed himself off the floor, happy to be able to move his legs.

"Hopefully," Bolzar agreed with a sigh.

Oswald stretched out his tight and sore muscles and followed Bolzar's gaze out of the window and into the street briefly, "What do you think my chances are of getting change back?"

"Almost none," Bolzar said, with a nod.

"And my clothes?"

"He'll be back with clothes... I just hope he pays for them," Bolzar said, and picked up the small box containing the pocket knife off of the table beside him and stood up with a grimace.

"Just in case though," Oswald said cautiously, "where's the other outfit that I left here?"

The water was hot and stung at his open sores, his face burned like fire and his blistered fingers felt like he had a handful of thorns. His hair was grimy with salt and dirt and despite the pain, the clean water and soap felt good against his skin. He carefully cleaned his elongated ears, feeling the small cut from the blade under his thumb and scowled to himself.

He lay back in the water soaking in the heat and started picking at his nails again, trying to get the dirt out from around the nail beds.

There was a single soft knock at the bathroom door and Oswald turned his head. The door cracked open and an arm reached in through the narrow opening with a handful of new clothes and set them on the table by the doorway. "Thanks," Oswald said, as the hand retreated and door was pulled shut.

He finished scrubbing at his limbs with the bar of soap and made sure that all of the suds were out of his hair before he pulled the drain. The water roared as it rushed out of the tub through the drain. He wiped the water droplets out of his face with a hand and stepped out of the tub, the air cold against his bare skin. He found a towel in the cupboard and tried to dry his wild hair and face before the rest of him.

The clothes on the table were dyed with rich color, something that Oswald wasn't accustomed to. The shirt was a vibrant green with a small, turned down collar and had a cross stitch in the front with pale strings, the pants were coal black and made of heavy material that felt soft to the touch.

Oswald put on his undershorts and put his new clothes on. They were very nice and he was happy to be in something both clean and warm. He pulled at the long sleeves to adjust them to his frame and patted at the pants to try and brush away a crease.

He looked in the mirror, besides needing to comb his hair, he felt that he looked better than he had expected. He supposed it was partly due to him getting used to his own swollen reflection, though many of the bruises had already started to fade away. He picked up the brush and tried to tame his wild curls without any more success than was usual. He shook his head violently and let the curls start to dry and bounce up out of his face on their own.

Nedtedrow and Bolzar were at the kitchen table, each of them taking chips of toffee off a plate at the center of the table.

Nedtedrow looked up with a smile, "Like them?"

"I do," Oswald said gratefully, "They're very nice. Thank you for getting them for me."

"You're welcome," he said, picking up a piece of toffee from the place and reaching his hand out to Oswald, "toffee?"

Oswald let out a knowing breath and smiled, happy to pay them back for the peaches he had eaten, "Sure," he said and took the candy and rolled it in his mouth. It was wonderful. He couldn't remember the last time that he had actually had a piece of candy. Not since his mother made it last, he supposed. He tucked the piece into his cheek so it would last longer and went to pick up his shoes from the floor in the hallway.

"So, what's your plan for the rest of the day?" Nedtedrow asked.

"I'm not sure," Oswald said, as he inspected his shoes routinely, "I thought it would take a lot longer to find you and I honestly thought I would have to be all over the city for one thing or another."

"Well if you don't do anything else, you should go to the market," Nedtedrow said, stuffing another piece of toffee into his mouth.

"I thought you said the market was going to close early," he said, setting his shoes down on the floor in front of him with the tongue's pulled forward.

"I did, and it will, but you should go," Nedtedrow said, picking pieces of toffee from his molars with a stubby finger. Oswald looked at him suspiciously and Nedtedrow put a hand up, "I know it's hard to believe but I actually *bought* the clothes."

"Then why should I go to the market?"

"You just should," he said cryptically.

Oswald pinched his brow together thoughtfully and put on his shoes, "Alright then," he adjusted the trim of his pant legs up over the top of his shoes and added hesitantly, "I'll see you both first thing tomorrow morning then?"

They both nodded, neither looking excited at the prospect of meeting the goddess, but neither did they look scared. It seemed more of a sacred moment for them and Oswald wondered if he were acting inappropriately by asking if they planned to be there. The silence was broken by Nedtedrow crunching loudly on the toffee that he had been sucking on for the past several minutes and Oswald nodded respectfully at the two men before making his way back out onto the street.

The day had taken on the clarity of running water and a comfortable temperature that made the suns warmth welcomed against his face. The city had a heaviness on it, and though people went about as they usually did, Oswald could feel the quiet and a general discomfort around him.

Some homes were now completely boarded up, wooden planks covering the windows and heavy locks on the doors. Oswald wondered how exactly that would keep the goddess out if she truly wanted in, but he decided it was for their comfort and passed them by.

As he walked, he made note of a few little shops that were not a part of the market. There was an apothecary, which looked as though it were rarely open, and a bakery which had its curtains drawn and a sign on the door that read 'closed until the departure of the Goddess'. There was one of the blacksmiths workshops, but it also looked as though no business was done there.

After a leisurely walk through the city, he finally found himself at the market. Many of the tents and shops were closed already, if they had been opened at all. The crowds were small and more polite than Oswald knew they usually were, weaving around the market streets like well knitted thread, rather than the chaotic fight for goods he had seen before.

He made note of a few tents as he went that he was sure he would like to come back to, including the clothing and wares he expected his new outfit had come from. A tent caught his eye and Oswald stared at it a moment before he realized what he was looking at.

There was a horseshoe shaped workbench with open basins at each end and a table stretched across the front of the tent in polished walnut. There was a chair within the workbench and the frame and roof of the tent were both solid and sealed tight from the weather. Canvas rolls were on each side of the roof for closing shop. It looked sort of like the one he had had back home.

"Hey!"

Oswald jumped and looked around spotting a copper skinned, dark haired man with a proud smile on his face.

"Mich," Oswald sighed putting his hand over his thundering heart, "You startled me."

"Is this good enough?" Mich asked with a prideful smile.

"What?" Oswald asked, and looked around absently.

"Your shop," Mitch said, with a grin gesturing back to the empty workshop, "That was the deal right?"

Oswald's jaw dropped open slightly. He looked back to the tent he had been admiring and then stared at Mich in disbelief, "I only expected a bench and four posts in the ground with a cheap tarp."

"Nah," Mitch said, shaking his head, "Anything I make, I want to be just as nice as these shoes."

"Thank you!" Oswald exclaimed now feeling as though he had permission to touch the fine workmanship, putting his hands on the perfectly sanded and treated wooden table with awe. He suddenly felt uncomfortable as he looked at how much was put into the workbench and the rest of the tent, "This is worth *so* much more than those shoes."

"It wasn't all me," Mich said, with a wide shouldered shrug.

Oswald turned around confused, "Who else helped?"

"Your new customers," he said with a grin, "They were eager to get you started and pitched in. They were mostly other shop owners around here. Friends of mine, including the blacksmith whose sons you saved. Some have even put in orders already and they bought the supplies from me, so we are more than even. Your tools and supplies are under the workbench in the drawers," he fished around in his pocket and pulled out a small steel key and held it out for Oswald to take.

Oswald took the key in astonishment and turned around and walked around the bench to the row of locked drawers. He unlocked each one and pulled the drawers open, shocked to see that each one was full of leatherworking tools and the cabinet to the side had various pieces of expensive leathers. A shelf had a box full of rubber and sealed jars of stain. He looked up with wide eyes, staring speechless at Mitch who stuck out his chest and nodded assuredly, "You're Gommorn's official Cobbler now."

Oswald sat in his new work chair and was surprised to find that it swiveled around. He laughed and spun the chair in a tight circle and watched the swirl of the market wobble in his head.

When the world steadied after a minute he launched himself off of the chair and back over to Mitch with an outstretched hand, "This is more than I ever thought I would have here. I can make anything with this."

"That's the idea," he boomed, "You have an entire city to work for."

"Thank you!"

Mitch took his hand heartily, his huge hand totally enveloping Oswald's and his firm grip locking in the handshake, "You're always welcome," he let go of Oswald's hand and dropped the last canvas roll at the front of his own shop. With a final nod and a friendly smile, he walked through the quickly dwindling crowd and out into the alleys of the city.

The street vendors, one by one, began wrapping up their wares and the city seemed to take a breath. A restful stillness began to settle over them like the shadows of the slowly sinking, early autumn sun.

Oswald locked up his new tools and supplies and tucked the key in his pocket and patted it through the cloth. He was afraid to trust the pocket, but knew he was being paranoid with his new generous gift. He touched the key one last time and stepped back out into the street.

Proudly he looked over his new shop, admiring every inch of craftsmanship and every moment it took to create it. He reached up and dropped the canvas lining around each side of the solid frame. He took one last glance at the tent, looking forward to the next morning he had free. He wanted nothing more than start working the leather and to be surrounded by familiar smells and the art of creating something.

His hands already knew the stitch he would use and the knot he would secure it with. He knew the stains he wanted to use first and was excited to work with Dragon hide. His fingers traced in the air the curve of the cuts he would use and they twitched with the comfortable memory of leatherwork.

He felt a joy in his heart that he had been missing and he suddenly felt much more at home.

Chapter Nineteen

The sun began to peak above the tree line, casting a stream of light from the ridge down to the city where an odd silence wavered in the air like morning fog. The city was still as its people stood at the south end of the city, watching the woods with apprehension. As the sun had crept higher in the sky, more and more people had come to join the growing crowd, each watching for the procession of the goddess.

The three high generals and their families stood at the front of the crowd with Oswald, Fred and Maria, and the other tribe Leaders at their side. Everyone was prepared to escort Fantasy and her guards to the town center and to welcome her to their great city.

The first movement over the hillside was a line of seven centaurs. In the center was Olivia, her chestnut color brightened by the dawn. On either side of her stood what looked to be a set of twins, black and white painted females with multi colored hair and dark skin. The other four were males, much larger than the females and each with their own unique shade of hair and fur. The atmosphere that they brought with them demanded silence and stillness, which the crowd didn't dare disobey.

They came forward into the city slowly and it became clear that each of them was armed with a sword and each of them had their own section of the crowd to oversee. Olivia came to stand closest to the center, near where Oswald stood, and he could see the bright shining scar on her palm where she had been healed from the sword wound and a sudden awe caught the air in his chest.

The next vision to come over the hillside was a mature, but young woman on the back of a white horse. She was fair and soft, with features that cast out shadows, and eyes that from any distance sent a chill into fluttering hearts. Porcelain fingers held the reigns gently, glass rings glittering on each elegant hand. Her hair glistened strangely, each individual strand of her hair was coated in a sheet of ice, catching the light in a way that made her look even more unnatural. It was spun, frozen, into a high and sophisticated bun atop her head and what strands strayed from the tie framed her face in regal beauty. She wore a pale blue dress made from lace and silk which hung across her body and flowed like crystal waters. Her shoes where as white as untouched snow and narrowly shaped, with embedded pearls strung into the design.

Fantasy stopped in front of the city with an expressionless face, her sharp crystalline eyes moved among the city and slowly everyone fell to their knees in reverence. When Fantasy had swept among the eyes of the city with her own, the centaurs all at once stepped aside as though they understood her thoughts.

She gracefully dismounted her steed, patting his muscular neck with knowing and released the reigns. The horse turned away with a snort and began to graze on a patch of grass behind her.

She turned to the city, the silk of her dress dancing around her ankles and the light reflecting off the frost on her hair. Her eyes drifted and slowly found a place among them, "Great city of Gommorn," her said, her voice was smooth and strong, and though she hardly spoke louder than she would have when speaking to someone directly in front of her, there was no doubt that every ear was able to hear her clearly, "Darkness looms with every passing day. Each of you have lost much, but know that this city, that each of you, will be the deciding factor in this war. I have come because I have foreseen the battle ahead. In the first warmth of the coming spring, when the first cherry apple tree blooms, Azar's army will march and will come to take this city. You must not let this happen."

The city took a collective breath but no one dared to look away from the goddess as she spoke, "You must be ready for this. Their numbers are far greater, but I assure you that you will not be alone. This war must end. I will be here for two days and I will meet with each person who comes forward, but know that my justice is swift and my grace must be deserved... Who among you will step forward now?"

No one moved.

After a few minutes a man, a Lieutenant, stood up from behind Ramif. He was human and looked to be in his thirties, clean shaven and in his military uniform. He looked up at Fantasy, holding his head low and wringing his hat in his hands. He trembled visibly as he slowly made his way forward. He stopped a few feet away from her and sank down to one knee, staring at the ground with frightened eyes.

Fantasy stepped forward gracefully.

He gasped in deeply as her delicate hand reached down and touched his chin, drawing it upward and forcing him to make eye contact with her. He shuddered for a moment and a thin smile fell across Fantasy's rubicund lips, "Jameson," she said kindly, "I will not harm you. It was not your fault that the war overcame you. There was nothing that you could have done to save them. No soul carries the depth of the same burden you carry with you. Your pain is great but I cannot heal that wound," she brushed a fearful tear away from his cheek with a slender thumb, "but within you lies a strength beyond measure, and a fire that cannot be contained. You will find that strength when you need it… Until that day," she said, withdrawing her hand from the side of his face. She gently pulled at his shoulder and helped him to his feet in front of her and a thickness took its place in the air, "Take this," she removed one of the two rings on her right hand and gripped it tight in her fist. When her fingers unwrapped, the glass band was no longer a ring but a small arrow, brilliantly shaped and made of solid gold with a pin on one side. She reached out to his chest and pinned the arrow above his heart onto the breast of the uniform, "It will give you the strength that you need until you are able to ignite the fire within you."

Tears flowed down his face in a steady stream, though his face remained firmly stoic, his shoulders trembling lightly. Fantasy let go of the pin and locked her crystalline eyes on his, the two of them silent. After a short while in the silence Jameson dropped to his knees, as if he could bare meeting her eyes no longer, and he bowed at her feet and sobbed into the gravel. She bent low and placed a hand on his back. His shuddering body stilled at her touch and he rested there and again stared into the dirt. Everyone knew that the conversation had not stopped, even though the silence was penetrative. He took in a deep breath before slowly pushing himself back up into a slouch and backing back into the crowd with wet eyes and weak legs.

Fantasy stood straight and tall again, her eyes now landing fixedly among the leaders, "Bolzar."

Oswald looked over and saw Bolzar's face go a sickening shade of grey that made him look as though his worst fears had climbed out of the sky. He stood up and wavered, looking closer and closer to collapsing. He took in an audible breath and limped forward and knelt down on his good leg. He swallowed hard and looked up into Fantasy's powerful stare.

"So much responsibility falls on you," she said, tilting her head slightly to the side and reaching out a hand, "but you are so determined to prove yourself, and you regret so much." A kind of pity crossed her face for an instant and she held her hand open in the air before her, but she didn't reach out to touch him as she had done for Jameson. Instead she waited for him.

Bolzar surveyed her eyes and the silence fell on them as well. He reluctantly followed silent orders and with a severe tremor in his fingers he began to unwrap his damaged hand. Raw meat, shiny pink flesh, and black scabs covered a large portion of his mangled hand. His three remaining fingers twitched involuntarily with the pain. He reached his hand up to her with fearful eyes and placed it in her outstretched palm.

"Prepare yourself," she said, with an odd distort in her voice.

Suddenly she gripped the wound in her hand, her fingers digging into the exposed flesh with a violent intensity. Bolzar took in a sharp breath which felt like a scream and he clenched his throat as his body clamped down on the air, unable to let a cry escape his chest.

Fantasy looked unfazed, and continued to dig at the wound with one hand, then brought her other hand over and started to do the same with it as well. Pieces of flesh fell from his hand as she worked at the wound and suddenly bone became visible through the meat, growing anew from the cleared pathway that Fantasy was working over. She continued to draw out the bones until the shape of the hand began to form.

Bolzar took in another gasp of air, bracing himself against the ground with his good hand, his mouth hanging open to the ground and a long string of drool dripping from hip open mouth. His shocked expression gasping at the air as if he were suffocating, his body convulsing occasionally with the odd sensation and the agony of the magic.

Blood poured from the wound as Fantasy continued tearing away pieces of skin and scar tissue. The white bones showed occasionally as she tore more and more of the muscle and nerve away from the center of the meat and as blood dripped wetly onto the ground at their feet. Joints began to form clearly and her fingers worked more rapidly to keep the bones clear of the original trauma.

Once the bones in his hand were regrown and looked complete, Fantasy closed both hands over the fresh bones, enveloping them in hers. She stooped down and pressed his hand, enveloped in her own, against her forehead forcefully. The city took in a collective breath and held it, watching.

A soft white light enveloped them like a pale and transparent mist that slowly settled against their skin and faded away into the morning sunlight. When she lowered her hands and stood up, she let one bloody hand fall to her side. The other hand opened and was supporting a perfectly formed and functional hand, where moments ago there had been butchered remains. She gripped his new hand tightly and he looked up from the ground disbelievingly with sweat beaded on his brow. She pulled him up to his feet and smiled, letting go of his hand gently.

Bolzar looked first at his hand and bent each of the fingers in turn, rotating his hand around in the air and admiring the new flesh. He took a small step and then suddenly looked down at his leg with wide, glassy eyes. He bent over and pulled up his pant leg, tearing off the bandages. Bright silver scars caught the light and no hint of a wound remained. He fell back onto the ground, sitting like a child in the dirt. He brought his newly repaired hand to his chest and he too began to cry with grateful, quiet tears.

Fantasy caught eyes with him one more time, "Your reward for your empathy and for your honest heart," she said, as she brushed one hand over the other and the blood on her hands fell away like a handful of grain.

"Thank you," Bolzar said, getting up off of the ground and quickly returning to his place in the line with awe, his eyes admiring his hand. After a few seconds, the stillness settled once more and all eyes were back on Fantasy.

Fantasy had locked her eyes on a man further back into the crowd. Heads turned. A man stood near the center of the gathering holding a damaged shoulder. The centaurs moved uncomfortably and Fantasy's stare shifted into an ominous glare, "Jeryl Tryt."

The man walked forward to the front where Fantasy stood but stopped shy at the intensity of the glare. They met eyes and something broke in the beauty of Fantasy, disrupted by the disgusted crumple of the skin on the bridge of her nose. She pointed a bloody finger to the ground at her feet and Jeryl complied by dropping to his knees and looking up expectantly.

"What is it that you want?" Fantasy asked sharply.

"My shoulder fixed my Goddess," he said, looking up to her and meeting her eyes for the first time up close.

"How dare you," she hissed. The man looked suddenly frightened and looked around nervously, "How dare you have the nerve to approach me and expect me to heal you? Expecting me to heal a wound given *because she didn't want to die*. That wound is nothing compared to what you deserve. It is NOTHING compared to what you have done!"

Jeryl looked as though his eyes were trying to pop out of his head and he tried to back away, falling back onto his hip and still trying to scramble away from her as her rage plumed. Fantasy took a sharp step forward for every inch that he crawled back until she stomped a foot down on the top of his ankle and pinned him to the spot, crushing the bones with her heel, "And it is *nothing* compared to what I will do," a different kind of magic changed the feel of the air and Jeryl's screams were stifled as if the sound had been pulled from his lungs, "Where are the bodies?" Fantasy demanded.

"I don't know what you are talking about," Jeryl pleaded.

"The people you've killed," she said placidly.

"What people?" he lied, panic saturating his voice.

"I can see your heart!" she bellowed, "I can see into your mind, to your soul, to everything you have ever done in your life! I *know* where they are. Tell THEM!" Fantasy demanded as she dug her heel into his ankle further and a sickening cracking sound snapped at the air with his magically stifled scream.

"I killed them," he admitted trying to free his broken ankle from under Fantasy's heel.

"Who?" she asked clearly.

He panted into the ground and tried to pull his foot free from under her without success. He clasped at the ground and cringed, "The — the Halbor sisters."

"How?" Fantasy hissed as coals burned in her eyes and the air between them thickened visibly.

"Please goddess," he panted.

"HOW?"

"I— strangled them," he gasped through stabs of pain.

"Now tell them where they are," she said slowly and clearly. The thickened air around them began to darken.

"The river!" he screamed, "They're in the hollow tree by the river!"

"How many?!" she bellowed over his screams.

"Three!" he shrieked.

Fantasy picked up her foot and when the magic silenced him again, she stepped back away from him. An icy cold pulsed out over them in a painful wave. Fantasy locked eyes with Jeryl and spoke sharply and with authority, "You will die."

Jeryl grabbed his chest, his body arching back off the ground in agony. His feet spilled the gravel and the dirt around him as he thrashed, blood leaking from both eyes and ears. He clawed at his own throat, turning in the dirt and fighting for a breath he could not take in. His face turned a deep red and then a sick unnatural purple. Fantasy tore her eyes from his body and suddenly the man lay still, dead at her feet.

She took in a deep breath and looked to one of the centaurs, a male with black hair and fur. He approached her without pause. "Go and bring back their bodies so that they can be laid to rest properly," she said, with authority and disgust. A second centaur came forward and reached down, he grabbed the man's foot and drug his body slowly out of the city, digging a path in the gravel with the man's body as he did so.

Fantasy sighed and her placid expression returned.

Slowly she looked back to the city gathered at her feet and not an eyelash fluttered. Not a person took in a breath, "You may disburse to your homes. I will find you when it is appropriate."

Oswald looked up and suddenly an ethereal voice echoed in his head, though he knew he hadn't heard it out loud.

Stay.

He looked around and noticed that a few of the Generals and tribal leaders had moved either. He supposed they had received the same message. They stayed kneeled before her until the entire city behind them had turned and fled back to their homes and the quiet had swept back around them.

"You may all stand if you wish," Fantasy said, sounding dampened though her expression remained unreadable. Everyone got up gently except for Fred and Maria, who remained sitting in the gravel but still meeting the eye level of many of the people around them.

Fantasy looked at Maria and stepped forward, "For your understanding nature..." she locked eyes with Maria and knelt down to touch the laceration on her thigh through her clothes. Her fingers gently traced the fabric leaving a pale misty heaviness over the place in their wake.

When the mist settled, Maria smiled, her sharp teeth pressed against her full lips. Fred and Maria linked their fingers together, "Thank you," they said together.

Fantasy smiled humbly, "Maria, I wish you to go home, Fred will stay with me for now. I assure you both that nothing like this wound will happen in this city again."

Maria nodded and quickly got up, rubbing at the place on her thigh and respectfully dismissing herself from the small remaining group. Fred stood and gave her a smile as she walked away, back into the maze of the city.

Fantasy placed a hand on Fred's forearm and his color drained slightly. She looked up at him reassuringly and he was able to take in a breath. Her eyes found his and Fred's anxiousness became more obvious through the quiet, "Your wife did not lose the child," she assured him reaching up to his thin narrow face at the end of her reach, placing her palm against his green cheek, "He is still healthy and well."

"He?" Fred said, looking suddenly as though he could run laps around the city, the color brightening back into his mossy skin. He took in a few excited breaths and smiled weakly.

"Yes," Fantasy smiled, removing her hand from his cheek, "He is well and should be born in late winter."

Fred's massive blue eyes began to well up and he laughed to himself, his thin blue lips stretching tight against his smile. He put a hand over his mouth and closed his eyes, "Thank you."

"You have a good heart," she said flatly, "but you should do well to control your temper. Keep friends nearby when you need support."

"Yes Ma'am," Fred said, bowing his head gratefully.

"Know also that your brothers live and that there still remains a Keernith mountain range untouched by this war," she said, and Fred nodded slowly, suddenly very interested in his hands.

Fantasy walked away from Fred slowly and slid her judgments throughout the gathering. She looked around and her crystalline eyes found General Loch. They exchanged silent thoughts and Fantasy smiled, charmed by something unheard. She gestured subtly for him to come forward.

Loch obeyed and walked towards her before kneeling back down on to one knee at her feet. She reached down and placed a hand on his head, pushing a few pieces of peppered hair through her fingers. He looked back up to her eyes and she smiled again, "There is no other man worth the respect you have earned for yourself through the years. No man but you. You have seen many battles and have never raised your blade unrighteously. You have a protective heart that has cost you much, even though the price was happily paid," she looked down to the stump of his right arm respectfully, "I cannot grow back your arm without you having to endure tremendous suffering…"

"I would never ask you to," Loch said, shaking his head lightly.

"I know," she said, with a twinkle in her eyes, "Besides, it would be unfair to your enemies if I were to do so," her face brightened with amusement for a moment and fell back to her more serious demeanor, "But I would heal you if you only wished me to do so."

"No, my Goddess," he said surely, "I have lived this way for many years now. I am used to it. I don't want it back."

She locked eyes with him and they came to a silent understanding, "Then allow me to remove the pain that it causes and to rebuild your battered joints."

Loch lifted himself and stood in front of her gratefully with soulful eyes. Fantasy brushed an icy lock of hair from her face, the ice shattering around the golden hair and new crystals began wrapping back around to hold the stand where she had placed it. She reached out to him with an open hand and placed it firmly against his chest. His eyes closed and he dropped his head to his chest feeling the magic break over him in waves. She drew back her hand and Loch opened his eyes, taking a step back and presenting her with a very low bow.

"You deserve more," she said firmly, but Loch shook his head gratefully and stepped back to his place among the generals.

She smiled and moved her way among them, her eyes deciding. They stopped on general Armond and flipped to Samuel who stood at his side and back, "Armond, your nobility and your bravery are legendary. To meet you in this point in your life and know your pure soul is an honor to me."

Armond looked shocked, if not appalled by the thought of the goddess admiring him and he tore his eyes away from her and sank down to one knee, and Samuel followed as quickly as he could to kneel with his father.

"Forgive me Fantasy but I am not worthy of your honor," Armond said, humbly.

"You are," she stated bluntly.

"I have done nothing for you," he said quietly, staring down at the ground at her feet.

"Just because you didn't think about it at the time, it does not make it nothing," she reached down and touched Samuel's head. Samuel froze as though a blade were at his throat and stared fixedly at his father. She drew her touch back to Armond and brushed a finger across his brow.

She spoke softly and stooped down low to meet his eyes once more, "Everything you have done already has shifted the balance in this war and some have secured a future where there would be none. Though no one but you and I know it all, history will remember everything and will look upon you fondly and your name will be known with greatness." Armond looked on, stone faced as she continued, "Now, however life is difficult and war is upon us all. Dark things are moving where they should not and the iron hand that can stop them rests with you. Keep that in mind and keep your son safe, he should not be alone anymore."

Armond's eyes widened fearfully in a distant understanding. They were silent for a moment before she turned to Samuel and touched his young face and drew up his chin to force him to meet her gaze.

"Samuel, you are far greater than you yet know," she held his gaze seriously, "You are skilled and intelligent but growing up is difficult without war in your daily life. When the battle comes and the soldiers leave, do not leave Gommorn with them."

"Why not?" Samuel asked dumbfounded, looking up to her solidly, "I'm a very skilled swordsman. I could help."

"It is more important that you remain in Gommorn." The two of them looked at each other as he took in the final word of the conversation and after a while Samuel nodded and lowered his head into a bow once more.

Fantasy moved further down the row and stopped at Satomi whose hair was up in a ponytail and lacking the spikes that people had become accustomed to. The two of them spoke in complete silence for several long minutes before Fantasy grabbed her shoulder comfortingly and moved forward.

Her eyes fell on Ramif who shuffled uncomfortably. He looked down at his son and told him to stay put and suddenly he and Fantasy began walking farther away from the group than had been normal up to that point.

There was a good distance between the two and the rest of them before a bright light hit the air around them and pulsed. The light obscured everything for a moment and solidified into a transparent golden box which enveloped them comfortably.

Ramif looked around from within and nodded solemnly before sinking down to one knee before her, bringing his hands together at his chin. They spoke aloud to one another, though not a sound escaped the golden room. The two of them talked for a few long minutes and Ramif occasionally looked around the room, seeing something that Oswald could not. It was clear to Oswald that the inside of that box looked very different to Ramif than the outside looked to him.

Some of the generals and leaders were now feeling comfortable enough to talk to one another very quietly, but Oswald's eyes stayed on Ramif and Fantasy.

They continued to talk and the more time that passed, the more uncomfortable Ramif began to look. He ripped his eyes away from her and shivered, shifting uncomfortably, suddenly looking lost and acutely aware of his own pain. Fantasy continued to speak and her own expression fell as Ramif continued to stare off into the ground at her feet.

Fantasy knelt down, crouching on the hillside with Ramif at the center of the golden veil. She reached out with a gentle hand and touched his bearded chin trying to turn his head to make eye contact with him as she had with the others. Ramif slowly lifted his head and turned out of her grip, pulling his face out of her hand with an agonized expression. He moved around her open hand and shifted so that he dropped to both knees and lowered himself further to the ground. He turned his elbows outward placing his hands flat in the dirt and leaned forward pressing his head down on the backs of his hands.

A desperately saddened expression took hold of Fantasy and she place her open hand on his back instead. She looked him over with a vigilant and omniscient aura about her. She rubbed his back softly and spoke to him in their own private place, her words clear to no one but Ramif.

After a while Ramif beat the ground with his fist, his skin flushing behind his black hair and shaking shoulders. He began to breathe heavily, sitting up only slightly, only enough get a momentary glance at the goddess before turning his head back to the grass he kneeled in. Fantasy looked nonplused by this and continued to speak. She shook her head slowly and pulled his ebony pony tail away from his back and slung it over one shoulder so that she could place a hand on the bare skin at the base of his neck.

Ramif's face looked up suddenly and Oswald could see the distorted face of loss and agony, the fear of her touch at his neck and the anger behind it all.

Fantasy moved quickly and gracefully, forcing herself to slide in front of him, finally looking him in the eye with the one hand still wrapped against the back of his neck for some form of control. She continued to speak and his breathing became more irregular. He tried to speak but it was obvious that he was having difficulty between struggled breaths.

Fantasy allowed him to speak for a while through battered breaths as Ramif sobbed. Fantasy drew their heads together, both of them touching at the forehead as the conversation continued. They both closed their eyes with their heads together and they spoke that way for a long time.

"What are you staring at?" Fred asked quietly.

"Oh," Oswald whispered back at him, looking up to meet his big blue eyes, "I was just watching."

"Watching what?" Fred asked suddenly confused.

"Fantasy."

"There is nothing there right now," Fred said, looking back out to the hillside concernedly, "They'll be back when they're finished."

"I know…" Oswald said, looking back to Ramif and Fantasy locked brow to brow on the ground in spiritual council, "I'm just watching."

Fred looked more concerned at this, but didn't say anything else on the subject, instead he put a large hand on Oswald's shoulder for a moment and walked back to speak with Armond.

Oswald watched as Fantasy tightened the hand at the back of Ramif's neck and pressed her palm at the center of his chest. They stilled for a breath and a hot red glow sank into the translucent room seeping out from the place where Fantasy's hand rested over his heart. The warm light faded and the two of them met each other's eyes again, speaking quietly.

When finally the two of them had said what it is that they had meant to, Fantasy dried his tears with the back of her hands and she drew him up to his feet to stand beside her. They stood for a moment as she allowed him time for composure.

As they stood Fantasy's eyes stole away from Ramif and locked suddenly with Oswald's through the translucent golden box.

Oswald felt cold for an instant and wondered if he were truly supposed to have been able to see them. He tore his eyes away for a second, but felt her stare in his chest. Only when the others around him began to stop talking and the air stiffened, did he follow their line of sight back to the hillside.

Oswald turned his head and saw the magical box glow in bright pulses of light and then begin to fade away from around them in the same way that it had appeared. Fantasy held her hand against Ramif's back casually as the two of them walked back to the group, neither holding any expression or hint as to what happened within the box. Her expression however ran cold and her eyes came once again back to Oswald.

The group slowly lowered themselves back down to kneel before her as the two of them approached from their seclusion. Oswald knew her eyes lay on him and kept his head still and found a place to fix his eyes in the gravel.

Fantasy left Ramif to stand with his son and then stepped deliberately towards Oswald.

He felt an invisible tug on his chin and he was forced to look up. They locked eyes again and Oswald felt as though a bucket of ice water had been poured into his stomach and he could almost feel her rummaging through his mind. She tilted her head a fraction and the ethereal voice resurfaced in his head, the invisible grip on his head holding him firmly in place.

You were able to see through the spell.

It was not a question or a conversation piece. It was angry and her voice was sharp in his mind.

I wasn't sure how developed your magic had become until now, and you dared to use it against my will. You may not have control of it yet but that is a minimal excuse for being so disrespectful. You were not meant to see his council. I bare no one's soul to the world nor do I speak what other ears need not to know.

Say nothing about it, not another word to anyone. These people need not to fear you any more than they already do. I have done what I can for you, but you must earn their trust. Truly, one of the more pressing reasons that I have come to Gommorn is to speak with you. I cannot do so around the others.

"Walk with me," she said firmly.

Chapter Twenty

The cold magic released him and he was able to move his head once more. Oswald looked around at the generals and then to the others with concern in his eyes. They in turn looked confused and troubled at Fantasy's demand.

You are making them nervous.

Oswald looked away from them and turned back to Fantasy who had her fingers intertwined at her waist and an impatient expression on her face.

Let's go.

She turned around and started walking back up the hillside in the direction that she had come. Oswald scrambled to his feet to follow along behind her and he gave a last backward glance to the group and he felt a magical tug at his head once more.

He followed her more quickly. They passed her white horse, still grazing peacefully at the grass, and crested the hill overlooking the valley to a place Oswald had never visited.

Many people in this city still fear you. Fear is a dangerous companion, as you have learned. It is best to air on the side of caution both in private and in public, though it is no better for you to fear them. You must find an understanding. Many people have already found trust in you where they did not expect to. Strive to be worthy of it.

The woods looked less wild in the valley, the trees had low hanging branches and the grass was fuller with less weeds and fewer pin bushes.

A few stray animals scattered as they approached, leaping back to their homes in the treetops or their burrows below. The tree that they came to after a short while was fruiting peta tree. The fruits on its branches were soft and rotting from the cold nights and Fantasy reached up with a long pale finger and touched the nearest fruit. The entire tree shuddered as though a fierce wind had tossed its branches aside and suddenly the fruits began to plump once more and the bright purple color of the skins deepened. She picked the fruit that she had touched and turned around, her entire demeanor changing and the stern expression melting away with an understanding of mortal life.

"Eat," she said softly, "I know you haven't eaten since yesterday morning."

Oswald took the fruit gratefully and wondered to himself if magic did anything to the way it would taste, "Thank you... I eat when I can."

"When you can afford it," she corrected, "Around here, especially now, when business is slow and it's difficult to make money, you need to know how to catch your own food." She cupped her hands and another ripe and rich peta fruit fell down into her opened palms. She brought it in close to her and took a delicate bite, "Matrim will teach you if you ask."

"I hadn't thought of that." Oswald said, daring to take a bite of the fruit. It was sweet and cold and his stomach was grateful for the food. He took another few big bites of the peta and felt impossibly full. He looked at the fruit and could not bring himself to take another bite. The magic had done something to it after all.

"You've made a good life here, if a meager one, for now," she took another bite of the fruit and seemed to be paying attention to something very far away. When she pulled her attention close she again, she noticed a fat raccoon on the ground behind her. She took a final bite and tossed the remains to the raccoon who grabbed it in its tiny hands and ran off with its prize looking elated.

"I have," Oswald said, feeling as though he were missing something from the conversation.

Fantasy turned to look at him and sighed. She walked up close to him and reached her pale hands up to his face and touched the swollen bruises with her long pale fingers, the sunlight glinting off of her remaining glass ring. Each place her fingers rested spread with a hot liquid-like warmth that burned gently before going cold. She reached up and touched each wound, each sore place on his head and neck, her fingers brushing his elongated ear to heal the small cut on its edge and moving back to his nose.

She took a hold of the bridge of his nose with two fingers and pinched hard. A hot wave of pain erupted through his face as he felt the broken bone in his nose shift into place and seal with a hot pain. The pain ebbed away and she lowered her hand.

When his face no longer felt hot or cold from the dwindling remains of magic, Fantasy turned her attention to his shoulder and a sharp stab of pain waxed and ebbed from her touch, penetrating deep into the bone and tendon. She continued to move her fingers further down his body, resting occasionally on a sore place and pressing magic into his skin. At the last bruise on his lower shin, she took ahold of his leg in a vicelike grip. Oswald felt a sharp stabbing pain in his bone for an instant and the pain subsided as she stood back up to meet his eyes again.

"You should take more precautions when you train. Wear leather beneath your armor," she looked unhappily over the places she had healed and added, "and don't pick fights anymore."

"Thank you," Oswald said, touching his own face gently with the tips of his fingers. It was no longer swollen and didn't hurt to the touch, "but this can't be why you brought me into the valley."

"No," she agreed.

"Why did you have to take me away from the others?" Oswald asked, an uneasy feeling creeping into his curiosity.

"Because your situation is far more complicated," she said, examining him with her crystal gaze, the bottomless depths of her eyes burrowing through him.

"Complicated?" he said, not entirely wanting to understand her meaning, "Everyone in this city has lost people in the war. Everyone has made mistakes."

"Not everyone refuses council," she said blankly. She looked away from him and gestured with a curl of her finger for him to continue walking with her. They stepped slowly through the underbrush.

"I haven't refused anything," Oswald said, perplexed by the statement.

"You do not want to soul search. You did not plead for forgiveness or understanding nor did you ask for anything when I looked into your heart. You are young and still developing your spirit and though you have suffered loss, you remain unbroken. You did not look to me for compassion or for relief from your hearts own measure of life."

"I was hurt when my village burned," Oswald said honestly, watching his footsteps as they walked aimlessly through the woods.

"But you were not broken," she said.

"I suppose not," he admitted shamefully, "maybe I should have been..."

"No," she said, staring into the far distance, "You just looked for more life instead of dwelling on death. For some people that is impossible."

"Why?"

"Loss is different for everyone," she said, as she locked her fingers together in front of her.

"And so is their council with you..." Oswald guessed.

"Yes," she said, with a small smile for the understanding between them.

"So why is it that we have to be so far out of the city?" Oswald asked again, looking back over his shoulder and judging the distance they had covered.

Fantasy stared at him, her face placid and her eyes unmoving against his face, "Because of the magic you possess."

"I don't have any magic," Oswald said, dumbfounded.

"You have enough magic, that just by your existence you will eventually bring back the magic of the elves to its people. You have a great deal of magic."

"I don't understand," he said, with a pause. He tried to look through her eyes but was unable to read anything and knew that in the same instant, his soul was bare to her, "I can't use magic, I can't do anything special... except make shoes."

"You already know that the magic of the elves was removed many generations ago by the Fantasy. Several lives ago, I assure you," she said, he elegant eyebrow raised as she glanced over to him, "The reason the magic was removed was because she was jealous of the Elven magic and what it could do," Oswald listened to her as her impossible crystal eyes sank deep into his soul as she spoke, "The elves used magic to create things. Not from the air or with alchemy, not conjuring magic but from within their own bodies. They created with absolute precision and speed. They made armor, carvings, intricate furniture and glasswork that was unrivaled throughout the world. They were craftsmen whose passion became magic."

"I make shoes…" Oswald said blankly, unable to accept what she was saying.

"Think for a moment," she ordered calmly, "Since the time when you understood the art of making shoes have you ever had to make a measurement for any customer?" he shook his head. "Have you ever made a poor cut in the leather or mistaken a stitch?" Again he shook his head. "And you never thought that it was strange… because it was natural to you."

"I use magic to make shoes?" Oswald clarified, hearing his own words and thinking of how ridiculous that sounded. He looked down at his simple leather work shoes and flexed his toes, thinking, "Why is that significant?"

"Because you are using the same magic now to learn the art of the sword. Once you have learned a new skill, it becomes second nature to you and there is no losing what you have learned. You can completely master the sword of Dashai by spring if you are willing to do so. You truly have the potential to do anything you wish, including" she said softly, "Making shoes."

"I could match skills with the generals?" Oswald asked with disbelief as he stepped over a stone in his path.

"No," she said, "You could very well surpass them," she placed a hand on his shoulder as they walked, "if you wanted to."

Oswald could hear the gallop of a centaur's hooves just out of his sight in the woods, keeping watch over them. He shook his head slowly, "How? They've spent their entire lives working to master the battlefield."

"They have," she agreed, "but you have more than elven magic in your blood as well."

"King Venhow?" Oswald asked apprehensively, his voice dragging unhappily.

"Yes."

"So he is my father?" he said, feeling suddenly sickened and disappointed.

"He is," she said, and nodded shortly, her expression unreadable, "and he has one of three the purest wizard bloodlines in the world."

"Can I ask you a quick question," Oswald asked, as he fidgeted with the hem of his shirt.

"Of course," she said, distantly.

"Why haven't you taken care of the problem with Venhow?" he asked, curiously, his eyes searching her porcelain features as the light caught on the ice in her hair.

She paused and looked at him intensely, "I am mortal," she said softly, "If I would perish in the battle, five-hundred years of darkness and chaos would follow before I could reincarnate into the world once more," she looked away from them and to the path at her feet, "As it is, a lifetime under a tyrant seems kinder," she took in a deep breath and added, "And he also has magic that protects him from me, a magic he obtained when he forged the sword of Dashai."

"So you couldn't do anything even if you wanted to?" Oswald asked quietly.

"No," she replied, "I may be able to stop him, but it is as likely that he would kill me in turn. Magic is complicated in itself, which is why you have to understand that you are using wizard's magic more each and every day you live, and if you don't learn how you are using it and how to control it, you will eventually harm someone," she brought him along the valley to a large boulder with a broken slab missing from the rock which made for a convenient place to sit. They both rested on the rock and watched as Olivia crossed the valley vigilantly and vanished back into the thicket.

"I couldn't hurt anyone, I don't use magic... unless I'm making shoes, I guess..." he said, still trying to wrap his head around the conversation.

"Not that you realize, but every day you do," she looked out into the distance again as though something kept calling for her attention, "In your entire life have you ever drawn a cold bath?"

"No," Oswald said confused, "our well lay over a hot spring."

"No, it didn't," she said distantly, "You have heated your own bath from the day you were old enough to draw it up yourself."

"That doesn't make sense."

"Magic comes easy to some," she said, trying to explain the concept, "But some have to work their entire lives, just to do something as simple as to heat a bath. You have done so since you could walk."

"But that's worthless… It isn't the kind of magic that people talk about," he said with a shrug.

"Just because you didn't kill anyone with it?" she said, with an elegantly arched eyebrow, "Or because it couldn't be seen from miles away?"

"Well…I meant…" Oswald muttered aimlessly.

"Not all magic can be seen with the naked eye, but the *effects* of magic *always* can."

"Alright," Oswald said, his mind spinning around the history of his own life, searching for things that he never thought of as strange before. He couldn't find anything, but after a while he realized that there were some things that other people found strange about him. Things he couldn't teach or describe to others, and he began to believe it.

"Your mother realized what was happening and what it meant for you, and she knew then it was time that you wear the pendant around your neck. She and her father came to me, late in my past life, when she knew she was with child, and I knew what you could become. I created that pendant to hide you from eyes that would do you harm."

Oswald pressed his lips together tightly as he thought about it, "Then how did Ramif find me the night before my trial?"

"You weren't wearing the pendant," she said, her eyes drawing down to the small knot under his shirt where the fairy lay, "You should always wear it; that is why I made it."

"I usually do," he said, thinking back through the days, "I do take it off sometimes though."

"That can be as dangerous for you as not knowing that you are using magic," she warned.

Oswald chewed on the inside of his lower lip. He looked out over the valley and frowned, "But heating bathwater I hardly consider dangerous, if it is magic."

"Heating bathwater isn't dangerous. Accidently using too much magic when training is," she shifted in her sear on the slab of stone and folded her hands in her lap, facing him, "You also draw energy from Dashai whenever you wield the blade and have the drive to win. When you command it to give you strength, it will. If you want the magic to burn, it does."

"I knew the sword was some kind of magic," Oswald said surely.

"The sword is cast of underworld steel and has a spell on it that reacts to the wielder so that only Kebana's may touch it," she reached out a hand and softly touched Oswald's upper arm, "The sword is cursed with fire but the magic it has is also an extension of your own. If it reacts too forcefully to *your* magic and you release it, it can be very deadly."

Oswald thought of the short fight with Ramif and the energy the sword had given him, "I thought most of that was in my head."

"No."

Oswald sighed resignedly and asked, "So which magic was it that allowed me to see through your spell today?"

"I'm not sure. Perhaps both kinds," she said, with vague interest, "It was a simple spell, but it is rare that I have to do anything more complicated to hide someone."

"Okay," he said, trying hard to understand, "How do I learn to control the magic?"

"By first identifying when you are using it. You can feel magic," she said, gripping his arm a little tighter, "Like a drive, an energy that you can't control. When you can feel yourself using magic you will start to understand how to use it and how to keep it contained. Pay attention to everything that you do for a while and when you can feel the magic, try to use it."

"But I thought people were afraid of me using magic," he said, confused.

"Try small things. Safe things," she said, spotting a hawk in a nearby tree and watching it thoughtfully as she spoke, "Whatever comes naturally to you. They will notice slowly, but they will get used to the idea as you do."

"What if I can't learn to control it?" Oswald asked apprehensively.

"If you don't try to learn to keep ahold of the magic, it can become explosive," she let go of his arm and her attention fell away from the hawk and back into his eyes. Her face fell unhappily, "I have had a vision of you killing a friend by accident."

Oswald felt his heart skip a beat, he couldn't imagine any situation that would come to that end, "But if I can control it," he said slowly, "Then what kind of power does that amount to?"

Fantasy closed her crystal eyes, her icy eyelashes glimmering in the now mid-day sun. She turned to him and opened her eyes slowly, "I will show you." She took in a deep breath and the air around them began to chill until the hairs on Oswald's body stood on end and the bitterness of the air bit at his cheeks.

The air darkened and wavered like a mirage between them until the daylight was stolen into darkness, the two of them suspended in a ball of effervescent shadow. When a roar began to thunder in the air and the magic became audible, Fantasy reached her arm between them and grabbed Oswald's face in her hand and suddenly threw him spinning backwards into the darkness, where everything became nothing and he could no longer see his own body.

The darkness faded slightly and a great midnight landscape started to take shape, the horizon line burdened with a great mountain and the hills littered with stones and fallen trees. A strip of flatland stretched to the distance and the sounds of war began to fill his ears. Screams hit the air and the shrieking of metal on metal rang in the dark.

The shapes of thousands of bodies, raging like ants on the battlefield, took shape below him and he realized he was observing the battle from the sky. Something hit the air like thunder and fire tore outward from the center of the open battlefield like ripples in a pond. Tribal roars of anger and screams carried up to him as the war raged below and the land rotated beneath him.

Hot flashes of color burned the air and white balls of light shot across the field with blood in its wake. Arrows flew through the night air whistling as they passed. The arrows suddenly came to a stop against an invisible barrier as if choked by time, hanging there suspended in darkness.

Nothing got through the circular barrier on one side as arrows, magic and fire easily crossed from the other. Figures began to fall to the onslaught, thrown to the ground in ruin.

Another figure ran at the barrier, gracefully dodging white balls of light as it went. It was then that Oswald spotted the distinct red blade in his hands below. The figure spun to avoid something dark below and brought the blade up to strike.

The blade reached up to the sky as the barrier became closer, sudden streaks of pure white lightning licking at the blade and arcing violently in wild bursts of electricity as it swung against the base of the barrier in a violent crash. The lightning traveled in forked arcs and the explosive band of magic snapped.

The barrier splintered, raining down liquid fire and scorching the land.

The battlefield began to fade away until the darkness was once again complete and all that remained of the war was the deafening roar that it carried. Soon it too was gone and Oswald was left alone in the darkness searching for any sign of light. He felt soft fingertips against his cheek and he tried hard to see its source when the shadows fell away and daylight brightened the forest around him. He looked back around the woods confused and dazed as he attempted to orient himself.

"Oswald," Fantasy said, dragging him back to reality. He blinked and focused his attention back on the glassy reflection of her icy hair and clear crystalline eyes.

Pain erupted around him blindingly, as though an axe were buried hilt deep into the crown of his head. He felt himself scream but could not hear it through the anguish. He remembered all at once the events of the day and struggled to understand exactly what had just happened. "There you are," she said, catching glimpse of his spirit returning to his eyes.

"What was that?" Oswald asked, holding his head in both hands, pressing them together, trying to hold the bones of his skull together as it felt like they were trying to tear away in pieces. He opened his eyes and it felt as though the non-existent blade in his head twisted. His stomach turned.

Fantasy's fingers brushed back through his hair, running along his scalp with a comforting and unnatural warmth. She brought her hand back to his forehead to repeat the motion and raked the pain away with her fingertips with her second and third pass. "That was the vision that brought me to Gommorn," she said, "It woke me from my sleep. Seconds later I had a vision of you on the executioner's block. That is when I sent Olivia to the city as quickly as she could travel."

"Thank you for that by the way," Oswald said genuinely, realizing that he had yet to thank her for it.

"It is difficult to place the hour on a vision. I wondered if Olivia would get there fast enough."

"It was close," he admitted. He sat up straight as Fantasy withdrew her hand from his head and dropped it into her lap. Oswald sighed, relieved to be rid of the pain in his head, "You sleep?" he asked curiously, rubbing his head. It felt bruised from the intensity of the pain that Fantasy had taken away for him.

"When I can," she said, sounding exhausted. Her features brightened, trying to mask her own expression in knowing he had noticed the tone in her voice, "But I never have to sleep if I choose not to."

He rubbed at his head a little while longer before he decided that it wasn't helping the bruised feeling and asked, "Do the visions hurt you like that?"

"They can," she said absently, "But it does not last but an instant for me. If you didn't have enough magic to handle it, that headache would have killed you."

"Good to know…" Oswald said uncomfortably, trying to distinguish any magic in his body. He couldn't.

She locked eyes with him again, her voice clear, "You have to come to grips with your magic."

"I'll try," he promised trying to remember the scene of the vision in his head. There was so much going on and he was unsure what it all meant, "What exactly did I just see?"

"It will be the battle that will decide who wins this war," she said, stressing the importance of it, "If Gommorn falls, there is no other stronghold that can take back the lands. If the army of Azar falls, then this war will end."

"How many wizards were there on the field? There was so much magic."

"Four."

"Including Venhow and myself?"

"Yes," she nodded.

"I thought wizard blood was rare," Oswald said, confused.

"Pure blood is," she corrected.

"Is that what I saw?"

"Not exactly. Two pure blooded wizards were there… and you."

"There was so much going on and it was no small amount of magic in that vision. If it wasn't all pure wizard's magic, and it wasn't elven… then, what was that?" he asked amazed by what lingered from the vision.

"Sometimes—" she explained, choosing her words carefully as she looked out into the woods, "—Very rarely — so rarely that I have not seen it happen in over three hundred years — magical blood is created within a body in times of great distress. This is called an Animus Wizard."

"And that was the fourth?" Oswald asked.

"Yes," she said absently.

"Then who was it?"

Fantasy's eyes narrowed and she looked over at him sternly, "You ask too many questions Oswald. If you were meant to know, I would have already told you."

"Forgive me," Oswald said quickly, realizing that he had nearly forgotten that he was talking to the Goddess herself. He bit down on his tongue and was afraid to continue the conversation.

Fantasy looked over once more and caught his line of sight, choosing the silence.

I know you. I know everything there is to know about who you are. I know your fears, your failures, your suffering and your dreams. I know your compassion and your drive and I sometimes can get glimpses of your future, all from within your eyes. I know in an instant how you feel and I know what it will take to break your spirit. But I will not share your soul with another, as I will not share another's with you.

When you want to know something personal, do you not ask that person directly? Show your friends and your fellows respect or I will teach it to you.

Oswald felt a sharp and sick discomfort in his gut and he was unsure if it was his nerves, or something else. He nodded and opened his mouth to speak, only to shut it again, his voice lost from his throat in a flutter of fear. Fantasy caught the fleeting thought as it passed through his mind and snatched it up as though she were pinching an autumn leaf from the air.

General Ramif is concerned with his reputation, he wished to confide in privacy, a privacy that was dishonored by you. Your curiosity did him a great disservice. Though he does not know that you saw him at his most vulnerable, and that I will not say anything to him unless he asks, you saw more than he wished anyone to. That is partially my fault, but you owe him some understanding and a great deal more respect.

I know that he is a difficult man, but if you try to see who he is, he will return the effort and try to learn who it is that you really are.

Your other friends are already trying to develop an understanding of you. That is why they are your friends.

War has many allies and many enemies. Choose wisely because it will mean the difference between life and death for more lives than just your own. Each action affects another whether you are able to see it or not.

People act very much in the same way as water. When a drip of water is dropped into a puddle, it disturbs every other drop, even though they are all made of the same life-force and the water began calm, one disturbance can rattle everything.

Know who will have your back when the time comes.

She stood up from the rock and began walking back to the city. Oswald decided not to follow her. He looked around through the forest thinking deeply about the morning's events.

A form rustled in the thicket and he caught glimpse of a centaur as Olivia made another pass around the valley floor.

Chapter Twenty-One

Venhow chewed on the end of his finger thoughtfully in the darkness, his mind unable to rest as it continued churning up pieces of an increasingly uncertain future. He spat out a piece of fingernail and sat up in his bed, frustrated. It had been days since Walt had made a report and he was growing more and more restless with every hour that passed. He finally decided that he could take no more of the silence and threw his covers away.

He leapt up from the bed, the stone floor cold against his feet. He snapped his fingers and a torch against the wall lit up suddenly, casting a dancing flame to light up the room. He went to the armoire, dressed quickly, and straightened his robe. He turned the corner and threw himself into the absolute shadow of the spiraled staircase.

His footsteps echoed against the stone walls and the sound of damp stone snapped with every step that he took. He passed through a long decorated hall and down another stairwell before he reached the main entry to the castle. A small torch burned from its place along the wall and the flames flickered nervously as he marched towards it. The fire tossed a bright coin of light on the wall and floor and reflected against the brass hinge of the main door as he threw out his arms. The large front doors burst open violently, smacking the stone walls with an explosive sound.

A man ran up the path, his armor clinking as he huffed his way up the hill, his eyes wide, "Your highness, what is it?"

"Come with me," Venhow ordered, "I need a report."

The guard nodded and turned after Venhow as the two of them walked briskly down the path. They wove around the courtyard to the back end of the citadel where a narrow tower stood, disconnected from the rest of the castle. Firelight flickered across a closed glass window on the ground floor.

"Stay here," Venhow ordered, and the guard turned and watched for motion on the pathway to secure the door to the tower.

Venhow turned and pressed his body on the heavy door and was annoyed to find it locked shut, "He did this just to piss me off," Venhow muttered under his breath as he flipped his hand over the wooden boards. He flushed the magic through the door and heard a heavy clatter from inside as the board popped out of its bracket. He pressed on the door again and it slid open.

Strange smells hung in the air, bitter and sharp. A smoke-filled fog rolled out of the door and burned at his eyes and nose. He coughed as he stepped into the assault of smoldering air and shut the door behind him quickly. The arid smoke began to dissipate once the door latched once more and Venhow walked around a large stack of books, weaving around artifacts and desks until he found Walt.

He was standing by a pedestal with a large book propped open and a flask of thick yellow fluid in one hand. He looked up unsurprised and unamused for a brief second before he returned to his reading. He skimmed a finger over the page, his long brown hair laying stingily in his face as he studied.

Venhow coughed out the last of the smoke roll and said dryly, "That was a very childish spell."

Walt stared intently at the flask full of liquid in his hand, "I didn't want to be disturbed."

"You never do," Venhow said, matter-of-factly.

"Then you should know," he said with a pause, lifting the flask and staring at the bottom of the glass, "That if I wanted to talk to you, that I would've found you."

"I can't wait anymore," Venhow snapped impatiently, "I need to know if you have an answer for me."

"I want a minute to go over this spell one more time," Walt said, scratching at his scuffled chin with one hand and still analyzing the potion in the other.

"And I want a report," Venhow said sternly.

"I'm not ready to give my report," he retorted moving the flask containing the yellow concoction over the nearby candle flame and watched it fixedly.

"It's beginning to drive me mad," Venhow said, looking up at a large book on the top of one of the many stacks that littered the tower and pulling it down into his arms. He began to thumb through pages with no real interest in what was on them, "There has to be a way to convince the Grimm to do what I want."

The liquid in the flask in Walt's hand began to spiral with a pink hue at its center. Walt quickly removed it from the heat and spun to the desk behind him, grabbing a pinch of herbs from a small bowl and quickly stuffing it into the solution. He grabbed a glass rod from the desk nearby and placed it in the flask, stirring the contents rapidly. The clinking of glass sang in the air as Walt counted under his breath, funneling his magic into the brew. After a short while, the herbs dissolved and the mixture faded away and thickened slightly. It began to settle over the short passage of time and it turned as clear as water through the glass. Walt smirked triumphantly.

"There is," Walt answered finally, taking the glass rod out of the flask and placing it carefully on the desk where it had been before.

"What is it?" Venhow demanded, sounding both excited and impatient. He snapped the book closed and placed it back on the top of the stack.

"This," Walt said, holding up the clear flask. He waved a hand over the neck of the glass and sealed the container with magic.

"I knew I could count on you," Venhow said, taking the flask out of his hand and looking it over thoughtfully, "What is this?"

"Very complicated," he answered, and snatched the flask back out of Venhow's hand, "And *very* delicate. This is the eighth batch I have had to make and this is the only one that reacted the way it was supposed to."

"Is it finished?" Vehnow asked hungrily.

"For the most part," Walt said vaguely, glancing back at the open book on the pedestal.

"So when can I use it?"

"It has to age for a month in complete darkness before it will be ready… and that's if I did it right," he paused for a bit looking down at the crystal clear vial carefully surveying the bottom for any sign of sediment, and smiled when he couldn't see anything but a clear vicious liquid, "Which I have."

"What exactly is it?" Venhow repeated.

"Terbran infused batronion oil cooked in griffin blood and magically titrated with sulfuric acid over a soft heat."

"How does it work?"

Walt looked at him impatiently, "Precisely as it's meant to. It's a barrier to the underworld."

"Are you absolutely sure that this will work?" Venhow asked as he leaned in to look greedily at the vial.

"I'm betting my life on it," Walt said seriously. He held up the concoction admiring his work before picking up a box from the shelf and placing the flask inside it. He closed the lid of the black box and sealed it tight. "Here," he handed the box to Venhow, "You should probably put it in the lower level of the castle somewhere until the moon is in its waxing quarter again."

"One month?"

"Then it will be ready," Walt promised him.

Venhow ran his fingers along the box and smiled wickedly, "One month."

Venhow watched the phases of the moon pass by anxiously, obsessing over death and its looming reaper. When the moon finally had risen over the mountain's crest, a sliver cut into the darkness, the galloping in his heart lead him down to the dungeon where the box lay hidden among the wide assortment of interrogation tools he had assembled over the years. He moved a large screw to one side, blood dried and flaking from its grooves, and he picked up the box that lay behind it in the shadowed corner.

He unsealed the lid and folded it away, surprised to see that its crystal clear color had clouded over the passing month. His excitement dribbled away and he gripped the bottle tightly. He ran back up the stairs and out into the courtyard with the flask in his hand and the moon's waxing light showing him a dim path as he made his way to the narrow tower.

Walt was standing in the path ahead of him, looking as though he had expected his appearance sooner.

"It clouded," Venhow said, a bitter discontentment in his voice as he walked the rest of the way up the path to where Walt stood.

"It was supposed to," Walt answered calmly, holding out a hand to take the potion from him.

Venhow handed the flask over and Walt looked at the thick fluid inside thoughtfully, occasionally giving it a swirl or turning the vial onto its side and judging how reactive it looked in the moonlight. He licked his chapped lips and lowered the potion slowly with a nod.

Walt looked unhappy but seemed assured of his own work, "It's the way it's supposed to be."

"Are we ready this time?" Venhow asked enthusiastically.

"Yes," Walt said, with his brow crumpled nervously, "but we need somewhere secluded. Somewhere we can leave it if we have to."

"There is a chamber in the South Wing of the castle that we don't use," Venhow suggested.

"Does it lock?"

"It'll lock if we want it to," Venhow retorted obviously, "I can weld the door shut if I have to."

"Yeah," Walt nodded again as if he couldn't think properly. He hadn't been able to sleep well, brooding over the potion and the stakes at hand, "You do have your gauntlet on you this time?"

"I do," Venhow said, touching the armored glove in his pocket through his robe, "They will expect me to have it. This time we'll be ready."

"We had better be," Walt grumbled. He seemed off balance by the situation, unwilling to call the beast back into a room with him, but he showed no sign of backing out, "lead the way."

The two of them made their way back down the path and into the castle through the front doors. Tonight all of the torches were lit and the soft light of the fires danced, though their light was of little comfort.

Walt looked around as they walked and noticed why the place seemed so empty, "Where's your skin changer?" he asked, he had yet to see one without the other somewhere nearby but for the last couple of weeks the persistent absence of her gave him a strange uneasiness.

"Still wounded," Venhow said, checking the halls for other people as he turned down the South wing.

"I would have thought she would have been healed well before now... They do heal extremely quickly, or am I mistaken?"

"They usually do, but she was in her true form," Venhow snapped over his shoulder accusatorily, "so she didn't have that magical barrier to protect her. It is also an underworld wound. It is something entirely different from anything either of us are used to healing."

"She *is* healing though?" Walt asked, suddenly more anxious about what they were about to do. He looked down at the potion and scrutinized it again to reassure himself.

Venhow didn't answer at first, winding down a very wide hall that branched off into separate staircases. He moved towards the one on the left, leading downward. He took in a deep breath and answered quietly, "Very slowly. She keeps falling in and out of a fever."

"As long as the fever keeps going away," Walt nodded to himself and studied the rooms and closed doors as he passed them, making a mental map of this side of the castle floor. They reached a bend in the hall where the corner swept around to left in a graceful arc and down another wing. At the end of the hall Venhow stopped and opened an old decorative steel door and gestured for Walt to go in first.

The room was bare except for an empty suit of armor standing decoratively at attention in the corner and a black and gold rug draped along the center of the room. Walt waited until he heard the click of the door and looked back to Venhow with a nod. He unstoppered the flask with a sharp flick of his fingers and waved his hand over the brew drawing the potion out of the bottle. It floated up in a liquid cloud, foggy and unstable.

He drew his fingers close to the hovering mass and suddenly forced his magic through the ends of his fingers as he tore his arms out quickly to his sides and the potion evaporated into a shimmering fog. Breathing heavily, he began to move his arms quickly trying to remain in control of the mist.

Venhow stepped to the other side and mimicked Walt's movements. Slowly the mist began to rest along the floor in the center of the room, coating the decorative rug. The two of them worked faster and built a barrier in the air, forcing the mist to create a wall that expanded across the room. The mist held in place for a second and faded away.

Walt put a hand up where the barrier was supposed to be and felt a gentle thickness to the air. He pressed against it with magic pulsing in his hands and felt the invisible barricade give slightly. He took in a calming breath and walked through the wall with ease, the magic forcing him to hold his breath as he passed through the barrier. Venhow followed and the two of them went to the edge of the rug where the stone floor lay bare.

Venhow pulled the pre mixed and measured combinations of herbs from a container in his pocket, setting it aside. He opened the thick paste and scooped it out, smearing it across the floor and filled in a large drawn circle with it. He dumped the herbs in its center and threw the container to the side. He opened a vial and smelled its contents, approved of its sour smell and poured the black potion on the pile of herbs. They sizzled against the floor and combined with the paste. Smoke began to roll up from the ground in a foamy mass.

Venhow stood up and put his hand into his robe pocket, sliding his hand into the gauntlet and clenching his fist, feeling the metal fingers click against one another. He pulled the silver dagger out of its place at his hip and handed it to Walt.

Walt took it reluctantly, looking down at the emerald on its hilt and wondering how many lives the blade had taken. He took in a slow, deep breath and hesitated with the silver blade laying against his palm. The silver glinted with the reflection of his own shaggy face, distorted in the gloss of the metal. He closed his eyes with a stifled wave of dread and he grasped his fist around the sharpened blade and drug the razor edge against the inside of his hand in a swift slash, feeling the flesh of his hand split open, hot with pain.

Walt held his shanking fist over the rolling smoke and opened his hand. He watched the steady, heavy, drips of blood from his torn palm slide down into the herbs on the floor. The smoke slowly turned a brighter red with each drop until it was satisfied and the smoke began to bellow upward into a noxious crimson pillar. Walt withdrew his hand and wrapped it tightly in a cloth from his pocket, staring intently at the floor.

They backed up, finding some comfort on the rug beneath their feet. A blackened arm slid from the smoke, parting the stone floor and pulling its large charred body up from the dark plume of red smoke. Its barbed back arched as it drew itself up out of the rock and into the circle. Its clawed feet flexed against the floor, scraping its claws along the stone with a sharp sound. It looked around the room to Walt with a malicious grin, "Couldn't wait to see my pretty face again?" it cackled, and moved forward heavily, its feet bordering against the edge of the rug.

"I couldn't," Venhow said, and the Grim rounded on him angrily, instantly recognizing his voice and snarling in bitter confirmation as its yellow eyes landed on his face.

Venhow took his gauntlet laden hand out of his pocket and flexed his fingers threateningly. The Grimm stared at the silver gauntlet and sneered, repulsed by the mere sight of it.

"I already told you, I won't work for you," it grumbled and rounded back on Walt, "How many years and for what?"

"I'm not making a deal," Walt said shakily, trying to keep his voice steady and sure.

"We are," Venhow said, drawing the burnt face back in his direction.

The Grimm gnarled his teeth and breathed angrily, smoke rolling out of the corners of its mouth, "I am not making a deal with you... you already belong to us."

"You may want to," Venhow coaxed grimly, "for this..." he pulled the gauntlet off of his hand and held it out in the air in front of him.

The Grimm looked at the gauntlet suspiciously, pondering the worth of the item, "No deal," it finally said slowly, still visibly intrigued by the offer, "I want what you owe me. I want my thousand years free of the wheel."

Venhow shook his head, "No chance," he said, and threw the gauntlet behind him and it hit the rug and rolled out beyond it where it clattered on the floor, "That's your offer. Take it or leave it."

"What is it that you want so badly this time?" it asked as it narrowed its yellow eyes behind the blackened sockets.

"I want a particular elf dead, he has my sword and I want it," Venhow said, with hatred in his voice, "Bring it back with his heart wrapped around my blade."

"An elf?" it asked uninterestedly.

"A half blood," Venhow corrected sharply, his every movement rolling with loathing.

"And the sword of Dashai?" it clarified with an upturned lip.

"Yes."

The Grimm snorted and a short plume of black smoke wafted out into the air, "You aren't as smart as they say," it said, eyeing the gauntlet on the floor knowing that it could easily reach it first. It played cautiously, not wanting to take it before it got what was owed, "That's too dangerous even for me. No deal. And *you*," it looked at Walt hungrily, "Called me and without even meaning to make me an offer. Very dishonorable of you. So I demand my blood offering for the consultation," it stared at Walt, the only person in the room he could touch, "No deal costs more blood."

Walt backed up quickly, the color draining from his face.

The Grimm lunged forward and caught Walt's lower leg with a claw. Walt rolled away from the impact feeling his pant leg tear as the claw tried to catch meat. He rolled again as he tried to put some distance between them and at the end of the roll he flipped back onto all fours. Heart pounding, he launched himself through the thick air and landed hard on his side against the stone floor. He looked up at the Grimm as it bounded forward with its lip curled and its long skeletal body pluming smoke along behind it.

Venhow pulled at the barrier as the Grimm hit the invisible wall with enough force to throw itself off its feet. It crumpled against the rug and looked up with its yellow eyes wild, enraged by the trickery. It roared and tucked its feet back under its massive black body.

Walt got back up to his feet and pushed against the other side of the wall as hard as he could, the two of them forcing the two loose ends of the barrier together. As the Grimm realized what was happening it leapt forward in a wide eyed rush. It hit the wall once more and the force of the Grimm's body smashed against the barrier as the two ends of the magic sealed together.

It panted from inside its small tomb and spun around angrily. It drug its talons through the air and left long white scrapes in the air along the border of the magic. The tears in the barrier sealed and the white marks in the air faded slowly as it fought in its cage.

It climbed the wall of the barrier and hit the roof of the container before kicking off of the ceiling and hitting the floor with a thud. It flailed against the ground trying to tear up the carpet but nothing happened. Nothing but white scrapes were left in any part of the makeshift prison, and those too faded into nothing. The barrier started filling up with the Grimm's smoke and even though it kept getting thicker, its yellow eyes pierced through the smolder hatefully.

"YOU DARE?!" the Grimm roared, thrashing against the walls.

Venhow laughed with grandeur, a maniacal satisfaction in his eyes. He walked up and stood with his face inches from the place where the magic bound the small space, still laughing at the Grimm cruelly. He smiled and watched the animal-like panic as it tried again to return to the underworld, pressing against the floor and without progress. It franticly searched for a seam or a weak place in the complex spell, working its talons into every inch of the magic.

It tore at a place near the ceiling of the tomb, leaving long white gouges that overlapped as they faded away. It threw itself into the place that it had been working on and the entire room rattled but the barrier didn't budge.

It rounded back to the edge of the magic and bared its teeth, its eyes swiveling around the room. It looked at Venhow and its charred face twisted.

"I will kill you!" it screamed, taking swings at the barricade and leaving white cuts in the air, "I will kill you both! I'm going to make a meal of you! I'm going to rip out your eyes, spill your guts on the floor and then tear out your heart and EAT IT!" it continued to rage against the walls for a while before slamming itself against the side facing Walt, its yellow eyes wide, "Let me out!"

"I'm sorry," Walt muttered unapologetically, "but I don't make deals with Grimms."

Its face distorted further and it screamed. The sound was nothing like the angry roar it had been bellowing but instead was a garbled guttural sound that made Walt's stomach rise up into his chest. When the sound faded away, the Grimm was back against the barrier at Venhow's side.

"What do you want?!" it screamed.

"A deal," Venhow said, with a grin.

"FINE!" the Grimm yelled with a hint of panic, "I'll take the gauntlet!"

"No, that offer expired," Venhow said, walking around the small circle and scooping the sharp fingered metal gauntlet up off of the ground. He put the gauntlet on and walked back to the

Grimm's panicked face, "Now the deal is, you agree to kill the elf for me, bring back my blade and I will let you go."

"NO!" the Grimm yelled trashing about in the smoky chamber.

"I can make it smaller," Venhow said dryly, pressing his bare hand against the viscous air and drawing his magic into it, pulling the walls in on all sides by several inches.

The Grimm screamed again at realizing that it could touch all sides of the prison now without moving. It turned in place, picking its talons against the walls and clawing at the ground.

"Ready to take the deal?" Venhow asked, with an amused eyebrow raised.

"I'll KILL you!" it shrieked with renewed energy, "HATE! I— HATE!" it was now hitting the barrier with its full body. It hit the wall and piece of its barbed back broke off in the air and hung there as though suspended by strings. It screamed again.

"Not enough?" Venhow asked, and he reached up and drew the walls in closer still.

The Grimm was now forced to remain on its hind feet from the confined space and bumped the walls as it tried to turn around, "LET ME OUT!"

"Or what?" Venhow asked tauntingly, "You can't touch me... but I can touch you," he put his right hand with the gauntlet through the barrier and snatched blindly through the smoke until he grabbed ahold of a thin forelimb. He pulled it against the barrier as hard as he could, digging the tips of the silver fingers into its blackened flesh.

It tore away from his grip, shredding its charcoal skin and drawing a clear substance from the open area. It guarded the wound, unable to back away any further from Venhow's reach. It pressed its body against the barrier and thrashed angrily, clawing up at the sides. It took in a deep breath and locked eyes with Venhow again, "FINE. It's a deal, just LET ME OUT!"

"An official deal?"

"On pain of death," the Grimm growled.

Venhow smiled agreeably and removed the gauntlet and held it out for Walt to wear as additional assurance. He bent low and tightened the dagger strap at his calf before stepping up to the magical wall. He put both hands in the thick air and pulled the barrier apart.

The Grimm shot out of its confinement and out into the open room, skidding on its clawed feet and dragging the talons on its forearms along the floor as it came to a stop. It turned around indignantly and scowled, "I need my blood offering from you."

Venhow smirked wickedly, "There is a dungeon below the main floor in the East Wing... Take your pick."

The Grimm returned the dark smile, "How generous... So who is this elf that I have the honor in killing?"

Chapter Twenty-Two

Oswald took a small, fine, blade and made a clean cut in the leather, marking the pattern in his head as he worked at a new order. He finished the cut and examined the piece approvingly looking back down to the leather and trying to feel the cut that he was making. He tried to understand the feel of the elven magic but didn't notice anything that he hadn't been used to his whole life. He tried to pay attention as he cut the sister piece but got distracted from his magic detection task, engrossed in his work.

"Excuse me," A woman knocked on the front counter of the shop.

Oswald set down the blade and pushed aside the cuts he had made in the leather. Getting up from the swivel chair in the center of the U shaped workbench, he caught whiff of something hot, "Hey, Matirm, take the rubber off the fire or it's going to burn."

"Yea' 'al right," Matrim said, getting up from his seat and putting down the leather stain and the piece he had been working with to lean over to the bowl. He took up the cloth nearby and scooted the bowl over out of the heat.

Oswald walked up to the counter and smiled brightly, "What can I do for you?"

"I need a pair of shoes," she said obviously, taking a lock of her light brown hair over her shoulder and rolling it in her hands nervously, "How much does it cost?"

"A whole pence if I get everything together but it will only cost half of that if you buy your leather from Mich and bring it to me," Oswald said, pointing to the tent next to him.

Mich looked up when he heard his name and gave the little woman a polite nod.

"What kind of leather do you need?" she asked, looking across the selection.

"Whatever you want me to use," Oswald said, with a shrug, "I haven't found a leather that I can't work with yet."

The woman smiled brightly and walked over to Mich's tent making her selection and paying for her wares. She brought back two silver fox hides and set them on the table with a gin, "Will this be enough?"

"It should be," Oswald said, looking it over, "Come around the table here and take off your shoes."

The woman blushed as she came around the corner, looking down at her bare feet. Her feet were dirty and calloused with a small cut on the side of her foot, "I haven't had shoes for about a year," she mumbled, "There hasn't been a cobbler here in a long time."

"Well, you'll have shoes now," Oswald promised, "I have to finish this order first and I have four others waiting but I'll push yours up since you need them so bad. You can pick them up late tomorrow afternoon."

"Thank you," she said gently, "Do you need to get measurements or anything?"

"No, I've done this for a long time," he said, with a kind, assuring smile, "So do you want dress shoes, sandals, casuals or boots?"

She looked at him blankly with a frozen smile, "I just need shoes."

"Casuals it is," he said, with an uplifted finger. He pulled a pencil out from behind his long ear and made a shorthand mark on the leather, "And your name is?"

"Laurie Coppers," she said quietly.

Oswald paused with his pencil over the leather's edge for a second and took in a breath, writing out the name, "That's a lovely name," he said, and put the pencil back behind his ear, "It should be ready tomorrow night," he repeated. He turned back to his workbench with the stiff leather hides and set them on the table next to Matrim and said, "Light stain."

"Yea'it'll be a minute," Matrim said, finishing the last of the dark stain on the steer hide he was working on.

"That's fine," Oswald said, walking back around the table to his chair, "Just make sure you clean off your hands when you switch stains. I have to finish this order first anyway."

The sun crawled across the sky as they worked, the autumn sunset highlighting the fine art of the leatherwork as he handed the pair of black boots across the table to a large man with wide jowls and beady eyes. He took the twelve silver coins that made the full pence, and shook the man's hand pleasantly, "It was nice doing business with you."

Oswald turned to Matrim whose cheek was discolored with stain where he must have scratched at his face at some point through the day. Oswald smiled understandingly at the sight and started picking through all of the coins that they had made throughout the day, and he held out a fistful of coins to Matrim.

"This is half of what we made today," Oswald said, dropping the pile into his open hands and pocketing his half of the money

"Really?" Matrim said, poking the coins around in his palm, "How much we get done today?"

"We finished two pairs and had three pickups from yesterday," Oswald said, as he moved back to the table, glancing at the supplies still out on the bench. He took the leathers and locked them away before pulling open the drawer for the blades.

"Wow. No wonder ya do this for a livin'. I've made mor' money in the las' couple a weeks than I've had in my whole life," he said, putting the coins into his pants pocket with the clatter of metal.

Oswald gathered the remaining items and finished putting his tools and supplies away. He locked the cabinets and slid his key into his pocket, "I never used to be able to get this much done. Without your help I would only get one pair finished a day. I'd still be behind on my debt orders from the shop itself."

"I's worth way mor' than one 'er two rabbits a day thas fa' sure," he said, and got up from his seat. He walked over to the water basin and dipped his hands in the water in an attempt to get the sticky remains of the stain out from between his fingers, with little success.

Oswald reopened one of the cabinets and grabbed a glass jar full of a paste he had made from the native plants. He held it out to Matrim, "Try that instead, and you have some on your face too."

Matrim pulled out a slab of the paste and scrubbed at his hands with it and felt the sticky surplus of stain separate from his fingers. He rinsed off the paste and looked at his hands. They were stained a deep tan but were no longer sticky or blotched, "Thanks." He took out a smaller amount and looked at his reflection in the water and worked at the spot on his cheek.

Oswald locked up the container and did a final sweep of the shop to be sure that everything was put away. A sudden troubled feeling overtook him and he paused.

"Everythin' alright?" Matrim asked, drying his face off with the inside of his shirt.

"Yeah," Oswald said, reaching up and pulling down the canvas tarp to the side of the shop, "Just had a weird feeling is all."

"Weird how?" Matrim asked, reaching up and getting the tarp on the far side, "Ya gettin' sick er som'thin'?"

"No," Oswald said, with a shrug, "Just one of those feelings... It's fine." They pulled down the tarp at the front and headed down the street towards The Burning Mill.

The tavern was warm and the smell of cooking food and alcohol was heavy in the air. Oswald picked at his plate of food and listened to the roar of the room. He tried to brush away an odd feeling as he surveyed his surroundings, it was a deep cold that felt like eyes in the dark. It had been an hour since Matrim left with a friend, but Oswald couldn't bring himself to leave.

Something seemed off balance. He looked around watchfully, hoping to see someone who might be able to settle his unease.

Ramif sat at the bar and was draining his fourth or fifth drink of the hour, becoming more withdrawn by the minute and beginning to sway at his seat, his face red and fixed in his glass.

Oswald looked around the tavern again not seeing anyone else he recognized and he knew it was too late for another of the generals to happen to come in. The hairs on the back of his neck stood on end and his stomach crawled for a few long seconds. He swallowed hard, picking up a bite and nibbling on another piece of bread, trying to suppress the discomfort.

A cold wash hit him and he felt suddenly like prey, cornered by something big. He felt a cold bead of sweat roll down the back of his neck.

He couldn't shake the strange feeling and got up from his seat. He looked around and walked up to the bar, dodging a thrown glass pint as it shot past his head, smashing against the wall along the way. A sudden fight broke out and Oswald watched as the guards left their posts and marched towards the two men as the fight began to escalate.

Ramif flipped his long black pony tail over his shoulder with the back of his hand to get it out of his way and tilted his glass. He rolled his fingertips on the bar slowly to give his hands something to do, ignoring the chaos of the room as if it were nothing more than a stiff breeze. He scratched at his beard with an unhappy scowl and leaned forward into his drink.

Oswald checked behind him one last time as he walked up the stool and took the open seat next to Ramif. He was feeling unwelcome in the seat, but was far more disturbed and put out of place by the feeling of being watched.

"What do you want?" Ramif slurred, not looking up from his drink.

"Advice," Oswald mumbled.

"Yeah?" he said, apathetically.

Oswald looked over at him, his discomfort pushing him forward as he fought to find anything to say that wouldn't sound stupid, "Something doesn't seem right."

Ramif tipped up his drink and took a long swallow, a small dribble sliding down into his braded beard, "Like what?" he mumbled wiping the drop of takwa from his beard with the back of his hand and still refusing to look away from his drink.

"I'm not sure. It just feels like something's wrong." Oswald said. He fidgeted and looked around the bar one more time, "My stomach keeps crawling."

Ramif knocked on the bar twice with his knuckles and Mill came over with two more glasses of his usual drink. He clunked them down onto the bar and took the empty glass from Ramif's hand.

Ramif grabbed one of the two drinks and pulled it in to him, "I'm supposed to trust the stomach of a man that can't hold one drink?" he belched and slid the other glass over the bar with a ringing sound and it stopped in front of Oswald.

Oswald looked down at the watery brown murk in his glass, his sinuses cringing at the assaulting smell of it. He lifted the glass to his lips and tried to hold his breath as he took a large swig of the drink. It burned like fire going down his throat and sent an involuntary shudder running through his back. He hit the bar with his palm as he coughed and choked down the drink.

A wide smile split across Ramif's red face, his eyes almost vanishing into his cheeks and his bright white teeth showed in the split of his grin. He chuckled amusedly into his drink as he caught a sidelong glimpse of Oswald's face as he had tried to swallow.

The sudden smile shocked Oswald and he was unsure what he was supposed to do with it. It was the first time Ramif had shown anything but anger around him, and now it seemed like the smile was unnatural on his face.

"Still feeling uneasy?" he slurred as he started on his new glass.

Oswald stopped and could still feel the edge of something sinister around him, "Yes."

"Then keep drinking," Ramif said, his smile fading away and taking another swig and hard swallow of the takwa, "It'll quit."

Oswald looked down into his glass and shook his head slowly, doubt just beyond the uncomfortable writhing of the unseen darkness, "I don't think it will."

"Give it a minute," Ramif said softly.

Oswald sighed and took another swig of the drink, unsure what else to do with the feeling. He shuddered again, the burn of the drink ripping at the back of his throat and burning a hot hole in his stomach. He cringed again and shook his head disgusted, "How can you drink this?"

"It gets better after a while," he said, with a smirk.

Oswald turned his glass on the bar and watched the fluid in the glass churn lightly. He waited for something that didn't happen and he felt the invisible eyes on him again. He turned around looking for whatever was making him feel this way. He didn't see anything unusual.

"What's bothering you, exactly?" Ramif asked, finally looking up from the bar at Oswald, "You're acting… twitchy."

"It feels like there's something… lurking…" Oswald said, as he took another glance over his shoulder.

"You're in the Burning Mill," Ramif snorted, "Something probably is."

"No," Oswald said, shaking his head and daring to take another sip of the takwa, surprised that the third mouthful wasn't as harsh as the first. He swallowed the drink away and started to feel a heat build up steadily in his chest, "It's not the same."

Ramif took a swiveled glance around the room, catching himself as he nearly toppled off of the stool. He pulled himself back upright and snatched his drink off of the counter and drained the rest of it like water. He set the glass back down clumsily and looked back to Oswald, "Fantasy told me, among other things," he slurred and he started to tip in his seat again but steadied himself against the bar, "that I should trust you," his red face darkened as he thought about his words. He shook his head once and he scowled, "I still don't."

"You don't have to trust me to listen to me," Oswald suggested tentatively, "I don't know what's going on but something isn't right."

"So why did you come to me?" Ramif asked, his dark eyes burrowing through the air.

"I don't know how to find anyone else," Oswald answered honestly.

He thought about this for a moment and a familiar sunken expression set into the lines of his face as an anger darkened glower, "Because I drink every night?" he asked dangerously, and he leaned forward in his seat. A few people sitting nearby got up and moved at the tone in his voice, "Do you know why? Do you have any idea what I have to do to sleep at night?" his hands clenched and his posture tensed.

Oswald shook his head fervently, "No, that isn't it, it's just that you were already here and no one else came in tonight and I thought that—"

"That you could get a rile out of me? That you could push me around and get me to jump through your hoops?" Ramif snapped poking Oswald sharply in the chest as he leaned further forward, "You want me to believe your little story so you can show me up again. Make a fool out of me when you can?"

"No," Oswald insisted, touching the place on his chest and getting up from the stool, uncomfortable with the distance between them as Ramif continued to inch in closer.

Ramif slid down off of his stool and grabbed a fistful of Oswald's shirt and pulled him down to meet his gaze, "You don't even know what the problem is. You just have a *feeling*. 'Something' is wrong... That feeling doesn't go away. I drink, because I want to forget... but it *never really* goes away, does it?" he pulled Oswald in closer, his breath sick with liquor.

"I don't know," Oswald mumbled.

"You don't know do you?" he barked, spraying Oswald with saliva and takwa through his fury, "You just want people to think you're more than the worthless bastard child that you are."

"I wanted to know what you thought," Oswald said desperately, trying to back out of his iron grip, "to know if you knew about anything weird going on."

"You don't even know what you are asking for!" he shouted, "You just wanted to piss me off!"

"I just wanted to ask for your help," Oswald said defensively, as he turned his head away from the heavy stench of alcohol and fought against Ramif's strength, "that's all, I swear!"

"Help with what?!" Ramif yelled.

There was a shift in the shadows outside of the tavern's window and Ramif snapped his head up. He let go of Oswald's shirt and looked suddenly like a wolf, his attention perked. He turned around and slowly slid his attention from one window to another.

Oswald opened his mouth to say something and Ramif smacked his hand across Oswald's mouth and held it there as he listened intently through the rustle of the room. His eyes caught another glimpse of something outside and his demeanor sobered up instantly. No one else seemed to notice the movement but Ramif dropped his hand from Oswald's mouth and walked forward with a sudden surprising steadiness to his steps. He made his way to the other end of the tavern and stood to the side of one of the rear windows as he looked out through the darkness.

His drink reddened face suddenly paled. He moved quickly, the rest of the patrons of the bar looked around confused as he swiftly cut his way back to the bar.

"The back door," Ramif demanded at Mill. The man's skinny face looked concerned at Ramif's sudden change in demeanor and he pointed behind himself into the kitchen. Ramif grabbed a seam of Oswald's shirt and pulled him along through the maze of pit fires and countertops until they reached the back exit.

He cracked the door open and took a quick survey of the alleyway. He gestured for Oswald to follow him and they slid out into the dark, not bothering to shut the door, afraid to make any noise.

Oswald followed Ramif through a maze of alleys with no clue exactly where they were or where they were headed. They made a few sharp turns, stopping occasionally and listening around in the darkness.

After a while they came to a stop at an ironwood home with stone corners and high windows. Ramif led him around to one of the rear walls of the building. He made a gesture for Oswald to tap on the window and then touched his finger against the wood sharply and repeated the pattern a few times.

Oswald reached up to the window and tapped the pattern that Ramif kept repeating against the wall. He stopped when Ramif held out an opened hand and looked around sharply as he tried to see through the darkness. After a few stilled breaths they heard something from inside and Ramif waved his hand moving around the building to the front door, which was now unlocked.

The two of them slid into the home through the shadow. A sharp spark of light startled Oswald before it was followed by the soft glow of a candle. The light flickered anxiously against General Armond's face as he pulled the door shut behind them and bolted the lock. He was wearing shorts but no shirt and looked as though he had just thrown himself out of the bed.

He looked at the two of them sternly and then fixed his eyes on Ramif, "What's going on? Another raid?"

"No," Ramif said, "I don't know what it is yet. There's something in the city."

"Something?" Armond asked, his brow drawn down perplexed and he looked over to Oswald for clarification.

"I don't know what," Oswald admitted, "but something doesn't feel right."

"It's nothing friendly," Ramif said certainly.

Armond frowned and looked back to Ramif with annoyance, "You're staggering drunk."

Ramif scowled, "Which doesn't mean that I didn't see it."

"Then what is it?" Armond asked impatiently, "It's not an animal?"

"No," Ramif said confidently.

"Then what?"

"I'm drunk," Ramif confessed, with hesitation in his voice, "It might have been a Marka looking for something to eat... but it looked more like..." he shook his head, his braided beard swaying in the dark, "It looked like a Grimm."

Armond's frown deepened, "Now I'm sure you're drunk. Why would a Grimm come here?"

Ramif took in a deep breath and glanced around Armond into the house, "You tell me."

Armond stopped as if frozen and took in a very shallow breath. He turned his head back towards the rear room of his home concern doubling up over his frustration, "You don't think it's here for Samuel?"

"How would I know?" Ramif said quietly.

"If it is a Grimm," Oswald interjected under his breath, "What can we do about it?"

"Not much," Armond said distantly. He shoved the candle into Ramif's hands who quickly pulled it away from his body, stroking his alcohol soaked beard nervously.

Armond vanished into the back of the house and there was a shuffle, a muffled voice and the sound of an opened door.

Armond walked back into the candle light with Samuel on his heels, rubbing sleep out of his eyes and looking confused. Armond took the familiar green bag off of his shoulder and tried to set it quietly on the floor. He took a second bag from around his back and set it alongside of the first. He knelt down and unzipped both bags which were filled with armor and swords.

Oswald caught glimpse of his red blade through the green canvas bag and stooped down, sliding it quietly out of its hiding place and strapping the sheath around his waist. He watched Armond pull out a sharp looking silver gauntlet and slide it over his left hand to take up his usual sword in the right, not bothering with the scabbard at all. Samuel picked up a sword still trying to shake himself awake, rubbing at his face occasionally.

Ramif took his pick of what was left, drawing out a short sword and standing remarkably steady on his feet. They stood still in the semi darkness, Samuel just now awake enough to form real sentences, "So what is going on?" he muttered.

He was answered by a hard solid impact to the roof of the building. Everyone flinched at the sound and watched the place on the ceiling as a heavy scraping sound slid its way along the boards. A loud snort rattled in the air. A sudden roll of smoke seeped through the boards of the roofing and the intense stench of ammonia mingled with it as it plumed into the house.

"It is a Grimm…" Ramif whispered, recognizing the stench following them.

"Outside!" Armond said sharply, shoving his son towards the door. Oswald unlatched the bolt and threw the door wide as the dark shadow of bones, spines, and blackened girth slid through the solid ceiling and landed with a heavy thud on the floor behind them. They raced out the door at each other's heels and slid out into the alleyway, racing out to the open road.

A deep unnatural rocky laugh echoed out after them.

They reached the open space of the main road and slid to a halt in the gravel as the rolling smoke merged in front of them. The city faded through the black haze and they backed up and whipped around, each trying to see the source through the smoke. Slowly they turned back to back and stared through the dark. They watched the darkness carefully and listened to the rolling cackle as it moved around them in all directions.

A shadow in the darkness moved and both Oswald and Ramif spotted the motion. They watched the spot closely for any movement, the smoke and darkness burning their eyes as they refused to blink or turn away from the place in the alley nearby.

The Grimm flexed its talons against the alleyway, quietly surveying the group. Its charred skin catching the darkness and clouding itself in a soft smoke as it shifted silently around to the other side of the tight circle, "There you are," it whispered ethereally, sending its voice around the group, pleased by the confusion it caused. It slid through the night, nearly invisible through the shifting shadow.

Oswald drew his sword from its scabbard, listening to its soft ring as it was freed. He held tight to the hilt and felt the deep warmth of it and the gentle tingle of magic as it gathered in his fingertips. His skin crawled and he tore his eyes away from the alleyway, instinctively finding a new place to watch. He looked back over his shoulder and could almost feel it moving, but he couldn't see anything.

After a few heavy breaths he spotted a place behind him where the smoke seemed thicker and a slow and subtle movement grabbed his attention.

It was standing down the street directly in front of Samuel, completely unseen in the center of the road through its smoky shroud.

Its yellow eyes caught the dim glow of the sliver of moonlight above, but only for an instant before they were swallowed up by the shadows.

Sure that he had spotted it Oswald turned his back on the alleyway he had been watching, and leaned in between Armond and Samuel, "It's right there," he said, as he pointed a finger between them and out to the street ahead. He didn't dare take his eyes off of the place he had seen it and he saw it move again in confirmation.

"Where?" Armond asked, trying to follow Oswald's pointed finger into the distance.

"Two houses down," Oswald whispered. The Grimm arched its barbed back, and this time Samuel saw it catch the light. Samuel started breathing irregularly, his grip clenching on the hilt of his sword. He spun his sword to the ready, loosening his shoulders and bracing himself.

"Hmmm," the Grimm let out a breath of smoke and stepped forward further into the street, "sharp eyes," it chuckled deeply again, not bothering to hide for the moment.

All four of them stepped out, each finding enough space to keep the beast at bay and watching its moves through the disorienting smoke. Oswald felt the sword heat suddenly and he tightened his grip.

The Grimm lowered itself closer to the ground and turned its head to stare at each of them in turn, "What a meal..." it taunted with a rocky laugh, "You aren't as hard to find as I thought you would be."

No one answered it. They stared at it, suddenly feeling the bitter cold of the night biting at their skin as they waited for it to move. It bared its teeth and growled as it looked them over, its yellow eyes stopping on Armond.

Ramif saw it turn its head turn away from him for an instant and he ran forward confidently, bringing his blade up across his body and braced. He arced the blade expertly as the Grimm turned its attention back to him with the snap of its head. Ramif's blade hit the beast in the side of its chest, slicing through air and cutting out from between the Grimm's eyes with a billow of black smoke. He regained control of the sword's swing with his eyes wide in surprise when his blade met no resistance as it passed through the Grimm.

The Grimm smirked, its yellow eyes cruel in the night. It swung an arm with precision and speed and wrapped its talons around Ramif's forearm squeezing it tight as it ripped the sword from his vicelike grip with its other hand. It threw the sword into the street behind them, breaking the air with the sharp sound of metal and stone. It brought its blackened face down close to Ramif's, bearing down harder on his trapped arm, "Nice try."

Ramif gritted his teeth, trying not to scream, as he felt the bones in his arm begin to bend against the pressure of its grip. It grinned and gripped down harder on his arm until something inside the meat of his arm popped wetly. Ramif's eyes widened and he grunted deeply and he took in a sharp breath through his clenched teeth.

It laughed and slowly sank a long burnt talon deep into the soft underside of his forearm. Ramif felt a sick wave sink into his body and a bitter cold seep into his core. The Grimm's venom slid into him, burning through his veins and washing out his eyes, blinding him from reality, fogging his head and sending him plunging into darkness.

The Grimm felt a forceful grip pull down at its barbed back and it let go of Ramif, dropping him to the street. Another forceful tug on its spiked back unbalanced it and it hit the ground awkwardly, pulled over onto its side. It kicked hard at the ground and was up in an instant and plumes of bitter smoke rolled out of its open mouth. It rounded angrily on Armond, its eyes landing on the silver gauntlet a loathing and lustful glint in its eyes, "You have it," it growled and launched forward viciously, careful to keep clear of the gauntlet.

It rushed forward and slammed into Armond's chest with the back of its arm. The force of the impact picked Armond up off of the ground and sent him rolling, head over heels, down the road.

Armond hit the street and his body rolled, scraping against the gravel as he tumbled. He felt the back of his head smack the wall of the alleyway and he came to a sudden stop, his head throbbing and his body slow to respond. His chest ached and a fire burned somewhere in his bones. He tried to fight his way clumsily to his feet and his balance failed and he pitched forward into the ground. He deliberately took in a few deep, slow, breaths and looked up into the smoke.

"Enough games," The Grimm roared and rounded back on Oswald and Samuel. It took a bounding leap as it dove forward and Samuel took a swing at it, his sword arced expertly and cut through air and smoke. Samuel dropped to all fours mid-swing and rolled under the Grimm quickly as its clawed back feet grazed his hair as it jumped over him.

The Grimm payed him no attention and focused in on its prey. It dug its back feet into the street, lengthening its stride and it cleared the distance to Oswald, its talons and clawed hind feet clicking against the stone.

Oswald's heart leapt up into his throat and he readjusted his grip and firmly placed his footing to the ground. The sword sent a sharp jolt through his body and Oswald swung the blade impulsively to defend himself. The blade made solid contact with the beast and it was thrown to one side of him.

The Grimm slid to a halt breathing heavily, pouring smoke and weeping a clear fluid from a gash at its shoulder, the fluid from its body caught the light in the faint shimmer of the moon. It looked down at its shoulder enraged, its yellow eyes coming back up to Oswald angrily. It roared and kicked up from the ground and leapt high into the air, flying over Oswald's head and it landed behind him.

Oswald spun around with his sword up defensively, catching a talon as it grazed passed his face, shocked at the speed at which the creature moved. He hooked the limb away from him and made another block as it swung with its other arm. He struggled to keep his footing as he was forced back, the impossible swings now shrouded in heavy smoke and darkness.

The blade sent another jolt through him and he responded to the sword, an understanding beginning to develop between himself and the magic.

He ducked and swung low, blindly into the smoke, trusting the blade. It swung clear through air the first swing but he felt a breeze cut next to his left ear as he had ducked to make the strike. He felt the magic push him to stand and made the second swing in the smoky blackness.

The second swing made contact again and this time it shrieked and Oswald felt the blade drag against bone, throwing the Grimm back to the ground where it rolled into the moonlit street. The Grimm was pluming smoke and grasping at the side of its heaving chest. Its charred body shuddered as it turned back to Oswald, its teeth bared with renewed hatred boiling in its blood.

It crouched low panting, its eyes now on the red blade.

Oswald held the sword, drawing the magic inward to himself and waiting for the beast to move. He saw a sudden movement and the glint of silver.

Armond ran around its side and jumped up, reaching with his gauntlet and caught flesh. He dug the silver fingers of the gauntlet deep into a solid grip on the back of its neck and pulled it down with all his strength.

Startled, the Grimm was pulled off balance, its face hitting the ground with a roar. Oswald ran forward as he saw Armond throw his weight against the charcoal giant and wrap his body around its throat. The silver gauntlet gripped the blackened flesh beneath him and held him against its body. The Grimm tried to roll, its long talons reaching out to tear Armond off of it.

Oswald saw an opening as its arm came up over its head and taking the sword in both hands he flipped the blade downward and drove it into its chest at an angle, the red blade sinking into the dark mass. Clear fluid began to pool beneath it as it made a clunky growl.

The Grimm arched its body against the ground and tried to take another weak and slow slash at the air before it let out a final smoky breath and stilled. Oswald and Armond looked at each other, both winded as their breath rose into the cold air.

Oswald grabbed the hilt of his sword and pulled it out of the Grimm's body, half expecting it to turn at him fiercely with its yellow eyes burning. He shook the sword and watery drips slid off the end of the blade. He slid it into his scabbard and looked back to the charred body and stared at it. It didn't move.

A very shaken and disturbed voice called through the darkness, "Is it dead?"

"I think it is," Armond answered, panting heavily and sounding surprised. He reached around his bare chest and held a black and purple bruise that expanded across his lower right side. He bent over the Grimm's charred face and stared into its yellow eyes, reflecting the sliver of moonlight in a way that made the world look glassy and distant. He put a hand at its neck, carefully avoiding its curled talons, and he tried to feel anything that would resemble life. It didn't move and he shook his head disbelievingly, "It's dead."

"Then I need help," Samuel said desperately, his voice cracking with a tone that made Armond go sheet white through the darkness, and made Oswald's stomach turn.

Chapter Twenty-Three

They ran through the darkness to where Samuel sat doubled over in the road.

Armond threw his sword aside, dropping the gauntlet as he fell to his knees beside him, "Son, what's wrong?" his voice broke anxiously, "Are you hurt?"

"No... I don't know what to do," Samuel said, on the verge of tears, his young face looking down beside him in horror.

Ramif lay on his back in the gravel beside him convulsing forcibly, his every muscle locking up every second or so, twisting his frame unnaturally and rolling his head into the road as his back arched angrily. His eyes were slid back into his head and a thick foam was building up at the corner of his mouth as he struggled to take in breaths through the seizure. He gasped wetly and shuddered.

The open wound on his forearm was black and deep, his veins standing up nearly out of his skin in a spider pattern, reaching outward from the puncture. Poisoned blood rolled out of his arm and over his convulsing body.

"Move," Armond commanded sharply. He slid up next to Ramif and rolled him onto his side, supporting his head with one hand and putting pressure on the wound with the other. Ramif continued to convulse against the ground but was able to take in a garbled breath as the foam slid out of his mouth and into the road, "Ramif, breathe," he demanded, "Take a breath!"

A deep rumbling sound rattled in Ramif's chest as he tried to take in a full breath, unable to breathe in more than a short spurt. He convulsed against the ground more violently and Armond let go of the wounded arm to try and protect his head from the rocky street. His tremors slowed as he fought for another ragged breath, his gut contracting and throwing up a foamy pool of blood-laced vomit onto the ground next to him.

Armond turned him further onto his side and felt the icy sweat drenching his body, "He's too cold," Armond said tensely, "we need to get him inside."

Ramif gasped for another breath, his eyes rolling deeper

into his head as his body arched back into the street, his chest rising up off the ground with a shudder as his arms flexed involuntarily.

"Help me get him back to the house," Armond ordered.

Oswald grabbed Ramif's legs and tried to get a good grip through the sharp seizures that were often taking ahold of him. Armond wrapped his arms around his torso, "Samuel hold his head up."

The three of them lifted Ramif up out of the street, surprised by the heavy weight of him despite his height.

They fought to keep ahold of him as he jerked in their arms occasionally as they made their way back down the alley to Armond's house. They came through the open front door into the overwhelming darkness of the home.

Oswald walked blindly forward through the building as Samuel and Armond led the way. They staggered back through another doorway and stopped.

"Set him here," Armond said, moving to the side and lowering him through the darkness. Oswald felt the soft cushion of a bed as he bent down slowly and let go of Ramif's legs, "Get a candle."

Samuel's clumsy steps staggered out of the room and back towards the front of the house.

Oswald felt a wild spasm kick him in the chest and he quickly put a hand up to try and keep Ramif from falling off of the bed through his tremors. Armond's arm knocked into his in the dark and it was clear that they were both thinking along the same lines. They heard him take in another difficult and ragged breath and they suddenly felt his body heave again beneath their supporting hands.

Armond moved suddenly and tried to support him better through the darkness until a trembling circle of light made its way into the room.

"Is that the only one you could find?" Armond asked, reaching out and taking the light from Samuel's trembling hands.

"I — I didn't — I," he stammered, his pale face gaunt in the candlelight. Visibly shaken, he stood frozen with his eyes wide and glassy.

"That's fine," Armond assured him gently and turned away from him. He leaned over the bed and looked into Ramif's pale and sweaty face, his eyes now shut in the dim light. He looked as sick as death but his tremors had slowed down to the occasional twitch.

Armond brought the candle down to his middle and surveyed the wide puncture wound and the unnatural bend in the center of his forearm. The spider like veins and sticky black poison deep in the wound stood out in the candlelight, an oily reflection that blended worryingly with the steady flow of blood.

"C—can I do anything??" Samuel whispered with a shudder.

"Find another candle," Armond said gently, "if you can."

"Wait," Oswald said, as an idea began to form, "we need to draw a bath," he suddenly felt driven, assured by the thought.

"We need more light," Armond insisted, confused by Oswald's outburst.

"No, I have an idea and we need to move faster than that poison," Oswald said sharply, and he sprang up to his feet.

"W-what should I do?" Samuel asked, unsure which order to follow.

"Is there a tub here?" Oswald asked.

"Yes…" Samuel said quietly, his hands shaking.

"Show me where," Oswald said firmly, and gave Armond what he hoped was a reassuring look as he followed Samuel out of the room through the darkened house and into another room nearby.

He reached blindly through the dark and felt the edge of the tub and followed it until he found the pipe and twisted the metal gear that closed the plug. After he heard the resounding clunk of the drain closing, he reached through the darkness with his fingers and found the grooved lever of the pump. He gripped the lever and immediately started pumping the water, putting all of his effort into filling the bath. After a few hard pulls on the lever he heard the water begin to flow into the empty bath.

"Go help your father move him in here," Oswald said, to the darkness behind him where he hoped Samuel still stood, "He needs to be in the water."

He heard footsteps turn from the room over the rush of water and the irony scent of it heating in the copper tub.

He felt the metal of the pump get hot as he heard the flow of water continue to rush into the tub, the flow of water into water churning as the level rose. He pumped at the well more forcefully listening to the heavy outpour and could feel the steam coming off the hot water. His hand slipped on the handle and he recovered quickly, trying to keep the momentum of the pump moving. Oswald heard the sound of heavy footsteps as Ramif was brought into the room.

Oswald moved out of the way and grabbed Ramif's head, supporting it as they lowered his now limp and cold body into the tub. The water level rose up to envelop him comfortingly. Oswald felt the water level stop at his chest and held his head steady against the rim of the tub.

"The water's hot," Samuel said, confused as he set Ramif's legs into the bath and pulled his dripping hands out of the tub.

"Now get the candle," Oswald said, ignoring the silent question and feeling more confident about his plan by the second, "and Armond, come and keep his head out of the water."

Armond obeyed apprehensively as he moved over in the dark and took over Oswald's place in the room. The soft rim of light passed closer in the hallway as Samuel came back with the candle, and lit the room with the shaky orange glow of the tiny flame.

Oswald stood at the side of the tub and grabbed the hilt of his sword. He drew the blade free of its scabbard and the ringing of metal caught Armond's attention instantly with a stare that could have stopped a dragon in its place.

"Trust me," Oswald pleaded quietly, meeting Armond's eyes and trying to loosen his posture encouragingly He bent over the tub and tried to see in the dim light. He reached a hand into the tub and disturbed the now bloody ribbon that streamed through the water as he grabbed ahold of Ramif's arm.

The bones moved unnaturally beneath his skin and the open wound looked as though it had expanded further in the few short minutes that Oswald had taken to fill the bath.

Oswald looked at the edge of his sword and saw the faint shimmer of the Grimm's watery blood still clinging to the red blade.

He swallowed hard and wondered whether its blood would work against the poison. He wondered too if he had enough magic to draw the poison from the wound if he had to, or even if he could. The doubt faded quickly with the intensifying heat of his sword in his hand and he knew he had to act quickly. His anxieties faded and he took in a calm breath.

He held up his sword and laid the face of the blade against the blackened hole torn into the arm and he quickly drug it down its full length hearing the sizzle of blistering skin and the stench of blood and burns as the Grimm's watery blood burned with the wound. Ramif seized involuntarily and fought for a breath.

Oswald looked up into Ramif's face, the distorted and sickly colored skin creasing in the twisted and pained expression in his aged face. He gently lowered the arm back into the water and he closed his eyes in concentration. He submerged his sword and both hands into the bloody hot water of the tub and he keept one hand on the hilt and the other against the wound.

He felt the tingling jolt of magic from the sword spill out into the water in sharp waves. Clenching his jaw, he felt the depth of the puncture and put pressure on the wound with his thumb. Oswald opened his eyes and watched as the black oily poison began to separate from the blood and it started to drift along the water's surface. He pressed harder on the open flesh and watched with renewed energy as more of the poison was drawn out into the water.

Ramif suddenly took in a clearer breath and began to tremble softly, his body too weak to convulse. Armond steadied his head and watched with rapt attention as the poison began to ooze out of the burn in small rivulets.

Oswald gripped the arm tighter and felt sick and sorry as he felt the bones shift again under his fingers, but he was encouraged by another gush of venom that rose lazily to the water's surface.

He worked on the wound, his concentration unbroken by the movement of the candle's glow or by the occasional twitch or jerk of Ramif's arm. He felt the water electrify with another wave of magic and he felt his energy fall away from him, suddenly drug down by the weight of the night.

Oswald watched as the last of the poison seeped from the wound and saw that the veins around it had settled back into his arm. The wound was dark and deep but had lost the black necrotic hue that it had a short while ago. He looked at the surface of the water which glistened black with the odd greasy reflection in the candlelight. He gently put the arm back into the hot water of the tub and let it rest against his body comfortably.

He breathed heavily, suddenly acutely aware of his exhaustion as he removed his sword from the tub and let it clatter softly to the floor, splashing water around it in a black and bloody ring. He grabbed the rim of the tub and turned around and he felt his knees weaken.

He slid down the side of the tub and sat on the floor next to his sword, his body aching numbly.

He panted against the tub and looked down at his hands, which were coated in venom, dirt, and blood. He sighed tiredly and took off his shirt as he sat on the floor, too tired to stand, and wiped the water and poison from his arms, unsure of what it might do if he left it there.

He turned his head back to Ramif wearily and lifted his eyes up to Armond's unreadable face, "We should get him out of the poison and get him cleaned up."

Armond and Samuel both stared at him quietly and neither moved.

Ramif shifted his body in the water and his voice grumbled something inaudible before he took in a full, clear, breath and slipping back out of consciousness.

Oswald looked up, his head feeling heavy and his body sore. He let out an exasperated breath when no one moved and he turned over onto his knees and then pushed himself back into a standing position. He picked up his already ruined shirt and tried to sweep the poison to one side of the tub as best as he could, soaking it into the cloth.

Armond reached in under Ramif's arms and lifted him out of the water where Oswald had cleared it of the poisonous coating, his clothes dripping bloody water onto the floor as he was pulled from the tub. He laid him down carefully in the middle of the bathroom floor and Samuel set down the candle and started pulling towels down off of a shelf nearby.

When Ramif was stripped dry and put into a clean set of clothes, they moved him back to the other bed again, which had needed fresh linens and another blanket.

Ramif was still pale and shaking lightly, but no longer having seizures. He was still cold to the touch and breathing quickly, but his breaths were now full and unlabored against the soft bed.

Armond looked down at his arm one more time and shook his head, thinking deeply about something serious. He frowned, "I need to set the bone before it swells up any more," he mumbled and grabbed Ramif's wrist and turned the arm as he tried to find the exact place of the break, "I'm going to need bandages and a splint." He looked up at Samuel who had already turned around and was rummaging around through drawers.

Armond got a vice grip on Ramif's wrist and took ahold of his upper arm near the elbow joint, "Hold him down," he said, looking at Oswald.

Oswald walked around the bed, suddenly unsure about the whole process. He put his hands on Ramif's shoulders and put a little weight against him. "More," Armond said firmly, and Oswald bent low, putting his forearms linked across his chest and pressed him hard into the bed. "Good, now just keep your chin clear in case he lifts his head up," Armond said, as he readjusted his grip on Ramif's wrist. Oswald tried to put distance between himself and Ramif but the position left little room for movement.

Armond took two quick sharp breaths, getting himself ready, and pulled suddenly against his wrist and pushed against his joint at the elbow. He continued to put more strength into the movement and Ramif's eyes shot open in shock. Suddenly the bones popped at the midpoint of his arm and Ramif opened his mouth wide and howled, his body tensing up reflexively. He let out another deep and rapid breath and fell back into unconsciousness.

Samuel rushed back into the room at the sudden scream, his hands full of bandages and four pine splints.

Armond held the arm in place as Samuel slid two pine slabs on either side of the break and they wrapped the arm as tightly as they could. The cotton mesh pulled the ironwood slabs taut against the newly set bone and covered the cauterized puncture wound. They secured the wrapping around his arm with a long pin and let his arm lay back onto the bed before they pulled the covers up over his limp shoulders.

"Just let him rest," Armond said tiredly, and he looked back towards Samuel and added, "You should rest too."

"I don't know if I can," Samuel said anxiously, looking at Ramif, "Is he going to be okay now?"

Armond looked back at Ramif's pale face and studied his

even breathing for a minute, "I think so. There isn't a whole lot more we can do for him right now. You should get some sleep, it's getting close to dawn."

"I don't want to just leave him there," Samuel said, as he watched Ramif.

"I'll watch over him," Armond promised, "Go to bed."

Samuel looked at them and nodded worriedly, "I'll try," he said, and shuffled towards the edge of the room anxiously, "You'll wake me up if something changes?"

"I will," Armond said reassuringly, and Samuel continued nodding to himself distantly as he wandered off back into the back room of the house. Armond looked at Oswald, "You should rest too. We can talk in the morning."

"At dawn?" Oswald asked.

"If that's what you want."

He nodded, "I need to get to the shop fairly early. I promised a woman I would finish her shoes by the afternoon."

Armond looked at him as if trying to decipher a puzzle, "That's really what you are worried about right now?"

"She really needs them…" Oswald said, and shrugged resignedly, "Besides, it's the only thing right now that I can do anything about. I can only try."

Armond looked at Oswald and crumpled his forehead in disbelief, "What more do you think that you could you do?"

"I don't know, but if I knew, I would," Oswald said, scratching the back of his head and trying to think of anything through the sleepy fog.

"You've done more than I thought was even possible," Armond said, watching him closely with narrowed eyes, "Grimm venom is supposed to be fatal within a couple of hours."

"You knew he was dying?" Oswald asked.

"Until you intervened…" Armond paused, and shook his head slowly, "I was sure that he would. I just wanted him to be in a home with friends instead of in the street," his frown deepened and he looked at Ramif attentively, "I don't know what you did exactly, but I'm grateful."

"I only did what felt right at the time," Oswald said uncomfortably.

"You did more than that," he said, looking at Oswald with an intense blue gaze that burned knowingly through the flicker of the candlelight.

Oswald took in a slow breath and tried to press away the worry and drug his eyes to the floor, refusing to make eye contact with Armond again. He swallowed hard and watched the dancing orange shadow that the flame cast on the grains of wood at his feet.

"Last I knew, elves couldn't use magic," Armond said softly.

Oswald looked at the candle and into its yellow fire, "I had to. It was the only thing that I could think of," Oswald rubbed his hands together uncomfortably, "I didn't know it was magic until recently."

The two of them sat quietly on the floor beside the bed for a while before Armond shook his head thoughtfully, seeming to make a silent decision and he said in conclusion to his own thoughts, "no one else has to know about it right now."

"I was told it's something that I've always had," Oswald mumbled quietly.

"And he's alive because of it," Armond said, and the deeper lines of his face softened, "He's a good friend of mine and he has been for a very long time."

Oswald dared to glance over to Armond curiously, "But you won't tell him about the magic?"

"No," Armond said, still slowly piecing together the night's events, "no one has to know," he repeated, "at least not right now," he looked at him, his blond hair and blue eyes catching in the firelight, "but he'll know what you did for him. I'll make sure of that."

"You don't have to," Oswald said dismissively, with a shake of his head, "It might just make him angry."

"You'd be surprised by his sense of honor," he said seriously, "he's really nothing like what you've seen of him so far," he readjusted himself against the floor and added quietly, "When he's sober."

"I know that," Oswald said, and looked at Ramif. His face fell with concern as he saw him jerk sharply under the blanket, "He and I might not get along very well, but I'll still do what I can to help him. If you think of anything I can do or if you need anything, let me know will you?"

"Why?" Armond asked, cautiously.

"Because he's a good man," Oswald said flatly, echoing back what others had told him, remembering the fleeting and genuine, beady eyed, smile and seeing for a brief moment the man behind it, "And it's the right thing to do."

"Then I will. Get some sleep," Armond said, "You won't get much rest if you don't."

Oswald felt a hand on his shoulder and it gave him a gentle shake. He took in a deep breath and picked his head up off of the floor, his eyes blurry with sleep and his bones heavy and stiff to move. He pushed himself back until he was sitting up and looked around the room with the faint glimmer of morning light shining in from the high window.

Ramif still lay in the bed on the other side of the room, unmoving. His breathing was rapid and his eyes were still closed.

Armond bent down next to Oswald and held out a glass of cold water and a biscuit.

"Thanks," Oswald said, taking them both and getting a real look at Armond since the attack. He was still wearing his shorts from the night and hadn't bothered to put on a shirt yet. His body was covered in bruises and a large portion of his right side and chest was swollen, purple, black, and red. He seemed to be guarding that side when he moved and was taking shallow breaths. Oswald suspected that several ribs were broken, though Armond showed very few signs that he was in pain.

Armond straightened up and turned around, his hair barely hid a wound on the back of his head and it looked clotted and angry. He bent over the bed and looked Ramif over slowly for any subtle change in his appearance. He stood up again and gestured for Oswald to follow him out of the room.

Oswald took a bite of the biscuit and stood up, walking slowly and quietly into the front of the house. The rooms were all well-organized with dressers and shelves keeping everything off of the floor but the chairs themselves. The walls were made of ironwood with stone corners at the edge of every room.

Armond lowered himself carefully into a chair that was turned so that he could still see into the bedroom to check on Ramif. Oswald took his place in the chair across from him and took a drink of the glass of water, realizing that his head ached and wondering how much Armond's must be hurting as well.

Armond shifted in his seat and looked away from the nearby bedroom and back to Oswald, "Can you be honest with me?" he asked bluntly, deep circles pulling down at his usually bright eyes.

"Of course," Oswald said apprehensively, taking another drink of the water.

"Completely?" his eyes burned daringly.

"Yes," Oswald said, setting his biscuit in his lap and sitting upright in his seat, "What's this all about?"

Armond looked at him, carefully studying the lines of his face as he asked, "What are you really?"

Oswald frowned, "What do you mean?"

"I won't tell a soul unless they need to know," he promised, "but I have to know the truth about a few things if I'm the one that is going to continue to train you."

"What kind of things?" he asked hesitantly.

"You are Venhow's son?" Armond asked, interlocking his fingers and resting his elbows on his legs.

"Yes, at least that's what I've been told," Oswald said, "...Fantasy included."

"Okay," Armond said, nonplused by the affirmation and he paused to glance back into the other room, "So you are an elf *and* you have pure wizards blood?"

"I guess so," Oswald said slowly.

"So you can do magic," Armond said, half asking, half stating his thoughts.

"Yes..."

Armond looked at him seriously, his eyebrows drawn together with a stern gaze, "How often do you use your magic?"

Oswald thought about it and sighed, unsure of the honest answer, "I guess every day."

"On what?"

"Little things," Oswald shrugged, "My work... training, I guess... nothing else specifically."

Armond nodded and fixed his eyes on him, unblinking, as if he were trying to catch a lie, "You use it every day, but can you control it?"

Oswald shifted uncomfortably and shook his head, "Not all of it."

"What do you mean 'not all of it'?" Armond asked, his

eyes narrowing slightly.

Oswald fidgeted with the glass of water in his hands and said carefully, "I have both elven and wizard's magic."

Armond looked him over searching for any sign of deception and found none. An expression crossed his face that looked like he was trying to remember something and he seemed frustrated with the thought he found. He rubbed at his face, feeling his stubbly chin and slid his hand around to the back of his neck and held it thoughtfully, "So, you do have both... I didn't think that was possible. Which one is it that you can't control?"

Oswald felt his cheeks flush slightly, "The elven magic. It's involuntary, instinctual. I can't seem to separate it from daily life, I'm so used to it that I can't identify when I use it."

"But the wizard's magic you can control?" he asked.

"When I have the sword," Oswald confirmed as he rolled the glass of water in his hands, "It's easier to feel wizards magic ... but when I don't have my sword I can't do much. I haven't figured out how to use it on my own yet... or how to stop it once it starts."

Armond looked down at his hands and then back to Oswald as he tried to understand the situation, "Like what?"

"Heating bath water mostly," he said slowly, "I can't seem to control that, it just happens, and sometimes the magic tries to protect me."

"How?"

"Like the feeling I got before the Grimm showed up. Hours before," Oswald said, shuddering lightly at the memory of the odd sensation of it, "That is why I went to Ramif. I couldn't figure out what the feeling was at first."

"You think it was magic?"

"I do now," Oswald said, and took a drink of the water, "but at the time it was just — odd."

Armond thought this over for a minute and nodded, "I don't think you should be without your sword anymore," he pointed back to the bathroom, "Make sure you have it with you when you leave. I didn't move it."

"Alright," Oswald said, trying to figure out the purpose of the conversation.

"One last thing," Armond said, his voice sharp, "It became very clear after a while that the Grimm was after you. Why?"

"I don't know," Oswald said honestly, locking eyes with Armond and holding his gaze.

Armond nodded and quietly accepted the answer as he looked back into the bedroom where Ramif lay and hadn't moved. "Alright," he got up from his chair with a faint wince, "Thank you for being honest," he sighed lightly and held his side briefly, "And I hope you understand if I don't train you for a couple of weeks."

"Your ribs are broken then?" Oswald said, concerned.

"They are," he said, "but if you need to keep training on schedule I'm sure that General Loch would be able to take over for me."

Oswald looked over curiously, "Is he really as good with a sword as everyone says?"

Armond's face split into a sudden smile and he raised an eyebrow, "You haven't gotten to see him yet?"

"No, I haven't," Oswald said, with interest.

He smiled softly, "Then you should definitely talk to him about training. I could be there but someone has to take care of Ramif until he's well."

"Doesn't he have a son?" Oswald asked.

"Isaiah," Armond said, his smile fading grimly, "and I'll have to send Samuel to bring him here. He isn't quite old enough to be on his own yet."

Oswald turned around to look into the bedroom, where Ramif lay still, "What are you going to tell him?"

"The truth," Armond said obviously, "at least what he needs to know of it."

Oswald watched as Ramif jerked harshly beneath the covers and lay still again, "Will he be okay seeing his father like that?"

"He's the son of a general," he said darkly, drawing his eyes towards the back of the house where Samuel slept, "I don't know if he'll be okay with it, but he'll understand. He knows that he's safe here."

Oswald set the glass of water down on the floor next to his chair and picked up the biscuit in his lap, "I assume you'll be here for a while then."

Armond nodded, "You're welcome to drop by if you need to."

"Or if you need anything," Oswald insisted.

"I'll find you," he agreed confidently, "There's an outfit of yours here from Bolzar's. I sent the neighbor out to find him and he came early. Now get dressed and go make that girl her shoes."

"Yes sir," Oswald said, with a tired half-smile, "And thank you." He got up and walked into the back of the house to retrieve his sword and scabbard from the floor.

Chapter Twenty-Four

Oswald thumped on the end of the punch, pitting the stitching holes around the lip of the vamp so he could pull the pieces together easier. The repetitive sound drew out the rest of the noise of the market which roared with rumors and fear. He was happy to hear the repeating thump beat out onto the table.

He moved to the next piece and continued rolling the leather and punching the stitching holes. He set down the punch and switched to a larger gauge. He picked up the pieces of facing and beat hard on the end of the handle to make deep holes for the eyelets. He finished punching the holes and put his tools aside.

He fished around for the threading and worked his hands into the container of needles and picked out a hooked needle with a narrow eye. He worked the stitching and watched the shape of the shoe come together with every bind and knot. He slid deeper into the focus on his work and the hours fell away to mid-day.

He set the finished silver fox hide shoes behind him on the counter and picked up the next order, checked his shorthand markings on the softened hide and picked up the blade. The blade slid across the leather as he cut out the sole, quarter, and tongue as well as their sister pieces that mirrored against the other shoe. He set them on the table and switched over to the new strip of hide.

He jumped when he heard his name, surprised by how close the voice was before he had noticed that anyone was there. He set down the blade he was working with and turned in his chair.

He looked up and saw Samuel, his black hair clean and combed with fresh clothes and dark tired circles under his teenaged blue eyes.

"Is everything alright?" Oswald asked, startled by his sudden appearance.

"Yes and no," Samuel said, shifting his eyes around the tent, "Dad said you know a lot about herbs?"

Oswald paused, "What do you need? What's wrong?"

Samuel looked stressed and tired but stood up straight, glancing at Matrim who was coated in various stains and leather fibers and then back to Oswald. He worked his narrow mouth with a put upon kind of sigh, "He's sick again, he's not as bad as he was… but he's in bad shape."

"What does he need?" Oswald asked, and stood up from his seat and grabbed a clean rag off the counter and began to wipe off his hands, trying to remove the stain and fibers.

"He has a fever… and…" Samuel shook his head looking scared for a fleeting second, "He's seeing things."

Oswald looked up, hopefully, "He's awake?"

"Sort of," Samuel said sadly, shoving his hands into his pockets and studying the ground beneath the shop.

"What kind of things is he seeing?" Oswald asked, and set down the rag.

Samuel opened his mouth to talk several times and closed his mouth again, obviously struggling with his words. He glanced over at Matrim again, shuffled his feet with a deepening frown and finally shook his head and threw up a hand despairingly. He turned away from Oswald and began to walk back out of the tent.

Oswald got up quickly, "Wait," he ran forward and grabbed his shoulder gently, "I can help."

Oswald looked over at Matrim, who was listening intently but not daring to ask, and said to him sharply, "Close up shop for me when Laurie picks up her shoes, and don't take any more orders," he took the key out of his pocket and handed it to Matrim.

"Sure…" Matrim said, worriedly, "Is everythin' 'al right?" he took the key slowly and dropped the key into his breast pocket.

"I hope so," Oswald said, walking away from his shop with Samuel.

When they had cut past the market and the crowd had died away, Oswald looked at Samuel who was watching his feet with an intensity that he knew must have been deliberate. They walked a little ways and Oswald looked at him again, "I need to know exactly what's going on to get the right herb."

Samuel took in a shaky breath, "I told you, he has a fever."

"You said he was seeing things," Oswald said, drawing his eyebrows together concernedly, "and what he's seeing does matter."

"Why?" Samuel asked, suddenly angry.

"I just need to know if they are real things or not," Oswald insisted, "Is he seeing people he knows, or is it like griffins made of purple snakes, or… is it something else?"

Samuel frowned and crossed his arms as they walked. He looked down at his feet and mumbled, "No, nothing like that."

"So he's seeing real things? Like flashbacks or—?"

"—Yeah, I guess," Samuel interrupted uncomfortably, and hung his head as he walked.

Oswald nodded, "Okay. When did the fever come on?"

"About an hour or so ago," he said, as he stuffed his hands deeper into his pockets.

Samuel's discomfort with the situation pulled against Oswald's stomach, "I'm sorry he's not doing well," Oswald said.

"Me too," he mumbled.

"You can get back to house to watch over him if you want to," Oswald offered, trying to look Samuel in the eyes, "I'll get what he needs and be there as soon as I can."

"I don't know..." Samuel said, looking up at Oswald in a brief sweep of his reddened eyes, "I want to be there for him, but I don't like not being able to help him through it. I just stand there and watch him suffer. I can't do anything... and it's awful."

Oswald's heart sank, "At least you're there for him."

"It doesn't mean anything if he doesn't know who I am," Samuel said, and he looked away down a nearby alley absently.

"He knows you," Oswald said, reassuringly, "and he'll remember that you were there, even if he doesn't recognize it right now."

"How do you know?" he asked, bitterly, taking his hands out of his pockets and crossing his arms.

"I don't know for sure," Oswald admitted with a gentle shrug, "But if I'm right about what he remembers, then wouldn't you want to be there?"

He thought about it for a while as they walked, staring down at his shoes, "Maybe you're right. I think I should be there anyway," he sighed and looked up at Oswald pleadingly, "Just hurry back to the house," he said, and turned down an alley that curved away in the other direction. He stopped after a few steps and looked back over his shoulder to add, "Please," he unfolded his arms, "And thank you."

They parted ways at the cut in the alley, each losing sight of the other in a matter of a few steps. Oswald went around buildings and walked down the unorganized curvature of the alleyways until he had found his way back around to the apothecary.

The little building was painted sky blue, chipped in places and worn from the rain and weather. Plants hung in the boxed windowsill and drooped over, hardly clinging to life, living off of the gentle warmth of the daylight and struggling to survive the change of the seasons.

The door was shut, but not locked, as he made his way into the shop. The heavy smell of cinnamon, herbs, and spices hit his senses as well as the stifling aroma of dirt and root saps. He cleared his throat and shut the door behind him.

"I'll be right there," a woman's voice called out from behind the counter, back somewhere in the depths of the building. She moved a few things around in the other room nosily before she made her way up to the front entrance.

She was shorter than Oswald, though not by much, with chestnut colored hair and dark eyes. Her dress was long and made of wool that was dyed a rich, dark, purple and was cut to allow movement while accentuating her soft frame. She had a heart shaped face and a contagious smile which she wore proudly, "What can I help you with?"

"A friend of mine is very sick."

"I'm sorry to hear that," she said genuinely, her smile fading away, "do you know what they're sick with?"

Oswald paused and picked his words carefully, "I know that I need dried Willow, Cajeput oil, Alam, and Agave leaves."

She thought about it for a bit and turned around to look through the bottles that lined the cabinet behind her, "A fever from a snake bite?" she guessed.

"Very close," Oswald said, suddenly intrigued, "I think it's as close as I can get anyway."

"So it's not a snake bite?" she said, putting a finger against her lower lip and looking through the vials.

"No, worse," Oswald said grimly.

"It's a poison then?"

"Of sorts," Oswald said, watching her as she rummaged through bottle after bottle on the shelf.

She looked over her shoulder at him with her lip drawn into her mouth as she chewed at it gently in thought, "Then what kind of poison is it?"

"Something you won't have a cure for," Oswald said, shaking his head.

"Try me," she taunted, with a sharp glint in her eyes. She fetched down a couple of glass bottles from the open cabinet and turned back to the counter. She set a few of the bottles down and turned back to the shelf once more.

Oswald shook his head more fervently at her enthusiasm and said in a quiet breath, "It was Grimm venom."

She stopped cold in her task with her fingers lingering on a black bottle, "Oh dear," she withdrew her hand from the cabinet and looked at him mournfully, "I can't help you with that. I should have listened to you. I'm so sorry," she looked flustered, her cheeks glowing a bright pink as she turned back to the cabinet.

"I didn't expect you to," Oswald said, "I'm hoping to help him with the fever and hallucinations until he works it out of his system."

She hesitated and put her hand over her chest thoughtfully, "I've never, in all of the books that I have read, heard of someone surviving the venom," she said sadly, "Please don't get your hopes up too high."

"He didn't get much," Oswald muttered, remembering the thick gleam of oily venom that had been drawn out of the wound. He tried to smile reassuringly but his smile faltered and she looked more uncomfortable. Oswald cleared his throat gently, "I just need the Willow powder, Cajeput oil, Alam and Agave so I can get back to him."

She reached up onto a higher shelf and picked down another bottle, setting four items on the countertop. She looked them over uneasily and she took a key from around her neck and unlocked another cabinet below the counter and pulled out a small black bottle with a white stopper.

She stared at the bottle, "Poppy oil may be more of what he needs now," she said, and tried not to look him in the eye as she set the bottle on the counter with the others that she had gathered.

Oswald's stomach flipped as he watched the tiny bottle slide to a stop beside the others, "You think he's dying," he said, feeling a wave of ice pour over him.

"Are you sure it was a Grimm?" she asked hopefully.

Oswald nodded, and her face slid into a beautiful and deep sadness. She looked at the bottle again and said slowly, "Then yes."

"There has to be something else that I can do," Oswald insisted as he stared at the black bottle.

"Just the poppy oil. It would take away his pain," she promised.

"So would the Willow and the Cajeput."

She shook her head, "It's not the same. He needs the poppy oil if he's as bad as you say."

Oswald pushed the tiny bottle out of the small collection of herbs and oils, "I'm not comfortable with that," he said, "It's too easy to give a man too much."

"He's already passing," she said, her eyes trying to portray her intent, "It will make what time he has left easier..."

"You don't know this man," Oswald said, beginning to get frustrated with her, "He's far too stubborn to die this way."

"Everyone dies," she said, trying to sound comforting.

"Not this way," Oswald said finally, "Do you have what I asked for?"

She nodded sadly and put the little black bottle back into the cabinet and locked the door. She looked around with the tip of her index finger between her teeth, thinking. She held up a hand and turned around into the back of the building. She shuffled around through drawers and glass bottles until she found what she was looking for.

She came back to the front of the shop with another bottle filled with a cloudy liquid. She sighed and set it on the counter, "Please, at least give him this."

"What is it?" he asked suspiciously.

"A mix of clove, and anise," she said, and added with a pleading look in her eyes, "And poppy oil, but it isn't nearly as strong as the pure oil."

Oswald shook his head again and said, "I don't want to give him that."

"Please," she begged, "It isn't strong enough to hurt him. The *entire bottle* wouldn't be too much for a typical man."

"You swear on its strength?" Oswald asked, as he glanced down at the new bottle of white cloudy liquid and considered what it meant.

"Yes," she said, holding it out to him.

He took the vial and rolled it in his fingers, "How much should I give him?"

"How big of a man are we talking about?" she asked.

Oswald put a hand out at the lower level of his chest as a visual, and said, "A dwarf, very fit."

She put her fingertip back into her mouth as she shifted her weight to one foot and chewed on her nail as she thought about it, "Give him a few drops at first, then a spoonful as he needs it."

"Alright," he said, looking back to the other vials and suddenly wondering if he would be able to get Ramif to chew on the Agave leaves or not.

She seemed to catch onto his line of thinking and she walked over to the bottles, putting a couple of them back and swapping them out for much smaller bottles of oils and concentrates, "This should work better," she said, sliding the bottles over to him, "Just a drop of each of the pure oils and a pinch of the willow powder under the tongue ever few hours."

"Thank you," Oswald said, digging out a small handful of coins, "How much do I owe you?"

She looked at the bottles, unsatisfied with the treatment, "Two silvers."

He handed her the coins and she picked up a stack of small paper squares, wrapping each of the bottles so that they wouldn't touch one another. She wrapped the covered bottles in another wrapping to hold them together, and tied it with a short twine.

"I hope he heals as well as you think," she said, handing him the package.

"He will," Oswald said, not giving himself room for doubt.

"My name is Sanna," she said softly, brushing a thin lock of chestnut hair from her face, "If you need anything else," she said, looking down at the locked cabinet, "Just ask."

"I will," Oswald promised, holding the package tightly as he walked out of the shop. He closed the door behind him and turned into the alleyway.

He sped up slowly as the thought of death loomed in his head. He hoped that she was wrong, but the discomfort in him boiled and he broke out into a run as he wove through the city, his heart thundering.

He reached the main road and his eyes caught a black shape burned awkwardly into the street where the Grimm had laid. He stared at it as he ran by and turned his attention into the last narrow path that became a familiar alleyway. He slowed down and tried to catch his breath as he made his way to the ironwood home. He fought to slow and steady his breathing as he gripped the package and knocked on the wooden frame.

Samuel opened the door and looked down at the paper wrapping in his hands hopefully, "Come in," he said, and stepped out of the way to let Oswald by. He closed and then bolted the door behind him.

Oswald looked around the room and quickly spotted a small, black haired child, sitting unhappily in a chair with an uneaten cookie in his lap. He looked up at Oswald with large dark eyes that were puffy and pink.

"Isaiah?" Oswald asked, and the boy nodded shortly. Oswald held up the little brown package and smiled at him warmly, "I have some medicine for your dad. Is that alright?"

"Yeah," the boy said, brightening a little but not moving from his place in the chair. He guessed that the boy must have been close to ten years old, his dwarven frame deceiving against the soft youth of his face.

"Alright then," Oswald said, and made his way back to the bedroom, leaving Samuel to sit with Isaiah.

Armond looked up at him when he walked in and twitched the hint of a smile before it fell back into concern. It must have been close to two days since Armond had gotten any sleep and he looked exhausted. He winced and braced his side firmly as he tried to turn his body in the chair.

"What did you bring?" he asked, glancing at the package in Oswald's hands.

"Something for his fever, something for the effects of the poison and something for pain," Oswald said, stepping closer to the bed.

"And that should help him?" Armond asked.

"I hope so," Oswald said, unwrapping the package and the individual bottles. He set them on the table at the bedside.

Ramif was drenched in sweat and so pale that in certain lights he looked grey in places. Oswald reached out and took off the wet wash cloth from his brow and put the back of his hand across his wet skin and felt an intense radiating heat. He put the cloth back on his head and watched his rapid breaths and the quickened beat of his heart through the veins in his neck.

"He's been asleep for a few minutes," Armond said, looking over the bottles, "Which of these were which?"

Oswald repeated the quick dosages and told him what each of the bottles were for. Armond nodded his understanding and opened the bottle that held the willow powder. He took a pinch of the white mixture and slipped the thumb of his other hand into Ramif's mouth to pry it open and shoved his tongue to one side. He dropped the pinch of powder into the pouch under his tongue and removed his hand from his mouth, brushing the remains of the powder from his fingers onto his pants.

Ramif made a disgusted face in his sleep, but didn't fight as Armond took the glass bar from each vial and dropped a dose of the oils into his mouth one at a time. He finished and put the tops back on the bottles with a sigh and sat back down in his chair slowly.

"You should rest," Oswald said, looking at the deep circles under Armond's eyes, "You haven't slept at all have you?"

Armond shook his head, "I'm fine."

"I can watch him as easy as you can," Oswald said, "You just gave him the herbs. He should get better soon. Let me watch him so you can sleep an hour."

"An hour," he repeated, running his hand through his hair, mulling over the concept of sleep, "You'll update me in an hour?"

Oswald nodded.

"Alright," he agreed, taking one final look at Ramif before he stood up slowly and walked out of the room but hesitated at the doorway, "I'll be resting in Samuels room for a bit then."

"I'll let you know if anything changes," Oswald said, taking the open chair beside the bed.

"I'm trusting you to," Armond said, and vanished around the corner.

Oswald listened to the sudden quiet of the house. The air was hushed except for the occasional piece of conversation that drifted in from the other room between the boys. He listened to them talk for a while, not hearing the actual words but listening to the fluctuation of their voices. Their conversation sped up and Oswald smiled, pleased by the sudden sound of Isaiah laughing.

Oswald looked down at his shoes and studied them passively. After turning his foot one way and then the other, he decided that he needed new soles for the shoes. All of the running he had been doing through town over the gravel and uneven ground had worn the leather unevenly and it was getting thin in places. He flexed his toes in the shoes trying to pass the time and checked the stitching of each seam, which was still fine.

When he figured that enough time had passed for the medicine to have worked its way through his body, he stood up to get another good look at him. He removed the wet washcloth from his forehead and felt the skin of his brow with the back of his hand. He sighed with relief at the dramatic drop in the fever. His skin was still warm and sweaty, but he was no longer hot enough to concern him.

He sat back down on the chair and watched his breathing, realizing that it had actually picked up pace and that he was breathing harder than he had been a few minutes ago. Oswald thought for a moment about waking Armond, but knew that if he woke him up that he would not go back to sleep again. He sat back and watched carefully, suddenly not daring to take his eyes off of Ramif, afraid that something would change again if he looked away.

Nothing happened for a while.

Oswald listened to Samuel and Isaiah continue to talk and watched he Ramif breathe. He began to think that it must be nearing the hour and stood up to make sure that the fever had not returned so that he could reassure Armond to sleep another hour.

He leaned over again and touched Ramif's face when his eyes popped open suddenly.

Startled, Oswald pulled his hand away and jumped a little. He took in a deep breath and leaned in to his line of sight, trying to get his attention. His eyes were blood shot and glassy with a fog to them that couldn't be seen, but obscured the soul within.

"Ramif?" Oswald said, snapping his fingers a few times and trying to get him to respond.

Ramif's eyes snapped over to him and something within him woke up, startled awake by the sight of him. His breathing deepened and quickened the longer he stared at Oswald's face. He was seeing him, but also seeing through him to somewhere far away.

"Hey," Oswald said, trying to get the glassy focus to come back from wherever he was, "Ramif, are you okay? Do you need something?"

He sat up suddenly, his face contorted and his movements were jerky and uncoordinated, "Who are you and what the hell are you doing in my house?" Ramif asked sharply, his voice strong and forceful.

"It's alright," Oswald said, trying to get him to calm down, "It's just me. We're at Armond's house right now."

"What are you doing here?" Ramif shouted, his voice suddenly both angry and afraid.

"You needed some herbs," Oswald said, offended by the tone of his voice, "I've only been here for a little while."

"Where is she?" Ramif's voice dropped to a trembling whisper and erupted again like volcanic ash, filling the room with fear and hatred, "Where is she!?"

"She who?" Oswald asked as he took a small step forward. He realized how far away his eyes were, lost into his own mind, and again he tried to bring him back, "Hey, Ramif, you need to calm down a little okay, you're hurt."

His eyes left Oswald and started darting around the room quickly seeing something that wasn't there and he sank into a panic, his hands searching for something in the bed that wasn't there. He looked back up at Oswald and a mixture of horror and rage overtook him. He threw himself forward off of the bed and launched himself at Oswald in a fevered attack and yelled, "Tell me where Niah is!"

Oswald threw his hands open and put them up in front of himself as quickly as he could, both trying to catch Ramif and keep him at arm's length. A sudden static swelled around him, adding thickness to the room and he felt the depth of the air break between his hands with an audible roar. He watched, stunned, as an invisible force took hold of Ramif, impacting him in the chest and he was hurled back into the bed and against the far wall.

Oswald's eyes were wide and he dropped his hands and his stomach rolled anxiously. He rushed forward, but Ramif backed against the wall, all of his anger gone and replaced by terror. His eyes were still distant and glassy as he shook his head and pressed his back against the wall tighter. He looked around absently and then back to Oswald, his lower lip trembling.

"I'm not going to hurt you," Oswald insisted, putting his left hand on his sword hilt and feeling another surge of magic which he suppressed into the blade, "You know me."

He looked away from Oswald and his gaze slowly drew down to his upturned and shaking hands, "No," he whispered as he continued to stare at his hands. His horror became anguish with a sound that could run blood cold, he howled and doubled over into his own arms through the scream.

Ramif looked up at Oswald with fear and despair.

"Ramif!" Oswald yelled, determined to bring him out of his fit, "Lord General!"

Ramif looked around, confused as Oswald knelt forward onto the bed with one knee. He grabbed Ramif's jaw, forcing him to look into his face and yelled, "I'm Oswald. You hate me, but you *aren't* afraid of me!" Ramif's breathing gradually slowed and his eyes began to focus.

"Come on, I'm not who you think I am," Oswald said, firming his grip against his jaw. Ramif tried to turn his head but Oswald held it tight in his hand, "You're no coward. LOOK AT ME!"

He looked into Oswald's emerald eyes for a long, slow, moment and the solid expression that was so commonplace in his features began to take hold. He began to lose the glossy sheen of distance in his eyes and he finally had a passing flicker of recognition show back at him.

He smacked Oswald's hand away from his face sharply with a disgusted and unhappy scowl, "Touch my beard again elf," he warned in his usual forceful tone, "And I will take your hand off."

Oswald smiled with an unexpected lightness to his chest and backed away.

"Dad!" Isaiah said brightly, and ran forward from the doorway. He clambered up into the bed and wrapped his arms around his neck, "You're okay!" Ramif held his son with his good arm and looked down at the other thoughtfully, as if he were trying to remember exactly what happened.

"I'm alright," Ramif grumbled, patting Isaiah's back comfortingly. He gently pushed him forward and set him on bed beside him. He turned his broken arm over in his lap and seemed to be piecing together his memory. He reached his good hand up and rubbed at his shoulder as he looked up to the doorway.

Oswald followed his gaze and saw both Armond and Samuel looking in. He wondered anxiously how long they had been there and what they had seen. They stepped into the bedroom and they both smiled at Ramif, relieved.

Armond sat in the chair by the bed and looked him over quickly, "How are you feeling?"

"Like shit," Ramif said grumpily, "It feels like someone ripped my skin off, beat it with rocks and put it back on…but I'll live," he looked up at Oswald, his expression unchanged, "What's he doing here?"

"He's been a lot of help," Armond said, gesturing over to him with a respectful tip of his head, "And I'm certain he saved your life."

"It's just a broken arm," he said bitterly.

"You know better than that," Armond said, looking at the bandage.

Ramif furrowed his brow with an unusual expression on his face and refused to make eye contact with Oswald. He put a hand over the burned wound under his bandage and chewed on his tongue. A sudden thought struck him and he looked up, "Samuel, are you alright?"

"Fine," Samuel said shortly, uncrossing his arms and offering a sigh and a smile, "I'm fine. Glad you're doing better."

Ramif looked around at the group a slightly confused, his stern eyes clear and the firm lines of his face set back into their place, "I must have been pretty bad off for you to bring my son here."

Isaiah scooted closer to him in the bed and Ramif thumped on his back supportively.

"A precaution," Armond said.

"We didn't know how long you would be out," Samuel said, crossing his arms again and looking a little uncomfortable, "So I went and got him this morning."

"Just one day?" he asked and they all nodded, "That isn't so bad then," he said dismissively. He tried to get up out of the bed and braced his arm against his body. As he got to his knees, the color drained from his face.

"Stay in the bed," Armond ordered calmly, "Just until you get something to eat."

"Why do I need to eat?" he asked, "I haven't done anything."

Armond closed his eyes brushing away the hours of seizures that were fresh in his mind and insisted, "You need to eat something. I can get you anything you want."

Ramif frowned, "I'd rather eat at the Burning Mill."

"I have the same food here," Armond said, frowning with a disapproving tone to his voice.

"I don't want it here," Ramif said sharply, "I think that I would feel better if I got out of the bed."

"Fine, get out of the bed, but stay here," Armond said firmly.

"No. I want to go to the Mill," Ramif growled.

Armond shook his head and said with a sigh, "I'll bring you a bottle of takwa, alright, and I'll get you something to eat."

"That wasn't my point," he snapped angrily.

"Look, you just woke up," Armond said, trying to sound reasonable, "And you have been in and out of a really unhealthy state until just a few minutes ago. For my peace of mind, please just stay here another night."

"But I need clothes too," he argued.

"You are wearing clothes," Armond said dully.

"But look what you've got me in," Ramif said, picking the shirt away from his body with his thumb and forefinger, "It's horrible."

"They're my clothes," Armond said, annoyed.

"I know," he said, pulling down at the cloth and looking revolted, "These shorts look like swamp boggers on me, and the shirt is so damned long it about reaches my knees, it's ridiculous."

"I can go and get you a set of your clothes," Armond muttered, "Would that make you happy?"

"No," Ramif grumbled, sitting back on the bed and leaning against the wall comfortably.

"You're never happy."

"No," Ramif agreed. He looked from Armond to Samuel and over to Isaiah before finally giving a sidelong glance to Oswald, "Fine. Takwa, dinner and my clothes and I'll stay tonight."

Armond smiled at the small victory, and Ramif gave him a small half-smile in return.

Oswald started walking towards the door and looked back at Ramif, "I'm glad you're doing better," he said. Ramif nodded, still not making eye contact with him as Oswald looked around at the others. He put a hand up in a short wave and walked out of the house, listening to the group of voices continue to argue behind him.

Chapter Twenty-Five

Oswald sat at the table next to Bolzar and set his plate of bread, cepa and poultry on the table in front of him. Nedtedrow reached across the table and helped himself to a slice off of Oswald's bread, sitting back comfortably and chewing on it as if it were his. Fred was leaning up against the wall in his seat thinking deeply about something, and Matrim was next to him with a plate of his own, picking through the pile of meat and piling the bones to one side.

"What are you guys doing here?" Oswald asked, curious at the unusual company.

"Looking for you," Bolzar said flatly, leaning forward in his seat and rubbing at his hand habitually.

Oswald looked at the odd assembly, "Is everything alright?"

"Everything's fine," Fred said deeply.

Everyone nodded in a passive agreement except for Matrim, who continued to pick at his food uninterestedly.

"I usually don't see you here," Oswald said, looking to Bolzar and offering him a piece of bread.

He held up his hand and declined the piece, "I don't like to eat here."

"Why not?" Oswald asked, picking up a thin slice of the grilled cepa with the bread and taking a bite.

"This place is just nothing but trouble," Bolzar said, as he looked around at the unsavory company of the tavern. He turned back to the table and tapped the fingers of his healed hand against the wood anxiously, "I try not to spend a lot of time here."

"I eat here almost every day," Oswald said, with a shrug, "I haven't had any problems with the people here yet. They aren't pleasant," he said, shaking his head lightly, "But they keep to themselves mostly."

"Yeah, they leave *you* alone," Bolzar snarked, looking up at Oswald with a raised eyebrow.

"What do you mean by that?" Oswald asked incredulously.

"People talk about you quite a bit," Fred added as he rolled his eyes over the tavern, "And there are a few serious rumors going around. People are afraid of you."

"I'm an elf," Oswald said, shifting in his seat uncomfortably, "Who makes shoes…"

"They're saying more than that," Bolzar said quietly.

Oswald shook his head and ignored the swell of magic burning at his fingertips. He had never been more than a cobbler until he had come to Gommorn, and now he wasn't so sure what he was anymore.

"I don't know about the rumors," Nedtedrow said, stuffing the last of the piece of bread into his cheek, "But I've seen you do some weird stuff."

Oswald looked over to Nedtedrow offended and asked, poking at another piece of cepa on his plate, "Weird? Like what?"

Nedtedrow smirked, "Climbing a pile of venom stones to grab a cursed sword is pretty high on the list."

"That was just stupid," Oswald said guiltily, looking down at Dashai, resting in the scabbard at his hip, "Not that I regret doing it."

"It was still weird," Nedtedrow insisted.

"But I'm not dangerous," Oswald said, in disbelief.

"You are getting deadly accurate with that blade," Fred said, scratching his long ear casually, "And fast enough that even the generals are having trouble with you in training every now and again."

"Those are lucky swings," Oswald lied, starting to feel more uncomfortable and overly anxious with all of the eyes on him, "They haven't told you that have they?"

"No," Fred said, linking his fingers together against his chest, "But I can see it."

"And not to put too much weight on it," Bolzar said reassuringly, "But you do look a lot like Venhow. About half of the people in this city have personally seen the worst of that man, and that's saying far more than any nightmare can."

Oswald shoveled a piece of poultry and cepa into his mouth forcefully. He chewed on the bite for a while and tried to swallow back his apprehension, "I don't want people to be scared of me," he said, decisively.

"It's better than no one being afraid of you," Nedtedrow said, with a shrug, "Most people hate me and I don't have a huge problem with that, but it doesn't exactly protect me."

Oswald looked away and shook his head, "I just don't understand how people can be afraid of me. You know that I wouldn't hurt anybody."

"We know that," Fred said, his deep voice difficult to hear over the sounds of the room. He pointed a long finger vaguely addressing the rest of the tavern, "But it's best that they don't."

"People aren't afraid of me," Bolzar said, looking around again, "And that can be dangerous in here."

"Then why are you here?" Oswald asked curiously, and trying not to sound unwelcoming.

"Because," Nedtedrow interrupted, taking another piece of bread from Oswald's plate, "He's nosy and always has to have answers."

"He asked me," Bolzar said, glaring at Nedtedrow, "And I'm not nosy. I did want to know whether it was true or not, however."

"If what was true?" Oswald asked, looking around the table with his brow furrowed.

"The new rumor," Nedtedrow said, shoveling the rest of his stolen slice of bread in his mouth, his cheek pouching out a bit as he fought to chew the mass.

Fred leaned forward. His long green arms and enormous hands easily took up half of the available space on the table as he leaned in close. He looked closely at Oswald and dropped his voice low and rough, "Is it true, what people have been saying all day long? I saw the burn myself but I don't know if I believe it or not yet."

"What?" Oswald asked, picking at the chicken and trying not to let anyone see the uneasiness on his face or the sudden tremor in his hands. He started to catch on to the direction of their questions and his heart thundered as his stomach rolled up into his throat.

Fred's pale blue eyes glistened with interest, "That there was a Grimm in the city?"

Oswald shrugged evasively, "Why are you asking me?" he asked, wanting less and less to do with the conversation's direction.

Matrim picked another bone clean and said, angrily, "'Cause they're sayin' you killed it."

Oswald looked up, taken aback by the unusually bitter attitude radiating from Matrim's usually happy demeanor. He looked around the table for a long time as everyone stared at him, "Yeah... I guess I did..." he said, feeling his face flush unnervingly.

"And you don't know why people are afraid of you?" Nedtedrow scoffed casually.

"It didn't happen the way you think," Oswald insisted, "and I wasn't the only one there."

"Then what did happen?" Fred asked curiously, his vicious face drawn into a curious scowl.

"I was here and something wasn't right so we left. We got to this house and it just showed up and dropped through the ceiling," Oswald said shakily, not hearing himself talk and not fully understanding his reaction to the memory. His stomach knotted slowly and the blood chilled in his arms and legs, "The next thing I knew we were in the street and there was smoke everywhere. It was — so fast and... nothing was touching it. It was like solid smoke. It came at me and I swung. I don't know what happened exactly, it happened so quickly and... Armond was there, I took a swing and then it was dead."

"When did this happen?" Bolzar asked concerned.

"Late last night."

"That doesn't make sense. You killed it? How?" Fred asked.

"It wasn't really me," Oswald said, flustered. The cold in his limbs crawled deeper into his body and his mouth went dry, "It was my sword," he said, putting a shaking hand on the hilt at his side, "For whatever reason, it's the only one that could touch it."

"Why didn' ya say somethin'?" Matrim asked angrily, "I worked wit' ya 'al mornin'. I knew somethin' wasn' right, you was too quiet. Ya could'a said somethin'."

"What could I have said?" Oswald asked becoming more upset and unable to think of a way to start a conversation like that.

"I dunno. Somethin', anythin'. I mean tha's serious shit! Why — Why was it here?" he asked, throwing his hands into the air before dropping them into his lap angrily.

"I don't know why," Oswald said, his eyes widening.

Matrim huffed and shook his head, "And why didn' ya tell me?"

"It didn't matter at the time and I was more worried about Ramif," Oswald said, and recognized his mistake as the words came out of his mouth. The whole table roared into questions all at once. He looked around trying to decipher the questions from the noise and they all slowly dwindled their attention back to him.

"What's wrong with the General?" Bolzar asked, with rapt attention.

"Just a broken arm right now, last I knew anyway," Oswald said, breathing heavily.

"How did that happen?" Fred asked.

"During the fight with the Grimm," Oswald said, swallowing nervously and unable to hide his shaking hands anymore.

"The Grimm hurt him?" Bolzar said alarmed, casting concerned glances at the others through more questions.

"He was alright when I left," Oswald said quickly.

"What happened?" Bolzar asked.

"Look," Oswald said, putting his head down and poking at his food, "He hates me enough the way that it is and I have a feeling that I need to stop. I'm sorry I said anything at all."

"But he's alright?" Bolzar asked, in confirmation, true concern etched into the lines between his eyes.

"Last I knew he was up and fine," Oswald said, taking a large bite of bread to end his side of the discussion. He gripped his sword tightly at his hip and felt short waves of magic suppress into the blade as he tried to understand why he felt so exposed.

His heart began to thunder against his chest and he felt like he wasn't getting enough air. The image of Ramif convulsing violently in the street suddenly began to haunt him and the knots in his stomach tightened. His mouth ran dry and he was having trouble swallowing the ball of bread in his mouth. His heart beat harder against his ribs and he could hear his heartbeat pulsing in his ears, pounding over the voices around him. They continued to barrage him with questions that he couldn't hear over his own heart. Slowly, they recognized his troubled expression and one at a time dropped the subject.

"You okay Oz?" Matrim said quietly, as he bent down low to the table to get a look at Oswald's downturned face, "Yur not lookin' that great."

Oswald looked up and tried to snap himself out of the emotional flashback. He rubbed his face in both hands for a second to try and drag himself back to the tavern and nodded, unable to hear his own voice through the pulse in his head, "Yeah. I'm fine. I think I'm just tired."

"No, you're not... I know that look," Bolzar said regretfully, with his blonde brow knitted together in a light frown, "Just take a deep breath and think about something else until it goes away," he put a firm hand on Oswald's back for a moment understandingly.

Oswald took in a deep breath, continuing to feel the electric sharpness of the magic sink through his palm and into the sword. An intense magic pulled away from his body as he gripped the hilt of his sword until his knuckles turned white. He held the deep breath and looked down at the floor. He looked at his shoes again and tried to decide what kind of leather he would replace the soles with.

After a few deep breaths and while of pondering his shoes as the others talked, he felt the magic ebb away from him and his heart began to pace itself normally again. The pounding in his head faded away one beat at a time and the grains in the wooden boards at his feet slowly came back into focus.

He looked up at the table when he felt more comfortable and ran a hand through his red curls, deciding in the moment that it was time that he cut his hair again. The others had finished talking about what they thought had happened with the Grimm, and were having conversations about plans for the day ahead.

Oswald looked up and met Fred's expression. It seemed as though he had been keeping a general watch over him as he had been trying to calm down. He asked a silent question with his eyes and Oswald nodded shortly that he was feeling better, to which Fred gave an encouraging, goblin smile.

He listened to the conversation shift to work and then back around again to food. He continued eating his dinner, taking small pinches of food until the knots in his stomach settled all the way and he was actually able to finish the meal.

Oswald looked out across the tavern and spotted Armond. He was leaning over the bar, talking to Mill who had retrieved a glass bottle of a dark liquid and was holding it out to him. Armond handed Mill a few coins for the bottle and spotted Oswald in the distance. He held up the bottle in greeting with one hand with a resigned and tired expression. Oswald acknowledged him with the short wave of a hand before he walked back out of the tavern.

"What do you think Oswald?"

He turned back to the conversation unsure when he had stopped listening, "About what?"

The sun peaked over the ridgeline and fell across the valley, reflecting over the heavy frost that had settled over the city each night for the last week solid. Oswald sat up in his bed, shivering from the bitter cold and unwilling to get out from under the blanket. He threw it off of him, reluctantly, and held his arms tight against his body as he forced himself to his feet.

The frost on the windows was thick and his breath hung in the air as he walked past Matrim in the bed across the room, trying carefully not to wake him up. He walked into the small bathroom and shut the door, turning to the small wooden water basin and the well pump and getting a few clean rags together.

He filled the basin, watching the steam roll off of the water into the bitter air. He threw off his dirty clothes and left them on the floor and looked at the fairy pendant around his neck and could hardly make out its fine details through the filth. He took the chain off and set the pendant carefully next to his folded pile of clean clothes on the small rickety table beside to him.

He took the washcloth and scrubbed the dirt and sweat off of his body as best as he could in the small basin. Enjoying the short time that the cloth was able to stay warm in the cold morning, he washed his face and dunked his head in the water for a quick scrub to rid himself of the salt in his hair. He shook the water out of his hair and dried off quickly, not wanting to stand in the cold for too long and got dressed as fast as he could manage.

He rolled up the sleeves of his shirt to his elbows and grabbed the fairy pendant, carefully washing it off in the hot water. He began to get the crawling feeling of being watched and he tried to clean faster. When he had gotten the last of the soot that had clung to its glass creases clean again, he slipped it back around his neck quickly and tucked it into his shirt keeping his hand over the pendant until the creeping sensation ebbed away.

He stepped into his shoes and pulled the laces tight, picking up a small bag and threw it over his shoulder. He picked up the sword and scabbard from the floor and strapped it to his waist as he walked out the front door into the harsh morning air. He made his way through the city and out to the edge of the valley to the clearing.

He spotted Loch at the bottom of the hill as he was finishing strapping on the last of his armor. Oswald watched out of curiosity as Loch used his teeth to tighten the armor straps onto his left forearm.

"Need any help with that?" Oswald asked, as he sped up to work out the cold from his body.

"Nope," Loch said, jerking his arm sharply to ensure the straps were tight enough, "I got it, thanks." He reached around and pulled the chainmail beneath his chest plate straight, making a metallic scraping sound as he fixed the bunched chain.

"Is it just us today?" Oswald asked.

"For a while," he said, now adjusting the angle of his scabbard, "The Lord General is going to be here after a while, probably General Armond and Samuel too at some point."

"General Ramif?" Oswald asked, surprised.

"Yes. I assume there isn't a problem with that," he said, with a warning tone to his voice.

"No sir," Oswald said, truthfully, "I'm just happy to hear that he's feeling better."

Loch looked him over suspiciously and agreed, obviously unaware of the entire string of events. Armond had kept his promise and Oswald was grateful for that.

Oswald took the small bag from off of his shoulder and tugged at the drawstring knot to open the bag. Inside were his leather pads he had recently made to go underneath his armor, along with a new piece, a leather cap with thick flaps that came down on either side of his head to protect his ears and his jawline in the atypical event of losing his helmet during practice.

Loch raised an eyebrow as he watched Oswald put on the under armor, but didn't say anything. When Oswald had finished he put on the chainmail and then the plating, getting faster at dawning the armor now that he had become fairly familiar with the process. The layers warmed him up and blocked out much of the cold, but he knew he would hate the armor by evening, because he always did.

Loch had lit a cigar and was smoking casually, leaning up against a small beach tree and watching a squirrel dart nervously through the woods, looking for the last of its food storage before winter. He watched Oswald finish up with the armor and while he was putting on his helmet, Loch took a final puff of the stumpy cigar and gave it a flip out to a dirt patch behind him.

"You think you're ready to train with me?" Loch asked, as he picked up his own helmet and secured it into place.

Oswald looked himself over and put a hand on the warmth of the sword's hilt, "I guess we're going to find out."

He smiled mischievously, "Alright then."

Loch stepped out into the open, choosing flat, even ground to begin with and he drew his sword with a sharp ringing sound. Loch's sword wasn't a typical training sword, like what Ramif and Armond had been using during practice, it was his own personal sword.

It was heavier and longer, with deep ribbing in the hilt for a trustworthy grip and a sharply tapered pommel. Its guard cross had an engraving in it that Oswald couldn't read from the distance and a fuller that grooved deep along the main body of the blade for easy retrieval. It was a war sword, and one that Oswald was certain had seen the heart of the battle field.

"Your sword is your partner out here," Loch said, following his line of sight and holding the blade to show off its detail, "It protects you. This one was my father's, one of the very last blades he made, and he made it for me. Not another one like it," he said, looking it over, "And it has served me well. Are you ready?"

Oswald drew his own sword, entranced by the morning sunlight on its rust red blade as it sang out into the air. He softened his knees and brought the blade across his body, readjusting his grip on the hilt until he found a secure and comfortable place for his fingers as he slowly let out a deep breath and watched as the warmth of it rose up in front of him. He nodded once.

Loch moved forward quickly, and instantly Oswald knew that he was out of his league.

Loch bent low as he moved and put power into the ground behind him, launching across the clearing in precise and calculated steps, his blade making tiny exact movements and corrections to his change in posture. He was nearly on top of him before Oswald had even fully turned to follow his motion, and with a dominant and unexpected strength, Loch made contact with his chest plate and threw him back onto the ground in one perfect swing.

Oswald lay on the ground, stunned for a second before he pushed himself up into a sitting position, looking at Loch in awe, "Wow."

"I was making a point," Loch said, looking down at him curiously, "Did you get it?"

"I got that you are every bit as good as they say you are," Oswald said, rolling his shoulder back and trying to stretch out the muscle in his chest as it tried to knot up where he had been hit.

"Close, but no," Loch said, "You'll get it by the end of the day. Get up."

Oswald shoved himself back up onto his feet and gripped his sword harder, now expecting the speed and power of his movements, determined to stay on his feet.

Loch went back to where he had started before and put his sword up, this time taking a slightly wider stance and angling his torso back slightly. His breath rose into the air and this time Oswald anticipated the charge, watching him take in a breath and hold it a fraction longer before he moved. His swift and defined mastery of the blade as he moved was terrifying and mesmerizing as he again cleared the distance in a flash.

Oswald caught the blade of the first strike and whipped it around him cleanly before he was able to take a narrow open strike of his own. Loch had been ready for it, and slid out of the way like water through netting. He twisted to one side, under the arc of Oswald's blade and made solid contact with the exact same place as the last strike, but this time he didn't strike hard enough to lie him flat on the ground. Oswald stumbled back and had the feeling that he had lightened the blow on purpose.

"You keep leaving that spot open," Loch said, sounding annoyed, "and I'm going to hit it every time until you either block it or until you actually make contact with my armor."

He was much more serious during training than Armond, and Oswald felt like he wasn't making any progress as each round ended quickly with a heavy blow against the same place every time. He was getting cramps in his chest from the repeated beating and he was getting more and more discouraged as nothing he tried worked to block the strike, and he was getting no closer to making a strike of his own.

After a while the Generals showed up and watched from the hillside amusedly as he continued to get beat down less than a couple of minutes into each fight.

"Learn the lesson yet?" Loch asked, looking down at Oswald lying flat on the ground again.

"I'm not good enough to train with you yet?" Oswald guessed breathlessly, feeling that it was the most honest thing he had guessed so far throughout the day.

"No," Loch said, disappointedly sliding his sword back into its scabbard so that he would have a free hand to help pull Oswald to his feet, "And you're actually doing very well. You really only seem to have the one weak spot in your defense," he glanced up at the hillside and added, "Let's take a break for a bit."

Oswald stood up with Loch's help and was breathing heavily. He put his sword in its scabbard and followed along behind Loch on the way to sit with the Generals.

Oswald took off his helmet and set it in the grass beside him as he flopped tiredly onto the dry grass.

"What the hell are you wearing?" Ramif asked mockingly, looking at the leather cap still setting over Oswald's head.

"Leather under armor," Oswald said, reaching up and taking off the cap and setting it alongside the helmet in the grass.

"Why?" Armond asked, looking at the piece oddly.

"Fantasy told me to wear leather under my armor when I train," Oswald shrugged, "I just finished making them yesterday."

Ramif snorted, "But I'll bet she didn't tell you to look like an ass."

"Ha ha," Oswald said, unamused, unlatching the chest plate so that he could rub out the bruised and cramping muscles in his chest.

"How are you two feeling today?" Loch asked, taking off his helmet and set it on the ground at his feet.

"Stronger," Ramif said, flexing the hand on his splinted arm, "Another two weeks or so and I'm going to call it healed. It isn't hurting so much and I've had no fever for several days. I'm doing well."

"Same here," Armond said, patting his chest gently, "Better every day."

"Where's Samuel?" Loch asked, rubbing at his face and feeling the grey stubble at his chin.

"He stayed home," Armond said, with a gentle frown, "He has some sort of stomach flu today. He should be fine by morning."

"Sorry to hear that" Loch said, "But I heard that it has been going around. I think it's the change in seasons, people tend to get sick this time of year."

"It's nothing serious," Armond said, dismissively, "No fever or anything, just sick."

"Matrim was sick with it yesterday," Oswald added.

"Is he better this morning?" Armond asked curiously.

"He was asleep when I left," Oswald shrugged, "But he was starting to feel better last night before he went to bed, so I would assume so."

"Well, a swift recovery to them both," Loch said politely, turning around and taking a seat on the hillside beside Armond.

"So how's his training going?" Armond asked.

"Good," Loch said, taking a cigar out of the pouch he had brought with him and sticking it between his teeth as he fished around for a match, "His stance is good, stamina's good," he mumbled through the cigar, finding a match and striking it on a textured patch of his armor near his stump of an arm, "Very quick reaction time," he lit the cigar and flicked away the match. He took in a drag of the thick smoke and pulled the cigar out of his mouth now gesturing with it as he spoke through the cloud, "his corrections are delayed and he brings his sword up too high when he dodges and leaves an open spot at his upper chest."

"Still hasn't fixed that, huh?" Armond asked.

"I'll beat it into him eventually," Loch said, "And once he closes that gap in his defenses, he'll be someone to be reckoned with."

"What are you talking about?" Oswald asked exhaustedly, "You've been kicking me around all day."

"Yes," Loch said, with a boastful smirk, "but I did actually have to try."

"Do you usually *not* have to try?" Oswald asked in disbelief.

"You don't seem to understand," Loch said, shaking his head, "Your offense is far beyond what you should know at this point in training."

"I haven't done anything at all yet today except get thrown to the ground," Oswald grumbled, rubbing harder at the soreness in his chest.

"You got a couple of shots in," Loch said, impressed.

"He did?" Armond asked, with raided eyebrows, "Did he make contact?"

"No," Loch said, puffing at the cigar, "Came close though."

"Really?" Armond looked over at Oswald and smiled mischievously, "Then maybe I'm being too easy on him."

"What?" Oswald asked, "I'm not getting beat up enough anymore?"

"I guess not," Armond said, with a grin, "You need to listen to Loch and get that defense straightened up. Try harder next round and keep your arms in when you move."

Ramif stood up slowly, holding his broken arm close to his body, and threw something gently at Oswald.

Oswald reached out and caught it, surprised by the sudden movement and looked it over. It was a deep purple peta fruit, "Where did you get this?" Oswald asked, curiously, "They're over a month out of season."

"Pewins," Ramif said shortly, lowering himself back down to his place on the cold hillside and taking a short moment to straighten the braid of his beard, "They came up from the south and passed through here a couple of days ago. I bought a box as they came through the city. That's the last of it. You like petas right?"

"I do," Oswald said, shocked by the sudden kindness, "Thank you."

"Don't mention it," Ramif said, digging into the bag at his side and pitching a wedge of cheese over to Loch who fumbled with the catch trying to keep the cigar in his mouth and not drop the cheese at the same time.

"Warn me next time," Loch said, mumbling through the cigar in frustration. He set the wedge of cheese in his lap and tried to decide which of the two he wanted to finish first. He decided on the cigar, and went back to finishing the last of the stub.

"Armond," Ramif said, looking back into the bag, "There's dried elk meat or bread left."

After the short meal Oswald felt better, and he put his leather cap back on, much to the amusement of Ramif and Armond, and then readjusted his helmet overtop of it.

"Are you ready?" Loch asked, drawing his sword and digging a foot into a small rut in the clearing. Oswald put his heels into the ground and softened his knees, leaning forward with his grip on his sword tight, the heat energizing his sore muscles. He nodded.

Loch came forward in a rush and swung his blade up.

Oswald spent more of his energy into trying to keep his sword closer to his body this time, blocking the sword with a tighter swing and moving faster because of it. He felt the magic begin to guide him and his body fell into the motions more smoothly. It seemed less like he was fighting the blade and as though he were more in tune with its range and movement using the new posture.

He took a quick swing at a small opening in Loch's defense.

Loch moved away from it smoothly, rolling his body away from the swing as he arched his blade again, this time aiming high at Oswald's shoulder. The blade swung up at a perfect angle as Loch brought his arm out and shifted his body closer to the ground as he moved through the weight of the swing.

Oswald watched the blade roll through the air and he reacted to the motion from the first movement of the sword. The blade grazed by, cutting through the air as Oswald dipped his shoulder down slightly feeling a jolt of magic as he remembered to keep his defense in line.

Oswald listened to the whisper of magic and swung the red blade low.

Loch saw the swing and jumped high, both feet clearing the blade by a hair's width before he landed hard back onto the ground and took a long high swing of his own into the open defense left in the wake of Oswald's wide swing.

Oswald leaned back and felt the tip of the blade catch his helmet and heard a light tearing sound. The helmet flew off of his head but he didn't have time to react. He caught the tip of Loch's sword with his blade and threw it aside forcefully, keeping his strokes short and accurate as he moved in closer.

Loch's face twisted in effort as he tried to regain the defense he had lost. He drug his sword across Oswald's with the hiss of metal as the two parted ways. He brought his blade back across his body and caught another quick strike from the red blade as it tore the air at his face and he forced it down out of the way and into the ground. He knew he didn't have time to pick his sword back up and he put all of his strength into a powerful kick and hit Oswald squarely in the gut which threw him back to the ground.

Loch was breathing heavily for the first time throughout the day. He looked down at Oswald confused and put his sword back into its scabbard.

Oswald rolled onto his side and guarded the sharp pain in his stomach and tried to catch the wind that had been knocked out of him. He gasped against the ground until he was able to catch his breath and slowly got back up to his feet. He rubbed at his gut, trying to make the pain in his stomach go away.

"Where did that come from?" Loch asked, looking down at Oswald quizzically.

"I just did what you told me," Oswald insisted breathlessly.

"You about had me that time," Loch said, in disbelief, his eyes wide and his drawn down in scrutiny.

"I missed," Oswald said, reaching down to pick up his sword. He slid it back into its scabbard and picked up his helmet. He took off the leather cap and saw a long tear along the side of the flap on one side. He touched the side of his face and was happy when he couldn't find a scratch and was very pleased with his new leather cap. He put the cap back on and then his helmet.

"You got closer than anyone's gotten in years," Loch said.

"You haven't gotten hit in years?" Oswald asked skeptically.

"No," Loch insisted seriously.

"There is a first time for everything," Oswald said, trying to be playful.

Loch didn't smile, "Were you holding back this morning?" Oswald shook his head and Loch seemed to be thinking something over. He chewed at the inside corner of his mouth and asked, "You got the point I was trying to make?"

Oswald nodded, "Defense comes first."

"And?"

"Don't underestimate your opponent."

Chapter Twenty-Six

A thick blanket of the first winter snowfall held the valley, the late afternoon sun reflecting off of the snow in a way that made the expanse of streets look like white rivers in the veins of the city. Smoke rolled out of chimneys and collected together in a light grey cloud that seemed to drift along overhead every day in a never-ending plume. The cold was biting and the beginning of winter promised a deeper cold to come.

Oswald locked up the stains and leathers last, Matrim hadn't come to the shop that morning for whatever reason, and he had been left to try and keep up with the increased workload for the season. He put the key into his pocket and poured a small amount of water onto the fire behind the desk. The fire hissed as it died away and billowed up a small tower of smoke.

Two of the tarps had already been pulled because of the cold, so he only had to pull down the tarp from the front of the tent. His fingers found a reservoir of new snow in the crease as he pulled down the tarp, pouring snow down his front. He shook away the snow that had fallen on him and walked down the street towards the Burning Mill, looking forward to the warm building itself.

He tucked his hands into his pockets and put his shoulders up next to his long ears trying to brace himself against the wind as stray snowflakes danced down into his face and perched themselves into his freshly cut red hair. He regretted the decision to cut his hair fairly quickly, as the cold front moved in and the bitter air bit at the base of his neck each time he walked outside. The tips of his ears began to burn against the wind and he tried to duck down further out of the random gusts of spinning snow but without success.

He took his left hand out of his pocket and moved his coat out of the way of his hidden sword, holding the hilt and taking in what warmth from it that he could. He turned down a narrow alleyway, feeling the wind cut away, blocked from the array of homes. He reached up and tried to warm up his ears as he continued through the crooked pathway.

"Hey Red!"

Oswald looked around, confused. The voice was familiar but he was having trouble finding its source. A skinny young face peeked around the corner of the alley behind him, his dark hair flaked with snow and his grin marked by a dark place where a tooth should have been.

"Matrim?" Oswald stopped and waited for him to catch up, "Where've you been all day?"

He caught up, brushing the snow out of his messy hair, "I've been out in the valley hunting with a friend."

"You catch anything?" Oswald asked, suspicious of something he couldn't quite put his finger on. He looked around thinking it may have been an onlooker making him uncomfortable. No one else was around.

"Got a snow bear," Matrim said proudly.

"Great," Oswald said, looking him over quickly, "Are we going to do anything with the hide? I bet we could get a lot of orders with that much."

"Whatever you want to do with it," Matrim shrugged, "I was more interested in the hunt so I told my friend he could take what he wanted."

"Which friend?"

"Todd," Matrim said quickly.

Oswald tried to think of a Todd but couldn't remember anyone with that name, "Really?" Oswald asked with a pause, "I guess I haven't met him yet."

Matrim shrugged noncommittally, "Probably not. No big deal."

"You feeling alright?" Oswald asked.

"Yeah, I'm fine," he said clearly, and Oswald realized what was bothering him. He was speaking clearly, his accent was gone and he was using full words when he spoke.

Oswald turned away from him trying to come up with as many reasons as he could as to why he would suddenly change his speech patterns. He couldn't come up with anything that would be considered 'fine'. A sharp jolt of magic slid up his arm and he tightened his grip on the hilt of his sword.

"Do you want to come see the bear?" Matrim asked, pointing a thumb over his shoulder towards the other end of the valley floor.

"Sure," Oswald said, drawing his coat tighter around his body and trying to shiver more visibly in the cold, "But I want to get something to eat first. Is that alright?"

"Yeah," Matrim said, looking disappointed, "Where do you want to eat?"

Oswald drew his brow down and looked back at Matrim, sure now that something was wrong. He felt the electric bite of the hilt at his palm and he forced it away, "The Burning Mill. How does that sound?"

"That's fine," Matrim said, looking around the city, "We need to hurry though or we will lose the light. It's hard to show off my game if it gets too dark."

"I would imagine so," Oswald said evasively, trying not to let the biting magic distract him and doing his best to look casual as they walked through the city. He looked back every so often seeing their tracks in the snow behind them and studied Matrim's face.

They walked around the alley corner and back into the main road where the wind picked up again. The sharp air stung at Oswald's ears and whipped snow around the back of his neck, but the breeze carried with it the smell of smoking food. They walked up to the tavern and went in out of the cold. Oswald looked at one of the guards as he walked in and gave him what he hoped was a warning expression as Matrim wandered in behind him.

"Go sit at our table and I'll get us something to eat," Oswald said, looking at Matrim and wondering if he knew where to go and sit or not.

"I'll just go with you," he said nonchalantly, brushing off the snow from his coat and out of his hair again.

"Okay," Oswald said, "So what do you want to eat?"

"I'm not really hungry," Matrim shrugged, "So anything's fine."

"Are you sick again?" Oswald asked, looking back at him as they reached the bar, still trying to figure out what was going on.

Mill walked over to the bar to meet them, his thin face sunken and tired looking, "What do you boys want this evening?"

"Rye bread and pork," Oswald said, looking back at Matrim and then added for himself, "And grilled potatoes with cepa."

Matrim followed him to the back table where Oswald took a seat facing the door, watching for anyone else he knew with the hope that he could get an answer from them. He set the two plates down on the table, his uncomfortable feeling encouraged as he watched Matrim choose the wrong plate and begin picking at the vegetables.

Oswald pulled the plate of pork and bread towards him and tried not to look nervous as he picked at the meat and put a strip onto a thin wedge of the rye bread. They ate quietly for a while and he felt some relief from the discomfort as he saw Ramif walk up to his usual seat at the bar and hoist himself up into the stool.

"I have to go and talk to the general for a second," Oswald said quickly, "I will be right back okay?"

"Yeah sure," Matrim said, picking up a slice of cepa and looking back over his shoulder his eyes grazing over the bar and not stopping anywhere near Ramif, "It is starting to get dark though so we need to get going soon."

"In just a minute," Oswald said, getting up from his chair and hurrying across the room. He leaned up against the bar next to Ramif who hung his head dreadfully at the sight of him.

"What is it this time?" Ramif asked, "I haven't even gotten my drink yet and you are already in trouble again."

"It's Matrim," Oswald said, "I need you to talk to him for just a minute if you would."

"I'm not the kid's dad," he said, putting a hand up and flagging down Mill who held up an empty glass in one hand in recognition and started looking for a bottle of takwa.

"No, it's nothing like that," Oswald said uncomfortably, "He's not himself."

"What do you want me to do about it?" Ramif asked, as Mill brought him his drink and set it on the bar in front of him. He picked up the glass and took a large swig before setting it back down on the counter.

"Please, just go and talk to him about anything, anything at all for just a few minutes. Something is very weird," Oswald said, trying to portray the odd feeling through his expression, "If I'm wrong I'll buy your drinks for a week."

Ramif looked at him with a raised eyebrow and took another quick drink of the takwa, "Alright, but I will hold you to that."

"I know and I mean it," Oswald insisted, "Just go and talk to him."

"Sure," Ramif slid down off of his seat and walked across the tavern and stopped at the table next to Matrim. Oswald watched them out of the corner of his eye, pretending to be busy but really counting the dark walnut grains in the bar between sidelong glances.

Ramif walked back to the bar and hauled himself back up into the seat. He took a long drink of the dark glass and swallowed hard as he looked down into the deep amber liquid and contemplated the short conversation, "Yeah, that's odd," he admitted, "Why is he talking like that all of the sudden?"

"I was hoping you would know," Oswald said, with a shake of his head.

Ramif looked at him and frowned, "Why do you think that I know everything about everyone?"

Oswald shrugged, "You've known him longer than I have so I thought you might have some idea as to what is going on here."

"I have known him for years," Ramif nodded shortly, "and that was weird, but I don't know what you want me to do about it."

"What should I do?" Oswald asked.

"I don't know," Ramif said, irritated, and drained the rest of his drink, "You just wanted me to talk to him. I did. You were right, he's not acting like himself. Now leave me alone."

"He keeps trying to get me to leave the city with him," Oswald said quietly, leaning forward on the bar.

Ramif paused with a wary look on his face, "Why?"

"He said that he and a friend hunted down a snow bear and he wants to show it to me. He's really insistent about it," Oswald paused and tapped his fingertips on the bar uncomfortably, "Do you know a kid named Todd?"

Ramif shook his head, "No, but I don't know everyone."

"I've never heard about a Todd before," Oswald said, still tapping on the bar, "and I don't think that the person sitting there is Matrim," he caught the look on Ramif's face and sighed exasperatedly, "I know that sounds impossible but I work with the kid every day and that just isn't him."

"Can you prove it?" Ramif asked.

"If we can find where Matrim really is or—" he thought for a minute, "—You haven't said my name when you were talking to him did you?"

"No," Ramif said curiously, "I asked if he had seen Loch around recently. He told me he hadn't but said that he thought he saw him near the market earlier today. I knew that wasn't possible. Loch was at the community building all day with me, and he isn't a man you can mistake easily in a crowd."

"I don't think that he knows my name," Oswald said thoughtfully, "When he caught up to me in the street he called me 'Red'. He's never done that before."

"So if he doesn't know your name then what do you want me to do?" Ramif asked, knocking on the bar for another drink.

"I haven't figured that out yet."

Ramif snorted disapprovingly as he straightened his braided beard, "Well you sure as hell aren't a good strategist."

Oswald held out a hand briefly, "I'm working on it, alright? What do *you* think we should do?"

Ramif stroked his braided beard, thinking deeply, "Well I obviously wouldn't leave the city with him," he looked up as Mill filed his glass and he stared at his drink, "Maybe he has something else going on with his head. Keep him here for as long as you can," he picked up the takwa and took a long drink, ultimately leaving the empty glass on the bar, "I'm going to find a medic."

"Alright," Oswald said, unwilling to return to the table, "I'll try to keep him here."

Ramif jumped down off of the stool and headed out of the bar quickly, but not drawing any attention to himself. Oswald stepped away from the bar and wandered back to the table, taking his time as he weaved through the chaos of an increasingly intoxicated group of patrons who had started to argue loudly between each other.

He took his seat back at the table with Matrim, who had pushed the plate away and hadn't finished his food, nor had he picked at Oswald's plate.

Oswald adjusted himself in the seat and slowly picked at the slab of pork, trying to take as long as he could with the rest of his dinner.

"So what did you have to talk to the General about anyway?" Matrim asked, interlacing his fingers on the table and watching Oswald studiously.

"I was just trying to find out when I have to go back to training again," he lied, feeling a familiar crawling sensation ripple through his skin. He touched the sword with his fingertips and tried hard to keep the magic that was building around him in check. A stein on a nearby table shattered suddenly and Oswald grabbed the hilt tighter wondering if he had been the culprit of the destruction, but tried to show no concern over the random act.

"And?" Matrim asked, curiously.

"I have to be there tomorrow morning," he said, truthfully and watched Matrim's tangled hands on the table twitch occasionally as if he were becoming impatient about something.

"At what time?" he asked.

"Dawn."

"Well, we should get moving then," Matrim said, sliding out of his chair and standing against the table, "You don't want to oversleep in the morning."

"No," Oswald said quickly, trying to come up with another reason to stay, but couldn't.

Matrim's face darkened knowingly and he slowly sank back into his chair, his expression changing to something that didn't resemble anything that Oswald had ever seen on Matrim's face before.

"Why not?" Matrim said sharply, "You said you wanted to get a look at the bear."

"I did," Oswald said uncomfortably, and he heard another glass shatter somewhere in the room, "But I haven't gotten my drink yet."

Matrim sat back in the chair with a scowl, "Elves don't drink," he crossed his arms and looked down his crooked nose, "What's the matter Red?"

Oswald felt his breath catch in his chest and the cold stare dared him quietly. He glanced at the door. He hadn't seen anyone come in yet and his nerves were getting the best of him.

"What's my name?" Oswald asked, locking eyes with the man across the table.

Matrim smirked, each of them now knowing what the other suspected. He reached around underneath his coat.

Oswald tightened his grip on his sword until the metal bit at his palm waiting for the draw of the dagger.

Matrim pulled out a grey cloth from an inside pocket, tucking a small orb back into the pocket that the handkerchief had been drawn from. He rubbed at his hands, thinking, before putting the cloth down on the table with a deep and dangerous frown, "Bawshade."

Oswald was shocked to hear his family name, and he hesitated, "My first name?"

The boy who looked like Matrim leaned across the table with sharp eyes.

The two of them held still, not daring to move. The boy grabbed the grey cloth slowly with a long finger and drug it across the table, fidgeting with the stitched corner, "What are you trying to say exactly?"

"I want you to tell me what my first name is," Oswald said tensely, "That should be very simple for you if you are who you look like."

"I don't know what you are trying to get at, but it isn't very funny," Matrim said, as he fidgeted with the cloth.

"No," Oswald agreed, "It's not."

A short and distant commotion broke the tension, but only for an instant as Oswald recognized the voice that was carrying across the room, "Why ya gotta' be draggin' me aroun' like dis for?" Matrim's voice echoed form the doorway. Oswald looked up and spotted Ramif, his hand gripped tight around Matrim's upper arm and pulling him forcefully to a clear line of sight to the table in the back of the tavern, "Oz? Wha's this about?" he took a closer look at the other boy who was sitting in his usual seat and his eyes widened, "Who is zat?"

Oswald's heart thundered and his cheeks flushed angrily as the other Matrim turned to look over his shoulder and made a disgusted face, "Well that makes things more difficult doesn't it?" he said angrily, "I knew I should have killed the brat first."

Oswald shot to his feet, tossing the chair to the floor behind him, and drew his sword. The metal sang loudly as it was freed, the red blade darkened by the torchlight and flickering with rage. The commotion of the tavern died away with the sound of ringing steel and all eyes had landed on the boy at the tip of the blade.

The boy looked down the end of the red blade hungrily and locked eyes with Oswald, an amused and slimy looking smile breaking across his face, "You know, it is a shame you had to expose me like this. Now a whole lot more people are going to have to die."

"No one will die today," Oswald commanded, the end of the blade steadily aimed at the hollow of the boy's neck, "Except perhaps you."

He let out a wicked laugh that had a kind of shrill waver behind it, "Big boy all of the sudden. Grew a pair in six months did we?"

"What are you talking about?" Oswald demanded, keeping his focus on any movement the boy made. He steadied the blade and locked his eyes on the unnatural expression on his face.

"Your village," the boy said, "You weren't nearly so brave when I burnt it to the ground."

"Who are you?" Oswald demanded.

The boy laughed again and slowly got taller, his face narrowed and his hair slid short. His eyes turned a cold grey with an intensity of death and his shoulders broadened. His nose straightened and his jawline drew deeper lines at his neck. The age of his face changed and the expression fell away to a sick satisfactory smirk. The man touched his face and took a slow glance around the tavern.

A sudden panic took hold of the room and people were suddenly clambering over each other to get out. Yells and fear flooded the building with the sound of flipping chairs the thunder of feet, covered with the sharp snap of breaking glass and panicked screams as they tore out into the city.

Oswald held his ground with the tip of his blade steady and he heard the metal ring of another sword through the chaos. Ramif had cleared the space and had stopped a few feet away, a contorted look of fear and anger twisted onto his face.

"Such a warm welcome," the man chortled.

"What do you want?" Oswald asked, frozen in place.

"I want my sword." the man said, eyeing the red blade.

"It's mine," Oswald insisted, tightening his grip on the hilt.

"It was never yours," the man said, darkly, clenching and unclenching his fists.

"Who are you?" Oswald repeated.

"It's Venhow," Ramif answered tensely, extremely fixated on the man's cold eyes.

"Do I know you?" Venhow said, suddenly amused as he turned to Ramif with a sick enjoyment, "You look familiar." He took a small step back away from the pointed swords, looking comfortable and not at all intimidated. He tapped on his narrow chin and brought his attention back down to Ramif with a gleam in his smile that made Oswald's heart sink. "I do know you, don't I?"

"You will," Ramif promised.

Venhow shook his head wickedly, "I already do," he smiled, remembering, "You spent a few weeks in Azar didn't you?" Ramif held his expression firm as Venhow continued, "No, not Azar... it was a stone craft home in the Dappler Mountains wasn't it?"

Ramif's cheeks darkened but he didn't move.

"Did you have a nice time? I did," Venhow said, as he laughed deeply to himself, "Tell me, have you ever *really* been able to get the blood off of your hands?"

Ramif's nostrils flared and his grip was so tight on the hilt of his sword that his hands were as white as bleached bone and bruises were starting to form along the inside of his palms. Venhow laughed again, bringing his eyes up past Ramif towards the doorway where General Loch, Lieutenant Jameson and General Armond burst into the open doorway with their swords at the ready.

Venhow looked around amusedly taking a quick count of who was still in the room, his gaze stopping on Matrim standing frozen at the bar, unarmed, and then back to Oswald and Ramif, "Five armed men and a teenager against me. Still not a fair fight, but closer," he laughed.

Lieutenant Jameson led the generals in their rush to the enclosed corner of the bar. He circled around to Oswald's other side with his sword balancing in the air and the golden arrow still pinned proudly against his uniform.

Venhow looked around at the sword tips, a semi-circle of five blades now pointed at his chest and he shook his head slowly, "You can't kill me... you just aren't fast enough."

In a blink, Venhow drew a dagger from his coat and ducked under the canopy of sharpened steel. Everyone moved in at once, trying to find their target as Venhow slid up against Jameson's side. He grabbed the guard of Jameson's sword with one hand, and hooked his wrist with the blade of the dagger with his other. In a clean sweep he tore open Jameson's wrist as he turned his body out of the trap and forced the sword out of Jameson's grip. He readjusted the hilt of the sword in his hand as he spun behind Jameson's back and threw him to the ground with a blunt strike against the back of his head. Venhow used Jameson's body as a launching point and leapt up and around Oswald.

They turned, in slow motion, watching as Venhow tore his way through the group, catching Oswald's head with the daggered hand and ripped the blade down, overbalancing him and tearing open his scalp near the crown of his head as he was pulled to the floor.

He pushed off of Oswald's arched back and turned in on Ramif in an instant.

Venhow took a swing with Jameson's sword and felt the block, the blades shrieking as they spun around one another. He blocked a quick strike and kicked a foot low at Ramif's shins, the power of the impact throwing his feet out from under him.

Ramif hit the floor, face first, as Venhow dove around him and locked blades with Armond. The two of them sealed an impenetrable glare and they shoved each other away. Armond took a clean shot down at his side.

Venhow ducked under the blade and took a swing of his own. He arced the sword in his hand upwards, splitting Armond's chin and sliding around behind him in a low sweep. He blocked a blow from Loch with one hand and buried the blade of his dagger into Armond's calf behind him with the other, simultaneously.

He pulled the dagger free, dripping with blood, and forced Loch's sword out of his face. Venhow leapt to his feet again as the swords slid to one side and he tackled Loch, ramming his shoulder into the center of his chest. The two of them went flying back into a table and Loch found footing quickly, pushing him away enough to take a quick swing that sliced open Venhow's face at an angle.

Venhow howled angrily and swept a foot around low, raising his blade high in a double strike. Loch blocked the sword but felt his feet come out from beneath him, and he was thrown to the ground in a defensive posture. Venhow threw the dagger as he rushed quickly away from the table, the blade missing its mark by a fraction and pinning Loch's shirt to the floor at his chest.

He locked eyes with Matrim as Loch and the others began to regain their momentum behind him. He cleared the distance and grabbed a handful of Matrim's hair as he tried to back behind the bar. Venhow tore his head back tight, and brought the base of the sword blade flush against the rapid pulse of his exposed throat.

"Enough!" Venhow yelled, a stream of blood seeping across his face as the flesh mended, stitching together before them as the separated skin filled in the space of exposed meat in his cheek. In only a few deep breaths the gash was gone but the blood was still there, slowly drying to mark the placement of the perfect strike.

Oswald put a hand up to his head, feeling the hot flow of blood from a three finger wide gouge in his scalp. He felt his stomach turn and he pressed the hilt of his sword against the wound and felt the hot gush of blood slow to a trickle. He looked up with blood glistening across the side of his head and down his face to the path of carnage.

Jameson had wrapped his wrist in his shirt and was holding it tight to try and stop the copious bleeding. Armond was leaving bloody foot prints as he moved, and a dribble of blood marked its path from his chin to his chest. Ramif stood next to Loch, each frozen in place and winded, trying to tend to less obvious wounds.

"That's enough," Venhow said again, taking an even tighter grip at Matrim's dark hair, "I want my sword."

"Don't hurt him," Oswald begged, staggering forward and trying to focus through the blinding headache, "Take it. Just take it." He flipped the sword over and held it out by the blade, the hilt, bloody, and facing out for him to take. His hands were slick with his own blood and the sword was shaking violently in his grip.

"In the scabbard," Venhow demanded, gesturing with his eyes, "And on the floor."

Oswald fumbled with his shaking hands to put the blade back in its holster. He slid the sword into its place and unhitched the scabbard form his belt, tossing it to the floor, "Let him go."

Venhow didn't answer, instead he kneed Matrim in the back of his leg and forced him to the ground, the swords fine edge cutting a thin slice in his throat, a small but steady stream of blood running down the blade. He looked at the group one at a time and his cold grey eyes stopped on Oswald, "Kick it closer."

Oswald put a foot on the scabbard and slid it across the wooden floor where it stopped right next to his foot.

He leaned into Matrim's ear and whispered warningly, "It wouldn't be wise to move." He kept the blade against his throat but let go of his head, reaching over with his now free hand and touching the scabbard with his fingertips quickly and pulling his hand back a few times before daring to take it up into his hand.

"You aren't Venhow," Oswald said blankly, understanding the apprehension of the burning blade, "What are you really?"

Venhow pulled the scabbard closer, unsure how to carry it now that it was in his hands. He looked around again and pressed harder against Matrim's adam's apple with the edge of the sword until he whined nervously with renewed blood, "Does that really matter right now?"

"No," Oswald admitted apologetically, "Please, just let him go."

"You're right," Venhow said, with a gruesome smile, "I should just let him go." He let go of the sword of Dashai in its scabbard and fished a small orb out from inside of his pocket. It was small and glassy with a foggy green liquid swirling around inside it, "A marsh orb is a much more fitting death for a city urchin like this," he pressed the orb against Matrim's tight lips through the flow of tears down his young face, "Don't you think?"

"Let him go!" Oswald demanded, and he felt the air around him thicken and the light in the room faded through a fog of black shadows.

Venhow smirked cruelly, and hooked his middle finger between Matrim's now torn lips in an effort to pry his mouth open. Matrim tried to turn his head away and the blade cut deeper into his neck, he cried out in surprise and pain and Venhow's finger caught between his molars holding his mouth open.

Matrim bit down hard on Venhow's finger but he hardly winced, rolling the orb to the part in his lips.

"I said let him go!" Oswald yelled, stepping forward into the thickened air and throwing a hand forward to grab the orb.

He felt the air hold his outstretched arm, and in that second his body decided what to do with the magic. He felt a tear begin to form in the air, like a crack in cold glass. He let go of the magic pulsing through his body, sending it into the rift in the air which he felt widen around his open hand with the building static.

A roar built up and a sharp impact rippled against the sudden shadows that drew into the room. The roar got louder and then snapped and the air shattered outward sending out a focused streak of lightening from the space between them. It lit up the room and cut a path directly into end of the sword and up through Venhow's arm. The two of them were thrown apart with a sharp bang, and Venhow spun up through the air and crashed into the bar limply.

The darkness faded away with the flash of light and Oswald ran forward and dropped to the ground next to Matrim who had gotten up onto his knees. Matrim was supporting his body with one hand and had the other at his throat but hadn't moved any further.

Ramif and Loch flew past them to the unconscious Venhow that lay against the foot of the bar. Its appearance hadn't changed and the two of them were working quickly to find a way to tie him up.

Oswald put a shaking hand under Matrim's arm for support and wrapped another around his chest as he tried to help him up to his feet. He could feel Matrim's heart fluttering erratically like a wild bird in a small cage, trying to break free.

"Matrim? Are you alright?" he watched the occasional drip of blood slide between his fingers at his throat down to a blackened tear in his shirt. A thin lightning patterned burn had carved a branching array of singed flesh across his chest and down his left shoulder. He was shaking intermittently and Oswald could tell he was trying to get control over his body through the tremors and the pain.

Matrim tried to talk, letting out a dry croak. He coughed and gripped tighter at the cut in the skin of his neck for support. He took in a stuttered breath, finally getting some control of his muscles, "O-Oz..." he stuttered, and slowly sat back on his feet. Carefully he pulled his hand away from the cut at his throat. It was bleeding steadily but didn't look deep, he put his hand back cautiously and tried to talk again but his voice failed.

"Move your hand," Oswald said, scrambling away on his hands and knees and grabbing his sword from the floor some distance away. He pulled the sword out of its scabbard and wiped off the hilt with his shirt, and gently moved his hand out of the way of the wound, "It's going to burn," he warned, and drew the pommel slowly across the gash.

Matrim gritted his teeth and groaned, but didn't move away from him as he finished pulling the sword along the skin, sealing the gouge and with the sizzle of burning flesh. The bleeding stopped. Oswald dropped the sword and looked at the cut and slid his eyes to the lightning burn which was radiating heat and weeping steadily. Matrim put a bloody hand over the worst of the burn and doubled over, focusing on his breathing and trying to calm the patter of his heart.

Oswald heard a pained grunt and turned his head and looked back at General Armond and Lieutenant Jameson behind him. The two of them were fighting over the wound around Jameson's wrist, the bleeding hadn't stopped and he was beginning to look pale.

Oswald grabbed his sword and got to his feet.

Jameson looked up, as Oswald stepped up between them and reached for the wound, and he pulled his hand away.

"I can help," Oswald said, keeping his hand outstretched.

"I don't need your help," Jameson said confidently, his firm voice betraying the snowy pallor of his face.

"I can seal it for you," Oswald said.

"I'll stitch it shut myself," Jameson insisted, "I just have to get my kit."

"Your kit?" Oswald asked, confused.

"My medic kit," he said, pressing his arm as hard as he could against his body.

"Where is it?" Armond asked.

"I left it at the community building," Jameson grumbled through gritted teeth, looking past Oswald to Ramif and Loch. They had tied up Venhow, who was still unconscious, with heavy twine from the kitchen in the back of the bar, and they each had an iron grip on one arm.

"How convenient," Ramif said, digging his fingertips into the meat of his arm, "I think that's exactly where we should take this thing."

Venhow opened his eyes, as if he had been resting, and looked around the room, surprised but casual about the situation.

He sat up against the back of the stone chair and felt his hands and feet bound back around the stone, the two bindings woven together in such a way that he couldn't move much more than his head.

Jameson sat in the corner of the marble room, his wrist facing upwards in his lap as he stitched long black knots into his broken skin. He cursed regularly through gritted teeth as he pulled the sections of skin together with each knot. Armond and Matrim sat nearby, each waiting for Jameson to finish so that he could look them over.

Ramif walked up to Venhow with a placid expression, "Comfortable?"

"Extremely," he said pleasantly, his grey eyes mocking.

"Who are you?" Ramif demanded.

"Whoever I want to be," he laughed softly, shrugging with one shoulder as best as he could through the tension of the bindings.

"What are you?" Ramif corrected, taking a step closer so that he could stare directly into his face.

"A wizard right now," he said obnoxiously, "but a trouble maker at heart."

Ramif picked up his sword and brandished it warningly, "Show me your real face."

"I don't think so," he said, with a slow shake of his head, as if he were doing no more than arguing the weather. He rolled back his shoulders and smirked.

"I wasn't asking," Ramif said, inching the blade closer.

"What, is this face not pretty enough for you?" he asked, coyly. Venhow's face slowly melted away. His brow narrowed and his eyes widened, the firm lines of the face slipping away into a softened round expression with full lips and a youthful gleam. Long black hair wrapped wistfully around her defined features with a harmonic grace in the quality of her voice, "Is this one any better dear?"

Ramif's expression dropped slightly as he looked over the familiar face. He looked lost, and stared at her for a long time, slowly remembering reality and his face hardened again. Anger flared up in him like a dry fire. He tightened his grip on the sword and his eyes sharpened. He gritted his teeth and leaned forward with one hand on the back of the chair and brought the blade tight against the hollow of her throat, "Not her face you son of a bitch! Show me yours!"

"Or what?" she yelled shrilly, "You'll cut out my heart?" she leaned into the blade purposefully drilling a small puncture into her skin and letting a drop of blood drizzle down into down into the curvature of her bust through the baggy shirt, "Haven't you already seen that?"

Ramif held the blade still but a heavy rapid pulse throbbed at the deep veins of his neck, "Stop it," he demanded.

She smirked, wallowing in the enjoyment of her talent of torment, "Why?" she pursed her black cherry lips and narrowed her eyes dauntingly, "you can't handle it? Couldn't you do it? Come on now, you want to cut out my heart while I'm wearing this face don't you?"

Ramif closed his eyes tight, "Stop."

She pressed her neck harder against the tip of the blade to put pressure on the sword until Ramif opened his eyes again and said, "You wanted her to die. You're happy she's gone aren't you?"

"Shut up!" Ramif shouted, blinking hard and fighting to keep eye contact with her.

"You didn't want me around anymore," she said, her tone changing rapidly. She opened her eyes wider and her eyes welled up with tears, "You didn't come home when the raid started. You left me on purpose!" she started taking sharp, rapid breaths and her frown deepened desperately, "You left me!"

"No I didn't!" he shouted, the end of his sword beginning to tremble as he withdrew it slightly from her.

"You wouldn't hurt me Ramif. You couldn't hurt me," she said, drawing her face in fearfully, piercing her bright amber eyes into Ramif, "Please, why am I here? You're hurting me! Let me go!"

"Stop it!" Ramif screamed, anger and fear boiling in his chest. He took in a deep breath and pressed against the blade again and made the small cut run heavier with fresh blood.

She screamed, her voice bouncing off of the marble walls. Ramif took an unsteady step back at the sound, dropping his sword to the floor with a clatter.

"You did this to me!" she yelled through sobs, twisting her face into one of horror, fear and betrayal, "Why wouldn't you save me? You could have saved me — You let him kill me!"

"No I didn't!" Ramif screamed, putting his hands up over his ears and pressing tightly against his skull.

"I suffered! IT'S YOUR FAULT—" A quick figure broke through the tight group and a sharp heavy impact silenced her screams.

Loch shook the pain from the hit out of his hand and watched the split at the end of her mouth seal shut in a matter of seconds, as if it had never been there. She spit out what little blood had seeped into her mouth onto the floor with a satisfied smile.

"Enough games," Loch said, "show us *your* face."

"What's the matter general, jealous?" she asked as she batted her eyes. Her face swiftly changed again into a young strong looking woman with soft cheeks and smooth features. Her dark hair became a sun catching, sandy, blonde and was now so long that it swept down into her lap, her eyes now a soft powder blue, "Do you want to play my game too?"

Loch grabbed her shirt and pulled her in as close as he could manage and the ties to the stone chair pulled taught at her limbs, "That shit won't work with me."

Her face softened and the pale blue eyes filled with tears again, "But Dad…" Loch let go of the shirt and punched her again, throwing her head back sharply.

She groaned quietly with her eyes shut tight as a sharp crackling sound popped in the air and the bones of her nose wriggled back into place under her skin. She opened her eyes and looked up at him, both impressed and amused, "That was pretty cold hearted."

"I said no more games," he said, as he pulled a knife out of his coat pocket and flicked it open.

"You don't like games?" she asked, and looked over at Ramif cruelly before she slid her eyes to Oswald with renewed hunger, "Do you?"

Oswald watched her, suddenly feeling the burning ache of the gash in his head intensify. He tried hard not to react as her face changed again and in a fluid motion her body became his and he looked at himself reflected in the mirror of the room, bound to the chair.

"They will put you here someday you know," his reflection told him, "Tied to a chair and left to rot. They don't trust you. Why would they? You're dangerous, just look what you've done already," he turned his head to look across the room where Jameson was tentatively guarding his freshly wrapped wrist as he was struggling to wrap the burns that were streaked jaggedly across Matrim's chest.

Loch leaned in and pressed the sharp end of the knife against his throat and whispered, "I won't say it again. I hate repeating myself."

The other Oswald rounded his face on Loch, trailing his eyes up his arm and staring hatefully at his age defined features, "You don't trust me. You know what happened back there and you're ignoring it. Aren't you going to say anything? You're afraid of me aren't you? Afraid of magic? You should be."

Loch sighed impassively and jammed the knife into his shoulder and let go, leaving the blade to hang there. The other Oswald yelled angrily, and his features shifted again, this time taking the form of a middle aged woman with bobbed brown hair, but the transition between the two was clumsy and stunted. She writhed, unable to heal with the knife stuck in place, and blood was pouring from the wound.

Loch leaned in again patiently, "I said that won't work with me. I want to see your real face Priie... That is your name isn't it? Priie?"

She drew in a sharp breath through pursed lips with a sour expression, "Naughty boy," she said, for the first time looking genuinely unhappy. She shifted around to try and get the knife out of her shoulder, and hissed darkly, "Where did you hear that from?"

"I heard that name the day I lost my arm. The day you took my arm," Loch corrected, and sank down to look her straight in the eye. He took ahold of the knife again but didn't pull it out of its place, "Someone was looking for you."

"And what makes you think that it was me?" she spat defensively, her eyes darting between Loch's face and the knife in her shoulder.

"Because," he said, ripping the knife out of the meat of her shoulder and taking a wide swing at her face with the blade. He made a quick, clean, cut across her forehead, which instantly began to pull together and seal, as did the deep puncture, only leaving streaks of blood behind, "goblins don't heal that quickly," he looked at her firmly, "And the one that took my arm did. I thought about it for years and never could quite put it together until now."

"There are lots of skin changers," she said dismissively, looking relieved to be finally rid of the knife.

"No, there aren't. Sombers don't heal like that," he said, turning the knife over in his hand, "You're the last of your kind aren't you?"

"Well, aren't you clever?" she whispered menacingly.

"Show me your face, Priie," Loch said again.

"That's never going to happen," she said firmly, shaking her head, "I'm protected this way."

"What if I were to peel your face off your bones? Would it show me what you looked like then?" Loch asked dangerously.

Priie shifted her eyes around as she thought over the threat. She made a silent decision and shook her head, "That wouldn't help you. You won't do it."

Loch wiped the blood off of his knife on the leg of his pants, snapped it shut and slid it back into his pocket with a shrug, "Then you'll die here."

Priie smirked and sat back in the chair looking bored, "You know you can't keep me here. Nowhere can hold me for long."

Loch pursed his lips and said dryly, "We'll see about that."

Ramif looked back to Oswald with a simmer of anger and shame hidden beneath the solid expression, "Come with me," he ordered, "We're going to clear out the weapons vault."

"Be sure to leave me a welcoming gift," Priie shouted out after them tauntingly.

It took Oswald, Ramif, Armond and Loch to move her from the chair to the cleared vault, each armed and each with a vice grip on a roped limb. They cut the bindings at her feet and left her hands wrapped behind her as they threw her into the small iron room. They pulled the door shut quickly and heard the bolt latch as she made impact with the inside of the door.

Oswald listened to the random impacts from within the vault as Loch bolted the door from the outside. He dropped the bar into place and turned the crank to secure the inner workings of the frame, the gears making a solid chunking sounds as they fitted into place.

"Thanks," Ramif said shortly, glancing up at Loch and running his fingers down his braided beard, "for earlier."

Loch looked down at him and shook his head, "I'm just sorry it took so long for me to do something about it," he looked down and flexed his fingers, watching the bruise that was beginning to swell on the knuckles of his hand.

"It shouldn't have been able to get to me," Ramif said apologetically, looking at the floor.

"Don't worry about it," Loch said, as he stepped away from the door, hearing the occasional impact from inside the room and looking back at it wearily, "That's a dark and cruel skill. It was bound to happen."

Ramif clenched his jaw, the muscles of his face working behind his skin, "It still shouldn't have," he said quietly.

"We all have regrets," Loch said supportively, "She just found yours first."

Ramif nodded at the floor as they walked.

Armond limped heavily over to Oswald and turned him away from the group. He walked him back towards a room on the far side of the building, near the weapons vault which was still thumping loudly.

"Is Matrim alright?" Oswald asked, trying to look back over his shoulder but couldn't see through the massive door to the far side.

"He's lost part of his hearing on the one side, his fingers are numb and his heart still isn't beating right," Armond reported and his lips pressed tightly together as he stared fixedly ahead.

"But he'll recover?" Oswald asked hopefully.

"I don't know," Armond said bluntly. He stopped at the door of the back room and struck a match, lighting a torch at the doorway, "but you just proved exactly how dangerous you are without your sword."

"I was trying to save him," Oswald said, suddenly feeling his stomach twist fearfully, "I didn't want to hurt him!"

"You just might have killed him in trying to save him," Armond said sharply, "It's a better passing than he would have had, but death is still death."

"You don't know that he will die though right?" Oswald asked pleadingly, his stomach and his heart fighting for the place in his throat, "He could be okay. He's been talking a bit and getting around…"

Armond looked at him seriously, "He was struck by lightning. If he lives it's because Jameson knows what he's doing."

Oswald felt sick and his head spun. He swallowed hard, trying to clear the heavy slab as it started to build in his throat. He gripped his sword tight and forced away the static in his chest.

Armond tried to soften his features but was having difficulty masking his frustration at the situation. He touched the stitching at his chin gingerly and moved his hand around to rub at his forehead, trying to massage away his racing thoughts. He took a deep breath and closed his eyes in the torchlight and said with a softer tone to his voice, "Your secret's out. We have to get your magic under control and we need to start now. I'll be honest with you, I don't have a clue where to start but we have to get it done. Give me your sword and let's see what you can do."

Chapter Twenty-Seven

Caleb leaned against the vault door, listening to the occasional voice as it floated along the marble walls to his post. He picked at his fingernails with a small pocket knife for a while to keep himself occupied as he patiently waited for the change of shift. He looked up as the echo of footsteps turned around the north side of the building and started in his direction.

A large man came through the wide door of the room, straightening his uniform and looking around casually. He walked up to the vault and seemed concerned with the silence.

"What's the night been like so far?" he asked.

"Very quiet," Caleb said, snapping his knife closed and thumbing it into his pocket.

"That's unusual," Vincent said, leaning down and inspecting the locks and gears of the vault carefully.

"I slid in some water a couple of hours ago," Caleb said, with a soft gesture of his head, "It's asleep. I guess three days of slamming around the vault finally wore it out."

"It didn't try anything weird?" Vincent asked cautiously.

Caleb shook his head, "No, it was just good timing today I guess."

"It must have been," Vincent said with a snort, scratching at the collar of his uniform, "Yesterday it charged the door as a troll when I opened it."

"You're lucky it didn't get out then," Caleb said, looking back to the door with his eyebrows raised.

Vincent grabbed the handle of the gear and tried to give it a tight turn, satisfied with the lock when the gear didn't budge, "Yeah. I guess when it can be anything, you have to be prepared for anything."

"That's hard to do sometimes. Just be careful what you say around it," Caleb said, lowering his voice softly, "It can hear you through the vault."

"How do you know that?" Vincent asked.

"Last night my wife came by and brought me something to eat. It was able to mimic her voice and yelled through the walls all night," Caleb frowned, "Tonight was easy though."

"So nothing really to report for this shift?"

"Nah," Caleb shook his head, "You want help with anything before I head home?"

"No," Vincent patted down his pockets to be sure that he had everything he needed, "I got it from here. You have the night watch again, right?"

"Yeah, I do," Caleb said, stepping away from the vault, "I'll be back at dusk."

"Alright," Vincent said, looking back at the vault and taking his post against the door, "Get some rest and I'll see you then."

Caleb smiled politely and walked out of the room, putting his hands into his pockets and fidgeting with the knife. He turned the corner into another hall and found his way to the wide front double doors of the building and shoved one open. The first morning sunlight shone in through the gap in the door and reflected up off of the disturbed snowbanks out in the street. The cold wind brushed against his face as he slid out of the building and closed the doors back into their place behind him.

He bundled up and passed the ornately carved pillars that encircled the entrance and down the shallow steps to the main road. He listened to the crunch of snow under his boots and the silence of winter as he made his way towards the northern edge of the city.

It was quiet, and the chill of the air burned his eyes. He passed a large man stepping out of his home, bundled up with layers of clothes. The man turned and smiled cheerfully.

"Hey, Caleb."

"Good morning," Caleb said curtly, returning the smile.

"What are you doing up so early?"

"I had a night watch for the generals."

"A night watch?" the man asked, closing the door to his home, "Is everything okay?"

"Yeah," Caleb nodded, "The Commanding General demanded secrecy so I can't really get into it, but everything's fine really."

"Well good. Where are you headed now?"

"Home."

The man frowned a bit, "I thought you lived on the other side of town."

"I do," Caleb insisted with a nod, "I thought I would stop at the graveyard before I turned in for the night, so I'm kind of doing a round trip of this side of the city this morning."

"Oh," the man sadly, "Has it been a year already?"

Caleb nodded, "This week."

"I'm sorry about that," the man said, wrapping his coat tighter against him in the cold, "It was a tragic thing, but sometimes it happens. How's Mary?"

"She's fine."

"I think I'm going to stop by and visit sometime soon," the man said thoughtfully, and added "If you don't mind... I haven't seen the kids for a while."

"Sure," Caleb said, "Just drop by. You know you're always welcome."

"Thanks," the man said, starting off in the opposite direction, "I'll see you soon then."

"Absolutely," Caleb waved at him and continued down the road. After a while the houses thinned out and the clearing gave way from gravel to dirt and the snow blanketed cemetery lay out in front of him. He walked through the rows of stones, not glancing at any of them as he went.

He reached the far end of the graveyard and continued on through it into the woods beyond, the sounds of his feet in the snow covered undergrowth changing into a muffled step. He peaked the hillside and began down the far slope. He wandered until the sun began to shine over the ridge with vigor and he broke out into a run.

Priie shifted her body from Caleb's military form and began to morph, her ribcage lengthened and the long bones of her arms and legs stretched to an abnormal shape and skeletal frame. Her face sunk in and her ears elongated. The fingers of her hands formed another joint and her skin began to change to a deep mossy green.

Her strides tripled with the new Keernith body and she found that she was able to cover an enormous amount of ground in very short time and the forest floor passed under her like swift storm clouds overhead.

She watched the forest trees change, each area favoring its own particular species. Rivers and streams were running smoothly with ice floats drifting by in the tossing waters as she tore across the province. She ran nonstop, as fast as she could manage, and noticed the sun creep over her and begin to fall again until the early dark of the winter swept away the telltale passing of time and she continued to run throughout the night. The stars glittered against the snow and the frost, lighting her way.

The sun rose and fell again to dusk before she found the crossroads of the providence and finally dared to rest. Exhausted, she found an evergreen tree with high branches and allowed her magic to fall. Her hair lengthened and turned to a fog white and stuck out at all angles and her porcelain skin became soft and fragile. Her entire body sighed with the relief of rest and the comfort of feeling her own skin. She stretched her wings as best as she could under the clothes, not wanting to bare them to the cold, and laid down against the dirt patch beneath the evergreen canopy.

She suddenly became acutely aware of her predicament.

She laid in the dirt and stared at the soft bristles of the tree, a conflicting turmoil of her thoughts began to fight within her. She felt this way often, but could never really bring herself to do anything about it. Frustration, anger, depression, hope and love all battled their constant war against her chest. Overwhelmingly it was fear that bound her to the ground as she thought.

She wondered, and yet knew, the welcome that she would receive back home when she came to him with neither the sword nor a triumphant story of bloodshed.

She closed her eyes and could almost feel the ache of Venhow's wrath in her bones already forming. She put a hand over her face and pushed a thick, coarse, lock of her hair out of her delicate face, her purple eyes able to see through the dwindling light with ease.

She dreaded going back.

In a way she never wanted to go back to him, but in another she always did, hoping to see the man that he had once been. She understood the consequences of each action and weighed them in her head. She wondered if death would finally be her sentence.

She shook her head against the ground knowing that death was the kindest command that Venhow ever gave, and knew also that she would never receive it. She felt trapped, cocooned by the evergreen and pinned down by life.

If she left, she knew that he would be able to find her and the anger he would have then would be nothing compared to the wrath of a single disappointment. If she didn't leave him now however, she knew she never would.

She let her thoughts roll until she gave in to sleep, the few short hours she allowed for rest full of worry and uncertain futures.

She woke up startled, and instantly hid herself. She snapped into the form of a dark haired woman and scrambled out into an inch of fresh snow that had fallen during the last few hours. It was still dark outside, the nearly full moon lighting the woods around her and hinting of dawn. She scrambled to her feet and looked around for what had woken her.

A goods wagon rolled down the narrow path, drawn by a black horse which turned with the clop of hooves at the crossroad. She ran to catch up with it, fumbling awkwardly in the soft powdered snow, she called out after it and it clattered to a stop.

A gruff looking man was at the reigns and looked her over with sharp and beady eyes, her body wrapped in Caleb's oversized clothing. He blinked down at her and frowned, "What is a little thing like you doing out in this weather so far from anywhere. It's dangerous for a woman to be alone out here you know."

"I know it's dangerous," she said, shivering in the night's cold breeze, "But it's still less dangerous than where I just came from I assure you. Where are you heading if I may ask?"

"Nowhere a pretty thing like you wants to go," he tightened the reigns and pointed ahead of him down the road, "I have to pass through Patterhead Gorge and then into Azar."

Priie smiled at him, "I have been running for two days and the cold is starting to get to me. Do you mind if I ride with you?"

He looked at her, concerned, but gave a short nod and held out a hand to help her up into the front seat next to him, "If you're sure that's where you want to go. I can drop you off anywhere along the way of course."

"No," she said, taking his hand and pulling herself up into the seat, "I'm heading to the central city of Azar myself."

"Why would you want to go there?" he asked, looking over at her incredulously. He snapped the reigns and the large black stallion snorted before starting back down the road, its glossy coat catching in the moonlight as it trotted along.

"My family's there," she said, sitting back in her seat and feeling the rumble of the wagon wheels against the road.

He looked her over cautiously, "What did you say you were running from?"

"I didn't," she said unhappily, looking out into the woods.

He frowned indignantly and watched the trail wind until the land began to flatten out and the snow faded away to a cold and bare landscape.

The sun rose slowly and the immensity of the gorge caught the light like the mouth of a great dragon, buttes jutting up from the canyon floor with ridged edges and the intense color of dragon fire. The red and yellow hues of the walls strung with black drags of volcanic rock and the history of death. Markers were placed along the path warning travelers of the wildlife and the intense flash floods during the rainy season. A single immense grave stone sat rigid in the canyon floor as they rolled slowly past it, thousands of names carved into the massive black stone.

"The great war left its mark on this place didn't it?" the man said, looking around as they passed through.

"All wars do," she commented dryly.

"I suppose that's true," he turned towards her and tightened the scarf around his neck, "All history leaves scars in the land. This one is just something a little different."

"Because it was carved by magic?" Priie asked, with an eyebrow raised.

"The great war was a wizard's war after all," the man said, looking down at the path, "People say that this gorge ran with a river of blood for a month."

"No," she corrected distantly, "but the flood waters did carry bodies and lost bones to the south for many years."

He glanced over at her interestedly, "You know your history."

"Of course," she said, looking at another shard of volcanic rock on the roadside as they rattled by, "History is littered with death, and death is just another part of life. Therefore I enjoy history when there is history worth learning."

"You're a strange woman," he said, looking back to the road and spotting a small spring in a rock pool up ahead, the water trickling lightly.

"Only if you don't know me well enough," she promised quietly.

They stopped and allowed the horse to drink and rest for a short while, sharing a small slice of bread and a handful of almonds before they were back onto the road. The sun crept through the sky and they continued out of the gorge and up into the flatlands, the towering horizon rolling up into the silhouette of Mt. Ire and the great city of Azar.

"Not far now," Priie said, both comforted and disturbed at the sight of the volcano in the distance, "We could be there by midnight."

"No," the man said, shaking his head and pulling on the reigns to lead the stallion off of the road and into a frosted glade, "My horse is strong but he needs a rest. We'll move again in the morning and be there tomorrow afternoon."

"I suppose I'll get the rest of the way there on foot then," she said, with a blank smile, "Thank you for the ride."

"Are you certain that you want to go into Azar? I don't think you understand what you are getting yourself into," he said warningly, "People don't come out of that city."

"You're going," she said, drawing her arched eyebrows down derisively.

"I'm going to the city's *border* for trade," he emphasized, "I have goods for the army. I'm not going into the city itself. People die there."

"People do," she agreed, and looked him in the eye with a warning gleaming behind her stare, "But I get along just fine."

"Do you know what you are doing?" he asked, concernedly.

"I always know what I'm doing," Priie said, regretfully staring at the volcano before her. She jumped down off of the wagon and continued down the road without a second glance back.

When she was sure that she was clearly out of anyone's line of sight, she removed the uniformed Gommorn military jacket and threw it against the side of the road, the cold biting at her skin through the thin undershirt. She slowly transformed back into a

Keernith body, the long green limbs swinging as she walked. She looked around one last time with her now elongated ears perked, listening down the road and hearing the silence of the evening. She took in a deep breath, her ribs now pressing tightly against the thin shirt with the dramatic change in size and she resolved to run the remaining distance to the city.

The city slowly grew as the hours passed and finally the base of the mountain sloped upwards and the lights of the castle windows could be seen flickering up along the high mountain side. A massive gate held fast to the walls of the city at the end of the road.

Two guards stepped forward into the night with their weapons drawn and sharp eyes glinting in the darkness. The larger of the two came close and looked her over, her goblin face set and well lined, a face that she had used often.

"Maurik," Priie said deeply, her voice deep and grating in the cold.

"Kyrat" he said, retuning the greeting and lowering his blade, "You've been gone a while. Anything interesting?"

"No good news," she grumbled back, "but I do need to speak with King Venhow."

"I assume he knows you're coming?" Maurik asked.

"Obviously," Priie said unhappily, looking back to the gate.

Maurik shrugged and gestured for the other goblin to open the gate, the large iron doors clicking as the gears turned and they groaned open into the city, "Alright then. Good luck with giving the King the bad news."

"I need it," Priie said darkly, making her way past the other goblin with a short nod of acknowledgement.

The city's roads were well paved and easier to travel on. She looked around at the lit candles in windows quickly being snuffed out as she walked by, a twinge of comfort in the safety of being feared. She made a straight path up the main road and watched the castle begin to tower. Each step brought the building higher up into the sky until she had to crane her neck to look up into the high tower where she knew he would be waiting.

Another guard at the castle door looked her over briefly and recognized the false features and opened the door for her. She ducked slightly, curling her back into the uncomfortable posture of the Keernith and hunched her way across the hall to the main staircase and hall after hall finding the familiar path to the spiraled tower staircase in the labyrinth of rooms and halls.

The musky smell of damp stone greeted her as she made her way up the staircase. She passed dim torches and could hear the distant muffled sound of voices. She hadn't expected him to have company at such a late hour. She stepped up to the door and listened with her goblin ears and recognized the other voice as Walt's.

She opened the door, not bothering to knock and was rounded on by two angry faces.

Venhow recognized her more quickly than did Walt and his expression softened, "Priie, it's good to see you. Close the door behind you, I'll be right there."

"Of course," she said, in her natural tone and allowed her magic to fall away again. The door shut with a loud thump and she tried not to eavesdrop as he and Walt continued their conversation. Instead she went to a cabinet nearby and found one of her tops, wanting the freedom to stretch her wings and the comfort a shirt woven with spells that would alter the fabric to fit her change in form.

She threw off the filthy clothes she had been wearing and quickly slipped into her own, shying away from Walt's curious flickering eyes.

She stretched her wings and fluttered them a few times to work out the tight feeling of their webbing and to enjoy the soft warm air of the chambered room. Her line of vision found the fireplace and she stepped closer, absorbing the warmth.

Venhow turned around and set his grey eyes on her frail features and a smile, fleeting, but smile nonetheless, flickered across his face, "So where is it?"

Priie looked down at the floor and braced herself, "Still in Gommorn."

There was a moment of silence as the concept slowly sank into his line of thought and an ember of anger began to flare, "I was sure that you would be able to handle it this time. You did at least kill the elf?"

"No," she said, quietly.

"Why?" Venhow said, a vein at his neck beginning to pulse harder against his skin.

"I didn't have a clear opportunity. When I found him he was already suspicious," she said uncomfortably.

"Why would he have been suspicious?" Venhow snapped, balling his hands into fists at his sides.

"It had something to do with the kid's dialect," she muttered, wringing her hands softly and tucking her wings in slightly, "I hadn't known about it until it was too late."

"And my sword?" he asked dangerously, his eyes narrowed.

"He still has it," she said, with an ashamed glance at the floor as she took a tentative step back, closer to the fireplace.

"How dare you come back to me with nothing!?" Venhow hissed.

"It was in my hand," she promised, her tight muscles and tense nerves waiting for his wrath.

"Then why don't you have it?!" he yelled, his face deepening in color.

"I never would have guessed he was that powerful. Something happened," she twisted one of her fingers anxiously, her purple eyes full of fear, "I had the sword and I was getting ready to leave with it. He filled the room with lightning and I woke up tied to a chair in the war room."

"You were caught!?" he howled viciously, as he stepped forward with his lips pinched together and his fists clenched, "What did you tell them?!"

"Nothing," she said, quickly shaking her head.

"What do they know?!" he cleared the room in a few long strides and threw the back of his hand across her face.

Priie swallowed and put a hand to the searing pain in the side of her face protectively. With her magic down she had to try harder to heal the wound, pressing her hand against the heat in her cheek, "Nothing," she said again, pleadingly, "I didn't tell them anything!"

He raised his arm again and she felt another strike against the same side of her head, the impact of the strike taking her up off of her feet and to the floor in a sprawled and painful heap. She tried to take in a rattled breath and saw his hand come up again and put an arm over her head protectively.

"Venhow!" Walt shouted, his voice echoing against the stone walls, "Stop it! Let her explain."

"How dare you," Venhow spat, lowering his fist and rounding on Walt, who looked unfazed by his anger, "This isn't your place."

Walt tucked his hands into his sleeves and scowled, "I'm here aren't I?"

"Damn you," Venhow said, turning back to Priie as she cowered against the ground at his feet.

Walt took a step forward with a distinct sharpness in his voice, "You hit her again and you and I are going to have problems," he said, with a coldness in his stare that had never been there before, "Take a breath and think about it."

Venhow stopped and looked down at Priie, his face placid. He thought about the situation carefully, as he tried to balance the force of his anger against Walt's abilities and power. The two of them stared at each other, unmoving, as the fire crackled in the hearth and pitched the occasional flare of sparks into the room.

Walt slid his hands out of the sleeves of his robe and flexed his fingers down at his side. Venhow took in a deep breath and scowled as his eyes lingered on the seriousness of Walt's face.

Finally Venhow lowered a steady and open hand, still breathing heavily with his rage, and lifted Priie to her feet gently. A glint of something resembling embarrassment crossed his eyes but he turned away from her and left her in the cold of his bitter silence.

Priie straightened her shirt uncomfortably and readjusted her wings, humiliated in the silence and unsure if she had the permission to continue speaking. She decided that she did, "They don't know anything. They don't know my face, I swear."

"How did they catch you?" Venhow demanded, his nostrils flaring as his anger continued to boil from a distance.

"The elf has found his magic," she said, with her eyes wide, "It's begun to develop and it's nothing like anything I've seen — except from the two of you," she added. She licked her lips, trying to meet Venhow's eyes, "It was a fully formed bolt of white lightning that he pulled out of thin air... and I don't think that he was trying very hard. If he gets full control of it, I think that even you'll have trouble against him."

Venhow took in a deep breath and tried to remain in control of his anger, "And what do you suggest we do about it? Obviously he's harder to kill than we thought."

"He killed a Grimm," Walt interjected, with a disdainful smirk, "You should have expected this."

Priie reached out an unsure hand and touched Venhow's shoulder. He looked at her coldly, but didn't withdraw from her touch. She looked between Walt and Venhow, and dared to share her opinion, "We need to take the city and we need to move now."

Venhow pondered the suggestion, "What exactly are we up against?"

"He's training with the three high Generals," she said tensely, "They're all in Gommorn, and they're more prepared than they should be. We need to take Azar's forces. All of them."

"Numbers, Priie," Venhow said, flickering his eyes around the room in thought, "How many people are we talking about?"

She chewed on her lip and pulled in her glossy wings as she tried to make an estimate, "The Brutes, the Dwarves, men from the South and what's left from the northern Harbored. Easily twenty thousand military men and women."

"That's nothing," Venhow said, dismissively.

"Please," she said, tightening her hold on his shoulder and trying to force eye contact, "Don't underestimate them."

He looked back at her thoughtfully, "General Armond is with them?"

"Yes," she said seriously.

He took in a deep breath and nodded understandingly, "Then all of our forces it is. We'll start moving them immediately and I'll lead them to victory myself," he looked to Walt expectantly, "and you'll come with me?"

"The battlefield isn't my place," Walt said flatly, "It's yours."

Venhow looked at him sternly, a harsh mixture of disappointment and anger in his cold grey eyes, "I need you there."

Walt shook his head, "I can't."

"Why not?" Venhow asked, drawing his brow down in scrutiny, "You told me that your services were mine. I need the extra security."

"It sounds like you do," Walt said, with a frown and an arced eyebrow.

"Then I expect you there."

"How long will it take to get everyone moving?" Walt asked, ignoring Venhow's stare and looking out the window towards the horizon and through the darkness.

"To bring all of the armies in together and be ready to march? Supplied?" Venhow thought out loud, trying to figure the time in his head, "Three months."

"And we can be ready by then?" Walt asked distantly.

"We will," Venhow said, looking back at Priie, "Go and wake General Skemir."

Chapter Twenty-Eight

Oswald tightened the scabbard against his waist and tried to sneak through the house to the front door, but caught a sharp movement in the corner of his eye as Matrim sat up in his bed. Oswald turned around, a heaviness on his shoulders as he caught sight of the bright purple and black burns across his chest and shoulder.

"Hey Oz," Matrim said, sounding stronger than he had been, "Ya haven' talked to me much. How's everythin' goin'? Are ya getting' it figyaed out?"

Oswald paused uncomfortably, "No. Armond said that he wants to try something new today though, so hopefully today will be better. How are you feeling?"

"Better," Matrim said, sounding unsure as he put a hand up to the edge of the burn and pressed on an unharmed place that the burn had wrapped around at his collarbone, "Jus' healin'"

"You know I didn't mean to hurt you, don't you?" Oswald said, fidgeting with the hilt of his sword and feeling guilty.

Matrim threw up a hand nonchalantly, "Yeah, I know. It wan't yur fault."

"I'm still sorry," Oswald muttered.

"Don' be," he said, with a painful shrug, holding tighter to the place on his chest, "Its betta than it coulda been. 'Sides, girls like scars right?"

"I guess so," Oswald said, with a weak smile, "That's going to be a nice one."

Matrim looked down at the forked lightning burn and gave a one sided smile, "Like no one else's fa sure."

"Is Jameson coming by again today?" Oswald asked, still staring at the burn unhappily.

"Supposed to," he said, with a nod, "He said he was gonna be by roun' noon."

"Alright," Oswald said, turning back to the door, "Do you want me to bring anything back when I'm done?"

"Nah," he said, leaning back onto the bed carefully.

"Get some rest," Oswald said, walking out of the front door and shutting it carefully behind him. The cold had deepened and a bitter sharpness swelled in the air. He pulled his coat around himself tightly and made his way through the snow covered city, stepping over patches of ice that glinted brightly against the road.

The community building shimmered in the morning sunlight and he saw Loch leaning up against the main doorway, his cigar pluming heavy clouds of smoke into the cold.

"You're late," he said, breathing out a roll of grey fog.

"Didn't mean to be," Oswald said apologetically, "I slept in on accident and Matrim caught me as I was trying to leave."

"Is he doing any better?"

"I think so," Oswald said, with a frown sinking into his features, "He wouldn't tell me if he wasn't though."

"He's a tough kid. I wouldn't worry about him too much," Loch said reassuringly, tipping his head towards the main doors of the building, "You should go ahead in. Fred and Armond are both waiting for you."

"Fred?"

"Yeah, he's going to try and help out," Loch said, taking another puff of the cigar, "It should be an interesting day," he smiled forebodingly and tapped the ashes off of the cigar as they hissed into the snow at his feet.

Oswald looked back at Loch apprehensively, and pulled the door open and stepped into the expansive front room of the building. He walked through the back room and turned down the hall, making his way through the dimly lit war room as he passed group of men huddled around a table. He passed on through the room and glanced at the door of the weapons vault, with a cold chill at his spine and the horrific memory of the slaughter they had found within.

He walked by the vault and continued on through the next set of doors. The room had a large metal cylinder at the far end of the room built onto a swivel with interlocking gears and a well-balanced pyramid of cannons sitting at its side. A sickeningly tart and bitter smell caught his senses and he recoiled slightly.

"What is that?" he asked, trying to ignore the burning in his sinuses.

"Dragon fire," Fred said happily, stepping away from Armond and the small table in the corner of the room. He walked over with an eerie grin, bearing his sharpened teeth between his blue lips as he thumped Oswald hard on the back in greeting. The thump jarred his shoulder and knocked the wind loose from his lungs.

"Why is there dragon fire in here?" Oswald coughed, trying to catch his breath back and rolling his shoulder to work out a muscle cramp that was threatening to seize up.

"Training," Fred said brightly, walking across the room towards the cannon.

"I think I'm missing something," Oswald said, trying to put the two together in his head, "What exactly are we doing today?"

Armond walked over to him, masking a limp in his right leg, with his hand out, "Give me your sword." Oswald removed the scabbard from his belt and held out the leather bound end of the metal sheath.

Armond took the bound end, carefully balancing the hilt in the air and walked it over to the small table where he had been keeping it over the last couple of days. He turned back to Oswald with a determined expression, "I think I have an idea on how to get a handle on this," he gestured for Oswald to follow him and he took him to the corner of the room where the walls were reinforced with steel plates, "You seem to have more of a reaction when you are confronted, right?"

"I suppose so," Oswald said hesitantly, "But it's still pretty unpredictable. I don't know if I can choose what happens yet."

"We'll see," Armond said sharply, "Stand right there."

"What's going on?" Oswald asked, his heart beating nervously.

Armond walked across the room, gingerly stepping with his injured leg, and he pointed back at the corner behind him where Oswald stood.

Fred laughed suddenly, far too happy with the situation, and grabbed the cannon, turning it on its base until it was aimed directly at Oswald.

Oswald understood immediately and his heart thundered, "Wait! You can't just—" There was a heavy plume of black fire as the cannon went off. He saw the iron ball leave the barrel and roll through the air directly at him. He threw up his hands in a panic and he felt the air thicken around him and pull the breath from his lungs as it solidified. The cannon ball impacted the air with a loud roar and dropped in front of him, hitting the stone floor and throwing chips of marble out in a sharp pattern.

"What the hell was that?!" Oswald screamed.

"It worked," Fred said, with a chortle that mingled with the ringing in his ears.

"You just fired a cannon at me!" Oswald shouted angrily.

"You're alright," Armond said aloofly, picking up another cannon ball and loading it down into the barrel as Fred picked up a container, pouring liquid dragon fire into the back end of the cannon, "That's what I thought would happen."

Oswald felt blood rush into his face as his heart thundered against his ribs, "You could have killed me!"

"Quit complaining," Armond said, lighting the cannon again. The dark fire rolled out of the barrel as another cannonball came raging across the room with a loud bang.

Oswald threw his hands up in the same way and felt the air respond again, the second iron ball came roaring into the barrier. It slowed in the air and turned around, smacking into the floor next to the last with the same explosive force.

"Stop it!" Oswald screamed, breathing heavily, "You can't just fire cannons at me!"

"Sure I can," Armond said, rolling another iron ball into the barrel.

"This isn't training! This is madness!"

"Shut up. You're getting the hang of it," Armond said, walking around the back of the cannon, letting Fred take over total use of it.

Six more cannonballs gradually piled at the ground around his feet and a small crater had begun to form in the floor where they had landed.

Oswald was having difficulty catching his breath, unable to breathe through the magically thick air and the heavy smog of dragon fire that was continually fogging out of the cannon. He held up a hand as he tried to ask for a moment to breathe. Fred stopped firing for a few minutes and allowed him to rest long enough for the room to quit dancing with bright sparklers in his vision. He leaned up against the steel paneled wall and closed his eyes waiting for the spinning to stop.

"Are you doing alright?" Armond called, from his place across the room.

"I can't breathe — very well — when — I'm doing that…" Oswald gasped.

"Why not?" Armond asked curiously.

"The air's — too thick to breathe — with the magic," Oswald said, swallowing hard and coughing at the dense smoke filled air.

"You are the one doing it," Armond said, with a shrug, "See what you can do about that."

Oswald bumped the back of his head against the wall lightly in frustration, "Don't you think I tried that?"

"Try harder…" Armond ordered, as he picked up the container of dragon fire, "We're loading the cannon."

"No!" Oswald argued heatedly, "I'm tired of being shot at!" He pushed away from the wall, his body tight and sore from bracing himself for so long. He walked away from the steel corner and headed for the door but he caught movement out of the corner of his eye and saw the barrel of the cannon following him as he walked. He heard the dragon fire ignite, followed by the tremendous explosion as the cannonball came hurtling towards the side of his head.

He rounded on the iron ball and reached one hand out into the air instinctively. The ball slid to a slow stop, spinning in the air. Oswald watched it and felt the continuous ripple of magic extend from his fingertips with awe. He turned his hand and the cannonball began to spin in another direction. He turned his hand the other way and watched the iron ball mimic his movements.

Something clicked and he felt a small understanding of the magic and how it reacted to his body and his mind. He relaxed and tried to keep up the flow of magic, keeping the ball hovering in mid-air. He rolled his fingers quickly and the ball began to spin more enthusiastically in the air until it began to whistle against the pressure of the air. He looked curiously to the steel wall and threw his arm to the side and the ball followed its path and shot across the room with the same force as the cannon. It hit the steel plate with a crash and the immense sound rang in his ears.

He looked up at Armond both shocked and pleased with the new understanding.

Armond looked surprised at the new development and uncrossed his arms. He took a few steps forward and called after him, "Do you think you can do that again?"

"Yeah," Oswald said, his blustering anger at the stressful morning fading away with his renewed sense of control over the situation, "Fire it again."

Fred lit the dragon fire and black flames spat the new iron ball through the air. He held out his hand more casually, this time feeling the magic run down his arm as he caught the ball. It hovered again, feet away from the end of his fingers but he could still somehow feel the heated metal and the subtle changes in its surface. He spun it with his fingers and launched it against the same place in the wall while trying to block out the deep reverberating sound of the impact.

"Good," Armond said, holding up a hand and signaling for Fred to stop reloading the cannon. He walked across the room quickly, the limp in his step only really noticeable with the increase in speed. He broke into an unsteady run and pulled a dagger out from his belt, and with the precision of a master, he threw the blade and the dagger spun in the air.

Oswald put his hands up through the thickened wall of air and he forced the air to give him room to breathe. Relieved with the small change to the barrier, he watched the spinning dagger stick into the air as if it had hit something wet and solid. He reached through the thickness and plucked the dagger out of the air.

"I think you are starting to figure it out," Armond said, as he stepped up to Oswald, reached over and took the dagger out of his hand, "Still angry?"

Oswald looked around at the room full of scattered cannonballs, "I still don't like that you were shooting a cannon at my face," he said honestly.

"I didn't think that you would enjoy it," he said, slipping the dagger back into his belt, "I asked if you still angry about it."

"No," Oswald said, now able to feel some of the magic in his body, "But how did you know that this would work?"

"I didn't," Armond said, looking serious, "I just noticed that both times that I've seen this particular kind of magic from you, it was because you were afraid. Who isn't afraid of getting shot in the face with a cannon?"

"That is a very poor excuse to try it," Oswald said bitterly.

Armond shrugged passively, "You weren't afraid of the last cannonball."

"No," he said looking over at it, "Because I'd gotten an idea of how the magic works."

"Or the dagger."

"Same magic, same concept," Oswald said.

"So you need something a little different then?" Armond asked distantly, his eyes flickering around the room as he got lost in his own train of thought.

"That isn't what I said," Oswald said quickly, not wanting to have to deal with anything more stressful, "I said that I figured out how to protect myself."

"To protect yourself..." Armond parroted back, as he walked over to the desk muttering to himself. He picked up a book and flipped through pages repeating the phrase and looking for something. He closed the book slowly in his hand, an idea forming and whittling its thought into his distinguished features. He set the book back down and scratched at his chin pensively, "Hey, Fred, when is Jameson going to be back here?"

Fred looked around trying to judge the amount of time that they had spent in the room so far, "I would think that he would be back any time now," Fred said, his voice grumbling deeply through the marble room.

"Take a break," Armond said, as he walked gingerly out of the doorway and into the next room over to join the group of men huddled around the war table.

Fred left his place and retrieved a long brush from against the wall and got down on his knees to start cleaning the inside of the barrel of the cannon. The occasional reactive puff of dragon smoke coughed out of the mouth of it as he began to scrub at the metal. He started sweeping out small piles of soot and Oswald looked around, not used to the concept of a non-food related break, and walked over to join him.

He sank down next to Fred and was impressed by the size and craftsmanship of the cannon itself. It was larger than he had expected it to be, next to Fred he hadn't thought much about the size of it, but kneeling beside it showed its true mass. It was iron and molded steel, wrapped and decorated with a bronze band at each end. The gears of the base all interlocked cleanly with the gears that turned the angle of the cannon and he was sure that it could swivel to any angle.

"This is a beautiful machine really," Oswald said thoughtfully, looking around for another brush and picking one up from behind the cannon. He found the place that Fred had been pouring the liquid dragon fire, lifted the hatch and started cleaning it from the side.

"I'm glad you think so," Fred said, with a deep rumble, "I built it."

Oswald held his breath as another short lived plume of smoke puffed out of the hatch at his face as the bitter, sour, smell of it irritated his eyes and nose. He blinked away the noxious fume and looked over with raised eyebrows, "Really? You made this by yourself?" he looked over the precision of the gears and the fine lines of it.

"Not solely," he said, sweeping another pile of soot out of the barrel, "Maria came up with the second set of cogs that run the inside of it there," he pointed inside the hatch to the dark interiors of the machine, "And that helps to separate the dragon fire from the cannonball until there is enough pressure built up from ignition then the gears spin and the fire hits the air and it goes off."

"Why does the fire have to be separated?" Oswald asked, trying to get a good look at the hatch as he brushed away the soot.

"Liquid dragon fire is too hot when it first ignites. It would burn off in layers as it hit the air because it's contained and it would melt the iron of the cannonball," Fred turned the brush upside down and started to clean the other side, reaching his arm into the hole to be able to clean down to the end of the shaft, "Basically it makes a mess."

"And she came up with how to fix that?"

"The original idea? No," Fred said, "But she did find a way to make it work better."

Oswald tapped the bristles of his brush on the floor and knocked out a pile of ash before he turned back to the small hatch and started scrubbing at it again, finally starting to see the underlying metal, "I had no idea you had this kind of expertise with machines."

"I told you that I build things," Fred said, as he pulled his long green arm out the barrel with a new pile of soot before sliding it back in up to his shoulder to continue cleaning.

"Building things can mean anything," Oswald said, fighting to sweep the soot up out of the angled hatch.

"Only if you don't know a goblin." Fred pulled his arm back out of the cannon leaving a black pile of ash to roll out of the mouth of the barrel at his knees. He set the brush down next to him and got back up to his feet, "That's enough for now. I don't know if the general is quite done with it or not."

"No offense, but I think I am," Oswald said, putting his brush down too, looking down at his arm and the entire front of his shirt, blackened with a fine layer of soot, "I've been shot at enough today."

"I'd hold off on that thought," Fred said, brushing himself off and rubbing at the black ash that coated his arm.

"Why?"

"I still have more cannonballs in the pile here," he said, with a nod to the ten or so remaining cannons behind them, "And if he's waiting for Jameson, then you're far from done with being shot at today."

Oswald dropped his head wearily and groaned, "Why does everyone want to shoot at me?"

"Because it's funny," Fred said, with a wide and pointy grin, landing a hearty thump against Oswald's shoulder.

The torchlights had been put out and the darkness of the solid room was complete but for what little streams of light were able to creep through the boarded windows. Oswald tried to see through the shadow but was having trouble discerning the faces of the circle of men moving around him in the overwhelming darkness. He caught the occasional sharp movement and was unsure where the shot would be coming from.

He held out his hands, moving them as he turned in the middle of the circle, trying to keep up his defense and having difficulty focusing on the magic while trying to find the assailant.

Jameson drew back the bow, the string resting against his cheek, crossing the corner of his mouth as he looked down the shaft of the arrow in the dark. His skin brushed the gold and black griffin fledging as he clenched his jaw and took in a deep breath, slowly letting it out and steading the bow. He let go of the string, the trajectory of the arrow spinning surely.

Oswald heard the cut of the arrow into the air and tried desperately to find its path but couldn't spot it. His heart thundered and he expanded the barrier in front of him tensely. Feeling the magic lead his body, he turned and felt a pressure in the air at the back of his neck. The barrier had failed behind him and he felt a sharp wave of panic. The static of magic built and released all at once and he heard a sharp crack behind his ear as the arrow shattered. The magic sent splinters of wood in every direction and hurtled the metal head of the arrow up into the ceiling where it imbedded itself into a fissure it had created in the stone.

Oswald put a hand at the back of his neck nervously and brushed pieces of the arrow off of the collar of his shirt and out of his hair. A flicker of anger took over, "That was too close! I'm not ready for this yet!"

Armond's voice echoed through the room, "You're not hurt and you've struck every arrow so far. You seem ready for this to me."

"No, I'm not. I can't handle much more of this!" Oswald picked a sharp end of a broken wedge of metal from his shirt and he threw it to the ground. He listened to the small piece click across the floor as it skipped and the sound was interrupted by the distinctive sound of another arrow being cut loose.

This time he sensed the movement and turned to it, anger taking place of the fear in his chest. He drew back his hand and felt a heat surround his fist like hot sunlight and threw a frustrated punch, hurtling the magic ahead of him as quickly as he could. He spotted the arrow in the reflection of a heated glow in the air. The arrow arched upwards in a tight swing and looped back in the direction that it had come. The fledging suddenly sparked heatedly and began to leave a smoky trail in the air behind it as it shot back towards its source.

Oswald recognized his mistake as he saw the reaction of the arrow to his anger, and his stomach churned. He reached for it with his magic and felt the back end of the arrow tip crookedly in the air before the magic faded out of his reach. The arrow's trajectory turned just enough that Jameson's quick reflexes were able to turn his head out of the way. The arrow whizzed by his face, rippling the air at his brow and missing his head by the width of a feather. It hit the far wall with a splintering crack.

"I'm sorry," Oswald said quickly, "Are you alright?"

"I'm fine," Jameson said, with a smolder of dislike and anger, brushing the lingering feeling of the current of air away from his face.

"I didn't know that it would do that," Oswald insisted.

A torch was lit along the wall by the door as Armond struck the match and the soft light gave some depth to the shadows of the room. Fred lit another and the destruction of the room became clear. Wooden splinters and arrowheads were scattered from one end of the room to the other like twigs across the forest floor, the occasional cannonball perched haphazardly among chips and dents in the stone.

"I think we're done for today," Armond said, sounding strained as he looked over Jameson from across the room to make sure that he was in fact unharmed.

"I didn't mean to redirect it. I didn't know," Oswald said again.

"Well, now you do," Jameson said sharply, holding his bow with white knuckled anger, "Try *not* to kill me next time."

"It was an accident!" Oswald spat back, his regret fading quickly.

"I bet it was!" Jameson said, through gritted teeth, posturing his shoulders and flaring his nostrils as he took a daring step forward.

"That's enough," Armond commanded, stopping the hinted escalation before it began, "It's done. Everyone's fine. Go home."

"Yes, sir," Jameson said, in a flat and dry tone. He took a final look back at Oswald as he passed by and went out the door with his bow and a harassed scowl.

Oswald swallowed and held his tongue.

"You too," Armond said to Oswald, "Get your sword. We're done for now."

"Yes, sir," Oswald said, resignedly walking over to the desk and picking up the scabbard, the heated hilt of the sword greeting him. He strapped the scabbard back to his belt and spotted Fred's long four knuckled green hand slip over his shoulder.

He glanced back up at his thin fierce looking face as it hovered over him. Fred looked at him reassuringly and said quietly, "Jameson won't stay mad. He never does."

"He does this often?" Oswald asked, putting his jacket on and covering his sword with a sharp pull of the fabric.

"Sometimes," Fred said, and looked back at the room's destruction, "That's a lot to get done in one day, you shouldn't be so discouraged."

"It's hard to feel good about being shot at," Oswald said, as he kicked a small piece of arrow out from under his foot.

"I imagine so," Fred said, picking up a cannonball up off of the floor nearby, "It was still more progress in one day than you've made all week. You feel like you have any more control over your magic?"

Oswald touched the hilt of the sword habitually and lifted his hand away, hardly feeling the difference in the surge of magic, "I do."

"Then it was a good day," he said pleasantly, picking up another cannonball and taking them to the far side of the room to begin building the pyramid again.

"I guess so," Oswald mumbled, ignoring the exhaustion in his bones and he started his way out of the building and back into the city streets, watching the early winter sunset over the crooked array of homes.

Chapter Twenty-Nine

Oswald handed a pair of double lined deer hide boots, high cut with black stitching over the counter into a tall skinny blond man in a pale coat. He took the small handful of coins and counted them out quickly before slipping them into his pocket and walking back to the workbench with a pleasant smile and polite gratitude.

He sat back down in his chair and swiveled the seat around to a pair of casual, black wingtips that he had been working on throughout the morning. He started wrapping the stitching together by pinching the leather bands tighter. He picked up the hooked needle and started working the new knots into the leather.

"Hey, Oz."

Oswald looked up from his stitching, pulled the knot tight and set down the bent needle on the work bench, "Matrim?" he got up from his seat and went to the front table of the shop where Matrim stood, wrapped in a heavy black coat, "Are you alright?"

"Yea' I'm fine," he said, with a smile, "I think I'm gunna start workin' wit ya again pretty soon."

"I need the help," Oswald said honestly, thinking of the backlog of orders he was having trouble keeping up with. He looked at Matrim and could see the healing burn across his neck shine a bright pink, mostly hidden beneath the collar of the coat. The burn from the sword had healed more quickly than the lightning burns, but still shined angrily in certain lights even though it no longer hurt him, "But I don't want you to do more than you think you should."

He wrapped the coat tighter around himself as a stiff breeze cut dry snow across his face, "I think I'll be al'righ. Jameson quit visiten' so I'm not worried 'bout it no more, 'sides I'm feelin' pretty good t'day."

Oswald smiled, "I'm glad you are feeling so good. I didn't expect to see you so far from the house yet."

"My chest don't hurt er nothin' no more and the burns is gettin' betta now so I — Oh! —" he looked up, suddenly remembering why he had come down to the market to begin with, "You need ta close up yer shop early an' come wit' me."

"Why?" Oswald asked, concerned.

"Nothin' ta get all worked up ova' er nothin' but ya gonna wanna see dis."

"See what?"

"Jus' come on" Matrim said, with a bright smile, "'ere, I'll help ya get dis stuff put up."

Oswald put the shoes he had been working on away, gathering tools, needles, and his other supplies and tossing them into their respective drawers. He pulled the rubber off of the fire and carefully stowed the bowl under the table, not bothering to lock it up. He put away the stains and leather and poured a little water on the fire and stepped away from the hissing smoke. He pulled on the cabinet doors to be sure that he had locked them and thumbed the key into his pocket.

Matrim reached up to pull the tarp down and sharply recoiled his left arm avoiding the pull of the skin around his burns. He quickly recovered, and pretended like he hadn't done it at all, as he pulled the tarp down with his other hand.

"So what is it that I have to come and see so quickly?" Oswald asked, bracing himself from the cold as another gust spun up a small storm of dry powdered snow around their feet as they walked.

"You'll see," Matrim said, tipping his head and gesturing down a narrow alley, "Be there in 'bout fi'teen minutes."

"Be where?" Oswald asked.

"Fred's house."

They cut around a particularly sharp angled building and stepped over an empty flower pot, watching the crooked path of the alley wind around the back of the city. He followed behind Matrim and watched the tall oddly shaped building creep around the alley in the distance.

They reached the high front door and Oswald put out a hand to knock on the door. Matrim grabbed his hand and shook his head slowly, pushing his arm away. He put a finger to his lips and went ahead and cracked the door open an inch.

A soft creak of a chair groaned through the room and slow footsteps reached the front door. Fred's long green fingers crept through the crack of the door as it was pulled open, he looked around the corner and smiled, stepping aside and waving them in.

Matrim walked in and Oswald followed, closing the door behind them. The house was warm and the sunlight broke through high windows for a dim and comfortable glow. He looked over at Fred curiously and spotted a thin swaddle of blanket bundled and held against his chest with one long green arm, his thin spiderlike fingers holding a moving figure within it securely.

Fred walked back over to the wooden chair and sank back into his seat as he shifted the swaddle of writhing blanket back down into his lap and nestled it between his knees. He looked up at the two of them with a prideful smile and curled a long finger in invitation.

Oswald walked over, trying to look over Fred's curled posture. He stepped a bit closer and looked in on the baby.

Its tiny body was a soft green, paler than Fred's with skeletal limbs and a wide chest and soft belly. Its elongated pointy ears were crumpled in and sealed flat against its skull, its eyes seemed unbearably large and its gums were lined with tiny white needle-like teeth that were surrounded by dark blue membranes. It yawned, deepening wrinkles in its tiny, strange, face.

Fred touched its little chest with a gentle finger and it squirmed, catching his finger with a wandering hand and holding it firmly. Fred leaned down and kissed the tiny, bony, hand that was wrapped around the end of his finger.

"What's his name?" Oswald asked quietly, and admiring the opportunity to see a newborn goblin, its unusual face both unfamiliar and charming.

"Gharettical," Fred said, his mouth filled with clicks and rolls as he pronounced it. He looked around at Oswald and Matrim with an understanding of the language barrier and corrected himself, "Grail."

"I've never seen anything like him," Oswald said honestly, "he's precious."

"Thank you," Fred said, looking back to the baby with misty eyes, "I believe so too." Grail blinked his huge eyes slowly and stretched in Fred's lap, its tiny legs pressing against the wrinkles in the blanket before getting comfortable again and slowing his blinks until he gave in to tiny sleep.

"When was he born?" Oswald asked.

"Last night," Fred said, slipping a fold of the blanket around to cover Grail's tummy.

"How's Maria?" Oswald asked, standing up straight and looking around the room.

"Good," he said, pointing at the stairwell, "She's upstairs sleeping."

A soft tap on the front door perked Fred's attention. Matrim went to the door first and peaked out into the cold, opening the door and letting in two more people before snapping out the cold breeze. Ramif straightened the long braid of his beard and Armond swept snow out of his short blonde hair as the two of them quietly stepped into the room.

"Welcome," Fred said quietly, scooping his hands under the baby and lifting him up where they both could see his little face, "Meet my son, Grail."

The two of them looked at the tiny swaddle of pale green bones and each managed a genuine smile at the strange sight.

"Congratulations," Ramif said, "And we thought that life was interesting with the two of you in the city. I can only imagine a goblin child."

"He looks like his father," Armond said pleasantly, reaching a hand out to the sleeping baby. He touched its tiny head, careful not to disturb its folded ears and drew his hand back as it wiggled lightly.

"He actually looks more like Maria," Fred said, touching its tiny chin.

Armond smiled, "Loch wants to see him too."

"Where is he?" Fred asked.

"Working," Armond said regretfully, "He's trying to get better communication between the divisions. He said that he'll be by later this evening if that is alright with you."

"Anytime," Fred assured him, "I don't sleep often and it's rare if not unheard of that Maria and I are both asleep at the same time," he tightened the thin blanket around Grail and added, "Especially now."

"How much sleep do ya norm'ly get?" Matrim asked curiously.

"Two or three hours a day," Fred said, with a shrug, "We don't sleep much —" he added, "Except for babies." He pulled the swaddle of blanket in close to his chest again and readjusted his long arm around the bundle protectively.

The echo of steps clicked against the walls as Maria came down the stairs and turned her head in on the houseful of people with a smile, her short blue hair mussed and her eyes heavy looking. She raised a hand in greeting and everyone smiled back at her.

"You're supposed to be resting," Fred said, concernedly.

"But we have company," she said gently.

"Were we too loud?" Fred asked, cradling his son.

Ramif reached up a hand and smacked Matrim across the back of his head.

Matrim looked down at him looking indignant, "What? I was bein' quiet! Wha' ya gotta be hittin' me for?" He took a quick smack at Ramif and missed his face, catching his shoulder as he moved. Ramif glared at him in a way that clearly would have ended in a fist fight if Matrim were feeling any better and if they had not been feet away from a newborn.

Fred scowled warningly at the two of them and the pleasant atmosphere quickly returned.

"No," Marila said, "No, you weren't loud, I just knew that people were here," her eyes flickered between the faces in the room, clearly recognizing the generals and pausing on Matrim, "Who is this?"

Matrim put a hand on his bad shoulder supporting the burn and bowed politely at her, beaming with a gap in his smile, "I'm Matrim. I work wit' Oz e'ry now an' 'gin and a friend a' Fred's."

She nodded unsure of exactly what he had said in the mess of his pattern of speech but smiled nonetheless, "I'm glad to meet you," she looked over at Oswald warmly, and said with another welcoming smile, "It's good to see you all."

Nedtedrow breathed in the first warm day of the winter's end, the dripping of melting snow pattering on the road as he walked through the wet and muddy city streets. He looked up at the faces of passersby as he went, occasionally ducking his head and weaving through alleyways as he cut his way around particular people.

He rubbed his thumb and forefinger together nervously with the indescribable need to take something. He looked around and spotted an open window in a nearby building. He walked over to it casually, looking around and measuring the risk of being caught.

No one was around and he stood near the window listening carefully.

There seemed to be no one home.

He stood on the tips of his toes and stuck his head into the open window curiously. He saw a comfortable set of furniture carved in soft white pine and a stack of papers with a quill and a small bottle of ink at its side. Beyond the main room he saw a basic kitchen and a shelf that was lined with glass figurines and rare geodes.

He grinned to himself and looked back over his shoulder, again checking the alleyway. He jumped and lifted his short and hefty frame through the open window, he caught a foot on the sill and quietly slipped into the house. He walked through the main room, while keeping an alert presence for the homeowner's return, as he headed for the shining shelf in the kitchen.

He picked up a small glass bird as it caught the light and reflected back in gold bands of sunlight. He slid it into his pocket as he looked passed a few other items that didn't catch his interest before he reached up and pulled down a cut geode, mesmerized by the glinting green crystals within. He wondered for a short time whether the crystals inside were, in fact, real emeralds and decided that it didn't matter. He slid it into a separate pocket, not wanting to damage the glass bird and was drawn by curiosity further into the house.

He peered into a bedroom and spotted a jewelry box and his fingers jumped anxiously as an overwhelming need overtook him. Before he realized it, he was opening the lid to the jewelry box and rummaging through the collection of silver and gold items. A particular piece caught his eye and he picked up a sturdy, white gold ring with an onyx band threaded through its center. He slid it onto one finger and then another until it stuck happily in place on his index finger, against the bold knuckle of his left hand.

He admired the ring in the light and then went back to digging through the box. The remaining pieces of jewelry in the box were all women's, narrow cut earrings and small ring bands, a broken necklace chain and a thin bracelet. He pulled out a pendant and inspected it closely, the golden ribbon wrapped snugly around a heart cut sapphire. He pondered its worth and set it back in the box casually.

The click of a lock echoed through the house.

Nedtedrow set down the jewelry box and bolted out of the bedroom and he turned down the hall to the room he had entered from. He spotted the open window and slid around the corner, noticing along the way that he was leaving a trail of muddy footsteps in his wake. He cursed under his breath as he heard a door open somewhere in the building as he reached the window and jumped out of it, like a rabbit out of a burning den. He landed clumsily and heard a loud, large, and angry man's voice charge behind him from within the house, heading for the open window and no doubt following muddy footprints.

Nedtedrow launched himself down the alley and listened to the hard smack of his feet on wet stone and the sheer of sliding shoes. He wound around the nearest house, cutting corners and taking new paths as often as he could manage, trying to avoid being seen or tracked down.

Buildings became blurred labyrinths of wood and stone in the alternating pathways as he flew by. He skidded to a hard stop after another sharp turn and rested his back against a nearby wall, panting heavily. He surveyed the narrow path while trying to catch his breath and holding the newly ringed hand against his soft belly greedily.

He listened hard and couldn't hear anything other than the sounds of the city bustling just down the road. He wondered where his random turns had brought him until he recognized a nearby building.

The market.

He took a deep breath and coughed, the sudden exertion taking its toll on him. He tried to compose himself and walked out of the alleyway from behind a vendor's shop and slid casually between the venues and out into the busy road.

He smiled politely at a few passersby and caught a vicious glare of the owner of one of his favorite shops. He ignored the watchful scowl and waved heartily at the man, thinking of the most wonderful toffees and tarts that the man sold. He thought for a moment about looping back and helping himself to a tart.

He stepped over a puddle in the street and caught a glimpse of a neatly displayed row of standing eagle quills and pretended to blindly bump the table. A few of the quills fell over off of the table and he scrambled to pick them up.

"I'm so sorry," he said, sounding genuine as he began to set up the display again, picking a long white quill and sliding it into his pocket without missing a beat or drawing suspicion as he set the rest of them back up where they had been.

The shop owner looked flustered as she straightened the line of quills from the far side of the table. Nedtedrow apologized again quickly and pretended to walk away embarrassed. He felt the objects hiding in his pockets merrily as he continued to watch for potential wares.

He heard a sharp and angry voice call his name and without a backwards glance he cut suddenly back out of the street and bolted through another alley, weaving around buildings until he felt safe again.

Such was the life of a thief.

He wandered around for a while, staring at the beauty of his new ring until he found another main road. He stuck his hand in his pocket to hide the small treasure and looked up.

Oswald spotted him at the same time, waving happily and wearing a smoldered dark grey suit. It was wide shouldered and seemed to fit very well, so well that Nedtedrow was sure that he must have had it custom made. To him however, it was the ugliest suit he had ever seen in his life and something he would expect an old man to wear to a funeral.

Oswald walked up to him, stepping carefully around muddy puddles as he walked.

"What is that?" Nedtedrow asked, pointing to the suit.

Oswald looked himself over and straightened out the fabric, "It's an elven twinset."

"It's as ugly as a dog's beard," Nedtedrow scoffed.

"It's traditional," Oswald said, affronted by the comment.

"Still ugly," Nedtedrow shrugged unapologetically, "Why are you wearing it anyway? Are you working in it or something?"

"No," Oswald said, still fussing over the fabric and trying to get it to lay correctly, now paranoid over the way that it looked, "I didn't have my shop open at all today."

Nedtedrow pressed his lips together and narrowed his eyes, "Surely you don't train in that?"

"No," Oswald said again, shaking his head.

"Then where are you going?" he asked, still trying to figure out the obnoxious outfit.

"Uh," Oswald paused, picking a red hair off of his lapel, "The apothecary."

"So you're sick," Nedtedrow said, with an understanding nod, "That explains the suit."

Oswald glared at him dejectedly, "No, I'm not sick, and this is a really nice suit!" he flustered restlessly with the jacket and shook his head, "I'm going to pick up Sanna. We have a date."

"Sanna?" Nedtedrow asked, wrinkling his nose, "The little potion woman?"

"She's an herbalist," Oswald corrected, "And yes."

Nedtedrow frowned in thought, "I thought you were sweet on Satomi."

Oswald shook his head passionately, "No! She broke my nose! Why would I want that?"

"Any woman will if you piss her off," Nedtedrow shrugged.

"I didn't do anything to piss her off, I just fainted," Oswald said and shook his head again, "Satomi's just always angry."

Nedtedrow shrugged, "At least that one was pretty."

"Sanna is absolutely gorgeous," Oswald argued, "and about as angry as a butterfly."

"There's something wrong with your eyes," Nedtedrow laughed rudely, "You just might be sick anyway. Maybe it's the height difference but I swear that woman has absolutely no butt from where I stand," he held up a hand defensively as his eyebrow raised, "All I can think of is how that woman can sit in a chair without carving her hips into the wood, it's got to be uncomfortable if you know what I mean."

"You're a terrible person, do you know that?" Oswald said, disgusted.

Nedtedrow shrugged in a noncommittal kind of way, "Yeah, I've heard that before. So what?"

Oswald snarled at him grossly, his voice full of admiration, "She's beautiful, smart and compassionate."

"And she has no butt, and her 'I'm angry' voice sounds like a dying hippogriff," he said, waving his hands in the air.

"She's not an angry woman," Oswald said, "I don't know where you're getting this."

"Try taking something from her shop. You'll hear it," he promised with a playful smile, "It, honest to the goddess, sounds like something is dying in her throat."

"You would know," Oswald said bitterly, "Look, I really like her —"

"—For some reason—"

"— And I want this date to go well. This is important to me, so I don't want to hear another word about it," Oswald finished, with a less than patient stare.

"Fine," Nedtedrow crossed his arms, "Where are you taking her anyway? Not the Burning Mill, I hope. Don't get me wrong, the food's great, but you might not want to take your date there."

"No," Oswald agreed sharply, "Absolutely not. We're going to the Jade Vine."

"Nice," Nedtedrow said, impressed, "But they aren't going to let you in like that."

"What? Why?" Oswald asked, looking down at his shoes.

"That mangy dog you're wearing," he said, pointing at the suit, "That's a nice place, you can't wear that."

"This is a nice suit!" Oswald said angrily.

"Yeah, sure," he shrugged, "And your girlfriend has no butt, but you can't say that I didn't tell you so when the time comes."

"You're an ass," Oswald snapped.

"I can be," Nedtedrow agreed fairly, "But at least I'm honest."

"An honest thief. Isn't that a contradiction in terms?"

Nedtedrow shook his head slowly, thinking about the question, "Depends on where you're from."

"How about reality?" Oswald said sarcastically.

"Nah," he said shortly, "I do like that place though."

"Where? The real world?" Oswald snarked.

"No," he said, pointing a thumb over his shoulder into the east side of the city, "The Jade Vine."

Oswald raised an eyebrow interestedly, "Oh, so you've been there before?"

"Oh yeah," he nodded, "You can really snatch some good silverware there, the good stuff too — if you can get in and out without someone catching you," he added.

"I'm *buying* her dinner, not robbing the place," Oswald said defensively, his brief good mood fading again.

"To each his own," he shrugged and looked down the street, spotting a familiar and unhappy face walking towards him. He decided he didn't want to risk being seen and stepped to the side in front of Oswald.

"Why do you steal stuff anyway?" Oswald asked, with a hint of sadness in his voice.

Nedtedrow thought about it, looking down at the street and rolling the ring on his finger contemplatively, "You know, I'm really not sure why. I just have to."

"You don't have to," Oswald argued softly, his face falling disappointedly, "Why do you do it?"

"I don't know," Nedtedrow said seriously, his expression dark. He shrugged and the seriousness slid away from him like driftwood in the river and he snapped back to his carefree attitude, "For the same reason you're determined to look like an idiot I suppose."

"You could at least try to be supportive," Oswald frowned.

"Yeah, I could," he said, looking around Oswald and judging the distance that the man had covered in a few seconds time. He realized the man was looking for someone, pausing to look down alleys as he walked, and Nedtedrow figured it was likely that he was being hunted down, "So, good luck on your date," he said quickly, bumping into Oswald as he started to make a quick path towards the alleyway again.

Oswald quickly felt his pocket and turned around heatedly, "Nedtedrow! I need that!"

"What?" he asked loudly, sounding offended as he turned back around.

"My wallet," Oswald snapped.

"What wallet?" he asked with a shrug, as he slid his hand into his pocket.

"The one in your hand," Oswald said, rolling his eyes.

Nedtedrow looked down into his clasped hand and smiled sheepishly, "Oh, that... I have no idea how that happened." He sounded half surprised by the small pouch in his hand and took it back to him quickly.

"Yeah, I bet," Oswald said, taking back the black leather pouch. He opened the wallet and did a sweep with his eyes, weighing the amount of coins in the leather pouch. He drew the string taught and slid it back into his pocket, "Go home before you get yourself into some real trouble."

"Good idea," Nedtedrow said, holding up a finger and eyeing the man walking down the street as he got closer and closer to where they stood. He turned quickly, putting his back to the man and vanishing back into the alley and around a wide based home, heading to the far side of town.

Chapter Thirty

Bolzar sat in his study with his thumb and forefinger pinching the bridge of his nose tightly as he attempted to force his mind to focus on the task at hand.

He took a deep breath as he organized his thoughts, prioritizing which problem demanded his total attention at that moment. He let go of the bridge of his nose and put the hand over his mouth tensely. He opened his eyes, sliding them over the pile of maps and documents that littered the angled table. He separated two overlying maps and trailed the river with his finger and tried to find another route for the army to travel that wouldn't bring them so close the Solber cliffs.

He knew it was an opportune place for an ambush and the risk was too high.

He also knew that he had to make a decision and send out the letter immediately, unsure of the consequences of his decision and the untold lives hanging in the balance at his fingertips.

He rubbed his face with his hands and retraced the river across the map, not wanting to diverge from the water source too far because of the current limitations, each person unable to travel with more than a day's water on their person at the current volume.

He sighed and sat back down in the chair again, reaching over and picking up a letter from Commander Erin and rereading the report carefully and mumbling through it as he read:

Lord General,

The southern troops have managed to reach the barracks at the Quillen boarder. 558 archers, 874 swordsmen, 390 Battleax wielders, 35 scouts, 140 dagger runners. Approximately two thousand additional men and women, to the previously reported 6,000 troops, who report with various intelligences of the Azarian army's departure from current bases. All of Azar's available troops are regrouping for war, confirmed P.O.W.

with further news of the termination of all raids both West and North of our position with orders from King Venhow. The cessation of the raids is concerning as is the number of reported enemy forces converging with ill intent against the great city of Gommorn.

We have requested further support from the South Eastern division of Brutes but have not received confirmation of their readiness to assist in the defense of your city.

We intend to march to the Solber cliffs and through to the field of to the convergence of the Wial and Azarian provinces where we will make camp and await your support to engage in the battle.

It is strongly believed that King Venhow himself will be leading the battle and has full intent to march on the next waning quarter moon, due to attack your city upon the new moon. The date of the army's departure from Azar has been confirmed by a P.O.W. the other has not been confirmed. We will leave the barracks as previously reported in 10 days unless we receive other orders from you by then.

Respectfully,

Lt. Commander Erin, Quillen Reserve

Bolzar read and reread the letter, turning it over in his hands and noting the wax seal and the date it was written. The letter was five days old and a man riding diligently on horseback would take three days to reach the Quillen camp with a reply.

He put his head in his hands and looked at the letter one last time before turning back to the maps and trying to find a suitable route that would be safer for both armies to travel separately, to avoid the risk of being flanked by gathering together before moving.

He knew he had to make a decision.

He chewed at his lip, looking down at his hand, still able to faintly see where the new and the old flesh met together. He rubbed at his new hand habitually and tried not to let his last military decision distract him from the impending situation.

A horrific flash of memory drug its corpse through his mind as brief moments of his time in the dungeons of Azar left bloody trails through his thoughts. Bloody trails and screams.

He shook his head and got up sharply from his chair and decided to pace round the desk as he pushed the darkness out of his head. He listened to his own footsteps on the wooden floor and allowed its steady pattern to remind him of the soft ticking of a metronome and let it swing back and forth in his mind as he walked.

He stopped and hovered over the map, wringing his brain over the painted landscape and slammed his hands into the desk on either side of it in frustration before going back to his steady pacing, cursing under his breath.

If he chose the mountain road to the East to cut around the cliffs it would add days to the journey. Days they didn't have. If they took that route it would be too easy for Azar's army to go around them and carve a deadly swath directly into Gommorn. There wouldn't be a city to take back.

If they cut to the West they would be moving over more rugged terrain with no water supply and no support. The western trail would also lead them dangerously close to territories that were already inhabited by enemy forces that may not have left their posts yet.

He knew that if they split the army to effectively rake the landscape forward as they came to converge on the intended battlefield, that there would be too few troops at its heart when the battle started. If King Venhow was in fact leading the army, it would be en masse.

He cursed again.

He didn't have enough information and he was further concerned by the last team of scouts that had been sent out and that they hadn't returned yet.

He paced back around to the front of the desk and stared harder at the map, willing it to give him the answers and angry when he still found no obvious solution to his dilemma.

"Twenty thousand men," Bolzar said to himself, as he looked across the desk, begging for anything that he may have overlooked, "It means the lives of twenty thousand men." He stared at the piles of information, now so troubled that he couldn't see the map or the letters through his own racing thoughts. It was a blur of paper and ink, hiding the answer he was looking for.

He hung his head and looked at the floor, holding on to the edge of the table.

He thought about the difference in time, Commander Erin was a few days further from Azar than they were, but they were also leaving over a week before Gommorn's army was due to leave the city. The time difference made no sense.

He sat at the table and pulled a blank sheet of paper in front of him, rummaging around for a quill and ink. He put the feather against his mouth and let the idea slide from the black ink bottle:

Lt. Commander Erin,

It has come to my attention that the risks associated with both of our armies taking the route through the Solber cliffs heavily outweigh the benefit of time. It is my official duty to inform you that your route is to be altered to the North East of the cliffs and around the mountain road. With the alterations in the pattern of our strike we are due to reach the Wial and Azarian borders roughly the same time on the day before the Azarian forces are due to reach the border.

Gommorn's forces will take the Solber Cliffside trail along the river's western fork as we have the numbers and adequate provisions and expertise to handle and address a potential problem should one arise. We appreciate your support and will see you at previously discussed campsite in eight days.

Adv. Bolzar Nolerkin the third of Saffermine

He read the letter over carefully and flipped the paper over, dating the back and folding it neatly. He slid the letter into his inner coat pocket and got up quickly, leaving the room and heading straight to the front door and out into the city.

He sped to a gentle run, pacing himself as he took the most direct route through to the heart of the city. The large marble pillars of the community building shone in the cool spring air, the smell of fresh rain seeping into his head as he ran. He passed the phoenix pillar and slowed down at the doorway just long enough to haul the heavy door open.

He stepped into the perpetually dark building and spotted Loch in a cluster of division commanders and lieutenants heatedly giving orders.

"The Lord General?" Bolzar asked loudly, over the noise.

Loch looked up with the aged lines of his face deep with the seriousness of his task, "Upstairs."

Bolzar turned on his heels and bolted up the marble stairway, weaving through the darkness and looking into bustling rooms full of uniformed men and women trying to organize for departure and to receive orders. He passed another room and looked in on Ramif, standing over his own table and rifling through letters and reports.

"Ramif?"

He looked up at Bolzar with stern and angry lines etched into his face. He recognized him quickly and the anger faded away slightly as he waved him into the room, "What do you want?"

"I need you to approve this," Bolzar said, and pulled the letter out of his pocket. He unfolded it and held it out for him to take, "It's my official decision on the route we should take."

Ramif took the letter and read it over shaking his head, "No," he said firmly, and handed the letter back as he picked up another report from his desk, "The valley at the cliffside is reported to be crawling with archers and traps. We're not going through there."

"That's our only option," Bolzar said, earnestly, "If we take any other route we leave the city exposed behind us or we have to go into battle with two days dry of any water. We can't win a war with disoriented troops."

Ramif looked up at him and back to the report, "I'm working on that."

Bolzar stepped closer to the desk, trying to remain respectful as he argued, "This decision has to be put through today. They're leaving the Quillen barracks in five days. This has to get to Commander Erin by then or they will end up going through the Solber Cliffs alone. They can't handle that."

"Neither can we," Ramif said definitively.

"Respectfully, General," Bolzar said, gripping the letter in his hand and looking at him with conviction, "I believe we can. I've been pouring over this for a while now and I think I have an idea on how we can get through without complications."

"Yeah?" Ramif asked noncommittally with a raised eyebrow, "How?"

"I think I've come up with a way to secure the ridgeline."

Ramif put down the report and stared at him, sizing him up, "How long have you thought about this idea of yours?"

Bolzar sighed and looked around the room embarrassedly, "It just came to me this morning."

Ramif rolled his eyes and thumbed through a stack of reports searching for one he couldn't seem to find, "Then why do you think I would approve it."

"Because it will work," he said slowly. He walked up to the table and put a hand on the desk with his letter in his fist, leaning in with desperate eyes, "You have to trust me."

"I do trust you," Ramif said, boring his eyes through him, "but Venhow already knows that we have to pass through that valley and he already has archers stationed there."

Bolzar nodded his understanding and asked, "How may?"

"We aren't sure. Our current estimate is around six hundred," Ramif said, dipping a quill into a bottle of ink and making a small note on a particular report before putting the quill back in its rest.

"So the scouts did make it back to the city then?" Bolzar asked, relieved by the information.

"One did," Ramif said grimly.

"Only one?"

"Yes, and he's being taken care of by Jameson around the clock until we are due to leave the city," he said, clenching his jaw, the muscles in his face working under his skin.

Bolzar paused, his relief sliding away to a sick apprehension, "What happened?"

Ramif looked at him and shook his head, "An ambush, so far as we can tell. He can't speak anymore and it's a wonder that he made it back alive at all."

"Why can't he talk?" Bolzar asked, not really wanting the answer.

Ramif drew his thumb across his throat slowly, drawing the line of the undoubted open wound he had seen.

"If he can't speak then how do you have an estimate on the number of archers stationed there?" Bolzar asked, trying to find support to his intentions.

"He wrote it down," Ramif said obviously.

"And in his condition you think that he's a reliable source?"

"He is, and he reported nearly six hundred archers," Ramif repeated.

Bolzar sighed and bit his lower lip tensely and ran his plan through his head again with the new information. He sighed and looked up at Ramif surely, "I still think we can make it through."

Ramif frowned and put the stack of papers he was rifling through back down on the desk. He pulled at his braded beard and looked at Bolzar sternly, "Then I'm listening."

"Send Fred and Bore ahead of us into the Solber forest at the cliff edge," he said clearly.

"You want me to send two men into foreign territory against an unknown number of enemy forces?" Ramif shook his head angrily, "I won't do it. It's a death sentence."

"No. It's not," Bolzar said, spreading his fingers and tapping the desk insistently as he explained, "both Fred and Bore are completely undetectable in that environment and if Fred is spotted he won't likely be a target until very late in the process."

"And then what?—" Ramif said, raising his voice and throwing up a hand disbelievingly, "He'll have no defense."

"Bore."

"Bore is a very unusual man and he is talented in hand to hand combat," Ramif agreed, the line of his jaw set tight as his eyes intensified against Bolzar's stare, "But I don't think that he can be considered a viable defense in this situation."

"If he's careful, they won't be able to see him there," Bolzar said, trying to think of anyone else who would be able to go with them but knowing that anyone else would give them away,

"He could stand in front of them and no one would know that he was there. With his condition he's a rare asset and he's absolutely a practical defense."

Ramif thought quietly for a long time, as he continually straightened the end of his beard. He looked over the desk of reports and nodded slowly, "Have you discussed this with either of them?"

"I came to you first," Bolzar explained.

"Put your head out in the hall and call Damien in here," Ramif ordered.

Bolzar did as he was told and a lanky, dark haired, young man came out of a nearby hall and marched stiffly into the room. He looked around watchfully, taking in everything with obvious discomfort in trying to find a place to put his eyes. He seemed afraid to be in the room with the Lord General and he swallowed back his anxiety with a firm and clear, "Yes sir?"

Ramif leaned across the desk and picked up a small map of the city, taking a quill and marking two X's over homes on the map. He put the quill back into its place and looked up at the man with a stony authority, "Go and retrieve these two men for me. No detours, no hesitation. Get someone else to help you if you must, but I need Fred and Bore brought here immediately."

Damien nodded sharply and took the map, giving it a short glance before turning out of the room, happy to be leaving the Lord General's company, and vanishing quickly down the hall.

Ramif sat in his chair and looked back to Bolzar, "You do have a plan?" he confirmed

"Yes," Bolzar said surely.

"Will it allow us to pass along the cliffside safely?" Ramif asked, closely watching Bolzar's expression as he answered.

"Yes," he said, with a pause, "If they're able to get this accomplished then we should have no trouble at all."

"If?" Ramif emphasized uncomfortably as he clenched his jaw and put a hand up to his mouth in thought, "And if they fail, you do understand what that will mean for us?"

"I do," Bolzar said, rubbing at his hand fearfully.

"And you still think that it's worth the risk?"

"I do," he repeated.

"You have *that* much faith in this instantaneous idea of yours that you are willing to risk us *all* to the dungeons of Azar?" Ramif confirmed sternly, his dark eyes unwavering.

Bolzar swallowed hard and suppressed a sharp flutter of panic. He took a slow breath and felt the hammering beat of his heart slow slightly, "Yes."

They both considered the repercussions of such a defeat and Ramif rolled his fingers as he tried to make the best decision. The sounds of people moving in and out of rooms and intense conversations passing through the halls of the building echoed against the marble walls. A messenger passed by them and reached an arm through the open door to slide another report into a small basket just inside the room.

Ramif looked up at the basket and ignored it for the moment, making a cautious decision, "If they both agree to your plan," Ramif said, looking over the letter that Bolzar had written on the desk in front of him, "I will approve you're action in Quillen."

"Thank you."

"—But *only* if they feel that they can accomplish this."

"I understand," Bolzar said quietly, "But if they refuse I still firmly recommend that we send a warning and a report to Commander Erin and divert their army to the North Eastern mountain trail."

"Agreed," Ramif said dryly.

Bolzar leaned up against the wall patiently, passing the following hour with collected thoughts and scenarios as Ramif went over the new report in silence.

A heavy-footed sound groaned mournfully in the halls and reverberated up the marble stairs. The slow thump of steps slowly drug across the marble towards the room.

They looked up as Bore walked into the room, his scaled and wooden body creaking as he moved. His skin was a brownish grey that mirrored an ash tree's bark in both texture and color with ridges that paved deep grooves up his body and crackled softly with his movements. He smiled, a thin fissure that cut across his appearance as he worked the muscles in his face. His eyes were slightly obscured by his scaly bark-like skin as his cheeks drew up, leaving the wet sparkle of his brown eyes the only hint of what had once been an elven body.

Bore reached out a deformed and widened hand, and took Bolzar's, shaking hands formally, the weight and grip of it similar to cold stone beaten by years of weathering. Bore released his grip and turned to Ramif, shaking his hand politely in turn.

"I'm in the Lord General's office on the brink of war," he said, with a voice that could have been mistaken for the low grumbling of a chair dragging across a hardwood floor, "That's either a very good thing, or you have very bad news," he straightened his back and stood still, hardly seeming alive, "So which is it?"

Ramif pushed himself up out of his chair and stood beside the table with an authoritative presence that filled the empty space in the room, "Bolzar has come up with a way for us to cut through the Solber Cliffside on the way to the campsite."

"That would save time," Bore said, suspiciously.

"But it can only be done if you and Fred are able to clear the way for the army to pass," Ramif reported.

"Clear the way?" Bore repeated questionably.

Ramif nodded, expecting the apprehension, "There are numerous reports of a large station of archers waiting for us to pass through the valley."

"How large?" he asked, creaking as he leaned back to look between the two of them.

"Around six hundred at last report," Ramif said firmly.

"And you need me for that," Bore groaned deeply, his voice lowering further, "And Fred? Is that all?"

"Yes," Ramif confirmed, "We would only send the two of you."

"Why?" he asked curiously, "What do you think we can do about it?"

Ramif looked at Bolzar for a moment and continued, "The physical and environmental advantage that the two of you would have along the ridgeline. Bolzar will discuss the plan with you in detail when Fred arrives."

Bore took in a calm breath that rasped against his wooden body and creaked a half-crooked smile, "Just me and Fred against a small army… Sounds like fun."

Chapter Thirty-One

The rugged hillside was slick as the rain poured down overhead, the mid-morning light brightening muddy paths as spring thunder rolled overhead. The clanking of his armor rubbed angrily against his rain soaked body as he climbed the hill. He repositioned his foot in the rocky ground, a fist sized stone coming lose under foot and rolling with sharp clicks as it collided with other rocks on its way to the bottom of the steep incline.

Fred moved a piece of cloth and put a hand against the pouch at his hip, making sure that it was still dry and well shielded from the hiss of the rain.

He found a sturdy place to put his foot and hoisted himself up a short but dangerous cliff and grabbed a root that had grown out of the face of the sharp and muddy drop in the hillside, and pulled his body up the ten foot rise with little to no effort. He stood on the level shelf at the top and looked around at the tall trees and the fresh brush of the rising ferns and waking shrubs.

The rain tapped insistently against the metal of his helmet and water ran in rivulets down the back of his neck and into the armor.

He walked along the ridgeline for a short time and came to the very edge of the cliff, the razor like drop cutting off into nothingness. He listened carefully as he leaned over the sheer drop and looked down the dramatic stone cliff, to the white and grey valley floor a hundred feet below. He admired the head spinning view for the simple beauty it was, and turned back to the sudden overgrowth of spring green leaves and the expansive ridgeline of the high forest.

He watched carefully at the foliage around him, knowing that Bore was among the shamble of broken limbs and healthy trees. Fred could feel Bore following him as he walked through the forest but he couldn't hear or see him through the sheets of continuous rain.

He trudged through mud and wet undergrowth for a while until he caught a glimpse of movement in the distance. He moved towards it confidently with an aura of authority as he took wide, lolloping strides, his goblin posture curled and casual.

A quick movement caught his attention and he turned towards it with his face contorted with his sharpened teeth gleaming behind his thin blue lips.

An arrow was nocked to the string of a bow, drawn and waiting release a short distance away. A middle aged man with black peppered hair and clear vision was staring down its string with his thin fingers locked around the arrow's fledging.

"Name and rank," the man demanded.

Fred snarled viciously, mustering up as much anger in his voice as he could manage and hearing himself spit his brother's name with disgust in his heart, "Maurik!"

The man lowered the bow and slowly reset the string but did not remove the arrow from its place. He took a few steps forward with his head cocked to one side, looking him over carefully, "Commander Maurik?"

Fred scowled, both engrossed and highly disappointed with how far his brother had ascended in the ranks, knowing exactly what he must have done to achieve the title, "Who else?"

"We weren't told you were coming," the man said, wearily.

"I'm sure they tell you everything don't they?" Fred said, mockingly. The man looked away, obviously embarrassed and frustrated. Fred split a false and daring smile, "I thought so," and passed the man, without another word.

He looked back after a few minutes of silence in the rain, and was not surprised by the sudden lack of the man's presence anywhere to be seen. He wondered if the man had gone back to his post or if he had moved back around to the main camp to report his presence.

He wondered too if he were a man that would be missed anytime soon, should his disappearance have not been by his own choice. He hoped to himself that Borc would have the restraint to wait and not to raise the alarm before he had even found the campsite.

He spotted another archer along his path, but didn't receive the same greeting. Instead, the man gave him a short glance and went back to picking blades of wet grass from the ground at his feet and continued peeling them into strips to pass the time, waiting for the sound of the bell from further up the trail that Fred knew would never be rung.

He began to hear voices through the trees, a dull rumble that he could hear over the beat of his heart in his ears. He took in a final calming breath, fixing his expression in a dark grimace as he saw movement between the trunks of a ring of wide oaks.

He walked into the camp and looked over the large group, most of the movement coming from men wandering between smaller cliques. He counted a total of six Keernith goblins among them, and he hoped that they would not be able to recognize that he was not his brother.

He tried to posture his back authoritatively without looking obvious, and found a man, sitting on a fallen log with a silver crest pinned to his uniform.

He stepped up to the man who looked up and raised his eyebrows thoughtfully. He stood up after looking him over for a minute and held out a hand, which Fred took with an iron grip.

"Commander," he said, respectfully, "It's good to have you here. We weren't expecting you. Are you here on official business?"

Fred locked his jaw and narrowed his deep blue eyes, "The communication around here is disappointing," he looked around at the group again and locked menacing eyes with a few men as they passed, each of them glancing down at the ground fearfully and they sped up as they walked passed him.

"A messenger came yesterday but it was a very simple report," the man said, apologetically, offering his seat on the log with an open hand and moving further down and sitting on a rougher place on the wood.

"Whose report was it?" Fred asked, grumpily.

"General Skemir's."

Fred shook his head with a hateful expression, "It would be," he growled.

"You two have trouble getting along?" the man asked, gesturing again to the seat on the log beside him.

"You could say that," Fred said unhappily.

The man rubbed his hands together as he looked up into Fred's green face, "So what can we do for you Commander?"

Fred sat down, feeling his wet armor rub at his knees and he tried to make himself comfortable in the rain, letting his posture fall casually, "I got tired of waiting around. I was hoping to spill some blood."

The man looked a little uncomfortable at first, and then nodded understandingly, picking the dirt out from under his fingernails, "Not a lot going on right here yet either. We should get a signal any day now."

"Both armies are moving now," Fred said truthfully, with a wicked, toothy grin that made the man snicker, "It won't be long."

"That's good," he said, sitting up straighter and looking up at the canopy of small leaves that hardly covered the small open area, "Any more of this rain and we're all going to start going mad. It hasn't stopped for three days."

"It's clearing up," Fred said, catching a whiff of something cooking. He watched two men in the distance feeding a low fire under a large cauldron of something steaming.

"You hungry?" the man asked, following his line of sight.

"I haven't eaten since I left," Fred said, "I wanted to get here before the fun started."

"Well, you aren't too late," he said, with a glance out over the forest, "We're just waiting for the bell."

"And dinner?" Fred asked, his stomach rumbling loudly.

"The food should be done fairly soon," he said, judging the time of day by the amount of light seeping through the clouds above.

Fred smelled at the air curiously, "What is it?"

The man shrugged with an unhappy grimace, "Gruel probably. We've been here for over a week and we are running low on our other supplies."

"I hate gruel," Fred grumbled, "but at least it's food."

"I know what you mean," the man said.

Fred surveyed the area again, "There are less of you here than were reported."

He shook his head, "No, there are five hundred, just not here right now. There are fifty taking shift on the ridge and the other hundred are in the valley floor still setting up the tripwires."

Fred snorted, masking his unease over the sudden complication, "They haven't finished the traps yet? It's been over a week. Are all of your men completely incompetent?"

The man looked up suddenly, a small amount of color fading away from his face, "It's the last one. They finished the others already."

"And that takes a hundred men?" Fred asked with a scowl.

"As a precaution," he said apologetically, trying to sound sure of his orders, "They're dangerous to set up and, like I said, we're still waiting for the signal to get into position," he swallowed worriedly at the deep set lines across Fred's brow.

"How many traps are there?" Fred asked, disapprovingly.

"Seven."

"They aren't all the same I hope." Fred said, warningly.

He shook his head quickly, "No, of course not. Two cannons, one rock fall, two dragon snares, venom stones in the creek bed, and a barbed pitfall."

"Not obvious?"

"No," he insisted, "We did it right."

"You'd better have," Fred growled. He made a mental note and tried to figure out how to find and mark them later without falling prey to the design. The man took the contemplative expression as a sign of approval and relaxed a bit.

"I'm sure we can eat now if you're interested," he said, still trying to win over his support.

"Your men don't all eat at the same time?" he asked, glancing around the camp.

"They do," he said, getting up from his place on the log, "after we eat."

Fred pursed his lips and nodded, getting up from his place as well. They walked over to the fire pit and the cooks stepped back, quickly retrieving a bowl for each of them from a large pile wrapped in burlap behind them. Fred watched as one of them ladled a generous portion into each bowl and added a spoon to each goopy bowl of pale grey paste.

Fred looked down at it distastefully and dipped his finger into the dish, tasting it with a sneer, "Hold this," he said to the cook, handing him the bowl and carefully picking a small salt rock out of the separated leather pouch at his hip, making sure that it was the right one. He took a pocket knife from his side and shaved white flakes onto the top of the gruel.

"What is that?" the man asked curiously.

"Salt," Fred said, finishing with the stone and moving to put it back into his bag.

"Do you mind?" the man asked, holding his hand out. Fred grinned internally, fighting to keep the locked scowl on his face as he slid his knife back into its place and passed the stone over into his hand and the man seasoned his bowl as well.

He reached back into the pouch and grabbed the larger grey and white stone from the other side of the bag at his hip, careful to touch as little of it as he could manage, and threw it into the pot and watched it sink into the goop.

"What are you doing?" the cook asked, sounding alarmed.

"Making this food eatable," Fred snapped viciously, taking the ladle angrily from the cook's free hand and pressing on the stone at the bottom of the pot, feeling it break apart unnaturally quickly and turned the food several times.

He felt the man behind him watching him carefully and the suspicion in the air was palpable.

Reluctantly, Fred dipped a finger into the pot and tasted the mixture, the salt just barely detectable and the poison untraceable in the mix. He swallowed, working the pieces of grit out if his angled teeth, anxiously regretting the need to have done so.

They seemed more comfortable with his tasting of the dish and didn't pry any further. He took back the real salt rock from the man behind him and slipped it into the now empty pouch and pulled the bowl of food from the cook's hand. He turned away from the pot without another thought as to what he had just done, not wanting to feed the mistrust of the cooks.

He sat back down on his place on the fallen log and started eating his bowl of gruel hungrily, wanting to put something on his stomach quickly before the poison could act. He hoped as he ate that it hadn't been enough to do anything at all but he felt his stomach already begin to knot uncomfortably.

The man sat next to him and took a bite of his bowl, "The salt definitely helps. Thanks."

Fred grunted in reply as he ate, looking up only once as the men began to line up for lunch as the cooks ladled out the tainted dish. He made a clear point not to pay too much attention to any of the other men, knowing the one beside him had to be the next highest ranking below Maurik.

He finished the bowl, scraping the last bite out of the bottom, and set it on the ground next to him, looking up only briefly as he watched a couple of goblins pass him with their dinner, saddened by their chosen fate.

"You can have more if you want," the man beside him said, gesturing with his spoon to the empty bowl on the ground.

"When it comes to gruel," Fred said, shaking his head, "One bowl is plenty. Maybe I'll find some mint root around here somewhere."

"That sounds good," the man said, picking at the last of his bowl as well, "Haven't had any of that in a long time. I never was very good at finding the right plant."

"It's not hard to spot," Fred said condescendingly.

"All the same, I've never really been good with plants."

"That's your loss," Fred said, interlocking his fingers and leaning on his arms, realizing that the rain had slowed for the moment. He looked out into the woods and wondered if he had seen Bore as something moved gently at the forest floor, unnoticed by anyone else. The movement vanished and he thought too, that perhaps he had seen an animal of some kind moving the undergrowth.

He sat, looking comfortable and bored and watched the field of men walk around for an hour or so, slowly beginning to feel the cramping in his stomach intensify into a true discomfort.

The man beside him got up and wandered around for a while, returning occasionally to ask if he needed or would like anything else that they had to offer. Fred continually shook his head each time, and stared fixedly out through the woods towards Gommorn. He worked his jaw and listened to the rain tap gently against the leaves around him and against the metal of his helmet.

The man passed by again and picked up Fred's bowl and he walked off through the intricate tapestry of men as they wove in and out of the clearing, rumbling with slow conversations. Fred listened for a while to the slowly dwindling conversations as a sharp and bitter pain began to spread in his stomach. He did his best to ignore it, his expression for the first time etched sinisterly without him having to force it.

He had to focus on every breath to keep from his pain being noticed, the dark look on his face keeping other people from walking up to him as he waited patiently for it to subside. He knew in the back of his mind that it wouldn't just go away. He took off his helmet, grateful to the cool air on the back of his neck as he scratched at his head to distract him from the gnawing feeling in his gut.

A man nearby grabbed at his stomach with a deep grimace as he walked by, trying to straighten his posture with obvious difficulty.

Fred stood up slowly, the pain doubling as he moved but he dared not stay put any longer. The campsite was becoming more and more quiet by the minute as the poison began to grip at their bodies.

He started to wander off towards the woods when he heard a voice behind him call after him sharply, "Commander Maurik!"

Fred closed his eyes trying to compose himself through his own pain as he turned back to the man he had been sitting with throughout the morning. The silver crest pinned to his uniform caught the light as he marched quickly in his direction, the scabbard of his sword at his side clicking against his armor.

"What?" Fred said sharply.

The man had a stony face and his eyes were unwavering, "Something isn't right here."

"What are you talking about?" Fred asked uninterestedly.

"My men are getting sick," he said, pointing back to the group accusatorily.

"Yeah?" Fred said, gritting his teeth and flexing his hand, ready to draw at the blade resting at his hip, "Tell the dogs to eat some grass and suck it up. We're supposed to be on guard."

The man suddenly looked taken aback and his attitude became less aggressive. He looked back at the camp as a foreboding quiet began to settle around them, "Do you know what it is?"

"Probably parasites. I've seen that stagnant pool you've been drinking from," Fred spat, "A bunch of morons, the lot of you."

"They've been fine until now," he said uncomfortably.

"That's how it happens," Fred shrugged, feeling a sudden sharp stab at his gut, "You think they're going to tell you if they've been shitting themselves?"

The man straightened up and looked around sharply as a collective retching sound began to fill the forest. He looked confused and seemed to be mulling over the possibilities of what could be happening. A pained scream cut through the camp and the man turned back around.

"*What is going on?!*" the man asked, racking his brain as he ran up quickly to the nearest man and put a hand on his back observantly as he doubled over, the first to vomit a bright red flow of blood, the vessels in his eyes broken, giving him a deathly appearance. The sick man dropped to his knees holding his stomach, a single drip of blood beginning to leak from his nose as he retched a generous cup of bright blood into the ferns.

"It has to be poison," the man whispered to himself, thinking hard about the salt stone that Fred had added to the pot. His nostrils flared and he stood up straight, rounding on Fred suddenly. He drew his sword and took a threatening step forward, "You poisoned my men! Who are you really?"

"Today," Fred said, grabbing the hilt of his sword, "I am death."

Fred drew his wickedly curved blade as the man charged forward and he knocked away the first swing as the blade marked the air. The man knew his sword and how to fight, but it was obvious that he had never done battle with a goblin. He moved clumsily and kept trying to take high strikes from a distance and Fred saw how each movement would end before the man had even made the swing.

Fred caught the second blow effortlessly and spun the sword in a tight circle, the curved tip of his blade locking against the guard of the sword and tearing it out of his hands. He slung the man's sword out of reach, freeing his own blade and took a fatal swing of his own, the arched tip dug into the man's chest with the smooth expert motion. It cut between his ribs and exited back through the front of his collar again, speared like a worm on a hook.

He put a foot up against the man's body and pulled hard, splitting his chest open to the air like the wide doors of a cabinet and exposing the bloody pink meat of his lungs with what remained of his torn heart as he fell.

An arrow cut the air unexpectedly and he felt a sharp and piercing pain radiate from his left shoulder and his armor no longer sat the way it should on his arm. He turned out of the line of sight and tore his way out of the camp, weaving through forest until he found a tree of sufficient girth to hide him for a moment.

He sheathed his bloody sword and unlatched the spaulder at his shoulder as he leaned against the tree with his right side and moved the piece of armor out of the way. Dark purple blood dripped from the end of the spaulder as he dropped it to the ground at his feet. An arrowhead was sticking out from the front of his chest, below his collarbone at the shoulder. The tip of the arrow was streaked with his blood. He took in several rapid, shallow, breaths as he took hold of the arrow.

He pulled on it, feeling the cold of it move through his body as it slowly inched through. He pulled at it harder, slowly moving the shaft through the meat and gritting his teeth hard through the blinding pain that was racking his body. He paused for a few more breaths and began to move it again, his hands shaking and his shoulder and chest screaming with the smallest movement of the arrow.

It squelched sickly as the fledging began to fold in, catching gurgles of blood and flesh as he grimaced. He readjusted his hand on the arrow shaft, the slick coating of purple blood making it difficult for him to get a solid grip on it. He felt the pain in his stomach surge again and pushed it away as he tightened his grip on the arrow and pulled it the rest of the way through his body, releasing it from his shoulder with a wet sound and renewing the flow of blood from the wound.

The pain changed slightly with the removal of the arrow, and he felt somehow more comfortable through the difference in the pain.

He threw the bloody arrow to the ground and put a hand over the open wound. His stomach lurched angrily and he vomited, dark strings of purple blood coming up with the contents of his stomach.

A wooden groan rattled nearby and Fred heard the rustle of brush.

"You didn't," Bore's voice came from behind him. He turned, holding his shoulder with a trembling hand. Bore blinked his dark eyes and his bark textured body grated as he moved forward a few more steps, coming up and blocking him from view from another angle. He grabbed Fred's hand and moved it away from the wound at his shoulder looking aggravated before letting him put it back in place and put a rough stony hand against the other side of it.

Fred coughed painfully and a drizzle of blood slid from the corner of his mouth. He wiped it away quickly with the back of his hand, fighting with his arm, unable to move properly because of the wound. He dropped his arm slowly to avoid straining his shoulder any further.

"Tell me you didn't," Bore said again, sounding far more disturbed with the close up view and scrutinizing his overall appearance, his rough and scaled face drawn in earnest concern.

"They didn't trust me," Fred panted, fighting to catch his breath and setting the back of his head against the tree that he was leaning against as his chest heaved unevenly, "I had to. It was the only way be sure."

"How much did you eat?!" Bore asked angrily, his deep voice creaking.

"Very little of what was poisoned," Fred assured him, "I think I'll be alright."

"You think?!" Bore snapped.

"I'm fine," Fred corrected heatedly, through another violent surge of pain.

"Hard ass!" Bore said bitterly, "Don't you dare lie to me."

"I don't lie to anyone," Fred said, through his locked jaw and held back another bout of nausea as he felt blood rise up in his throat. He bent over and coughed it up, gagging on the taste of it in his mouth.

"Yeah, I see that," Bore snorted.

"Really," he said, trying to believe himself but feeling better with each time his stomach emptied, "I should be fine."

Bore cursed again as an arrow splintered against his back, shattering harmlessly against his strange body. He turned his head around and spotted the archer, "I'll get him. I'm going to rip his arms off for you," Bore said, angrily. He let go of Fred's shoulder and turned to face the man. In a blink he had torn through the woods like a raging beast and Fred looked back out into the woods as he rested against the tree.

A horrific scream pierced the air and died away quickly.

Fred set his jaw and swallowed away another stab of pain in his stomach, only now recognizing the distant death screams of hundreds of men behind him as their stomachs were eaten away by the poison, hitting the acid and burning through their bodies.

He felt another wave of pain and he doubled over, vomiting up the entire contents of his stomach with poison and a large amount of blood. He felt the damage left behind, but felt relief with its absence, the burning pang of his gut somehow preferable to the knives that had been there before.

He worked his tongue around the inside of his mouth, gathering what he could and spitting it out onto a nearby plant.

Bore trudged back, sloughing blood from his wooden hands looking disgusted at the sight of it on his body. He looked back to Fred and saw the large amount of fresh blood shimmering on the ground and cursed.

"That was the last of it I think," Fred said dismissively, pushing himself away from the tree and feeling the wet slickness of blood under his armor.

"The last of what? Your blood?" Bore snapped.

"The poison," Fred barked, putting a hand on his stomach and feeling the burn but no longer in unbearable pain, "I said, I'm fine."

"I heard you the first time," Bore said, rolling his eyes.

Fred decided to ignore his attitude and wiped his mouth again and said tiredly, "There are a hundred more men in the valley and fifty more along the ridgeline."

"No there's not," Bore argued defiantly.

"The officer told me that they there were," Fred said sharply.

"There were," Bore said with a shallow expression, "And now there's not. I took care of it already."

Fred stared at him in disbelief, "You already took out a hundred and fifty men?"

"More or less," Bore said, with a light shrug that groaned with his movements, "Setting up a rock fall can be very treacherous."

"Quit bragging," Fred said, forcing a smile.

"What's there to brag about?" Bore snorted, "You just took out the rest of them. If anything I'm falling behind in my numbers. There's still a few stragglers but I'll find them."

"Are you sure?"

Bore grinned, the thin line of his mouth creeping up and blocking his eyes behind his raised skin, "Besides, if you get shot again I'm going to have to carry your giant butt back to Gommorn and I don't want to do that."

"So you're being selfish," Fred joked, bracing his shoulder through the pain.

"Absolutely," he said, with a grin.

"Then what do I get to do?" Fred panted, as a warm rush of blood slid between his fingers.

Bore pointed back to the camp, "Go ahead and start the signal fire for the Lord General. I've still got some nit picking to do around here," he turned around and started off towards the ridgeline and looked back pointing a wooden finger at Fred accusatorily, "Don't do anything stupid this time."

Fred pushed away from the tree and walked slowly back to the campsite, an irony stench in the air that circulated with death and vomit. He stepped over bodies, occasionally driving his curved sword down into them as he walked, stilling the subtle movements as some clung to the last breaths of life. He walked over to the fire pit and kicked over the nearly empty kettle of poisoned food, letting it clatter dully to the ground as it rolled away and stopped in a pool of blood against the open, dead eyes of the cook.

He stooped down by the burning pit and drew his dagger from his hip and held it out over the open fire, trying to keep his fingers away from the licking flames. He watched the tip of the metal turn black and then begin to get a soft red glow to it. He pulled it back from the fire and pressed the heated blade against his shoulder and let out a muffled cry as his skin sizzled. He closed his eyes and balled his fist tightly, waiting for the pain to ebb away slightly.

When he could manage to take in a steady, shallow breath, he put the metal tip of the blade back into the fire and waited. When the blade had heated again he braced himself and reached around the back of his shoulder where the arrow had entered at his back and pressed the blade against his weeping flesh again, rocking back and forth for a few short seconds until he couldn't take the pain anymore and pulled it back off of the wound.

He waited again for his body to find an equilibrium in the balance of life and pain and stuck his pocket knife into the ground so that it would cool off quicker. He looked around the mass grave that littered the ground around him, the small river of blood that he had created met in forked streams and pooled in thick clots at the low areas of the clearing.

He looked up at the clean sky, the clouds covering from horizon to horizon but no longer raining. He put a hand at his heavy heart and closed his eyes to the unattractive sight and smell that lingered around him like the markings of the plague.

He pulled the knife out of the ground and touched it tentatively, feeling the heat from it but not being burned. He slid it back into its holster smoothly and forced himself up off of the ground.

Fred stretched out his long legs and glanced at his shoulder, the bleeding slowed and sealed. He walked over to a nearby area and started dragging wet logs into the fire, picking sizes that he could pick up and carry with his unscathed arm. He fanned the fire as it rolled with white smoke and began to die out. When they didn't catch fire after a while, he regretfully began to add bodies, one at a time to the pyre.

They began to burn more readily than the wet wood and he continued to drag the fresh corpses into the pit until a tower of black and horrifically putrid smoke rose readily up out of the canopy above him. The smell of burning flesh mingled into the sour air and carried the signal high above the tree line and rolled southward in the wind.

Chapter Thirty-Two

Ramif looked out over the not too distant horizon where the sheer cliff face caught the midday light among the low land of the valley floor. The dark plume of smoke began to billow up from beyond the edge of the ridgeline in a tower of rolling black smoke that expanded across the pale white and clouded sky.

He watched the spot intensely, waiting for the signal and hoping for good news.

He watched the smoke stack for a while and finally he saw the break in the tower as it separated into two clear sections, another fire had been set nearby the first and formed a separate pillar of black smoke.

He smiled arrogantly, relief lifting from somewhere in the back of his mind. He stroked his braded beard and watched for a while longer, waiting for a third fire anxiously, counting the time as he waited for a signal that did not come. He nodded proudly to himself, silently thanking Bolzar as he turned away from the hilltop and headed to the bottom of the hill. His feet slid on the wet ground as he went until the ground leveled out beneath him.

He sped up slightly and jogged though the woods to the edge of the expansive fields where he looked out over massive land full of waiting soldiers, talking quietly between each other. The sea of armor and men stretched out in front of him. He worked his way across the field with his hand in the air.

Armond saw that he was back at the edge of the forest and watched as he clearly put an open hand in the air, closed it and opened it again. Armond sighed with relief and took a horn from his pack. He pursed his lips and sounded the all clear, getting the attention of the men and quieting their conversations.

Armond waited for Ramif to take his position in front of the far column of soldiers before he sounded the horn again, each of them leading one side of the huge wall of armored men.

Ramif stood in his place at the front of the column and took in a deep breath that would carry his voice into the fields over the sound of the horn, "Let's move!"

The collective clinking of armor and the pounding of feet on wet ground echoed behind him as they marched across the fields to where the valley floor flattened out and the soil became stony.

The crunch of rocks under their feet sounded with the echo of shifting metal. The land around them became more rugged as they passed the sparse woods and shade into the vast rocky terrain. The sun peaked through the clouds and beat against their armor and heated the metal uncomfortably before it finally faded back into the sea of overcast sky.

The white crown of the cliffs crept closer with each step until they could see down the path of the valley. The cliffs rose high into the air, looming like the dull blade of a guillotine over their heads as they passed slowly into the mouth of the valley. The expansive white and grey stones of the cliff stretched out into the distance where a bend in the path cut into their line of sight.

They entered the valley floor and the muddy and slick rocks beneath them were difficult to walk on and occasionally a hard clink of metal would signal that someone had lost footing in the mud-covered ground.

After a while of marching through the valley, an obstinate and assaulting sound of clicking armor and irate voices grabbed Ramif's attention, and he turned angrily back to the troops to see Oswald stumbling through the ranks to force his way to the front.

"What are you doing?" Ramif barked.

Oswald fought gracelessly through the front line and hurried forward as anger flushed darkly in Ramif's face. He ignored the look and said quickly, "You're not going to like this but we have to stop."

"Why?" Ramif demanded, with sharp eyes and a vein rising at his temple.

Oswald moved anxiously and looked around the canyon, "Something isn't right here."

Ramif's nostrils flared dangerously, "I should just kill you. I really just should. Every time you've said that someone's almost died," he said, narrowing his eyes as they continued forward.

"None of which were my fault," Oswald insisted, his face pale as his eyes flickered around the rock face of the cliff, "I know when something is going to happen, I don't cause the problem."

"I'm not convinced of that," Ramif grumbled.

"You should be by now," Oswald said, his eyes pleading, "We need to stop."

Ramif snorted and stared ahead into the canyon watchfully and said, "You're nothing but trouble."

"But have I been wrong yet?" Oswald asked, running ahead of Ramif a few steps and walking backwards awkwardly, trying to keep eye contact as he moved, "I know you don't like me, and that's fine, but for your men, please... I've been shot at enough in the last couple of months to know what that particular magic feels like. You know that."

"Do you think there's still an ambush?" Ramif asked, looking up the high cliff and still seeing light wisps of smoke catch in the wind overhead.

"I don't know," Oswald said, uncomfortably, "Just let me go on ahead a little and I'll find out what's going on."

"And then what?"

"I'll do what I can to take care of it," he said, brushing his fingers over the red hilt of his sword and not feeling a difference in the magic flow.

Ramif twisted his face angrily, not wanting to stop in the valley at all. He cursed, knowing that they were pinned between the cliffs and that an ambush would be horrific. He slowed down and put his hand in the air and stomped his foot, "Halt!" The army stuttered to a stop unexpectedly with the clatter of metal that rippled back through the valley.

Ramif looked sternly at Oswald, the lines of his face set deeply on his brow, "Fine," he said sharply, "We'll be five minutes behind you, and no more."

Oswald nodded and turned away from them as he jogged cautiously forward and around a faint bend in the path ahead before vanishing from their line of sight.

Ramif looked back across the valley to Armond who looked confused. Ramif shrugged exaggeratedly and pointed off after Oswald with a noncommittal shake of his head. He counted minutes and gave the all clear again to Armond and the army began to move again with the sound of the horn.

They reached the bend in the valley path and a ground shattering explosion of cannon fire rattled the cliffside ahead of them. A rock slid from its place in the cliff and fell down to a stop to where Oswald stood, with his hands out and forcing it to settle at his feet where two cannon balls lay. Oswald turned when the boulder came to a standstill to glance back at the group. He looked up ahead of himself in the path and put a hand up, waving an all clear before slipping further ahead of the army as they moved forward again, though this time at a slower pace.

Ramif sighed as they moved through the valley and watched the ground as he stepped around the cannon balls and came upon disturbed ground where a trap had been exposed. He spotted a pit in the ground full of metal spears that stuck up from the bottom of the massive hole. He turned and ordered men around the pit and continued forward.

They crossed triggered snares every hour or so as they marched safely through the white canyon.

Ramif looked ahead to a huge pile of fallen stones where Oswald stood, waiting for them. They walked up to the rockslide and Ramif was able to see portions of dozens of crushed bodies beneath the large stones. He looked at Oswald curiously as he came close enough to speak with him.

"It wasn't me," Oswald said, at the look on Ramif's face. He looked down at a broken and deformed hand that was sticking out from the nearest stone, "This was already here."

"Good," Ramif said shortly, "Are we clear then?"

"I think so," Oswald nodded.

Ramif locked eyes with him and gave a short, respectful nod, before saying quietly, "Then get back in rank."

"Yes sir," Oswald said, and fell back into the lines, clumsily knocking through the front row and disturbing the group as he went back into his place.

Ramif looked around and rolled his eyes as he tried to ignore the noise. He searched for an easier way around the high collection of boulders and saw none, "We're going to have to go over," he muttered to himself. He looked back at the massive collection of his army and waved them forward as he found a sturdy path and started leading them up the rock fall. He reached the top and started cautiously down the other side, stepping over the occasional body mingled in the debris. The sound of unorganized steps and gritting armor plates followed along behind him.

They crawled over the rockslide and continued through the valley until the cliff began to shrink alongside them and an opening at the mouth of the valley brought them back to a smooth path.

The relentless march of men followed him until the low falling sun lit the open field. He turned and ordered the camp to set up and watched the steady flow of men and women pass around him into the campsite to their predesignated tasks. A man on horseback trotted up beside him and dismounted, holding on to the reigns.

"Lord General," he said, in greeting. He removed the horses bit and patted its muscular neck as it bent its head low to graze on the fresh alfalfa in the field.

"Tanner," Ramif replied, "Report?"

"The Quillen army will be here to join us through the night. There were no complications with their travel moving through the mountains. They weren't expected there," he said, openly relieved at his own message.

"Anything further?"

"Not yet sir," Tanner said, looking out into the distance, "I'm still waiting for the second group to return."

"Find me when they do."

"Certainly," Tanner said, and patted his horse again before he took the reign and led him further out into the field. Ramif walked through the bustle of people and found General Armond and General Loch among the swathe of men.

The two of them looked over as he joined the group.

"Has anyone heard from Fred or Bore yet?" Ramif asked.

Loch shook his head as he lit the cigar plugged between his teeth. He shook the match and threw it into the wet grass and took his cigar between his fingers as he let out a dense cloud of smoke. Armond backed out of the smoke's path and shook his head as well, "No, we haven't."

"I wonder what's taking them so long," Ramif grumbled.

Loch puffed at his cigar with a light hearted shrug, "I wouldn't worry about them. They set the signal fire for an all clear right? Just two?"

Ramif nodded, "It wasn't a distress signal, so I assume it all went well. It isn't like them to run late though. They should have met us here already."

"They will," Loch said casually, "If they had any trouble we would have known about it by now, don't you think?"

"I'm not sure," Ramif said, looking back the way they had come, "You never really know with those two. There may have been more men there than we had thought."

Armond looked over at Ramif, surprised, "Surely you didn't send them out blind?" he asked.

Ramif worked his jaw in thought, "I gave them all the information we had," he said regretfully, and remembered back to the rock fall at the end of the mouth of the canyon. He wondered passively if there had been a complication that they didn't want to report to him.

"What about the scouts?"

Ramif looked back up at Armond, "No word yet."

A heavy-footed crackling sound popped through the air, mingled with the metallic clinking of armor as Bore slunk forward through the group towards them.

"There you are," Ramif said critically, both relieved and irritated at the sight of him, "I was beginning to worry."

"*Sorry* for being late," Bore grumbled unapologetically, brazenly tipping his head to one side.

Ramif looked past Bore into the sea of men and waited to see the towering form of a goblin through the mass of rising tents, "Where's Fred?"

Bore creaked forward and looked away ruefully, "Still at the edge of the Solber cliffs."

The generals stopped and looked at him with pause.

"What happened?" Loch asked, picking the cigar out of his mouth suddenly.

"The gork got himself hurt," Bore said angrily, his wooden features locked stiffly, blocking the shine of his eyes. He gestured with a flip of his hand back towards the path and cursed openly in frustration.

"How?" Loch asked, concernedly.

"He's stupid," Bore spat, with a deepening frown, "He ate some of the poison so they would eat it," he said, waving his arm heatedly through the air, "And then he got himself shot with an arrow just to top it all off."

"Is he alright?" Armond asked quickly.

"No!" Bore said irritably, "he keeps telling me he's fine, but the man's got more blood outside his body than in."

"And you left him there?!" Ramif barked, stepping forward, his face reddening.

Bore threw his arms up exasperatedly, his limbs cracking loudly as he yelled, "He wouldn't let me stay!"

"What kind of condition is he in?" Loch asked, ashing the cigar sharply as he pinched his lips together in thought.

"He swears he's going to be alright," Bore said bitterly, putting a hand behind his head and scratching at his bark-like skin, "But he's having trouble breathing now from the arrow wound, and he's started vomiting blood again," he shook his head, distressed, and said reluctantly, "I don't know if there's anything I can even do for him."

"How much of the poison did he eat?" Armond asked.

Bore shrugged, "He won't tell me exactly. 'A taste' is what he keeps saying," he paused and let out a heavy breath, "But I don't know for sure."

"Why would he do that?" Loch asked, thinking as he stared at the burning ember of his cigar.

Bore picked at a rough place on his face nervously, "He said they didn't trust him enough."

Armond put his face in a hand and rubbed at his eyes, "You have to go back."

"He made me leave," Bore said, persistently, "Because I *had to* come and tell you not to drink out of the creek bed. They poisoned the water supply around the valley. All of your water has to come out of the river."

Loch cursed and threw down his cigar quickly as he turned on his heels and raced through the horde to the far side of the field, warning people loudly as he went.

Ramif took a sudden sharp step towards Bore, "You could have started with that!" Ramif reprimanded.

"No, I couldn't have," Bore said, shaking his head angrily, "You kept asking me questions!"

"You could have said something sooner!" he shouted.

"Like you wouldn't have yelled at me for that too?" Bore said, frustrated, throwing out his rough arms and taking a heavy step forward so that he loomed over Ramif. He bent down to look him in the eye and twisted his wooden features.

"Watch yourself," Ramif warned, gritting his teeth and holding his ground, "And get out of my face!"

"What are you going to do about it?" Bore taunted, beating a stony fist against his solid chest with a dull thump.

"I should teach you a lesson," Ramif said darkly, the pulse at his temple visible through the deepening red of his face.

"You can't hurt me!" Bore hissed viciously, balling his heavy hand into a tight fist.

"I could set your insubordinate ass on fire!" Ramif snapped.

Bore snorted dismissively, "I dare you."

Armond drew his sword slowly, and held it out between them to keep them apart. He gently pushed the face of the sword against Bore and forced him away from Ramif as he stepped between the two of them.

"The water is poisoned," Armond said, looking at Bore and trying to bring him back to the current situation, "Is there anything else we need to know?"

"No," Bore said defiantly, trying to look around Armond's body to Ramif, "That's it."

Armond took his water bladder off of his shoulder and pushed it authoritatively up against Bore's wooden chest, "Then go back to Fred and make him drink as much water as he can. Make him eat some charcoal too," he let go as Bore took the bag and watched him closely as their eyes locked, "It might not help now, but try it anyway," he gave Bore a serious look that communicated the disparity of Fred's predicament, and commanded with a nod to the south, "Go."

"Yes sir," Bore said, dropping his anger for worry and looking at the bag gratefully with his iron grip around the strap. He turned with determination in his long strides and ran back towards the distant cliffs.

"Damn," Armond muttered, watching as Bore vanished back out into the line of woods behind them. He turned to Ramif and rolled his eyes impatiently as he passed him to go and help Loch warn the troops.

Ramif let his anger smolder out, pacing through the camp as the sun set and the creeping darkness of evening reached over them. The sky darkened, casting the fields in a blue grey haze that hinted at a dark night.

Thunder rolled somewhere in the distance.

"Lord General!" A panicked man tore through the camp towards him.

Ramif turned to Tanner with interest, "What is it?"

"My men just returned," he panted.

"And?"

Tanner pointed back around towards the Azarian boarder, "They're almost here."

"Who?" Ramif asked, following his pointed finger with his eyes.

"Azar," Tanner said, his face glistening with sweat.

Ramif's face fell and his heart skipped a beat, "Already?" he asked, alarmed at the sudden change.

"Yes sir," Tanner said, blankly waiting for orders.

Ramif looked around the camp, "How far?"

"No more than an hour away," he said, his face stoic.

Ramif felt his heart hammer against his ribs and nodded once, moving quickly, "IN ARMS!" he bellowed, over the crowd.

There was a sudden stir of startled expressions at the order. He repeated himself and watched as people began to scramble for their armor and weapons. He strode hurriedly to the edge of the field as he continued to give the order.

Loch and Armond met him at the front of the field, "They're early?" Armond asked.

"They are nearly here," Ramif said tensely, "We don't have a choice, we have to move now."

Loch and Armond tore off into the massive throngs of men and began to help organize them to march. It wasn't long before everyone was at attention, thousands of eyes on him, a sudden stillness that only came with the moment of war. He drew his sword and held it into the air as he spoke over the deafening silence.

"Azar's forces are nearly here! The battle hangs over us in this hour!" the silence rang, "They marched in the night and meant to catch us off guard! THEY FAILED!" the army roared with the clatter of metal, "They wanted us tired and weak! WE ARE NOT! They tried to set traps for us because THEY FEAR US!" the roar of battle hit the air energetically, "They want our home! THEY CANNOT HAVE IT!" the men approved with a collective yell, "We WILL defend our people and each other! We ARE strong! We ARE fearless! Today WE ARE DEATH!" the anger of the men grew again in loud agreement as he continued, "King Venhow wants this land. HE WILL BE STOPPED TONIGHT! *WE* WILL END THIS!" The battle cry of the army now was so loud that he had to pause to be heard over the roar of the voices, "HE WILL FAIL, BECAUSE GOMMORN'S FORCES — WILL — NOT — YEILD!"

He turned his back to the raging army and began the final march into the eve of battle.

The steady beat of armor marched through the rolling fields and hills, covering what distance they could in the night's cover. The cool air was still as they crossed through the land, watchfully.

Their army stopped as defined rows of the Azarian army crested the hill in the distance and the dim moonlight glinted on dark armor as they marched forward to meet them.

Ramif let them clear the distance slowly, hearing the thunder of their armor as they approached. When the distance became reasonable he raised his sword to the air again and dropped the blade forward. The army bellowed as they charged forward.

Azar's army sped to a clear run and there was a harsh metallic sound as the two armies collided in the center of the field.

Ramif caught the eye of a man on the front line and they quickly locked blades. He sank under a high swing and arced his blade, feeling the armor plate at the man's ribs separate at contact. He drove the sword in deep and pulled the blade back out of the man's body as he reached for the wound. Ramif advanced, stabbing in an upward slice at the man's throat, piercing the fine mesh and with a hard sweep the man's head was torn from his body with a thick ribbon of blood flying into the air around them.

The severed head dropped away from his body and wetly landed on the ground with wide, open eyes.

The man's body fell on top of the occupied helmet, pouring blood over the grass at Ramif's feet as he stepped over the body and pressed forward into the frenzy of battle.

Another man made eye contact with him from a short distance away, the white band at his shoulder catching the light in the semi-darkness. Ramif brought up his sword, his hands biting on the hilt with his muscles tight as he took an open swing at the man's face. He felt the twinge of iron reverberate up his arms as the blades met.

Ramif stepped aside as the commander's blade marked its path and he moved around the swing and brought his body in close enough for a strike. He rammed the hilt of his sword up into his stomach, hard and repositioned his footing. He felt the air slice near his head as the man took another swing through his gasping breaths.

Ramif shifted his body, spotting a weakness in his defense and he turned his sword over and brought the tip of the blade into a crease of the commander's armor under his arm at a tight angle.

The man howled and withdrew his arm as he regained his balance and kicked at Ramif with the heel of his foot.

Ramif took the advantage of his height to duck under the kick, grabbing the foot with one hand and pushing it up into the air. The resistance of the armor didn't give him the range of motion he needed to catch his balance, and the man landed flat on his back with a loud grunt.

Ramif released the foot and took his sword in both hands as he spun with his blade and he drove it into the commander's exposed belly.

He screamed, grasping at the sword blade desperately. Ramif pulled out the blade and drove it in again, at another angle and the man jerked and sputtered up blood without a scream to be had. He pulled out the blood coated blade with a slick sound and moved on, charging deeper into the battle.

Ramif felt an arrow whizz by him but ignored the hiss of air to lock his eyes on a new target.

A Keernith goblin drew his sword from a soldier's body, dropping it lifelessly to the ground with a dark grin. The goblin turned on him, its eyes glinting.

Ramif tightened his grip on his sword.

The goblin stepped forward, his curved blade dripping with fresh blood. He snarled, raising his blue lip and baring his sharpened teeth with the malicious points of their narrow edges reflecting in the dark like daggers. He smirked as he took a sudden wide step forward and brought the blade in at Ramif with an insatiable hunger in his eyes.

Ramif blocked the blade, careful not to let the two swords remain in contact for very long. He knocked it away and came in closer, blocking another strike to clear the distance between them. He felt the curved blade catch at his side and he rolled back and away from it as it scraped across his armor plate teasingly. He took a low swing at the goblin's knees and watched satisfactorily as he was forced to move back quickly and he lowered his guard.

Ramif swung again, this time high, catching the goblin's face and tearing it open, throwing his head back sharply on impact. He tried to recover, now distracted form his wound and Ramif took a shot at his exposed arm. He felt the armor slide away with the precision of the cut and the sudden but brief resistance of bone as the arm came clean off at the elbow and the sword dropped with the clasped green forearm still clinging to the hilt.

The goblin roared, holding the stump of an arm against his body and pulled a knife from his side, stabbing blindly through the blood in its eyes. Ramif avoided the knife and swiftly spun around the goblin, he gathered his strength and drove the sword up into its back with a weighted shove.

He twisted the blade and felt something inside his body pop. Ramif withdrew his sword violently and watched as the goblin dropped slowly to the ground, barely clinging to the last moments of life.

Ramif turned and left him to die, marking his next victim with the blood of the last.

He felt a heavy blade come down on his shoulder from behind, rattling his bones and tearing at his muscle with the weight of the blow. He turned quickly with his sword in hand and jabbed upward, finding the mark and peeling through the plating. The man's body jerked up off the ground with the force of the stab and fell further onto the blade.

Ramif removed the sword angrily, the hot pain in his shoulder radiating up into his neck. He watched the man fall and moved his arm, recognizing the feeling of torn muscle and he screwed up his face in pain.

He turned his anger onto the nearest person and swung the blade out and slit the throat of the man cleanly in a blur as he rounded on another.

The new target's eyes went wide as the carnage in Ramif's wake became apparent and he turned and ran from him.

Ramif followed after him quickly, his feet beating the ground as he began to close the distance between them. He pulled his dagger from his side holster at his hip and threw it, watching the graceful spinning of its weight as the razor edge and its handle twirled around one another. It found its mark and stuck fast in the back of the man's neck.

The man slowly stumbled to a stop and grasped back for the handle of the dagger. Ramif cleared the remaining distance and drove his sword deep into his back feeling the pulse of his heart stop through the metal in his hand.

He pulled out the sword with a wet sucking sound, letting the body fall. He bent over and pulled the dagger from the man's neck and he slid the blood smeared blade back into its holster.

His gaze fell quickly on another goblin and he felt the wave of adrenaline hit his bones, driving him forward with a vengeance. He charged with his sword brought up across his body at the ready as the goblin bent low to the ground and swung at his feet. Ramif jumped the wicked blade and arced his sword.

His sword tore through the air and collided with the goblin's helmet, ripping it free from his head and sending it out into the darkness.

He landed hard on his feet as the goblin's sword slid through the air and missed his shoulder. It stood upright again its face contorted with rage. It turned the blade around in its hand and brought it back down at Ramif's face.

He caught the blade with his own and the clatter of metal rang sharply as the two swords collided through another strike. The goblin took a sure footed step and brought a fist hard to the soft open side plate of Ramif's armor, a sick crack echoing in his chest as his rib broke under the large green fist.

He grimaced and swung hard at the goblin's open shoulder and feet his sword tear through a fine layer of muscle and sinew. The glint of the goblin's blade caught in the shadow of the moonlight and he spun to catch it, tossing the path of the sword high over his head. He watched it pass over him and spotted another exposed area in the goblin's armor.

He spun the blade and circled around. The power in the swing coursed through his body and he felt it make contact as the sword penetrated the armor at the side of its gut. Ramif pushed at the hilt and felt the end of the stroke come against the metal plating near its core. He drew back his sword and ducked under another clumsy blow, slow and uncoordinated.

The goblin braced its side, dark purple blood stained its teeth as it drew back its upper lip and scowled at him. It huffed, fueled by pain and anger, and rose its curved blade up into the air again.

Ramif threw himself back and watched the tip of the goblins blade slide down, grazing the side of his face with a fine, hair-thin slice at his cheek. He moved under the follow through of the swing and stabbed up, sinking his blade into the base of the goblins jaw. He pushed it up through stiff tissue and bone and into the depths of its skull.

Its weight dropped instantly to the cold, damp ground and Ramif had to work against the splintered bone to retrieve his sword again. He took in a short shallow breath through the pain in his side, and looked out over the field of battle.

Chapter Thirty-Three

Jameson nocked an arrow, drawing the string to his cheek and staring down the shaft of the arrow. He fixed both eyes on his target and took in a slow and steady breath and held it as he set the tip of the arrowhead on its mark. He let out the breath slowly through pursed lips and released his fingers on the string as the arrow spiraled through the dark.

He followed the spinning fledging with his eyes and watched it imbed itself in the eye of a man down the field. He crumpled like a puppet with its strings cut and hit the ground, dead.

He scanned around him as he pulled another arrow from the quiver and nocked it back to the string smoothly.

He drew back the bow and felt the string on his cheek and the tension in his arm as he readjusted the string's positioning slightly. He lined up the target with a balanced breath and let go, feeling the string of the arrow depart his face with the soft hiss of the shot. It stuck stiffly out of the back of a goblin a short distance away. The goblin did not crumple and instead rounded angrily on him, his eyes flickering through the field of soldiers and landing on the bow and then Jameson.

It made its way towards him, its back postured and an iron mace in its hand.

Jameson knocked another arrow and drew back. He released the arrow to the wind and the goblin moved with lightning reflexes, tipping its head out of the shot. The arrow sliced its ear cleanly but the goblin didn't even seem to notice as the arrow followed through and fell out into the night behind it.

It had come too close to take another shot with the bow.

Jameson spun the bow back behind him and into a holster angled on his back, and drew his sword with the ring of steel. The goblin swung the mace and Jameson had no choice but to dodge the shot as it rumbled in the air, unable to block the weight of it. He moved quickly as the goblin brought the second swing down towards the top of his head.

He kicked off with one foot as he jumped back, spinning his body out of the way as the mace slid by his back and passed on through to hit the ground, spitting up dirt with the sound of its immense weight and the goblin's strength.

Jameson found footing and swung his sword, knowing that the goblin would have no choice but to hesitate as he picked his weapon back up from the ground. The blade slid up the armor, leaving a white scrape in the metal until it passed the goblin's chest plate and exploded up into its face.

The goblin's jaw split open wide with shattered bone and blood raining into the air.

Jameson turned the swing around with the shock in its face and put his weight into the swing until the end of his sword shattered into the side of its skull. The blade tore through its bone like a fine axe through cheap wood. The sword freed itself out the other side of the goblin's face as its enormous body sagged into the field at his feet.

He looked around quickly and sheathed his sword before retrieving his bow from his back and fetching out another arrow. He nocked it to the string and scanned the battle through the darkness.

Another archer on the distant hillside was firing out in their direction. He judged the distance and decided that the shot was too far to take at his current position. He headed closer.

His feet moved through the battle, his body occasionally dodging the glinting swing of a sword as he passed through, determined to find the man he had marked for his arrow.

The sound of the battle crashed occasionally and assaulted his ears with the scraping of metal and the guttural sounds of looming death and pain.

He leapt over an armored body lying awkwardly on the ground and landed smoothly, picking up momentum as he came closer. He slid under a high swing as a man tried to engage him as he passed by and continued on until he was able to find an open place to take his new shot.

The arrow fitted into its place against the string, finding its rest as the cold of the arrow chilled the end of his finger as he supported its side. He drew the arrow back and fixed the tip of his arrow at the end of his sight at the other archer. He released the shot confidently, feeling his mark in the distance as it flew straight and true. He listened and thought he heard the wet and heavy smack of the arrow in its target.

He drew back another arrow and scanned the field with it.

A dark skinned, blonde, woman caught his attention and he watched her for a moment. Her long hair was braided down her back with a heavily spiked tie at its end. She spun gracefully and ferociously through the battlefield, arcs of blood and bone in her wake as she expertly tore her way through the center of the field.

He watched her spin her body around quickly throwing her hair out high behind her, the spikes in her braid grazing a nearby man's face as a distraction as she finished the tight spin and brought her blade around to pin him through with her sword. She drove it in down through the collar bone at the hollow of the armor and peeled it back out of his body, missing not a step as she plowed her way into the next person in her line of sight.

Jameson smiled at the sight, not sure why it amused him so. Suddenly he spotted another target for his arrow, looking away from Satomi's hypnotizing grace of battle, and drifting the arrowhead in front of him so that it cut a line through the intended path. He let go and watched it spiral out through the night.

He watched the body drop and reached into his quiver, his fingers brushing the soft fledging of three remaining arrows. He looked around the bloody field, trying to remember where he had dropped the last archer, intending to replenish his supply.

He made his way towards the hillside and was cut off by a massive goblin. He tried to put the bow at his back but didn't have time as the goblin threw a long arm into his chest, and he was picked up off of the ground and hurtled through the air.

The bow flew up and out of sight.

He landed hard in a curdled pool of cold blood and fought back up to his feet as the goblin cleared the distance again.

Jameson drew his sword quickly and tried to find stable footing in the blood soaked grass.

The goblin grinned at him, showing a heavy scar across its lower lip that trailed down its chin in a wide band that reflected glossily in what little light there was. The pale yellow-green hue of the scar stood out against the thin blue lips and dark green skin as he smirked.

"Well, well," the goblin snickered, "If it isn't my old friend."

Jameson felt a wave run cold in his blood. He swallowed back the fear and tightened his grip on the sword, anger boiling below the surface.

"How long has it been?" the goblin asked, licking the scar at its lip with a blue tongue.

Jameson clenched his jaw and pushed the question away, refusing to speak with the green demon as his crimson eyes narrowed in on him vengefully. The goblin began to walk in a slow circle around Jameson who compensated, not daring to turn his back to the beast.

They circled each other tensely.

The goblin's red eyes lingered on the sword in Jameson's hand as it continued to smile smugly, "A year ago, wasn't it?" again Jameson did not answer as he spoke, "If you want revenge, you'll have to give your life for it."

Jameson moved to one side and took a swing as the goblin moved to block, the two blades singing as they rubbed against one another in passing.

A dormant rage began to build in Jameson's chest; an anger that fueled something within him, deep in the caverns of his heart. He drew back his sword and waited for an opening. His heart pulsed in his head and it marked the steady beat, like a drum to his fluid movements as they continued to circle each other.

The goblin moved in quickly with a downward strike which Jameson caught in mid swing. He set his feet into the ground and made a strike of his own, lurching the sword up at the goblin's center.

The goblin slid away from the blade and curved its own, catching a piece of armor plating against Jameson's forearm. The hit picked up the plate and snapped it back as the blade released the armor, narrowly missing the muscle beneath.

Jameson took another opening and swung the sword low, this time feeling the graze of the sword edge make light contact with the goblin's thigh before it was able to catch the blade with a hard block, ringing steel as he was forced away.

He took another strike, and another in quick succession, each time meeting the disappointing feel of steel on steel. His sword craved the give of the goblin's flesh, but only the sharp song of the blades intertwining met his ears. He lunged, trying to move in closer, but couldn't as the goblin swung sharply each time he tried, forcing him back to slick and unsteady footing in the wet sloth of the earth.

"Come now," the goblin chortled, "You have to do better than that."

The curved blade cut around and Jameson was barely able to knock away the blow, the blades disconnecting and sending the jagged tip passing in front of his eyes by a single breath of night between himself and the razor edge.

He moved in as the blade passed across his face and swung hard. The goblin moved out of the way and snarled. It spun its blade and caught the guard of Jameson's sword with its hooked edge, dragging him in close and locking the swords together in an immovable knot.

They both fought against the tangled blades and the goblin's strength pushed against him, forcing his feet to slide in the mud and blood as he was heaved back a step. Jameson tried to regain footing in the slick ground and felt a stone under the ball of his foot and balanced his weight on it. He regained some control with the small piece of solid ground under foot, and gritted his teeth as he pushed back against the goblin's blade and forced it further away from his face.

The goblin breathed out sharply through its bared narrow teeth, an angry string of spit flying into the air. They locked eyes, each knotting their muscles against the other in battle for the firmly interlaced swords.

The goblin's red eyes glinted, "When you see your little girl in hell," it leaned in closer with a sickening twitch of its mouth and hissed, "Tell her I miss her screams."

Jameson's stomach churned revoltingly and his heart began to gallop, the horse of his buried rage charging forward to the sound of war, with murderous intent focused on the bloody red eyes before him. He felt the beast of wrath break in his body like a splintering bone, the sharp edges infecting his breathing, his strength, and the air around him as it became a palpable dense mass of his energy.

The goblin locked the trunk of its body and shoved hard taking one hand from its sword and seizing the hilt of Jameson's. It gripped its hand tightly like an iron binding over his hand and it twisted its wrists, wrenching at Jameson's fingers and taking both swords. The goblin kicked a massive heel into Jameson's chest and flattened him into the ground.

Jameson saw the glint of the two swords as they separated, the goblin's red eyes like burning coals in the darkest caves.

Jameson felt something happen within the explosion in his chest, a sudden release of drive that welled up into his head and slid down into his feet. He rolled to dodge a downward stab of his own sword in the goblin's green hand and heard it sink into the ground beside him. The strange feeling expanded out to the ends of his fingers and the hairs on his body stood on end.

Jameson heard a crack of thunder reverberate from within his chest and expand out into the field. He rounded back on the goblin, getting up to his feet as another crashing thunderbolt exploded from within him, rattling his armor and lighting the ground at his feet. The grass around him instantly caught on fire in a circle of righteous fury, welling out in waves as the energy within him flowed heavily with his rage.

He drew an arrow from his quiver, the fledging and wooden shaft setting ablaze in his hand at his first touch.

He walked fixedly, dodging a swing of the sword as he rammed the arrowhead into the goblin's gut with his hand. He jerked on the shaft of the arrow aggressively and watched fear begin to ebb into the goblin's dark face.

He pushed on the arrow again, feeling a hot flow of blood seep over his hand as it sank deeper into its body.

The goblin's face contorted with anger and pain that could stand nothing against what Jameson had felt

He twisted the arrow as another bout of thunder rolled through him and the goblin caught on fire like dry timber. The goblin screamed intensely, an unearthly sound like no other on the planet, as the flames expanded within its core and licked up its body beneath the armor. It dropped the swords and tried to back away from Jameson's grip on the arrow.

He would not release it.

Jameson watched closely as the green flesh began to melt away from its face through the yellow flicker of the fire, exposing dark muscle and black ribbons of charred remains over white bone, contorted in horror and pain.

Finally, Jameson let go of the arrow and picked up his sword form the ground. The waves of energy pouring from his chest ran hot white flames down the length of his sword like running water until the entirety of the sword was lit like a torch.

He rounded back on the goblin with a cold expression.

"That's for my daughter," he breathed darkly, staring down at the blackened flesh of the goblin's face, "And this is for me."

He turned the fiery sword on the writhing goblin and ran the white hot blade into its chest. The sizzle of burning flesh and blood assaulted him as smoke rolled from the goblin's burnt skin. He leaned his weight into the sword and inched it forward slowly, as he watched the red fire of the goblin's eyes as its life slowly began to fade and die away, glazed in the release of death.

He pulled out the sword, his mind fogged in a nothingness of numb wrath as he looked up at the circle of eyes on him. The white fire of his sword reflecting in their eyes.

Jameson straightened his back and watched the men around him back away.

He walked, his muscles shaking through his firm stride as the sudden magic in his blood seeped into every inch of his body and he jerked reactively as it coursed through him. The field and grass set on fire in his wake as he walked, each step burning in a brightly lit, fiery, footprint before dying away to scorched ground behind him.

The sudden magic jolted at the muscles in his arms and legs as he moved forward, a wide path cutting before him as men moved clearly out of his way in fear.

He looked ahead of him.

One man did not move.

A shaggy man with mousey hair that strung limply in his face stood in his way, his wide shoulders covered with simple clothing. He had no weapon and he smiled, his narrow chest breathing steadily. Walt took a step forward, flexing his hands as Jameson came towards him.

Jameson felt his body tremor sharply as he took another step, leaving a fiery footprint behind him.

The two stared at each other for a long moment and the biting anger within Jameson took hold of his body and he swung the fiery blade from a distance, slinging a stream of bright liquid fire from the end of his sword.

The fire slid through the air, lighting Walt's unkempt features momentarily as he threw his arm wide and the liquid fire ignited into hot red flames as it was thrown up and away from him in a blaze that rose into the air and died away into the darkness.

"An Animus Wizard," Walt said, interestedly, "How very rare you are. And what a shame to kill."

Jameson renewed his grip on the sword and charged forward jerkily, the liquid fire on his blade brightening as he took another swing. Walt slid a hand between himself and the sword, spitting the fire up and into the air where it rained around them, he turned his body and directly released a pulse of air that shattered the wind and forcibly pushed Jameson back.

Jameson's feet slid as he was forced away, scorching new ground with the fire that rolled from his body. He found his footing and ran forward again as he began to regain control of his muscles and he started to get used to the surge of the fire within him.

He spun the blade in his hands, turning the sword over his head with the fire dancing on the tips of his fingers playfully and he felt no damage or sensation to the caress of it. As the blade spun, it slung the liquid fire in a wide circle overhead, setting the ground ablaze at it landed in white hot drips before it ignited to an intense inferno, forcing Walt back.

He marked a place on Walt's chest and swung his blade into the ground, sinking it into the dirt and lifting hot rocks into the air, throwing them, coated in white fire, to the intended mark.

Walt spun his arms in front of him and watched as the stones exploded into the air like shrapnel.

Jameson spun again, sinking his sword into the ground and spitting up more rocks that hurtled ahead of him as he slung white drips of light and fire around him. The shrapnel of exploding rocks and fire filled the air as he continued to sink his sword into the ground and launch the stones, keeping Walt occupied as he crept closer. When he had closed the distance, he thrusted the sword into Walt's circle of movement.

Walt bent away from the sword and sank back to the ground, avoiding the blade and with one hand supporting his weight, he spun his foot in a wide circle and released a pulse of solid air. The magic hit the ground beneath Jameson's feet and broke the ground, pitching him up into the air.

He landed flat on his back, disorientated, as the air was forced out of his lungs and lights danced in front of his eyes.

Walt leapt to his feet as Jameson hit the ground and he brought his hands out wide and pulled them together quickly, condensing the air between his open hands until his palms beat together forming a bright light and heat that directed down into Jameson's face, blinding him.

Jameson blinked at the nothingness left from his useless, burning eyes, and rolled back onto his stomach. He got to his knees with his sword up defensively and scrambled to his feet, holding on to his sword for dear life and listening closely to the crackle of the fire that he could no longer see.

He swung the blade over his head in a swift circle, feeling rather than seeing the magic, as it slung out liquid fire in fine ribbons. He felt the fire ignite and the heat that it gave off, warming the left side of his face.

He turned on the feeling and swung his blade again, taking blind swings in the air and feeling the magic ignite the fire and feeling how close he was by how quickly through his strokes the heat expanded around him and following the heat.

He swung again and felt the hot singe of fire against his face, and knew he was close enough to strike. He ducked and spun the sword low at Walt's legs and then cut it up at a sharp angle that was meant to cross his body. He felt the air thicken and fought against it, forcing his blade to swing through it and he felt a satisfying slip of cutting flesh as he slid the blade across Walt's outstretched arm.

Walt stumbled back in surprise as he tried to reinforce the barrier between them. Jameson fought against the magic and he started to bore his way through the invisible wall, spitting liquid white fire as his sword broke the magic.

Walt turned as the barrier broke and ran back a short distance, quickly working his hands around each other, rolling his wrists as though trying to balance a ball of water on the back of his dominant hand as the other worked around it. A solid ball of yellow light formed beneath his hand and condensed until he could feel the static burning at his palm.

Jameson tore through the remains of the barrier and spun his blade over his head again, waiting for the feel of the burst of heat that did not come.

Walt staggered clear of the fire, his concentration focused on the ball of light in his hands and threw it forward. The ball hissed angrily as it shot through the air.

Jameson heard the sound and reflexively brought his sword up in a swing to block it, feeling it make contact with something, the sword stopping short in midair. A strange sensation filled his body and stole the breath from his lungs as the magic drew in and exploded violently around his sword. The intensity of the concussion as the magic exploded collided with his head and sent him spinning through the air.

Jameson fell face down with a hard crack into the ground, the fire around him dying away as he fell still in the field.

Walt walked forward cautiously, breathing heavily as he looked down at Jameson's lifeless form in the mud. He stopped over the body and shook his head disgustedly and muttered to himself, "So much talent. Such a shame he's here."

He looked back at Jameson one last time and wandered over the scorched ground and back into the raging battle.

Chapter Thirty-Four

An arrow split the air at his face, whipping by as it landed fast in the hip of the man beside him. The man cried out and stumbled forward trying to pull the barbed head of the arrow back out the way that it came in, grasping the bloody shaft and grimacing.

Armond passed him into the depth of the battle, finding another target, his sword drawn and his jaw set.

He wove around an entangled mass of flying blades and saw a bright flash of yellow light whizz down from a distant hill, and an explosion of armor and blood sprayed into the air.

He moved towards its source and was stopped short by a commander in black trimmed armor, swinging his sword into his path. Armond stepped back and found sure footing, blocking the next swing as he smoothly wrapped his blade into the man's lacking defense and forcing him back. He swung the blade high, expecting the response as the man brought his hands up to block it, exposing his center.

Armond drew the dagger at his side and moved cleanly under the man's sword as he held it aloft, stabbing the dagger into the man's side. He withdrew the blade and repeatedly stabbed at the open place at the man's armor. He slid around the injured side and dropped his sword low as he drew it back to his body and moved around to the man's back. He swiftly slid the sword in between the metal plates of his armor and shoved as blood poured down the grooved fuller and he drove it in deeper.

He pulled out his sword with a wet sucking sound and turned as another flash of light went off in the distance, hearing its crash over the collapse of armor.

He started off again towards the hill, taking clean sweeps at unguarded throats as he went.

Another man stepped in front of his warpath.

He was unarmed and did not wear armor, a thin stream of blood staining his forearm. He seemed unfazed by his presence and Armond gave him pause. He stopped in his tracks and he and Walt exchanged knowing glances.

"You're a wizard," Armond said, surveying the basic clothes and searching for a weapon that was not there.

Walt put his hands at his sides, palms facing up with a bored and bothered expression that made Armond's heart beat harder against his ribs, "What can I say? I'm blessed," Walt said placidly.

Armond gripped the hilt of his sword until the metal bit into his hands, watching Walt's bemused expression carefully. He took in a deep breath, "Don't be so sure just yet."

"And why not?" Walt asked, with a small smile.

"Because it won't save you," Armond said, as he rolled the hilt of his sword in his fingers tightly.

Walt snickered, "I suppose you think you can beat me?"

"I know that I can," Armond said.

Walt's smile widened, "Then this should be enlightening."

Armond moved quickly, raising his blade as he ran forward.

Walt threw an arm out and the ground rumbled as he turned his body and drew his other arm up at a sharp angle, the rumble breaking the ground apart as though it had been hit from beneath. Cracks began to form under the soil at Armond's feet as he ran to clear the remaining distance.

Armond moved quickly as the solid field he stood on lifted away from the face of the earth. He slid to a sudden stop with the shifting of the dirt under his boots and felt the ground begin to lift into the air.

There was a sudden upsurge of the land and he had the feeling of being suspended before it dropped suddenly and deep fissures cut unevenly into the ground, spidering around him as they crept further out into the battlefield like cracks in cold glass.

He stumbled with the sudden drop and caught himself quickly as he fought to keep his footing, the sharp rivets and creases that had been torn in the soil making the landscape a dangerous place to run through. He watched attentively as Walt snickered, obviously playing games.

Armond smoothly grabbed the dagger at his side and threw it hard, watching it spin towards Walt's shabby, self-righteous face.

Walt drew back a balled fist and punched at the dagger which spun in the air and turned, flying like a dart back at

Armond who, recognizing the motion, was able to duck as it few past his head and into the dark field behind him.

Walt raised an eyebrow and smiled, "First time that's happened."

Armond studied the uneven terrain, following the sharp fissures in the soil with his eyes and returned the smile as he found a solid path, "Then you don't know me very well."

"Indeed," Walt said, with intrigue, "I'm meeting a lot of interesting people today."

"I'll be the last," Armond promised.

Walt laughed, it was a pleasant sound and without menace, "Confidence. I like it," his amused expression fell slightly and he gestured for Armond to come in closer, "Let's see it then."

Armond didn't move, not wanting to give him the advantage of expecting his strike, instead he spun his sword tauntingly and readied himself, carefully watching the movement of Walt's body and trying to interpret the motions.

Walt twisted his hand sharply and Armond felt a sharp tug at the sword. He gripped it tighter.

Walt gave him a charming half smile and widened his footing slightly, bending his knees and turning his hands out in the air before him, his hands sweeping in opposite directions in a swift and deliberate bend with his fingers catching the solid air.

Armond felt his feet pull out from under him and his head swung down suddenly. He was lifted from the ground and spun like a wheel in the air before he dropped back to the ground, hard. He tried not to let the shock of the motion show on his face as he grabbed his sword again, confused and dizzy, as he got back up to his feet.

He readied himself again, and again Walt laughed enchantingly with a hint of encouragement in his voice, "You are determined aren't you? No wonder you're a general."

"I've spent sixteen years waiting for today," Armond warned him, breathing heavily as the world began to settle in his vision.

"Waiting for battle?" he asked bewilderedly, "Most men avoid war if they can."

"Waiting for *this* battle."

"And what does this battle mean to you, exactly?" Walt asked, with honest curiosity, flexing his fingers and waiting for Armond to move.

Armond clenched his jaw, "The last day of Venhow's reign."

Walt looked at him in thought for a moment, "Sounds serious. How can you be so sure that will be today?"

"Because I will make it so," Armond said, flickering his eyes to the hillside as a bright flash of light rippled downward into the battle.

Walt crossed his arms for a second before letting them drop and scratching the side of his face contemplatively, "You're serious."

"I am," Armond said tensely, "And right now, you're in my way."

"I suppose I am," Walt said, as he looked back over his shoulder to the hill top.

Armond took the distraction to his advantage and charged, clearing the ground with his pre-marked path, stepping over and around the deep fissures in the ground and closing the distance in two short breaths. Walt turned in surprise and threw his hands out, but too slowly.

Armond slashed the blade against Walt's chest, tearing open skin and muscle before the magic struck him with the force of a falling tree and sent him hurtling back into the ground. He fought for his breath as he scrambled back up to his feet, a heavy ringing in his ears as the pounding in his head faded slightly.

He stood with his sword resting on the ground, the hilt loose in his hand from the blow. He picked it back up as his senses came back to him and looked up at Walt.

Walt had a hand on the gash at his chest, breathing heavily, blood weeping through his fingers and soaking his clothes. He looked at Armond with a mixture of confusion and awe. He swallowed, not daring to look away again, and said, "I didn't give you near enough credit," he pulled his hand away from the wound and looked at it thoughtfully before turning his eyes back on Armond, "Who are you anyway?"

Armond tensed the muscles in his arms again, bracing the sword defensively across his body as they stared at each other intensely, "Commanding General Armond of the Kings First Army."

Walt tipped his head in confusion and pointed his hand back to the hill behind him, his eyes not leaving Armond's, "You are an Azarian?"

"I was," Armond corrected.

"Then that's your king," he said, gesturing back at the hill where the magic lit the sky again, "You're fighting against him?"

"That is a tyrant," Armond spat, "That is *not* my King. *My* king will be crowned when that savage is dead."

"Your King?" Walt asked curiously.

"The true King."

Walt's face fell dramatically into a sudden realization, his eyes wide, "So he is alive?" he muttered and seemed to be thinking things through. He came to a silent decision and shook his head, "It doesn't matter. Venhow is King."

"Not for long," Armond snapped, trying to gather his energy through the dull ache in his body. He charged forward again, putting power into the uneven ground.

Walt threw up his hand and brought it down across his body at an angle, spreading his fingers as the air solidified. The magic formed as it met Armond's flesh and a wide cut split across his brow and down his temple, exposing bone and smacking him down to one knee forcefully.

Armond took in a sharp breath through the burning pain and he launched back up into his charge without hesitation, blinking the hot flow of blood out of his eyes. He swung his sword up at Walt and watched as he moved gracefully out of its path. He swung again and felt the sword hit solid air as Walt threw up his open hands protectively.

He drew back the sword and moved in for another strike, the tip of the blade aimed at Walt's heart. He felt it hit the barrier again and pressed into the magic forcefully and the sword began to slide through it.

Walt felt the barrier break and give way suddenly. The defense broke and he moved out of the path of the driving sword, with fear in his eyes.

Armond brought the sword up again with resolve.

Walt moved quickly, his hand dragging magic as he hit the armor plating at Armond's forearm as the blade began its path downward. The metal armor buckled under the pressure and broke, and a sharp end of the plating imbedded itself deep into the flesh and bone of his arm.

Armond cried out sharply, taking up the sword in his other hand as he brought the broken arm tight against his body and he made another swing.

Walt let a powerful pulse of magic course through him and pressed both hands hard against Armond's chest plate. He watched as Armond was hurtled back, tumbling head over heels, dropping his sword a distance away as his body crunched into the ground.

Walt stood there breathing heavily, watching in disbelief as Armond began to stir and got back up to his feet, his face dripping with blood and his eyes a stony cold blue that peered into him through the distance.

Armond started forward again, his eyes on the sword between them.

"Leave it!" Walt shouted angrily, not wanting Armond to close the distance again.

Armond ignored him, the tenacity in his face lined with blood and a fearless resolve hung in the air around him as he continued forward.

Walt watched as Armond stooped for the sword and he quickly began to roll his wrists, one over the other. The solid yellow ball of light began to form, condensing into a solid mass that gleamed like sunlight.

Armond picked up his sword and charged forward again.

Walt took aim and drew back his hands to fire at the general.

A sudden wet sound cut through him as the magic fired, missing its intended path and exploding in the air above the two of them.

Armond picked himself up off of the ground, stunned by the explosion, and looked up at Walt. A glistening blade was sticking out from his stomach, streaked with thick lines of blood. The sword retracted from his body and Walt fell to his knees, holding the gruesome wound in his hands and revealing Loch's age lined face behind him.

Loch drew the sword up high over his head for a death blow and Walt held a shaking and bloody hand in the air over his head, "Wait," he breathed coarsely.

"Stop!" Armond ordered, catching the look on Walt's face.

Loch lowered the sword slowly as Armond struggled to get up off of the ground and staggered forward.

"Why?" Loch asked confused.

"I can help you," Walt said wetly, a drizzle of blood seeping from the corner of his mouth.

"Isn't it late for that?" Loch said grimly.

Walt held his stomach, realizing that he could not feel or move his legs anymore. He took in a pained breath, "I didn't want to be here in the first place."

Armond stopped in front of him with his sword gripped tightly in his uninjured hand, the blade tip aimed clearly as he stooped down in front of Walt, their eyes meeting, "Then why did you do this? Why did you come?"

Walt's body shook visibly with the pain as he breathed through the sharpness of the wound, "He convinced me to."

"Who?"

"Venhow," he breathed, his teeth lined with blood as he spoke, a drip of blood from his mouth falling from the end of his rugged chin, "We were friends once," he panted for a second as sweat began to glisten on his brow, "But he isn't the man he was when I knew him last. He changed somewhere along the line." Walt swallowed and tried to straighten up to look at Loch, unable to move enough to do so and looked back at Armond respectfully, "He was like you once. A strong and determined man. I don't know what changed."

"It doesn't matter," Loch said, "He could've been a saint, but he's a monster now."

Walt let out a muffled cry, his eyes unfocused as he held at his bleeding gut, "I know that now. I've seen it. Something's not right in his head anymore. He enjoys death," he took a pained breath, "And he revels in suffering."

"He has to be stopped," Armond said, firmly.

Walt closed his eyes tightly and nodded.

"You said you could help?" Loch redirected him as he listened to his uneven breaths as Walt panted harshly.

"Yes," he said with a grimace, and spoke with his voice shaking, "I abhor unnecessary bloodshed," he gasped as the sweat began to roll down his face and the back of his neck, soaking into his shirt, "I don't care who wins this battle," he said honestly, "But if you kill the Keernith generals, it will save many lives on both sides."

"How's that?" Armond asked, with interest.

Walt gasped again and looked back to his wound and then to Armond working his tongue in his mouth as he fought to form words, "The goblins follow their leaders. The generals follow Venhow," he took a few rapid and shallow breaths with a shudder of pain, "The goblins will stop fighting if their generals are dead."

"How can we tell who the generals are?" Loch asked, stooping down to look at Walt beside Armond, keeping a watchful eye on their raging surroundings.

"They wear black and gold crests on the pauldrons of their armor," he explained, pressing harder on the hot wound in his abdomen and shuddering stiffly. As he curled up tighter trying to brace himself, a chain slid from the collar of his shirt. A gold and jade pendant swung out into the air, marked in blood and swaying mournfully.

"All of them?" Loch confirmed.

"Yes," Walt said, as he licked his lips and looked down at the ground with saddened eyes, "do it quickly," he grimaced, his face twisting in agony, "stop this madness."

"If you hate killing so much then why did you fight me?" Armond asked harshly.

Walt huffed as a ribbon of blood slid from his mouth, "To save you."

"That makes no sense," Loch said sharply.

"I didn't want to hurt anyone," he promised.

"You tried to kill me," Armond said darkly, his confidence in the man waning.

"No, I didn't," he insisted passionately.

"What about that?" Loch asked, gesturing to Armond's mangled arm and the heavily opened gash cut across his head, the bone still exposed through the pouring blood.

Walt gasped for breath in short bursts, fighting to speak, "You were too fast," he groaned, "and you kept breaking my magic. I didn't want to die either," he paused and swallowed hard,

"I never thought that you would keep getting up. You were supposed to be unconscious."

"That doesn't make sense!" Loch barked again.

Walt shook his head, "It does. I haven't killed anyone tonight."

"I don't believe you," Loch said flatly.

"You don't have to. I wouldn't either," he moaned through gritted teeth, and rocked back and forth on the ground slowly, "Anyone I have fought, every one that I have come across, I have knocked out. It is the best thing that I could do. If they look dead they won't have to die," he looked at Armond pleadingly, "If they do die, it was not because that's what I had in mind."

"Why are you telling us this?" Armond asked, his blue eyes fixed on Walt's.

"Because," he said weakly, "I don't want to be the monster. I never did. I just wanted it all to be over," he clenched his jaw and leaned forward as new blood slid out of the corner of his mouth and dripped into the cloth of his shirt.

Armond and Loch looked at each other with silent questions.

"How can we trust you?" Armond prodded.

"I don't have a reason to lie anymore," he answered, his voice cracking as his body shuddered with pain, "Because it doesn't matter."

"What doesn't?" Loch asked, leaning forward.

"My life," he answered weakly, "My body is dying. What good would it do me to lie now?"

"Loyalty?" Armond suggested.

Walt laughed mockingly through the pain, a spurt of blood flying from his mouth as he closed his eyes, shaking his head, "I have no loyalties to anyone but myself," he opened his eyes and looked mournfully at Armond, "I never have. I'm worthless that way."

"I'm sorry for your pain," Armond said, looking down at the seeping wound.

"It won't last," Walt promised quietly, looking down at the swinging jade pendant with a cold shudder.

"I can ease your passing," Loch offered, trying to sound supportive and still struggling with what Walt had said.

"No," he breathed roughly, trying to take in a steady breath, "Leave me in peace."

Armond and Loch exchanged glances and Walt laughed shortly, stopping from the assault of pain, his face grey as ash, "I couldn't move if I wanted to, my legs are as good as gone and I don't have the will or the strength for my magic. Just leave me. Please."

"Alright," Armond said, meeting his eyes for a final time, "I promise we'll end this quickly."

Walt gave a short nod and looked to the ground, curling around his wound and shaking in the night as Loch and Armond stood up and walked away from him into the clatter of war.

They walked a short distance in thought, listening to the rattle of iron and the sharp impact of steel as it clattered around them.

"Do you think he was lying?" Loch asked.

"No, I don't," Armond said definitively, bracing his arm tighter against his body.

"Then what are your orders?" Loch asked, as he worked his fingers over the hilt of his sword, loosening his joints.

"We have generals to find."

Loch looked down at Armond's mangled forearm, the metal shards sticking out of the meat oddly, "Do you think you can handle it?"

Armond forced a smile and tightened his grip on the hilt of his sword, "You manage with one arm, so can I."

"I'm used to it," Loch said seriously, as he thought it over, his lips curled up smugly, "Besides, I'm faster than you are."

"I'll be fine," Armond said, wiping the blood from his face.

"You would say that with an arrow in your eye," Loch said, with a thin smile.

"And it would still be true," Armond said determinedly.

"Should I go with you then?"

Armond shook his head, "We'll be faster if we split up."

"What about Venhow?" Loch asked, glancing behind him.

Armond looked to the hilltop as strips of light arced down into the mass, "He'll have to wait. If the wizard's right then we need to take out the generals first."

They looked around as a horn blasted out over the field. It's trumpeting call echoing into the fray. It sounded again as a new army of men charged in from the far side of the field.

"And now the Quillens are here," Loch said triumphantly, "Let's finish this."

Armond smiled exhaustedly, "I'll find you when it's over."

They each tore off along different paths, weaving through the renewed energy of the battle, searching through the dark for black and gold crests among the chaos.

Chapter Thirty-Five

Oswald took in the warmth of the sword, hearing the bellow of a horn somewhere in the distance and trying to remember what that was supposed to mean.

He felt the ripple of magic crawl through his skin and he turned with his sword up reflexively as a man with an axe swung. He felt the power of the blow rattle in his bones as he blocked it clumsily.

He staggered back with wide eyes as the axe cut into the air again. He ducked under it quickly and tried to take a swing and felt nothing as his red blade parted the air. The axe came around again and he lunged back, not sure if he would be able to block its weight again or not. He waited patiently, his heart thundering as the man lifted the axe into the air over his head.

He spun aside as the axe fell, bringing up his sword and meeting the soft meat of the man's neck, severing it cleanly in a full swing. The head and the body both fell, the head rolling grossly into the grass as the skin around each end of the wound continued to hiss from the magic of the sword.

Oswald's stomach churned. He had been prepared to fight, but had never been ready for the carnage of battle. He looked away from the seepage of blood from the meat of the open neck, the white bone of the man's spine showing, like a snapped stick jutting out from a hunk of raw roast. He gagged on the smell of scorched flesh and blood as he turned away, officially losing his appetite for any kind of meat.

He looked up as a man charged him, the crest of a Lieutenant glinting, his sword laying level with the ground as he ran.

Oswald noticed a few things wrong with the way the man approached him and he felt suddenly grateful for the intensive training he had endured. He turned to one side, catching the end of the sword with his own and spinning it up out of his way. He brought down the red blade and felt it crash into the Lieutenant's armor at the shoulder.

The man recovered quickly and swung his sword back at Oswald with anger in his eyes.

Oswald blocked the strike and stabbed at an open place in his defense, the same place that he had so many times left unguarded. He drove the sword into the gap in the armor at the man's shoulder and sliced through tendon before dragging the blade back out into the night. The man screamed and moved to attack with a weak and uncoordinated swing as he fought to use the torn arm properly.

Oswald blocked another swing and moved in through the sluggish motion, driving the sword between two plates in the chest of his armor and parting in between his ribs with a wet hiss from the sword. Oswald jerked hard on the blade and watched as the man fell backwards into the field, the sword freeing itself from his body as he fell.

Oswald shook his sword, trying to run the blood off of it so he wouldn't have to keep looking at it. He gave up after a few seconds and sighed, grateful that the sword was already stained a rust red and that he didn't notice it as readily.

He looked up into the clashing of metal on metal that expanded across the hills and the open fields and heard a shrill scream pierce the air like metal on glass.

He shuddered at the sound of it.

The scream died away as quickly as it had appeared and he found himself standing in the field listening for another sound, unsure what he was waiting for. He picked up his sword, the weight of it beginning to drag down at him as the battle raged on, an enthusiasm bursting into the energy of his surroundings as something happened in the distance.

He moved forward, not wanting to stand over the corpses around him any longer and his stomach twisted at the sight of them as he walked by.

Oswald made his way steadily through the roar of gnashing metal and blood. An odd feeling began to pull at him and he followed the tug of the magic as it urged him in another direction, cutting around to his left where the ground became more unstable, the soft mud sinking up around his boots as he walked.

He fought through the low lying area and saw a goblin rise from a low place in the field with a straight sword marked with hot blood that steamed into the cool night air.

It looked at him slowly and smiled. Its sharpened teeth gleamed wickedly and a glint in the amber eyes caught his attention as a flash of magic lit the air as it met a place down the field and exploded into bright arcs of fire.

The goblin turned on him, no hurry in its steps as it loomed closer, its heavy feet sinking into the mud as it strode confidently forward, long heated breaths rising into the air.

It lifted its sword with a smug sense of knowing and Oswald gripped his own in waiting.

He watched the goblin swing, the blade moving with the speed of a snapping jaw, biting at the space between them as Oswald blocked the strike. The two blades hissed on contact.

Oswald tried to take a step through the mud and found that his movements were slowed with the soft ground. The goblin didn't seem to mind the terrain and took another strike down at him from its high shoulders. Oswald struggled to work his feet to steady his stance in the mud as he brought up his sword to meet the goblin's bloody blade in the air.

Oswald felt his sword respond as he tightened his command of its hilt and reacted to the magic. He spun in the mud and took a low swing which was caught by the goblin's unnaturally fast reflexes. He felt his sword get thrown to the side and he tensed his muscles to keep control of it, trying to keep the sword up across his body and his arms in.

The blade swept at his face and he ducked to one side, tightening his legs and fighting for balance. He swung up at the goblin's elbow as its blade passed over his head and he felt it impact the armor.

Unfazed, the goblin moved its feet and danced around him, faster than he was in the muddy soil. He felt the magic surge, tingling in sharp pricks at the back of his neck and he dropped down to one knee in the wet ground, hearing the blade whistle in the air over his head.

He spun around, cutting footpaths in the field and he swung his sword again, this time blindly, unable to move as fast as the goblin.

His sword made contact with the steel again and he heard it hiss as it hit metal and slid across the plating.

The goblin stabbed down at him and he felt the sopping ground hold fast at his feet like bindings that rooted him to the spot. He released the crawl of magic in his chest with his sword held out and he watched as the goblin's sword hit a barrier over him and the blade passed to one side, narrowly missing his trapped leg in the mud.

He jerked at his leg hard and felt the suction of the ground release him.

The goblin swung again and he took a swift step forward, bringing up his red blade and cutting it away. Oswald moved in closer, his shoulder within a hair's breadth of the goblin's body, and felt a hard punch hit his side, the armor clinking as the goblin released the sword with one hand and belted him off balance. He hit the ground and rolled instinctively as the glint of the blade sank into the ground beside him.

Oswald got to his feet, breathing heavily.

The sword swept in the air again and he blocked it, the rattle of the swing beating his bones. He ducked low and put all of his effort into a sharp step forward as he swung the blade high.

The red edge of the swords blade hit the goblin's face and tore open flesh, parting the skin and muscle from the bleached bone beneath.

The goblin kicked him with a flat footed heel, smashing powerfully into his chest, and he lost his footing in the mud and fell onto his back with a wet slap. He looked up and his heart dropped as the goblin smiled down at him, the open wound on its face pulling together as fibers of flesh wove together on its own until the skin finally connected and sealed shut around the streak of purple blood that marked where the gash had been.

"Well, hello again," Priie said tauntingly, as she wiped the drip of blood away from her freshly healed, and goblin hidden face, and repositioned her grip on her sword.

Oswald's heart thundered and his breath caught in his throat as he slid in the mud, trying to stand in an effort to put a wider distance between the two of them.

Priie took a wide step forward and swung the sword in her goblin form like a force of nature, and the blade caught on his armor and pitched him like a corkscrew back into the ground.

Oswald breathed in sharply, a sudden bout of panic catching in his chest as the magic within him began to gather. He watched the sword slide down at his face from above and he rolled again, barely missing the heavy thump of the blade into the wet ground.

He flew to his feet and turned in the mud, catching another swing with a hard block and feeling the blade respond to his magic as it was again suppressed by the distraction of the sword at his face. The metal of the two swords hissed in passing as Priie spun in place, gathering momentum and streaming the razor edge towards the core of his body.

He blocked it again, breathing heavily and feeling the cold beading of sweat begin to gather at the nape of his neck as his breath rose in the dark air.

The steel of the swords clashed again as another streak of magical light opened up the sky and exploded in the distance, illuminating the field in hot light for a short moment before it died away, taking with it the cover of the night vision of his eyes.

He trusted his sword as he waited for his night vision to return and moved with it, feeling and hearing the clamor of metal and the impact of each blow reverberate in his head. The feel of each redirected strike clashed with the exhaustion of his body and bruised his bones.

Oswald began to see the movements again through the dark and caught another swing, desperate for a rest.

The goblin Priie, grinned.

He knew he couldn't match her speed and that his strength was fading. He ran his thoughts as the sound of ringing steel crossed paths again in front of him as he blocked another hard swing. He pushed her back and tried again to take a swing at the goblin throat and he felt the steel of his sword get forced away from her again.

His feet slid in the mud suddenly.

The mud.

He saw the glint of the edge of the sword aim towards his face and he dropped to the ground in revelation.

He sank his hands and his sword deep in the mud at his feet and sent a single hot wave of magic into the ground like a thunderclap, the water in the ground heating instantly at the touch of the magic.

Each drop of water was drawn forward into the ground at her feet as it rapidly began to boil in a fraction of a second. He breathed out sharply and pulled his hands out of the now dry ground at his fingertips and pulled the water to the surface where it evaporated into a scalding cloud of steam that boiled up her body and shrouded him from her, as she howled at the sudden agonizing pain on her feet.

Oswald ran forward with all of his strength, his feet now landing thunderously on dry ground as he cleared the distance and took a sharp swing into the steam. He felt contact with the goblin arm and watched the sword fly up into the air.

He reached up a hand and caught it with his magic and threw his arm down, the sword following his movements, its blade pointed down. It cut through the cloud of steam and he heard the wet smack of the sword against a body. It continued to drive downward and caught on the metal plating of her armor and slammed her forcibly into the ground.

The steam rose into the air, revealing a convulsing goblin body, gored through the heart and pinned to the earth by the sword it had wielded a moment before.

Oswald walked up to Priie as she tried to move, the sword buried to the hilt in the goblin's chest and imbedded into the dry ground immovably. She writhed like a spider caught beneath a boot and he drew his red sword up high, blade down, and stabbed the second blade through her chest again and again until her body lay still at his feet.

He stared at the raw meat of the wounds, waiting for them to heal.

When nothing stirred within the body for a long time, he became more aware of a voice in the field behind him, calling him by name. He turned to the voice and scanned the darkness but couldn't see anything.

He heard it again, and walked towards the sound slowly. Cautiously, he looked back at Priie's body pinned to the ground, just to be sure that she had not moved.

He looked across a wide area, filled with corpses, death and silence. A woman's voice called after him weakly, "Is it dead?"

Oswald looked back at the goblin body, as cold as iron, and still pinned against the ground like a statue of death, "I think so," he said, tentatively.

"Help me..."

He looked out to the large ring of Azarian corpses and spotted a weak movement as a glossy red hand reached into the air, "Oswald..."

He could hardly recognize her from the dead lying around her, blood coated her chest and her arms so heavily that the color of her skin had become wet blood except for a few copper colored streaks of skin yet uncovered by the red stain. Her hair was caked in mud, grass and blood so thickly that he only knew it was blonde because he had seen it before.

Satomi lay sprawled in the field, propped up and leaning on the corpse of an Azarian commander. Both of her arms were wrapped around her middle and shining with bright red rivers of her blood.

Oswald knelt down beside her, a heaviness in his chest holding tight against the pulse of his heart. He swallowed and leaned in closer.

She looked at him with a glassy sheen in her eyes.

"Let me see it," Oswald said gently, taking one of her slick and bloody hands in his.

She moved slowly and cautiously, unfolding both of her arms away from the grotesque wound. She had been split open across her abdomen and the wound was so deep that her flesh hardly held her body together. The gash wrapped all the way across her stomach, tearing from her side and around against an exposed lower rib. He could see through the broken armor and shreds of meat that her intestines were threatening to fall out of her body as she moved, bulging outward with the sharp action of her breathing.

He felt the blood drain from his face with a cold wash of horror and nausea that rippled in the pit of his stomach. He put her arms back across the gross evisceration of her body, his hands shaking and a despair welling up in him.

"I — I can't help you," he said gravely, looking back up into her eyes, "There's nothing I can do for you."

She grabbed his arm with one hand and pulled him closer to her. He was surprised by the amount of strength she still had and the force of her grip on his arm. She stared at him hard, her face stiff and unexpressive, "Yes there is."

Oswald looked down at the hidden wound behind her blood soaked arm and shook his head slowly, a sorrow seeping into his body and his hands began to shake gently as the grief welled up within him. He swallowed back as a heavy slab slid into his throat, "I don't have that kind of magic. I can't."

Her grip on his arm intensified and she looked at him as an angry tear flowed down her face, mingling with her blood, "That isn't what I said," she whispered and her nostrils flared in pain and her breathing quickened as her eyes flickered to his sword.

Oswald looked at her, confused, a sudden anxiety fluttering in his heart as he came to realize what she was asking for. He blinked away a thin streak of sweat that burned as it rolled down into his eyes. He shook his head again, "No."

She pulled on his arm harder and looked at the red sword at his side, the blade stained and glinting in the darkness. She gritted her teeth and took a shallow breath, "Finish me."

"I can't," Oswald insisted, as he tried to pull his arm free from her vice like grip.

"You have to," she said quietly, as her tears began to flow more readily, her face stoic and her lips steady as she spoke, "It's cruel to leave me here."

"I — I won't leave you... I promise," he said, searching her blood soaked body with wide eyes and trying to find another way to help her, "But... I won't — I can't."

"You would be doing me a service," she insisted, pulling at his arm and making him look into her eyes.

"No," he begged, his heart thundering in his chest in a horrified and grieved panic, "I can't do that."

"Coward," she spat angrily, her lips trembling and her body shaking both from pain and from the cold touch of death in the night air, "I can't survive this," she closed her eyes despairingly, and held her body together with a rigid arm as she panted unevenly, "Give me the dignity of a quick death."

He shook his head again as his anxiety turned to blind fear, the hot slab in his throat thickening as he fought to speak through it, "I couldn't... I couldn't live with that."

"But you would let me suffer?" she asked, her fingers biting down into his arm around the armor plate, the metal edge of the armor cutting into her hand.

"No," Oswald whispered quietly, "I wouldn't do that either," he fought with the emotions in his chest and his body began to shake more violently, his arms jerking under her hand, "I — I don't know what to do."

"Kill me," she said softly, her eyes pleading with him. She fought through her pain and struggled to keep her expression placid as the corners of her mouth drew down sharply and the muscles in her face twitched, "please."

"I…" Oswald choked back his terror and swallowed, his eyes burning as his tears mingled with his sweat.

"Please," she asked again, letting go of his arm and reaching up to his armor. She unlatched the armor on one side of his shoulder so that it hung loose on one side and exposed the bare skin of his arm.

Oswald watched her closely as she reached a trembling hand under the armor of her calf and ripped something loose. She pulled out the rust colored and heavily segmented body of the brain leach from under her armored calf and it squirmed in her bloody hand, its head resembling a flat and barbed arrow with a dark underside.

"What are you doing?" Oswald asked apprehensively.

"His name is Nile," she said weakly, and she shoved the barbed head of the thing into the tight muscle of his upper arm.

He felt a hot wave of pain bite at his arm and he grunted, breathing through the discomfort. The pain ebbed away gradually into a gentle tingling that comforted him somehow. He looked up from the strange parasite back into her weak and bloody face.

"Take care of him," she said gently, "he's very old."

Oswald looked to the brain leach, too distracted to dwell on its presence and looked back to Satomi, who looked genuinely sad to be without the strange pet, "I will," Oswald said uncertainly.

"And, Ember," she said, through a shallow and pained breath, "My cat, will need an owner."

"I can't take care of that cat," Oswald said, desperately.

"No," she agreed softly, her eyes falling away from him slightly, "My father will take her…" she looked out into the distance glossily for a moment before looking back to the brain leach buried in Oswald's arm, "Nile will tell you where to find him."

"Tell me?" Oswald asked, confused, and he looked down at the worm in his shoulder.

She nodded weakly and she tried to lean forward, with a mangled expression of fear and agony, she cried out suddenly. She fell back against the body beneath her, holding in her guts as she fought with one arm to pull something from around her neck. She got it loose after a short struggle, and the metal crest freed itself from her armor and she slid the chain around her head and held it out to him. Her bloody hand shook in the air, gripping the silver chain of the pendant as she held it up.

"Take it," she told him.

"No — I can't take that," Oswald said sadly, understanding the importance of the crest to the Naddow family, and the significance that it held in the Brute community.

Her hand quivered as she continued to hold it out to him, her eyes fixed on his, "You will. For your service," she said clearly, "I can give it to anyone I deem worthy of our honor."

"I haven't earned that honor," Oswald said feebly.

"*For your service*," she repeated firmly, and held it out as she stared at him insistently.

Oswald took it regretfully and put it around his neck, tucking it into his armor with the fairy pendant, the bloody metal cold and wet on his skin.

She swallowed as she forced back the sorrow in her eyes and she looked at the sword longingly, "please…"

Oswald picked up his sword, the heat no longer a comfort, but a distraction, as he knelt beside her. The heat bit at his hand sharply as he readjusted his fingers around the hilt, fighting to keep the blade steady as it hovered in the air.

Satomi reached out and grabbed the end of the blade and set its sharpened edge over her heart.

Oswald held it there, breathing heavily and trying not to let the deep sadness break over him as he heard her skin hiss against the magic of the sword.

He held on to the hilt of the sword with one hand and took the back of her head with the other and pulled her forehead against his supportively, feeling the cold of her damp skin against his brow. He closed his eyes tightly, took in a deep breath and put his weight into the sword, feeling it glide smoothly through her body in a quick and graceful movement.

Oswald held her head in his hand and kept his brow against hers as the sword passed through her. He clenched his jaw for the heavy feeling of the slab in his throat and he slowly looked up into her face as a single tear slid down her cheek, the soul vacant from her glassy eyes.

"I'm sorry," he whispered mournfully, feeling the heat of a tear stream down the end of his nose, his voice rough and stiff, "I'm so sorry, Satomi," he tightened his grip on the hilt of his sword and pulled it back out, the force of it lifting her body slightly. His stomach knotted as a painfully cold feeling washed over him. He slowly let go of her head as it slid out of his hand limply, sinking back onto her shoulders.

The sword slid out of his grip, clattering unsteadily against the armor of her sprawled legs beside him. He pulled his hands into his lap and looked down at them through the darkness as they trembled, stained red, and empty but for the dwindling heat of her cooling blood in his palms.

He fought back a sob and looked back at her lifeless beauty. He doubled forward on the ground and took in a sharp and uneven breath as he tried to choke down his grief.

The hot anguish of his heartache churned inside him and he felt the horror and remorse of what he had done rise suddenly in him. It burned in his body, tearing him open somewhere on the inside, and he screamed angrily into the night, not sure what else he could do with the invisible pain.

He heard his own voice, his scream, echo back to him in the night as he fought for a breath through his aching sobs. The sharp sounds of his breathing scraped at the air as he struggled with his body, trying to stumble to his feet through the weakness in his soul. He steadied his feet underneath himself and reached an unsteady hand down for the blood soaked sword and the feel of it in his hand again, ignited a wisp of vengeance in his chest.

A flash of light exploded from behind him in the distance and his grief suddenly began to slide away into an intense rage, like the flow of water from a breaking dam. The anger flooded his vision as his pulse blurred the lines of his surroundings, obscuring his eyes from the field. He took in a deep breath and his vision refocused slowly as his heart punched at his ribs. The light began to fade from the distant explosion and he rounded on the magic, his eyes fixing on the hilltop.

Chapter Thirty-Six

Oswald took his sword in a death grip and walked heavily towards the hilltop as another flash of light shot down the hill.

He took in slow, deep breaths, allowing the magic to build in his body and feeling the electric static drive him forward through the chaos, not letting his eyes waver from his new target.

A sword arced at him in the dark and he turned away from it and threw his hand out to one side feeling the hard punch of the magic leave his fingertips. He picked up speed until he felt the cool night air cut at his face as he ran.

The hilltop crept closer and he saw arrows fly overhead and stop dead in the air. A shimmer of magic caught the light as people were stopped at its border, some angry and others confused. He felt a renewed surge of anger as the static built.

He pushed his feet hard into the ground, propelling himself forward in the darkness, the magic of his sword drawing a thick darkness around him as he swiftly approached the barrier.

"Move!"

He watched as men parted in front of him, away from the magic and the deepening thickness of the air.

A sharp white light began to pull up from the ground and arced through the darkness. It drew up around the end of the red blade and grew into a blinding halo as he lunged forward. The hairs on his body stood on end and a painful tingling sensation spread up his arm and into his body as the electricity continued to build.

He squared his shoulders as he reached the barrier and spun his body in a tight circle to gather momentum as he turned. He released the magic as he swung at the magic and he watched the lightning fully form in the condensed darkness before him.

It branched out from the end of the sword as he made contact with the invisible wall and the lightning climbed up into the air and spread across the battlefield, traveling along the magic and lighting the entire field as clear as day throughout the brief flash of its travel.

The sword broke through the magic and he felt it shatter like thin glass before it collapsed into a fire that rained down in front of him and marked where the barrier had been drawn, burning the ground and seeping into the earth. The sound of the fire snapped at his feet as he stepped across its path to the base of the hill.

He looked up the hill and saw a dark figure draw back a hand as a light formed at his side and was thrown in his direction.

Oswald threw out a hand and the light exploded between them. He ran up the hill, his feet beating the ground to the pulse of his heart.

Another ball of light shot down at him and he threw his arm out wide, sending the magic down into the side of the hill. Dirt flew up beside him from the impact in a small fountain of earth, and he ran up the incline as another streak of light formed and came down at him. Again he redirected it to the ground and this time passed its impact into the ground, hearing the explosion behind him as he closed the distance.

He gathered the darkness and felt the electricity build in him again, pulling it up out of the ground at his feet. The light gathered around him again and he swung his sword hard, throwing the immense white streak of lighting at the figure on the hilltop.

Venhow's enraged face was briefly lit by the pulse of light from the bolt as it streaked up the remaining distance directly at his body.

Oswald watched as Venhow turned his hands in a sharp circle and the lightning forked around him, streaming up into the air. The lightning reached up into the cloud cover with long fingers of white light and traveled through the blanket above them in a flickering strobe of fragmented plasma.

Oswald drove his anger to the top of the hill, his hands biting on the hilt of the red sword, a hot energy passing into his tired muscles and giving him the strength he demanded. He swung at Venhow's black armor, aiming for the hollow at his neck.

Venhow moved swiftly back and threw out his arms and a hard hit of magic drove Oswald back a few steps and knocked the sword from its intended path. He drew his sword with the sharp ring of steel, the intricate Azarian carvings on the gossamer steel glinted in reflection of the desperate hatred in his cold grey eyes.

Venhow blocked as Oswald took another swing, the red blade sparking angrily as the two blades collided, and the magic within them began dueling through contact.

They pulled the angry swords apart to the dim flicker of metallic sparks.

The red blade came up again to the ring of steel and another sharp punch of magic that threw his sword to one side and beat at his lungs, rattling the air inside him as he turned, unaffected by its impact through his rage.

Oswald moved cleanly into another swing, the expert motion taking Venhow slightly off guard. The magic of his sword clashed hotly against the onyx plating on his armor, catching him at the shoulder and barely missing his head as the follow through of the swing slid through the air.

A visible anger washed over Venhow's face as he returned with a sharp stab of his sword.

Oswald released his magic as he turned away from the end of the sword, pushing it outward and Venhow was taken off of his feet and thrown back on the small plateau of the hill. He hit the ground and rolled a short distance, securing his grip on his sword as he staggered to his feet as Oswald pounded after him.

The two blades met in the air again and hot sparks of fire and magic spat from the metal.

Venhow shoved him back and a bright light gathered quickly in his hand and was thrown forward the short distance. Oswald responded, unable to move fast enough to redirect it and instead ignited the magic.

A concussive explosion expanded between them as the shock wave rippled outward and they both were thrown out into the darkness.

Oswald hit the hillside, digging his toes into the ground to stop from rolling back down to the bottom of the hill, his fingers catching the ground. He got up and ran back towards the crest of the hill, ready for anything as Venhow took the high ground first.

Oswald watched carefully as Venhow drug the tip of his sword quickly across the ground in front of him and stomped his foot, pressing his hands forward with the sword in one expert motion. The ground broke open and an upwards spout of lava grew from within the ground to a wall of heat and fire taller than any goblin. The intense heat radiating from it burned at his eyes.

The fiery tsunami rolled forward gathering momentum and crashing quickly towards him, the heat of it approaching singeing the ends of his hair.

Instinctively, Oswald drove the end of his sword into the ground, pulling up the earth and water around him in a sharp angled shield. The lava splashed up around the barricade in molten drops that caught the wet grass on fire as it touched the hillside.

Oswald drew more water from the ground and up into the hillside to reinforce his shield. The lava hardened with a sharp hiss as it touched the cold ground and water as he continued to draw the moisture out of the soil. His grip on the sword began tearing his palms as he poured his magic into it.

The hot sharp rock of the hardened lava steamed into the air.

Another blast of light hit the small barricade and sent sharp fragments of the heated rock up into the air, the pieces grazing the side of his face as they flew by.

Oswald stood quickly and pulled the sword back out of the ground, spinning it to the ready as he watched a rock fly through the air at him. He threw a hard punch at the stone, sending his magic ahead of him and hurtling it back the way it had come.

Venhow moved in a blink, the Azarian sword slicing up through the air and splitting the large rock in two, each half of the stone diverting to either side of him and hitting the ground behind him with a satisfying thud.

Oswald ran around the sharp shards of volcanic rock and made his way to Venhow's side, dodging a streak of light and swung his sword again, the two blades reacting more viciously with each connecting strike. Sharp fragments of light and heat spat out into the air and the wind itself kicked up in the static electricity in the air, sending branches of lightning into the sky above them.

He let go of his red blade with one hand and pulled up his arm with his palm to the sky, pulling the ground loose at Venhow's feet and flipping him over onto his back.

Oswald immediately turned the blade of the sword down and drove it towards Venhow's chest as he lay sprawled on the crest of the hill.

Venhow pushed his magic into the hill and slid his body forcibly across the ground, dragging himself away from the fatal strike.

Oswald corrected for the sudden movement and his blade caught through the armor at his calf, tearing through flesh as Venhow threw himself out of the path.

Oswald felt the sword drag across dense fabric, feeling a pop through the reverberation of the metal as the sword cut a deep gash in both the meat of Venhow's leg and broke loose a dagger holster from its place on his leg. The heavy holster stayed on the ground, pinned under the red blade as Venhow's magic slowed him to a stop a short distance away.

Venhow got to his feet with a bloody stream running down his leg and he looked down to the holster on the ground, a sharp bout of panic in his eyes for a fleeting second and he shouted with fear and anger in his voice, "No!"

Oswald picked up his sword and charged him, stepping on the holster as he sprinted forward and took a sharp swing towards his now weakened leg.

Venhow swung his sword tightly and caught the blow at the last second. The two swords bit at each other, now sparking so energetically that it was difficult to pull them back apart, the metal drawn almost magnetically as they hit one another.

Venhow pressed against Oswald's strength as the blades shot bright sparks out into the space between them, arcing with fire and lightning. He released a hard burst of magic and threw up his arms while he pressed against the red sword. The pulse of magic exploded with the force of a cannon, hitting Oswald in the chest and sending him flying up into the air.

Oswald felt his body crunch into the ground, knocking the wind out of his lungs as he felt his sword fly out of his hand and he rolled uncontrollably down the hill. He put out his arms, trying to stop his relentless tumble. His leg hit a rock as he rolled and a sharp jab of pain shot up his body as he was jarred inside of his armor. He spread his legs out to stop the roll and dug his toes into the ground and slid to a stop about halfway down the hill.

Oswald looked up as Venhow threw both fists into the ground at the crest of the hill and the earth underneath him rumbled and began to fall away.

Oswald watched frozen as tons of dislodged ground slid down towards him, an unstoppable tidal wave of dirt and stones. He braced himself as the wave hit and he felt his body being thrown around in the musty darkness of the rolling landslide. The deafening roar of the sound of the landslide mounted in his ears as he was tossed violently in the dark. Rocks and roots beat at him as he was mercilessly flogged by the earth.

He felt a sudden stop as he reached the bottom of the hill, surrounded by darkness and dirt.

The crushing weight of it pushed in at him from all sides as he heard the last of the ground roll to a stop around him. He tried to take in a breath, realizing that his mouth and nose were both filled with soil.

His lungs ached for air and his heart pounded as he tried to move against the crushing weight of the landslide.

Nothing budged.

A panic started to build in him as the weight of the ground above and around him began to crush and compress at his bones. The soil settled every time he tried to move and became harder and denser against his body.

He listened to a final stone roll down somewhere overhead across the ground above him.

The thought of being buried alive strangled an extreme and sudden bout of panic in him and his heart beat harder.

Light began to dance in front of his eyes and he tried to work the dirt out of his mouth with little success and in the ever compressing depths of the ground there was nowhere to move the dirt to. He worked out what he could and began to gag on the now loose clots of the fine granules in his mouth.

There was no air in the immensity of the crushing darkness, just the unbearable weight of the ground around him and the fear of death.

A burning pain began shooting up from his limbs and in his chest through the hot flashing lights in his eyes, begging for air. He felt a hot pressure build in his head, everything he had left in him trying to breathe through the dirt.

He tried to move anything, hoping that the ground somewhere, anywhere would give.

It didn't.

A true fear and the sudden realization of imminent of death washed into the intensifying pain and the darkness seemed complete.

"Calm down or we both die."

Oswald heard the voice and thought that perhaps madness often fell before death, unable to comprehend the odd inner sound of it in his head.

"Get a grip! Get out."

Oswald tried to calm himself and gathered what magic he could through the limited energy and pain in his body. He released the pulse of magic out from him in a sharp wave and felt a sudden relief as the top layer of ground above him was thrown away.

He felt his fingers break into the cold night air through the layer of soil and he began to dig himself out as quickly as he could, shoving piles of stones and dirt away from his body as he uncovered enough of his head and chest to sit up slightly in the ground.

He immediately put his fingers in his mouth and began to clear away the rest of the remaining dirt, gagging and coughing coarsely on the dirt as he gasped for desperate breaths of air. He felt his mouth filling waves of saliva as he fought for breaths while trying to clear his mouth and lungs from the last grits of the soil.

He climbed out the rest of the way out of his hole in the fresh landslide, pulling his feet free with some difficulty and looked up the hill.

Venhow was franticly trying to find a way to fix the torn dagger holster, preoccupied with his task and attempting to put it back into place.

Oswald roughly coughed up the last of the dirt and spotted the hilt of his sword sticking up from the loose ground a few feet away. He scrambled to his feet, the cold air abrasive in his raw and burning lungs, and ran to where it rested. He grabbed it and pulled hard, wriggling it loose and feeling the familiar warmth of it in his hands.

Oswald looked out to the quiet around him to the field of battle, which had all but stilled. All eyes were lingering on him, and he returned his attention to Venhow, who was still distracted at repairing the strap on his leg.

He turned back to the hill, the energy from the sword masking the pain in his body as he sprinted up the now unsteady incline.

Venhow looked down the hill and spotted Oswald as he ran towards him. A burst of anger and anxiety flooded within him and he stood up with the holster in one hand and picked up his sword in the other.

Oswald huffed up the hill and spun his sword in the air as he passed magic through the blade, creating a whip of condensed air. He swung the blade hard and the magic around it snapped out harshly.

Venhow threw up his hands defensively forming a wall around him. There was a hard crack as the air cut into his small barrier and sliced his hand open across the knuckles. He let out a startled wave of magic, trying to force more distance between the two of them but Oswald pressed through the blast with a sharp anticipating cut of the sword and magic.

The concussion wave fell away and Venhow rolled his wrists over one another quickly forming a ball of bright light. He aimed the shot and threw it forward.

Oswald reached out his hand forcefully, his fingers spread and his palm cupped and the ball of light stopped in the air in front of him. He took in a sharp breath and threw it back with a burst of confidence and energy, a new idea sparking in his mind and running forward quickly in the path of the magic.

Venhow took a startled step back and was forced to drop both his sword and the holster, each of them dropping on to the disturbed ground as he watched the magic return to him with renewed force. He caught it and threw it haphazardly out to his side and his eyes went wide when he realized that Oswald was suddenly within arm's reach.

The red blade sliced across his face, tearing open his bottom lip and grazing up the length of it, barely missing the white of his eye as it passed.

Venhow balled his hand into a fist, the pain and hatred taking control of his body. He swung his fist at Oswald and released his magic. The impact of the blast was more intense than any magic that had come before it.

Oswald felt his feet come up off of the ground and felt his bones break as the metal plating of his armor took the blow and caved in at the chest. His body snapped like brittle wood at the force of it, his ribs rubbing loosely in his body as he breathed and a sharp and vicious pain racked through him. Each splintered shard of his ribs made its own wound within him and he screamed as he landed hard back onto the ground. The broken bones jarred and raw.

Venhow laughed through the rolling blood down his face, a cold sound that shook through his heavy breathing, triumph gleaming in his eyes. He picked up the sword he had been using at his feet and stepped forward arrogantly, "I guess if you want something done," he said breathlessly, his tone full of conceit that merged with the smug satisfaction in the curvature of his grin, "You've got to do it yourself."

Oswald felt the hilt of the red sword under his body and he watched Venhow's feet as he walked confidently towards him. He was wearing wizard's shoes, a thin leather that allowed for better conduction to the earth. His right foot lifted from the ground and Oswald saw the sole of the shoe part from the rest of it with torn stitching.

Venhow lifted his Azarian sword into the air, blade down and lunged at him.

Oswald rolled over his broken ribs to a new explosion of pain, moving through its blinding hold on him as the blade sank into the ground where he had been lying. He pulled the dagger from his side as he rolled and drove it down through the battered shoe with everything he had, pinning Venhow's foot to the ground.

He moved quickly, rolling the hilt of the sword into his hands from under him and he turned the blade up as he rose to his feet. The end of the red blade drove up through the black armor, parting the plates and driving straight into Venhow's chest at his heart.

Oswald pushed against the sword again angrily, hot blood pouring down the blade as Venhow's wide grey eyes went glassy. He pulled the sword out of Venhow's chest with a sharp jerk and watched as he stumbled back a step, fighting against the throws of death.

A sudden burst of purple and fuchsia light erupted up out of the ground forming a bright beam that broke the sky as the dawn began to light the field in the misty green haze of morning.

The beam of light flickered and faded away as Venhow sank to his knees, still holding his sword in a death grip.

The ground thundered and opened up beside him.

A long black curl of smoke rose from the divide in the earth and a black taloned hand clawed up from its depths. Black charred skin and bony features climbed through the ground, the smoky black barbs on its back heaving as it rose up out of the fissure, dragging the rest of its body up with it as it came.

The Grimm looked from Oswald to Venhow and grinned wickedly, its gaze falling on the torn and broken dagger strap on the ground a short distance away.

It looked back to Oswald in scrutiny, "You're the one who killed my brother," it said, through a plume of black smoke, its yellow eyes drifting to the red sword. It looked back to Venhow who was dragging himself across the ground, away from the Grimm in a bloody path of bent grass. The Grimm took a wide step and placed a clawed foot over his legs, pinning him down before he looked back to Oswald with narrowed eyes, "...We've been hunting this man for a long time. Now we can retrieve our debt," it breathed gratefully, "Thank you. I believe that you and I will agree that we're even then, shall we? My brother's death forgiven, for the debt due to us finally paid," it said, with a tip of its flat skeletal face angling down towards Venhow.

Oswald nodded uncomfortably as the Grimm split a wide, charred grin.

It reached out and roughly snatched a claw to the side of Venhow's leg and wrapped the black talons around the unprotected calf. It backed into the part in the ground and drug him through the opening into the ground.

The fissure in the earth lit briefly as Venhow clawed at the blood stained grass, writhing against the massive black body of the Grimm as it sunk deeper into the ground. In a final sweep of the taloned hand the two of them were swallowed by smoke and both of them disappeared into the underworld.

The break in the ground pulled together and sealed itself as they vanished with the smell of ammonia and sulfurous smoke it its wake. The penetrating silence of the battlefield lingered in waiting as Oswald straightened up at the crest of the hill and turned his back wearily on the charred grass that marked the underworld's path.

Oswald braced his side through a new explosion of pain as he twisted and looked out over the field where many eyes had turned to meet his.

He gritted his teeth and breathed through the broken ribs, feeling the bone fragments shift. The morning light began to break and he held the bloody red blade high into the air, the light catching it in sharp relief, and the roar of victory erupted from Gommorn's army.

Chapter Thirty-Seven

The immense halls of the castle of Azar were opened up to the midday light, streaming beams of sun through the open doors and from the drawn curtains of the high windows. Golden light of the bright spring day and the warmth that followed streamed in through the elegant building and reflected on the black and silver streaked marble floor.

Oswald sat in clean clothes, the heavy fabric of a white shirt over his bandaged ribs. The cleaned silver crest of the Naddow family gleamed in the light, hanging in accompaniment of the glistening glass fairy pendant on his chest.

He shifted in the padded seat as a man walked through the front doors, one of many who had done so in the past several days, and knelt on the floor in front of him respectfully.

"I can't begin to tell you how grateful I'm to you," the man said, looking more to the floor than to Oswald.

"Please get up," Oswald said, rubbing at his brow.

The man stood with a smile, wringing his hands uncomfortably, "The city hasn't been this way for fifteen years," he said thankfully.

"It should never have been anything less," Oswald said, shaking his head at the horrors that had been told to him, "I'm glad that things have gotten better," he said truthfully, not liking the amount of attention that he had been receiving.

"They have," the man said, with a smile, "The guards are gone. We don't have to hide anymore. We have food and peace of mind."

"Is there anything that I can do for you?" Oswald offered, not sure exactly what the man wanted with his company.

"No," the man said, and sank back down to one knee, much to Oswald's disapproval, and looked up at him in reverence, "I know my services may not be much," he said humbly, "But anything you ask of me will be yours."

Oswald sighed in frustration. He waved his hand sharply, gesturing for the man to stand again, "So you want something to do to help the city?"

"Yes," the man said, getting back to his feet, uncomfortable standing in front of Oswald.

"The only thing that you can do for me is help spread the peace. If you would please tell people of this city to stop threatening my Keernith friends, I would appreciate it," Oswald said, glancing past the man out to the open front doors of the castle, "They're just trying to help set things right before they go home."

"Yes, sir," the man said with a nod, and smiled, happy to be put to a task.

Oswald braced himself against the chair, holding his ribs as he stood, "Let me walk you out."

The man seemed horrified at the idea but didn't protest as Oswald stepped up beside him. They turned towards the wide front doors and walked up to the bright daylight. The man gave him a curt bow and walked on out towards the city as Oswald watched his elongated shadow creep across the courtyard and out into the sunlight.

Quickly, Oswald rushed over to the door and fought through the dull pain in his chest as he struggled to shut the heavy doors, not wanting anyone else to come and pay him reverence.

"Why do people keep doing this?" Oswald mumbled to himself as the door finally creaked shut.

"Because you're their king now."

"No, I'm not!" Oswald said, and looked down to the rust colored segmented body of Nile the brain leach, still perched on his arm. The beaded body curled tighter around his arm comfortably.

"Rules of conquest," Nile replied in his head, *"You're the son of the last King of Azar. Not to mention you killed him in battle and that is a clear cut way to become the new king."*

"I don't like this," Oswald grumbled, walking back to his chair at the end of the great hall, "I don't want to be king."

"They need someone," Nile replied dryly.

Oswald looked down to the brain leach and scowled, "They don't need me."

"You seem to be doing an okay job. Far better than the last ruler they had, if I'm not mistaken," Nile replied passively.

"Venhow hardly counted as a king, he was a psychotic tyrant," he said, stepping back up the short platform. He held the arm of the chair to lower himself back into the seat with a sigh.

"So there is no way that you could do any worse as king than he did. An improvement is still and improvement." Nile's voice drug through his head, *"Don't you think?"*

"That isn't helpful…" Oswald complained.

"And?"

"At least I'm not that bad."

"No," Nile replied sharply with a hint of condescension, *"That was my point. King Oswald of Azar."*

"I am not the king!" Oswald shouted, staring angrily down at Nile as he twisted his strange body tauntingly before he rewrapped his tail around his arm in a beaded band.

"Which is why everyone keeps treating you like the king? And why you keep answering them?"

"What am I supposed to do?" Oswald griped, throwing his hands up in the air in frustration, "I can't just ignore everyone."

"You could if you wanted to." Nile replied with a smile in his tone, *"The king can pretty much do what he wants."*

Oswald frowned, "You're obnoxious."

"Why thank you… and you're a whiny bastard."

"Shut up," Oswald snapped exhaustedly, placing his face in his hands and staring at the floor between his knees.

Armond walked up behind him and sat in the nearby chair with a raised eyebrow, "Talking to yourself are you?"

"No," Oswald said embarrassedly, looking up, surprised by the sudden company.

Armond's arm was held tight in a sling, wrapped from fingers to shoulder in heavy bandages. He looked tired but comfortable and at some sort of peace, with a calm and pleasant expression on his face.

"Then what are you doing?" Armond asked, surveying him with amusement.

Oswald gestured to Nile and held his arm out so that Armond could see him more clearly and he gave a sheepish smile, "I'm trying to figure out what is going on around here, but he keeps interjecting into my thoughts."

"They do that," Armond said, with a genuine smile, "What are you trying to figure out?"

"People keep treating me either like I'm going to kill them at any second or they keep kneeling at my feet and start groveling," Oswald said, his brow knitted, "I can't stand it."

"It's making you uncomfortable?" Armond asked.

"You can say that again."

"I don't like all the attention," Oswald explained.

"That's because you're a strange thing." Nile commented.

Armond leaned forward in the chair beside him with a one armed shrug, "It wasn't a small victory after all. You saved millions of people from a brutal man. They're allowed to be grateful to you."

Oswald rubbed at his face anxiously, "I don't want their gratitude, I want to go home."

"You would just hide in a hole forever if you could wouldn't you? It won't kill you to be a little empathetic to these people for a little while." Nile retorted.

"Stop it. You're confusing me," Oswald said, exasperatedly down at Nile.

"You know I can hear you without you saying anything out loud..." Nile replied, trying to sound helpful.

"Yeah, that's great," Oswald said annoyed, as Armond smirked with an amused turn of his lips. Oswald held a hand out in frustration, "I'm sorry, Armond. What were you saying?"

Armond laughed shortly and shook his head, "The dungeon is cleared. All of the war prisoners have been set free, wounds treated, and the entire palace has been gutted."

"Good," Oswald said, awkwardly glancing around the great hall, "When can we go home?"

"This is your home now."

"No, Gommorn is my home," Oswald insisted.

"You are going to have to get over this eventually, you know. The tyrant king is finally dead. These people are free from his cruelty but there's still a lot that needs to be done to set things the way that they should be. You have to quit being a big baby about it and help these people."

"Shut up!" Oswald yelled suddenly, still not used to having the extra voice in his head.

"You'll get used to him," Armond snickered, sitting back in his chair slightly.

"He's driving me crazy," Oswald said, pinching the bridge of his nose.

"He's a rare creature," Armond said, looking down at the strange parasite, "You'll come to an understanding soon enough. I promise."

"Great," Oswald said unhappily, "Until then I just sound like I'm going mad."

Armond laughed lightly again and nodded, "Yes you do."

"I just want to go home to Sanna and my workshop," Oswald said, wallowing in a deep pool of homesickness.

"Gommorn would be happy to have you back," Armond said with a pause, "I'm sure your friends miss you."

"What do you mean 'would be'?" Oswald asked, catching the tone in his voice.

"Desiring to or aspiring for something as used in context. He's suggesting that you won't be going back anytime soon."

"That doesn't make any sense," Oswald said, down at Nile, "Why not?"

"As I have been saying repeatedly," Nile said impatiently, *"You — are — the — king."*

"I already said 'no'," Oswald barked and sat back in his chair bitterly, "I don't want to stay here."

Armond's face fell slightly and he leaned further back in his chair as he chewed on his tongue thoughtfully, "Azar needs a king, and it's your right to be that king if you chose to."

"No," Oswald said emphatically, "I don't want to be a king. I can't be."

"You would make a good king," Armond said seriously.

"No I wouldn't," Oswald argued gesturing around the halls of the castle with wide eyes, "I don't have a clue how to do anything. I don't know how to talk with dignitaries or how to take care of an empire! I make shoes."

"Yeah, a lot of information on shoes in here."

Oswald looked down at Nile with wide eyes, "You seriously have to stop talking. You are making me look crazy."

"You're making yourself look crazy. You don't have to talk to me out loud you know."

Oswald put his face in his hands and sighed heavily.

"Fine. I'll be quiet."

"Thank you," Oswald whispered exasperatedly through his hands.

Armond grinned and leaned forward, putting a supportive hand on Oswald's shoulder, "A good king just needs to be able to put his people before himself."

Oswald dropped his hands and shook his head, "I don't want to be king. I don't want that kind of responsibility."

"You don't think you could handle it?" he asked quizzically.

"I — Maybe..." Oswald let out an exasperated breath and looked up through his fingers, "I don't know. I don't really want to find out."

"Are you absolutely certain?" Armond asked, with a sympathetic smile.

"Yes," Oswald said firmly, "I do not want to be King."

Armond patted him on the back reassuringly and sat back in his chair again with a gentle smile, "If you absolutely refuse...There is an alternate."

"A what?" Oswald said, looking up at Armond hopefully, catching a glimpse of pride in his sky blue eyes.

"An alternate. Another member of the royal family that has rights to the throne."

"Who?" Oswald asked curiously.

Armond sighed with a small smile, "My son, Samuel."

"Your son?" Oswald asked trying to piece the puzzle together in his head.

"He both is... and is not my son," Armond explained. He readjusted the sling at his wrapped arm and looked at Oswald seriously, "Before Venhow took the throne I was the King's first general. I was supposed to protect and care for the royal family as well as oversee Azar's army."

"How old are you?" Oswald asked, surprised by the gentleness of his aging.

Armond scowled and continued to explain himself, "When the King became ill, I never left his side until he passed away. I hadn't realized how involved Venhow had become in the Queen's council. She came down with the same strange plague as the King and then her son's began to die in very suspicious ways."

He paused, lost in the past and looked around the great hall absently, "I thought that Venhow had something to do with it all but I didn't know for sure until the night he was crowned King. I was told that the children had killed themselves in grief over losing their mother and father."

He scowled angrily, "I knew it was a lie," he sat quietly for a minute and continued, "I took care of those boys. When Venhow was crowned, I gathered the guards that were loyal to the royal family and we tried to overtake the castle. I stole one of Venhow's magical gauntlets, afraid that we would be caught and thinking it was my only defense against him."

"Did the gauntlet help?" Oswald asked curiously.

Armond shook his head and looked down at his hand as he worked the fingers on his injured arm, "I didn't have to use it. I don't even know if it would have worked or not. I never found out. He was preoccupied with my men."

"They were keeping him away from you," Oswald said sadly, lowering his eyes to the floor, "Weren't they?"

Armond nodded somberly, "My men were all killed but I was able to break into the nursery and save the King's last surviving son. He was only a baby at the time, hardly able to crawl. It was my job to protect the royal family, and for the most part I had failed."

"But you were able to save Samuel," Oswald finished in awe, a respect in his emerald eyes.

Armond nodded, "We moved from city to city for a while. Eventually I hid him in Gommorn and I raised him as my son to protect him. I lost a lot of people to keep him hidden."

"Does he know?" Oswald asked, reading the look on Armond's face clearly.

"No." Armond said, looking up at the high marble ceiling.

Oswald shifted in his seat, "Why didn't you ever tell him?"

"Because I love him," Armond said obviously, turning back to Oswald, "It was safer for him not to know and I had the chance to instill in him the will to help and protect others. To keep him away from the pressure of what he was meant to be. I wanted him to be able to be a child. To have fun, make his own decisions and to find who he is as a man without all of that hanging over his head."

"That makes sense," Oswald agreed with a nod.

"I hoped that I was making the right choices," Armond said, and looked up to the high window as a cloud broke the sunlight and a gloom filled the great hall for a few seconds until the sunlight peeked back through the window.

"It sounds like you did," Oswald assured him with a kind smile, "You gave him a normal life."

"The life of a General's son," Armond said, and huffed disapprovingly, "It wasn't exactly what he needed, but it was what I was able to provide for him."

"You're a remarkable man, Armond," Oswald said honestly, "And you have raised a very intelligent boy."

"He is still just a boy," Armond said, fidgeting with the sling on his arm uncomfortably.

"But Samuel is the true king?" Oswald asked.

"You both have claims to the throne," Armond said, as he looked at Oswald, his sky blue eyes clear and concerned.

"But I don't want it," Oswald said again.

"I know," Armond said sadly, "I'm just not sure how to tell him."

"He'll make a far better King than I ever would," Oswald promised, "He's a wonderful man, he's strong willed, kind and compassionate."

"And a defiant, angst ridden seventeen year old," Armond added, drawing his brow down in deep ridges.

Oswald laughed but stopped short and clutched at his side as a sharp pain stabbed through his chest. He put a hand over the heavy bandages and let his smile slip back into place, "That goes away."

"It does," Armond agreed, slipping a smile in return, "But do you think that he would be able to take on the responsibilities of a king at his age?"

Oswald thought for a moment and nodded, "I do."

Armond hung his head and closed his eyes, "Then what do I tell him? I've been his father for over sixteen years. It'll change everything."

Oswald shook his head with a light hearted sigh, "You'll always be his father. You raised him. Knowing what you've told me won't take away his love and respect for you," he assured him.

"How do you know?" Armond asked anxiously.

"Because that doesn't just go away. You've been there for him through his entire life. You teach him, care for him, and protect him. That doesn't go away because you aren't his father."

"And what if it does go away?" Armond asked through a wave of sorrow.

Oswald leaned forward in his seat and rubbed his fingertips together. He licked his lips and his smile sank a little, "Then he will still be your king and he will still be your son, and you'll love him anyway."

Armond's blue eyes reddened slightly and he choked back a tear. He smiled with a short nod and looked back at Oswald with respect and understanding, "You would make a great King."

"I'm a much better cobbler," Oswald assured him.

"That you are," Armond said, getting up out of the chair stiffly. He rubbed at his face with his free hand and took in a deep, clear breath.

"Well at least you have something going for you," Nile snarked.

Oswald looked down at Nile and scowled as he curled tighter around his arm, "I thought you said that you were going to stop talking."

"I lied." Nile replied defiantly.

Armond smiled at him weakly, trying to regain his sense of humor for the situation, "You may be a great cobbler but you may begin to lose business if you keep talking to yourself. People will think you're mad."

"I'm not talking to myself," Oswald said, in frustration, "Nile just won't stop talking. It's his fault. It's going to take a while for me to figure out how to either ignore him or be able to follow two separate lines of thought."

"It's not my fault you aren't smart enough to keep your mouth shut."

Oswald rolled his eyes, "Well, I'm not exactly used to having you ramble at me all the time, now am I?"

"Again. I can hear your thoughts without your mouth working, dumb elf."

"I'll talk if I want to," Oswald said rudely, blushing a little as he looked back up at Armond, "I'm sorry. He's very distracting."

Armond smiled down at him and took a few slow steps down from the small platform. He turned back around and said resolutely, "Give him time. You'll figure out how to communicate with him better after a while. I have faith in you." He walked away from Oswald and started towards the front door to the courtyard.

"Where are you going?" Oswald asked, not wanting to be left alone with Nile for company.

Armond shrugged with his head down slightly as he turned. He continued to walk slowly backwards towards the door and said, "It seems like I don't have a choice. So I'm going to talk to Samuel."

"He's here? I thought he was in Gommorn."

"He was," Armond said with a nod, "He got here this morning on horseback. Fred brought him for me."

"How is Fred?" Oswald asked concernedly, "I haven't seen him."

Armond smiled, "He's doing better every day."

"I'm happy to hear that," Oswald said, relieved.

"So am I."

As Armond lifted his hand and waved goodbye, Oswald called out after him, "You shouldn't worry about what to tell him so much, and you shouldn't be afraid of how he'll react. He'll understand as long as he hears it from you. He has to."

Armond turned back with a bright smile and another short wave, "You really would have made a great king," he repeated, "But since you're so certain about not wanting it, we do still have something else to consider," he said with a pause, "We need a Royal Sorcerer for the wizards court," he held up a hand to stop Oswald's protests, "Just so you have something to think about when you go back home," he turned through the doorway and wandered slowly out into the brightly lit city.

Chapter Thirty-Eight

Fantasy stood at the side of the throne, her frozen hair catching the light as it came through the high, open windows. Her fair skin and fine pale blue dress shone in the morning light, intensifying the reflection of the sun on the golden crown in her hands.

Samuel sat in the throne, his young eyes anxious but his face regal and sure. He sat up straight in the chair patiently, looking across the hall to the faces around him.

Oswald stood next to Ramif along the side of the hall opposite Jameson and Loch. Between them stood Fred, Bore, Satomi's father Hadem Naddow, Bolzar and a female Dwarf Lord named Iksa. Beyond them stood other members of important families, mingled faces of strong men and women, all rising in support of the new king.

Armond stood on the other side of the throne, across from Fantasy, his arm healed and his eyes beaming with a pride that could be felt across the city.

Fantasy stepped forward with the crown resting between her hands.

"Samuel Navar Ghraner, Last son of King Edward the Second of Azar," Fantasy paused as Samuel rose out of the throne and knelt before her on the marble floor, his coronation uniform creasing as he moved. The regal black and blue trimming of the suit, accented in silver, glinted in the light. He turned his head upwards and looked up into her crystalline eyes as she spoke, "Do you swear to serve this country in honor and nobility?"

"I do," Samuel said, his eyes never wavering from hers.

"Will you strive to be worthy of the trust of your people? To be fair in judgement and pure of spirit, putting first your duties to the protection and splendor of the lives of your people through all the days of your life?"

"I will," he promised.

"Will you lead your people with strength and compassion? Showing the mercy, justice, and honesty of your heart to all those who come to you in need?"

"I will."

"Do you swear to preserve the rights of your people, through all cultures and lands that you govern in this new era of peace and understanding?"

"I swear," Samuel said soulfully.

"Then before the gathered leaders of your people, I do now crown and christen you King Samuel the First, of Azar," she lowered the crown onto his head, the gold glinting against his black hair, "Rise," Fantasy commanded, lowering her hand to him.

Samuel took her hand gently and stood as she wrapped her fingers around his, meeting his eyes with a gentle smile and a silent conversation. They stood quietly for several long minutes and Samuel smiled proudly back at her. She let go of his hand and Samuel took his seat on the throne gracefully.

"Your new King!" Fantasy announced loudly.

The hall burst in polite and enthusiastic applause.

Armond stepped down from his place beside the throne and knelt down on one knee with his head bowed and prideful tears in his eyes.

Oswald knelt down on one knee in his place in the hall and every other person throughout the assembly followed suit.

"Long live the King!" Ramif bellowed.

The hall erupted in agreement, quoting back, "LONG LIVE THE KING!"

Samuel looked around, astonished by the sudden exclamation, "Thank you," he said loudly, getting to his feet and looking over the kneeling assembly, "I will always strive to be worthy of your honor and your respect. Please rise."

They did as they were asked.

Samuel smiled brightly and squared his shoulders as he raised a polite hand to gesture to the great hall, "I hope that you will all stay and make yourselves comfortable in my home. There will be a banquet served shortly, please help yourself," he said, and lowered his arm to his side, "I would also like to come and thank each of you personally for coming and for your support at some point through the evening. Enjoy."

Samuel waited for the assembly to disburse around the castle grounds and he turned to Armond with a stern expression, his eyebrows drawn together and his jaw tight.

"I never," Samuel emphasized, as he stepped down from the rise in the platform to look Armond in the eye, "Want to see you kneel before me again."

Armond looked hurt and confused at the outburst, the deeper lines of his face drawing inward, "You're my king."

"And you're my father," Samuel said softly, meeting his gaze, "It doesn't feel right. You don't have to."

"I don't have to," Armond said, "I didn't think that you would have made me," he paused, the sense of pride back in his eyes, "But I love you."

"I love you too," Samuel said, with a warm smile.

"I took an oath many years ago," Armond said, and looked thoughtfully over the glint of gold that peeked between the locks of black hair on Samuel's head.

"Yeah?"

"To protect and serve the royal family," he said humbly, placing a hand on Samuel's shoulder.

"You already have," Samuel said gratefully.

"For a total of twenty five years," he nodded.

"I wouldn't expect you to stay here if you didn't want to. You could go back home to Gommorn," Samuel said.

Armond shook his head, "Azar was my home. It will be again."

"And what would you do here?" Samuel asked, looking out to the throng of gathered people as they talked amongst one another in small, polite groups.

"I'll protect you as I always have," Armond promised, "I'll take up my old position as the king's first general, if you'll allow it, and take care of your family too someday. Until the day I die."

"You won't keep watch over me every day I hope," Samuel said, with a mischievous smile.

Armond laughed brightly with a shrug, "We'll see. Go," he said, tipping his head out towards the great hall, "You have a lot of people that are waiting to talk to you."

Samuel smiled at Armond and stepped down the marble landing to the hall and walked over to where Oswald was standing and talking with Fred. As Samuel approached, Fred tipped his head respectfully and shuffled off to speak with Armond.

"Your highness," Oswald said, turning towards him and bowing respectfully.

"If you drop to one knee, I'll kick you," Samuel warned.

Oswald looked confused by the thought as he straightened up again, "Why would you do that?"

Samuel sighed and fiddled with the cufflink on his left sleeve, "There are five men that I never want to kneel before me, and you're one of them."

"Why?" Oswald asked, startled.

"Several reasons," Samuel said seriously, "Not the least of which is that you should have been king and you turned it down."

"You'll make a far better one," Oswald said surely, without an ounce of regret in his decision.

"You would have been fine too," he retorted.

"I didn't want it," Oswald confessed, with a half-hearted shrug, "It's too confining for me. I miss home."

"I suppose it is," Samuel said, "But it needs to be done."

Oswald smiled, "And that's the difference between me and you. I'm selfish. I'm not strong enough to lead an empire."

Samuel shook his head, "I wouldn't say that at all, but either way... My point is that you will never have to bow to me, and I wanted you to know that."

"Why? It shows loyalty," Oswald said.

"You saved Ramif once," he said reflectively, a shadow of the memory fleeting across his deep blue eyes, "I'm extremely grateful for that. You stopped a Grimm, and you were the one who killed Venhow and then you gave up your crown..." he paused and said quietly, "I don't want to see a man that I respect so much kneel in front of me on the ground."

Oswald raised his eyebrows, "I'm honored."

"But don't get cocky about it," Samuel said, with a smile.

"I won't," Oswald promised.

Samuel grinned and walked out into the hall, shaking hands and greeting people as he passed along the great hall towards where Ramif had wandered off to.

"Well that was fun. What now?"

Oswald looked down at the lump in the arm of his suit that was Nile and rolled his eyes, thankful that he had been respectful and quiet until now, "Let's go home."

Oswald pulled a few silver coins out of his wallet and handed them over to the shop owner. He pulled the string on the wallet tight and tucked it back into his pocket and took the bouquet of deep maroon, summer lilies, from their place on the market table. He smiled at the shop owner and thanked him as he turned away from the stand and out into the streets of Gommorn.

He wove among the bustling crowd as they elbowed their way through the street until a hand grabbed his shoulder briefly from behind. He turned, surprised by the sudden greeting, and saw a familiar, thin, gangly face with a grin that marked a gap in his teeth.

"Hey Oz," Matrim said brightly, "I thought dat waz you. When d'ya get back?"

"Today," he said with a smile, readjusting the stems of the bouquet in his hand, "and very happy to be back."

Matrim eyed the flowers and smirked, "So, I see yas busy, so I won' take long, but I got sum'tin fer ya." He reached into his back pocket and pulled out a stained and wrinkled piece of paper, which he held out for him to take.

Oswald took the paper and unfolded it. He pulled gently at the corners as they stuck together in places through the stain on the folds and flipped it open. It had names scrawled on every inch of the page with short notes scribbled around them in places until the paper had no available space to write anything at all, "What is this?" Oswald asked, turning the page over in his hand.

"Yer orders, 'o'course," Matrim said, sticking his hands in his pockets, "I don' know how ta do anythin' else but I got da leathers stained 'n all, ready fer ya. Mos' of 'em paid in advance too, so I got ya money waitin' fer ya at the house."

"Matrim," Oswald said, with his mouth hanging open slightly, "This is over fifty orders!"

"Yeah," Matrim nodded, "We gonna be busy fer a while."

"I'd say so," Oswald said, stuffing the paper into his back pocket with a heavy sigh, "I'm going to need help catching up with these... Do you think that you're ready to learn how to make shoes?"

Matrim's eyes went wide and his grin broadened, "Yeah!"

Oswald smiled tiredly, thinking of the list in his pocket, "Then I will see you first thing in the morning?"

"Absolutely," Matrim said brightly. He waved as he turned to leave and said over his shoulder as he headed back out of the market, "Break a dawn, and I'll see ya then."

Oswald waved at him and felt a hard impact against his back. He stumbled forward and turned around.

Nedtedrow was short of breath and pale with his mouth hanging open as he panted, "Hey, Oswald, glad you're back — I'm in over my head this time! — Cover for me!" he said, and started running off past him.

Oswald touched his pocket and hollered, "My wallet!"

"Yeah, no problem," Nedtedrow said quickly, and he threw the small pouch of coins back to him and ran off into the crowd like a rabbit through brush.

Oswald caught the wallet and shook his head slowly as he watched Nedtedrow vanish off into the city. He turned around and spotted three very large men shouldering their way through the market in his direction, their heavy brows drawn down and their eyes narrowed.

The largest of the three men stopped in front of Oswald and grumbled, "Where did he go?"

Oswald ignored the man and sighed as he opened his wallet, intending to count the coins. Not a coin was out of place and on top of the pile in the leather pouch was an onyx ring with a silver band through its center. Oswald reached into the wallet and pulled out the ring, holding it up for the man to see, "Is this what you were looking for?"

"Yes," the man said bitterly, snatching the ring out of his fingers and holding it in an iron fist, "Now where did the stupid little thief go?"

"You got your ring back," Oswald said sharply, "There's no harm done. Leave him alone."

"The thief was in my house!" the man shouted, looming over him with his two friends stepping closer on either side, "Who do you think you are anyway?" he spat, inching into Oswald's face, his beady eyes piercing.

Oswald fought back a laugh, "I'm an elf, a cobbler, and a wizard. Who are you?"

The man paused and took a step back, looking over his face closely as recognition began to sink into his features, "...So you're Oswald?"

Oswald smiled with a short nod, "Yes, and that little thief is my friend. You got your ring back, so leave him alone."

The man looked at him closely and his friends backed away as well. After a moment his anger faded away and he worked the corners of his mouth thoughtfully, "No harm done I suppose," he muttered and held out a threatening finger that Oswald couldn't help but smirk at as he continued, "But keep that thief out of my home!"

Oswald forced a one-sided smile, "I'll do what I can," he assured him, and watched at the three men turned around and made their way back through the throng of people. He shook his head and readjusted his grip on the flowers in his hand as he turned and made his way down the nearby alleyway.

The faded sign of the apothecary rocked in the wind in the distance and the chipped blue paint of the building caught the light as he came closer. His heart thundered in his chest as he stepped up to the short set of stairs and stared at the sign.

He knocked on the blue door sharply and hid the bundle of fresh flowers behind his back as he heard her footsteps shuffle through the shop. The click of her shoes on the wooden floor trotted forward and the door opened.

He held out the flowers with an ecstatic grin, "For you, my dear."

Sanna's face split into a wide smile and she leapt off the slight rise in the steps of her home with a squeal, knocking the flowers aside and wrapping her arms around him.

He took her in his arms tightly, his arms linked around her back as he held her. She wouldn't let go of him and it was the best feeling he'd ever had.

Being missed and being loved.

He held her tighter and breathed in the smell of cinnamon and spices that always seemed to cling to her. The intense feeling of her arms holding him so tightly settled his fears and calmed his soul. He held her for a long time, rejoicing in the comfort of her arms.

"You're back," she mumbled into the crook of his neck.

"I'm back," he said warmly, "and I'm never going to leave you again."

She grabbed the back of his head and pressed her lips to his passionately. They clung to each other as he returned the kiss and they parted gently after a long moment.

She looked into his green eyes softly, a playful gleam in her eyes, "Never?"

"Never," he promised with a soft smile.

She brushed her thumb across the side of his face, and Oswald smiled, glowing in the light of her. They interlaced their fingers and walked back up the steps and into the small blue house full of cinnamon, herbs, and spices.

Made in the USA
Charleston, SC
29 October 2015